ASSASSIN!

Time slowed as Carrie watched the Sholan aligning his gun on them. Around her she heard loud shouts, but the words were too slow to make sense. She glimpsed figures running toward the gunman. She knew they wouldn't be in time. Even thoughts were too slow now.

She leaned against Kusac, trying to push him and herself out of the line of fire, but he was too heavy. She was trapped like a butterfly on a board, waiting for the pin to descend.

Light lanced toward them. Almost at the same moment she spied a second Sholan releasing a shot that hit their attacker, sending him crashing to the ground.

Helplessly, she watched the light accelerate toward her. Then it hit, knocking her backward. . . .

DAW Books
is proud to present
LISANNE NORMAN'S
SHOLAN ALLIANCE Novels:

TURNING POINT (#1)

FORTUNE'S WHEEL (#2)

FORTUNE'S WHEEL

LISANNE NORMAN

DAW BOOKS, INC.
DONALD A. WOLLHEIM, FOUNDER
375 Hudson Street, New York, NY 10014

ELIZABETH R. WOLLHEIM
SHEILA E. GILBERT
PUBLISHERS

First Printing, August 1995

3   4   5   6   7   8   9

DAW TRADEMARK REGISTERED
U.S. PAT. OFF. AND FOREIGN COUNTRIES
—MARCA REGISTRADA.
HECHO EN U.S.A.

PRINTED IN THE U.S.A.

For my son Kai, and my brother Richard, who enrich my days by sharing with me their unique outlook on life, and because I love them both dearly.

With special thanks to the following people and their expertise,

Sholan Medical Guild Master	- June Third
Commander of the Sholan Forces	- John Quadling
Adjutant & Adviser to the Commander	- Gina Quadling
Sholan Tactical Commander	- Steve Barrett
Sholan Technical Commander	- Andrew Stephenson
Sholan Brotherhood sub-Guild Master	- Les Heasman
Sholan Telepath Guild Master	- Sherry Ward
Sholan Communications sub-Commanders	- Linda Apperley
	- Judith Faul
Sholan Research & Development	- Merlin
Sholan Catering	- Mike Hawkes

PART I

KHALOSSA

Prologue

Adjutant Myak pressed the chime on the outside of Commander Raguul's private quarters and waited. He could have used the comm, but both he and the Commander preferred the personal touch. As the door slid open, he stifled a yawn, extending his claws to scratch vigorously behind his left ear. He'd get no more sleep that night either. The starship *Khalossa* was already on Yellow 2 alert.

Commander Raguul lay propped up on one elbow, regarding him balefully. The set of his ears showed his irritation at being disturbed in the middle of his night.

"Yes, Myak?"

"The duty crew thought you'd like to know we've just received a transmission from the *Sirroki*, sir."

"The *Sirroki*?" Raguul frowned, ears flicking briefly. "She's the one that missed the rendezvous in the sixth quadrant, isn't she?"

"That's right, sir. You just posted her as officially missing."

"You didn't wake me just for that, surely. What was it this time? Not more freak storms?"

"Not this time, sir. They've found the Others." Myak could hardly keep his tail from swaying with pleasure.

Raguul sat up. "Found them?"

"Yes, sir. The *Sirroki* was shot down by them on a planet designated as KX 1311. Our people are in hiding with a second group of aliens and request that we go to their aid."

"Natives, eh?"

"Not natives, sir, colonists, a new species. Sub-Commander Kolem thought you might want to hear the original transmission yourself."

Raguul was already out of bed and dressing. "Tell me about the Others," he ordered as he pressed the seals on his jacket.

"They've a substantial base on the planet, plus two domed cities and garrison posts at each of the four colony towns. They're capable of putting up a formidable resistance."

"Has—whatzisname—transmitted the locations of these occupied zones?" demanded the Commander, fumbling with his belt.

Myak moved forward to help him. "Captain Garras, sir. Communications is still decoding the message, but we believe so."

"These colonists, what're they like?"

"They're upright and bilateral like us, and there's a telepath among them," said Myak, stepping back as he finished with the Commander's belt.

Raguul's tail began to flick as his ears and head swiveled round to look at Myak. "Telepaths, you say."

"Yes, sir. It seems that our telepath has formed a link to one of the female colonists."

"Has he now?" Raguul took the brush Myak was holding out toward him and, flattening his ears out of the way, ran it cursorily across the top of his head. He handed it back to his adjutant.

"Apparently, sir," said Myak, returning the brush to the night table.

"Any more tactical details such as the numbers of the Others on the planet, their firepower, capabilities of their craft?"

"There could be, sir. As I said, they're still decoding the message," replied Myak, following the Commander out.

"Has a course been set for KX 1311?"

"They're waiting for your orders, sir."

"Tell the bridge to have a chart of sector six set up on the main screen."

When Raguul reached the bridge, it was humming with suppressed excitement. Sub-Commander Kolem rose from his seat, offering it to the Commander. With a nod of thanks, Raguul sat down.

"Have you finished decoding the message?" he asked.

"Just finished, sir," said Communications. "Putting it on audio now."

Raguul and his bridge crew sat and listened to the voice of Mito Rralgu, the communications officer from the scouter

Sirroki. Though terse, the message held all the information they had hoped it would.

Getting to his feet again, Raguul turned to Sub-Commander Kolem. "I want yourself, Tactics, Weapons, and Sub-Commander Chaazu in my briefing room today at the fourth hour. See that the chart of sector six is set up on the holo-table. Keep the ship on Yellow 2 alert and ensure Chaazu gets the message. With a week of transit time ahead of us, I want those ground troops of his ready before we reach KX 1311."

"Yes, sir."

"In the meantime, relay that message to my comm. Sholan High Command will want to hear it. The bridge is yours."

"Aye, sir."

* * *

Raguul was finishing his meal in the bridge mess when he was paged through the comm system.

"Approaching KX 1311 now, sir," said Sub-Commander Kolem's voice.

With a growl of annoyance, he gulped down his mug of c'shar and got to his feet. Changing his mind, he turned and neatly speared the remaining piece of meat with a clawtip. These disturbed meals weren't doing his gut-ache any good. Up until a week ago this had been a boring, routine mission. He had a feeling it wasn't going to last. Mop-up operations had a way of getting very messy.

Kolem rose and stood aside for the Commander.

Raguul waved him back. "Sit, sit. I'll stand for now," he said, looking at the view screen displaying the KX 1311 system. "I presume there's no sign yet of that back-up we were promised?"

"Not yet, sir."

A sudden burst of sound filled the bridge, then stopped.

"Our long-range scanners have activated a coded message from the life pod, sir," said the comm officer.

"Get onto it immediately," said Raguul.

"I'm picking up an incoming signal in sector five, sir," said Navigation. "It's an Alliance fleet identity. They should be on screen any moment now."

A portion of the upper right-hand quadrant of the screen appeared to waver, then steady as a group of ships materialized out of jump.

"Identities coming in now, sir. Battleship *Cheku,* accompanied by the cruisers *T'chelu, Rryabi, Vriji,* and the *Vek'ihk,* a Sumaan craft."

"Signal from the *Cheku,* sir," said the secondary communications officer. "*Cheku*'s comm officer says Commander Vroozoi wishes to speak to you in private. He adds that the tanker and escort ships are following."

"Patch it through to my briefing room," said Raguul, turning away from the screen.

"Force Commander," said Raguul, a flick of his ears acknowledging the other's superior rank. "What can I do for you?"

"Raguul. I see you struck it lucky this time," said Vroozoi. "High Command says you've found a den of these Others."

"Yes, Commander. As you know, our report says there are only a few thousand of them on the planet. Though I doubt we'll need all your firepower, it's still comforting to have it. We aren't equipped for an extended military campaign."

"Each to his own, eh, Raguul?" Vroozoi dropped his mouth in a lazy smile. "That's why we're here." His tone changed and became sharper, more businesslike. "I want you to join me an hour from now for a tactical briefing. You'll get a copy of your new orders then. Your assault craft will remain on the *Khalossa,* but they and their crews will form an integrated part of my task force. Once the planet has been secured, you'll be in charge of the diplomatic side. I'll see you within the hour," he said, reaching forward to close the channel.

Raguul frowned at the comm. He'd come across Vroozoi before. An ambitious male, that one, determined to climb as high as he could within the forces. Rumor had it that there were more than a few people who had had the misfortune to be between him and what he wanted. Their shattered careers littered his past like fallen leaves. Raguul didn't intend to become one of them.

He sighed and, leaning forward, paged Myak, requesting him to join him. Switching off the comm, he got to his feet and headed back to his bridge.

Sub-Lieutenant Draz looked up from the scanner display as the Commander reentered the bridge. "Scans show no signals going in or out. I'd hazard a guess that our people have done some heavy damage to their coastal base. The Others appear to be blind and deaf."

"Let's hope you're right. The last thing we want is a prolonged campaign. I'll take that seat now, Kolem," he said. "Order my shuttle made ready. I'm to join Vroozoi on the *Cheku* within the hour."

"Yes, sir," said Kolem, hurriedly standing up and moving to one side.

"Message decoded, sir. It's for our resident Leskas," said the communications officer.

"What?" Raguul swung round to face him.

"It's from the *Sirroki*'s telepath, Kusac Alda, to our Leska pair."

"You said that," said Raguul testily. "What's it say?"

"It's security coded, sir," the comm officer said apologetically.

"Then pass it on, and tell them I expect an explanation," said Raguul, pressing his hand to his stomach as a stab of pain hit him. He grimaced as he kneaded his gut to relieve the pressure. He just knew this mission was going to be messy. Some people had weather-wise joints. He had a trouble-predicting gut.

"Message incoming from Shola, sir," called out the secondary comm officer.

Raguul stifled a groan. This was all he needed. "I'll take it on the main screen. Patch it through."

The image of Chief Commander Chuz of the Sholan High Command replaced the view of KX 1311.

"Commander Raguul," he said, ears flicking in acknowledgment. "You've located the Others."

"Yes, Chief Commander Chuz. We've located some of them at least. Seems they were using this planet as a hospital and R & R base. They call themselves Valtegans. I'll be able to tell you more when we're in contact with our people on the surface."

"I want information from these Valtegans as soon as possible, Raguul; so does Alien Relations. I've put you in charge of interrogating all prisoners. I want to know as a matter of urgency why they destroyed our colony worlds. AlRel also wants information collected on this new species of natives. Get your First Contact people onto that. Send us the results of the *Sirroki*'s debriefing as soon as you have it;

at least it'll give us a starting point." He stopped talking to glance briefly to one side.

"I've been asked to remind you to convey the message from Konis Aldatan to Kusac Alda as soon as possible. Until we received your report regarding the *Sirroki* and the Others, Konis had no idea where his son was. Kusac disappeared a year ago and hasn't been in touch since."

"I'll pass the message on, Chief Commander."

"Good. Keep me informed of your progress." The screen went blank.

A glass of white liquid appeared in front of Raguul. He took it gratefully from Myak. "Thank you," he said, downing the contents and handing the empty glass back to his adjutant. "Couldn't you make it taste more palatable?" he asked.

"I'm afraid not, sir. I'd have to see the dispensary about that."

"Then do it, please. I've a feeling I'm going to be taking a lot of this vile brew."

"Rhian and Askad, our resident Leska pair, are waiting, sir," said Myak.

"Send them in."

The two telepaths came onto the bridge. One look at the set of their ears and Raguul knew their news was not good.

"Commander, we're here to report on the message we received from the life pod. It was from Kusac Alda, telepath on the *Sirroki*," said Rhian, the female.

Raguul nodded and waited.

Rhian looked at Askad.

"Well?" prompted Raguul. "One of you had better tell me!"

"Kusac's requested our intercession on behalf of his Leska," said Askad.

Raguul frowned at them, his ears flicking briefly. "His Leska, you say. As far as I'm aware, he doesn't have a Leska. Myak, what do you know about this?"

"We have him listed as a grade five telepath, Commander. At that basic a level of talent they don't form Leska Links," replied his adjutant.

"I'm afraid he has one now, Commander," said Askad. "His Leska isn't a Sholan, she's one of the people who live on the planet. A Terran."

Raguul closed his eyes. "His Leska is an alien?"

"Yes, sir. He's asked that we meet him on Keiss and . . ." began Rhian.

"Keiss?"

"What they call their world, sir. He wants us to meet him on Keiss and take charge of his Leska. He's afraid of her being seen as a specimen for the Medics to study. Apparently she's a healer."

Raguul took a deep breath and opened his eyes. "What in Vartra's name is he trying to do?" The question was rhetorical. "We meet another telepathic species for the first time in five hundred years and he goes and forms a Leska Link to one of them without even a by your leave! They haven't even been investigated yet! Surely even the densest cub would be aware of the diplomatic implications. I'll have his hide on my wall for this!" he promised grimly.

"Commander, you can't create a Leska Link," said Rhian. "It's a gift from the Gods. It just happens to you, you have no power over it."

"He's not responsible for forming the link, Commander," said Askad.

Raguul let loose a string of invectives. "Then you'd better get permission from Mentor Mnya to go down to this . . . Keiss . . . when it's been secured!"

"Yes, sir."

"See to it now. Dismissed!"

When they'd left, he turned to Myak. "This situation has all the makings of a powder keg ready to blow up under us. What the hell is Kusac playing at? With his background he should know better!"

"Oh, it gets better, sir," said Myak quietly. "While Rhian and Askad were with you, contact was established with Captain Garras of the *Sirroki*. He's requested an armed escort for his first officer who is under arrest for mutiny. He Challenged Kusac Alda against orders. This same male is making allegations against Kusac of mentally controlling this Terran female and forcing her to become his Leska for sexual reasons. I know, sir," he said, seeing his Commander's eye ridges go up. "That means Kusac and his Leska will have to face a Telepath Guild hearing."

"As you said, it gets better by the minute," said Raguul testily. "The Gods know what Vroozoi will make of all this! So Kusac's a runaway, is he? Well, at least he's shown more spirit than most telepaths! His father's going to create some grief for us when he learns his son's Leska is an alien. Perhaps we'll all be lucky and it won't be a permanent link. She isn't a Sholan, after all."

"If he claims she's his Leska, I'd believe it, sir," said Myak. "Telepaths don't make mistakes like that, and I'll warrant he's no fifth grade either. May I also suggest it might be politic not to mention anything about his Leska to his father for the moment? We need to debrief the *Sirroki* crew, establish a liaison with these new aliens, and assess them and their telepaths before we can think about dealing with clan matters."

"I think that's a very sound suggestion, Myak,," said the Commander. "Deal with matters on a priority basis. We are on a war alert, after all. I take it I can leave the matter of his father in your capable hands?"

Myak closed his eyes and forced his tail to stay still. "Of course, sir," he said faintly.

"Excuse me, Commander," Draz interrupted. "Your shuttle is ready, sir."

Raguul got to his feet. "You're coming with me, Myak. If Vroozoi has heard this transmission, I'll need all your abilities to talk my way out of him insisting on getting involved in this."

"It would be extremely unfortunate if Force Commander Vroozoi were to become involved," said Myak, following him from the bridge into the lift. "However, as you say, sir, this matter is potentially explosive. Knowing the Force Commander's reputation, I think he'll be more than glad to leave it to you."

"Let's hope you're right. Main landing bay," Raguul ordered as the elevator doors closed.

* * *

Three days had passed since they'd rendezvoused with the *Cheku*. They had been days during which Raguul would have preferred to have denned with a spine-covered wild hog. Luckily, true to Myak's prediction, the one problem they had avoided was the one concerning Kusac and his alien Leska.

Raguul entered the bridge, taking over from Sub-Commander Zyan. The main wall screen showed the progress of their assault on Keiss.

"Are the ground troops ready?"

"Yes, sir. The drop vehicles launch in one minute, followed by the assault cruisers and destroyers," replied Sub-Commander Chen at Tactics. "The strikers will launch last."

"Put the *Cheku*'s bridge comm on audio."

"Yes, sir. Switching to audio now," said Communications.

"I presume we have the full tactical and weapons crew on the bridge?"

"Yes, sir," said Chen. "My people came on duty two hours ago."

"Ready and waiting, sir," said Khodi from Weapons.

The bridge crew sat watching the main screen as the heavy troop carriers were launched. Surrounded by their attendant swarm of assault craft, they headed inexorably toward the planet's surface. Onboard the *Khalossa,* Raguul felt theirs was the more difficult task: that of waiting for the outcome of the battle below. Both they and the *Cheku* were to remain within planetary range of Keiss, monitoring the system in case of incoming alien craft. Supporting them were the thirteen escort destroyers.

"Trying to locate the *Sirroki*'s crew now, sir," said the comm.

Chapter 1

"I think you'd better come and see this for yourselves," called Davis from his concealed position at the mouth of the cave.

Garras, sitting near the entrance, pricked his ears, turning to face the circle of daylight.

Mito leaped to her feet and ran outside. "They've come!" she yelled, her voice all but drowned out by the now audible sound of high level airborne vehicles. There was a general rush to the cave mouth as everyone surged into the open to stare up at the approaching craft. Even as they watched, a group of them banked toward the Valtegan base, the faint glow of energy weapons lancing down. Plumes of smoke began to rise, accompanied by the sounds of distant explosions.

"All right!" yelled Davies, waving his rifle in the air as a salute to the avenging craft.

"My God, the sky's almost black with them," said Skinner, watching as more vehicles headed out toward Geshader and Tashkerra.

"They certainly know where they're going," said Nelson. He turned to Mito. "Just what did you put in that message?"

"The location of every strategic Valtegan unit," she said smugly. "It seems they got the message correctly."

"Get under cover," ordered Skinner. "We're far from safe yet, this is only the beginning." He pointed to the south where some Valtegan craft had just taken to the air. "If they see us, we've nowhere to hide. Believe me, within hours this planet will be crawling with Valtegans trying to escape capture. Get moving!" he bellowed as everyone hesitated, torn between a desire to watch the forthcoming aerial battle and the need to remain hidden.

There was a mad scramble to get back under cover and to secure a good vantage point at the mouth of the cave. Garras took advantage of the confusion to have a quiet word with Skinner, who glanced sharply at Guynor, then nodded. Casually, he went over to Anders and Hughes, drawing them aside. A few words with them and they returned to the group at the cave mouth, flanking Guynor on either side.

Having observed the interchange, Kusac limped over to where Carrie stood on tiptoe, trying vainly to see over the heads of Jo, Edwards, and Davies.

"I told you they would come," he said, placing a hand on her shoulder.

"You were right," she said, her tone somber. "Time doesn't stop for anyone."

Kusac tightened his grasp reassuringly. "You see your future up there in the skies, not Sholan war craft. I understand," he said.

Come, it's safer if we move away from them, he sent, nodding in the direction of Guynor. Anders and Hughes had just taken hold of the Sholan male, placing him under close arrest.

Now the Khalossa is here, Garras doesn't trust Guynor's parole. His hatred of us is so strong he may not wait for the results of my hearing or his court martial before deciding to take the law into his own hands.

Carrie turned away from the cave mouth, moving out from under his hand.

"I wish I had your confidence in the future," she said, unwilling to look at him.

Acutely aware of her growing unease and withdrawal from him over the last few days, Kusac took her by the arm, urging her farther into the cave with him. He led her past the group gathered round the Sholan transmitter, toward an empty table at the far side of the main cave, sensing as he did so her reluctance to be alone with him.

Carrie, I think it's time we talked.

For a moment he felt her resist. Then, as he eased himself down with his back to the wall, she slipped onto the bench facing him. Inwardly he sighed, trying to block his annoyance over yet another of her unsubtle hints that she was a person in her own right, apart from him.

"I prefer to vocalize," she said in Sholan.

Kusac shrugged, leaning his elbows on the table. "It makes no difference to me," he said mildly. "I said it was time to talk, and it is. I know you can shield some things from our Leska bond, and should I choose to pry, I could probably find out what." He held up his hand to forestall her as he felt the indignation and denial that rose to her lips.

"I choose instead to ask you," he continued. "So tell me why this is the first time in three days that we've been alone."

Carrie examined her hands. "I'm not avoiding you, Kusac," she said at length.

"True," he agreed amicably. "You're just avoiding being alone with me."

"I'm not really. I only want to spend what time I have left on Keiss with my own people. It came as a shock to realize how soon I would be leaving everything I know behind, and how much there was to leave."

"You've said these words before, Carrie. While I recognize their truth, I'm listening for the words you've not spoken."

Carrie looked up with a faint smile. "I forgot that half truths aren't possible between us."

The smile faded and she sighed, reaching for his hand. She held it between both of hers, stroking the dark fur before turning it over to look at his palm. It was much like hers, flesh-colored, the fingers long and narrow. The sharp tipped claws were retracted now.

"You know what I feel about you, Kusac," she said, as he turned his hand to clasp one of hers. "Our Link makes it impossible for me to hide it, and I know what you feel for me. Your conviction that our Leska bond must be like the Sholan one—linked as life-mates, body and mind—frightens me."

His hand tightened on hers, claws automatically coming out, to be retracted almost as soon as they touched her.

"Do you wish the Link hadn't been forged?" he asked, trying to keep his voice and thoughts neutral.

"No," she replied quickly, frowning. "I don't wish it undone, but I wish I had had a choice! It seems that all my life other people or circumstances have dictated what I do. Just for once I'd like to have some say in the matter."

"What do you want to do?" he asked, cursing inwardly as his tail gave an involuntary flick against her legs. "Do you want to remain on Keiss?"

"I don't want to stay here," she said. "No, I intend to leave with you. Apart from anything else, we have to attend your guild hearing and Guynor's court-martial. I wouldn't let you go through those alone no matter what I felt for you."

"Thank you," he said dryly.

"So much has happened since we left my home," she said, her eyes taking on a distant look. "Do you realize it was only about a month ago? Who could guess so much could happen in so short a time?"

She came back to the present, giving herself a little shake, a gesture that was almost Sholan.

"I just need some time to adjust to the changes in my life, to decide what I want to do." She looked intently at him. "Could you do that? Would you let me have some time to myself?"

"If it means so much to you, then take the time that you need," he said, carefully keeping his voice level.

"Thank you," she said quietly. "I know what this costs you." She released his hand and rose from the table, smiling before she left.

Left alone, Kusac clenched his hands into fists, his claws drawing blood from his palms. The pain stopped him thinking, stopped her picking up the worry that would otherwise be in his mind. Facts about telepathic links, Leska Links in particular, were what he needed. The Telepath Guild's files on board the *Khalossa* held the information. Once there he could access them; then he would know for sure what at least a normal Sholan Leska Link entailed.

For now he needed a distraction, something to do to keep his mind occupied. If only Vanna's medikit carried some psychic suppressants, he could have escaped the constant awareness of Carrie that was rubbing his senses raw. Her decision to keep him at a distance mentally and physically was exacerbating his situation. Unfortunately, investigatory teams like theirs didn't normally include telepaths, so the drug wasn't contained in the standard medikit.

He heard a cry of pleasure from the direction of the transmitter and looked up.

"We're in contact with the *Khalossa!*" shouted Vanna, catching his eye.

Kusac grinned and, unclenching his hands, pushed himself to his feet and went over to join them.

"How're things going?" he asked her.

"Fine. Six or seven Valtegan ships made it off planet, but

were tracked by our craft. Two have been allowed through the cordon, the others were destroyed."

"Why let two through?"

She shrugged. "I presume to warn the Valtegans that their R and R planet has been returned to its rightful owners."

Kusac digested this for a moment. "Surely they'll retaliate?"

"Garras thinks not," said Mito. "If they used Keiss as a relaxation base, then it must be far enough from their war zone to be safe. Being at war, they won't want to start another one with us, will they? It would split their resources."

"I expect they'll leave well alone now that they know there are two races capable of retaliating in this sector of space," said Garras.

"Any other news?" Kusac asked him.

"They plan to airlift us out of here as soon as possible and take us to Seaport to rendezvous with the Tarran leaders. They're sending down our top negotiators to begin the treaty talks."

"Seaport's a good choice. Part of the original Terran craft is there with their computer records and transmitters. Any news about the Terran colony ship?"

"They've sent a message for two escort ships to meet it and bring it directly here," said Vanna. "Keiss is shortly going to seem very crowded."

Kusac nodded. "Life moves on," he said.

Vanna frowned as she looked at him. "That's a strange thing to say."

"It just seems a very rapid solution for a problem that was almost insurmountable a few weeks ago."

"You're being too profound," she said, showing her teeth in a wide Sholan grin.

"There're two personal messages for you, Kusac," said Mito, looking up at him, a strange expression on her face.

"Personal?" repeated Kusac, looking startled.

"Yes. Rhian and Askad, Leska telepaths on board the *Khalossa,* thank you for the message and say that all has been arranged and they will meet you at Seaport."

"Ah," said Kusac, glancing sideways at Garras, ears flicking with embarrassment, but the Captain appeared engrossed in listening to the transmission.

"And your father says he is glad you are well. He says he

awaits with interest the pleasure of meeting you and your Leska."

Kusac took a deep breath. "Damn!" he swore.

All the eyes of the little group were now on him.

"Is there some problem?" asked Vanna quietly.

"Just more complications I could do without," he said, sitting down beside her and stretching out his injured leg. "I'd hoped to tell him myself. I should have known better."

"How, in a military emergency such as this, could he get a message through from Shola?" asked Mito.

"How did he know you'd found a Leska?" asked Vanna. "Did someone on the *Khalossa* inform him?"

"I don't know," said Kusac, shrugging. "Just leave it, please."

"It seems there's more to you than meets the eye," said Garras, glancing appraisingly at him before returning his attention to the transmitter.

"He must know someone important to be able to use the military communications to send a personal message during a state of war," Mito continued, unwilling to leave the matter alone.

"I said enough, Mito!" said Kusac, standing up. "Captain, I claim a telepath's privilege of solitude. I need to leave the cave. Have I permission to go?" he asked curtly.

Garras glanced briefly at Vanna, obtaining an almost imperceptible movement of her ears in assent. The risk of him encountering Valtegans on the run was outweighed by his need for solitude.

"Granted. If you find game while you're out, it would make a welcome change to our diet."

Kusac nodded and, spinning round, left, barely aware of Carrie's startled reaction to his outburst.

* * *

By late afternoon, a Sholan craft arrived to ferry them to Seaport. They landed in the square in front of the *Eureka*. It was a huge metal edifice, only a fraction of its former height but still dominating every other building in Seaport. Skai and the other guerrillas headed off to the local inn, Skinner accompanying Carrie and the Sholans through the entrance.

Garras stopped briefly to talk to the Sholan guards inside, handing Guynor over to their custody. That done, Skinner led the way, passing by the elevators to the upper levels where the communications and records departments were housed, heading for the room that had been the Terrans' council hall before the advent of the Valtegans.

It still bore the scars of the occupation, but had been returned to the semblance of human use by the local townsfolk. A huge carved wooden table sat in the center of the room surrounded by chairs. At the far end of the table, a small group of Sholans and Terrans sat. They looked up as the new arrivals entered.

"Carrie! Richard!" called their father, getting to his feet and coming forward to meet them.

Richard threw Carrie a rueful glance.

"I didn't think we could avoid him for long," he said quietly.

"What possessed him to bring David, too?" she said.

Kusac stepped closer to her. "David's here?"

She looked up at him. "Yes, but don't worry. I can handle him."

Kusac flicked his ears in irritation. "I dislike him. The man is cruel and self-opinionated."

"Carrie," her father said, hugging her when they reached him. "You shouldn't have left like that. We were extremely worried about you. Thank God Richard found you."

"I was fine, Dad. I had Kusac with me," she said, returning the hug.

"Ah, yes. Kusac." Peter Hamilton regarded him critically.

Kusac bore her father's appraisal patiently, knowing it was only the first of many obstacles that he and Carrie would have to face. Briefly, his viewpoint altered, and he saw himself through both his Leska's and her father's eyes. Tall, dark-furred, and fairly powerfully built, the pointed ears added to his feline look. The face was humanoid yet still catlike with vertically slitted amber eyes set above high cheek bones. The nose and mouth, though bifurcated like a feline's, appeared more humanoid.

A wave of dizziness hit him along with the realization that Carrie was making sure her father saw the person that he was rather than the animal he had impersonated during his stay at the Inn. Then his vision cleared and he sensed her father's conclusion that his appearance, despite the heavy musculature that hinted at a strength beyond that of the Terrans, was pleasing rather than threatening.

Gods, cub, you need to learn some subtlety! he sent.

Time for that later, she replied.

Her father was nodding and holding out his hand. "It seems we owe you everything. Had it not been for you, we wouldn't yet be free of the Valtegans. Been wounded again, I see," he said, looking at the bandage around Kusac's thigh.

Kusac took the hand, holding it lightly and releasing himself before Peter Hamilton's grasp triggered his claws.

"It's almost healed," he said. "I owe your family my life. It seemed a fair exchange."

Peter Hamilton smiled and turned back to his children.

"Richard, I see you've managed to keep body and soul together."

Richard grinned. "Just about," he said.

Her father turned to allow David to join the group.

"I've brought someone with me who's very anxious to see you, Carrie," he said.

"Hello, Carrie," said David. "You really shouldn't have left so precipitously, you know. Not exactly a mature act, was it, to cause so much distress? Still, you're back with us now." He stepped forward to give her a perfunctory kiss on the cheek.

"Hello, David," she said, sidestepping him to stand beside Kusac. "I see you haven't changed. You shouldn't have bothered to come, you know. We said our good-byes the day I left Valleytown."

David stopped abruptly, an angry look crossing his face.

"Carrie, that's hardly any way to talk to someone who's been as concerned over you as David has," scolded her father.

"I don't give a damn what David thinks or feels, Father. I want nothing to do with him. He needn't stay on my account."

Let's leave, Kusac, she sent.

Kusac put an arm around her waist, drawing her to one side. He inclined his head briefly to her father.

"You will excuse us, sir, but we have to see my commanding officer. I'm sure you understand that Clan matters have to come second to duty."

He drew her toward where the Sholans were grouped together round a section of the table, aware of her father's and David's puzzled anger at their abrupt dismissal.

"Carrie, come back," her father called. "You shouldn't be

here. These are important discussions, not some social event."

She stopped, turning to face him again.

"I am here officially, with the Sholans. I have another mental link, this time with Kusac. It makes me part of his ship's crew now."

"Mental link?" said her father, confused.

"A link like I had with Elise. I told you I wasn't returning home and I meant it," she said, her voice and face unyielding. "When the ship leaves Keiss, I'm going, too."

"What nonsense is this, Carrie? Just because you looked after Kusac and helped him find the rest of his crew doesn't mean his people want you on their ship. That's work for the diplomats, not you. It's time for you to return home to your family and friends."

"I have no friends on Keiss, and you were prepared to barter me to David against my wishes for the sake of the family."

"That's different . . ." he began.

"Yes, it is. This is what I choose to do."

Kusac's heart began to lighten. Maybe there was hope for them after all.

"Don't talk utter rubbish, girl," her father stormed. "You'll do as you're told!"

A voice from behind interrupted them, the heavily accented Sholan breaking the angry group apart.

Kusac released Carrie and turning sharply, saluted the officer behind him. There followed a brief interchange before Kusac turned back to them.

"Sub-Commander Zyan asks that this discussion be delayed until we join the others. There are many facts that need to be investigated before the matter can be fully resolved. He also asks that I act as interpreter until I have imprinted the knowledge of your language to a telepath from the *Khalossa* who will then remain with you as your permanent interpreter."

"Telepath? Language imprint?" echoed Mr. Hamilton, looking thoroughly confused and exasperated. "I'm afraid I don't understand. And what's all this got to do with Carrie?"

"I'm sorry but I have to ask you to respect our security. This matter is not for public discussion," said Kusac, throwing an evil openmouthed grin at David.

"As one of the leaders of the Terran community on Keiss,

I am sure you are aware of the need to keep certain matters confidential. If you would rejoin our people at the table?" Kusac stepped back, indicating that Carrie's father should return to his place.

David moved to follow him, but before Kusac could bar his way, Richard reached out and grasped him by the arm.

"Sorry, mate, but if I'm not included, then you certainly aren't."

David tried to shake free. "Anything that concerns Carrie concerns me," he blustered.

Richard forcibly led David away as Kusac escorted Carrie after her father and the Sholan officer.

"I think my sister has already made her opinion of you clear," said Richard, his voice drowning out David's complaints. "No matter what deal you and Dad have hatched, if you go near her again, you'll not only have Kusac to deal with but me as well."

Once the group around the table was settled again, Kusac performed the various introductions, nodding briefly when he introduced Rhian and Askad, the Leska telepaths.

Sub-Commander Zyan began to talk, and Kusac turned again to Carrie's father.

"The Sub-Commander wishes to touch on the matter of your daughter, since he wants to get Clan matters dealt with first."

"He realizes you do not have a recognized Telepath Guild amongst your people, so he asks that you bear with us and accept what we say until the matter can be proved to you."

"Very well, but I still don't see how it involves Carrie."

Kusac relayed his answer to the Sub-Commander, waiting for his reply.

"Your daughter is not only a powerful telepath, but a healer," said Zyan through Kusac. "Telepaths are in a minority amongst our people, but healers are even rarer. As well as that, she has developed a mental link with one of our personnel—myself," he continued.

"Leska bondings happen occasionally amongst Sholans, but never before has there been one with a member of an Alien race. In fact, we have never come across another telepathic race until now. It is important, therefore, that we assess and study what gifts your daughter has, how it is possible that she should have a link with one of our people, and the benefits to both our species."

"That's impossible," her father said flatly.

"I assure you it has happened, Mr. Hamilton," murmured Kusac, still listening to the Sub-Commander.

"Your daughter will go aboard the *Khalossa* with our resident Leskas, Rhian and Askad," Kusac indicated the two Sholans sitting to one side of him, "who will help the Tutors assess her abilities. Since the matter also involves a Sholan, I'm afraid we have to insist."

Mr. Hamilton took a deep breath. "Insist is rather a strong word."

"Had you the facilities and personnel capable of making this assessment, we would assist you on Keiss. Since you have not, then it must be done on the *Khalossa*," said Zyan, through Kusac.

"How do I know my daughter will be . . ."

"She'll be safe," interrupted Kusac, glancing at Zyan. "I would let no harm come to her, believe me."

Skinner leaned forward.

"We haven't any choice, Hamilton. They're a reasonable lot, they won't harm her; Kusac will see to that."

Peter Hamilton looked sharply from Skinner to Kusac. "There's something here I'm missing. What is it? What kind of link do you have with my daughter?"

"I'm linked to her like Elise was, Mr. Hamilton. If they harm her, believe me, I will feel it. No one will harm her. She's important to both of us, and to both our species. We place a very high value on telepaths and healers."

The Sub-Commander interrupted again. After a brief conversation, Kusac turned back to Skinner and Mr. Hamilton.

"It'll be tomorrow morning before a shuttle returns to the *Khalossa,* and Carrie will be on board with the rest of the crew from the *Sirroki*. Once the preliminary talks are finished here, Sub-Commander Zyan will return to the ship, but that won't be for several days yet. When he does, you're welcome to accompany him and see your daughter for yourself."

Mr. Hamilton hesitated briefly. "I have no option, do I? I take it you'll be returning with Carrie?" he asked Kusac.

"Yes."

"Then I'll have to trust you to look after her for me."

Kusac relayed the answer.

"Since your daughter isn't involved in any of the other matters we have to discuss, Rhian will escort her to the inn across the road where our people are being billeted. We can arrange for any personal items she might want to take with her to be collected from her home. An armed scouter and an escort can take them to Valleytown should she wish it."

"I've nothing I want to take," said Carrie, looking bleakly at her father as she rose to leave.

Kusac reached up to touch her hand comfortingly as she passed.

"I hardly recognize her," her father said, watching her walk away with the Sholan female. "That's not the girl I raised. What happened to her out in the forest?" he asked Skinner.

Skinner glanced briefly at Kusac. "She grew up, Peter," he said. "They all do. They grow up and away from you, which is as it should be. She was never cut out to be a colonist, you know. You kept her too long as it was. Let her go now."

"The Sub-Commander would like to turn to other issues now," interrupted Kusac. "Have you been briefed on the matter of your ship, the *Erasmus?*"

Mr. Hamilton nodded, reluctantly turning away from Skinner.

"A message was sent to one of our vessels in that sector of space, and two ships have been dispatched to escort it to Keiss. It should be here within a week."

"A week!" he exclaimed.

"Our technology is more advanced than yours," said Kusac, with a deprecating gesture. "It's suggested that you don't contact the ship until it's in orbit around Keiss, then presumably you have a coded signal to waken the various personnel on board."

Skinner nodded.

"We also need to contact your home planet so as to make parallel treaty negotiations with Earth as well. A deep space relay will be arranged to enable you to contact Earth using your own transmitter. Once you've appraised them of the situation here, we can arrange for one of our ships to call there and bring the necessary personnel to Keiss. Our flagship, the *Khalossa,* will be stationed in permanent orbit here to protect you until such time as between us we have organized a defensive force not only for this area of space, but also your home planet."

And so it continued until late into the night.

* * *

The next morning, Kusac was dug out of his makeshift bed by Mito with the news that the incoming shuttle had landed and he was needed to imprint the telepath. That done, he went in search of Carrie and food. Linking with her, he found her across the road at the inn where they had met Skai.

It had been requisitioned for Sholan use, and was serving as their main canteen and accommodation area. Carrie was sitting with Vanna, Mito, and Garras.

He joined them, ordering a meal when the innkeeper's daughter came to the table.

"How did the talks go?" asked Vanna.

Kusac wrinkled his nose in disgust. "I don't think I could work with the Diplomatic Guild," he said. "All facts and dancing round the truth. Not the easiest or most interesting of work."

"Well, it's nothing to do with us any more. It's back to the ship in a few hours, and the usual routine."

Kusac shook his head. "We're in permanent orbit here for some time."

"Ah, protection duty and routine search flights," said Vanna.

"To say nothing of flushing out the last of the Valtegans still loose on the planet," agreed Mito.

"The troops will handle that," said Garras. "Could be interesting. Hunting another intelligent species for the first time will provide an unusual challenge. I've found out that the Valtegans have been making suicide attacks on our troops and the few they've managed to pin down have killed themselves rather than be taken captive."

"Why would they do that?" asked Carrie.

"We won't know until we can ask one of them," said Garras. "It could be conditioning or it could be a racial characteristic. Did they display any hive creature attributes? You've been exposed to them longer than we have."

"They acted as independent beings rather than part of a group mind, but how do you begin to study an alien race anyway?"

"That's the job of our first contact teams. Doubtless AlRel will send some personnel down from the *Khalossa*," said Vanna.

"AlRel?"

"Alien Relations."

"To assess us or them?" asked Carrie.

"Both," grinned Vanna. "You don't think they'll take our humble words for what we think of you, do you? Oh, they'll debrief us and note our conclusions and findings, but that will have to be backed up by hard facts from a team of specialists."

Kusac's meal arrived and he began eat.

"They're taking Guynor on board the shuttle," said Mito, glancing through the window. "It can't be long until we leave."

All heads turned to look as Guynor, under an armed escort of two soldiers, was led into the waiting craft.

"What's likely to happen to him?" asked Carrie.

"Mutiny when on a war footing; that at least will be a dishonorable discharge," said Mito.

"No," said Garras, looking at Kusac. "It's more serious than that. There are ... political complications."

Kusac looked away and toyed with his food. "My fault, then," he murmured.

"Nothing to do with you in a way. I found out he was from Khyaal, one of the two colonies destroyed by the Valtegans," said Garras. "When we crashed on Keiss and realized that we'd found the Others, that was when his attitude changed. I presume it was because he was powerless to hit back at the beings who had destroyed not only his family, but his world. Then you two arrived. It gave him the perfect opportunity to release his pent up xenophobia on you."

Garras sighed. "He was a capable officer, but we can do without his attitude in the Forces."

"And the political implications?" prompted Mito.

"I can't discuss that matter with you since the court-martial is still pending," said Garras, refusing to be drawn any further.

"By the way, I was none too pleased that you sent a message to the ship without my knowledge," he said to Kusac. "Had you told me your fears for Carrie, I would have had no objections, but I thought you could have trusted my judgment a little better."

Kusac dipped his head, flattening his ears backward in apology.

"Well, it's done now," Garras said, somewhat mollified. He checked his wrist unit, noting the time. "I want everyone on board the shuttle in ten minutes," he said, rising to leave. "Carrie, Rhian and Askad will meet you there. I would suggest you take your leave of your father before it gets any later."

Kusac watched her go, aware that she was still maintaining the distance between them despite what she'd said to her father the night before. Well, he'd promised her some space; he'd have to wait now until she came to him.

"Is Carrie all right?" asked Vanna quietly. "I know how difficult a time this is for her."

"She's coping," he said, pushing his plate away. "She just needs a little space at the moment."

Vanna grunted. "She doesn't know her own mind. She's subject to the same fears as us and responds to the same reassurances. What she really needs is you beside her to lean on."

"I'll deal with it my way, Vanna," said Kusac, getting up.

* * *

Carrie boarded the shuttle first with Rhian and Askad, sitting at the rear of the craft. The Leska couple sat together, opposite her, leaving the seat beside her empty, presumably for Kusac.

A sense of isolation swept over her all of a sudden. Around her were only Sholans, not one of them familiar. The only one she knew, Guynor, was in the forward area under close guard. She thanked whichever Gods were looking after her that she hadn't had to pass him.

Human voices and footsteps sounded on the gangway and she cautiously peered over the seat in front. It was a group of her people, including Skai. Under her breath she cursed, watching them move to the front section. What the hell was Skai, not to mention the others, doing going up to the *Khalossa?*

Ducking back out of sight, she lowered her mental shield, trying to sense what they were saying. Before she could, she picked up the crew of the *Sirroki* boarding, including Kusac.

With relief, she sent a thought to greet him, feeling his surprise, followed by a resulting wave of pleasure. Almost as if she were using her eyes, she could "see" him pushing through his friends to reach her.

He stopped by the seat, towering over her as he looked down.

Can I join you? he asked.

She smiled up at him, the relief apparent in her face as she nodded.

Kusac sat beside her, eyes narrowing.

What's upset you? he sent.

Nothing. I'm just glad you're here. From up front the Terran voices seemed loud and harsh in comparison to the low sounds of the Sholan conversations around her.

Kusac put his arm across her shoulders, drawing her up against him. *There's nothing to worry about,* he sent reassuringly. *You won't be alone. I'll be there, as will your other friends.*

I know. She relaxed against him, letting her barriers down a little and closing her eyes as she felt his low purr begin. Exhausted by the effort of keeping the block against him up and fielding her father's questions and demands, she felt herself nodding off to sleep.

Kusac felt her consciousness drift. As she began to slowly collapse against him, he moved closer, easing her down till she lay sleeping across his lap. Automatically his hand went to stroke her hair, fingertips gently touching her cheek. His need for her flared and this time it took more concentration than before to push it to the back of his mind where he could contain it.

A low chuckle from Askad drew his attention as the shuttle door was sealed for takeoff. He looked over at the other male.

I can see that being of different species isn't a problem to you or your Leska, Askad sent. *The Link is already working its magic.*

No, not the Link, Kusac replied. *This is ours, the Link only enhances what we have.*

Even better. It'll make life easier for you both.

Her mind seems very similar to ours, Rhian ventured. *Perhaps being with us on the* Khalossa *will not be as large a step as you feared.*

Perhaps. There hasn't been time for us to get to know each other properly yet, replied Kusac, ears flicking briefly.

What's to know? Your minds are Linked, aren't they? You

are aware of each other's feelings and strong surface thoughts; there is no need to know more, chided Askad.

Our Link is stronger than that. I know all her thoughts, I feel all her fears and joys as if they were mine. She's become a part of me now. His attention was on Carrie, and he missed the apprehensive look that the two Sholans exchanged.

Then the problems must be lessened with such close understanding, sent Rhian.

Must they? I know that what she calls pain will hurt me, that what she thinks of as love, so do I, but the rest. . . . His thoughts trailed off into a silence that was filled by the humming of the engines.

* * *

Chyad waited impatiently for Maikoe to open the door.

"The rumors were true," he said, before she had a chance to greet him.

"What rumors?" She moved aside to let him enter.

He nodded cursorily at the others as he stepped over them toward the chair that Kaedoe hastily vacated. "The ones about the Terrans coming on board," he said, turning to face her as she let the door slide closed. "I traveled up in the elevator with one of them, a female."

"What are they like up close?" She returned to her seat.

"They smell strange," he said, perching on the edge of the chair. "Like us but different. Unsettling. This one was either small or a youngling. Her face was flatter than ours and her skin is hairless except for on her head."

"Hm," she said, looking thoughtful as she picked up her mug. "Oh, help yourself to a drink if you want one."

Chyad got up and went to the dispenser.

"I've just been telling the others about my interesting day," she said.

"What did you find out?" he asked, returning to his seat.

"There were Terran collaborators. Mostly their females, many of whom went to work in the domed cities. The female telepath was one of them. I'll bet it was her you saw."

Chyad grunted in disgust.

"Naisha found out that one of the *Sirroki* crew is facing a court-martial for Challenging their own telepath."

"Who?"

"Guynor," said Naisha. "You remember him, surely? He's one of us. He came from Khyaal."

"I saw them taking someone off the shuttle under guard. Thought he looked familiar, but I couldn't place him. Why'd he Challenge the telepath?"

Maikoe put her mug down and sat back in her chair. "He Challenged the female first, but he was stopped, so he Challenged the telepath instead. He went all the way, too: a Death Challenge, no less."

Chyad sat forward, ears pricking with interest. "For what?"

"Because of the female Terran. He accused him of using his talent to make her pair with him."

"And did he?"

Maikoe shrugged. "The trooper I spoke to didn't know any more."

"I don't like it, Maikoe," he said, shaking his head. "Why didn't the Valtegans kill the Terrans? They killed everyone on Khyaal and Szurtha. What was different here on this world? I have a strong feeling that this could be a trap. Allying ourselves with the Terrans could be the worst thing we've ever done. There are bound to be collaborators still on the planet, and having betrayed their own kind once, they won't have any qualms about betraying us."

"This world has fewer people on it," volunteered Khay. "It could simply be that they didn't see the few Terrans here as a threat."

"I don't agree with that," said Ngalu. "If they let them live, there has to be a reason. I think Chyad's right. They could be laying low, ready to signal the Valtegans when they think we're at our most vulnerable."

"There's got to be something we can do," said Maikoe. "There's an official get-together for those of us who lost family in the seventh level mess in an hour's time. Maybe if enough of us protest about this treaty, they'll listen to us."

"Don't hold your breath," said Chyad. "In fact, don't say anything about how we feel if you go to the meeting. If we want to do something about this treaty, then we'll have to do it ourselves, and we can't do anything with the military protectorate looking over our shoulders. Believe me, if they get the faintest notion about how we feel, the protectorate will have us in the brig so fast our feet won't touch the ground."

Naisha looked uncomfortably at the others. "Look, I think we might be overreacting," she said. "We've no proof that these Terrans are in league with the Valtegans. They'd been here for years before our colonies were destroyed. The Terrans could be victims just as our families were."

Chyad took a swig of his drink and put the mug back on the table. "You could be right, Naisha," he conceded. "What we need more than anything else is reliable information. Most of us work in different departments. Let's see what we can find out. Does anyone know any of the *Sirroki*'s crew?" He looked at the other five people in Maikoe's crowded room.

"I've flown with Mito Rralgu before," said Maikoe, "but I wouldn't say I really know her. Khay has, too."

Khay looked over at her in surprise. "I don't remember her," he said.

"Just take my word for it," Maikoe said.

"Well, see if you can get the chance to talk to her. The rest of you, see what gossip you can substantiate. Jakule," he said, turning to the only trooper in the room. "You see what you can find out from any of your cronies running ground patrol duties."

Jakule nodded. "I'll see if I can get down planetside to talk to some of the Terrans," he said.

"Just do as you're asked, Jakule," said Chyad, his tone sharp. "I don't want you drawing attention to yourself. Ask your friends in the smoke den, see what they know. They must have managed to set up some black market deals in new narcotics by now." His tone was full of contempt. "You'd better get on your way if you plan to make that meeting," he said, looking round the rest of them. "I'll be in touch. Remember, say nothing to anyone else at this moment, and let me know if you hear anyone else talking out against the treaty or the Terrans."

He waited till they'd gone before getting up to fetch another mug of c'shar.

"What are you planning?" asked Maikoe, following him with her eyes. "You agreed far too readily with Naisha."

"One or two of the others believe we're right, but they're all easily led," he said. "I meant what I said. If we want to stop this treaty, we'll have to do it ourselves."

"You haven't answered my question. What do you plan to do?" she repeated.

"I'm thinking that the quickest way to stop the talks is for there to be a Terran death on the *Khalossa*."

Maikoe's mouth fell open in shock. "You plan to kill one of them?" Her voice came out almost as a squeak.

Chyad frowned. "These talks aren't going to take long. Can you think of a better or quicker way?"

"Aah, um. I haven't actually been thinking along those lines," she admitted.

"Then start thinking that way now, because I can't see any act more guaranteed to make the Terrans back out of the talks."

"It sounds like a suicide mission, Chyad," she said. "I don't feel like departing this life yet, thank you."

He drained his mug. "I've no intention of getting us caught. That's why I told them to say nothing of how they feel at this meeting. I'll get in touch with you tomorrow. There're one or two people I need to speak to. Try to find out where your friend Mito is and have a word with her. See what she thinks of the Terrans' relations with the Valtegans."

"Why are you so against the treaty?"

"Because I know the Terrans are in league with the Valtegans."

* * *

As the shuttle set down in the landing bay, Carrie woke, yawning and stretching.

"Why are my arms and legs never long enough when I want to stretch them?" she asked, stifling another yawn.

Kusac opened his mouth in a grin, the outer edges of which were beginning to curve, Terran style. "Are you sure you have no Sholan blood, cub?" he asked with a deep purr as he sat up.

Maybe it's catching, she sent with a grin of her own. "Where do we go now?"

"You go with Rhian and Askad for the moment. I'll have to accompany Captain Garras and the others for a debriefing. I'll join you as soon as I can."

The *Sirroki* crew left the shuttle last, accompanied by Rhian and Askad. Carrie hesitated briefly at the top of the ramp, then Kusac's steadying hand was there to reassure her as they stepped out into the chill and glare of the landing bay. As the cold air struck her, she shivered, remembering the last time she'd been in a spaceship. It was as cold here as it had been on the cryo level on the *Eureka*.

This isn't the Eureka, *Carrie,* Kusac sent. *We don't have cryogenics on board. What happened to your mother can't happen here.*

I know, she replied, giving herself a small shake. *I'm all right.*

It was with relief that she noted there was no sign of the Terrans. All around her was the hustle and bustle of the various craft being serviced and refueled. At the far end of the bay, through a group of disembarking Sholans, she saw the retreating backs of Guynor and his guards.

We're holding the others up, he sent gently, his hand tightening on her arm briefly.

She nodded and made her way down the gangway with him. At the bottom of the ramp her meager bag of possessions lay waiting for her.

Vanna sniffed the air dramatically as they all headed across the bay to the main exit.

"Gods, but it's good to be home again!" she said. "The familiar smells of reprocessed air, my own room, a shower, and a comfy bed! Shall we meet up for a meal in an hour or two?" she asked, looking first at Carrie then at Kusac.

"Sounds good," said Carrie.

Kusac nodded.

"Rec level mess?" asked Vanna, as they stopped outside the elevator, waiting for it to return to their level.

Reluctantly, Kusac nodded again.

The doors slid open and they stood back, waiting for those on it to leave. Carrie moved surreptitiously behind Kusac, trying to avoid the openly curious looks.

They piled into the lift, crowding toward the back of it to make space for the pilot and crew of one of the shuttles.

Sensing Carrie's need to orient herself, as well as her slowly rising tide of panic, Kusac leaned down to speak to her. "We docked on the lower level bay, our main one. Now we're going up to the ship level where we change elevators."

"Ship level?"

"The ship has two types of levels. The first thirteen are where our ground forces live and work, the levels above that are the ship levels, where all the officers, pilots and those involved in running the *Khalossa* live."

"Why separate levels? Aren't you allowed to mix?"

"Yes, of course, but apart from the main mess and the concourse where the supply store and the bars are, the troopers tend to stick to themselves. Being ground troops, they don't have a lot in common with us."

The doors opened, and Rhian touched Carrie gently on the arm, drawing her attention. "This is our level," she said.

Panic welled up and she was unable to take that first step away from Kusac's side. She looked up at him.

"I'll join you as soon as I'm finished," he reassured her. "You'll be fine with Rhian and Askad."

"I'll see you later, too. You won't get rid of me that easily!" joked Vanna as Carrie took a deep breath and followed the Leska pair out.

The doors closed and they continued on up to the administrative level.

"Is going to the rec level mess so soon a good idea?" Kusac asked, his voice low. "Wouldn't one of the smaller mess areas be better?"

Vanna shook her head. "She'll have to mix with the rest of the ship's crew soon enough, Kusac. Now is as good a time as any."

"I think it's too soon," he said. "Everything we do is being rushed. Too much too soon," he repeated.

Vanna shrugged. "The decision is yours, Kusac. You know her better."

"That's just it, I don't," he said tersely.

* * *

Though the rest were dismissed after only a few hours of grueling questioning, Kusac's continued presence was requested by the officiating member of the Alien Relations Guild. Half an hour later he made his way to the nearest communicator booth with the official's words still ringing in his ears.

"Have you any idea of the political implications involved in your Link with this human girl? You have? Well, I'm glad to hear it, because I'll want a full explanation of why and how it happened from you and the Telepath Guild within the next few days! Her father is their equivalent of a planetary governor, and I'll wager he'll be none too impressed when he realizes the connotations of your association with his only daughter. Nor will he be overly pleased to discover she's now part of the Sholan Forces because of that association!"

That was the least of what he'd said. Even the memory of the interview made Kusac wince. He keyed in the code for

Rhian's quarters but received a busy signal, then a message from Askad saying Rhian and Carrie were waiting for him in his room.

Cursing, he headed downward. He should have arranged to meet them in their quarters rather than let them assume she was moving in with him. With her human frontier colonist morals . . . Within five minutes he was palming open the door.

Rhian rose as he entered. "You were quicker than we anticipated," she said. "I expected you to be another couple of hours at least. I'll see you both later, once you've settled in."

"Isn't this your room?" asked Carrie, looking from Rhian to Kusac.

"Good gracious, no!" she said with a laugh. "This is a single room. You'll be moved to Leska quarters but probably not till tomorrow."

"I thought I was staying with you," said Carrie, getting up from the chair. "No one said anything about me living with Kusac. I can't do it. I won't." There was a rising note of panic in her voice.

Rhian hesitated, sending a puzzled look in Kusac's direction.

"It's all right, Carrie," said Kusac, remaining where he was by the door. "There's no need for you to stay here. It was just assumed that you would. I'm sure Rhian wouldn't mind you living with them for a few days till we sort things out."

She's not ready for this yet. She needs a little time to get used to our ways, he sent to Rhian. *Can't she stay with you?*

"Of course you can stay with us," said Rhian, "if you're sure that's what you want?"

"Yes," said Carrie, grabbing her bag before the Sholan female changed her mind. Then, as she realized the implications, she looked at Kusac. "It isn't that I don't . . ." she faltered.

Kusac made a dismissive gesture with his hand, tail flicking briefly. "It's all right, cub," he said. "I understand. Stay a few days with Rhian and Askad till you know your own mind better."

"If we're going to meet up with your friends at the mess, we'd better hurry," said Rhian. "I'll have her there in about an hour, Kusac."

Kusac shut the door behind them, tail twitching in annoyance as he walked over to the bathroom. Unfastening his belt, he pressed the seals on his jacket, taking it off and flinging it on his bed in passing. He was tired, mentally and physically tired, of trying to understand Carrie and keep pace with her moods.

He'd studied the Touiban and Chemerian cultures and even worked with them for a while, but that had been on Shola and those aliens had been experienced space travelers. She was not. He'd never been involved in First Contact before. Studied it, yes, but the reality was entirely different, especially when the alien involved was his Leska.

Despite their Link, despite their closeness, every forward step he tried to take with her was like moving through a thornbush. He needed time to think through what he'd picked up about her culture during his stay with her in Valleytown and compare it with the memories he had assimilated from her. Maybe then he could anticipate the problems before they appeared. At the moment they seemed to stumble from one crisis to another and that was no way to build a relationship. Perhaps some time on his own was what he needed, too.

He stepped into the shower, turned on the water, and reached for the soap container. What was Carrie's problem anyway? They both knew how they felt about each other, so why the difficulty over their pairing? Her people took one partner for life and though his didn't, he was offering her the same. She wouldn't lose status among Sholans by being his Leska, quite the opposite. It was considered a mark of favor by the Gods, Vartra in particular, to have a Leska. But an alien Leska? How would that affect his life?

He sighed, stopping that line of thought and letting the hot water sluice over him, washing the soap and grime away and easing some of the tension from his muscles.

His mind began to drift again. Leskas. Now that he was back on board the *Khalossa* he could find out what a Leska link involved. Hurriedly, he switched off the water and, grabbing a towel, headed back into his bedroom. Switching on the desk comm, he keyed in his ident and logged into the Telepath Guild library for their files on Leskas.

He toweled himself absently as he scanned through the general information; then, as the subject divided into detailed topics, he found that certain files were sealed.

Damn! That boded ill. It was even more vital that he have

access to those files. He sat down, weighing the risk of discovery now against the certainty that his identity was going to come out into the open within a few days. Resolutely he punched in his own security code, opening up the remainder of the files. As he read further, he forgot everything else.

A chime sounded from the comm and he blinked, taken by surprise. Reaching out, he keyed in the vidiphone channel; Vanna's face came on the screen.

"Is everything all right, Kusac?" she asked, an ear twitching in concern. "Carrie's already here with us. Are you coming?"

Mentally he gave himself a shake. "Yes. I'll be there in ten minutes," he said. "Sorry."

She nodded. "See you."

The screen blanked, returning him to his files. He closed the channel and switched off, realizing with a shiver that he was still damp.

Picking up the discarded towel, he began to rub himself vigorously but it did nothing to dispel the chill he felt inside.

* * *

Rhian and Askad lived on level 20. Their quarters were the more spacious ones reserved for Leska pairs and boasted a small lounge and two bedrooms. Carrie was shown to a room the same size as Kusac's had been.

"You have the room with the bath," said Rhian, indicating a door to the rear of the bedroom.

"How come you have two bedrooms?" Carrie asked, dumping her bag on the floor.

"This is Askad's room, when he chooses to use it," Rhian said, stuffing the contents of a couple of drawers into a cupboard. "You can use these while you're here. I have the larger room, which we're both using at present."

She moved over to the wardrobe, clearing a space for her unexpected guest there, too. "Why should we want separate rooms?" Rhian turned round to look at Carrie, cocking her head on one side, ears turning in her direction. "Why not? We have our own lives to lead, and occasionally one of us meets someone nice with whom we wish to spend a few days or weeks."

Misinterpreting her startled look, Rhian grinned in the openmouthed Sholan style. "We work for Alien Relations," she said. "I can pick up very little from you telepathically as yet, but the 'Why?' was so loud I think even the untalented could have heard you!"

She handed Carried a thick toweling robe. "Here, go and have a bath. After a month living rough, I'm sure you're feeling itchy and uncomfortable. Admin will catch up with you in a day or two and make sure you're issued with all the essentials. I'll lend you what you need till then." With that she was gone, leaving Carrie to her own devices.

The bathroom was easily navigated, and though there wasn't the time for a long soak, she emerged feeling refreshed and clean for the first time in several weeks. As she toweled her hair, she came back through to the bedroom.

An oval bed dominated the room. Gingerly, she sat on the edge of it, half afraid she would roll into the central bowl-shaped depression. Unbidden, an image of a curled-up sleeping Sholan sprang to mind. The memories from Kusac were blending into hers now as she began to experience life in his culture. It was unsettling.

She sensed Rhian outside the door before she heard the knock.

Carrie opened the door, admitting Rhian and an armful of brightly colored clothes.

"I have some clothes I can lend you until you have the time to buy your own," she said.

"I've brought some things with me, thanks," Carrie said.

"Let me show you anyway," said Rhian, depositing her bundle on the bed. "Certain plain colors denote the guilds and can't be worn by anyone other than guild members. As a telepath, you are entitled to wear purple like us and it would be wise to be seen wearing it from the first so everyone is aware of your status."

"What status?" asked Carrie, an edge to her voice. "Do I have to proclaim to the world I'm part of a Leska team?"

"The color only tells others you are of the Telepath Guild," said Rhian calmly, her tail giving an involuntary twitch. "When the guild grades you, you'll wear a mark of rank on your uniform. Next to it will be the symbol 'L' to show you are part of a Leska pair. It is necessary," she said, her voice rising as Carrie opened her mouth to protest. "Should there be an accident, they'll know that you have a partner nearby who must also be found. You'll need to wear that badge on your leisure clothes, too. All this will be explained to you later, not now."

Carrie subsided, muttering. "Kusac's already told me." She knew Rhian was not the one to argue with over this.

"Look," said the Sholan female, reaching out fleetingly to touch Carrie on the arm. "You are a new species. Do you really think news of your telepathic abilities and your Link to one of our people hasn't already spread throughout the ship? We've been in space for seven months now. It has been boring beyond belief until we arrived here. The events on Keiss, with you and Kusac as the central characters, will be the subject of gossip for a long time to come. What does a small insignia on your collar matter more or less? If you fight all our customs before you understand them, you'll wear yourself out to no purpose. Now, come on," she said persuasively. "You're about to go and enjoy your first real Sholan meal with friends. Let's choose something nice for you to wear."

Despite her protests, Carrie let herself be persuaded into borrowing some of the less brightly colored clothes to augment her rather drab trousers. Those she refused to leave off. Finally she chose a long blue overtunic with panels split to mid thigh and a contrasting undertunic.

"Hm," said Rhian, regarding her critically. "It's longer on you because of your lack of height. Just as well you don't have a tail," she grinned, picking a purple sash off the bed and tying it round Carrie's waist. "That's better," she said. "It matches the edging on the tunic."

"Rhian, we're only meeting up for a meal," said Carrie, exasperated by the fuss the Sholan was making over her clothing.

"Meals, and first impressions, are important," chided the older female. "You will blend in more if you dress like us. Besides, Kusac will like what you're wearing," she said. "In fact, even though your legs are covered, the robe still enhances them enough to interest more males than just him, I'll warrant! Now come, or we'll be late."

As Rhian grabbed her by the wrist and towed her into the lounge where Askad was waiting, Carrie made a low noise of disgust. She felt overdressed by her standards to say the least, and only hoped that Rhian knew what she was doing. Still, both she and her Leska were now wearing casual clothes of a similar style.

* * *

The trip to the mess hadn't been as bad as she'd feared. There had been many curious glances, but they were just that, nothing more.

"Now you see why I suggested you wear Sholan clothes," whispered Rhian as they joined Vanna and Garras at a small table in the quieter area of the large room. "You are just the Terran Telepath to them, and naturally you would be in the company of other telepaths."

Rhian was right. Dressed as she was, she blended in amidst the colorfully dressed Sholans. She was glad to sit down and let the general hubbub of noise wash over her. In the more familiar company of Vanna and Garras—Mito having been unable to come—Carrie began to relax.

Kusac arrived, fur still damp from his shower. He took the seat between Carrie and Rhian.

"Sorry I'm late, I had some business to attend to," he apologized.

"Your first meal back on the *Khalossa* and you didn't even bother changing," scolded Vanna.

"It is a clean jacket. I didn't want to keep you waiting any longer," he said, turning to Carrie, his hand briefly touching hers in greeting.

"It's as well you didn't," said Garras, an amused look on his face. "You might not have had a Leska waiting for you. We've had to fend off at least two hopeful young males."

"Excuse me?" said Carrie, startled.

"Pheromones," stated Vanna. "Jo has to be right."

"Are you trying to tell me . . . ? You mean they weren't just being friendly?"

"They were being very friendly, until we suggested they leave," said Askad with a grin.

"How could they!" exclaimed Carrie. "Surely they know I have a Leska," she faltered, glancing at Kusac.

"There's no need to take offense," said Rhian, puzzled by the human female's reaction. "They were very careful to behave courteously."

"Carrie's people form a bond with only one person," said Kusac quietly.

"Ah, like the Touibans," said Askad.

"No harm was done, Carrie, nor insult intended," said Vanna, leaning forward to pat the girl reassuringly on the hand. "In fact, the opposite."

"I said more than Kusac would find you attractive, didn't I?" said Rhian with a laugh that bordered on a purr.

"Let's get some food," said Kusac abruptly, getting to his feet and waiting for Carrie to join him.

Confused, she reached out for him as she got to her feet. Mentally and physically, he lent a steadying hand.

It's the Sholan way, cub, he sent. *Look at the memories you gained from me when we Linked the first time. You'll understand it better now. Vanna or Rhian can tell you more about our ways. Ask them.*

Are your women often approached like this?

It depends. Often they do the approaching, too. He hesitated. *There are ways I can prevent this happening if you wish.*

I wish! Do it now.

No one will approach you when we're together, he said, his hand tightening on hers. *We'll talk of other ways later.*

Reassured, she moved closer to him as they approached the serving area.

"Did Rhian lend you those clothes?" he asked. "You look really good in them. They suit you."

"She wanted me to wear the Telepath Guild colors."

"Sensible. It gives you the protection of my guild from the first. Now, let's see what they've got to eat today," he said, stopping at a board of glowing cursive script.

The meals she'd shared with them so far hadn't prepared her for the food on the *Khalossa*. The Sholan diet was rich in meats, but the variety of sauces they were either cooked in or served with was extensive. Vegetables and fruit were numerous, too.

After they'd eaten, they made their way from the mess through to the main concourse, the communal leisure area of the *Khalossa*. It was very different from what she had seen of the ship so far. Here was no narrow corridor of identical doorways all painted a utilitarian restful gray.

The first thing that struck Carrie about the concourse, apart from how large and open it was, was the view. The blackness of space lit by a myriad of tiny pinpoints of light gleamed beyond the transparent wall. She could only stand and stare in wonder as the limitless vista called to something deep in her soul.

She reached out, fingers tentatively touching the window. In her mind she could feel Kusac's gentle amusement.

This is why you and I left our home, he sent, his hand closing on her shoulder. *A new life and new worlds among the stars.*

It's so beautiful, I had no idea!

How could you, tied to one world? He gestured with his other hand toward the stars. *That's where the future lies, and we're part of it.*

Yes, she sighed, laying both palms against the cool surface. *No barriers to stop us, just the vastness of space before us. I don't think I could bear to leave it.*

"I don't want to hurry you," said Vanna's voice from behind them, "but you've been starstruck now for the last ten minutes! Do you think we could leave now? I'd rather like to get a drink."

"I'm sorry, Vanna," said Carrie, turning around. "It's just so beautiful!"

"I gathered you were somewhat impressed by it when your eyes glazed over and you started stalking across the concourse. It was as if nothing else existed, the way you were prepared to walk through anyone in your way!"

"I didn't," said Carrie aghast, looking round in embarrassment. Sholans sitting around the tables by the window were regarding their little group with indulgent amusement.

Put your shield up, cub, came Kusac's warning. *They aren't laughing at you, they're just enjoying your pleasure. It reminds them of their first time in space.*

Carrie concentrated on building a mental barrier as they moved off toward one of the doorways with tables and chairs outside it.

"Where are we?" she asked.

"This is called the concourse," said Garras. "Over there are the main stores for both ship levels. That's where we get all the day-to-day essentials like brushes, soap—stuff like that."

"Over there," said Vanna, pointing to the opposite side, "that's where you get the few luxury items that the *Khalossa* carries. Hair decorations, cosmetics, some leisure clothes, snack foods—things that make life a little more varied on a starship like this."

"In the center they sell memory cubes for the comms and the notepads, ones with books on them," said Kusac.

"Books? What kind of books?"

"Whatever you want," said Vanna. "Some are stories told

by our leading storytellers, others you read yourself. You can get them on any subject you want. Like the clothing, if they haven't got it in, they can order it for delivery on the next supply ship."

"Would you like to go into the store?" asked Rhian.

"No, thanks," she said, moving closer to Kusac as she became aware that she was the focus of many curious looks. Suddenly the concourse seemed full of people. A headache was building and all she wanted to do was sit down in a quiet area away from the noise and bustle.

Remember your shield, cub, sent Kusac, picking up her distress.

As she strengthened her barrier again, the headache began to fade and the noise seemed to lessen.

"It's shift change," said Vanna. "That's why it's gotten so busy. Let's get settled before all the seats are gone."

The bar was not dissimilar to her father's, having a long counter with several tall stools placed beside it as well as the surrounding tables and chairs. They chose to sit at the counter, the six of them forming a little knot at one end. Perhaps because of the semifamiliar surroundings, or perhaps because of the company, she finally found herself slipping back into the easier relationship she'd had with Kusac before the raid on the Valtegan base. She'd found a referent to counter the culture shock that had suddenly begun to hit her.

Since leaving Rhian's and Askad's quarters, she'd been watching the Sholans, trying to see them as a people now that she had the opportunity. They were gregarious, liking to be in groups rather than couples. As Vanna and Kusac had said, there were far more males than females but that didn't stop their clothing from being on the flamboyant side. Her outfit was nothing spectacular compared to some.

They were also a highly tactile species, as she had already guessed. Within their groups, they frequently touched their partners or friends. The exceptions were her telepath companions. She'd already picked up Rhian's and Askad's reluctance to touch anyone not of their guild, but they showed their affection for their friends in the featherlight touch of fingers against their cheeks.

The same was true with Kusac, though tonight he touched no one but her, his hand straying frequently to where hers lay on the counter. His need to touch her, as if for reassurance she was there—not to mention her growing reciprocal need—was no more than others were doing.

She sat quietly, sipping the rather heady drink she'd been given and listened to them discussing the reports they were due to hand in to the Admin office in the morning. She leaned against Kusac, pleased when he put an arm around her shoulders, his fingertips gently stroking her neck for a moment or two.

"Kusac, what happens when you've to go back to work?" she asked. "What do I do? Come to think of it, what do you do?"

"We're on leave for the moment," he said. "After what we went through on Keiss, we've been given ten days off."

"You've got longer," said Askad. "New Leska pairs get an extra five days, fifteen in all, so as to get to know their partner better. During that time they meet with their Tutor to assess their working capabilities. Once that's been done, then they're reassigned to appropriate duties. I presume the same will happen with you."

"What do telepaths do on the *Khalossa?* What do you do?"

"I don't so much do, as work with people and advise them about what needs doing," he said vaguely, keeping his eyes turned away from Rhian and Askad.

"Yes, what have you been doing, Kusac?" asked Rhian, her tone a little sharp. "You're wearing a grade five badge, but I'll warrant that isn't your true level."

"It was suggested that I needed the experience, so I've been working with the military protectorate in the troop levels. You know the sort of thing," he said. "Assessing situations and advising what level of telepath is needed to defuse any potential trouble. Glorified crowd control."

"Hm," said Rhian, obviously not convinced. "It'll be interesting to see what you're doing three weeks from now."

"You want to know what we do," said Vanna from across the curve of the bartop. "Well, I'm up in the medical section taking my turn in the wards with any of the injured or ill, or I'm in the labs running tests. I was included on the *Sirroki* because it was on a three-month mission, and they needed a medic on board."

"I pilot scouters," said Garras. "Normally I'd be plying the trade routes for my clan, but I was drafted in to fly the scouters doing reconnaissance and survey work. Again, I'll be on leave for the next few days. After that, who knows what they'll find for me to do?"

"It's not exactly leave," said Vanna. "We've still to be properly debriefed. AlRel will want to talk to us, then they'll want us to have medicals. The Telepathic Medics have scheduled a session for you tomorrow morning, Carrie. It won't be too much of an ordeal as they've been told you're a healer. That means no psych profiles and a minimal physical examination. Rhian and I will be with you, so you won't have to go through it alone," she reassured her. She looked over at Kusac. "Your session is in the afternoon."

"Are they afraid I'm carrying some strange germs or something?" asked Carrie.

"No, of course not," she laughed. "We all went through decontam as we came off the shuttle. You're a new species, they want some tissue and blood samples so they can run their batteries of tests. If you take ill, they have to know how you'll respond to our drugs. They also need to key your physiology into the computers so we know how to reproduce your blood, plasma—all those things."

Underlying Vanna's voice, Carrie was aware of the sound of Terrans coming into the bar.

"Why do they want to see me?" asked Kusac.

"They don't, I do," said Vanna. "I'm curious to see if there have been any chemical changes in your brain because of your Link. And I want to check on your leg wound. The bandage needs changing."

Kusac frowned thoughtfully.

Carrie meanwhile had leaned back to glance quickly toward the door. It was Skai and the rest of the Terran party. She ducked back against Kusac, trying to make herself invisible in the faint hope they wouldn't recognize her. Several of the Sholan women she'd seen wore their hair long.

Skai spotted Vanna and called out a friendly greeting just as Kusac picked up Carrie's distress.

"I hear there's a Terran woman on board," said a loud voice, "keeping company with one of your males."

Kusac, leaning down toward Carrie, froze.

"That's him," said Lawson, the owner of the voice as he walked over toward them. "The telepath. Found one of your own kind instead, eh?" His ribald laugh died as Kusac turned to face him, exposing Carrie.

"So they were right," Lawson continued, his voice low

and full of venom. "You're the one from Geshader. Bloody little no-good tramp!"

Kusac began to snarl, lips pulled back to expose his large and deadly canines. "How dare you talk to my Leska like that."

Skai tried to pull him back. "Leave it, Lawson. You met her sister, not Carrie."

"So?" said the man belligerently, pulling away. "Some bloody family they are! Both of them no better than ..."

"Shut up, Lawson!" said Anders, cutting him short and trying to step between him and Kusac. "You've had too much to drink. Leave them be, they aren't harming anyone. It's none of your business."

Carrie moved back, trying frantically to get off her stool. Fear and anger warred in her in equal proportions, and she knew Kusac could feel it.

"No, I won't shut up," said Lawson, staggering slightly as he pulled free of Skai for the second time. "I want to know why she keeps screwing aliens! Is she a pervert or something?"

Skai backed off, trying to catch Carrie's eye, but it was Vanna who was staring at him.

"Nothing to do with me, honestly," he said, spreading his arms.

Anders grabbed for Lawson as the fourth member of their group ran to help. Together they tried to haul him back toward the door.

As Kusac leaped off his stool, Carrie lost her balance and tumbled off to be caught by Garras. She was thrust unceremoniously toward Vanna as he left the bar to circle round the side of the angry group.

Slowly Kusac padded over to where Anders and Perry had managed to haul Lawson. He was in a half crouch, tail lashing, ears so flat and to the side they were almost lost against his black fur. The hair across his neck and shoulders was raised and from his narrowed eyes, the pupils glowed red.

Carrie sensed Lawson through Kusac's huntersight. He had focused on his prey with the concentration and single-mindedness of a telepath. His need to kill this ... person ... for such a mortal insult was paramount.

"Garras!" Carrie called out frantically. "For God's sake, stop him! He's Hunting!"

Kusac stood before the human, trying to force back the

tide of anger racing through his blood. At his sides his hands clenched, fresh pain shooting through his already injured palms, but by doing that he managed to keep his claws retracted. He'd had enough of Terran bigotry.

Lawson, with the strength of the drunk, pulled free of the two men and crouched down in a parody of Kusac's stance. The large man spread his arms. "Come on, kitty. What're you going to do, eh?"

"He'll do nothing," sneered Norris, who till now had kept out of it. "He's got no guts, he's only a Telepath! They can't fight. Stupid bitch couldn't even choose a real cat!"

The angry group had spread to the center of the room by now. Around them, the Sholans were hurriedly leaping out of the way, one or two of the braver souls hauling the nearest tables clear.

Instinct suddenly took over and Kusac lashed out at Lawson's head. The human went sprawling, crashing into Anders, then staggering to a halt against a table.

Kusac leaped after him only to find Garras there first. The Captain pushed Kusac back, then caught the blow intended for the telepath in a fist twice the size of Lawson's. With his other fist he landed a blow of his own, hitting the Terran on the jaw and felling him like a male rhakla. The two Sholans exchanged a brief glance, then turned to face the other Terrans.

"First bar brawl?" Garras asked Kusac with humor, keeping his eyes on their opponents. "Enjoy it, just get out of the hunter/kill mode," he growled, landing Kusac a stinging blow across the ears.

"Hey!" said Kusac, shaking his head and blinking, but it had had the desired effect. The killing urge had gone. Perversely, he wished it hadn't.

Skai and Anders, hands held up at shoulder level to show their neutral state, were backing off, leaving Perry and Norris. Hurriedly, Perry joined them.

Likewise, Garras moved away from Kusac.

"Well, now," Norris drawled, looking round. "Looks like it's just you and me."

Kusac's mind was suddenly swamped by Carrie's memories of his last fight, the Death Challenge that Guynor had called. Mentally he called Rhian, telling her to get Carrie out of there and back to their quarters, then he blanked his Leska out.

Norris took advantage of his apparent hesitation and came barreling in, determined to get as close as possible before the deadly claws could get him.

The first blow caught Kusac in the stomach, winding him and causing him to double up. This gave Norris the opportunity to land a couple of punches before Kusac was able to recover enough to retaliate.

Shoving him backward, Kusac swung at the Terran's head but missed and hit him a glancing blow on the shoulder instead. His hand drew back ready to try again, then he was roughly seized from behind.

"Enough!" a voice bellowed in his ear as his arms were pulled backward and pinned behind him. He remained still as the security personnel pounced on Norris, Garras, and the Terrans.

Oblivious to his own situation, Kusac sent again to Rhian, demanding to know if they had gotten clear before security arrived.

We're clear and on our way home, she replied.

* * *

They were hauled before Sub-Commander Kolem, who didn't take kindly to the incident. After a blistering dressing-down to Sholans and Terrans alike—relayed to the latter group by the senior telepath translator on duty—they were dismissed. The Terrans, in the custody of two security guards, were escorted to their quarters to remain there until the following day. Garras and Kusac remained behind.

"Just what the hell do you think you're doing?" demanded Sub-Commander Kolem. "You were the ones who contacted these people first, the ones who gave them an impression—Vartra help us!—of all Sholans! You lived with them, fought for them, made a trade agreement with them," his eyes pinned Garras at this, "started peace negotiations with them, and now you engage them in a barroom brawl!"

Garras flinched from the glare, ears lowering.

Kolem got to his feet and began pacing, tail flicking from side to side in barely suppressed fury. "Never in all my years in the Forces have I had to discipline a ship's Captain or a telepath for brawling. What in hell am I supposed to do with you?" he demanded of Kusac.

Silence.

"Are you listening to me?"

Kusac nodded, eyes beginning to glaze noticeably.

Kolem grunted and began pacing again. "We've barely begun negotiations with Hamilton, and your Link to his daughter has weakened our position. He isn't yet aware of the implications of that bond, but he's damned suspicious and displeased about it. Your actions today could have jeopardized the treaty before it's even been drafted!" He stopped in front of Kusac again. "With your background, there is no excuse for this kind of behavior. Of all people, I should have been able to rely on you to keep the peace!"

Angrily, he returned to his desk. "Garras, brawling like a junior officer is not what I expect from a Captain of your seniority, even if you have been drafted in from the Merchants. Your leave is canceled. You'll return to duty on your next scheduled shift. Till then you're confined to your quarters," he snapped.

"Sub-Commander," interrupted Adjutant Myak, moving forward to catch Kusac as he began to sway. "His Leska is in severe distress. She's broadcasting on a wide band, every telepath will be picking her up. Look at him," he said as Kusac gratefully leaned against him. "He's taking little of this in because of her mental state."

Kolem made an exasperated noise. "Get him out of here! See he joins her. And fetch the medic, the one who was with them on Keiss. I want that Terran female calmed down now before the Telepath Guild starts its complaints! Kusac's confined to quarters until further notice."

"Yes, sir," said Myak, assisting Kusac through to the outer office. "I'll see to it personally."

When Garras left, Kolem turned to Draz, head of Security. "What was the fracas about?"

"Species prejudice from two of the Terrans, sir. Specifically comments relating to the nature of the relationship between our crewman and the human female."

"Who was responsible for the Terrans' orientation program? They should have picked up those sort of attitudes then and dealt with them so that this sort of situation couldn't occur!"

"Apparently it hasn't taken place yet, sir. It's scheduled for the sixth hour tomorrow. Unfortunately, I was not informed of this, or I would have ordered that the Terrans be confined to their quarters till then."

"Find out who's responsible. I'll nail their hides to the

wall," growled Kolem, flinging himself into his seat. "Right now the fate of this sector of space hangs in the balance. We must secure this treaty, or the Alliance remains vulnerable to further Valtegan attacks. If anything happens to Kusac or his Leska, we could have more trouble than you or I could imagine, both from Shola and from Keiss, and we're stuck right in the middle of it."

He shook his head. "A telepath with an alien Leska, a telepath who now initiates fights! The Commander is just going to love this." He sighed. "You'd better prepare a report for Commander Raguul as soon as possible. See that someone from your department escorts Kusac and his Leska to meals until we've transferred them to Leska quarters. At least he has her company."

"Apparently not, sir. My people tell me that she's staying with the Leska pair, Rhian and Askad."

Kolem lifted an eyebrow in surprise. "I presume the guild is aware of this?"

"Yes, sir. They have their own people watching them."

"Poor devils. They can't make a move without someone seeing it. Well, I suppose it's the price they have to pay for their Link."

"Yes, sir," said Draz dubiously.

"Contact the guild anyway, Draz. I want them to find out why I suddenly have a territorial male telepath on my crew. Commander Raguul will shortly be asking me the same question, and I want to have an answer for him."

"Yes, sir."

* * *

Vanna was leaving as Kusac arrived with Myak. "I was coming to look for you," she said to him. "I'll take care of him, Lieutenant, if you have no objections?"

"Certainly, Physician Kijishi," said Myak, disentangling himself from Kusac's arm and letting her take his weight.

Vanna raised an eye ridge at the Lieutenant, ears swiveling toward him as she wrapped an arm round Kusac's waist.

"Commander Raguul would like to see you as soon as is convenient," Myak said quietly to her before he left.

When he'd gone, Kusac pulled himself upright, leaning against the door frame. "Promotion?" he asked tiredly.

"And how," said Vanna. "I wonder what the cost is. That sort of promotion doesn't come cheap. Never mind that. I've given Carrie a suppressant. It should take full effect in about fifteen or so minutes. Can you cope for now, or do you need one, too?"

He shook his head. "I'll manage," he said. "It's only making me light-headed now. The nausea's stopped." He started to move slowly toward the doors at the far end of the room. "Which room is she in?"

"On the right. I'll wait for you," she said, her professional eye picking up the tinge of white that meant his nictitating lids were showing at the edges of his eyes.

So great was the turmoil in her mind that Carrie remained unaware of his presence until he sat down on the bed beside her.

As she turned round, he took her hands in his.

It's all right. I'm here and safe, and so are you, he sent.

"I've had enough, Kusac," she said. "I can't take any more of this reaction to us. When we're alone like this, it's fine, we're all that matters. With others around . . ." Her shoulders lifted in a shrug. "Your people are all right. It's mine that are the problem." A tear ran down her cheek.

"Don't cry, cub," he said, tilting her chin to wipe the tear away. "The Terrans won't be on board for long. I'll make sure we stay away from them if you prefer." His hand moved to the back of her neck, gently soothing the tight muscles, thinking relaxation into her body. He could feel the drug beginning to work as her thoughts became gradually weaker.

"Can't you see that it shouldn't have to be like this?" she said. "Why can't they accept that we have a loving friendship and just leave us alone?"

There was an edge of hysteria to her voice that troubled him.

"A little more than a friendship," he murmured, as his eyes were unconsciously drawn to her throat. Long and slender, it was a neck that many a Sholan female would kill for. He caught himself and looked back to her face.

Another tear, quickly followed by a third, was falling.

"They won't let us have anything, Kusac," she said. "All we really have is this damned link. I wish it had never happened!"

"This isn't like you, cub," he said, encircling her in his arms and drawing her close. "I know you don't really mean that. We have the Link, yes, but we also have each other."

He nuzzled her chin upward, this time licking her tears away.

He felt her stiffen slightly; then, as he continued to lick her cheek, she relaxed. Her hands came up to rest on his arms and her fingertips began to push through the thick pile of his fur seeking the skin beneath.

He kissed her, letting his feelings for her come to the surface of his mind, slowly at first, waiting till she accepted them. This time, for a wonder, she did and he felt her mind begin to quiet and respond to him.

He let his hand stray across her arm, then down her back to her thigh, enjoying the clean muscular feel of her limbs. Differences between their species there were, but she possessed many of the qualities Sholan males looked for in their women.

The compulsion born of their Link had built so gradually in him this time that only now did he realize it was there. He felt it echoed in her as hesitantly her fingers searched for the seal on his jacket. His hand guided her as she opened it, then as she laid her head against his chest, he began to untie the sash around her tunic.

Cautiously, he slid his hand across the bare skin of her back. Perhaps finally they could resolve the physical side of their Link.

She froze, her mind losing its softness and becoming brittle again as she pulled back from him, a look of panic on her face.

Kusac released her instantly. "What is it? What's wrong?"

"This isn't us, Kusac, it's the damned link," she said, a catch in her voice as she continued to back away from him. "I won't be driven by this compulsion!"

"You've got it confused, cub," he said, forcing himself to remain calm. "The compulsion only enhances what we feel for each other. If our emotions weren't involved, there would be no worrying over whether what we feel is us or the Link. Pairing is only the mechanism that brings Leskas close enough so they can work as a bonded team. It's part of their working relationship. You're worrying over something that is too small to matter."

"It's important to me," she said, fetching up against the wall at the head of the bed. "I've lived too long with other people's illusions of what I am and what I should be. I want to know what's real for me."

She pulled her legs up, wrapping her arms protectively round them. "My head is full of memories that aren't mine, Kusac. They're yours, yet they feel as real to me as if I'd lived them. Maybe it's easier for you with your training, but that coupled with being always aware of what you're thinking and doing means I'm losing myself and becoming only 'us,' and it frightens me!"

"That's because the Link is still incomplete, Carrie," he said. "We need to pair to make it complete, and then it will be easier, I promise."

"How can you know?" she demanded. "You've never had a Leska before."

"I checked it out in the guild's files," he said.

"Theory! What do they know about us or our link? I'm an alien, or hadn't you noticed?" she said caustically.

"I'd noticed," he said, suppressing his anger. "Were you Sholan, we wouldn't be having this discussion. There are no guarantees, Carrie, you know that. I can only tell you what is known about Leska Links."

He sighed and got to his feet. "This is getting us nowhere. We can't go on like this, Leska. I can't cope with any more of this, it's too painful for both of us. You know what I feel for you and you know what I have to offer. If you want me, you come. You've got four days in which to decide; I can't give you any longer. If your answer is no, then somehow I'll find a way to break the Link. It should be possible since, as you reminded me, you're an alien, not a Sholan."

Stopping at the door to fasten his jacket, he turned back to her. "You aren't a youngling, Carrie. You're a grown female among your own kind. Find out what your heart wants, what is really important to you, not what your intellect says should be. Just see you don't leave it too long, or I may not be there for you when you finally make your decision."

As he closed the door behind him, Vanna looked up.

"Where're Rhian and Askad?" he asked.

"In the other room, keeping out of the way of Carrie's broadcast. How is she? Even with the slight differences in her system the drug should have taken effect by now."

"The drug's working. I can feel her presence in my mind, but that's all. She's emotionally overwrought at the moment, Vanna. I think it best she remains here tonight. Rhian has agreed," he said, making his way across the room toward her.

"What's wrong?" she asked sharply, getting to her feet as she saw the set of his ears.

"Nothing. I'm just tired, that's all."

"I don't believe that for a moment," she said, reaching up to touch his cheek. "You've got a nasty bruise coming there. Let me see to it."

He pulled away from her, going to the door. "I'm fine. Look, I've got to go. I'm confined to quarters because of the fight." He touched the door sensor, waiting for it to open. "I'll see you later."

"I'm finished here," she said, following him. "Don't forget that appointment at the medical section tomorrow afternoon."

* * *

Carrie sat looking bleakly at the door. Well, she'd gotten what she'd asked for. Her mind was quiet, just an awareness of a faint pressure that was Kusac, none of his thoughts. He'd given her the time and space that she'd asked for.

She sat there, going over in her mind what he'd said about the link. Unbidden, memories of time spent studying and practicing linking in to medics, to Chemerians and Touibans all came flooding in, demanding to be sorted and relearned by her. Whatever she chose, there would always be Kusac's memories. Her headache began to return as, panicking, she fought to control them, to push them down to a level where they wouldn't intrude on her consciousness.

". . . the Link is still incomplete." She heard the echo of his voice as finally she succeeded, knowing it was only a temporary victory. Instinctively, she reached for him but met only solitude and the pain flaring behind her eyes.

Chapter 2

Brother Dzaka had taken the seat reserved for him in the front row. Rhuso, one of the Telepath Guild tutors, had requested that he attend this unofficial gathering of those who'd lost clansfolk on the colony worlds of Khyaal and Szurtha. Already the meeting had given him cause for disquiet. Despite the counseling that had been given to all the relatives of those who had died, this small group of about twenty people had still not come to terms with their loss. The nuances of feelings he was experiencing from some of those gathered in the room were causing him concern.

Traditionally, only telepaths could become priests, but few telepaths entered the priesthood and those who did, didn't want to serve in the Forces. Consequently, the religious needs of the ships were often met by lay brothers like himself. A member of the Brotherhood of Vartra, Sub-Guild of the Warrior's, his position on the ship not to mention in society, was as ambiguous as the God Vartra Himself. Patron of both the Warrior and the Telepath Guilds, Vartra represented the ability of the warrior to fight for peace, then, like the telepaths, lay aside his weapons as one unable to fight. Theologians had argued for centuries as to whether the God was depicted laying his weapons down, or had halted in the act of picking them up. Dzaka had never been able to decide.

Unbidden, the God's image came to his mind's eye as powerfully as if he stood before the massive carved statue in the Brotherhood's temple.

Gentle laughter echoed in his mind. He knew it well, and the voice that spoke to him.

Well, Dzakayini—little-one-brought-in-from-the-cold! Here you are again. You'll find no answer in staring at my image: look within yourself, that is where your harmony lies!

The laughter and the image faded, leaving him sitting there shaking because of the rebuke. It was no God-Vision and he knew it, but just the same ... Lieutenant Nuada was trying to field questions from several angry individuals.

"I want to know why we haven't been given any real details concerning what happened," a young trooper was saying. "It's the inalienable right of surviving Clan members to be allowed to bury their relatives. We've been denied that right and given no concrete reasons for it! There might even be survivors!"

"There were no survivors, and you've been told that it would be impossible to identify the dead," said Nuada. "The devastation was global. There was no warning. People died where they were—in the streets, in their homes, at work."

"If they died in their homes, then all I need to do is go to my Clan's land. I'm not asking a lot, only that I be allowed to at least visit my home and bury my dead."

Dzaka looked at the trooper. Still a youngling, barely into adulthood. Tears of frustration and loss were trickling down the sides of his nose.

"I'm afraid that's impossible," began the Lieutenant. Dzaka stood up and turned round to face the room of angry and grieving Sholans.

"You feel angry and cheated because you haven't been given enough information, do you? You can't believe that your Clans are gone, your loved ones dead? 'But they were there yesterday,' I hear you say. 'How can they be gone?' " He stopped, aware that his own voice was rising in anger, an anger that should not be directed at his own people.

"You need to see for yourself that there is no chance of survivors," he said quietly, looking round the stunned faces of the young trainees and the few older career people. "I can understand, but thank the Gods that you haven't seen it for yourselves. You want facts? Then I'll give them to you, and when you wake in the night sweating and crying out for your loved ones, don't curse me for telling you!" He stopped to catch his breath.

"Brother Dzaka, I don't think ..." began Nuada.

"No, you don't think," said Dzaka. "They need to know. We of the Brotherhood were called in from the first when the scale of the ... destruction ... was realized. It was as Nuada said, bodies everywhere. They lay where they'd fallen—on the streets, in the stores, in the still smoldering wrecks of vehicles gone out of control. There was no dignity in their deaths. They lay as if an angry giant had finished his game and had tossed his toy people away." He stopped, noticing that the younger ones had their ears laid back in distress. Well, they were getting what they'd demanded.

"Some buildings had been hit by falling vehicles and were still blazing when we landed. The stench of burning flesh and decomposing bodies filled the air and made us retch." He looked round the room again, picking out the previously vociferous youngster.

"But do you know what really brought the devastation home to us?" he asked, pinning the youngling to his seat with a look. "The silence. Not a bird, not an insect. Nothing. However they were killed, it was immediate and without warning. The only life left on those two worlds was microscopic—bacteria. No higher life survived, and we have no idea how it was done."

"That's classified, Brother Dzaka," said Lieutenant Nuada sharply.

Dzaka turned round. "Who the hell are they going to tell, Nuada?" he demanded. "Each other? Rumor is doing more harm." He turned back to his silent audience.

"We can't tell how it was done because of the damage caused by the deaths. It could have been nerve gas that dissipated within a few hours. It could have been an air attack—we just can't tell yet."

"What's being done to discover the cause?" asked a grizzled officer wearing the green flash of the Communications Guild on his shoulder.

"All the samples we needed were taken during our first, and last, visit. There were a hundred teams working at different locations on each planet," said Dzaka. "The samples are still being analyzed back on Nijidi, the orbiting science lab."

"What is being done about ... seeing to the dead?" asked one of the young females, her voice barely audible.

Dzaka glanced at Nuada.

"There's no point in withholding that information from them since you've told them everything else," the Lieutenant said resignedly.

"A network of large incendiary devices was placed on each world. We detonated them simultaneously. When the global fires finally cease, we may be able to start reseeding the two worlds with life-forms from Shola and our remaining colony, Khoma."

"That could take hundreds of years!" exclaimed someone.

"There's no rush," said Nuada dryly. "We haven't the population now to warrant another colony."

There was a stunned silence as this last fact was absorbed. Now they finally understood that two worlds and millions of inhabitants had really died.

"I pray that now you can let your loved ones go," said Dzaka. "They have been cremated as custom demands, and, believe me, prayers were said. The manner of their deaths may have been ignoble, an act of cowardice against them by an enemy unwilling to face a fair fight, but we sent them to the Gods with all the honors of Warriors. Their names and Clans are listed in the Hall of Remembrance in the Governor's palace. Already the work of ensuring that no Clan is allowed to die out has begun. Relatives are being contacted—they'll be in touch with you soon—and, where possible, Clan Leaders are being appointed from the main family line. If this isn't possible, the nearest relative will be appointed. When the time is right for expansion, your Clans will be offered prime places on new worlds. This information will be posted to the comms of all the families involved within the next few days. There is no more we can do, except mourn with you."

There was nothing more to say, and within a couple of minutes the room had emptied.

Dzaka sat down heavily. His imagination and memory were too strong for his own good. While he spoke, he had been reliving the scenes on Khyaal. They would remain with him forever because he'd lost his own family on Szurtha.

At length, Nuada broke the silence. "I'll have to report this to the Commander."

"So report me," he said tiredly. "I don't really care. The only way to convince them their clansfolk were dead was to tell them. What I saw made me grateful that I didn't have to visit Szurtha."

"Don't think me unsympathetic," said the other, his tone gentle. "I have no option, you know that."

Dzaka nodded. "I was asked to close the matter as quickly as possible. I think I've done that. I'd be surprised if they tell anyone else what they heard tonight. No one in their right mind would wish to cause another that much grief. I still wake in the dead of night, and it's been four months now."

Nnya, I should have been with you, I should have been there! The ache of her loss welled up again. He would give his life just to see her, touch her, one more time. Yes, he knew how those others felt.

* * *

"Commander Vroozoi," said Raguul, keeping his temper in check. "I'm glad you could spare the time to talk to me."

"One of the disadvantages of command," said Vroozoi. "Never enough time, as you'll find out one day, eh, Raguul?" His mouth opened in an expansive, toothy smile. "Now, what was your problem?"

With a supreme effort of willpower, Raguul managed to keep his ears from moving. *Damn you,* he thought angrily. *You're my problem!*

"Commander, I believe you have another Valtegan captive," he said. "When can I expect him to be sent to the *Khalossa* for questioning?"

"My dear fellow, what makes you think he'll be coming over to you for questioning?" Vroozoi arched an eye ridge in surprise.

"Questioning the captives is my province," Raguul replied stiffly. "Chief Commander Chuz made that clear to me."

"He did?" Vroozoi managed to convey extreme surprise. "Then once the planet is considered secure, I'll make sure any captives are conveyed directly to you. At the moment, with everybody still on maximum alert, they are naturally being brought here since the craft conveying them off-planet are from the *Cheku*."

"Then when will I get an opportunity to interrogate your prisoner?"

Vroozoi looked regretfully out of the screen at Raguul. "I'm afraid that won't be possible, Commander Raguul. Once again the prisoner has decided that suicide is a preferable option to captivity."

"That's the third one dead in as many days," said Raguul, his voice tight with suppressed anger he could no longer completely contain. "Perhaps your interrogators are a little overenthusiastic?"

Vroozoi frowned. "Let me be sure I've got you right, Raguul. Are you inferring my officers are to blame?"

"Far from it, Commander," Raguul said through gritted teeth. He hated having to stalk around this male, watching what he said. "After all, your officers aren't trained in the diplomatic niceties as mine are. As you said, each to his own."

"I hear the treaty talks are hitting a few problems, and then there's your rogue telepath and his human Leska," Vroozoi drawled, absently arching his hands so his clawtips touched. "Perhaps you'd do better to solve your diplomatic problems and leave the other matters to me." In one fluid move, he reached forward and blanked the screen.

"Damn him!" swore Raguul, his fist thumping the desk. "That bastard isn't going to let me forget about the Aldatan cub! How in all the hells am I supposed to do my job when Vroozoi blocks me at every opportunity?"

"Commander, ignore him," said Myak soothingly, bringing over a mug of c'shar and putting it down in front of him. "He's trying to get you wound up."

Raguul growled deep in his throat before taking a drink. "I know what he's up to. He thinks if he interrogates the Valtegan captives, he'll be the one to get the information High Command wants. He's after another promotion!"

"I'm sure you're right, sir," said Myak, moving round to sort the papers on his Commander's desk. "May I suggest that a call to Alien Relations on Shola might expedite the situation? A suggestion that the true situation on Keiss is well under control may also help, shall we say, facilitate the removal of the *Cheku* and Fleet Commander Vroozoi back to sector eleven."

Raguul looked sideways at Myak. "Perhaps you'd like to make that call."

Myak's ears flicked backward, then righted themselves. "Ah, yes. Perhaps a message from our AlRel department would be more appropriate," he said hurriedly. "Shall I see to it, Commander?"

"Yes. As soon as possible."

A klaxon began to blare. "All personnel to battle stations. Commander Raguul to the bridge. All personnel to battle stations."

"What the hell . . . ?" muttered Raguul, pushing his chair back and heading for the door at a run.

* * *

For three days they'd lain silent amongst the debris surrounding the dead planet on the outermost reaches of Keiss' solar system. Their craft the *M'ijikk,* wasn't large, certainly not up to defending itself against either of the two starships that had suddenly arrived several days ago.

M'ezozakk had the four prisoners dragged up to the command room to look at the alien craft, hoping by their reactions to discover if they were of the same species. They certainly didn't belong to the pale humans. They weren't capable of that level of technology. He thought he'd seen a spark of recognition in the eyes of one of them, but it had quickly died when he'd tried to question them.

Communicating with them was almost impossible. They'd refused food and drink until he'd ordered them force-fed; they were prepared to die rather than talk. These captives were his one edge over his enemies, and he had to have them beaten almost senseless to get a sound out of them. They lay chained in the Shrine Room, as much for their own safety as from his sense of foreboding regarding them. His men, like all those from the fighting class, were riddled with superstitious fears and saw these furred captives as demons incarnate, hating them with an almost psychotic fury.

Born to the leading tribe on M'Zull, he knew better. But even he, who normally only paid the barest courtesy demanded to the priests, had found his footsteps leading him to the Shrine. Like the priests, he had looked to the dark shape they revered for answers. None had been forthcoming. The dull faces of the cuboid remained as enigmatic as ever, its surface neither absorbing nor reflecting light, belonging neither to this world nor the next.

As he left, he nudged the nearest captive with his toe. It moved slightly, curling tighter round itself. On the filthy uniform jacket, he could see the flash of purple on the shoulder that told him it was one of the two small ones—females, the priests said. What kind of species let their females walk freely outside the nest? They were as contemptible as the humans, deserving of the sickly hatchlings they were bound to produce when allowed to breed without check.

Irritated, he kicked it this time, sending it sprawling.

A priest, all but concealed beneath his blood-red robes, glided unctuously forward, "General, the creature is chained. Do you wish me to release it?"

M'ezozakk leaned down and picked the creature up by the

scruff of the neck, lifting her clear of the floor. A faint mewl escaped her as she tried to reach behind her to the hand gripping her neck.

"Yes," he snapped, raising his head crest in anger. "I'll try one more time to get sense out of it!" He set his captive's feet on the ground, ignoring the hands that clutched at his arm for support.

The priest approached the General, bowing low, and reached out to the collar round the captive's neck. Using his long nonretractable claws, he punched a combination into the lock that held the end of the chain. Released, it fell heavily to the deck floor.

Transferring his grip to the collar, M'ezozakk dragged the creature along the corridor to the command center.

They'd been running on emergency power till now, feeding just enough to the view screens every few hours so that they could monitor the situation around Keiss. His current predicament was unenviable, but at least he'd survived so far. Had his ship not been called away from this sector, he'd have been a sitting target when this enemy fleet had arrived.

He flung the creature on the floor at the base of his seat and turned to look at the main screen.

"Divert power to the forward scanner," he ordered. The lighting dimmed as the screen came on line, showing the *Cheku* and the *Khalossa* surrounded by their small fleet of cruisers floating starkly against the blackness of space.

"The passive scanners have shown that all is quiet for the moment, General. They sent out a patrol over an hour ago," said his first officer.

He sat down in his chair and reached forward, pulling the female up on her knees. Cupping the back of her head with his hand, he forced her to look at the screen. He pointed to the two craft. "Yours?" he asked, prodding her in the chest.

The inner nictitating lids were almost closed. She could barely see the screen.

Still holding her by the back of her head, he shook her until she finally mewled with pain and fear. Again he forced her to look at the screen and repeated his question, tightening the grip on her head and neck until he felt his talons pierce her flesh, then he eased off.

"Yours?" he demanded.

The inner lids closed and she went limp in his grasp. Disgusted, he pushed her away, letting her lie where she fell. He was sure that these ships belonged to her species, the same species whose planet he had helped destroy.

When he'd intercepted the small craft, he'd ordered it disabled so they could take captives. He'd intended to use them to add to his already strong position back home on M'Zull. He came from the ruling family—only a cousin to be sure— but his discovery of this world twelve years ago had ensured that his branch reached prominence in the Royal Court. Now he'd lost it all. The fact that he'd survived would be an embarrassment to his family. It was one they'd rectify by his murder—and call it an execution—if he didn't commit suicide as tradition demanded.

Somehow death had no appeal for him, which left him with very few options for the future. His crew would support him because his defeat was theirs and they would likewise be condemned to death. He had a plan, an audacious one worthy of the Emperor himself, if he could pull it off.

He stilled his hand, aware that he'd been tapping his claws on the armrest, an unacceptable sign of weakness. His men were twitchy enough without that. His plan was a double bluff, but first he had to hide the Holy object. He might appear to defect, but he couldn't allow his family's sacred totem to fall into the enemy's hands, and he would need to recover it before they could return to M'Zull. The captives were of no use to him now, but he knew where he could trade them for supplies, and hide the totem at the same time.

"Power up," he ordered, his mind finally made up. To wait longer was only to deny the obvious. The whole plan was fraught with danger, but this first step was the most daunting.

* * *

Raguul looked on in disbelief as the ship came careening out of the asteroid belt and headed for deep space, the fighters from the *Khalossa* instantly following.

"Where the hell did that come from?" he demanded, watching as the foremost craft fired on the intruder.

"It must have been hiding in-system since we arrived, sir," said Tactical. "Nothing could have come in since then without our noticing it. We called you when we detected its engines coming on-line."

Another hit was scored on the fleeing craft, then there was

a blossom of light as it went into jump, igniting the fighter behind it.

"Gods!" swore Raguul. "It's gone!"

"We've lost fighter *Delta One,* sir," said Tactics quietly.

"Message from the *Cheku,* sir," said Communications. "Fleet Commander Vroozoi is demanding a report concerning your engagement with the hostile craft."

Raguul began to smile as he saw the fighters and destroyers from the *Cheku* reach his own craft. "He wasn't quite as prepared as he thought he was," he said softly. "Tell Fleet Commander Vroozoi he'll have my report after I've spoken to Sholan High Command," he said briskly, getting to his feet and heading off to his briefing room. He was going to enjoy making this call. "Raise HQ on the comm for me," he ordered. "Kolem, you have the bridge."

"Aye, sir."

* * *

The next afternoon Kusac arrived at the medical section for his appointment with Vanna. He was directed to one of the smaller diagnostic and treatment rooms.

"On your own?" she said with a grin, getting up to welcome him. "How did you manage to get rid of your Security escort?"

He touched her hand fleetingly in greeting. "I gave my promise. I'm only leaving my quarters for the hearings and this."

She indicated the examination couch. "What about food? Are you eating in your room?"

Kusac eyed the array of gimbal-mounted scanning devices nestling neatly against the wall. He sat down reluctantly, then eased his legs up onto the couch. "The food's adequate."

"How long is this supposed to go on?" she asked, cutting the soiled bandage free. "They can't keep you isolated from the rest of us for long because of the psychological effects."

"Till after the hearings, at least. Beyond that I have no idea. Security says it's for our own protection, nothing more," he said, leaning forward to look at his thigh in an effort to show an interest he didn't feel.

"Protection from what? Guynor is in the brig," she said, gently examining the barely visible gash. "It's coming along nicely, thank goodness. I'll run an ultrasound scan to check how it's healing below the surface."

She reached for the small hand scanner that lay on the end of the couch near her. "I really don't like field medicine," she admitted. "Energy weapon wounds can easily turn nasty without the proper treatment, and I was afraid we'd have problems with yours because of my lack of equipment. Pity Carrie couldn't repeat the work she did on your shoulder, but she did manage to accelerate the healing very nicely." She passed the scanner over his leg, checking the readings.

"You're doing fine," she confirmed. "I'll just give you a short burst of ultrasound, then redo the dressing. It's going to be painful for some time."

Returning the scanner to her desk, she picked up a sealed pack. "Did you hear about all the excitement last night?" she asked.

"No. What happened?"

"Apparently a Valtegan ship has been hiding in-system since we arrived. Last night it made a run for it."

"Did it escape?"

"Afraid so. It went into jump, taking one of our fighters with it. By the way, next time you come, I'll be in my new room," she said, ripping the pack open. "They're working on it now."

Placing the pad over the wound, she quickly and efficiently rebound the injury. "It's in keeping with my new status as a Physician. Now, lie back, I want to run some scans on your brain chemistry."

He lay down and stared at the ceiling, blinking as he tried to avoid looking at the bright overhead lights. He was on edge and he knew it. Thankfully Vanna was in a chatty mood which meant he didn't have to make an effort with conversation.

"Headache?" she asked, swinging the scanner out and over his head, effectively blocking out the brightness.

He could see his face mirrored in the interior of the device. His inner eyelids were showing again.

"A bit," he admitted. "A dull ache behind my eyes."

"Photosensitive?"

He nodded, instantly regretting it.

"Keep your head still, please," she said, her voice becoming a little distant as she moved away from the scanner.

He heard her working at her keyboard.

"How long?"

"Since yesterday evening."

"What I expected. Same with Carrie. I'll give you something for it before you leave."

"Anything on the scan?" he asked.

"You've got a basic knowledge of medicine as it applies to telepaths, haven't you?" she asked.

"Fair," he admitted. "I studied with the medics in the guild. It's not my calling, though."

"Well, there's increased activity in the thalamus region," she said. "Which is what I expected as that's the area concerned with memory. Again, I found the same with Carrie. I presume it's due to the mental exchange you experienced when you bonded to each other. The chemical levels are out of synch—in fact, yours are worse than Carrie's, but that may well be due to the species difference rather than anything else. You actually exchanged memories, didn't you?"

He made a sound of assent as he heard her moving around again.

"You're also showing a small weight loss since your last physical, but considering what we've all been through in the last couple of months, I'm not surprised," she said, a hint of humor in her voice. "Everything else is normal. I'd like to do regular checks on you both, so I can monitor your vital signs. If there are any changes at all, I want to be able to identify them as soon as possible."

"Are you expecting any problems?" he asked, picking up her concern despite the lightness of her voice.

"Not expecting, I just want to be prepared. I need to have established base-line readings I can trust."

He heard her footsteps come toward him, then the scanner was swung back. "Kusac," she said, looking down at him. "Do you know anything about the Leska Links that wouldn't be in the medical files? Any Telepath Guild information we might not have?"

"I presume our guilds have always shared relevant information," he said, swaying slightly as he sat up. The dizzy spells were coming more often now. This was the third time it had happened today.

Vanna steadied him, helping him swing his legs over the side of the couch. "That's some headache you've got!" she said sympathetically. "The Telepath Guild Medics occasionally treat Leskas themselves, presumably because there are certain conditions they don't want us in Medical to know about." She went over to a cupboard and, selecting a medicine container, began dispensing some pills into a small bottle.

"If you are aware of anything, I'd appreciate it if you told me because, the Gods help you, I'm literally the only expert we have on Terran telepath physiology, and what affects Carrie affects you. I need cross-guild knowledge which your guild won't even admit it has! This is too new and too important to be bound up by the restrictions of our separate guilds."

"You probably know more about it than I do, Vanna," he said, trying not to sound evasive as held out his hand for the bottle.

Her eyes flicked across his face, assessing his answer. "Fair enough. Don't take these on an empty stomach. I've put my personal contact number on the label. If you need me, page me anytime. I'll see you again in four days. I'd like it to be sooner, but your guild hearing is tomorrow and we all have the court-martial the following day. I don't envisage any substantial differences will show up sooner than that."

"I'll get in touch if there's a problem," he said, pocketing the bottle and pushing himself off the couch.

Vanna watched him leave. As he reached the door, she called out to him.

"Kusac!"

He stopped and turned round.

"You and Carrie take it easy, hear me? This Link is a tremendous upheaval for both of you. It'll take a lot of adjustment. Remember, I'm here as your friend, not just as a medic."

"Thank you, Vanna," he said, touched by her concern even though it posed a problem for him. "We'll take it easy, don't worry."

The walk back from the medical section tired him out, and it was with relief that he sealed his door behind him. He'd slept badly the night before, partly because of working late on his reports for Sub-Commander Kolem and the guild and partly because of the unfamiliar silence in his mind.

He'd woken uncharacteristically late for him and had spent what had been left of the morning making rough notes on what he'd read of the physical and psychological effects of a normal Leska Link and correlating it against his personal experiences.

The pattern of the Link's development was similar, but the degree of dependence and depth of their continual shared experiences, both mental and physical, was already far in excess of the Sholan Links.

His mental world was still silent, but he knew it was not due to the effects of drugs. Carrie had managed somehow to block their link in a way that he couldn't figure. That in itself was an achievement that marked her Talents as substantially different from those of Sholans. He needed to do some more work on this, but his headache had reached the state where all he really wanted to do was lie down.

Absentmindedly, he scratched a vague itch on his thigh, then another on his neck. Moments later, he stopped in the middle of vigorously clawing himself behind the ears and cursed. The last thing he wanted to do was start grooming, but if he didn't, the itching would drive him mad.

Discarding his jacket and belt as he went, he made for the drawers where he kept his brush. Using the minimum effort, he was shocked to find that after only a few strokes he had to clean the bristles. He was shedding, and quite heavily. Something was very wrong with him. As he drew the brush through the fur between his ears, a wave of dizziness made him reel, and he reached out to the unit beside him to stop himself from falling.

My hair's growing, he/she thought, drawing the brush through its length, watching the sunlight bring out the copper glints in the blonde before stopping to untangle a snarl. The memory faded.

Shaken, he put the brush down. What the hell was happening to him? Nothing like this had been on even the sealed files that he'd read. Was this a product of the increased activity Vanna's scans had shown? On unsteady legs he went over to his bed and sat down. Carrie had mentioned flashes of his memories intruding into her consciousness. No wonder she'd been frightened. It was unnerving enough to constantly share your every thought with another, let alone being unable to tell where you began and she ended. Even though the light level in his room was set low, it was too bright for him now. The headache had spread and every movement sent stabbing pain straight through his skull.

I need to record this, he thought. *Father needs to know.*

A wave of nausea swept through him. He lay down, the desire to do anything other than sleep leaving him abruptly. *Gods, are the next three days going to be like this?* he thought.

* * *

Vanna and Garras were sitting in the main bar on the concourse enjoying a quiet drink.

"May I join you?" said a voice.

Vanna looked up to see Mito slide into the seat opposite them.

"Surely," she said, concealing her surprise. Mito struck her as one who wouldn't normally seek out their more staid company.

"Will you join us in a drink?" asked Garras. "I was just about to order another for us."

Mito hesitated. "No, I won't," she said. "I can see you've just come off duty, Captain. I don't want to take up your leisure time."

"Then what can we do for you?" he asked, raising an eye ridge quizzically.

"I've been talking to Anders," she said, ears twitching faintly with embarrassment.

"And?" prompted Vanna as she hesitated.

"Well, it may be something or nothing," she said. "Apparently, yesterday Skai was asked by one of our people about the incident involving Kusac and Guynor."

Vanna's ears swiveled round toward Mito. She felt Garras' tail flick once, warningly, against her leg.

"Go on," said Garras.

"He wanted to know about the Challenge," Mito said. "Details like what Guynor's grounds were, the allegations he made against Kusac, and did Skai think they were true."

"It's not unreasonable to assume that Guynor had some friends on the *Khalossa* and that they should want to know what happened on Keiss. After all, he is being held in solitary except for seeing his legal representative. They can't ask him directly."

Mito nodded. "I thought that myself, but why ask the Terran? Why not ask one of us?"

"I'm sure it's nothing, Mito, but I'll look into it if you

like," he said, finishing off his drink and getting to his feet. "Are you sure I can't get you something?"

"No, thank you," she said, getting up also. "I have to go. I've arranged to meet friends shortly."

"Oh, before you leave," said Garras. "Skai didn't get the name of this person, did he?"

"I'm afraid not. He said he hasn't yet learned to identify anyone but us. He did remember the male was brown in color," she said, an amused tone creeping into her voice, "but he was out of uniform, so Skai couldn't even tell me which guild he belonged to."

Vanna sat there in a state of extreme agitation until Garras returned bearing two large spirit glasses. He placed one in front of her.

"It's a Chemerian M'ikkoe. Drink it slowly," he said, sitting back down. "We need it," he said grimly, seeing her surprise. "I have a feeling we've got a large problem on our hands."

* * *

The incoming call light on his comm was blinking when he returned from his visit to the nearby village. Settling himself at his desk, he tapped the accept key and waited.

The image resolved to show the face of his one-time Leader from the Brotherhood.

"Ghezu. To what do I owe the dubious pleasure of your call?" he asked, his voice a soft purr.

"Your status has been reactivated. We've a contract for you."

He could sense the terseness in the other's voice. "I don't think so," he murmured. "The Brotherhood and I parted company a long time ago."

"I want to renew our relationship about as much as you do," said Ghezu. "I have no choice. This contract comes from the highest level."

Dispassionately, he watched the Sub-Guild Master's ears move fractionally. Another would have missed it, but not him.

"You no longer have any jurisdiction over me, Ghezu."

"Your association with the Brotherhood never ends, Tallinu, you know that. You owe me a debt, and I'm calling it in now."

"It was in our mutual interests that our ... association ... was terminated," he reminded him.

"You're the only person capable of handling a job of this complexity. It's also one that will appeal to you."

He raised an eye ridge. "Tell me about it," he said abruptly. "I guarantee nothing, but tell me about it."

"You know the Others have been located, and with them another species that may be friendly toward us." Ghezu stopped.

"Go on." None of this was news so far.

"There's a telepath among them, and one of our males has formed a Link with her. A Leska Link."

He had to force his mind into stillness lest he give himself away. "Her people have been fighting the Others." It was a statement. "She can fight."

Ghezu nodded.

Realization hit him like a cold shower. "So can he!"

"Retirement hasn't dulled your senses," Ghezu said dryly. "Yes, they can both fight. I don't need to tell you the political implications of this, do I?"

He shook his head.

"We need you to assess the situation and then take appropriate action within the scope of your contract. The agreement will be delivered to you in person at the temple in Valsgarth. Your employer wishes to talk to you in person and will meet you there at the twenty-second hour. You leave from the shuttleport at dawn."

"If I accept, it will be as a free-lance operative." He watched Ghezu's eyes narrow. A flick of his left ear affirmed his grudging consent.

"Agreed, but I expect to be kept informed of all developments."

"Then I'll take the contract," he said. "It comes from the highest source, you said."

"That information will be on the contract." Ghezu's voice was cold. "No comm is completely secure."

Tallinu refused the bait. As the Sub-Guild Master reached to cut the connection, he forestalled him.

"Ghezu, this pays my debt. Understood? I owe you nothing after this."

Ghezu's face darkened. "Agreed," he snarled before blanking the screen.

"The years haven't taught you subtlety," said the priest,

continuing to survey the distant snow-topped mountains on the other side of the Kysubi Plains. "You still don't know how to handle him, do you?"

"I'd like to see you do better," Ghezu growled as he pushed his chair back impatiently. "You know I didn't want to use him at all. That was your idea. He's too dangerous, too much of a loner."

"I agree," said Lijou, turning away from the window. "Unfortunately, he's also the only one capable of thinking on his feet. What a pity you had to alienate him all those years ago."

"It was him or me, Lijou. There's only room for one leader in the Brotherhood," Ghezu replied angrily. "I won fair and square."

"You won," agreed the priest, walking over to the desk and picking up his mug of c'shar. "What you did was, shall we say, unethical?"

"Ethics be damned! The Brotherhood stands outside the normal bounds of ethics, always has. It's the result that counts."

"Not quite, Ghezu," said Lijou quietly, taking a sip of his drink. "You want to be thankful that he wasn't as ambitious as you were, and that he still follows the code of the Brotherhood."

"I had no choice, Lijou! He kept disobeying my orders and carrying out contracts his own way. He had to go."

"Or die."

Ghezu regarded him stonily. "We were friends, once."

"Yes," said Lijou, looking him calmly in the eyes. "He would have made a good Guild Master, combining as he does the best of both disciplines. Still, it wasn't to be. He's as inflexible as you are in his own way, and who's to say you aren't the better leader?"

"I don't think I like your inference, Lijou," he said, turning his back on him and walking toward the door. He hesitated, hand on the doorknob. "He was the popular choice among the students, but he didn't have what it took to be a Master, and as his friend, I knew that. So did he." He turned round to face Lijou again.

"The Brotherhood has never been stronger than it is now. My intelligence network is spread wider than it was under Loedd. Because of that, we've heard about what's happened to one of the telepaths on the *Khalossa* and his Link to a new species. When there's been news of new artifacts found at one of the ruined cities, we've been there to—liberate—some of them without suspicion before the senior members of the Telepath Guild have arrived to destroy them. Don't forget what has been achieved in your desire to criticize my ethics, Lijou. I'm sure Vartra would not be so damning of me."

"I'm not trying to destroy your achievements, Ghezu. As your priest, I'm merely reminding you that you're mortal and can make mistakes. Tallinu is right for the job, trust me. He still serves our God."

"Oh, I know that," he said dryly, "and I believe he'll do the job, but on his terms, not ours."

"Times are changing, Ghezu. These two people on the *Khalossa* represent a new force that will upset the order we've lived under since the Cataclysm. They could be the sign we've been waiting for."

"They could be our destruction, have you thought of that? Tallinu couldn't be controlled. If they can't be, what then?"

"You answer your own question," he said, pointing to the crystal cube lying on the desk. "His orders are explicit. He'll do what needs to be done."

* * *

An insistent tone dragged Kusac from the depths of sleep. Bleary-eyed, he tried to focus on the timepiece set into the wall opposite the bed. He'd slept the clock round. The door sounded again, more insistent this time, and with an effort he rose and dragged himself to his feet. His head was still pounding, yet he felt curiously light-headed. He made his way to the door and pressed the communication button.

"Who's it?" he growled.

"It's Rhian, Kusac," came the answer.

The door slid open, admitting Rhian.

"Are you all right?" she asked, moving over to him as he made his way slowly to the nearest chair. Her face creased with concern. "You don't look well."

"Fine. Jus' woke up, tha's all," he slurred, trying to wave her away. His mouth felt like it was full of cotton wool and all he wanted to do was to go back to sleep.

"When did you last eat?" she asked sharply, going over to the small drink dispenser in the far corner of the room.

"Uh, when we all went to the mess," he mumbled, trying to keep his eyes open.

"That was two days ago!" she said, carrying a mug back over to him. "No wonder you feel so ill. Here, drink this."

She wrapped his unresisting hand around the container and forced him to lift it to his mouth.

"What is it?" he asked suspiciously, moving his head just enough to avoid it.

"Protein drink," she replied, holding the mug to his lips again.

This time he drank, taking the mug from her with an unsteady hand.

She watched him finish. "You look a bit more alert now," she said, noticing that some of the dullness had left his eyes.

"Sorry," he apologized, ears flicking with embarrassment as he tried to concentrate on what he was saying. "I'm not exactly being hospitable, am I?" He looked away, turning the cup over in his hands. "I haven't even thanked you for your help, and for looking after Carrie."

Rhian made a dismissive gesture. "I'm only glad we were here. Your fears weren't groundless, you know. You did the right thing."

Kusac looked up at her, his eyes so bleak she almost shrank from them as involuntarily she picked up his thoughts and realized he wasn't thinking about the medics on the *Khalossa,* but about the events on Keiss.

"Did I? I wonder."

"You did," she said, retreating behind a mental barrier, unwilling to be exposed to his private innermost fears. "You couldn't let the girl die. You did what you had to. No one could fault you."

Kusac made a small noise of denial.

Rhian leaned forward and took the mug out of his hands, putting it down firmly on the floor.

"I know what you're going through," she said gently, taking him by the hands and letting him feel her concern and sympathy. "Remember, Carrie isn't a Sholan, she hasn't even had a guild education. She has grown up in ignorance of her Talent and knows nothing of our ways and customs— how could it be otherwise?" She stopped, making sure he was taking in what she said.

"We're telling her that not only has she to turn her back on her Clan, leave her home planet, and live alone of her kind among an alien race, but that this strange telepathic bond that she now has means she must also be paired with you for life. This is no easy thing, even for one of our own people. Think how much more daunting it is for her, despite her love for you."

Kusac stirred, withdrawing his hands from hers to avoid the mental contact.

"She loves you," said Rhian. "Don't doubt that."

Kusac broke the short silence. "It isn't easy for me to fly in the face of convention either. I've had to make similar decisions."

"It's never easy to be the first, Kusac," she said with compassion, getting up to pull another chair over beside him. "Give her space and time to get used to us, as you yourself suggested. I know you need to see her, to touch and love her. It's the same with Askad and me." She smiled briefly. "Time doesn't dim the Leska bond, you know. I do know how hard it is for you to be physically apart. At least you two have the time to wait, unlike Sholan Leska pairs."

Kusac said nothing for a while.

"What brought you here?" he asked at length.

Rhian looked at her wrist, making an exclamation of annoyance.

"I came to fetch you for your guild hearing! If we hurry, we'll just make it in time." She bent down to pick up his jacket and belt. "Here, put these on."

Tiredly, he got to his feet and dressed.

"What about the court-martial? When is it?"

"Surely you haven't forgotten! It's tomorrow. You and the rest of the crew of the *Sirroki* will be called to give evidence. Personnel should have sent a reminder to your comm."

She went over to check, tearing off several printouts and scanning them for the correct one.

"It's here," she said, putting it on the desk. "Read it when you get back. It's at the fifth hour tomorrow. Now let's leave before you're late," she said, herding him toward the door.

* * *

Rhian left him at the Mentor's office on the fifteenth level and returned to her quarters.

"How is he?" her mate asked.

Rhian shook her head. "Not too good. He's exhibiting

some of the signs of Contact Deprivation you'd expect because of their separation. We'll need to keep an eye on him,
Askad. At least he has the mental link to the girl. If it
weren't for that, then I would be worried indeed. How is
Carrie?"

"Trying to look brighter than she feels, if I pick up her
emotions correctly. This isn't the first time she has been
bonded, remember. She was linked to her sister and all she
got from their relationship was pain. I'm not surprised she's
suddenly unsure now that she has time to think coherently.
Still, that doesn't explain her wish to remain with us."

"That's their affair, Askad, not ours. We will need to
watch them both closely, though. She's is spending too much
time alone."

* * *

Kusac was ushered through the formal office into the
Mentor's inner retreat, a warm room pleasantly furnished in
dark colors with several large, high-backed and slightly concave chairs.

The Mentor, titular head of the Telepath Guild on the
Khalossa, rose to greet him, her long purple robes rustling
as she advanced, palm held out in greeting.

"You must be Kusac Alda," she said.

Kusac briefly touched the Mentor's palm with his, nodding assent.

"I'm afraid I haven't met you before, but I believe you
have kept in touch with your tutor over the six months
you've been aboard the *Khalossa.*

"I have, Mentor," Kusac answered, glancing toward where
his tutor sat in one of the other chairs.

"Good. I like to know my telepaths have the confidence in
their tutors to seek them out when they need help or advice.
Please, sit down." She indicated a fourth seat. "This is not
a formal hearing, despite what you may have heard to the
contrary."

Kusac moved over to the chair, sinking into its depths, a
look of surprise crossing his face.

The Mentor laughed. "Those chairs take everyone by surprise," she said. "I like my comfort, and as senior telepath
on this vessel, I make shameful use of my privileged position to obtain it." She returned to her seat, picking up a
sheaf of papers from a low table beside her.

"The administrative and pastoral side of my work on a vessel this size would surprise you. We all need an escape, a bolt-hole where we can shut the world out and be ourselves. This is mine."

"I'm honored that you should invite me in here, rather than in your office," murmured Kusac, beginning to relax.

The Mentor shot him a penetrating look. "The positions are slightly reversed, but we won't go into that at this moment," she said urbanely.

"It seems events are catching up with me," said Kusac dryly.

"We can't escape our destiny for long. It has a habit of taking us unawares. Which brings me nicely to the matter in hand" she said. "Give him a cup of c'shar, Rhuso," she said, scanning the notes in her hand. "The other tutor is Terno, from the twenty-fifth level."

Terno nodded as Kusac's tutor rose and went over to the brewing unit on a side table.

"Will you have a cup?" he asked. "It's fresh, not the dried muck the rest of us have to drink." He grinned briefly.

"Please."

"As far as I can ascertain from talking to your Captain, the gist of Guynor's Blood Rite Challenge hinged on the fact that he accused you of forcing a Leska bond on an alien female and mentally manipulating her for sexual purposes. These acts he claimed were against the good of Shola. Is this essentially correct?"

"More or less," agreed Kusac, ears dipping in acute embarrassment as he accepted the delicate mug from Rhuso.

"Leaving aside the fact that a Leska bond cannot be forced on anyone, did you take advantage of her mentally?"

"No, Mentor," he replied, keeping a tight rein on his shields even though he knew that here among his own kind, there would be no check on his honesty. It was his physical condition he was trying to conceal at the moment. The light-headedness was returning and he was deadly tired.

"Then tell us what happened from the moment of your crash on Keiss."

Kusac took a gulp of his drink, hoping that it would help him to stay alert.

"I was wounded during the attack. The others pulled me clear of the wreck. Leaving our dead on board, they detonated the craft to conceal the nature of our appearance from anyone on the planet." He stopped for a moment.

"We were attacked before we could leave the area, and lost another crew member in the fight. His body, along with those of the Valtegans who had attacked us, was placed in the burning craft and I was left under cover while Captain Garras and the others made their escape.

"I managed to crawl far enough away from the vehicle to remain hidden when the Valtegans arrived in force and started combing the area for survivors."

"Why were you left?" interrupted Rhuso.

"I was the only wounded survivor. If they'd tried to take me with them, I would have slowed the whole party down. There was too much chance of us all being caught if I hadn't remained."

"Please continue," said the Mentor.

"The pain heightened my senses, and the following day I was aware of another telepath not too far distant."

"The Terran."

"Yes, Carrie. When I first picked up her thoughts, I assumed she was dying." He stopped, reliving again the agony and fear he had felt in her during those first moments of contact. "I quickly realized that it was her sister, not her, who was dying and that in some way they were linked mentally—not as telepaths, but I didn't find that out till later."

"How had they been linked?" asked the Mentor.

Kusac seemed to have left the reality of the *Khalossa* and was once more back on Keiss, his leg afire with the pain of a deep gash caused by a flying piece of metal debris.

"Her sister felt no pain, it was Carrie who suffered for her. Elise was working undercover for their Resistance in the main Valtegan pleasure city. She had been caught and was being tortured. She was too afraid to let Carrie go at the last and nearly dragged her down into death."

"This was when you sensed her," the Mentor said quietly.

"Yes. I reached out and held her, pulling her back from the brink, telling her she was not alone, that I would always be with her," he whispered, beginning to shiver uncontrollably as her memories flooded through him. The acrid smell of blood filled his nostrils.

"That moment has gone, Kusac. You didn't lose her. She

is here now, safe on this vessel," said the quiet, almost hypnotic voice.

Kusac blinked, returning slowly to the present, but not quite to reality.

"You saved her life. What then?"

"When she had recovered, I used the link we still had to find her. My wound was infected and I needed medical help. I could only get it from her, so I made my way to the settlement where she lived."

He took a deep breath. "When she found me, I'll admit I probed the surface of her mind, picking up my resemblance to the forest cats on Keiss, and her memory of a pet animal she had owned on Earth. It, too, was a cat, and in color resembled me. I exploited these facts, making her and her family assume I was merely one of the wild cats."

"What did you do while you were recuperating at their estate?"

"The link was still there, much stronger now we were physically close. She had no idea that it was me she was linked to. In fact she seemed strangely incurious. She's very Talented, and had begun trying to probe the Valtegans' minds. I had to teach her or she would have given herself away through her ineptness."

The Mentor nodded, her face unreadable. "Then she left her Clan."

"Her father was trying to pressurize her into a marriage she didn't want. We left her home with the intention of trying to find the guerrillas so she could join them. The first night she used what I realized was her full potential for the first time to force me to go hunting for her. She put a very effective compulsion onto me," he said wryly.

"It seems she is indeed a Talented lady," said the Mentor.

"As I was in mid-leap for my prey, her mind sent out a call for help so powerful that it felled me on the spot. Without thinking, I demanded the nature of the danger—she was being attacked by a scouting party of four Valtegans—and headed back to our camp. That was the point at which I first suspected that we had become Leska bonded." He fell silent.

"What did you do to the Valtegans?" asked the Mentor.

Kusac looked up. "I killed them," he said, surprised at his need to answer the question.

"Didn't that strike you as strange?"

"Not particularly. I thought of them as animals, the way

they were behaving. And they threatened the life of my Leska."

He fell silent again, waiting for the next question.

"What prompted you to help the girl in the first place?" asked Terno.

Kusac glanced at him, reality beginning to fade a little again. The whole situation had an air of the surreal about it. For him there had been no thought of doing anything but help her.

"Her pain was greater than mine," he said.

"I think the reason why he did it is obvious," said the Mentor quietly. "I feel that given the uniqueness of the situation, I would have to say that you acted in a manner that brings you only credit. However, the nature of your bond will need further study. I suggest we send the two of you to the guild on Shola where they have the people and equipment to do it. Are you in agreement?"

There were nods of assent from the two tutors.

"As to Guynor's charges, your story is virtually identical to Carrie's. In our opinion, there is no charge to answer. Someone of your background and training," she gave Kusac a hard look, "would be incapable of making a decision that went against the interests of either your Clan or the Telepath Guild, which is why this has been an informal chat rather than a hearing. On a vessel of this size, justice has to be seen to be done, even if there is no need for action." The Mentor shuffled through her papers again.

"As to your Leska bonding with the girl, I see you have not yet consummated it." She looked up at Kusac. "There is no reason why you can't. We are physically compatible according to the medical report. Just remember that since she is of a different species, you have a duty as an only son to provide the Clan with heirs."

"I am rarely allowed to forget my duties," Kusac murmured, ears flicking.

"I'm afraid this time you can't avoid it. As for the incident with Guynor, we are interested in the fact that as a telepath, you not only fought a Challenge against someone physically stronger than you, but actually managed to beat him. This is something no telepath has done for many generations, and why our guild was declared inviolable and exempt from Challenge rites. I also have the details of your brawl in the bar on the concourse," she said wryly. "Since you seem to have broken free of the normal telepath's inhibitions regarding violence, you'll have to be constantly on your guard not to react accordingly."

"I can't understand Guynor's attitude in issuing a Blood Rite Challenge against a telepath in the first place," said Terno. "To think that your Link with the Terran girl was a crime against Shola was madness in itself." He shook his head in puzzlement.

"I had no option but to fight," Kusac muttered, trying to concentrate on what he was saying. The room was so pleasantly warm that he was finding himself drifting off while trying to control the vague sense of disorientation he felt.

"Guynor leaped on me and I found myself fighting for my life. What would you have had me do? Lie there and get chewed to death?"

"Hardly," said the Mentor. "I would have expected the rest of the crew to go to your aid. Apparently they didn't because they saw you were able to handle him, and they don't fully appreciate what we go through when we even have to witness a Challenge. Except for you, that is, judging by the calm way you said you dispatched four Valtegans."

"Didn't you feel any pain when you were fighting?" asked Rhuso.

"Only my own," said Kusac. "Were you told Carrie is also a healer? That's the reason why I bear no wounds from the Challenge."

"It seems we have much to learn about your bond. Carrie obviously has no trauma concerned with fighting from what she told us of the battle at the Valtegan base, and you now seem to have only a residual one. It appears that there's an element of crossover between your Talents. You seem to be learning some of her attitudes and abilities. This also needs studying, another reason why we are advising that you both be returned to the guild on Shola."

The Mentor stood up. "I don't think there is any need to detain you further, Kusac. As we have said, there is no charge for you to answer. You are free to come and go as you will within the ship. The Commander has lifted your confinement. You and Carrie will receive your orders within the next few days. There is a lot of administrative work to be done at present, and your case isn't pressing."

She smiled briefly at him. "Should you need any advice, then feel free to call on your tutor. He will make himself available to you immediately. If necessary, he can contact me, but I don't foresee any problems." She held out her palm again as Kusac rose to his feet.

Kusac returned the gesture and, thanking the Mentor and tutors, left.

"I think we have to agree that there was something more than coincidence at work here," said Rhuso, once the door was closed.

"I agree," said the Mentor. "Suddenly we have a female, a member of a species that doesn't recognize telepathy, Linked to one of our people. Why? Could it be because both of them were rendered temporarily vulnerable to each other's minds by the extreme pain they were both suffering?"

"It's a reasonable hypothesis and fits what we know so far about them," said Terno.

"Till now we have believed the Leska Link exists as a form of natural selection, bonding strong Talents together with biological imperatives to breed. So why would one form between these two when they aren't genetically compatible?" asked Rhuso.

"This is what I hope the guild on Shola will discover," said the Mentor.

"Sensing an alien on even a fairly basic level takes several years of study for those of us who work with Alien Relations," said Terno pensively, "yet they are both capable of doing it immediately."

"You forget that we now know Kusac has one of the most powerful Talents on our records," said the Mentor. "He has also spent several years training in Alien Relations. All this makes it more likely that he would have the knowledge and the potential to read alien minds easily."

"I am also most concerned as to the matter of his lack of inhibition to fight. It's virtually inbred in us as telepaths. Does he now lack this because the girl does? Why should there be the crossover of her Talents to him? This doesn't happen with Sholan Leska Links."

"What tests can we do to try and chart her abilities, or even Kusac's now?" asked Rhuso. "We have more questions than answers."

"If the guild adapts their basic tests for grading, then at least we can rate her level on our current knowledge. Beyond that, we will have to see how they react to life. Since the Cataclysm our Talent has enabled us to survive more easily than those who lack it. I expect the same is true of the Terrans, even if they have suffered no such major disaster in their past as we did. Therefore, by seeing how they react to daily situations, we can gauge what they're doing."

"That assumes one of our people can follow their thought patterns," grunted Terno. "I couldn't read anything from Kusac while he was here. The barrier he had up, though unsophisticated, was too tight to allow any penetration. If his mind is altering and becoming more like hers, I doubt any of us will be able to follow their thoughts unless they wish it, not even the Clan Lord himself!"

"Then we do what I recommended. We enlist their help. I believe they will have as great an incentive to wish to understand their Link as we do. That's why I suggested to the Commander that their confinement to quarters be dropped. Without exterior stimulus, there will be no need for them to explore their Talents," said the Mentor. "Continue to keep them under surveillance, and remember who you are dealing with. Use at least three telepaths at any given time and warn them to refrain from communicating with each other. Make sure each has a legitimate reason for being in the area. I can't shake the certainty that there is something at work here that we cannot comprehend, and we must control it. The impact on our society of telepaths who can fight could be catastrophic. We can't allow the old fears of us to resurface."

"Vartra knows what this is all in aid of!" said Terno. "I'm just glad that I'm not the Clan Lord or the Guild Master!"

"Perhaps you have the right of it," the Mentor said slowly. "Vartra may be the only one who does know the purpose of this Link."

* * *

The cold air of the corridor served to waken Kusac and dispel the feelings of unreality but started him shivering once more. Moving as quickly as his injured leg allowed, he headed for the elevator down to his level and the sanctuary of his room.

Once inside, he lowered the lighting to a vague ambiance and turned up the heating. Gradually the warmth began to seep back into his body. Going over to the dispenser he selected a glass of water. Sipping it slowly, he sat down in front of the comm. There were more messages for him. Tearing them off, he tried to scan the list, but his eyes refused to focus properly. Exasperated, he held the paper farther away, managing at last to read the names of the callers. No one important. He tossed it aside, letting it slide off the desk and drift to the floor.

Switching on the comm with its flare of bright screen triggered the headache that had been lurking ominously since he woke. He winced, turning the brightness down to the point where he could just see his text.

Lifting his glass, he swallowed a little more water. As it hit his stomach, the nausea returned. His hand shook as he replaced the glass and closed his eyes. He had to finish the file now. If he left it any longer, he might not be capable of doing so.

He lifted his head, squinted at the screen, and moved his hands to the keyboard. Claws extended, he began tapping in the information, aware as he did so that every joint and muscle in his body ached, particularly his hands. Maybe he was coming down with some virus and all these physical symptoms had nothing to do with his Link. Possible, but he doubted it. It was more likely due to the stress caused by the situation he found himself in.

Another wave of nausea hit him and he stopped, waiting till it had passed. What the hell was he doing to himself? All this to give her the right to choose when there was no choice to make! He must be mad to get involved with any female, let alone her, to the point where her principles mattered more than his life. Denying a Leska Link would never occur to any Sholan. It happened and you accepted it, with or without pleasure. For him it had been easy. Why, in the God's name, couldn't she decide?

Memories jostled for attention, a flash of them sitting against a tree in the forest, her head on his chest minutes after the Leska Link had formed; s/he looking at him through the flames of the campfire, realizing he was not the animal s/he had thought; the smell and taste of blood in his mouth during the fight with Guynor; after the Challenge when he explained what he knew of the Link; when s/he reached out to touch the awful wound in his/her shoulder . . . The images continued, flashing so quickly before his eyes that he barely saw them.

Moaning, he put his hands to his head, turning his thoughts inward as desperately he tried to make them stop. Gradually they slowed, finally ceasing, leaving him in a state of total confusion. Lowering his hands, he opened his eyes and looked around. The room appeared unfamiliar. Where was this and why was the comm on? The hands lying on the desk were covered in black fur. Yes, he was the furred one. As he looked, the fur faded, leaving a lightly tanned bare arm, the fingers tipped with paler nails, not dark claws.

He leaped to his feet, sending the chair flying backward. Forcing the terror aside, he tried to focus on the here-and-now, fighting to push the rogue images deep into his subconscious where they belonged while around him the room appeared to darken, then lighten perceptibly.

I'm Kusac, I'm in my quarters, he kept repeating as he rested his hands on his desk in an effort to anchor his physical senses.

The disorientation eased until he knew where and who he was once more. Trembling with the aftereffects, he bent down and retrieved his chair. His head throbbed with the exertion.

Was Carrie experiencing this, too, and was she coping? At this moment, frankly, he was beyond caring. He sat down and continued laboriously to finish recording his data. Finally done, he indexed the file to Vanna's personal comm, date-sealing it to a time three days hence. He'd done more than could be realistically expected of anyone in his circumstances.

Closing down the comm, he eyed the glass of water. His mouth was so dry that swallowing hurt. Maybe in a minute he thought, his head drooping forward in exhaustion. He was too tired to stay where he was, too tired to move.

With a start he came to, realizing that he'd fallen asleep at the desk. Picking up the glass, he staggered toward the bed, placing his drink on the unit by the head of the bed. Sitting down, he undressed, then programmed in an alarm for the following day. He couldn't afford to be late for the court-martial. Reluctantly, he picked up the glass and took a mouthful, waiting for the resulting nausea. He wasn't disappointed. When it passed, hands slick with sweat, he rolled into the depression in the center and let himself fall into unconsciousness.

* * *

The craft began to emerge from hyperspace on the outskirts of Keiss' solar system. An observer watching the quadrant would have seen it waver briefly as it continued its course inbound, skipping in and out of real-time like a stone skimmed across the water.

The shock waves of its brief emergences were picked up onboard the *Khalossa* almost immediately.

"I'm detecting what looks like an incoming craft, sir, but it's disappeared," said the navigator on duty. "There it is again!"

Sub-Commander Kolem looked up from his ops board. "Have you a visual on it?"

"Not yet, sir. I've never seen anything flick in and out of jump like that before."

"The craft is signaling to us on our frequency, sir," interrupted the communications officer. "It's one of ours. Code Three, Nine, Five, Zero, Red."

"Predict its next point of entry and try to get a fix on it. Relay your board to the main viewer."

"Relaying now, sir."

The main viewer lit up showing the outermost planets of Keiss' solar system. In one corner a flickering image formed into the outlines of a slim craft. A moment later it flickered and was gone.

"Got it, sir! Enhanced image replay now on screen."

The sleekly functional lines of an interstellar to atmosphere vehicle filled the center of the screen.

"By all the Gods," swore Kolem, staring at it, "They've finally done it! A Stealth multipurpose fighter! If we'd had half a dozen of those at the start of this mission, we'd have found Keiss and liberated it sooner, without the need for Vroozoi!"

"Message being transmitted on our security channel, sir," said communications. "They repeat, Code Three, Nine, Five, Zero, Red, and request permission for priority docking in our upper bay."

"Acknowledge, then relay the message to Commander Raguul," said Kolem, still watching the screen as the view switched back to real-time and the unmarked craft re-emerged, this time to stay.

Commander Raguul's voice rang out through the comm. "Clear the upper docking bay of all personnel except those with top security rating. See that the route from there to my office is secure. Sub-Commander Kolem, report to the docking bay yourself with Sub-Lieutenant Draz. Raguul out."

"You heard the Commander, snap to it," said Kolem, getting out of his seat. "Page Draz and get him to meet me at the docking bay. The bridge is in your hands, Sub-Commander Rreba," he said, passing the science officer.

"Sub-Commander! The *Cheku* is demanding to know what's happening."

Kolem stopped and turned back to face the bridge crew. With a wide grin he said, "Tell the *Cheku* that the information they're requesting is highly confidential. We're not at liberty to divulge it to them because they lack the security clearance."

From behind the reinforced viewing screen in the gallery they watched the predatory vehicle move steadily to the turntable landing pad. It hovered briefly before descending, the high-pitched whine of the engines dying away to almost nothing.

Bay doors sealed and the small deficit in air pressure made good, the craft's hatch opened as Kolem and Draz crossed the metal floor toward it.

The Captain was dressed in the black fatigues worn by the Warrior Guild when on active duty in space.

"I'm Sub-Commander Kolem and this is Sub-Lieutenant Draz, head of Security. We'll escort you to our Commander."

"Our security needs have been seen to?" the Captain asked, giving a brief nod to each of the two officers.

"All has been done as you requested," confirmed Draz.

"Good. Our job was to convey our passenger to you. This we've done. We'll need to refuel before we can depart."

Kolem beckoned to the group of males at the far side of the hanger.

"They'll see to your needs," he said.

The Captain acknowledged this with a flick of his ears, then turned to beckon his passenger out.

From the hatchway emerged a figure heavily concealed by a voluminous cloak and hood of gray. His head inclined toward them.

"Welcome aboard the *Khalossa*," said Sub-Commander Kolem. "If you follow us, we'll take you to Commander Raguul."

As the figure moved silently toward them, vague memories stirred in Kolem's mind. He glanced at Draz who responded with a minute flick of one ear. Like all senior officers in the Forces, they had served time at the Warrior Guild. They knew a member of the Brotherhood when they saw one.

Once a year the Brothers called at the guild to check over the students about to graduate. The cadets viewed their arrival with a mixture of hope and fear. To be singled out to join their elite Warrior force was an honor one was never sure one really wanted.

The journey down to the twenty-first level was made in silence. Their visitor obviously had no wish to communicate with them. As they preceded him along the corridor, both were aware of the fur on their neck and shoulders beginning to rise at his unnatural silence: not even his footfall could be heard. It was with relief that they delivered him to the Commander's office.

Commander Raguul's adjutant opened the door. "Thank you, Sub-Commander Kolem. The Commander wishes you to return to the bridge," said Myak. "Sub-Lieutenant Draz, would you join us, please?"

As the door closed, the visitor threw back his hood and, reaching into a pocket, withdrew a crystal cube. Walking to the Commander's desk, he handed it over to him.

"This contains my employer's instructions," he said, his voice notable only in that it had a slight highland burr to it. "You are to see that you facilitate those instructions, Commander."

Raguul regarded the cube, then the person, as his unexpected guest removed his cloak and threw it over the back of the chair opposite.

He wore a tunic of grey over which sat a jacket not unlike the Sholan Forces one, also in gray, bearing a red flash over his right shoulder. From the utility belt hung, among other things, an energy pulse pistol.

"I don't take kindly to being given orders on my own ship," said Raguul. "You have no business coming here." His ear flicked with annoyance. He knew without reading the cube that the male before him was one of the special operatives.

His visitor sat, face and ears imperturbable. "I suggest you read the orders now," he said.

Raguul leaned forward and inserted the cube into the viewer, scanning the data it disclosed. He removed it, handing it back across the desk.

"It seems you are correct," said Raguul, sitting back in his seat again, a slight opening of his mouth showing his faint amusement. "You have arrived at an opportune time, but you'll find the situation somewhat different from what you expected."

The visitor shrugged. "I was chosen because I am flexible. No problem is insurmountable."

"Hmm," said Raguul, not convinced. "Since this problem is now out of my hands, I'll leave you with Draz. He'll bring you up to date, and should you need any extra personnel, he'll be able to advise you."

"I'd like the briefing first, then some clothes and accommodation. I was forced to leave immediately to fit in with the *Striker*'s schedule."

"My adjutant, Myak," Raguul nodded in his direction, "will take your requirements and see they are brought to you as soon as possible."

Raguul leaned forward. "Just remember, Brother," he said, "I am in ultimate command out here. I will be kept informed of what is happening, and I will have no conflict of interests in this matter. It is sensitive enough."

"My interests are confined to one area only, Commander. I accepted this mission because of the challenge it offered."

"Oh, you'll find it a challenge, believe me," said Raguul. "Draz, give our guest every cooperation. See he's quartered where he wishes and set up a secure line of communication between the two of you. When his clothing arrives, escort him to his quarters. You can use my outer office for the moment." He rose and eased himself out from behind his desk. "Now if you'll excuse me, gentlemen, I'm going back to bed."

As the door shut behind Draz and their guest, Myak selected the appropriate data cubes from the Commander's desk.

Raguul muttered darkly as he crossed to the door at the rear of his office.

"Pardon, sir?"

"I said, damned Brotherhood of Vartra! How they can claim to be priestly is beyond me! They give our guild a bad name!"

"They are a fully recognized sub-sect of the Warrior Guild, sir," said Myak. "Their abilities as special assault forces are invaluable."

"I still don't like having him on board. We can handle the situation ourselves." A pained look crossed his face and he pressed his hand to his stomach. "Get me something for my indigestion, Myak."

"Considering the political implications of the situation, perhaps his presence is a blessing in disguise, sir," said Myak, going to a cupboard on the far side of the room. "At least it's one less problem for you to worry about."

"You may be right," he muttered. "Did you pick up anything from him?"

"No, sir. His mind is as well disciplined as his body. He gives nothing away," said Myak, returning with a glass of white liquid.

Raguul grunted, accepting his medicine. "We'll see. When does the *Cheku* leave?"

"Tomorrow, at the eighth hour, sir, once the system defense vehicles arrive."

"Well, we managed to twist Vroozoi's tail nicely, Myak," he chuckled, handing the glass back to him. "Missing that Valtegan starship has halted his rapid progress, much to the delight of a lot of people in the Forces. I reckon that our officers will be able to dine out on that story for a good few years to come."

Myak grinned. "Yes, sir. I believe he's also highly displeased at the arrival of a Stealth fighter under orders kept secret from him."

Raguul got to his feet and stretched. "Life's tough up at the top, Myak. He'll have to learn to live with disappointment like the rest of us!"

* * *

Guynor's hearing seemed to pass in a world of half-reality for Kusac. The buzzer had actually succeeded in waking him. He had taken a fresh jacket out of his wardrobe and made a futile attempt at grooming himself since he didn't have the time or inclination to take a shower.

Rhian had arranged it so that he and Carrie waited separately, neither of them needing to be in the anteroom with the rest of the crew from the *Sirroki*.

Somehow he managed to negotiate the corridors and elevators until he was at the military judicial section of the ship. He was shown into a small bare room and told he would be called when his evidence was required.

The narrow seat was almost enough to keep him awake, the way it aggravated the aches he felt in every joint. He had managed to reduce his headache to a dull ache but found he had to force himself to get to his feet and pace around the room every few minutes to stop himself from nodding off.

Finally someone came for him and he was ushered into the courtroom. Facing him was a large semicircular table behind which sat the four presiding officers. To either side were the tables for the Prosecution and the Defense. Kusac was led over to the prosecuting side and asked to sit in the chair set there for the witness.

From the other side of the room, Guynor cast him a glance of pure hate.

"Would the witness please state his full name and rank for the records," directed the Prosecuting Officer.

"Kusac Alda, Telepath Fifth Grade, of the survey ship, *Khalossa*," he replied.

The Sub-Commander chairing the court looked up from his notes.

"Sir, I realize that you chose to join this ship without the benefit of rank, but for the legal purposes of this court, it is necessary that you state your full name and rank."

Guynor looked up sharply, as did the officer conducting his defense.

"Kusac Aldatan, Liegen of Valsgarth Estate, Telepath First Grade, serving on the survey ship *Khalossa*," he said quietly, staring down at his hands. Well, he'd expected no less. The wonder was that he hadn't been approached before now.

A chair scraped back noisily. Kusac looked over to where Guynor sat slumped forward onto the table.

"Sub-Commander, sir, could I ask for a five minute recess with my client in view of the fact we were not aware of the witness' full identity?" asked the Defense Counsel.

The Sub-Commander turned to his fellow officers, exchanging a few brief words with them before turning back to the Defense.

"The court will adjourn for five minutes to allow counsel to confer with his client."

"Thank you," said the officer, gathering his papers and following Guynor and his guards.

Guynor stopped, sending a look of glowering hostility in Kusac's direction. *I know you can hear me, you bastard,* came the thought with all the cold fury Guynor was capable of projecting. *I'll get you for setting me up like this!* The guards tugged him on and he was led from the room.

As the presiding officers filed out of the door behind their table, the Prosecutor came over to Kusac.

"Liegen Aldatan," he said, bowing his head. "It's my pleasure to represent you. I expected that reaction from the defense when they heard your true rank. We should have no trouble in getting a conviction."

Anger was burning away some of the fog from Kusac's brain.

"Someone's life is at stake here now," he said with suppressed fury. "I don't want his death! Who gave out the details of my identity?"

"I don't know, Liegen," he stuttered, backing away slightly. "The information was in my brief, and obviously the Sub-Commander's. Knowledge of your identity is restricted at the moment, not to go beyond the doors of this court."

"Why wasn't the defense told?"

"Court procedure, Liegen. It's part of the prosecution's case. It wouldn't have changed anything," he said hurriedly, seeing Kusac's mounting anger. "He's guilty on two counts. Issuing a Challenge against a superior officer's orders in a time of war, and issuing a Challenge to a telepath with intent to kill. Those alone warrant the death penalty, without taking your rank into account."

Kusac growled and turned away.

"Leave me," he snapped.

The officer was only too glad to put a table between him and the outraged lord.

The door in front of Kusac opened and the four officers returned. Moments later, Guynor entered with his counsel. He looked like a man who knew he was facing death. Despite his mental barrier, Kusac could still feel the waves of hate emanating from him.

"Court is now resumed," said the Sub-Commander.

The Defense stood up. "Sir, we withdraw our defense."

"What, entirely?" asked the Sub-Commander, shocked out of his ritual responses.

The officer smiled faintly. "Yes, sir. Entirely." He sat down again.

"You do realize we have to proceed with the prosecution evidence?"

"Yes, we do."

"Very well. Proceed," the Sub-Commander said to the Prosecution.

"Liegen Aldatan, could you tell us in your own words what happened on the evening of . . ."

Kusac felt a hand shaking him awake. "You're wanted in the courtroom again, sir," said a voice.

He groaned, trying to shake the fog out of his mind, and staggered to his feet, feeling a hand catch him.

"You all right, sir?" the young rating asked.

"I'm fine," he said. "Let's just get this farce over with."

At the back of the courtroom stood Carrie, flanked by Rhian and Askad and the crew of the *Sirroki*. Kusac was led to the prosecution's table and asked to sit beside the officer while the court announced its decision.

"Guynor Chanda, First Officer of the *Sirroki*, you have been found guilty on two counts," the Sub-Commander said, reading from his report. "On the first count that you disobeyed a superior officer's order while in a war situation, and on the second count that you, with intent to kill, issued an unlawful Challenge against a telepath. This charge was duly altered to one of Attempted Murder.

"The charge of Challenging a superior officer cannot in fairness be leveled against you. Since you voluntarily gave up your right to defense, do you wish to make a statement before sentence is passed?"

Guynor rose to his feet.

"Only to say that this court may have judged against me, but time will prove that I acted correctly in issuing the Challenge in spite of his rank! I still say that he," he said, face contorted by hate as he swung round to point an accusing finger at Kusac, "acts against the interests of our race when he lies with his alien whore! I warn you again, Kusac, keep looking behind you! If I can't get you, others will!" He sat down abruptly.

The Sub-Commander drew his breath in sharply.

"You forget yourself," he snapped. "Had I known you intended to further insult not only the injured party in this trial, but also an honored addition to our crew, I would not have allowed you to speak. The penalty for your actions is death. The sentence will be carried out at dawn tomorrow."

The Defending Officer rose hurriedly to his feet.

"On behalf of my client, I would like to appeal to the court to allow him the right to die with honor, by his own hand."

"Denied. There is nothing honorable about your client. He is a dangerous and deluded man, and I will personally make sure the sentence is carried out."

"But, sir . . ."

"I said denied! He has just restated his desire to kill one of the most important people on this vessel. There will be no chances taken over this execution."

The Sub-Commander rose to his feet and stalked out, leaving the courtroom standing in stunned silence.

Askad made his way over to where Kusac sat.

"Get me out of this circus," he said, his voice barely audible.

Askad helped him to his feet, pushing a way through his stunned crewmates until they were clear of the courtroom.

Kusac leaned against the wall, clutching his stomach as it cramped up on him.

"You're ill. I'm getting Vanna," said Askad, moving away.

Kusac grabbed hold of him. "No," he said. "It'll pass. It's just a reaction to what I've witnessed in there today."

Askad hesitated as Kusac began to straighten up and breathe more easily.

"See? It's gone already."

"It wasn't that much of a circus, Kusac. He did get justice, you know. What else could the court do when he virtually promised to murder you if he got the chance?"

"I dealt with him once, I can do it again. Next time I'd be prepared."

"Why should you have to? It comes down to your and Carrie's deaths or his. He isn't going to settle for less than killing you. No, they made the right decision."

"Well, I don't think so!"

"Then what would you have done?" asked Askad, just as angrily.

The fight left Kusac. "I really don't know," he replied tiredly. "Look, I'm going back to my room. Today has been too much for me. See Carrie is all right, will you?"

"Shouldn't you speak to her while she's here?"

"No. When she's ready, she'll come to me."

"I think you're making a mistake. You should make the first move."

"Everyone thinks they know my business better than me!" he growled, jerking himself free.

As he made his way to the elevator, someone grasped him by the arm, pulling him to a halt.

"Kusac! It's me, Vanna. Why didn't you wait and talk to us?"

Kusac stared at the medic for a few seconds before he recognized her.

"Vanna," he said. "Good to see you."

"Kusac, what's wrong?" she asked, reaching up to touch his face briefly. "Are the headaches worse? Are you feeling ill?"

He smiled vaguely. "Not ill, just tired." He pulled himself together with an obvious effort. "The court-martial, it took a lot out of me."

"I'm not surprised," she replied sympathetically. "How's Carrie? She rushed off, too."

"Carrie? Oh, she's well, I think."

"Don't you know?" she asked sharply.

"I haven't seen much of her lately. Look, I must go," he said, beginning to move away from her. "I really do need to rest. As you said, the headache is still with me."

"Then why haven't you been in touch? Obviously you need something stronger for the pain."

"If I still have it tomorrow, I promise I'll call you."

Vanna watched him walk away, a worried look on her face.

No sooner had he shut the door and taken off his jacket than the tone sounded.

"Who is it?"

"It's Carrie."

Kusac opened the door, looking at her silently. "You look well," he said after a moment, noticing that again she wore Sholan clothes. With her long fair hair, it made her appear even more exotic than usual.

"Kusac, may I come in?" she asked, looking nervously to either side of her.

Silently, he moved away from the doorway toward the center of the room. "Sit down," he said, indicating a chair.

She shook her head. "I've only come for a minute. I think I'm starting a cold or something," she said. "I've had these terrible headaches and pains in my joints. Vanna gave me something for it, and it helps a bit." When he didn't reply, she stood looking around the room, obviously unsure what to say next.

"What can I do for you, Carrie?"

She turned to look at him again. "I had to come," she said.

"Why?" he asked, realizing through the haze of pain from his headache that he was only vaguely curious.

"I miss you," she said. "I realized that when I saw you today." Hesitantly, she came over to him.

As if from a distance he noticed that her hand was trembling as she reached out to touch his shoulder. Her fingers stroked his fur, pushing as always past it to the skin underneath. A tremor ran through him, one so strong she couldn't fail to notice it.

She moved closer, resting her head against his chest, her hand moving to touch his neck.

Kusac breathed in sharply, closing his eyes as he tried to counteract the stab of agony that lanced through his head. Her scent was strong in his nostrils, and like her presence, all but unbearable. His hand came up to touch her waist, almost but not quite daring to hold her close. He touched her face fleetingly with his other hand, jerking it away as a spasm of nausea wracked his body.

"Carrie," he said harshly in Terran, "you've no idea what you're doing to me. I'm no different from your own males, and your presence is stretching my self-control beyond endurance." He pushed her away. "You don't know what it costs me to say this, but leave me now and don't return unless you intend to stay."

She stood there, what little color there was draining from her face. "I thought you'd be glad to see me," she whispered.

"Gods, I offer you myself and you can't decide! Yes," he hissed, baring his teeth at her and making her step back in shock. "I am glad to see you! You've had your time to choose, now it's all but run out. For Vartra's sake, make up your mind, girl! Either stay or go!"

Carrie stumbled to the door and, fumbling with the release mechanism, ran out into the corridor leaving it open behind her.

Still shaking, Kusac sealed it. His legs gave way and he sank down into a crouch, head in his hands, fighting the spasms in his stomach. At last, his body under some sort of control, he staggered to the bed, rolling into the concave depression as the images started to flicker through his mind. He tried not to fight it this time, there was no longer any point. He began, finally, to let go.

Heedless of the curious eyes of the Sholans around her, Carried fled to the safety of Rhian's and Askad's quarters. She punched the entry code into the lock, pushing through the gap as soon as the door began to open, sealing it behind her almost immediately. Quickly, she sent a probe round the apartment. She was alone. Stumbling into her room like Kusac, she flung herself on her bed, only to have to rise moments later to rush to the bathroom, retching.

The attack over, she sat up, wiping her clammy forehead with a towel. She hadn't been feeling well these last few days, but this was probably just a reaction to the stresses of the day. Going into the main room, she chose a glass of water from the dispenser and returned to her bedroom. She pulled the cover off the bed and wrapping it round herself, sat down and sipped the water. She was still trembling, but now she felt chilled to the bone and her head had begun to throb again.

She tried to think about Kusac, about their Link, but her thoughts kept wriggling away from her like so many serpents to be replaced by flashes of memories. S/he saw her floundering through the snow toward her/him, grateful at last for the help he/she needed to stop the pain and fever; she/he stood against a tree, surrounded by four Valtegans intent on amusing themselves before killing her, then he/she erupted into the clearing, laying about with deadly claws. Faster and faster flicked the images until, her mind bruised beyond coping, she collapsed.

Chapter 3

Anonymous in his Forces uniform with its green flash of the Communications Guild, Tallinu had ambled off to find his quarters and store his gear. Draz had sent one of his security officers down to the stores on the concourse to collect everything he'd need while Myak adjusted the ship's records to not only list him on the payroll, but to show that he'd been on board for several months. Tallinu handed him a set of personnel records and, within moments, his cover was complete.

An hour or so at his comm and he'd acquired all the relevant data that he needed. Switching it off, he stood up and stretched each muscle group in turn. It was a good job he'd kept in shape over the last ten years. He was stiff and tired. *Striker* might be fast but it was damned uncomfortable. As well as that, his body was on Sholan time, not ship time. It was another six hours before he could call it a day.

Going up to the Admin level on the twenty-first floor, he made his way to the small shrine. Next door to it was the office used by the priest—in this case, the Brother—for their more secular duties. He opened the door and went in.

"I'll be with you in a moment," said the Brother, peering round the doorway of his inner sanctum. He froze, staring at his visitor.

"It looks like I can't call you Dzakayini anymore," he drawled, flicking a coin toward him.

Dzaka's hand reached out instinctively and caught it. "The guild coin," he said. "I knew they were sending someone, but I never dreamed it would be you." He came into the room and, hesitating, handed the coin back to Tallinu.

"Is that all the greeting I get?" he asked, eye ridge raised. Before he'd finished speaking, Dzaka was embracing him.

"It's been so long," said Dzaka, as Tallinu returned the gesture. "I didn't know Ghezu had reinstated you."

"He hasn't, exactly," he said, sitting down on one of the lounge chairs. "I accepted the contract as a free-lance operative. I have all the guild privileges, and a free hand in this one. Now I know why."

"C'shar?" Dzaka asked, moving back into the inner room. "I'd just put some on when you arrived."

"Please. I was sorry to hear about your mate, Nnya. I know what a terrible blow it must have been to you."

"I can't talk about it yet," he said, his voice bleak. "Did you get my report? Is that why you're here?"

"Partially," Tallinu admitted. "I need you to bring me up to date not only on these potential troublemakers, but also on what you've found out about this mismatched Leska pair. I'm here to assess the situation concerning them."

Dzaka nodded to himself as he brought out the mugs and set one down in front of Tallinu. "I thought as much. You know it's got Mentor Mnya in a sweat, don't you? To say nothing of the Commander? He's got his adjutant, Myak, fielding her father and Konis Aldatan, which isn't an easy thing to do considering the situation. No one wants to tell him about his son."

"I'm not surprised. And Mnya? What's got her so worried? The cross-species Link, or the fact they can fight?"

"The fact they can fight," he said, sitting down. "She's afraid that fear of them will start up the post-Cataclysm pogroms again, when telepaths were hunted down and murdered because of their Talent."

Tallinu made a noise of disgust. "The fear of the telepaths back then was because the ordinary people thought they'd caused the Cataclysm."

"I know. There's no reason for her to think that could ever happen again. It's one thing for a race emerging from global destruction to be paranoid and superstitious, but not now, a thousand years later."

"Enough of Mnya's paranoia. Tell me about this group of xenophobic younglings."

"They're not exactly xenophobic. Their logic's a little more complex. There're another two Brothers on the *Khalossa,* and one of them tried to infiltrate their little group but failed. Most of them have known each other for some time, and they aren't about to admit strangers into their confidence now."

"I hear you ruffled some fur the other night at a meeting

for those who'd lost family on Szurtha and Khyaal," said Tallinu, relaxing back into his chair.

"I did, rather," Dzaka admitted ruefully. "Tutor Rhuso told me to put this issue to rest once and for all, so I did. I told them what it was like. Before I did, though, I was sitting beside several of that little group and their attitude—then and later—had me worried. It wasn't what they said, because they sat there and just listened. You know how it is, I get a feel for the mood, and I didn't like theirs one bit, especially the one called Chyad."

"Carry on," he said, picking up his mug and taking a drink from it.

* * *

"Kaid, it's good to see you again," said Garras, slipping into the seat opposite his friend. "You got my message, then. I didn't expect to see you quite so soon."

A glass was pushed across the table toward him. "Friends come first. Your message coincided with one from the guild. I was able to combine the two."

Garras lifted the glass gratefully, taking a long drink. "Thanks. I've just come off duty and I needed that. I'm breaking in a new crew."

"I hear you had bad luck with your last one."

"News gets around fast," grunted Garras.

"Particularly when it's news like this."

"What's being said?"

"Chitchat about the Terrans, especially the new Telepath you brought back with you. How she's formed a Leska Link with one of your crew. And of course, Guynor's Challenge and the court-martial resulting from it."

"That it?"

He nodded, taking a sip from his own glass. "What's left?"

"Depends how you look at it," said Garras. "One hell of a lot from what I can see."

"So. Tell me."

* * *

Vanna had spent an hour trying to find Garras. She finally tracked him down in the main bar on the concourse. Stopping at the doorway, she looked around the crowed area, trying to spot Garras' grizzled head. Not old, she reminded herself with a faint grin, just mature.

Catching sight of him at the far corner, she headed over, threading her way through the crowded tables. As she got closer, she noticed his companion get up and leave.

"Where's your friend gone?" she asked, slipping into the vacated seat against the wall.

"He's due on shift," said Garras. "What brings you down here at this time of day?"

"The need for familiar company," she said. "I look around at these people and I don't know them anymore. It's as if they were ..." She stopped, lost for a word.

"Alien?"

"Yes, alien. It's as if they're only playing at what we actually experienced. They ask what happened and when I tell them, they don't understand."

"This is their first real taste of war, Vanna. Apart from policing the odd border dispute between the Touibans and the Chemerians, the Forces don't see any real action. We've lived years of their placid existence in three months, and in a way they resent it."

"I don't know about that, but they seem to think it was exciting. Being holed up in that cave for weeks on end, not knowing if we'd ever get off-planet isn't my idea of excitement!"

"Nor that of any sane person who's actually experienced it," he said soothingly. "Now, what did you really want to see me about?"

Vanna glanced up at him. "I'm beginning to think telepathy is catching," she said wryly. "I'm worried about Kusac and Carrie. I wondered if you'd heard from either of them."

"Me? Why should they contact me?" he asked, cocking his head to one side in surprise.

"No reason really, just a faint hope," she shrugged, looking down at the table again. "After what we've been through, it's natural to want to remain together because of the shared experiences. Especially when no one else understands them," she said with a flash of humor.

Garras looked up and managed to catch the eye of a bartender. Beckoning him over, he handed him his empty glass. "The same again," he said. "Vanna?"

"Oh, c'shar please."

He turned back to her. "Why are you worrying about them?"

"Carrie is still at Rhian's."

"Leskas don't always live together," he said reasonably.

"I know that," she said, her tone almost sharp. "But Kusac looked pretty rough when we saw him yesterday after the court-martial. He's had constant severe headaches since the night you two had your fight in the bar. So has Carrie. Something isn't right."

Garras frowned, ears twitching slightly. "You're not being very specific. Are you concerned that one or both of them is ill, or that they are apart?"

"I can't be more specific. It's more of a hunch, a gut feeling," she said, concentrating on dipping a clawtip in a small puddle of drink on the table. "After living with them on Keiss, I seem to sense when something's not right."

"So that's what you meant by telepathy being catching," he said with an attempt at levity.

She ignored his comment, waiting till the bartender had placed the drinks in front of them. "From what I've been able to find out about Leskas, they need to be together every five days. Be it biological imperative or a psychological need to renew the closeness between them, they need that twenty-six hours together. Kusac and Carrie haven't been alone together as far as I know since Guynor's Challenge. That was sixteen days ago by my reckoning. That's not right or normal for Leskas."

"What's normal for the first Sholan and Terran Leska pair?"

Vanna's ears dipped briefly to the side as she shot him an angry look. She returned to drawing patterns in the spilled drink with her clawtip.

"Drink your c'shar," said Garras placatingly. "When are you due to see him next?"

"Tomorrow," she said.

"Not much is likely to happen between now and then even if you're right. If he's ill, he'll call you. So will she."

"I suppose so," Vanna said reluctantly.

Garras sighed. "If you're that bothered, call him."

"I can't," she said, looking up. "It would be an invasion of his privacy. They're on leave at the moment, so they can adjust to their Link."

"Maybe being so closely involved with them wasn't such

a good idea after all," said Garras, reaching out to place his hand on top of hers comfortingly.

"I'm the only one who can do the job at present," she said.

"Then train someone to take over."

"It would take too long, and most of what I know is based on intuition. I can't teach anyone else that."

"Have you managed to get any more information from the Telepath Guild?"

"None. They say we have all the relevant data we need, but I don't believe them."

"Why would they lie about it? They must realize that Kusac and Carrie are more important than keeping guild secrets. You're letting your imagination get the better of you."

"Maybe you're right," she said. "I'm probably looking on the dark side. I was up in my lab this morning when they brought Guynor in, and it's left me feeling down."

"That's probably what's at the base of your 'gut feeling.' Guynor's death."

"You're probably right. This is the first execution there's been on the *Khalossa* in the five years I've served on her. On top of that, he was a colleague of mine."

"The death of someone you know always makes you aware of your own mortality," he said, tightening his grip on her hand. "At least you know he was guilty of attempted murder."

"That doesn't really help, and that's the worst part."

The intercom chimed melodiously. "Vanna Kyjishi to Med level, lab three."

"I've got to go," she said, withdrawing her hand and standing up. "It could be them."

"Do you want to meet later?" Garras asked, looking up at her. "If you're feeling that low, company would be good therapy."

She hesitated. "I'll get back to you, if I may."

"Leave a message on my comm," he said. "Personnel will give you the code. I'll authorize it with them."

Vanna hurried into her office, going straight to the comm. The monitor glowed red in the left corner, indicating a message.

She keyed in the command for a hard copy and the unit erupted into life, spitting sheets of paper into the tray. Picking up the first sheet, she scanned the top, wondering what could have been so urgent as to necessitate her being paged.

At the top it read, "Kusac Aldatan to Vanna Kyjishi" and was dated for the following day's transmission.

Frowning, she sat down to read it. She soon realized that here was the information she was lacking—the medical data that the Telepath Guild claimed didn't exist.

Grabbing a medikit, she rifled through its contents, adding extra ampoules for the hypoderm gun. In her haste, she dropped one. It fell to the floor, smashing and spreading its contents round her feet.

Swearing, she hopped out of the way, yelling for one of the nurses to clean it up. The last thing she needed now was a cut foot.

Less haste, she told herself as she cursed Kusac in every direction for being a fool.

Replacing the broken ampoule, she snapped the case shut, heading at a run for the nearest elevator.

When it stopped, she shoved her way out, upsetting several people in the process. She went down the corridor at full lope until she reached Rhian's and Askad's quarters. She punched the chime, tail lashing impatiently from side to side as she waited.

* * *

Raguul switched off the comm and looked up at Myak. "Where is she?" he asked succinctly.

"Still at the quarters of Rhian and Askad, our other Leska pair."

"And our runaway?"

"He's in his quarters," replied Myak, heading unobtrusively toward the cupboard in the far wall.

"I want her here, in my office in an hour's time," Raguul said. "I want the Mentor here now. This Link of theirs has to be dissolved."

"I'm afraid that's not possible, sir," siad Myak, coming back across the room to the Commander and offering him his medicine.

"I didn't ask for that," said Raguul, nonetheless automatically taking it from him. "What do you mean it isn't possible?"

"I can contact the Mentor without difficulty, but the Terran girl, I'm afraid not. There's some kind of medical emergency involving both of them. I don't have any details at present, but it's being dealt with. Doubtless the Mentor will be able to tell you more when she arrives."

Raguul gave him a pained look, then drank the contents of the glass. He handed it back to Myak without a word.

Myak ushered in the Mentor.

"Commander," she said, taking the chair beside the desk. "How can I help you?"

"First, what's all this about a medical emergency involving Kusac and Carrie?"

Mnya smiled. "Nothing that hasn't been satisfactorily dealt with."

Raguul blinked, surprised. "I expect you don't intend to discuss it any further," he said, "but I expect a full report on it tomorrow. Meanwhile, you're aware that we've opened negotiations with the Terran's home world, Earth, aren't you?"

"I had heard that everything was progressing well."

"It was with Keiss, until Earth became aware of two things. Keiss' independent status and the fact that we have a Terran female, daughter of Hamilton, the planetary Governor, on board."

The Mentor looked puzzled. "I fail to see a problem."

"The Terrans wish to retain absolute control over all negotiations. They and only they will make the treaty with us. Keiss is their colony and will do as it's told. Hamilton is having none of it; he's holding out for independence. Earth threatens to cut negotiations completely if we make a treaty with Hamilton."

"What does Alien Relations say?"

"That we deal with Keiss."

"And Earth?"

"We point out that their participation in guarding their sector of space from possible Valtegan incursions would be useful, but not necessary to the Alliance. Basically, they can sink or swim on their own."

"Harsh words," murmured the Mentor.

"Oh, they'll come round. That isn't the real problem. While Earth was arguing with Hamilton, they pointed out that we are holding his daughter as a hostage. Hamilton has now demanded the immediate return of his daughter or he'll cut off all negotiations with us."

"This is unfortunate."

Myak returned bearing mugs of c'shar.

"Thanks," grunted Raguul, taking his. "You might as well remain," he said, nodding to a companion chair by the Mentor. "This is more than unfortunate. The whole treaty now hangs in the balance because of their damned link!"

"It's hardly their fault, Commander," said the Mentor, taking a sip of her drink before placing the mug on the desk.

"Mnya, that Link has got to be dissolved. I have to return the female to her planet," Raguul said, leaning forward, ears flicking.

"Impossible. It's too late now, even if there had been anything we could have done."

"Dammit, Mnya! It's a cross-species Link, not even a real one! There has to be some way to break it. Can't you people do something to her mind, shut it down or something?"

"Have you any idea what you're suggesting, Raguul?" the Mentor asked, her anger evident in the set of ears and eyes. "That is tantamount to blinding and deafening an unTalented person! The girl has done nothing wrong to deserve such a punishment even if it could be done! And what about Kusac? Do we just 'shut him down,' too? The shock of doing that could kill them both!"

"If it saved the treaty, I'd order it. Without her Talent, Kusac would no longer be Linked to her which would get rid of our other problem. She has to be returned to Keiss, and on her own. Find a way to do it."

"Their Link is as real as any Sholan Leska Link."

"I don't think you're considering the political or military consequences if we don't return her, Mnya. And Kusac must remain here. His father is trying to get his service in the Forces terminated," said Raguul. "Hard though it is, this has to be done."

"Raguul, you are the one ignoring the political consequences," said Mnya stiffly. "When I said it's impossible, I meant it cannot be done, unless you want to return two corpses!"

"Come off it, Mnya," said the Commander, sitting back in his seat. "I know you want to study her Talent, but the treaty has to come first. If you wanted to, you could find a way to do it, I'm sure."

"Raguul, kindly grant me the courtesy of believing I know my own craft," said Mnya, her tone biting. "By now their

Link is complete. Their minds are working as one, in a way no Sholan Leska Link does! This Link of theirs is abnormal, yes, in its intensity. They have exchanged Talents and memories to a degree never known by our guild before!" She leaned forward. "As for the politics, do you really want to return Hamilton's daughter to him as a corpse? And Konis Aldatan's son? Head of Alien Relations, Lord of the Sixteen Telepath Clans? Return his son dead because of a treaty? I'm sure he'd understand," she said sarcastically. "So will Rhyasha. She's got two other children, after all. One of them can be heir instead of Kusac. I'd understand perfectly if I were them."

Raguul flinched. "Konis doesn't know about their Link as yet."

"Well, I'm not going to tell him!" she said tartly. "You're being foolish in the extreme to even think of risking their lives. In their case there can be no doubt that if one of them dies, you'll lose them both. Take that as a certainty."

"How can you be so sure?" demanded Raguul, regaining a little of his equilibrium. "You haven't had time to verify all that you've told me."

"I don't need to. Kusac did it. I received a locked and dated file that he had intended for the physician, Vanna Kyjishi. I've no idea how it landed on my desk, but I'm damned glad it did! It puts paid utterly to lunatic suggestions like yours!"

"There's no need to be offensive, Mnya," sighed Raguul. "So, like it or not, we're stuck with their Link. What the hell do I do about Hamilton?"

"Tell him. Once he knows, he won't risk her life either."

"I'm not going to tell him!"

"Ha! So who is?" demanded Mnya.

They sat and looked at each other in silence. "Excuse me," said Myak. Taken by surprise, they both looked round at him.

"Why not let them tell their own fathers? That's what would normally happen with our people. I should imagine it's the same for the Terrans. Kusac will definitely want to speak to his father himself, and probably Carrie's as well."

Raguul's expression relaxed into one of relief. "What could be more natural? The female is, after all, only Kusac's Leska. It's not as if he's contracted to her as a mate."

"I for one will be glad not to have to face Konis' anger,"

she said candidly. "What about Hamilton? He's going to take none too kindly to his daughter having a relationship with Kusac. At least Konis has dealt extensively with aliens. It won't be quite such a shock to him."

"If the female talks to her father and makes it clear she intends to stay with Kusac, then he'll have to accept it."

"If we had an official reception, Hamilton could come and see her for himself. He would know it was her decision and nothing to do with the treaty negotiations," ventured Myak.

"It might work," said Mnya thoughtfully. "If we adapt our Attitude Indoctrination sessions to cover that, it should answer most of the problems Hamilton will come up against over their relationship."

"Myak, contact the girl and Kusac. Have them come up here so we can contact Hamilton and then Clan Lord Aldatan on the comm. The sooner it's done, the better."

"No, Raguul," interrupted Mnya. "They're together now. Leave them. It's the first of their Link days. Stall Hamilton and the Clan Lord for now. Myak can think up many reasons, he's good at that. I know from personal experience," she said, grinning.

Myak lowered his ears, refusing to look at the Mentor in the face.

"Yes, at least you have the grace to be embarrassed about it! Give them till tomorrow, then if their parents call, inform them and let them deal with it in their own way," she said, picking up her drink.

* * *

At last Rhian answered the door.

"I need to see Carrie now," said Vanna.

"I'm afraid Carrie has shut herself in her room. She won't see anyone."

"Tough. She'll see me," said Vanna grimly, pushing past Rhian and heading for Carrie's door.

"Vanna, this is an invasion of her privacy, not to mention ours," Rhian called out as she followed her. "You have no right to intrude. Askad, tell her."

Vanna ignored her and tried the door handle. "It's locked."

Askad got up from the chair and came over, putting a hand on Vanna's arm to gently restrain her.

"What's this all about, Vanna? If you tell us, perhaps we can help."

"I have to see Carrie now. She's ill. Let me in."

"How do you know? Surely we'd have been aware of it."

"You're wasting my time!" she said angrily. "Just take my word for it and open the door!"

"Not without some proof, Vanna," said Askad.

"Someone dumped a file of Kusac's into my comm. It details the symptoms he's been suffering over the last four days. They both need medical attention fast, and I need to start with her. She's been blocking the Link since the fight in the bar!"

"What? But that's impossible," said Rhian, shocked.

"Apparently not for our Terran. Now will you open this bloody door?" Vanna demanded, pulling away from Askad. "If you don't believe me, try to reach her."

"Very well." Rhian shut her eyes and reached for Carrie's mind. With a shocked exclamation, she stared round-eyed at Vanna.

"I can barely sense her! Askad, get the door open," she ordered her mate.

Askad moved the females aside and, lifting his foot, gave the door a hefty kick. It burst open, spilling the three of them into the room.

Rhian ran over to the bed, placing her hand on Carrie's forehead. "Her skin is clammy."

"Can you reach her?" asked Askad, his voice a calming influence.

"She's there, thank the Gods, but what has the stupid child done? I can't sense Kusac's presence at all."

"The shielding in the room . . ." began Vanna, depositing her medikit on the bed.

"No barrier to a Leska bond," said Askad curtly.

"Can you do anything?" Vanna asked, loading the hypoderm and leaving it ready.

"I don't know," said Rhian anxiously. "It's generations since we've had any trouble with a Leska pair. Everyone knows the danger signals and watches for them."

"Everyone except Carrie," said Vanna angrily, pushing her out of the way.

"She was told!" said Rhian hotly. "She said Kusac had warned her of the dangers."

"What else did she say?" Vanna demanded, checking the

unconscious girl's pulse and thumbing back her eyelids. "Probably that she didn't believe him!" She looked up at the other two. "What game have they been playing with each other? The same one that started on Keiss?" She placed the hypoderm against Carrie's neck and pressed the trigger.

"If you mean she wanted time to accustom herself to . . ."

Vanna let loose a few expletives as she pulled the cover off Carrie. "She was accustomed to us on Keiss! She's suffering from plain, old-fashioned fear. You heard the medics say she has yet to mate. I'd lay odds that unlike us she has inhibitions about pairing for the first time."

Bodily lifting the girl with one hand, she landed her a stinging slap across the face with the other.

"Carrie! You can hear me," she said, slapping the other cheek. "Wake up, Carrie!"

Rhian grabbed at her arm, but Askad stopped her. "She knows what she's doing. She is a medic."

"Carrie, wake up," chanted Vanna, administering another couple of slaps.

Carrie moaned, turning her head away to avoid the blows. Vanna began to shake her.

"Come on, Carrie. I know you can hear me," she said. "If you two want to help, get me a protein drink for her."

"Leave me," mumbled Carrie. "I want to sleep. I don't want a drink."

"You can't sleep, cub. You must wake up." Another couple of slaps and Carrie's eyes opened blearily.

"Vanna? What are you doing here?" she asked.

"Trying to save your life."

"My life?" echoed Carrie, trying to focus her eyes. "Nothing wrong with me, I'm just tired."

Vanna shook her again, taking the cup from Rhian.

"Here, drink this."

Carrie choked on the first mouthful but managed to swallow most of the drink.

"What have you done to Kusac?" Vanna demanded, handing the cup to Rhian and letting Carrie lie back again.

"Kusac? I haven't done anything," she said wearily. "Is something wrong with him?"

"You've blocked your Link, Carrie. Take that barrier down now. Rhian can't sense Kusac in your mind."

"In my mind?" she asked, trying to push herself upright.

"Remove the block now, Carrie," repeated Vanna.

Carrie brushed her hair out of her eyes and looked at her. "I shielded him out," she mumbled. "I had to think."

"Oh, Gods," moaned Rhian, sinking down onto the bed.

"Get that shield down. Reach for him," said Askad urgently, bending down beside her. "Find him quickly."

"All . . . all right," Carrie stammered, lowering her mental shields. "He's not there! Where is he? What's happened?" she demanded wildly, trying to get to her feet despite the overwhelming weakness that seemed to have her in its grasp. She stumbled and Vanna caught her.

"When you shielded yourself against the Leska bond, it put both your lives in jeopardy," said Askad grimly. "You may be lucky. We might find him still alive, but I doubt it."

"I only wanted to make up my own mind," Carrie whispered, the lethargy and disorientation washing over her again, "not be forced into another bond."

"Make up your mind!" exclaimed Vanna, giving her another shake. "What's to make up your mind about? You're Leskas, there is no alternative but death for you and him! Kusac didn't tell you that though, did he?"

Releasing her, she whirled to face Askad. "And what were you thinking of?" she demanded. "How could you let her believe she had a choice? Even with Sholans the Link is indissoluble."

"It was Kusac's decision, not ours," he replied, picking Carrie up in his arms and striding toward the door. "We were as much in the dark as you. We haven't the time to argue over this now, Kusac should be our main concern."

"You've let them play with each other's lives," Vanna said with suppressed fury as she followed him out. "They aren't some damned experiment, they're my friends!"

Askad set the pace, running in a distance-consuming lope, Carrie hanging like a limp doll in his grasp.

The corridor on Kusac's level was busy at this time and their passage was hindered by the reluctance of people to move. Vanna impatiently pushed to the front, shoving aside anyone who got in her way. Startled Sholans lined their route, their mouths open in amazement as they stared at the alien figure lying supine in Askad's arms.

Carrie drifted in and out of consciousness, aware only that try as she might, she couldn't sense Kusac.

They reached the door at last. Askad deposited Carrie unceremoniously on her feet, leaving Vanna and Rhian to catch her.

"You can't kick that door down," said Vanna dryly. "How are we going to get in?"

Askad looked around.

"We haven't time to get the combination from Personnel," he said. "I need something to use as a lever."

"Here, take Carrie," said Vanna, pushing the girl against Rhian and dumping her medikit down. "I'll be back in a moment. I have a friend on this level who might be able to help." With that she sped up the corridor, returning within a few minutes carrying an energy pistol. Taking careful aim at the locking mechanism, she pressed the trigger. The lock exploded in a shower of splinters, sending the door sliding back a couple of precious centimeters.

Askad grabbed the edge and pulled, oblivious to the crowd of scandalized people beginning to gather round them.

"Medical emergency," said Vanna, holding up her case for them to see before pushing her way past Askad into the room. She rushed over to the still form on the bed, checking for pulse and breathing.

"He's still alive," she said briefly. "Bring Carrie over," She opened the case and searched for the hypoderm and the drugs. Fitting in an ampoule, she applied it to Kusac's neck. Laying it aside, she felt again for his pulse, counting the beats, praying that the stimulant would work.

"Where shall I put her?" asked Askad.

"Beside him." She looked at Carrie as Askad laid her on the bed next to Kusac.

"You want a choice, Carrie? Well, here it is. Does Kusac live or die? Your choice is that simple," she said. "You might survive the shock of his death because you were able to cut off the Link, but I wouldn't bet on it."

Carrie reached out to touch Kusac's face. "He's so cold."

Vanna prepared the hypoderm again.

"He's dying, Carrie, that's why he's cold. He risked his life giving you the right to choose. You can't put it off any longer." She continued to monitor Kusac's pulse. "Are you going to stay with him, or shall I call the morgue to collect your bodies?"

Carrie looked at her in shock, then turned back to Kusac. "Do something about that door, would you, Rhian?"

Vanna said, trying to keep her voice calm. "No need to let the curious know what's going on."

She felt a faint shudder run through Kusac's body, and his pulse began to increase slightly. Again she pressed the hypoderm to his neck, giving him a second shot.

"Touch him properly, girl," Askad ordered Carrie. "Hasn't anyone told you anything about Links? He needs to know you're physically there. Why do you think we avoid touching those outside our guild? Flesh carries its own messages to us, ones as potent as those of the mind link."

Leaning over him, Carrie pressed her hands on either side of Kusac's head, her hair brushing his face.

"Search for him, Carrie," urged Rhian. "You know his mind. Follow him to where he's hiding."

Carrie, weeping silently now, reached into Kusac's mind, finding it like an empty shell. She began to search, fighting her fatigue and using every ounce of power, desperate to find some small part of him that she could still reach.

"Will it work?" she heard Vanna ask as if from a great distance.

"I don't know," replied Rhian. "It must. The alternative is unthinkable."

To those watching, it seemed that Carrie must fail. Sweat broke out on her forehead and she seemed to falter. Suddenly Kusac's chest rose in a deep breath, then another.

"He's coming out of it," exclaimed Vanna, releasing his wrist. "Thank the Gods!"

Kusac's outer eyelids fluttered, revealing the inner nictitating ones beginning to recede. His hand moved spasmodically, trying to brush his face but he touched Carrie. He grasped her hand, holding it so tightly his claws pressed into her.

"Carrie?" His voice was hoarse and weak.

"Kusac, thank God you're all right! Why the hell didn't you tell me what you were doing?" she demanded, laughing and crying all at once with relief and anger. "I would never have let you risk your life like that!"

Kusac shifted under her weight, moving himself to one side, still keeping a tight grip on her hand.

Picking up her case, Vanna signaled the others. Silently and unnoticed, they made their way outside, making sure the door was at least closed if not locked.

"I think everything will be all right now," she sighed,

leaning against the wall for support, feeling emotionally and physically drained.

"Gods, if you'd been any later!" Rhian said.

"Didn't you realize something was very wrong? You're telepaths, and Leskas, surely you must have noticed something!"

"We noticed some physical symptoms because of the separation, but we had no idea she had blocked their mental Link. The Gods alone know how she did that! Kusac just asked us to look after her, saying he wanted her to come to terms with the situation. I had no idea that Link deprivation would be so severe for them. How could we have known? How could we have guessed that no one had told her enough about her Link."

"He knew what was happening," said Vanna. "He knew exactly what game he was playing." She shook her head.

"He took a terrible risk," agreed Askad. "He miscalculated badly. They were beyond helping themselves. She couldn't go to him."

Vanna looked at him sharply. "He took no risk. He intended to die if she wouldn't have him. If you don't realize that, you don't know Kusac. That file he made, it wasn't supposed to reach me till tomorrow. By then it would have been too late." Her expression softened. "Look, I'm sorry I said what I did about experiments, but I care deeply for both of them."

"There's nothing to forgive," said Rhian.

"I'll come back and check on them tomorrow," Vanna said, moving off.

"Let us know how they are," Askad called after her.

Vanna raised her hand in acknowledgment.

* * *

"Do you stay?" he asked, his voice still hoarse, eyes alight with a feral glow she had never seen before.

"Yes," she whispered, only too aware of the warmth and pressure of the hand that held her wrist. She now realized his touch, his thoughts, literally were life itself to her, as hers were to him.

Letting her go, with an obvious effort Kusac pushed himself into a sitting position, his eyes never leaving her. Already he felt stronger just from touching her; his mind felt clearer and the nausea had gone.

To have given up hope, then to wake to this ... he could hardly believe it was real. His hand shook as he reached out, gently pulling her face closer to his. His cheek touched hers, his tongue finding her ears. Small, almost Sholan sounds escaped her as she moved her head slightly from side to side, trying to elude him, his touch too intense to bear. He turned his attention to her neck.

Now she recognized the sensations that came flooding through her. She felt his arm pressing against her back, urging her closer. Her eyelids began to close as the insistence of her body to respond overtook her conscious will.

She needed to hold him, to feel him warm and alive. She'd come so close to losing him forever—it didn't bear remembering. Her hands went to his sides, traveling across his lean ribs to the muscles of his back, feeling their subtle differences rippling under her touch.

He stopped, and felt her relax back against his arm. Her eyes had a heaviness about them which he immediately recognized as a signal common to Humans and Sholans alike. His hands went to her shoulders. A slight pressure on both seals, a gentle tug, and her tabard dropped to the bed.

He could feel the compulsion starting to build in both of them, increasing, if possible, his need for her. As yet she hadn't noticed it. No matter. She would soon enough. He began to exploit the different textures of his tongue on her neck: first the gentler tip, then the rougher midsection. All the while his fingers were working loose the fastenings on her shirt.

Carrie was lost in the sudden surge of sensations till she realized that it wasn't her but their Link. About to pull back, she stopped, eyes opening wide in shock as she felt his hand close on her naked breast, his fingers and mind reveling in its soft roundness.

His other arm was behind her, making sure she couldn't pull away. The knowledge that Sholan females only had breasts while nursing their young came to her as did his enjoyment of this pleasure forbidden to single males like himself—males still young enough to be driven by their biological need to find a female willing to carry their cubs.

She blinked, disoriented, as she felt his mouth replace his hand and his teeth gently close on her nipple.

A soft moan of pleasure escaped her lips and the tension left her body as suddenly as it had come. As her reaction swept through him, Kusac found himself suddenly light-headed. The nagging doubt that had been worrying him was partially laid to rest when her hands began to clench almost painfully on his shoulders. This couldn't be her first time, not the way she was responding.

Lifting his head, he pulled at her shirt, only to realize it was held on because of her grip on him. Reaching up, he disengaged her hands, eliciting small noises of distress from her until he'd tugged the shirt off and released her. Sliding his hands down her sides, he pushed her last garment free before taking her in his arms and drawing her down onto the bed by his side.

With her heightened sensitivity, the silky feel of his fur against her bare skin started her trembling uncontrollably. Hesitantly, she put her hand against his chest, running her fingers through the longer fur. She could feel his heart racing. His smell enveloped her—deep, musky, male—of that there was no doubt! Tipping her head back slightly, she looked up at him through half-opened eyes.

Wherever they touched, he was intensely aware of her, every hair on his body suddenly sending messages rich with sensuality. He ran his hand down her back, coming to rest on her hip, savoring her smooth alienness with more than his fingers. Gods! He'd forgotten how *small* she was! Hardly larger than a youngling.

This close her scent was stronger, a sharp, sweet musk unique to her. Her throat was curved toward him now, a signal to which his body automatically responded. He moved his arm, taking her by the scruff of the neck and drawing her head farther backward. With a low growl, his jaws closed over her throat, canines pressing into her flesh as he completed his part in the ritually submissive gesture she had begun.

She lay still now, waiting, eyes closed. Against his mouth he could feel her pulse beating in time with his own. Kusac began to purr, a deep sound of pleasure that made his whole body vibrate. She knew the response!

He was done waiting. He'd already waited longer than any other Sholan would have for their Leska. Releasing her, he rolled her onto her back, looming over her momentarily as he pushed her thighs apart with his knee.

Lowering himself onto her, he remembered he'd wanted to take it slowly with her the first time, let them both discover the pleasures of a Leska Link, for it was as new to him as her. In giving her the choice, he'd lost it for himself. Now it was too late. The days of Link deprivation and his own need, coupled with the compulsion to mate was too strong in both of them.

As he matched his larger frame to hers, Carrie's hand came up to ward him off.

Kusac grasped her hand in his, pushing it through the longer fur on his belly till it reached his erection.

She tried to pull back, panic radiating from her, but he forced her hand around him.

Feral eyes, black as night with only the narrowest amber ring, glittered down at her. "No. Not this time," he said, his voice still hoarse. "You chose to stay."

Carrie, eyes fully dilated with sudden fear, looked up at him, seeing only his animal need.

Her fear battered at his mind until, with an effort, he released her wrist, moving his hand up to touch her cheek gently, the feral glow dimming.

"Why do you still fear me physically?" he asked softly. "You know what I feel for you. I would never hurt you. Can't you trust me?"

Her answer was immediate and devastating for both of them. Without warning, he felt himself within her, the shock of that final intimate contact making him gasp. Automatically, he pushed forward only to be brought up short by a physical barrier. Confused, he tried to draw back but found Carrie's hands clasped around his hips. Then as the secondary phase of his erection was triggered and he felt himself swell inside her, he was lost, his senses and his body exploding forward into hers. It was as a fully aroused Sholan male that he took his Human Leska, not hearing her brief cry of pain in that first moment.

His hands moved to clutch her shoulders, claws flexing out as he held onto her.

She responded with an ardor neither of them had anticipated, her need taking them both to higher and higher levels of sensuality.

His grip slipped down to her back and as their minds were swept out of their bodies, they finally merged physically and mentally, completing their Link.

When it came, their climax of shared sensations was shattering. He shuddered, all but spent, but for her it continued. She clutched him close, her need fueling his until he found himself aroused once more despite his tiredness.

Finally, spent and lightheaded, they lay, limbs entwined, as gradually their minds began to separate.

No female I've ever known could be like you, he thought, lying with his life-mate clasped in his arms. *There could never be anyone else now.*

He rolled onto his side, pulling her with him. Putting a hand behind her head for support, he began kissing her, using a mixture of gentle Sholan bites as well as his tongue in the Terran style she had shown him before.

"So long I've waited for this," he said releasing her and running a gentle finger along her cheek and down the curves of breast and hip.

The glow of contentment and love that enfolded him was all the answer he needed.

"You're all the mate I could want, cub," he said.

Carrie touched his mouth with her hand. "After knowing you, I could never want anyone else," she whispered as he caught her fingers in his mouth and began licking them. While they lay there like this, it was as if no one else in the world existed, she thought.

Why didn't you tell me you had never paired before? If I'd known how afraid you were, I could have helped.

It was against everything I'd been taught to believe, she sent. *Stick to your own kind I was told. But they aren't my own kind. To them I'm as alien as you.*

He rubbed his cheek against the top of her head. "The Terrans have hurt you for the last time," he said. "I won't let it happen again." He stopped talking as she rested her head against his chest.

She could feel him purring again, a low sound of pure pleasure.

"It never occurred to me this would be your first time," he said. "Pairing is something we do from puberty onward. I never thought it wouldn't be the same for you. No wonder you were afraid to take an alien lover."

Carrie looked up at him, brown eyes serious. "Kusac, we're Leskas. Nothing about you could be alien to me."

His arms tightened around her for a moment, then relaxed. The last few days were catching up with them. Now the need for urgency had been satisfied, he could feel a warm lassitude begin to spread through both of them.

He came to suddenly, the unfamiliar warmth and touch of another body disorienting him, until he remembered. Her head still rested on his chest and her arm curved round his waist. Her smooth skin looked so frail and vulnerable against his dark fur. He moved his hand to touch her cheek and as he did so, her eyes flickered and opened.

"We've been asleep," she said, her voice blurry.

"So we have," he agreed. "I think we should get up."

She made a small noise of denial and closed her eyes firmly, snuggling closer and holding him tightly.

"I need a shower," he said. "I'm itching all over." There was no response. He reached down to her ribs and began to tickle her.

"Hey! Stop that!" she squealed, moving quickly away from him. "That's unfair!"

Kusac grinned, canines flashing against his dark fur. He sat up and reached across for her. "A shower," he said, hauling her to her feet, "we both need one, and something to eat would be a good idea."

Keeping hold of her hand, he towed Carrie toward the shower room, opening the cubicle door.

It wasn't unlike the ones she vaguely remembered from Earth, but instead of only an overhead faucet, the water also came from jets set into the walls.

They stood in the water, enjoying its invigorating warmth until Kusac picked up a container of soap.

Hold out your hands, he sent, squeezing some of the liquid onto them when she did. *Much more fun having someone scrub you,* he added as he began to smooth the soap over her shoulders.

In a short space of time, they found themselves once more locked in each other's arms sharing a kiss. This time it was Kusac who bared his throat to his life-mate. Water sluiced unnoticed over fur and flesh as they joined again, this time with no fears to conquer.

Both half-drowned, Kusac helped Carrie to her feet then turned the shower off. He shook himself, sending droplets of water flying everywhere. Reaching out of the cubicle for a towel, he wrapped it around Carrie, ignoring her protestations and began rubbing her vigorously before getting a second towel for himself.

He sensed her giggles before he heard them and sent a questioning thought toward her.

A hand came out from the depths of her towel to smooth the hair between his ears.

He grinned back and flicked a switch set into the outer wall, sending hot air blowing round them.

Carrie raised her eyebrows.

"Fur takes longer to dry than your skin," he said, throwing his damp towel on the floor outside.

Carrie let her towel fall and stepping forward, ran her hands across his chest, her eyes becoming heavy-lidded again.

Kusac put his hands on top of hers. "I think you like my fur," he said, stopping her gently.

"Mm," she said, trying to move her hands again. "It's so soft, and so much a part of you."

This time he caught both of her hands in one of his and planted a fair approximation of a kiss on her forehead.

"Later. We need to eat and sleep," he purred quietly. "If you continue, we'll be awake all night."

Carrie sighed as he released her hands. "I suppose you're right. We have a lifetime ahead of us."

She bent to pick up the towel, giving her hair a quick rub before letting the warm air finish the job for her.

Kusac meanwhile had disposed of the wet towels and was checking the saturated bandage round his thigh. He undid it, surprised to see his wound had healed to the point where there was only a bright pink scar showing through the shaved fur surrounding it. He tossed the dressing in the disposal unit and obtained fresh bedding from another cupboard.

"Now whose hair is sticking up on end?" he teased as she lifted her head up, letting her hair cascade around her shoulders.

As he went through to the other room, Carrie looked

around for a mirror. Finding one above the basin, she ran her fingers through her hair, pushing the longer strands back from her fringe. Her hand stilled as she looked at her face in the mirror. Dark brows arched beneath her hair, brown eyes looking back at herself calmly. The slightly upturned nose was unchanged, so was her mouth. She still looked the same, nothing had outwardly altered.

She'd just shared lovemaking with an alien. Didn't it show? Couldn't everyone tell just by looking at her? She turned her face this way and that. On her neck she could see something, a little bruise and teeth marks. She put her fingers up to it. Apart from that, nothing had changed—except how she felt inside. Perhaps that was worse, that she'd enjoyed it and she loved him. Yes, she'd had her choice, and she'd chosen to live—with her alien lover. It would hurt her father, but then his reaction would hurt her. She shied away from that thought. She'd chosen her life, now she meant to live it to the full among the Sholans.

She became aware of Kusac's image in the mirror and dropped her hand.

"Is it so important to you that no one knows?" he asked in her language. His mind felt still, sadness hovering on its edges.

"Here on the *Khalossa*, among your people, no, it doesn't matter," she said slowly. "Those who know us—Vanna, the others from the *Sirroki*, as well as Rhian and Askad—couldn't understand why we weren't already lovers. They see nothing strange or wrong between us."

His next question hung in the air, louder because it was unasked.

I see only you, she sent.

"What of your people?"

She hesitated. "I don't know," she said at length, looking down at where her hands rested on the basin. "Need they know?" Raising her hand, she looked at him again in the mirror.

This time he looked away.

"It depends on you," he said quietly in Sholan, leaning back against the wall. "I told you that the choice was yours. Our Link places certain restrictions on us, but within those you're free to lead your own life, one separate from me should you wish. You could take a partner from your own kind and let others see us only as friends and colleagues."

She digested this for a moment, trying to sense what he felt, but his thoughts were still firmly under control. Hers were not.

"What do you want, Kusac?"

He looked back, startled by her question. "Me?" He took a deep breath, slowly shaking his head. "Cub, my wishes would cloud your choice."

She waited, her eyes holding his in the reflection. Could she bear being only his friend? Was that what he wanted? What did love mean to him anyway, the same as it did for her? Was there someone else?

"What do I mean to you, Kusac? Tell me what you want," she whispered.

"There's no one else, only you. I want you beside me always." His voice was low, almost a growl. "I want you as my life-mate, not just my Leska. That's my choice!" He stepped forward, his hands curling round the sides of her shoulders as he held her close, his cheek against hers.

Blonde hair lay against black, skin against fur, a mingling of peoples and minds. She turned round to face him.

"Are you sure? Think of what you may have to give up for me." She searched his face, reading his expression, the set of his ears.

His eyes began to glow, taking on a luminous quality. "Anything I have to give up isn't worth having if you aren't beside me."

The love she felt now was fierce and protective.

"Then let them all know we're one," she said as he held her close.

"We're one," he echoed, ears flicking in startlement at her unconscious use of the phrase. He damped the thought firmly.

As she moved her head, he saw the bruise. Reaching out, he touched it, then her cheek with his fingertips.

"I'm sorry I was rough, cub, but you made me wait so long," he said ruefully. "I'm afraid I also scratched your back and shoulders. I checked them when we showered. They should be all right, but we'll get Vanna to look at them in the morning."

"No!"

"You don't need to worry, it's me she'll scold," he said. "I felt your fear . . . but I thought it was because I'm Sholan, not a human like you."

"That least of all," she said with a chuckle. "I probably shouldn't admit it, but the fact you're Sholan only made me more curious!"

He laughed, holding her closer till she winced in pain as he pressed against the scratches.

"I promise to take it slowly next time," he said, bending down to gently bite at her lips before progressing to one of his kisses. "You use Sholan body language, so I responded instinctively."

"Is it a problem?"

"No, I wouldn't say so, would you?" he asked, his voice soft as liquid velvet. His hand strayed down to her breast. "I'll show you what I like, and learn what pleases you."

"I thought you wanted to sleep," she murmured, relaxing against him.

"Did I?" She found herself swung into his arms as if she weighed nothing.

He grinned down at her. "Now why did I say that? I think we've both spent enough time asleep over the last few days, don't you? Besides, it'll be fun to start those lessons now," he said, carrying her through to the bedroom.

"Oh? Wasn't I good enough for you, then?" she asked as he pulled back the cover, laying her down in the central bowl of the bed.

He climbed in beside her, passing his hand over the bedside light sensor, dimming it to an intimate faint glow.

Leaning across her, he began to run his tongue across her cheek.

"Cub, the first time was more than I dared hope it would be." He could feel her starting to remember it with as much pleasure.

"The second was fun—and wet!" she laughed.

"This time we'll enjoy each other slowly," he purred, his eyes glinting with mischief as his tail curled around her leg.

Chapter 4

Vanna stirred, opening her eyes and looking blearily around the unfamiliar room. Where the hell was she? She ought to know, the smell was familiar. Uncurling, she instantly regretted it as her vision swam. She groaned, triggering off the headache.

A glass of frothing liquid swam into view and gratefully she grabbed it, swallowing the contents. It hit her stomach, instantly settling the incipient nausea.

"Better?" asked Garras, sitting down beside her.

She handed him the glass, remaining still for a moment till the drug dealt with the rest of her hangover. "Thanks," she mumbled. "How'd I get here?"

"We came back together," he said. "You were sitting drinking in the rec bar on your own last night, and I thought you needed company."

"What did we do?"

"Talked mostly."

"I'm afraid I don't really remember anything," she said ruefully. "I think I overdid it."

"Just a little," he said with a grin, reaching down to touch her cheek. "I didn't expect you to remember much."

"That bad, huh?" Her headache had dulled to a vague ache by now so she risked sitting up.

Garras' arm was there to support her. "You'll feel better when you've eaten."

"No food yet," she said with a shudder. "I'll have a c'shar, though."

He got up and went over to the dispenser, returning with two faintly steaming mugs. He handed one to her before getting back into bed.

She took several large mouthfuls before her thirst was quenched. "Whatever was I drinking last night, Garras?"

"Would you believe Terran coffee?"

"You're kidding!" she said. "It's had *this* effect on me?"

"They make it too strong in the rec bar."

"Oh. And it made me talkative?" she asked, giving him a sidelong glance.

"Moderately," he replied, taking a drink himself.

Vanna checked her wrist unit. "Gods, is that the time? I've got to go!" she said, finishing her drink with a gulp. Putting the mug down on the bedside unit, she swung her legs over the side and began scrabbling among the clothes on the floor for her uniform.

As she fastened her belt, she was aware of Garras watching her. She risked a glance in his direction. He was getting up. Deciding discretion was the better part of valor, she headed for the door.

"Bye," she said, putting her hand on the sensor.

Garras' hand closed over hers, preventing her from activating it.

"Vanna, wait. You aren't in that much of a hurry. I'd be surprised if our two friends go anywhere today," he said, turning her around to face him.

Acutely embarrassed, Vanna tried hard to keep her ears upright. Her tail tip flicked against her legs. What *had* she said the night before?

"Don't neglect your own life because you care for them," he said. "Start training someone to take over from you now, before it becomes too complex for you to leave. There'll be other chances for you to work in xenobiology. You're getting too involved for your own good."

"I want to work with them, Garras," she said quietly. "I like them both."

"I know, and I understand. I want you to come back here tonight," he said. "Spend your off-duty time with me, Vanna. I like your company a lot." His hand cupped her cheek, fingers caressing her ear briefly. "Don't decide now, just think about what I'm saying."

She hesitated, then nodded. "I need to make sure they eat after what they've been through. We'll use the mess on their level. Do you want to join us?"

"I'll be there. I won't be able to stay for long, I'm afraid. I've some business to attend to."

"In an hour, then," she said, turning to go.

* * *

"The AlRel lectures are nothing more than thinly disguised thought control, and if you can't see that, it just proves my point," said Chyad angrily.

"If they're controlling what we think, then how come you don't agree with me?" Khay demanded.

"I don't go to the lectures," he said, dropping his voice. "You think I want my head filled with their subliminal messages?"

"They wouldn't dare!" said Naisha.

"I don't believe it either," said Kaedoe. "If what you say is true, then how did you manage to avoid the talks?"

"There are ways, but that's not the real issue. What should be concerning you is whether or not we're going to sit back and let Shola make a treaty with these Terrans. Did anyone manage to find out anything?" Chyad asked, pinning each of them with a hard look.

"I managed to speak to one of the Terrans," Kaedoe mumbled, looking away from the larger male.

"You did? Excellent," said Chyad, his tone now a delighted purr. "Someone with some initiative. What did you find out?"

"Mostly what we already knew. The Valtegans arrived there twelve years ago, overpowering the humans very quickly because they didn't have any real means of defense. Those who could, escaped to the hills and woodlands where they tried to fight back. The remainder were made to help build the two cities and the base."

"What about Guynor?"

"He hated the Terran female from the start, according to the human," said Kaedoe.

"So the Valtegans built themselves a base here with the help of the Terrans, and once they were well established, they set out to destroy anyone who got in their way—namely us," said Chyad.

"I think you're assuming too much," said Naisha, shifting uneasily in her seat.

Chyad turned an angry glare on her. "What am I assuming?" he demanded. "Did the human tell Kaedoe about the Valtegans trying to destroy their colony on Keiss, or of his home world being destroyed the way our two worlds were? No, he . . ."

"There's Mito," said Maikoe, grabbing hold of Chyad's arm, "from the *Sirroki*."

Chyad glanced across the concourse in the direction Maikoe indicated. "Go and see if you can get her to join us," he said. "Let's see if she can tell us any more about the humans."

Mito was restless and troubled. Despite her companionship with Guynor while they'd been on Keiss, she hadn't really been involved with him on any serious basis. Though she believed it justified, his execution had shocked her. Looking at the vastness of space had always helped her cope with moments of crisis in the past and she hoped today wouldn't be an exception.

She was brought to an abrupt halt as a stocky female of about average height stepped in front of her.

"Mito," she said, her voice as bright and enthusiastic as her tunic. "We were just talking about you. Do come and join us," she said, taking her by the arm. "We're dying to hear about your adventure on the planet below us."

Bewildered, Mito looked again at the ginger-haired face with its tightly braided plait of pale hair as she let herself be guided over to a group of half a dozen people sitting by the viewing window.

"Do I know you?" she asked the female.

"Oh, yes," said Maikoe, mouth opening in a friendly smile. "When I was first posted here a year ago, we flew a couple of missions together on the *Sirroki* before I was allocated the captaincy of the *Alanti*."

Chyad stood up to greet her. "Maikoe mentioned that she knew you," he said. "It's nice to meet you. I'm Chyad, and these are Naisha, Khay, Kaedoe and Jakule." He indicated the rest of the group. "Please, join us. We've heard so many rumors of what happened to you all on Keiss. It would be nice to hear the truth."

Still taken aback, Mito sat down on the seat Chyad indicated. Dutifully, she recounted the main details of their experiences on Keiss.

"Tell me again why the Valtegans didn't destroy the Terran colony," said Chyad.

"I told you, we don't know for sure, but from what Carrie said they used the small Terran population as captive labor to help them build the two domed cities where they housed their injured and the soldiers on leave. They were like indoor towns. She said sometimes the troops would come out to see the settlements, behaving like people on leave in a strange town. Keiss was an R & R world for them," she repeated.

"Did you see their domed cities?"

"No, I only saw their base."

"Anyone here flown over those cities?" asked Chyad, turning to the others.

"Yes, I did," said Khay. "Not much left of them now, though. Just broken husks."

Chyad nodded. "What about the base? What went on there?"

"That's where their deep space communicator and landing pad were. Supplies and the injured arrived there and were ferried to the domes."

"Did you see any of these injured Valtegans?" asked Maikoe, getting up from her seat at the adjacent table. She tapped Khay on he shoulder, jerking her head to one side indicating he should take her seat. He moved and she slid into his place.

"You're asking as many questions as the Sub-Commander did!" Mito complained, ears and tail flicking. "What is this, some kind of informal debriefing? Yes, I saw injured Valtegans arriving from space. I spent three days in that stinking swamp recording their computer transmissions!"

"What sort of injuries were they? Energy weapons, projectiles?" prompted Maikoe.

"Not projectiles," Mito said. "A lot of burns—what you'd expect from a space battle. Look, what's this all about? What're you trying to find out?"

"Why the Valtegans didn't kill all the Terrans—not only on Keiss, but on their home world, too," said Chyad. "I, for one, don't like it. This smells of a conspiracy between the Valtegans and the Terrans."

"Don't be ridiculous! For a start, the Terrans fought with us when we attacked the base."

"That doesn't mean that most of the Terrans aren't collaborating with them," said Chyad. "They didn't say anything about there being a Valtegan star ship in the solar system, did they?"

"They didn't know about it!" Mito said. "Neither did we until you arrived. If you're that concerned, ask the Terrans! Several of the ones who came into the base with us are on board at the moment."

"They'll only tell us the official line," said Maikoe dismissively. "Besides, every species has its dissidents. The ones you met up with are probably them. Don't you find it too much of a coincidence that we lose Khyaal and Szurtha to the Others, then stumble over a new species of aliens who have coexisted with them on the same planet for twelve years?"

"I'd be more likely to ask what it was that made them kill our people out of hand like that!" replied Mito tartly. "Especially since they'd coexisted with the humans for so long!"

"No," insisted Chyad. "You're wrong. Our people died rather than help the Valtegans. Not the humans, they gave in. Guynor had the right of it. We don't need the Terrans. A treaty with them will only bring the destruction of the Valtegans down on us again."

Mito made a noise of disgust and got up. "You're as mad as Guynor was," she said. "I refuse to discuss it with you. I'm leaving."

Chyad watched her walk away. "How can she be so blind to what's happening? Why can't she can't see what's under her nose? Dammit! We need someone with communications skills."

"Why?" asked Khay.

"I've a friend on the *Rhyaki*—the ship that's on its way to Earth—who's prepared to send us information on the humans. Information that might otherwise be kept secret. If we had someone on the bridge who could intercept a message before it reached the comm ..."

Maikoe sighed. "I'll have another try with her. We may have said too much already though. She could be a danger to us now."

"I'll have an eye kept on her," agreed Chyad.

"I didn't realize there were so many of us," said Naisha.

"There aren't. The more there are, the greater the chance is of someone backing out and telling the military protectors or security."

A figure came running toward them from one of the elevators, skidding to a stop when she reached them. She waved a piece of paper at Chyad.

"Got it! They just posted the findings of Guynor's court-martial."

Chyad took it from her, scanning it quickly. "Guynor's been executed. When so many of us died on Khyaal, what

right have they to take the lives of the survivors?" he asked
angrily. "And guess what? The telepath that Guynor Challenged is no less than the Clan Lord's son! I'll bet he pulled
rank to get a conviction. The charge was changed from one
of wrongful Challenge to one of attempted murder. If this
Kusac has a link to one of the Terrans, then he's as much of
a collaborator as she is. Killing a traitor has never been
called murder before!"

"Let me get this right," said Maikoe, wrinkling her nose
in thought. "The Telepath Clan Lord's son is the one who
has a Leska Link with the Terran female, the daughter of the
Governor of this mud ball beneath us. Yes?"

"That's right. Now wouldn't it be tragic if the treaty negotiations were disrupted by the deaths of these two?" he said
thoughtfully, folding the paper up and placing it in one of
his pockets.

"Now you really *are* talking rubbish, Chyad," said
Kaedoe. "How the hell would killing them stop the treaty?"

"We want this treaty stopped, don't we?" he demanded,
looking round the half a dozen people present. Several heads
nodded in assent.

"If we take Kusac and his Leska out, the two sides will be
at each other's throats within hours, arguing over who's to
blame. The treaty wouldn't stand a chance."

"Just how do you plan to creep up on telepaths without
them being aware of you?" demanded Naisha, leaning forward and tapping a claw on the table in front of Chyad.
"Even if you do manage it, how are you going to kill them
without being caught?"

"Easy," said Maikoe. "We know that among the Terrans
are at least two who are anti-Sholan; specifically, they dislike our Clan Lord's son and his Link to one of their females. If we can get one of them to work with us, we should
be able to dupe him into killing Kusac. The shock of his
death would certainly kill the Terran female."

"I like it," said Jakule, grinning.

"So do I," nodded Chyad. "Nice and simple, the best idea
we've come up with yet. We can see to it that one of us kills
the Terran as soon as he's succeeded—after all he's a dangerous assassin, isn't he? No loose ends if we do it right."

"Come on, Chyad. You're being unrealistic. Where are we
even going to get pistols from?" asked Ngalu. "They're all

counted back into the armory when we return from duty on Keiss."

"Pistols are easy," said Jakule. "I got the contacts."

Chyad shot him an angry look. "You'll leave that to me, Jakule. We need to keep a low profile from now on. No attracting attention to ourselves. You hear me?"

Jakule flicked his ears in grudging assent.

"You still haven't said how you're going to get anyone near enough the telepaths to shoot them without their intentions being picked up," reminded Kaedoe.

"We create a diversion," said Maikoe. "A spontaneous brawl nearby should catch everyone's attention."

"That's what we'll go for, then," said Chyad decisively. "Are we all agreed?" He looked round the little group, staring at them each in turn until they nodded. "Then I'll see to getting weapons. Maikoe, you have another try at recruiting Mito. She would be invaluable in approaching the Terrans, especially as she knows them personally. Try not to arouse her suspicions any more than we already have, though."

Maikoe nodded.

"Ngalu, Naisha, and Khay, you'll be responsible for finding out where the two telepaths are living. Doubtless they'll have moved them to Leska quarters by now. Watch them, work out any patterns of movement. Find out where they go to eat and drink. Let's give it a week. By then we should have enough information to start planning."

"Why wait a week?" demanded Jakule. "Do it now, before the treaty is signed."

"Jakule, we do it my way," said Chyad, fixing a hard look on the other male. "I want no trouble from you, hear me? Just do what you're told, nothing more."

"You haven't given me anything to do," he complained, tail flicking violently from side to side.

"You've been told to keep a low profile, that's your job now. Keep your hands in your own pockets and stay away from the smoke bar! You get some of that smoke in you and you're a danger to everyone. Because Security is up to all your little tricks, I can't give you anything else to do till nearer the time. Just stay out of trouble, or I'll deal with you myself, understand me?"

Jakule looked away from Chyad's hard eyes. "No one trusts me," he said. "You told me to ask my smoke friends for information. Now you're telling me to stay away from them."

Chyad bit his tongue. No point in antagonizing him further, his moods were too unpredictable. He still had his uses, though, not least of which was the fact he was their main link to the troopers in the lower decks.

"Did you find out anything from them?"

"No," he muttered. "I can't until I pay them what I owe. If I don't get the money soon, they'll come after me, they said."

"Gods!" Chyad exclaimed angrily. "That's all I need, you marked out for a beating! That's really going to attract attention to you, isn't it? The last thing we need is the military protectorate sniffing around you! How much do you owe? Twenty? Thirty?"

"Fifty-six."

Chyad reached into his pocket and slammed a handful of coins down on the table. "Take this for now. I want it back next payday or you'll find out just how bad an enemy I can be."

He looked up at the others as Jakule hurriedly scooped the coins into his hand and pocketed them. "Right, we'll meet here in two days time, sixteenth hour?"

In ones and twos the little group dispersed. Several tables along, the sleeping male stirred, putting his hand up to his ear to remove the miniature amplifier. It had been an informative hour. Getting slowly to his feet, he strolled off down the concourse, sniffing the air, searching for a particular scent. Finding it, he began to track.

* * *

The comm chimed as he was about to leave. With an exclamation of annoyance, Garras went over to his desk and activated the unit.

"Kaid?" he said uncertainly.

"Can you join me in the level thirty-nine viewing lounge in ten minutes? I need you to introduce me to one of your last crew. The female, Mito."

Garras hesitated. "I can't stay, I have an appointment."

"Give me ten minutes, that's all I need." The line went dead.

* * *

Kaid was waiting for him when the elevator doors opened. "What's so urgent?" he asked.

Kaid took him by the arm, drawing him along the corridor to the lounge. "I want an introduction to Mito. I need you to stay with us for a few minutes, that's all." He flashed a quick grin. "You can join your young lady then."

Garras grunted. "You haven't changed. Even at the guild you always knew everything that went on."

His friend shrugged. "I just keep my ear to the ground."

Garras grunted again. "What's this all about?"

"Later. Just introduce me to Mito," he murmured as they approached her table.

"Mito, can we join you?" asked Garras, stopping opposite her.

She looked up, ears tipping round and backward in surprise. "Captain Garras. Yes, of course. Please, sit down."

"This is Kaid, an old friend of mine. Mito was my communications officer on the *Sirroki*," said Garras as they sat.

"Garras told me about your work with the Valtegan computer programs. Very professional. I hear that you're still working on them in Linguistics," said Kaid. "How's it progressing?"

Mito's facial expressions went from annoyed through surprised to delighted. "You heard about my work? Do you know you're the first person I've met since my return that's been interested in what we achieved on Keiss?"

"Communications is one of my fields," said Kaid. "Can I get you a c'shar?" he asked, looking over to the service counter where they sold c'shar and other hot beverages as well as various snacks.

"I'd love one," she said.

"Garras?"

"I'm afraid I have to go," he said, standing up. "I'll catch you both later."

* * *

He woke in stages, at first thinking he was dreaming as gentle fingers moved across the heavy muscles of his neck and shoulders. Remembering the utter despair and ache of loneliness inside from the days before, he turned his mind inward again, not wishing to lose this dream.

A feather touch on his thigh made his leg twitch, bringing

him nearer to wakefulness again. The sensation continued, moving up toward his hip.

This time he lay still, his mind barely registering his wakefulness as he carefully probed to find out who or what was disturbing his sleep.

Carrie? he thought incredulously. Then he remembered.

Now fully awake, he continued to feign sleep, eyes open just enough to watch her in the almost dark room. There was a half smile on her face as her hand gently played with the longer fur that coated his belly and groin. No dream then, she was here. The worst was over. Closing his eyes again, he moved restlessly as if still asleep, fetching up lying on his back.

She waited a moment, then sidled closer till they touched, her hand growing bolder as her teeth gently captured his jawline and cheek. She released him laughing, her face looking down at his.

I can feel your pulse, she sent, her thought almost a purr. *It matches mine.*

Kusac opened his eyes, his mouth reaching for hers. The kiss was more Terran now as his tongue touched hers and his hands clasped round her hips, bringing her body down to meet his.

"Is it any wonder?" he growled, nipping her ear with his front teeth. "Your presence is enough, cub," he said, his voice trailing off as they joined again with all the urgency of the night before.

Gradually Carrie became aware of a loud banging on the door.

Ignore it. She sensed Kusac push the thought aside from their minds.

The knocking continued, its insistence beginning to dominate Carrie's senses and draw her mind away from his.

"Kusac," she said, but he pulled her down against him and began to gently bite at her lips to silence her. He had no intention of being diverted by the door or anything else.

The door, she sent as he rolled her over on her back, continuing his efforts to reclaim her total attention.

"Sorry, I didn't mean to disturb you," said Vanna.

Carrie froze, then in a flurry of pale limbs grabbed the cover around herself and disappeared under it.

Kusac lay beside the pile of bedding for a moment then, ears and tail flicking, looked over toward the door.

"Vanna," he said. "Couldn't it have waited?"

"I'm sorry," she said, backing through the partially open door, "I was worried when you didn't answer. I wanted to make sure you were both all right."

"You needn't go now," he said, sitting up. "What do you mean, are we all right?" he asked.

Vanna slid the door shut and approached the bed, stopping at the end of it. "You both look a lot better," she said. "How do you feel?"

Kusac regarded her with puzzlement. "I'm fine, Vanna. Is there any reason why I shouldn't be?"

Putting her medikit on the floor, Vanna walked round to sit beside him, taking hold of his arm.

"Don't you remember what happened last night?" she asked, looking at her wrist unit.

Kusac's glance flicked to the anonymous lump that was Carrie, then back.

"Before that," grinned Vanna, letting him go. "Let me check your eyes, please."

"What's all this about, Vanna? I know I was ill, but surely you're overreacting," he said as she gently checked the color of his eyelids.

"You're fine," she said, getting up and moving round to Carrie's side to make the same checks. "You, too, cub," she said, waiting till a somewhat red-faced Carrie emerged.

"There don't seem to be any lasting effects from your experiences that I can see, but I'd like you to report to my lab tomorrow morning so I can run more extensive tests."

"Vanna!" exclaimed Kusac, exasperated.

She settled on the end of the bed, regarding them both. "You were pretty out of it," she said to Kusac. "I'm not surprised you didn't notice us."

"Notice you?"

"Rhian, Askad, and I brought Carrie to you last night," she said. "Didn't you tell him, Carrie? Perhaps you were too busy to talk much." She grinned again.

"Sounds like all the world and his cousin was here last night minding our business," he muttered.

Carrie flushed again and anchoring the cover round her, climbed out of bed. Reaching for her clothes she beat a hasty retreat to the bathroom.

Still confused, Kusac got out of bed and headed for the drink dispenser.

"Will you join us in a cup of c'shar?" he asked.

"With pleasure," Vanna replied, turning back to look at him. "You'll have to be more gentle with her, Kusac," she said. "Remember, her skin is more fragile than ours and will break easily."

The blank look on his face faded and his tail and ears flicked with acute embarrassment. "I told her you would scold me," he said. "I was too urgent, I know, but I'd waited a long time for her to decide, Vanna."

"I know you did," she said gently as he handed her a drink.

"I wish I'd known sooner what she was afraid of. It's going to take a little time to get used to all the cultural differences between us."

"Knowing wouldn't have helped, Kusac. She was too afraid of what she felt for you and the way the Link amplified it to think coherently until she realized you were dying. We were barely in time as it was. She was so ill she couldn't have come to you even if she'd wanted to. What in Vartra's name possessed you to play games with your lives?"

"The stakes were very high. Without all of her, part of me was already dead," he replied, returning with two more cups. Setting one on the floor, he sat beside her. "I couldn't live with only seeing her every five days, not when our Link bound us so closely even then. I thought the separation hardly seemed to affect her, and because she'd blocked our Link completely, I had no way of finding out. I hoped that as a Terran she would be immune somehow. It seems I was wrong."

"You were," said Vanna. "Both of you came close to dying."

"How close were we?" he asked quietly, avoiding her eyes by looking into the depths of his cup.

"Too damned close, Kusac," she said.

He sensed her sharp fear as she remembered.

"Don't ever frighten me like that again." She reached out and ruffled the longer fur between his ears, making him grin.

"Another place, another time, eh, Vanna?" he said, giving her a sidelong glance.

Vanna smiled. "Come looking for me when she needs to choose a father for her children," she said. "Oh, I know I'm not from the Telepath Clan, but there have been a few wild Talents in our family."

Kusac frowned briefly. He didn't want to think of that. Clan duties lay well ahead in the future for both of them. "How did you know what was happening to us?" he asked, changing the subject.

"Someone was sensible enough to dump your file on my desk yesterday," she said, "and a damned good thing they did, too. Now enough of this," she said brightly, draining her cup. "You've got your first meal to have and quarters to move, and it's already past second mealtime!"

"Why do we have to move quarters?" asked Carrie, emerging from the bathroom with the cover over her arm and a brush in her hand.

Kusac rose and took the brush from her. "I'll do that for you," he said, turning her round.

"Have you forgotten that we had to shoot the lock off the door last night?" reminded Vanna. "Besides, now you're together, you will need larger accommodation."

"Do you mean anyone could have walked in last night . . ." began Kusac, glancing round as he ran the brush through Carrie's hair.

"If they did, they didn't disturb you, did they? Come on, let's eat."

Kusac shook his head. "I want a quick shower first," he said firmly, handing the brush to Carrie. "There's a cup of c'shar for you," he said to her, catching hold of her long enough to attack her neck and ears. He set her down on her feet again and disappeared into the bathroom.

Embarrassed, Carrie started to spread the cover over the bed—anything to avoid looking at Vanna. Eventually, the other female called her over.

"Your drink will be cold."

Carrie joined Vanna, picking up her drink.

"Vanna," she said hesitantly, "I don't know how to say this, but . . ."

"I know," she said, patting Carrie's hand. "Next time, just listen to Kusac. He knows what he's talking about."

"He knew the risk he was taking all along. Why didn't he tell me?"

"It would have influenced your choice, you know that. But it's in the past now, you made your decision last night."

Carrie smiled faintly. "I'll still have to face my father in a few days. I'm not going to enjoy that."

"Will there be trouble?" Vanna asked.

"Oh, yes," said Carrie. "I'm his daughter, I won't be allowed to frustrate his plans for me. What I want is irrelevant."

"Wouldn't it be easier to let our people tell him?"

"Yes, but I've got to do it myself," she said firmly.

* * *

Garras was waiting for them when they arrived. Vanna greeted him with a smile and gentle touch to his neck. He put his arm round her shoulders and they followed Kusac and Carrie into the small mess.

The meal over, they were finishing their c'shar when Garras drew Kusac's attention to a male hovering nearby.

"Kusac, I think Myak wants to talk to you," he said.

Kusac looked up. The Commander's adjutant. Frowning, he got to his feet and went over to him.

"Liegen Aldatan," the Sholan said, crossing his forearms over his chest and inclining his head. "I'm Adjutant Myak, assistant to Commander Raguul. There is a call from the Clan Lord, your father. If you would accompany me to the communications office on this level . . . ?"

Kusac nodded. "I'll tell my companions where I'm going."

He returned to the table, ears and tail flicking in annoyance.

"Kusac, why did he salute you?" asked Vanna.

"Later. I have a call to answer." He reached out to touch Carrie's cheek. "I won't be long," he said, his expression softening.

Carrie watched him leave with Myak.

"He's annoyed and distressed at the same time, that's all I can sense," she said. "Who'd be calling him?"

"I don't know," said Garras slowly, "but I can guess. I think you should prepare yourself for the fact that Kusac isn't just a telepath but a high-ranking civilian, never mind his true military rank."

Carrie looked at him in surprise.

"What do you mean?"

"I'm just remembering little things, like that message from his father when the *Khalossa* arrived, and at the court-martial when the Sub-Commander said that the more serious charge of Challenging an Officer of too superior a grade

couldn't fairly be leveled against Guynor. I have a feeling
that Kusac is a member of a Clan Leader's family."

"Does that make a difference?"

Vanna frowned slightly, her nose wrinkling.

"It might cause you more problems, but on the other hand,
it could make life easier. You'll just have to take it as it
comes."

Myak ushered Kusac into the communications office,
showing him into a smaller room that had obviously been
hurriedly vacated to ensure he could take his call in privacy.

Kusac sat at the table while Myak activated the unit. Mentally, he constructed a barrier deep below his conscious
thoughts where he could conduct this conversation without
Carrie picking it up, and without his father being able to
read him. He was not looking forward to it. Nearly a year
had passed since they'd last spoken.

"I'll be waiting outside for you, Liegen," Myak said, bowing before leaving.

The screen began to clear and Kusac's father appeared.

"Kusac, what in all the names of hell have you been
doing?" the Clan Lord thundered without preamble.

"Nothing, Father."

"Don't give me nothing! When I can pick up your distress
from here on Shola, I know something is wrong! I demand
to be told what."

"You might be the most powerful telepath on Shola, Father, but how can you possibly be picking up my mental
state from that far away? Surely you're mistaking me for
someone else."

"I didn't train you to be a fool, boy," his father growled.
"When I started picking you up through your increased Talent, I knew the Gods had blessed you with a Leska, but
these last few days have been indescribable, despite the di-
luting effect of the distances involved! You should know I'm
up to my ears in work with this Sholan/Keissian treaty at the
moment. I can't afford to be distracted like this. You haven't
been foolish enough to try and refuse the Leska bond, have
you?"

Kusac closed his eyes briefly. What to do? Tell him now,
or let him discover it for himself when they landed on
Shola?

"I'm waiting for an answer," came the angry prompt.

He opened his eyes again. "Father, grant me the basic

privilege of privacy. You have no right to pick up my emotions and demand an explanation. I'm not a child, nor am I your pupil. All I will tell you for now is that there were ... complications, which have now been resolved."

"They had better be," his father grumbled. "I'll grant that everything's quiet now, but I'll thank you to take better care of yourself in the future. I've requested that your military service be curtailed because of your civilian rank. You've spent enough time on this foolish desire of yours to live without the duties or privileges of your position. It wasn't until this incident occurred that I knew where to find you."

"Father, I ..."

"Don't interrupt me, Kusac. I know you were seriously injured on Keiss, and I also have my suspicions about the last few days, but enough is enough. It's time for you to resume your duties. You are heir to your mother's Clan, and because your Talent is second only to mine, you are a contender as heir to the leadership of the Clans, and I'm not prepared to let you risk your life any further on this nonsense."

Kusac sat silently. There was nothing much he could say in the face of his father's determination.

"Besides, your mother misses you, as do your sisters," his father said, softening at last. "She and I concur in this matter. You will return home at the earliest opportunity."

"I will be returning, Father," sighed Kusac, ears flicking despite his efforts to stop them. "But I have guild matters to attend to before I can come to the estate."

"The Commander has told me of your orders. Apparently your Leska has abilities that are unusual. Something about her being a healer, too," he said.

Kusac nodded. "Yes, she's a powerful telepath, and an unusual Leska."

"Well and good. See to your duties at the guild first, but visit us as soon as you can. I wish to meet this Leska of yours. Her mind has an unusual flavor to it—in fact, I found her so meshed with you that it was difficult to sense her as an individual. I can't remember coming across so complete a Link before. I presume the complications you mention concern that, so I'll request a report regarding them from your Mentor. If you're having abnormal difficulties concerning your Link, then I should know what they are. I may be able to help."

Even now he has to pry between the lines of my life,

Kusac thought angrily. *When he finds out she's Terran, it'll get worse.*

"I don't need any help, Father. We can deal with it ourselves. I'll contact you from the guild house," he said.

"Very well. By the way, Rala sends her greetings. If you would marry and father children of your own, then some of the weight of being Clan Heir would devolve from your shoulders. It's a matter to think on if you find your rank too restricting. Now you have a Leska, this marriage shouldn't prove the burden you feared."

Kusac closed his eyes again tiredly. Maintaining the block was taking a lot of energy he didn't yet have. "Father, you know I dislike the female. I refuse to talk of marriage at the present. There is plenty of time for such things."

His father sighed. "You're as obstinate as I was at your age. I will see you presently."

"Fare you well, Father," said Kusac as the screen blanked.

Too many duties and too many problems, that had been what had driven him to leave home and enlist in the military as an ordinary telepath. Now it seemed there was no escape from the future that fate had mapped out for him.

Resignedly, he got to his feet and left the office. Myak was waiting outside.

"If you're ready, Liegen, I'll show you and your Leska to your new quarters."

"We've got to pack first," said Kusac as they made their way back to the mess.

"All has been seen to, Liegen," said Myak. "The Commander ordered Personnel to collect the few items belonging to your Leska from Rhian's and Askad's quarters and take them to your new rooms. Yours are already there."

"Why the haste? Where are our quarters?"

"Your present quarters are not secure, Liegen. Your new ones are on the same level, corridor seven."

Kusac headed back to where Vanna and Carrie were still waiting.

"Garras had to leave. He sends his apologies," said Vanna.

"Is something wrong?" asked Carrie, looking up at him.

"I'll tell you later. Adjutant Myak is waiting to take us to our new quarters."

* * *

Jakule lounged against the corridor wall by the elevator. From here he had a clear view of corridor seven. Bloody Chyad! Who'd elected him leader anyway? No one had asked him his opinion. He'd show them that he could be trusted. He'd get the information on the telepaths before Ngalu and the others. He snorted. Keep away from the smoke bar! What harm did a little smoke do? Made him feel good, more awake. He'd show that tree-climbing bastard that he could do as good a job as anyone else!

He stiffened as he saw a small group of people heading toward him. It included the Terran female. They stopped to talk to someone, then entered a room. The one they'd talked to was coming toward him now. Jakule kept his head down as he went past. The stranger hardly spared him a glance before entering the elevator.

Jakule relaxed. He could stay for an hour before he had to leave for his shift.

* * *

As they stopped in front of their new quarters, the door beside them opened. Hearing the noise, Kusac glanced round.

"Just moving in?" asked the male, sealing his own door. "You'll like it here. It's a quiet corridor, unlike some. You must be Kusac Aldatan," he said, holding out his hand, palm upward.

Despite his natural caution, Kusac found himself briefly touching the male's hand in greeting.

"And you have to be Carrie Hamilton," the stranger said, holding his hand out to her. "I'm Kaid."

Hesitantly Carrie reached out to touch his fingers.

"See you around," he said, ears giving a little flick of acknowledgment before he left.

Curiously Kusac watched him head up the corridor, then turned back to Myak.

"If you touch the locking plate with your hand, Liegen, I'll key in your palm print. The same for your Leska."

Vanna looked sharply at Kusac but said nothing.

This done, Myak left them.

By the elevator, Jakule was getting restless. All this waiting was boring, he liked action. They weren't going anywhere if they'd just moved in. There was no point in him hanging around. He glanced at his wrist chronometer. If he left now, he had time for a quick cone in the smoke bar. He'd stalk them later, when he came off duty. Someone was coming out of their room. Myak! Turning, he dashed toward the elevator, managing to jump in as the doors began to close.

* * *

"Thank you for seeing me, Commander," said the Brother, moving silently over to the seat by the desk.

"You said the matter was urgent."

"Not urgent," he demurred. "Active. You have a small dissident faction building. An anti-Terran group made up in the main by people from Khyaal and Szurtha. As yet it is not a problem, but it could be in the future."

Raguul raised an eyeridge. "You have been busy," he said. "Tell me more."

"There appear to be two ringleaders. One Chyad, from Engineering, the other Maikoe, a pilot. Among their followers is a male called Jakule, a known troublemaker who has been up on charges twice for being under the influence of recreational drugs while on duty. At present I know of only six of them."

Raguul stirred in his chair, making himself more comfortable. His stomach was constantly bothering him these days, what with the worries of the treaty negotiations and the added complications of the mixed Leskas. It seemed there was another one to add to what promised to be an ever-increasing list.

"Go on," he said.

"Their aim is to negate any possible treaty between the Terrans and us by bringing about the deaths of the new Leska pair, Kusac and Carrie. This they plan to do by involving the Terrans in their conspiracy and priming one of them to kill Kusac, thus plunging both species into war."

"Neat," said Raguul, nodding. "What's the basis of their complaint against the Terrans?"

"The fact that they're still alive, as is their home world. Their reasoning is that the humans are collaborating with the Valtegans and the destruction of our two worlds proves this. They see the main collaborator as Carrie Hamilton, and Kusac Aldatan as an accessory because of his Link to her. Although they're few in number, I consider them a real threat to the treaty if they can enlist the anti-Sholan Terran support and proceed with their plan. However, even if they succeeded in killing them, they would ultimately fail in trying to create a war between our species. The Terrans are effectively planet bound."

"Do you think they'll get the support?" asked Raguul, shifting uneasily. "I hadn't thought there was any anti-Sholan feeling among the humans on Keiss."

"It's possible. I want to wait and see. There may well be more in the group, at present I don't know. My sources on the planet only report an individual here and there with a particular gripe against us, nothing more. I'd like to leave this for the moment and see how it develops. The only way we'll be able to identify those involved is by allowing them to rally round Chyad. That way when we strike, we can get them all."

"This involves putting our pair out as bait."

"Yes," Tallinu said. "My remit from the Brotherhood, countersigned by Sub-Guild Master Ghezu, gives me that authorization. Does it present a problem?"

"Depends on you," growled Raguul.

"I want them exposed for the moment," said Tallinu. "Besides," he grinned mirthlessly, "it allows your Telepath Guild to measure their new Talents in a life-threatening situation."

"You tread too fine an edge," said Raguul stonily, eyes glittering, ears swiveling sideward. "See you don't miscalculate this or *your* hide will be on the wall, not mine. I can't afford to lose the Terran girl without good reason."

"Understood, but stop it now and it will crop up again like a weed with broken roots left in the soil. Let it come near to flower, then uproot it, and you've caught it all."

"Your authorization is higher than mine, but take what reasonable steps are necessary to eradicate this situation on my clearance too. This treaty is too important to lose. It could be more crucial to Shola than any other we have."

Tallinu inclined his head. "I'm well aware of what hangs in the balance here, Commander. You need to accelerate the crew program of Attitude Indoctrination. It will do a lot to counter any possible spread of this xenophobia. I strongly suggest you advise Sholan High Command of the need to repeat the program on all starships, particularly the *Rhyaki,* and until it is complete, restrict all outgoing and incoming communications. Hopefully we can isolate this on the *Khalossa* where we can eradicate it."

"Your advice is noted. I'll see our Mentor liaises with Alien Relations in this."

Another brief nod. "Your chief of security's cooperation is appreciated. I'm drawing on his expertise for the extra people I need."

"Somehow I don't think these matters were anticipated when you received your brief," said Raguul.

"The contract, like my authorization, is flexible," murmured the Brother.

"Yes," sighed Raguul. "Just keep me informed." He watched the other walk to the door before calling out. "Wait," he said. "Tell me why you do it."

Surprised, Tallinu stopped and turned round.

"Why did you choose to become a Brother? What made you give up your Clan and live on the edge of the law?"

"I was chosen by the God. When that happens to a Warrior, you know he or she has no option but to accept the Brotherhood's invitation," he replied quietly. "Who else could step outside the laws of Shola to interpret the laws of the Gods and do what must be done? The protectorate can't, they're the guardians of all the civil laws. There is only us."

"Then let's pray Vartra sees fit to protect these two."

Tallinu inclined his head and turned once more to leave.

* * *

"You were seen!" said Chyad with barely contained fury. "Don't lie to me! I told you to keep a low profile, and what do you do? Stalk them outside their new quarters with Myak around! Of all the bloody stupid things to do!" He paced up and down Jakule's small room, tail lashing from side to side in extreme anger. He'd had to interrupt his negotiations for weapons to get hold of the little worm before he went out on duty in the scouter patrols.

"I left before he could have seen me," blustered Jakule.

"You were seen!" Chyad stopped and turned on the hapless male. "From now on, do *exactly* as you're told and keep out of sight. You cross me again, and I'll see you wake up in hell. I promise you that," he said, his voice low and spiked with venom as he slammed the door behind him.

Jakule began to mutter angrily to himself as he went over to the drawer unit in his room.

"Who the hell does he think he is, ordering me around like that? I'll show him. Threaten me, would he?" He pulled out the bottom drawer, taking it free of its runners and laying it on the floor. From the cavity it left, he drew out an energy pistol. He turned it over in his hands, pulling the power pack out to check that it was fully charged, checking the trigger mechanism. Reloading it, from the same place he collected two spare battery packs. Concealing the pistol and the spares inside his jacket, he returned the drawer to its place.

* * *

Vanna hesitated at the doorway. "I think I'd better leave you two to get settled in on your own," she said.

"No, do come in," said Carrie, stopping in her prowl round their new quarters.

Kusac turned to look at the medic, immediately knowing what was wrong. As she started to back away, his hand shot out and he grasped her firmly by the wrist, claws touching but not penetrating.

"No," he said. "We need you, Vanna. Carrie needs you. I'm not going to let your prejudices about rank stand in the way." He pulled her into the room, sealing the door behind her. "Now sit down and listen to me before you make up your mind." He released his grip to push her over to one of the easy chairs, making her sit down.

Head on one side, Carrie watched him. This was a different aspect of his nature; one she had not seen before. She moved over to join him on the settee.

"Yes, you're right," he said, sitting opposite Vanna. "I am Clan Lord Aldatan's son. That's why I left Shola about a year ago and joined the Forces under an assumed name. I'd had enough, Vanna," he said, reaching out to draw Carrie to his side. "I wanted, and still want, an ordinary life, not one as the son of the elected Lord of the Sixteen Telepath Clans, Head of Alien Relations and member of the Sholan High Council. As well as that, being firstborn, I'm my mother's heir. There was nowhere for me to have my own life, only the one that custom dictated I lead as Clan Heir. Gods, I want to *live* my life, not spend it tied to duty and tradition! My father enjoys it. I don't and never have!" He stopped, catching her eyes with his.

"During our mission on the *Sirroki*, you befriended me,"

he continued. "Since then ... I don't have to tell you, I know. The call I got, it was from my father. Somehow he's been tuned in on the edges of our Link and has picked up certain feelings from me over the last few days. That's how he knew I had a Leska."

"Then he must have been aware of how near death you were," said Vanna.

"Probably. He also claims to have known I was injured on Keiss. I think he's trying to guilt trip me into worrying that he'll suffer mentally for everything I do. He's applying to have my service in the Forces terminated because of my rank and has ordered me to return home at the first opportunity." He gave a small shrug. "The irony is we're being posted back to the guild on Shola anyway."

"I hadn't heard," Vanna murmured.

"They've said they can't even begin to chart Carrie's Talents on board the *Khalossa,* so they've asked the guild to do it. Then there's our Link," he said, glancing at Carrie curled up beside him. "How long before the other Clans demand that the Heir of the Aldatans should step down because he has an alien Leska? I don't give a damn about the title or the position; I'd rather stay in the Forces. Here I have my own life and friends, Vanna. You can see that our future is uncertain to say the least."

No, not us. Never that, he sent to Carrie as he felt her sudden fear. "I haven't many friends, Vanna, neither has Carrie. We need every one we have. While I still have the title and the power it brings, I can use it to make things a little easier for us in the future. When we leave for Shola, will you come with us as our personal physician?"

They felt her incredulity at being asked, and her indecision.

"No one on Shola knows anything about Carrie's species," he said. "Only you."

"It would give you the opportunity to do what you want," said Carrie. "You'd have me as a captive specimen!"

Vanna's ears dipped and she radiated acute embarrassment.

Carrie laughed. "No, I'm not offended, I never was," she said. "I'm as curious about you as you are about me."

"Come as an equal, a friend, that's what I'm asking," he said. "Will you at least think about it?"

Slowly she nodded, getting to her feet. "I'll think about it, but I have to go now. This has all been rather a lot to take in."

She stopped at the door. "Remember your appointment," she said. "Tenth hour tomorrow, and check out the food dispenser. It prepares more elaborate meals in Leska quarters to compensate for your Link needs."

"Thanks, Vanna. We'll see you tomorrow."

"Do you think she'll come?" asked Carrie after she'd left. "Is it fair of us to ask her when she's just formed an attachment to Garras?"

"She's the only one who can make that decision, cub," he said.

Chapter 5

"Well, I wondered when you'd show up again," said the older of the two pilots, leaning back in his seat. "Go and get a couple more drinks in, Chima. Tallinu?"

He gave a negative flick of his ears as he slipped into the seat opposite them. "Just c'shar, please."

The pilot waited till his companion had left. "I knew they'd bring you back for this one, they couldn't afford not to. One of your specialties, isn't it? Observe, evaluate, recruit or destroy—isn't that how it goes?"

"You've grown cynical over the years, Rulla," he said. "This one isn't that simple."

"Did I say it was? Ghezu and Lijou want them, the Telepath Guild isn't sure. They're running scared because of Kusac's high profile. They can't just make him disappear, can they?"

Tallinu shrugged. "I've only two remits to dance between, Rulla. What the Telepaths want is no concern of mine at the present."

"Then there's you," said Rulla softly as he leaned forward across the table. "Tallinu's tune. What is it this time, eh, old friend?"

Tallinu looked over the other's head. "Chima's coming."

"Sod Chima, he's one of us. I know you. The God's been walking through our halls again: Brothers have been having visions. What's Vartra been saying to you? Why did you take this contract?"

"Your drink, Rulla," said Chima, setting the glass in front of him. "Your c'shar." He placed the mug in front of Tallinu then returned to the bar for his own drink.

"Why, Tallinu?" he insisted. "I know why it's important to Ghezu—important enough to forget the past. But you? I thought nothing would make you forgive what he did to Dzaka, and you."

Tallinu reached for his mug, but Rulla's hand caught his, trapping it on the table between them.

"Some of us still prefer to follow the God rather than the figurehead, Tallinu. It may be that our visions coincide."

Tallinu carefully withdrew his hand and continued to reach for his mug as Chima returned to his seat. He could still feel Rulla's eyes searching his face as the other sat back abruptly.

"I see your fosterling's on board," said Chima, taking a sip of his drink. "He's making a good lay priest. A little unstable since he lost Nnya, but that's to be expected, especially since he had to go down to Khyaal."

"Given time, he'll come to terms with her loss," said Tallinu. "His sensitivity was what led to him being abandoned in the first place."

"The God knows what his Clanfolk were thinking of to leave him on our doorstep in the middle of winter," said Rulla. "We aren't exactly known for taking in foundlings."

Tallinu made a noise of agreement as he put his mug down. "I need you to keep your ears open for any rumblings against the humans," he said. "I know you've tried to infiltrate Chyad's group, Chima, but leave it now. I'm in the process of getting someone undercover there and I don't want anything putting them at risk."

"You mean Chyad and Maikoe's little group?" said Chima. "He's been snouting around muttering darkly about collaborators among the humans. No one's listening to him, though. The Attitude Indoctrination program seems to be working—except with us," he said with a flash of humor. "Our training negates it."

"See what you can find out. The area I need a contact in is the troop section. Jakule is the name of the one trooper they've managed to attract. He's a fine specimen. Been up on charges concerning the misuse of recreational drugs and theft."

Rulla nodded. "I know him. I've been working the troop area myself in my off duty time. Nothing much of interest, just the usual. I presume you know about the local drink—coffee?"

Getting a nod in agreement, he continued. "They're trying to get a small black market trade going to undercut what the main rec bar sells it for, but they aren't doing too well. The growers have got contracts for their harvests already. They have managed to find something else, though. A sweet-tasting brown substance. Acts as some kind of sexual pallia-tive which, considering the number of young males under thirty that we've got on board, is all to the good. The pro-tectors and security are turning a blind eye to that one. In fact, I heard the Chief Protector has actually made sure that there are sufficient supplies available to the black market-eers!"

Tallinu raised an eyebrow in surprise. "The qwenes won't appreciate that. What's it called?"

"Chocolate."

"Haven't heard of it yet. Well, life belowdecks is as usual, then, as you said." He finished his c'shar and stood up. "I've got to go now. You know how to get in touch with me if you've anything to report."

"There're one or two others of us on board," said Rulla.

"I know. I'll be in touch with them as and when I need to."

* * *

Jakule hadn't turned up for his shift. He'd contacted his unit, reporting in sick so no one would be looking for him. Instead he'd spent the ensuing hours scrounging drinks in the rec bar with his off-duty cronies. His backbone stiffened by the alcohol, he'd moved on, padding around the smaller bars and areas where he knew Chyad was frequently to be found. His luck was out. Not even a faint scent of him.

His feet led him unerringly to his favorite smoke haunt, a small bar on the outer limit of the concourse. It was squeezed between the section of the main bar that was mainly used by ground troops like himself, and the elevator up to the main mess.

The smoke bar was legal, just, as long as no one from se-curity came in when the "special" cones were being used. It was a dingy, dark dive of a place, the walls stained brown by the constant smoke. Tables were scattered randomly around, the center of each holding the pottery dish in which the smokers burned their cones.

There was a group of people there that he knew. He loped over, hoping they would let him join their table, then he no-ticed Kheszi. Damn! He'd hoped to avoid him. It meant he would have less money to spend on smoke.

"What you doing here, Jakule?" asked the large male with

the notched ear as Jakule hovered a few feet from the table. "You got that money you owe me yet? You'll get no more smoke if you haven't."

"I've got it, Kheszi," he said, delving into his pocket and bringing out a handful of coins. "See, it's all here." He placed it on the table in front of him.

"Count it, Tayn," said the large one, ignoring the money and continuing to look at Jakule.

"All there," was the pronouncement.

"Good. I like debts paid promptly. It means I don't have to get nasty, and you know I hate that," he said with a flick of the scarred ear.

"Who's got a light pocket tonight, Jakule?" laughed one of the others. "One day your hand'll come out minus your fingers!"

There was general ribald laughter as Jakule's ears flattened in embarrassment. His tail flicked spasmodically as if beyond his control.

"You want something more, Jakule?" asked Kheszi.

"I want some smoke, Kheszi," said Jakule, trying to gather his shredded self-control and get his ears upright again.

"Can you pay for it?"

Jakule nodded.

Kheszi raked him with his eyes. "Can you cope with smoke? You look like you already spent too much time in the bars."

Again the chorus of laughter as Jakule's tail flicked in resentment.

"I can cope," he muttered. "I'm not that far gone."

"Money where I can see it."

Jakule shoved his hand into another pocket and put the coins in front of Kheszi.

Kheszi nodded to Tayn. A cone flew through the air toward Jakule. He just managed to catch it.

"You're slipping, lad," said Kheszi. "See you are up to coping. I don't want to have to disturb one of my males to throw you out."

Jakule backed off and headed for a table near the door. His hands were sweating and his tongue felt swollen in his mouth. Bloody Kheszi! Treated him like dirt. There was no need for it. He was a good customer, always paid his money.

Well, maybe once or twice it had taken longer than usual to settle with Kheszi, but he wasn't the only one!

Shaking, he sat down and placed the cone in the burner. He took one of the stick ignitors from the pile and dragged it along the side of the pottery dish, lighting the cone with the resulting flame. The cone flared yellow for a few seconds till he blew it out, then settled down to burn with a red glow. Jakule pulled the dish closer, inhaling the aromatic smoke, feeling his mood lift immediately. He plotted his revenge on all the Chyads and Kheszis of his world, knowing they would be unable to stand up to his lightning skill and tactics in a Challenge.

His hand strayed to his inside pocket, lovingly feeling the lines of the gun. With this he didn't even need to Challenge them. One shot and they would be gone.

* * *

Though she had been on leave for the last five days, Mito had chosen to go into the linguistics lab for a couple of half-shifts to continue her work on the Valtegan computer data. Once more she'd been working with the Terran female Jo, finding in her a kindred spirit. Now she was taking the last two days off before starting her regular shifts again.

She was browsing round the one luxury store on the *Khalossa* when Maikoe approached her.

"Mito, I was hoping I'd run into you," the other female said. "I'm sorry you got upset yesterday. You have to excuse Chyad. He's from Khyaal and finding out what happened to Guynor distressed him. There are very few of us left from the colony worlds. To lose yet another was a hard blow to all of us."

Mito grunted, continuing to pick up various hair ornaments and examine them.

"Look, I'd like to talk to you," said Maikoe, taking her by the arm. "Can we go for a c'shar somewhere?"

Shaking the other female's hand free, Mito made her selection and delving into a pocket in her tabard, passed her card over to the storekeeper. "When I'm finished," she said, waiting for her beaded ribbons to be packaged and her card returned. The transaction complete, she turned round and began walking out of the store.

"Come on, Mito. Be reasonable," said Maikoe, catching hold of her again. "The cafe serves fresh c'shar. My treat."

Mito let herself be gently pulled toward the cafe. Once through the door, Maikoe led her to one of the tables that boasted soft easy chairs.

"Two c'shars," she said to the waiter as he came over to them.

"What do you want?" asked Mito, settling herself carefully so as not to crush the overtunic she wore.

"Just to explain about yesterday," said Maikoe.

"There's nothing to explain," said Mito. "I've never heard such lunatic suggestions in my life. The Terrans on Keiss have suffered a great deal at the hands of the Valtegans."

"The ones you met. What about the home world? You don't know what goes on there, do you? What if the Valtegans had a treaty with them, and Keiss was used to send the human dissidents to. Not an R & R planet, but a prison planet instead?"

Mito sat for a moment before answering. "It's possible," she admitted, "but unlikely."

"Say it is true, what then? The Valtegans would have a back door to Alliance space and could wipe us out before we knew we'd been attacked, just like Khyaal and Szurtha."

"In which case, a treaty with Keiss is to our advantage, isn't it? It's the one with Earth that could cause us harm."

"Exactly."

"We know nothing about their home world," she said slowly. "How can we make decisions on major issues like treaties if we haven't even visited them?"

"You're beginning to understand what worries us," said Maikoe.

Mito could see the female visibly relaxing now in her seat. She regarded her calmly. "What is it you want me to do?"

"We need information. Rumor has it the *Rhyaki* will be sent to Earth. We need our own communication link with them so we can get information that the authorities would rather we didn't have."

Mito laughed. "You're not asking a lot, are you?"

"We have a contact on the *Rhyaki*. He'll get hold of a small transmitter to send coded signals to us. We need you to intercept them before the bridge picks them up. We can arrange to have them sent when you're on bridge duty."

"I presume you also want me to send replies."

"Yes, but not from the bridge. You're still working mainly in the lab, aren't you? No active duty?"

"None. My work on the Valtegan programs is vital. We have a deep space transmission which we've partially deciphered that includes mention of the navigation crystal from the *Sirroki*. The Commander wants it translated as a matter of urgency so we know whether or not the Valtegans managed to access our data."

"I didn't realize you'd lost it," said Maikoe quietly. "That's worrying news."

"Isn't it just," said Mito with only a trace of sarcasm. "I'll be going planetside in a few weeks to study the remains of the Valtegan communication equipment. They've got a specialist team on it already. If they find anything useful to me, then I'll be down there for a long time."

Their drinks arrived, and Mito watched Maikoe sit in silence for a few minutes digesting her news.

"You'll be working with the Terrans on Keiss, won't you?"

"I'm working with them already."

"Would you find out what you can about their home world? See if they knew anything about the Valtegans prior to their arrival here."

"Maikoe, what the Keissian Terrans know about their home world is already ancient history," said Mito, enjoying being able to put down this oh-so-confident female, even if she wasn't aware it was being done.

"What do you mean?"

"The Terrans traveled here in cryogenic suspension because they have no jump drive. It took them the Gods know how many years to get here. Add on the time they've been here, and the fact they don't have deep space transmitters and you'll realize what they know could be anything up to fifty years out of date! The Valtegans could have taken over their world for all they know!"

"Have they?" asked Maikoe sharply.

Mito hesitated. "Not to our knowledge. It's confidential information at present, but we're already deep into negotiations with Earth as well as Keiss. If the Valtegans are there, they're letting the Terrans run all their own communications with us, which is unlikely."

"I have to agree with you on that," said Maikoe thoughtfully. "Still, I'd like to meet some of these Terrans and talk to them myself."

Mito shook her head. "No chance. They're only allowed to see people with a special permit. You must have noticed a lack of them in public since the brawl in the bar."

"I did wonder where they were," admitted Maikoe. "How do you get a security clearance then?"

"You don't," she said bluntly. "They're only here for a couple more days, then they return to Keiss. I can get in to see them, though. So can the others they work with and some of the senior officers."

"Why such tight security? We've never bothered with it before when we've had visiting aliens."

"Don't ask me," Mito shrugged. "Probably because they disgraced themselves by starting a fight."

"What do you think of one of our people having a telepathic link and a relationship with an alien?"

Mito took a sip of her drink. "Why not? Some of the Terrans are all right, just like some of us are all right and some are real bastards. I've got my eye on one of them myself."

"You're kidding!" exclaimed Maikoe, shocked out of her role as mediator for Chyad.

"No, I'm not. You haven't met them yet. Wait till you do."

"But one of them was responsible for Guynor's death."

"No, Guynor was responsible for his own execution," said Mito, banging her mug down on the table. "Just remember that. He chose to try and Challenge a Terran female, a civilian without our height, our claws, or our fur to protect her! He disobeyed Garras' order to leave her alone and when Vanna stopped him, he turned on Kusac, a telepath!"

Her eyes glittered at the other female. "He broke every rule in the book. They had no option but to execute him. I know, I was there. He was a fool, Maikoe, not a martyr, and I shall say so to anyone who'll listen."

Maikoe pulled back warily. "I didn't realize you felt so strongly about it," she said.

"I do. I've got a career in the Forces and I don't intend to jeopardize it on crackpot schemes. I'll talk to the Terrans for you, I will probably help you encode and decode your messages, I may even send and receive them, but only if I am convinced it's to gather more information about the Earth Terrans and if it doesn't put my career on the line."

"Thanks," said Maikoe, still unsure of Mito's temper. "I'll get in touch with you in a day or two."

"You do that. You can leave a message for me at the linguistics lab," said Mito, getting up.

"I think a personal one would be safer," said Maikoe, her voice tailing to nothing as Mito swept out into the concourse.

* * *

They were meeting Vanna and Garras on the concourse for second meal. Carrie was waiting for Kusac to finish dressing. He was digging in drawers for a belt to go round the tunic he was wearing. Various items were being flung on the bed as he muttered darkly about Personnel moving his belongings without his permission, and that they might at least have had the courtesy to keep them in the same order.

A bronze torc flew through the air to land with a clunk on the floor. Dodging a flying brush, Carrie bent to pick it up.

"Ah, found it!" he said, emerging from the chaos he had created.

"This is nice, what is it?" she asked, turning the torc over in her hands and examining the relief pattern on it.

Kusac fastened his belt as he came over to her. "The torc? It was a coming of age present from my parents."

"What's the design?" she asked, passing it back to him.

"A double sunburst. The sign for our family." He looked at it for a moment then moved to put it away.

"Why not wear it? I've seen other males wearing them, and females." She felt his reluctance.

"It'll be recognized," he said, tail tip gently flicking from side to side. "It's not something I want people to know."

"They know already, so why not wear it?"

Twisting it open, he put it on, turning it so the wider middle section with the sunburst was at the front. He shivered slightly at the bite of the cold metal.

Carrie surveyed him critically. "It looks good," she said, getting up from the chair. "Now let's go before Vanna and Garras decide we aren't coming."

"We should get some clothes for you today," said Kusac as they left their rooms and headed down the corridor.

"Sholan clothes suit you and I want to see you in something nice of your own."

"I'm not going to object," she said. "I've never bought clothes before. They were distributed from a central store at Seaport. One size fits all, one style suits all," she grinned, taking him by the hand as they stood waiting for the elevator.

"We'll see if we can persuade Vanna and Garras into going shopping first, then," said Kusac as the doors opened.

The elevator was almost empty, only two males and a female were in it. As they went down to the fourteenth level, Carrie was acutely aware of their curious looks. She turned round to smile at them, surprising them into embarrassed grins.

Stop teasing them, Kusac sent, his tone full of laughter. *They aren't used to Terran grins.*

I didn't show all my teeth, she replied as the doors opened on their level.

* * *

Jakule had finished his cone and would dearly have liked another, but even with his increased confidence he couldn't face another bout of Kheszi's brand of humiliation. All these males, they treated him as if he was nobody. One day, he'd show them, just wait, they'd see! Who was it he wanted to see? Chyad, that was it. Bastard, coming into his room and threatening him like that! Who'd he think he was anyway? Just some jumped-up greasy mechanic, that was all. He, Jakule, was one of the ground troops. They risked their lives while people like him sat safely in their little metal shuttles flying backward and forward, safe from the enemy on the ground.

It was about time someone showed Chyad what it was really like, and he was going to be the one to do it! Palming his gun out of the inside pocket, he pushed it into one of the large side ones. Now it was within easy reach. He staggered slightly as he got to his feet, and holding onto the tables he passed, he made for the door.

"What did you give him, Tayn?" asked Kheszi, watching him leave.

"A special," grinned Tayn. "Cut with that moss extract."

Kheszi turned back to look at him, snarling in anger. "You bloody idiot!" he said, landing him a vicious blow across the side of his head. "That stuff doesn't mix with alcohol, and he's been drinking! Follow him, make sure he doesn't get into trouble. Get him to his quarters if you can. Keep him there any way you want. Knock him out if you have to. A couple of hours should do it. Now get!"

Blinking back the tears of pain that sprang to his eyes, Tayn headed after Jakule.

He could see him heading down the concourse. He was moving fast for someone who had been staggering when he got up.

* * *

Chyad knew through his grapevine that Jakule was on the loose. He also knew where to find him. That little bugger was getting to be more of a problem than he was worth, he thought grimly as he made his way down the concourse toward the smoke bar. Him and his bloody habit! They should clean up that area, get rid of the illegal substances. A person could get enough out of the drinks and the legal smoke without wanting more. It had no place onboard.

* * *

As they came out of the elevator, Carrie saw Vanna and Garras sitting on a bench waiting for them.

Still there, she sent as Kusac put his arm across her shoulders. She waved, attracting their attention.

"Do you mind if we go shopping first?" asked Carrie. "I'd like to get some clothes of my own," she said. "Rhian has very kindly loaned me some, but I'd like some that fit me."

"Not a problem," said Vanna, "so long as we've eaten in time to go to my lab. We have an appointment there."

* * *

Jakule stopped. There was Chyad, right in front of him. He'd show the bastard! It would be the last time he talked to him or anyone else like that! He pulled the gun from his pocket, raised it up and pointed it at Chyad, then froze. It was the Terran female and her Leska.

From behind Tayn saw him stop, saw the flash of metal that was the gun. Gods, he was going to use it! He started to run, knowing there wasn't time, that he was too far away!

* * *

Time slowed in that inevitable way it has when something is about to happen. Carrie had experienced it before. She watched as the Sholan moved fractionally, realigning his gun on them. Around her she heard loud shouts, but the words were too slow to make sense. With peripheral vision she saw figures moving toward them, running toward the gunman. She knew they wouldn't be in time. Even thoughts were too slow now.

She leaned against Kusac, trying to push him and herself out of the line of fire, but he was too heavy. She was trapped like a butterfly on a board, waiting for the pin to descend.

Light lanced toward them. Almost at the same moment off to one side she saw a second Sholan release a shot, hitting their attacker, sending him crashing to the ground. Helplessly she watched the light accelerate toward her, then it hit, knocking her backward to land in a heap on the ground.

From nowhere, people appeared, descending on the fallen body of Jakule and around Carrie and Kusac, forming a living barrier between them and any further assailants.

She lay there stunned, looking up at the ceiling above, then Kusac and Vanna were by her side.

"She's all right," said Vanna, clamping her hand over the wound on her arm. "Just call Medical. I'll see to her."

Are you all right? demanded Kusac, kneeling beside her. *I can't sense any pain.*

It doesn't hurt. She was aware of being surrounded by people on every side. It was difficult to breathe, she felt claustrophobic.

Kusac got to his feet and started pushing them back. "Get back! You're causing more harm than good," he said. "We need room!"

He knelt down again, suddenly feeling an agonizing pain in his right arm. His head began to swim, then he felt her black out.

"I think the pain's just hit her," said Vanna.

"I know," said Kusac, his voice tight.

"You, too? Shit! Hang in there and try to block it. She can't feel anything for the present. Where the hell's the on-duty medic team? They shouldn't take this long."

"You hold her arm, I'll carry her," said Kusac, reaching down to pick her up.

"I don't want her moved, Kusac," said Vanna, but he ignored her.

* * *

Chyad stood rooted to the spot for several seconds, hardly able to take in what had happened. As Jakule fell, he saw Tayn standing beyond. The other skidded to a stop, staring at him with wide eyes, then turned tail and ran in the opposite direction.

Jakule had been coming for him, Chyad realized with a shock. He began to growl low in his throat. That damned smoke bar! What the hell had they given him? He'd blown everything now, the stupid son of a she-jegget! Then he saw the security people moving. Where the hell had they all come from? His blood ran cold as he realized the extent of the unseen protection that surrounded the Terran female and her Leska. His people had picked up none of it. They were all amateurs compared with this.

Turning, he headed back the way he'd come. Maybe it was just as well the runt had flipped like that. Now he knew the full extent of what they were taking on. At least no one could tie this to him and his friends.

The klaxon had brought everyone out into the concourse, and a hand grabbed at him as he pushed through the crowd.

"Chyad! Wait!"

It was Maikoe. He pulled free, slowing slightly to let her catch up with him.

"What happened? Why's the alarm going off?" she demanded.

"Jakule shot the Terran female. The energy flare set off the alarm."

"Hey, stop a minute," she said, hauling on his arm. "Jakule shot her?" she asked incredulously. "Why would he do a stupid thing like that?"

"He wasn't after her, he was after me," said Chyad. "The Terran just happened to come into his line of sight and he changed his mind."

"Gods, you were lucky! What about the Terran? Is she dead? What happened to Jakule?"

"I don't know, I couldn't see for the security people around her." He stopped and grabbed her, pulling her back against a store front.

"You should have seen them, Maikoe! There must have been upward of half a dozen of them rushing forward!" He shook his head, beginning to realize just how narrow an escape he'd had, not only from Jakule but from Security. "Jakule's dead. One of the guards took him out."

"At least he can't tell them anything," said Maikoe. "What the hell did you do to him to make him come after you with a gun?"

"He was watching their corridor when they moved into their new quarters. Myak saw him. I told him to stay out of sight."

"Are you sure Myak saw him?"

"Positive!" growled Chyad, pulling away from her. "I'm getting out of here. If you've any sense, you'll do the same. I'll contact you when things have calmed down. Tell the others to do the same."

* * *

The emergency team arrived back at her lab five minutes after they did. The comments Vanna threw at them over her shoulder as she worked were brief and to the point.

"Where the hell were you? An emergency team shouldn't take fifteen minutes to reach their patient! By then they're likely dead! I'm ordering drills for all of you as of tomorrow morning at eighth hour. See you're here on time. If you don't improve, I'll have your rank reversed to ward orderlies! Now get out of here!"

She glanced up at Kusac, her tail still swaying from side to side in anger. "You're in my way, too," she said abruptly.

"I'm not leaving," he said from his position by Carrie's head.

"It's not serious, Kusac. Just a flesh wound. There's no need for you to stay. Go and join Garras outside."

He ignored her, staying where he was.

"Don't you trust me?" she asked as she finished wrapping a dressing over the wound.

"Don't be ridiculous," he said.

"She's staying here overnight so that I can monitor her," warned Vanna, collecting her various implements. "I want to be sure she doesn't go into shock."

"I'm not leaving," he repeated.

"You can't stay."

"Then neither does she."

"Aren't you carrying this a little too far?" she asked quietly.

"Gods, Vanna, I've just found her! I could have lost her

out there, and you ask me to leave her here on her own?" He shook his head. "No, I'm staying."

Vanna looked at him across the limp form of Carrie. There was a determined look on his face. She had a sudden feeling she was going to get to know it well. "I give in," she sighed. "Stay if you must, but I don't know where I'm going to put you."

"You'll find somewhere," said Kusac with a faint grin.

"Don't bet on it," she said, leaving the treatment room.

* * *

"Well," growled Raguul to the Brother, "not to put too fine a point on it, you bungled that one."

"On the contrary. He only got off one shot which, considering he was a wild card, is acceptable. Even your telepaths didn't pick him up because he changed his target at the last moment."

"I don't consider it acceptable."

"Commander, it is impossible to guard anyone against an unexpected attack. Given the circumstances, everyone concerned acted with speed and efficiency to protect them. I destroyed the threat. Have you had the lab report on Jakule yet?" he asked, changing the topic.

Raguul grunted assent and pushed the folder over to the Brother with a clawtip. "You were right. Drugs and alcohol pushed him over the edge."

Tallinu picked up the file and quickly scanned the contents. "His intended victim was Chyad, the leader of the dissidents."

"So you said. He's still at liberty as you requested. The smoke bar has been cleared, and those responsible are in the cells."

Tallinu nodded. "I don't want Chyad to know we're on to him yet. I've got an informant in the group now. It should be interesting to see what comes out of this."

"Interesting isn't the word I'd choose," said Raguul. "I'm having them moved. I don't care what your plans are, I cannot put either of them at risk again. They'll spend the rest of their stay on the *Khalossa* in one of the ambassadorial suites, which is where they should be anyway considering Kusac Aldatan's rank. In future, they'll go nowhere without personal bodyguards."

"As you wish," said Tallinu. "I have to warn you that if

you do this, though, you run the risk of not being able to eliminate this dissidence at the root."

"We'll all face that problem when we come to it," growled Raguul. "One way or another I want that gang rounded up now. If you don't, then I will. I won't risk their lives again. Gods, their parents are the major negotiators in this treaty!"

"Very well. I'll need thirty-six hours."

Raguul nodded with relief. "Draz tells me you've organized the security at Physician Vanna's lab."

"I've placed two males, Meral and Sevrin, on personal guard duty outside their room, with another at every corridor junction and elevator in that section. They're on two-hour shifts to maximize their efficiency. Has High Command isolated all our ships and started the Attitude Indoctrination program?"

"It's been done, both in space and on Shola and Khoma. There have been no other reports of dissent against the humans."

As he left the Commander's office, Tallinu stopped to talk to Myak.

"How is the indoctrination program proceeding? Did you get your guild's aid?"

Myak looked up at him, his eyes unblinking. "The Telepath Guild has included some subliminal messages for us in both the standard Attitude Indoctrination program and the Basic Ethnography. We're using it at present on those due to go down to Keiss. It appears to be working. Quite a few of our personnel seem to be enjoying the lectures, in fact."

"No crises of conscience, then, Myak?"

Myak blinked once. "No, Brother Tallinu. Not in this case. Too much hangs in the balance. You are more in touch with the Gods than us, you should know this."

"Oh, I do, my friend. I do. Vartra has a lot to answer for."

* * *

"I thought you wanted to run some tests on them today," said Garras as they left the medical section.

"That can wait," said Vanna tiredly. "I need to eat."

"Then let's have . . . third meal," said Garras, checking his wrist unit. "Why don't we go to my quarters and call the restaurants? We can get them to send something over."

"Sounds good. I need to relax, not sit in the mess or a restaurant."

Though hungry, Vanna picked her way through her meal. Finally, when they sat with cups of c'shar, Garras asked her what was wrong.

Vanna sighed. "I've been offered a new job."

"Let me guess. When Kusac and Carrie leave for Shola, they want you to accompany them."

Vanna looked up at him, startled. "How did you guess?"

"Not difficult. It's the logical thing to do. You've told me their lives depend on each other, so he'd be foolish to leave behind the only Sholan medic with any idea of how to treat his Leska. And Kusac's no fool."

"I'd like to go," she said.

"It's your decision, Vanna. Personal physician to the heir of the Aldatan Clan, and a contender for the leadership of the Sixteen Telepath Clans isn't a job to be turned down lightly."

"He's concerned he may not remain the heir for long when his parents find out about his Leska."

"I doubt that," said Garras. "It would look very bad for the Head of Alien Relations to disinherit his son because he has an alien Leska."

Vanna shrugged. "It doesn't affect my decision anyway. The problem is, I also want to stay."

"Oh?"

"Yes," she said.

"May I ask why?"

"I've got friends I don't want to leave behind. Good friends," she said, looking up at him.

He reached down to touch her cheek. "Now you're getting sentimental," he said gently. "You mustn't let sentiment stand in the way of the life you want. Just be sure that it's what you really want."

"Shola's a long way from here."

"My duties are likely to keep me on the surface of Keiss for some time. With you here doing research, we wouldn't see much of each other. If you go, I can visit when I'm on leave. I'm due one soon. I have Clan matters to attend to regarding my trade agreement with Skinner over coffee."

Vanna grinned. "You crafty so and so! You've been planning it!"

Garras' ears dipped slightly. "Let's say I anticipated your

leaving and was hoping rather than planning that I would have a reason to visit you. Now come up off the floor. It's too far down for me at my age."

"Your age!" she scoffed, uncurling herself and joining him on the settee. "You're hardly an ancient!"

Garras made a grab for her, catching her by the scruff. "You go with Kusac and Carrie to Shola if that's what you want," he said as he licked the insides of her ears, making her squirm, "just so long as I can visit you and have you to myself for a while."

"I promise, I promise!" she said, laughing.

* * *

The maintenance communicator chimed. "Ngalu, report to sector three landing bay. They have a breached oxygen pipe."

"On my way," responded Ngalu picking up her tool kit and emergency air supply. Slinging the portable breather unit over her shoulders, she loped off to the nearest servicing elevator.

The landing bay was aft of the ship and housed a quarter of the available eight-person scout ships that were flying patrols over Keiss and throughout that sector of space. The bay doors were currently open, the faint blue glow of the force field that kept the atmosphere in lending an eerie cyanic glow to the parked vehicles.

All nonessential personnel had vacated the area before she arrived; only the chief engineer on duty remained.

"Where's the problem?" she asked as she joined him at his station.

His ears flicked to the bay doors. "Over there. Looks like one of the scouters may have caught it as they entered. I'm in the process of topping up the liquid oxygen levels so the blow-out detectors are disabled. I've stopped the refueling sequence, but there's still liquid in the system."

She looked over to the open doors, eyes narrowing to focus on the array of pipes to the left.

"I see it," she said, catching sight of the thin stream of gas as it emerged from the break into the warmer atmosphere of the landing bay.

"Can you isolate the pipe manually?"

He shook his head. "Not from here. I'll have to go up to the gallery to access those controls."

"Do it, then. I don't want to run the risk of a fire down here. Let's have the bay doors shut."

"Not possible. There's a patrol due to land in fifteen minutes."

"Advise the bridge of the problem in case we need to reroute them. We'll do it by the book. I want this area depressurized. I don't anticipate any problems, but there's no point in chancing fate with those fuel lines in operation. I'll give you the signal when I'm ready."

While the engineer proceeded to route his controls up to the gallery, Ngalu went over to the lockers. Putting her repair kit down, she pulled out an emergency pressure suit. Releasing her breather unit, she placed it in the locker out of the way. By the time she'd climbed into the suit and sealed her helmet, the engineer's voice was audible over her comm unit.

"Oxygen feed line has been isolated, Maintenance. I'm ready to depressurize on your command."

"Depressurize now," said Ngalu, picking up her kit and making her way over to the bay doors.

As she approached the breached pipe, she could see the slight rime of frost surrounding the crack. The stream of gas was lessening now that it had been isolated.

She reached out to touch it. There was a bright flash followed by a searing pain in her chest, then darkness.

* * *

When Vanna returned to the medical section the next morning, she found Kusac curled up beside Carrie. She reached out and shook him awake.

His eyes flicked open, and Carrie began to stir.

"How is she?" Vanna asked. "Did she have a peaceful night?"

"She woke in pain, so the nurse gave us the pills you'd left," said Kusac, blinking in an effort to wake.

"I notice your leg hasn't been bothering you."

"It stopped hurting so I took the dressing off a couple of days ago," he said.

"There's no point in having a personal physician if you don't do what she says," said Vanna, checking the logbook on the nightstand.

"You'll come?" asked Kusac, lifting his head up to look at her.

"I'll come," she agreed.

"I'm glad. And Garras?"

Her ears flicked in a mixture of embarrassment and annoyance. "Doesn't anyone around you get a private life?" she asked.

"I haven't used my . . ."

"Hey, I'm only teasing," she said quickly. "He'll visit me."

"I don't need to look," he said. "You both have a contentment you lacked before."

Carrie woke, eyes flying open in panic till she got her bearings and realized Kusac was with her.

"Maybe you were right after all, Kusac," said Vanna quietly. "How do you feel this morning, Carrie?" she asked.

"Bruised and sore," she said, sitting up. "And hungry."

"Your arm will hurt for all that it's a shallow wound." Vanna put a small container on the stand beside her. "Take one of these when you need it, but no more than six in a day," she warned. "They're the same tablets you had before. They should help. Now if you two will get up, Myak is waiting to talk to you."

"Myak?" said Kusac in surprise as he slid out from under the cover. "What's it about?"

Vanna shook her head. "You'll have to ask him."

"Can someone pass me my clothes, please?" asked Carrie.

Kusac went over to the chair for them. *Clothing taboos,* he sent on a tight thought in Vanna's direction.

A startled look came over her face.

Kusac went back to Carrie with them. "I'll be outside with Myak," he said, touching her cheek lightly.

"Moving again?" said Kusac incredulously. "Why?"

"For your safety, Liegen," said Myak.

"Where?"

"One of the ambassadorial suites."

"No. I refuse. We'll stay where we are."

"Orders, Liegen. Commander Raguul sends his regrets at the circumstances that make it necessary, but it is the only place we can guarantee your safety until the matter is dealt with."

"Who was the male that shot at us?" he demanded. "Did you get him?"

"He was a member of the ground forces, a petty criminal.

He was given a recreational drug cut with a dangerous narcotic and wasn't in his right mind when he encountered you and your Leska, Liegen. He's dead. One of our men killed him as he shot at you."

"So what remains to be dealt with?"

"I'm afraid I'm not at liberty to tell you, Liegen," said Myak firmly. "I have with me your adjutant, Kaid. He'll act in an assistance capacity in any way you need him. He will also accompany you when you leave for Shola." He beckoned Kaid forward.

Kusac looked at him briefly, then back at Myak. "This is ridiculous. I don't need an adjutant, nor do I need to move into the ambassadorial rooms! Either I'm a member of this crew without the rank to justify having an adjutant, or I'm a civilian who does. Which am I, Myak?"

"Your rank is Lieutenant because your grade is first among the telepaths. Your records have been altered accordingly," said Myak stiffly. "Your Leska has the same rank, and for the moment shares your grade until the guild has assessed her. Therefore, your status within the Forces demands you have an adjutant."

"Ye Gods," swore Kusac, turning away from them. "Tell the Commander I will follow his orders under duress! And stop calling me 'Liegen'!"

"Yes, sir," said Myak. "I will leave you in the capable hands of Kaid." He flashed Kaid a quick look then left.

Kusac turned around to look at Kaid. His eyes narrowed. "Haven't I met you before? You look familiar."

"Yes, sir. I was living in the quarters next door to you," said Kaid.

"Well, we're stuck with this ludicrous situation, so we'd better make the best of it," Kusac sighed, responding at last to Carrie's calming influence.

A moment later she emerged with Vanna. "I'm going to have to get some new clothes," she said ruefully. "Rhian's tunic was ruined, so Vanna kindly lent me this one for now, but I'll need some of my own."

"We'll see to it," promised Kusac.

"I'm fine," she said, responding to his unasked question. "Are they sure the gunman was under the influence of drugs? He wasn't another Guynor, was he?"

"I give you my word that neither of you was the intended victim," said Kaid.

Kusac regarded him for a moment. "Well, let's get on with this move, then," he said, tail flicking.

As the elevator opened and they stepped out, they were stopped by armed guards carrying energy rifles. Kaid flashed his pass at them and they stepped back to their posts.

"This is ridiculous," muttered Kusac, taking Carrie by the arm.

"It is standard security for this level, sir," Kaid explained. "We have the Chemerian Ambassador on board at present."

Kusac grunted in reply, slightly mollified.

Kaid stopped in front of a door flanked by two more armed guards. Over their heavy leather jackets they wore ritual swords strapped to their backs with body harnesses. On the right shoulder of each was the Warrior Guild flash of red. Each one carried an energy weapon holstered to his belt as well as a rifle.

"What are they doing here?" Kusac asked icily, aware of Carrie's sudden fear.

"The Commander appointed them as personal bodyguards to you and your Leska," murmured Kaid. "At present, you are the two most important people on board the *Khalossa,* a bridge between Shola and the Keissian Terrans."

"I don't care who appointed you, you are dismissed," Kusac ordered them, his voice full of barely controlled fury.

"I'm afraid you can't dismiss them, Liegen Aldatan. I'm sure you're only too aware of the consequences should anything happen to either of you. Had the attacker been successful yesterday, we could now be at war with the Terrans. If you had been accompanied by guards yesterday, then your Leska might never have sustained an injury at all."

Carrie's thoughts penetrated his anger at last. *Kusac, let's leave it for now,* she sent. *I'll be glad of them for the moment.*

They'll follow us around everywhere, drawing attention to us. We'll never have any privacy.

They're outside the door. Once we're inside, we're alone. If you're worried about them being noticed, ask for one in a Forces uniform to accompany us, rather than two in Warrior's gear.

Kusac gave her a surprised look. *If you feel safer with them around, and the Commander will agree, I suppose I could live with it.*

He turned to Kaid. "Would you lead the way in?"

The entrance hall was large and sparsely furnished with hard-backed chairs set against the walls and occasional low tables between them. A corridor led through to the interior area.

"Kaid ..." began Kusac, his hackles beginning to rise again despite Carrie's calming influence.

"You presented us with the problem, Liegen Aldatan," came the urbane reply. "We've merely tried to solve it to the best of our ability. Where else but in the Ambassadorial Quarters can we house you in the utmost security? I assure you it was not chosen for reasons of your rank."

Kusac shot him a fulminating glance. He hadn't expected the *Khalossa* to have staterooms on board comparable to those in the Governor of Shola's palace.

"If you have any more surprises like these in store for me, I suggest you tell me now," he growled.

Only the rigidity of Kaid's ears betrayed the fact that he was aware of the need to proceed with caution. The male in front of him could not be pushed further. Being a telepath, he couldn't be manipulated or coerced into cooperating.

"None, sir, save for a formal reception tomorrow to welcome the visiting Terran dignitaries. Your Consort's father will be there," he said, inclining his head toward Carrie.

"Never again refer to the Liegena Carrie as a Consort," snarled Kusac, baring his teeth. "That I will have understood from the outset." He took a step toward Kaid.

Ears flattening slightly in apology, Kaid backed away, crossing his arms over his chest and bowing low. "It shall be as you wish, Liegen Aldatan. No insult was intended."

Kusac let some of his anger drain away, aware not only that he was blaming the adjutant for a situation that was beyond his control but that he was adding to Carrie's anxiety. As it was, she was afraid of coming face-to-face with her father.

"I'm sorry, Kaid. I hate all this," he said, indicating their surroundings. "Your job, as far as I'm concerned, is to keep this world as far away from us as possible. I like things simple and straightforward."

"It shall be as my Liegen wishes," Kaid said.

"Please show us the rest of the suite."

Kaid led them through the various rooms, explaining that the *Khalossa* had several of these suites, each one capable of being environmentally adapted for the Chemer and the Sumaan as well as Touibans or Sholan dignitaries when they were guests on the vessel.

As they returned to the ample lounge, Kusac steered Carrie over to the settee.

Rest. You're looking tired, he sent.

"In fact, sir," continued Kaid, "from tomorrow, Liegena Carrie's father and the rest of the Terran party will be resident in a suite nearby."

"I think it would be best if Mr. Hamilton was kept at a distance," said Kusac.

Carrie nodded. "Tomorrow evening is soon enough. Perhaps at a public function I can avoid having him ask questions I don't want to answer."

"I'll see to it, Liegena."

"Thank you. Will we meet any Chemer and Sumaan?" she asked.

"You'll meet the Chemerian Ambassador tomorrow evening, Liegena, along with his Sumaan bodyguard."

"It should be quite a gathering," said Kusac dryly.

Kaid tried not to smile. "The suite is equipped with kitchens and there is a food dispenser with an extensive menu. The data terminal and your desk are there," he said, pointing to a corner of the lounge, "and a secretary will be available if you wish one. A female rating can also be provided to help Liegena Carrie for tomorrow evening and she'll be on hand at any time should she be needed. I have a room at the rear and I'm in charge of the smooth running of the whole, and here to see your personal wishes are met, Liegen."

Kusac sat down beside Carrie. "What about a personal medic?"

"Medic?" echoed the startled adjutant.

"Medic," repeated Kusac. "After yesterday's incident I want a personal medic who'll accompany us to Shola. If my Leska took ill, who would treat her? One of our medics with no knowledge of her physiology? What provision has been made to cover that?"

"Ah, none, Liegen," said Kaid, caught without an answer.

"Then I suggest you look into it."

"Do you have someone in mind?"

"Physician Vanna Kyjishi."

Kaid looked thoughtfully at him. "I'm sure it could be arranged, if Physician Kyjishi wishes it."

"I've already asked her, and she's agreed."

"I will attend to the matter immediately, sir," said Kaid.

"One other item. The bodyguard. I refuse to be followed about by those two in Warriors' dress. If we must have them, then get them wearing an ordinary military uniform, something to make them blend in with everyone else."

Kaid's jaw dropped in a slight grin for the second time that day. "Certainly, sir. There should be no problem in doing that at all."

Chapter 6

Tallinu lay looking up at the ceiling. He was due to send in a report, to his employer if not to the Brotherhood. The time was fast approaching when he'd have to make his evaluation of the situation, even if he didn't share it with Ghezu and Lijou. Was Kusac's just one of the rare rogue talents that turned up every few years? What about the human? She was a totally unknown quantity. How could he begin to assess her? Usually it was more clear-cut, with either the Talent or the owner so unstable that there was no option but to terminate. That was one of the reasons why traditionally the Brotherhood had to work outside the law, so the Telepath Guild could order these terminations without considering themselves murderers. In the remainder of cases, and by far the rarer, the person under observation simply disappeared.

But this unlikely pair? Rulla hadn't been that far off the mark with his guesses. He, Tallinu, knew something was about to happen, something that would affect all their lives. Was it them—this human female and one of their males? Was it their lives—or deaths—that would change everything? It could be either. The God knew Shola needed changes. For too long the Telepath Guilds had been the real power behind the world council, the Telepath Guild of Valsgarth in particular. Telepaths might represent a tiny proportion of the population, but the old fears of them, though buried deep now, were still there. So the guild ruled from behind the scenes: that power had to be broken one day soon if their society was to evolve. Guild Master Esken of Valsgarth didn't like change.

With a sigh, he got up. So the God was walking the halls of the Dzahai Stronghold, was He? Maybe it was time for him to visit the temple again. Perhaps the familiar sounds of the rituals and the smell of the incense would let him achieve that state of mind where the God could reach him.

* * *

Chyad's comm beeped at him from the corner of his room. Going over to the desk, he sat down and activated the vidiphone link.

"Kaedoe, I thought I told you not to call me," Chyad began, but the other cut him short.

"Have you heard the news? There's been an accident in the shuttle bay. An explosion. Naisha and Khay were working on it when it blew. They're dead, Chyad. Like Ngalu. That's three of us gone. I tell you, they're on to us."

"Kaedoe, stop panicking," said Chyad, forcing his ears to stay upright. The news had shocked him. "There's nothing for anyone to find out, remember? Now tell me what happened."

"I don't know. I tried to contact Khay and was told he'd had an accident. When I went to Personnel, they told me he and Naisha had been killed while working on an engine fault in a shuttle. It's not a coincidence, Chyad. They're after us. We've got to get out of here!" Kaedoe's ears were flat with fear.

"Kaedoe, pull yourself together," said Chyad. "You should hear what you're saying! You're talking absolute rubbish. The Forces don't have people blown up, they arrest them. We've done nothing but talk, and talk isn't illegal. Just carry on normally, and stay calm."

"What about Ngalu?" Kaedoe demanded, his voice getting more frantic.

"A freak accident. They're investigating her death, they'll investigate Khay's and Naisha's, too. There would be a cover-up if the authorities were involved. Just keep your head and everything will be fine. Now I have to go. Remember, just stay calm and try to forget about it."

Chyad cut the connection. Kaedoe's news had worried him more than he dared let on. He needed to see Maikoe. It was still possible it was a bizarre coincidence. Six months ago, a scouter had blown in the central landing bay, taking a crew of eight with it. There hadn't been enough wreckage left to be absolutely sure what had caused it.

He felt a shiver run up his spine. Getting up, he headed for the door. Maybe Kaedoe was right and getting out was the sensible thing to do.

* * *

Commander Raguul had been handed the report of the second freak accident in sixteen hours.

"So this one is as inconclusive as the other," he said to Myak.

"Yes, sir. There were no fragments from the conduit found in Ngalu's chest, yet her suit had been ripped open by something. Even allowing that the breach exposed the outer casing to liquid oxygen, it shouldn't fracture like that."

"And the actual cause of death?"

"Explosive decompression," said Myak.

"Messy. What about the shuttle accident?"

"The engine compartment where the two crew members were working is just so much molten slag fused around their bodies. Even taking the volatiles on board into account, there shouldn't have been that large an explosion or that much heat present."

Raguul looked at Myak and handed him the files. "I want these incidents tidied up satisfactorily. I'm sure you can see to it. I also want the Brother contacted immediately. This has gone far enough. I expected these people to be brought into custody."

"I'm afraid I can't contact him, Commander," said Myak, taking the papers from him. "He's involved in the final phase of his orders." He began to move unobtrusively toward the cupboard.

"That's not acceptable, Myak," snapped the Commander, a pained look coming on his face. "Yes! Get me my bloody medicine, but get me that damned male here as soon as possible!"

"Yes, Commander," said Myak.

* * *

Vanna had called on Kusac and Carrie in the midafternoon of the following day to check on Carrie's injury. It had only been a shallow flesh wound and with the help of the drugs she'd used, was already beginning to heal. She'd declined an invitation to accompany them to the reception as she had just moved into her new medical lab and wanted to finish organizing everything to her satisfaction.

Evening came, and with it the need to get ready for the reception. Carrie sat grooming Kusac until his fur shone almost black in the subdued lighting of the bedroom. The fur on his head, much more like hair now it had begun to grow again, had a slight spring to it unlike the rest of his coat. She ran the brush through it, enjoying watching the way it coiled free of the bristles.

Kusac turned over onto his back. "I won't have any left if you brush me any longer," he said, reaching out to take a handful of her long fair hair. "Yours feels so soft, and the color is unlike any shade of ours."

"The differences seem to bring us closer," said Carrie, rubbing her palm against his chest.

He reached up to pull her nearer just as a discreet knock sounded at the door.

"Damn!" he swore, the mood broken. "I told you having others around would ruin our privacy."

"We haven't had much of that yet," said Carrie ruefully, moving away from him and pulling her robe tighter.

"Enter," said Kusac, sitting up.

Kaid opened the door. "Could I have a word with you in private, sir?" he asked.

Ears pricking in surprise, Kusac got up and followed him out into the lounge.

"What is it?" he asked, closing the door behind him.

"I thought you might like to know that a barque from Shola is docking in the main bay. Your mother, Clan Leader Aldatan, is on board and is requesting that you meet her."

Kusac stood looking at Kaid. "My mother? Here?"

"Yes, sir."

He stood there, his mind numbed by surprise.

"It would be better to meet her there, sir, rather than let her arrive here alone," prompted Kaid.

"Yes. You're right," he said, turning back to the bedroom. He hadn't had time to discuss it with Carrie before, and now it was too late. There wasn't time. Gods, why did events rush upon them like this! He pushed a barrier to the front of his mind, knowing what he must do before his mother arrived.

"What's wrong?" Carrie asked.

He went over to her, his hands going up to the torc round his neck. "I've got to go out for a while, there's some business I have to attend to. You stay here and rest," he said. Sitting down, he took his torc off and held it out toward her. "I want you to wear this tonight," he said.

She looked at him, puzzlement foremost in her mind. "Are you sure?" she asked, taking it from him.

He nodded. "Will you wear it for me?"

"I'd love to, if you're sure you don't mind me borrowing it," she said, turning it over in her hands.

"Let me." Taking it back from her, he held the ends apart and looped it round her neck. "It's a gift. I want you to keep it," he said, pulling her close to kiss her briefly. "It will look good with your clothes for this evening."

"What's going on, Kusac?" she said, putting her hand up to touch the warm metal as he moved away from her to pick up his uniform. "You're blocking your thoughts again."

"I've some personal business to attend to, that's all. I won't be long," he said, concentrating on putting on his jacket and buckling his belt over it. "You rest, I'll be back shortly. A sleep would do you good. After all, we didn't get much last night!" he grinned, sending relaxing thoughts to her.

She returned the smile, the tension visibly leaving her as she curled up on the bed.

He left the room to rejoin Kaid. One of the Warriors was waiting with him.

"This is Meral. He'll accompany you, Liegen."

"Not dressed like that he won't!" said Kusac. "I thought we'd agreed they should wear an ordinary uniform."

"Tonight is an official reception, they need to be traditionally dressed. Besides, it's a fitting escort for you to go to greet your mother, sir." Kaid said.

"I haven't got time to argue," growled Kusac, heading for the door closely followed by Meral.

They reached the bay as his mother was disembarking. His thoughts were in such confusion that he hadn't had time to think about what he was going to say to her. At the moment she was in conversation with Sub-Commander Kolem and Myak.

Gods! He had to tell her about Carrie before they did. He hurried forward.

She turned immediately to look at him and he was aware of her gentle touch at the edges of his mind. They stopped a few feet apart while she studied him carefully, then she stepped forward, her long robes rustling softly as she walked.

"Kusac." She held her hands out to him and he came forward to take them in his.

"Mother," he said. "What brings you here?"

"I'm here as the chief negotiator from Alien Relations," she said. "Your father is needed at home, so the duty fell to me. Besides," she smiled, "I thought you would rather see me than him." She put her arm through his and drew him toward the exit.

"Yes, Myak," she said, letting her voice drift over her shoulder to the adjutant as he padded along behind her, followed by her attendant. "I will let you escort me to my quarters, after I have visited with my son. For the moment, you can see to Miosh. Now tell me about your Leska," she said, hugging Kusac's arm. "Through your father I have felt the echo of her mind, but only just. Is she young? Is she pretty? Come, I want to know it all. How did you meet her?"

"Not here, Mother. I'll tell you all of it, I promise. Wouldn't you rather go to your own suite first and freshen up after your journey?" he asked, looking round for Myak.

"No, I wouldn't," she said frankly. "You've been gone for over a year." She stopped, taking his face in her hands. "You left in the night with no warning, leaving no word of where you had gone. No news of you in nearly a year, my son," she said. "I want to be with you now." She released him, stepping back to study him more closely.

You've grown thin. No, you've grown up in the last year. I can see marks of suffering on your face. She touched his cheek briefly with her hand then linked her arm in his again.

"This Leska of yours, you're in love with her, aren't you? I see it in your face and I can feel it in your mind. You've finally met the female who means everything to you. I'm glad."

"Mother," he said, "please, we've got to talk first. I need to explain . . ."

"We'll talk," she said, drawing him inexorably on to the elevator. "But first I will meet your Leska."

Meral and Myak accompanied them, leaving Miosh to organize the ratings who were seeing to the luggage. Like Kusac, they traveled up in silence, he listening to his mother's chatter about his sisters. It would have given him time to think had he been capable of it, but his mind remained blank. Now that the moment was here, he found himself with nothing to say.

As they entered the suite, he turned to her again. "Mother . . ." he began.

"Well come, my Liege," said Kaid.

"Kaid," she said, with a faint flick of an ear as she swept past him toward the bedroom.

Kusac sent a look of panic at Kaid who merely raised an eye ridge. For the first time Kusac sensed the other's mind, feeling the faintest touch of ironic humor at his predicament. He hurried over to the door, managing to slap his hand over the control panel before her.

"Wait, Mother," he said firmly. "We must talk first."

She stopped, and he felt her take in the set of his ears and the anxious flicking of his tail. She shook her head. "No. I will meet her first," she said equally firmly.

"Why?"

She locked eyes with him. "Because you are so protective of her."

They stood like this for several moments, then Kusac looked away. Moving his hand, he pressed the control. The door slid open.

Carrie lay asleep in the center of the bed.

"So this is your Terran," his mother said, stepping into the room and going over to look down at her.

"No, this is my Leska." Kusac moved to sit protectively beside her.

His mother bent down and reached out her hand toward the girl's face.

Kusac tensed, but her fingers barely touched Carrie's cheek.

Have you lost your trust of me, Kusac? she asked before moving a finger down to the torc that glinted at the human female's throat.

"So," she said, straightening up and looking across at him. "I knew I was right."

He nodded, reaching out to touch Carrie as she stirred and began to wake.

His mother turned and moved toward a nearby chair. "This explains everything," she said.

"I'm sure it does," he said. "But I really don't care any more, Mother. All I want is her."

Carrie stirred and feeling his touch turned to him, still more asleep than awake. "You're back," she said, reaching out to pull him close. Then she froze, sensing the other person in the room.

"We've company," said Kusac quietly, his face only inches from hers.

Who?

My mother.

Oh, damn, I'm sorry. She let him go.

Kusac sat back, giving her room to move. She sat up and, keeping a tight rein on her thoughts, tied the belt on her robe and turned to face his mother.

His arms came round her, holding her close to him for reassurance.

Eyes as amber as Kusac's looked calmly back at them.

"Mother . . ."

She raised her hand, motioning him to silence.

Through their shared Link they both felt her gently touch Carrie's mind as her eyes flicked first across the girl's face then her son's.

Anger began to flare in Carrie. "He's done nothing wrong," she said. "You've no right to judge us."

"No, he's done nothing wrong," said Rhyasha slowly, letting her mental touch fade. "Had he acted otherwise, he wouldn't be my son."

Carrie felt the tension suddenly evaporate from Kusac as his mother held out her hand toward Carrie. *Come, let me greet you properly,* she sent.

Kusac released her, urging her to go.

There was nothing for it but to scramble in an undignified fashion across the bed to the other side. Swinging her legs round, she stood up, unsure what to do next.

Rhyasha went to her, sweeping the Terran into a warm embrace, her cheek touching Carrie's briefly. "Well come, Carrie," she said, her voice a low purr in the girl's ear before she let her go. "Cub, is it?" she asked Kusac, returning to her chair. "Then cub she'll be to me. Now, Kusac, we'll talk. Once you have ordered some c'shar for us."

As he went to the door to speak to Kaid, Kusac relaxed all but one of the barriers in his mind. It was a relief knowing he needn't fight against his mother.

Carrie sat on the edge of the bed, trying not to stare. Kusac's mother was striking to look at, the amber color of her eyes being echoed in her fur. Her hair, lighter by several shades, was long and worn in a mass of tiny braids into which had been woven silver beads. Her robe of light purple was plain, its color relieved by an edge of silver at the neck and wrists.

Kusac returned, bearing a tray with three mugs on it.

"Ah, they've anticipated us," said Rhyasha as he passed one to her.

"Kaid says we only have an hour before we need to get ready," he said, passing a mug to Carrie before taking the last one himself. Putting the tray down, he sat on the floor and leaned against her.

"Rubbish," said his mother. "We'll take what time we need. I've only just arrived, after all. Myak can see that they delay the start for us."

"How did you know about Carrie?" Kusac asked.

Rhyasha put her mug down on the table beside her. "For the last three or four months, your father has been picking up stray images which he was convinced came from you. He was unable to make sense of them until nearly three weeks ago when they became even stronger. Between us we were able to pinpoint them to here. Your father contacted the *Khalossa* and was able to ascertain that you were among the crew." She picked up the mug again, taking a drink from it.

"Then a week ago when it became obvious that the negotiations were getting into problems, it was decided I should come here in an official capacity. That was when we both sensed you and your Leska."

Kusac's ears flattened and he glanced away from his mother to Carrie.

"Your father and I had been sent the initial reports concerning your crew's first contact with the humans living on the planet, including details of the injured crewman who had been helped by one of the Terrans. Then he spoke to you."

She hesitated a moment before continuing. "Your Link is unique, Kusac, in more ways than the obvious one. The feel of your minds is different. There was just enough of an alien quality then for me to realize that perhaps your Leska wasn't Sholan, especially when we heard that there was a Terran telepath. Now that quality is stronger."

Kusac frowned. "The alien feel?"

"Yes, I'm afraid so. I felt it when I met you in the landing bay. Your minds are so closely bound together now that you no longer feel completely Sholan. I've never known a Leska pair so completely Linked as you are."

"Carrie has many more talents than we have," he said slowly, "and some of them have crossed over to me. We've done things I never dreamed possible, like finding the pod in the swamp and contacting our crew. I've compared our Link to the normal Sholan Leska Links and the differences are marked. Perhaps that's what you're sensing."

"It may be," she agreed. "I'd like to see a copy of your findings. I can study them during my stay on Keiss."

"I'll see you get a copy."

Rhyasha looked at Carrie and smiled. "So, cub, you would be part of our world, would you?"

Mother, don't mention it yet, Kusac sent to her using the private Link they'd always shared. *I've told her nothing of my life at home.*

But your commitment . . .

My commitment is to her, no one else, and she accepted it, he sent firmly. *You've touched her mind, you know what she feels for me. Let that be enough for now.*

As you wish.

"I don't have much option, do I?" Carrie said. "But, yes, it's what I want."

"I came here as much to meet you as to lead the negotiations with Keiss," Rhyasha said. "I needed to know what you felt for each other. I know now. You'll need all that fighting spirit you both have if you are ever to have the life you want. You realize that, don't you?" she said, looking at them each in turn.

"I don't just mean your father, Kusac, I'm referring to the Forces and our guild. Already the reports mention the potential military benefits of telepaths who can easily sense and read alien minds and who can also fight. They'll try to use you for their own ends, running endless tests and studies on you till you're no more than jeggets in a maze to them. Don't let this happen."

"We'll be careful," said Kusac. "I'd already anticipated that." He felt Carrie's concern and mentally reassured her.

She nodded. "I was sure you would. You always plan ahead carefully."

"Except this time," he said wryly, looking up at Carrie. "This cub came at me unexpectedly."

Rhyasha laughed. "You were the one who felt life was too predictable! Are you complaining now that it isn't?"

"No, not at all. You know that."

His mother stood. "Miosh is reminding me that we must get ready for this reception. We'll talk again later. Come and give me another hug. I've missed you."

Kusac rose and went to her.

"You, too, Carrie," she said. "You're part of our lives now."

Carrie went to her, sensing through her Link his mother's genuine liking of her son's mate.

"Call me Rhyasha, cub," she said, once more touching her cheek to the girl's face as she held them both close.

"You can walk me to my suite, Kusac," she said, releasing them and moving toward the door.

Meral and Myak accompanied them at a discreet distance.

"You've placed me in a very awkward position, Kusac. I'll stand by your decision for tonight," she said, "but you must tell your father yourself, and soon. I don't want him knowing that I've given public approval to your actions and kept it from him. Once you've done that, I'll help you all I can."

No words were needed to convey his thanks.

"I have to ask you if you're sure this is what you really want," she said.

"I lived with Carrie and her family for six weeks before we left their village, and all that time she thought I was only an animal because on Keiss there are forest cats that resemble us," he said. "I got to know her well during that time, and I found myself attracted to her. When I finally told her who I was, she had to see me as a person not an animal before her feelings could come to the surface."

He glanced sideways at his mother. "What we feel for each other isn't something that happened suddenly. It isn't because of our Link either," he said, coming to a stop. "I know exactly what I'm doing, Mother, exactly what I'm giving up."

"I know," she sighed, reaching out to touch his cheek. "but I needed to hear you say it. Now go back to your Leska before she comes charging out to your rescue," she smiled. "I like her, Kusac. Vartra has indeed blessed you, even if she is Terran. There's a lot about her that is almost Sholan."

"More than you think," he grinned.

"Off with you, scamp!" she said, laughing. "Go and get ready for this charade we have to play out for the dignitaries. I'll send Miosh over to help Carrie get ready."

"I don't think she'll need any help," he said.

"Perhaps not, but having another female around to help you look your best for your first public appearance is very calming, believe me. Now go. I'll see you shortly."

* * *

Raguul hated wearing his dress uniform, so his temper was none too mellow by the time Myak had finished fastening his baldric over the sleeveless red tabard.

"My shirt's caught now," he grumbled, tugging ineffectually at the black cloth.

Myak came to the rescue, easing the shirt free at the shoulders, then tugging the cuffs at the bottom of the full sleeves.

"Try that, Commander," he said, standing back.

Raguul flexed his shoulders experimentally then nodded. "That's better, thank you."

Myak handed him the knife first, followed by the single sword which, as a Commander, he could wear at his side.

Raguul adjusted the weapons till they sat comfortably over his hips. "Right, I'm ready," he said.

"A moment, Commander," said Myak, bending down to adjust the lengths of the tunic panels so they hung level with his knees.

The Commander's tail flicked in annoyance. "Come on, Myak. You're being over-fussy."

"If you wouldn't mind holding your tail still, sir, I'd be a lot quicker," said Myak quietly. "There, I'm done."

"You said Clan Leader Aldatan was at ease with her son when you showed them to her quarters?"

"Yes, sir. She was laughing as he left her."

"Gods, this whole situation is like a container of explosives about to blow up under us! At least they seem to have made their peace over his Leska. What about Hamilton? Did you make sure he attended the Attitude Indoctrination lecture when he arrived?"

"Yes, sir. He was there along with the other visiting Terrans."

"He hasn't said any more about that male he wanted to bring—what was his name? The one we refused."

"David Elliot, sir. No, apart from his initial complaint, nothing more has been said."

"Vartra be praised you recognized the name, Myak. The

last thing we needed was the human girl's betrothed here tonight."

"She wasn't betrothed to him. From what I understand of their social setup, they can choose their own life partners. Her father chose hers for her without her consent."

"No matter. Considering their strange views on sexual matters, we've enough problems brewing with her father. We don't need the added complication of that male as well." He looked sharply at Myak. "You realize this whole situation could still explode in our faces?"

"I know, sir."

"Did you manage to pick up anything more from the Clan Leader?"

Myak gave him a reproving look. "You know I won't probe for information, sir. Besides, I would have found nothing if I'd tried. The Clan Leader has a formidable talent."

Raguul grunted. "Well, let's be off. I want to get there early."

* * *

Kusac returned to their suite feeling a lot calmer about the forthcoming reception. Carrie was sitting on the edge of the bed finishing her drink. He sniffed the air, nose wrinkling till he recognized it.

"Do I smell coffee?" he asked. "Don't tell me they've had the sense to program it into the food dispensers."

"Kaid had it done for us," she said. "C'shar just isn't the same. Do you want some?" she asked, getting up.

"Please. I'm sorry I had to spring my mother's arrival on you like that, but I didn't know she was coming," he said, taking his uniform off and going over to the wardrobe. "I didn't want to worry you because I hoped she'd go to her own rooms first."

"She had to know sometime," said Carrie, handing him his mug. "She didn't seem to dislike me."

"Far from it," he said, taking a drink. "She said she likes you and finds you very Sholan. She's sending Miosh over to help you look your best so you'll be more relaxed at the reception."

"That was kind," murmured Carrie, moving over to the other end of the wardrobe to get her clothes.

There was a knock at the door. Kusac opened it.

"The attendant says she's here to help the Liegena, sir," said Kaid.

His mother's subtlety wasn't lost on Kusac and he sent a quick thought in her direction.

I will enjoy watching the discomfiture of our people at tonight's gathering, she sent. *They won't know how to react!*

With a grin, Kusac let Miosh in and returned to the wardrobe to get the clothes he was wearing. Kaid remained to help him while Carrie and Miosh went into the adjacent bedroom.

Understandably, Carrie hadn't felt like going back down to the concourse to shop for clothes so they had taken advantage of Kaid's suggestion to have the storekeeper bring a selection up to their suite. Kusac had made sure she'd chosen several different outfits, telling her not to worry about the cost.

For the reception she'd chosen a deep blue split-paneled robe which they'd had edged with a dark purple border. Shoes had proved a problem until she remembered the pair of simple black slippers that were among the few things she'd had sent from home. Round her waist was a plain black leather belt with a dagger hanging from it.

"Why the dagger?" she asked, coming back into their bedroom.

"Ceremonial." Kusac was digging in his drawer for an arm bracelet. "It harkens back to our less peaceful days, and looks good to the peasants," he added with wry humor.

Kaid winced at the sarcastic tone.

"Well, what reason would you give?" Kusac asked him.

"It goes back to those days, certainly. The years after the Cataclysm, when no one went unarmed. The size of the knife shows that it has devolved from a sword, and that though more peaceful now, we're prepared to fight should the need arise."

"Neat, and it has the ring of truth to it," said Kusac, slipping the bracelet over his shirt to sit snugly above his elbow. "It sounds very like one of the Warriors' maxims to me."

Kaid shrugged and moved forward to hand Kusac his belt.

"Well, I'm ready," Carrie said, standing up. His mother's attendant gave a final twitch to the folds of her robe, then stood back.

"The Clan Leader sent this for you to wear tonight," murmured Miosh, taking a sleeveless black over-robe out of the package she'd been carrying. She held it out for Carrie to put on.

Kusac heard a slight intake of breath from Kaid and looked up at her. He nodded his head slowly, the presence of the black over-robe not lost on him either.

"The Terran part of me knows how your own people will admire you tonight," he said. "The Sholan loves your beauty. Cub, you look wonderful, and you've got legs!"

Carrie grinned, running her hands down the front of the split-paneled dress that almost, but not quite, hid her bare legs.

"The styles are so flattering," she said. "I've never had anything like this to wear before, nor the occasion to wear it."

She looked appraisingly at him. He wore a shorter version of her tunic but in a soft olive color with a white full-sleeved shirt on beneath. The purple border of his guild was on the hem and neck of the tunic.

"Come to think of it, I've never seen you in anything other than your uniform. You look pretty good yourself. What do the colors signify?"

Kusac looked down at himself. "Nothing particularly," he said. "I just happen to like them. They're the clothes I brought with me."

"The Clan Leader sent a robe for you also, Liegen," said the attendant, handing the garment to Kaid.

"My mother is nothing if not thorough," said Kusac ruefully, taking it from her and putting it on.

"What's the significance of the black robe?" she asked. "I ought to know, but I can't find the memory of it."

"Worn as an outer robe it's our Clan color," said Kusac. "Well, we might as well get this over with," he said, putting his arm round Carrie's waist. "Let me guess, Kaid. We have an honor guard to escort us there, right?"

"Tomorrow you will have your Warriors in military uniform, Liegen. For tonight, you must be seen to have a proper honor guard. Your mother will have one, too."

"It's as well all Leskas don't have these problems," said Kusac as they crossed the lounge toward the door, "else there would be very few Leska pairs."

"There haven't been many Leskas amongst the Clan Leader's immediate family, Liegen," murmured Kaid.

* * *

"Commander, you said my daughter would be here tonight. Where is she?" asked Peter Hamilton.

"She'll be here, Mr. Hamilton," Raguul assured him. "They have been unavoidably delayed I'm afraid."

"They?" he asked sharply. "Who's they?"

"She's with Liegen Aldatan's mother at present," interrupted Myak, coming to his Commander's rescue. "They'll be here shortly, sir."

"This isn't good enough, Commander. Whenever I've tried to contact my daughter, I'm told she's busy or can't be found. I want to know why you appear to be frustrating my attempts to see her."

"Mr. Hamilton, on a ship the size of the *Khalossa* it's just not possible to know where everyone is at a given time," said Raguul.

"I'm sorry to interrupt, Commander, but I have a message for you," said Myak. "The Chemerian Ambassador wishes to see you urgently." Myak pointedly stood waiting for Commander Raguul to follow him.

"Do excuse me, Mr. Hamilton," said Raguul, taking his leave. "Myak, thank you," he said as soon as they were out of earshot. "Hamilton's really beginning to annoy me. Find someone to keep him occupied for now. We should have held this tomorrow and let him have tonight to speak to his daughter!"

"We couldn't do that, sir. Tomorrow is their Link day. Have you forgotten they need every fifth day to themselves?"

Raguul muttered darkly under his breath as he went over to the Chemerian. Myak headed off to find Jo to keep Mr. Hamilton occupied if not entertained.

* * *

They went down to the reception suite in the company of Rhyasha and her guard.

I see we're presenting a united front, Mother, sent Kusac.

They'll gossip anyway. As well give them a good reason, she answered imperturbably.

"I'm not sure I want to go, Kusac," said Carrie quietly. "I don't think I can cope with my father yet."

"You'll do fine," said Rhyasha, taking her hand and patting it reassuringly. "We're with you tonight and eventually your father has to return to Keiss while you remain here with Kusac. It's only for a few hours." She looped her arm through Carrie's and smiled down at her.

Kusac took her other hand. "He can't make you do what he wants any more, just remember that. If you keep your shield up, it'll help you feel calmer."

They entered the reception suite like that, Carrie arm in arm with her mother, Kusac holding her other hand.

Commander Raguul, flanked by the ever attentive Myak, came forward to greet them.

"Clan Leader Aldatan," he said, inclining his head toward her. "Well come to the *Khalossa*." As he turned to Carrie and Kusac, his ears twitched briefly.

"Commander, I don't think you've met my son and his Leska yet," Rhyasha said smoothly. "Liegen Kusac Aldatan and Liegena Carrie."

Kusac and his mother were well aware of the Sholans' re-action to her words. Like it or not, she had placed Carrie firmly under the protection of the Aldatan Clan and given her blessing to their relationship. They had to accept it and act accordingly.

"Liegen, Liegena," said Raguul with a nod to each of them. He turned back to Rhyasha. "Let me introduce you to the Terrans, Clan Leader," he said.

I'm here if you need me, she sent to both of them as she moved off in the company of the Commander.

Kusac put his arm round Carrie's waist and nodded to-ward where Garras stood talking to Mito and Anders.

"Let's join them," he said, drawing her over in their direc-tion. Kaid followed them while Meral and Sevrin stood back near the door, watching them from a distance.

Carrie was beginning to feel decidedly ill-at-ease. She had caught a glimpse of her father across the room as Rhyasha was escorted over to him. He caught her eye for a moment, then had to look away as the Commander began to talk to him.

In hiding her fears from Kusac and his mother she had left herself open to her father, and now his feelings came flood-ing over her. For a moment she saw Kusac through his eyes, was aware of the alienness of him not only in the fact that he resembled a furred animal, but in his height and strength compared to the fragility of his only daughter. His fear for her physical safety swamped her, and with a shudder she blocked him out.

The residue of his reaction remained with her, though, and she found herself feeling alienated from everyone—Terrans and Sholans alike.

Garras looked up as they approached. His eyes narrowed slightly and his pupils contracted to slits as he caught sight of Kaid behind them.

Kusac sensed his recognition and glanced at Kaid, motioning him forward. "You know each other?"

"We met during basic training at the Warrior Guild, sir," said Kaid, taking the lead.

Kusac glanced from one to the other.

Garras is concerned, sent Carrie. *Kaid is as always.*

"Kaid, there's no need for you to be on duty," said Kusac. "Enjoy yourself. Someone ought to," he added with a flick of his ears and a slight grin.

"Carrie, don't you look grand!" said a voice from behind her.

She turned round to hug her brother. "Richard! I didn't expect to see you."

"Jack's here," he said. "Come and talk to him. You don't mind, do you, Kusac?"

"Not at all," he said.

"Quite the secretive one, aren't you?" said Garras as they watched her walk away with her brother, Sevrin following at a respectful distance.

"Your entrance caused quite a stir. No one was expecting that. Still, if you have the backing of your family, there should be no insurmountable problems."

"I've yet to speak to my father," said Kusac, turning back to him.

"Carrie's father is about somewhere," said Anders. "I'd watch out for him if I were you. He's got a stubborn look to him tonight."

"Thanks for the warning," said Kusac. "Mito, nice to see you."

"Kusac," she said, putting a hand on Anders' arm. "I heard about the shooting. Carrie's all right?"

"She's fine. The injury was minor, thankfully."

"Watch yourselves," she said, her tone serious. "I'm afraid that Guynor's threat wasn't empty."

Kusac looked puzzled. "I'm sorry, Mito, but I don't see

the connection. The man who shot Carrie was after someone else. He was under the influence of illegal drugs."

"He was from Khyaal, like Guynor," said Mito. "Just be careful, that's all."

"Anders, why don't you take Mito over to the buffet to get something to eat." A tone of command underlay Garras' suggestion.

"Yes, sir," said Anders, drawing Mito away.

"Is there anything I should know?" Kusac asked Garras. "Or is Mito being her usual melodramatic self?"

"Probably just Mito," said Garras. "I should think you've enough to contend with tonight without dealing with imaginary problems."

"I think I could do with a drink," said Kusac. "What about you?"

"I've got one, thanks."

Kusac made his way over to one of the long tables and asked for a glass of wine—supplied by the Terrans, the rating who served him said. Wanting a little peace and quiet, he ambled toward an empty chair—one of the comfortable ones.

"Liegen Aldatan," said a voice at his elbow.

Looking round, he found himself face-to-face with the Commander. He inclined his head. "Sir."

"We haven't met properly, but already I feel I know you through the piles of paperwork that you've generated," said Raguul.

"Me?" Kusac asked, surprised.

"You. You've no idea how much red tape your father has torn apart, trying to get your military status rescinded."

Kusac sighed. "I've a fair idea."

"Oh? Then you might not be displeased to find that the Commander-in-Chief has refused him."

"Really?" Kusac's ears pricked up.

The Commander nodded. "We feel that taking all the circumstances into account, the best thing we can do is place you on indefinite leave on Shola. You were training for Alien Relations, weren't you?"

Kusac nodded in agreement.

"You'll be able to finish your training there."

"Why go to all that bother?" he asked, frowning.

"Because of your Leska and her ability to fight. You seem to have absorbed some of her attitudes, and quite frankly, telepaths who can take part in combat situations could be an advantage to us. I don't say we have a need for them at the moment, but should that need arise, I want to be able to recall you both at any time."

"Which is why we need to go to the guild to work on our Link and find its limitations. I can see it all now. I'm afraid I have to say that I don't approve of the military using telepaths in combat, Commander."

"You're already working for the military, Liegen. However, don't prejudge a situation that hasn't yet occurred and may never do so."

He turned to look in Carrie's direction. "Speaking of Leskas, was that a wise move?" he asked, nodding toward her. "I believe your father has other plans even if your mother lends her support."

"I have plans, too, Commander," Kusac said quietly.

"I hope you know what you're taking on."

"What do you think?" Kusac asked, looking unblinkingly at him.

"I think you'll win, Liegen Aldatan," he said abruptly. "Your actions so far demonstrate honor if not wisdom. I wish you success."

Kusac flicked his ears in thanks.

"When do we leave for Shola?"

"When I have a craft free to send you," the Commander said, moving away. "Oh, I thought you'd like to know that you can have your physician. I consider it a very wise move on your part." He smiled, then headed for the buffet table.

Preoccupied by what the Commander had said, Kusac didn't realize he was being approached until a hand clapped him on the shoulder, almost making him jump out of his skin.

"Kusac," said a cheery Terran voice. "I'm glad to see my poor doctoring returned you to full health."

"Jack Reynolds?" said Kusac, slipping politely out from under the hand and turning to greet the Terran.

"Aye, no doubt you remember me," he said grinning, "but I had to have you pointed out to me by Carrie. You aren't the only one here with black fur, you know, and with your upright posture and clothing you look totally different. How you put up with my poking and prodding, I'll never know. You were probably heartily sick of it long before I was finished."

"Not at all," said Kusac. "I was extremely grateful to you for saving my life. I'm very glad to have the opportunity to thank you in person."

"Think nothing of it, lad. I thought you were far too patient for a forest cat even then," said Jack. "I'll have to rewrite all my notes on Keissian felines now!"

"I seem to be creating quite a pile of paperwork wherever I go," said Kusac wryly.

"Eh? Oh, you and Carrie. Yes, I gather you've caused quite a stir among your own people, not to mention ours. Tell me more about this Link you have."

"It's just a telepathic Link," said Kusac.

Jack shot him a piercing glance. "Just, eh? Don't give me that, laddie. I saw the two of you arriving. Can't think when I've seen a cozier pair so obviously at ease with each other."

Kusac glanced around sharply, mentally scanning to see if any other Terrans had overheard them. He took Jack by the arm, drawing the doctor toward a quiet corner of the room which boasted two empty chairs.

"I knew there was more to it," said Jack in a satisfied tone as he lowered his bulk into one of the chairs. He grimaced as he sank back in the seat. "This furniture definitely wasn't made for the likes of me," he said, eyeing his slightly rotund frame. "But you lot, it's just a treat for you. You can curl up in them. Now, tell me about you and Carrie."

"The Link is telepathic, but it's total. A blending of mind and body," said Kusac, leaning forward so he could speak quietly.

"How? Tell me more about it. I've been convinced all along that Carrie's talents could be explained scientifically."

"I don't know the mechanics, only the effects. We're constantly in communication with each other. Our minds are never alone."

"How on Earth do you keep your own identity?"

"We do have our own thoughts," he said, "but there is some overlap, of course. We need time to see how it will develop, because what we have isn't a normal Leska Link, it's far more intense."

"Hm. You said body and mind. Is pain the only physical sensation you share?"

Kusac frowned, sitting back a little. "Our Link's very different from what Carrie and Elise shared," he said. "The body is made up of senses, and ours ... communicate ... on a physical level, confirming and consolidating the mental Link. Every fifth day the Link draws us together physically so our minds can merge totally. The experiences we've each acquired are then sorted into our separate memories where we can assimilate and understand them. Without that closeness, our minds couldn't cope with the Link. It would literally overload our systems and kill us. It's analogous to the body needing sleep so the mind can file all the experiences of the day."

"This Link sounds like it should be avoided if at all possible," said Jack, shaking his head. "I assume that whatever happens to you, happens to her, just as it did with her sister."

Kusac's tail flicked, his ears trying to fold down. "No," he said sharply. "Not like her sister. I have more to give her. Elise gave only pain."

Jack leaned forward, frowning in concern as he patted Kusac on the hand. "Now, don't take me wrong. I never meant that. I can see you care about her. I do have a personal interest in you both, you know."

Kusac relaxed slightly, again moving away from Jack's hand.

"What is it?" asked Jack, picking up on the gesture. "Have I done something I shouldn't? Your people seem to be free of many of our taboos. Don't you touch unless you're related?"

Kusac grinned. "The scientist at work again. Yes, we're very tactile but telepaths are a rule unto themselves. We don't like being touched unless we invite that intimacy. I told you, our bodies sense as much as our minds. Imagine being touched by someone who dislikes you. You can't avoid sensing all that hate directed toward you." Kusac wrinkled his nose. "It's far from pleasant."

"That sounds more of a disability than an advantage," said Jack, sipping his drink. "I suppose your own people know better than to touch you. I'm sorry if I caused you any distress."

Kusac shook his head. "Only a little discomfort," he said.

"Can you pick up knowledge through your telepathy?"

"Oh, yes, but it doesn't give you the experience to use it. It has its limitations."

"Have you picked up anything about our culture from Carrie, other than what you saw when you lived with us?"

"I know everything she knows," said Kusac, "as Carrie does with me."

"Then you two are the only people with a working knowledge and understanding of both our cultures. I hear you're being posted back to Shola. It would make sense to pass on that knowledge to someone before you leave."

"To you?" grinned Kusac. "Certainly, Jack. Come and see us tomorrow and I'll arrange for you to meet our First Contact team personally. You'll be the leading Terran xenobiologist yet!" he laughed.

"Good," grinned Jack. "It's refreshing not to have to conceal one's small ambitions. Quite a glittering gathering, isn't it?" he said, looking around the room. "Your people have a barbaric splendor tonight."

Though slightly smaller than the average Sholan, the Terrans stood out because of their more sober clothing.

"Everyone is wearing ceremonial clothes," said Kusac. "We dress for show, not warmth or nudity taboos like you."

"What about that fellow," said Jack, nodding at the Warrior standing resplendent in black and red near Kusac's chair.

"Bodyguard," said Kusac briefly. "One of the Warrior Guild."

"I notice Carrie has one, too."

"We keep getting told we're a bridge between our species and they can't afford to take any chances with our safety," said Kusac tiredly.

"Have there been threats against you?" asked Jack, looking worried.

"No, none. In fact, most people present are untroubled by our bond. Most Sholans, that is," he amended. "There was an incident on Keiss concerning one of the crew of our scouter and myself, but that was dealt with several days ago."

"What happened?"

"I'm sorry," said Kusac tersely, "I don't wish to go over the incident again."

Jack nodded, content to leave the matter. "I wish I could say our people are being more tolerant of you two, but some of them aren't."

"David," said Kusac quietly.

"Yes. He's trying to cause trouble by stirring up sympathy

for himself over what he sees as your interference between him and Carrie."

"Is anyone believing him?"

"One or two who are here tonight are half-convinced he has a genuine grievance, but in the main, no. However . . ."

"Carrie's father?" asked Kusac, taking a drink from his glass.

Jack nodded.

"He intends to have the truth from you tonight."

"I was afraid of that," said Kusac, running a hand through his hair in annoyance.

"If I can offer some advice, go to him first. Take him aside and tell him privately because there's no way you can soften the situation for him, and he'll let everyone know how displeased he is."

"Perhaps I should introduce him to my father first and tell them together," Kusac grinned mirthlessly. "They don't sound very different."

"Fathers aren't, essentially," said Jack. "I'll come, too, if you want. Perhaps I can explain the situation in a way that will ease matters."

Kusac nodded, turning his head as he caught sight of a heavily armed Sumaan approaching him.

"It looks like the Chemerian Ambassador wants me," he said. "I hope it's nothing more than curiosity."

"He's a bit too like the Valtegans for my taste," muttered Jack, looking suspiciously at the tall reptilian being coming toward them.

The Sumaan stood six feet tall to his shoulders. A sinuous neck which extended his height another two feet, was topped by a large crested head. He walked upright, his muscular legs like pillars above feet with nonretractable claws. His powerful arms ended in mobile clawed hands with three fingers and an opposable thumb. Behind him his tail, almost as thick as his thorax, was carried several inches off the ground.

"I wouldn't say that," said Kusac. "The only common factor is that they're both reptilian. Even their skin color is different. His is more of an earth-brown color. He's a Sumaan, the hired bodyguard. The Chemerian is the small furred being in the chair by the other guard."

Jack glanced back to the Chemerian, noting the small robed body perched in the chair. Large dark eyes regarded them intently, then looked away to blink rapidly. The semi-circular ears set on either side of the face quivered, almost folding over themselves before the ambassador managed to straighten them.

"They don't like maintaining eye contact for long," said Kusac. "They interpret it as confrontational. It's one of the few ways to unsettle them without even trying."

The Sumaan stopped in front of them, effectively blocking their view of his employer. Curving his neck down so his face was level with Kusac's, he addressed him in halting Sholan while displaying a formidable array of teeth.

"Liegen Aldatan, Ambassador Taira demands you and Terran female."

"Tell the Ambassador we will approach his presence shortly," said Kusac.

The Sumaan's tongue flicked briefly out toward Jack. Then, turning back to Kusac, he raised his hand in salute and left. They watched him threading his way back to his diminutive employer, trying to prevent his heavy tail from knocking into anyone.

"They live partially underground and their eyes see in the infrared range. As you can see, they're built for speed and strength. The Chemerians, on the other hand, live in cities constructed in the upper branches of the trees that cover their world. They have few needs in common so they don't compete with each other for resources or planets to colonize. It makes the Sumaan the perfect mercenaries for such a paranoid species."

Jack sighed. "Before tonight I almost wished I was going to Shola with you. Now there are all these exotic new people to meet and study right here!"

Kusac laughed and got to his feet. "I can see I'll have to make sure you get access to our data on the Sumaan and Chemerians, too! Nice to see you again, Jack. If I need your help tonight, I'll call. Otherwise I'll see you tomorrow morning in our suite about the third hour."

He made his way over to where Carrie was talking to Skinner.

"Have you come to take care of her yourself?" asked the Captain. "I'm running out of excuses to keep her out of her father's clutches."

"I'm afraid it's duty that calls," he said, touching Carrie's cheek gently with a finger as she smiled up at him. He turned to Skinner.

"The Chemerian Ambassador wishes to meet us. Have you been through that scrutiny yet?"

Skinner grimaced. "Unfortunately. They're almost rude with their curiosity, or is it just because we're the new boys?"

"No, they're like that with everyone. The trick in dealing with them is to be that bit more arrogant and unconcerned than they are. Didn't someone brief you?" he asked, a frown appearing between his eyes.

"No, but you seem to be pretty well-informed."

"A Clan Lord's son is involved in interspecies diplomacy from an early age," said Kusac. "It was one of my more interesting duties."

Skinner narrowed his eyes. "Quite the dark horse, aren't you?" he said as Kusac turned to go.

Kusac grinned and inclined his head, turning away. He drew Carrie's arm through his as they walked toward the diminutive Chemerian Ambassador who sat curled in a chair, flanked by his two massive Sumaan guards.

Someone stepped in front of them. "I want a word with you two," he said in Terran.

Kusac sized up the tall middle-aged man in front of him. "Mr. Hamilton, may I suggest we leave this conversation until tomorrow," he said, aware of Carrie's sudden wave of fear.

"I want to talk now, not tomorrow."

"This is neither the right place nor time," said Kusac. "It's a public gathering and several of the Sholans present understand your language, not to mention your own party. Our presence has been requested by the Chemerian Ambassador."

"I'm the Terran Ambassador and I insist on talking to you here and now," Mr. Hamilton said angrily, his face flushing above his beard as he reached out to catch Kusac by the arm.

Instantly, the warriors stepped forward, swords drawn and pointed at the Terran. With a curt gesture, Kusac dismissed them.

Though obviously rattled by the guards' instant reaction, Hamilton was by no means intimidated and kept hold of Kusac's arm.

"If you insist, Mr. Hamilton, but shall we go to one of the

smaller rooms here?" Kusac suggested, releasing Carrie's arm in order to disengage himself from her father's grip.

Leave us, cub. He's in an unreasonable mood. There's no need for you to be involved in this scene, Kusac sent quickly.

Carrie began to back away.

"You stay where you are, miss!" her father said, not taking his eyes off Kusac. "I've several things I want to say to you, too."

Kusac sighed. "Very well, Mr. Hamilton, since you seem determined to deal with this in public, what is it you want?"

"I want to know exactly what's going on between you two," he said angrily. "There's a conspiracy of silence here. No one will tell me anything about either of you. Just what little game are you playing?"

Carrie stood there, her anger building as she realized she was almost incidental to their row.

"We aren't playing any games, Mr. Hamilton. Your daughter and I share a telepathic Link known as a Leska bond. You've been told that."

Her father made an angry gesture. "Don't give me that rubbish! There's no such thing as telepathy! Every time I've seen you together you've been touching her! What's your interest in her?"

Kusac was peripherally aware of Jack Reynolds and Skinner, and from farther away, his mother, heading over toward them.

"I've told you, she's my Leska. We're Linked together, mind and body as one."

"So you do have a physical interest in her!" He swung round on Carrie. "As for you, how could you get involved with him? He's an alien, not one of us. He doesn't even look human ..." he began.

Jack put a restraining hand on his arm. "Easy, Peter. Watch what you're saying. Apart from your daughter, you're insulting the son of the Sholan Ambassador."

Peter Hamilton shook him off roughly. "I don't care who he is! I have no intention of letting this relationship between him and my daughter continue," he said, beside himself with rage. "I hope you're pleased with yourself, my girl! You've completely ruined your reputation. No decent man would have you now!"

Carrie stepped forward, her face white with fury. "You

won't let me?" she demanded, her voice shaking. "The choice isn't yours to make!"

Kusac felt her pulling on their Link, felt the energy start to swirl between them.

"No, Carrie, don't!" he cried, feeling reality start to fade briefly as he was physically tugged toward her. He could feel the power continue to build as she began to tap into the other people in the room.

There was a cry of pain as the Sholan interpreter, another telepath, crumpled to the floor.

He saw Carrie's father reach for her. "Leave her alone!" he said, his voice sharp with the fear of what could happen if she initiated a total mental merging. He fought the Link's domination of his senses, trying not to let it control his body as he was forced, against his will, to move closer to her.

"What the hell's happening?" demanded Skinner, holding his head as he, like everyone else present in the room, experienced the onset of a stabbing headache.

Kusac felt himself being physically pulled nearer and nearer to the maelstrom of Carrie's anger. He tried looking for a way to break the gestalt Link, but all he sensed now was Carrie changing.

Her body had begun to shimmer. He saw a strange almost rippling effect that made him feel nauseous. Her anger built in him, reaching a white-hot pitch then, abruptly, the shimmering stopped.

A honey-colored fur began to spread over her hands and face as the lines of her body altered subtly, becoming longer, more feline. For a moment she stood there, a Terran overlaid with Sholan features as Kusac finally reached her side.

In a voice that was pure Sholan, she shouted an angry phrase.

Shocked to the core, Kusac saw his own hands changing, too, starting to lose their fur and claws, becoming Terran.

Then, as suddenly as it had begun, it was over. Carrie, once more Terran, slumped unconscious against him. As he staggered under her unexpected weight, Skinner put out a hand to steady them.

"Don't touch them!" said Rhyasha, hitting his hand violently out of the way. "They're still too closely Linked. Your touch could kill them both!"

Stumbling to his knees, Kusac grasped Carrie tightly.

"Get Vanna," he said, his voice harsh with fear. When everyone hesitated, he lifted his head looking round them as if at strangers. "Get Vanna now!" he roared, his voice a fullthroated Sholan cry.

Chapter 7

The Sholans stood rigid with fear. It was a legend come to life! Carrie had quoted the words last spoken by Khadulah Aldatan, which had resulted in the fatal Challenge that changed forever the laws regarding telepaths.

The Warriors came to their senses first. Sevrin left at a run while Meral and Kaid tried to push back the crowd that was gathering round Kusac and Carrie.

Jack bent down beside him. "Kusac, let me look at her. I've been her doctor for years, I know her system well."

"No! No one touches her till Vanna arrives," he replied, baring his teeth and raising his hackles. He gathered her unconscious form closer, her blonde hair spilling across his knees onto the floor beneath them.

"What's her mental state, Kusac?" demanded the Mentor, also crouching down. "Can you still sense her? Did that power backlash through her?"

Rhyasha motioned to Kaid. "Get the suite cleared of everyone but us," she ordered. "Mnya, don't be a fool. Even I can sense her presence. Kusac, what can you feel through your Link?"

"She's unconscious. I can feel her presence but nothing else. I don't know if she's been burnt out." His voice caught and he laid his head against Carrie's. "The gestalt phase has gone now."

"It's happened before? Why wasn't that in your notes?" demanded his mother as she crouched beside him.

Kusac looked blankly at her. "You didn't tell me you'd had them."

"Tell me about the gestalt," she said, ignoring his comment.

"I can't. We don't know what it is. I couldn't find a reference to it anywhere in the guild files."

"What triggers it?"

Kusac's eyes began to focus on her. "Why are you bothering me about this? I don't want to talk, I want Vanna!"

"What triggers it, Kusac?" his mother insisted.

"I don't know!" he said angrily. "Now leave me alone!"

"I'm trying to help," Rhyasha said more gently, her hand touching his cheek now that she knew he was no longer in rapport with Carrie. "If I know what's happened, then I may be able to do something."

The room was emptying steadily with only a few people now remaining. Peter Hamilton pushed through the group around them to kneel beside Kusac and his daughter.

"What in God's name have you done to her?" he whispered, putting out a tentative hand to touch her.

Kusac snarled and bared his teeth at him, ready to snap at the reaching hand.

Jack pulled him back. "Don't interfere, Peter. They know what they're doing. I haven't the foggiest what's even happened, let alone how to treat her."

Kusac took a deep breath and forced his lips back down. "Mr. Hamilton," he said in Terran, looking up at him. "I've done nothing to your daughter. It was you who angered and upset her, you who triggered our gestalt Link. Even I don't know what's happened to her. If you'd done as I asked and left the matter until tomorrow, this need never have happened! You're responsible, not me!"

"Mr. Hamilton . . ." began Myak, touching the Terran on the arm to get his attention.

Kusac interrupted him. "If you can't accept that our relationship is more important to us than the breaking of your petty taboos and morals, then I'm sorry for you, but you won't make us ashamed of our love! Commander," he added, lapsing back to Sholan. "Get him out of here! I refuse to have Carrie exposed to his presence. I don't care what it takes, keep him out of our way!"

Raguul made a sign to Myak. "My office, now."

Myak nodded, turning to Mr. Hamilton and taking him by the arm. "I think you'd better come with me, Mr. Hamilton. Your daughter will be well cared for, but the fewer people around her, the better."

Her father got to his feet and reluctantly turned to leave. "What did she say?" he asked. "When she spoke, what did she say?"

"She used an archaic form of Sholan, spoken only for ritual purposes now. She said, 'Refuse me, and I'll Challenge the Clan,' " said Myak as he led him away.

"How did she know that? Who told her?"

"She has Kusac's memories," said Myak as the door closed behind them.

"Our Attitude program isn't working well enough with the Terrans," Raguul said to the Mentor. "Someone should have anticipated this problem. You and the First Contact Team have slipped up somewhere." He gave Mnya a hard look. "I thought you'd dealt with this specific issue in the Terran program."

Mnya got to her feet. "So did we, Commander. Obviously it didn't work on him. We'll need to rethink our approach. Clan Leader, can I call on your skills to help us? I think we're going to need to tailor something specific for Mr. Hamilton."

Rhyasha nodded. "Of course. Janahi has regained consciousness," she said, looking round to see one of the stewards helping the telepath to his feet. "Carrie drained him of energy, but he'll have recovered by tomorrow. I was just able to prevent her draining the rest of us." She turned back to her son. "How do you feel, Kusac?"

"I don't want to talk," he said tensely. "Just get Vanna."

"She's here," the Mentor said as the physician rushed over to them.

At a glance, Vanna took in the knots of people still grouped nearby. "Get this room cleared. I want no one here but the Terran doctor and yourself," she said brusquely to the Mentor. She pushed past Rhyasha to get to Kusac and Carrie. "Leave unless you're needed by the Mentor," she said.

"I'm his mother," said Rhyasha, moving out of Vanna's way. "I'd prefer to stay."

"Then stay out of my way," she said, squatting down beside them. "What happened, Kusac?"

He looked up, holding out his hand. Reluctantly she took it, closing her eyes at the flood of information that suddenly assaulted her mind. He released her, waiting while she sorted through the new memories, trying to make sense of them.

Not wise, Kusac, murmured his mother. *She isn't a full Telepath.*

I haven't time to explain, and she has a minimal Talent.

Vanna sighed and reached out to take Carrie's pulse. Leaning forward, she checked her eyes. She gave a gasp of shock. "Gods, her eyes have changed! They're like ours!"

A stunned silence greeted her remark. The Mentor moved closer again, squatting down to get a better view.

"She is changing, Vanna. There's something happening and I can't stop it," said Kusac, fear in his voice and written in every line of his body. "I can feel it, like a tingling going through her." He held her even more closely, his ears flat and laid to the side, the fur on his tail bushed out.

"Kusac, keep your fear under control," said his mother taking him by the shoulder and shaking him firmly. "You know better than that!"

He jerked free, turning to snarl at her, a feral look on his face.

"Kusac, control yourself! I can't sense anything happening. I need to touch her. Let me feel it for myself," said his mother.

Kusac looked at her. Taking a deep breath, he shook his head several times in an attempt to push back the fear. His eyes began to lose the glowing haunted look as he forced himself to be calm. With an effort, he managed a nod of assent.

"Give me your hand, too," Rhyasha said after a moment. "Yes, she's tuned in to your body rates, Kusac—breathing when you do, her heartbeat the same as yours. Ah, now I can feel the tingling. It's as though her whole body's been charged with energy." She let go of them quickly, giving her hands a little shake. "I've never come across anything like it before. I'm sorry, Kusac, I don't know what's happening either. I think Vanna's medical equipment will be of more help."

"Is she becoming Sholan?" asked Kusac, his ears still flicking. "Surely her anger couldn't have driven her to that."

"Kusac, you'll need to let me see her," said Vanna. "I can't examine her when you're holding her so close."

With obvious reluctance, Kusac relaxed his grasp, letting Vanna straighten Carrie's limbs so she could examine her properly.

Quickly, she began checking Carrie for any other obvious changes. "I didn't know telepaths could change themselves."

"We can't," said Kusac, "but there's a legend of shape-changers in Carrie's culture."

"I think it's more that she was identifying so closely with you that briefly she appeared to be Sholan," said his mother. "Our medics can create visible auras, and you managed to create the illusion of being Valtegan, didn't you?"

"What about me? It's happened to me, too. When I touched her just now I began to change, too."

"It's probably one of those crossovers from the Link that we were talking about a few days ago," said Mnya.

Finished, Vanna sat back on her heels. "As far as I can see, apart from her eyes, externally she's still Terran. I can't do any more for her here, so I want you both—yes, both," Vanna emphasized as Kusac looked up in surprise, "in my lab on monitors. If something is happening to either of you, I want to be the first to know."

"I'll send for a medical team," said the Mentor, standing up.

"No need," said Vanna. "Earlier today I organized a twenty-six-hour emergency team with access to the Terran data. I alerted them before I left. They should be waiting in my new lab."

"Efficient," murmured Rhyasha.

Kusac shifted Carrie's limp form until he held her comfortably in his arms before getting slowly to his feet. "Which way?" he asked.

"I'll lead," said Vanna, picking up her medikit.

"Shouldn't you get a trolley or something?" asked Jack, silent until now because of his inability to follow the conversation in Sholan.

Vanna looked at him wryly. "There would be no point, Mr. Reynolds. Kusac wouldn't put her down even if we had one. I'll have trouble enough as it is getting him to lay her on the bed and get into a separate one himself."

"I see," he said, with a slight smile. "He's that protective of her, is he? What can I do to help?"

"I intend to hook them up to monitors to check their telemetry, then run a series of tests on their blood, hormone levels, and genetic typing. I want to see what, if anything, is changing. You can help me with the Terran data."

"I saw Carrie's eyes. How the hell did that happen?"

Vanna took Jack by the arm and led him in front of Kusac. "Carrie's a healer. I saw the wound on Kusac's shoulder vanish in one day. If she has the ability to do that, who's to say that she can't alter herself—and him."

"There's a big difference between closing a wound and creating new tissue," said Jack skeptically.

"Kusac's wound was comprised of several deep tears caused by Guynor's teeth ripping his flesh in a Challenge. Carrie regenerated the tissue, she didn't just seal a cut! For whatever reasons, Carrie has acquired eyes with vertical pupils and nictitating inner lids. I don't know if they are fully functional or not, but tests will reveal that. Who knows what can happen when two alien minds merge so completely? I just pray it doesn't destroy them both," she said as they entered the elevator up to the medical section.

Kusac's mother held Kaid back as Meral and Sevrin followed Kusac out. "They'll be safe for the moment with them. I need to talk to you."

"As my Liege wishes," said Kaid. "May I suggest that I contact you shortly? I have commitments within the next few hours that I can't easily put off."

"Very well," said Rhyasha. "But see you don't leave it any longer."

Kaid followed the others for a few meters, then as they passed one of the washroom facilities, he ducked inside. Checking to make sure it was empty, he dug a small communicator from his pocket and keyed in to Dzaka's comm.

"Dzaka," he said. "Seven, nine, Green, zero. Location level fourteen, six by twenty-four. Single male, identity known."

"Confirmed. Problems?"

"Delays, nothing more. I'll be in touch. Out." Pocketing the device, he slipped back out into the corridor.

Vanna ushered Kusac into the intensive care area and while Jack prowled around the lab, fascinated, they undressed Carrie, placing her on the raised formfitting couch. Seeing the torc, Vanna looked over at Kusac, the shock visible on her face.

He shook his head. "Leave it on," he said. "It's hers now. She accepted it when I offered it to her."

He hovered at the side of the bed as Vanna turned away from him and switched on the monitors, then lowered the hood over Carrie's body, leaving only her head exposed.

Checking the readings, she spoke to the two nurses on duty, giving them instructions for the tests she wanted to run.

"Now you," she said, turning back to Kusac.

Kaid came into the room on silent feet and took up a position by the door.

"What can you tell from the readings?" asked Kusac, pointing to the displays above the bed.

"Only what we know already," said Vanna. "She hasn't passed from unconsciousness into sleep yet, and her respiration and pulse are nearer Sholan rate than Terran. Once I've settled you, I'll set up a brain scan to see what electrical and chemical activity there is. All I can say is her vital signs are stable at the moment."

"I've got something I must do first, Vanna," he said. "It'll take about a quarter of an hour, then I'll do anything you ask."

Vanna flicked her ears. "Are you actually trusting her alone with me?" she asked in mock disbelief.

Kusac frowned, his nose wrinkling. "Of course I trust you. It'll only be for a short while." He looked across at Kaid, beckoning him over. "I want you to stay here till I get back. Make sure no one else comes into this area, especially her father—he just might try to do something foolish. Do what is necessary if she's threatened in any way."

Kaid's ears flicked sideways. "I know what to do, Liegen," he murmured. "I have Meral and Sevrin on guard outside, too."

Kusac nodded. "Get a telepath to imprint Jack now," he said to Vanna. "It'll make your work a lot easier. Have your medical knowledge transferred, too, then he can assess the Sholan data properly. Get someone to call the Mentor and say I authorized it."

Vanna nodded. "That makes sense. Remember, only a quarter of an hour," she warned as he left.

* * *

Sub-Commander Kolem and Mr. Hamilton had just left the Commander's office. Raguul sat back in his chair and looked up at the ceiling.

"Not the medicine this time, Myak. Get me some of that Chemerian spirit—you know the stuff I mean," he said tiredly.

"Certainly, sir." Myak went to the cupboard reserved for drinks.

"That was one job I didn't want to do, Myak. I'm not even a father! What the hell do I know about daughters?"

"Your explanation sounded excellent, sir," said Myak, pouring the Commander a generous measure.

Raguul grunted. "Well, it's Mnya's problem now, and I wish her well of it! Gods, what a shambles! Who'd have thought he'd row with her in public like that?"

"It fits in with their culture, Commander." Myak handed him the glass. "Unlike us they don't attempt to control strong personal emotions in public. They don't appear to have a sense of pride in how they behave. For them it's more important to stand up belligerently for what they believe in, and try to get what they want that way."

Raguul downed the contents of the glass and handed it back to Myak. "You've been working on the orientation program," he said.

"As an unofficial member of the Alien Relations team, my insight has been asked for. They were particularly interested in my comments as I see a great deal of the other species in my service with you."

He took the glass and went back to the cupboard to refill it. "The Mentor should be able to deal with the rest of Mr. Hamilton's questions tonight. If we don't start the talks for another day or two, it gives the guild and First Contact time to get their revised program together."

"Schedule a briefing with the section heads for the sixth hour tomorrow. We'll discuss it then. All we need is for her father to accept the situation, he doesn't need to like it, damnit! I expect Konis Aldatan will have a great deal to say about it, too."

"The Clan Leader seems to be giving them her blessing, sir," said Myak putting the full glass and the bottle down in front of the Commander.

Raguul eyed the bottle, then Myak, before picking up the glass. "That was a turn up for the books. Who'd have thought she'd back them in public, and so soon?"

"She knows her son, Commander," said Myak. "He'll have the Terran as his mate whether his family wishes it or not, and if she doesn't go with him on this, she'll lose him. She won't risk that."

"Despite the problems his Link to the human girl has

caused us, I liked what little I saw of him tonight. I hope the politics of those groundlings on Keiss and Shola don't spoil what they have. I have a feeling their only chance for the life they want may well be with us."

He picked up the bottle in his free hand and got to his feet. "I'll see you in the morning, Myak. We'll see what we can salvage out of tonight's shambles at the briefing tomorrow. Your idea to delay the talks has a lot of merit. Perhaps as well as a new orientation program, a tour of the *Khalossa* would do some good. Let her father and the others see how we live up here. Trying to understand a culture in isolation from its people isn't easy."

* * *

As Dzaka changed from his robes into a tunic of neutral color, he ran several scenarios through his mind. Deciding on one, he sat down at his desk and keyed in to Kaedoe's comm. It was a matter of a few moments to patch into the unit and check whether Kaedoe was in and if he was using the comm. Good, he was there, and even better, the comm wasn't in use. He set the message down, making it suitably cryptic, then hesitated. Deciding a name wasn't needed, he pressed the transmit key. Now all he had to do was wait for him in the empty smoke bar.

* * *

Followed by Meral, Kusac headed to the communications office on the floor below.

"Liegen Aldatan," said the Sholan on duty, leaping to his feet and saluting. "What can we do for you?"

"Get me a personal line to the Clan Lord Aldatan on Shola," Kusac said.

"I'll have to go through the Commander's office," said the junior officer, punching a series of numerals into his keyboard. "A communications block has been imposed on all ships."

"Just make it quick." Kusac paced up and down the office impatiently. "I'm sure the Commander will authorize the call."

"He has. I'm being connected now, Liegen Aldatan. If you would take the call in that office there," he pointed to a small clear-paneled room across the corridor.

Kusac nodded and went over to the room. He sat at the

desk, switched the comm on and waited. No point this time in trying to conceal anything from his father.

"Kusac, have you any idea what time it is?" asked his father, rubbing his eyes and trying not to yawn. "I trust this isn't just a personal call."

"No, Father, it isn't," he said. "There's something I should have told you this morning."

"What was that?" Konis asked, trying and failing to smother an enormous yawn.

"It concerns one of the Terrans from Keiss."

"Oh?" said his father, all trace of tiredness vanishing. "What about this Terran?"

"My Leska is a female Terran, not a Sholan," he said, his voice brittle.

There was a lengthy silence. Kusac cursed inwardly that he was unable to pick up even the faintest nuance of what his father was thinking.

"A Terran, you say."

"Yes. I've just had to deal with her father an hour ago. They have a less casual attitude to pairing than us, and I didn't enjoy our talk. I want you to realize that I don't intend to go through similar arguments with you."

"I see," said his father slowly.

"Either you accept her, or we won't return to Shola," said Kusac.

"Which particular Terran is your Leska?" his father asked, keeping his voice carefully neutral.

"The current Ambassador's daughter, the one who saved my life on Keiss."

"Ah, I can see your problem," sighed the Clan Lord.

"Then you'll understand my position. I won't have her insulted and hurt any more," Kusac said, the residue of his anger with Peter Hamilton sounding in his voice.

His father flicked his ears sideways, angrier still. "You've met with prejudice from the Terrans? I hope our people didn't have the same attitude."

"No. Those we've met have only been concerned for us."

"May the Gods be thanked for that! I wondered why my reports seemed to be lacking certain areas of information. Now I know. It seems that many people have been making it their business to see that you and your Leska are protected. From what, I wonder. My anger? You seem to assume so."

"Father, I can't stay much longer. Stop playing your word games with me. Tell me straight, will you accept her or not?" demanded Kusac, irritated.

"She's your Leska. Whether she is Terran or Sholan, the bond is irrefutable. She'll be welcome here. I presume your mother has met her?"

"Yes."

"Then I'll speak to her tomorrow. I can't say it's what I'd wished for you, Kusac, but the Gods bless us as they choose. I take it that your relationship with this Terran girl has also caused problems with the treaty talks."

"I've no idea, Father. I'm not involved in them."

Konis nodded. "Very well. Your mother can brief me tomorrow. As I said before, I shall look forward to meeting your Leska—what is her name?"

"Carrie Hamilton."

"I'll look forward to meeting your Carrie when the time comes. I presume that's why you have business at the guild."

Kusac nodded.

"See to it that I'm now sent full reports on the Keissian situation, and all matters concerning you and Carrie. Unless you clear it, I assume no one will tell me," he said dryly.

"I'll see it's done. Good night, Father, and thank you," he said, beginning to breathe more easily.

"Good night, Kusac."

* * *

Rhyasha sat in her room at her mirror while Miosh, her friend and attendant, unbraided the beads from her hair.

"I should call Vanna now," she said. "I know they're in good hands with her, but I'm worried, Miosh."

"It will take an hour or two to run the tests," said Miosh soothingly. "By then there should be some news."

"When she changed, Miosh, her eyes remained Sholan! What are these Terrans that they can alter their appearance like that? What kind of Talents have they?"

"There's bound to be a rational explanation for it, Rhyasha, you know that," she said soothingly, beginning to draw the brush through her hair. "When they go to the guild, they'll chart her Talents. It won't seem so strange once we understand them."

Rhyasha sighed. Miosh's rhythmic brushing was working

its usual magic. "I know you're right. I can't help but worry; he's my son."

"Yes, and he has to find his own way in the world. He's a fully grown male now."

"Did I tell you she spoke the words used by Khadulah? I pray this isn't a bad omen for them."

"Yes, you told me, but it was the Terran who said them to her father, not your son to you. It can't possibly be an omen for you or Kusac. You're fretting over nothing, Rhyasha. From what you said of her father's behavior, she's the one who will have to turn her back on her Clan if she wants your son."

"I hadn't thought of it like that," she said pensively. "I'm sure you're right. If it were an omen, the Gods would surely send it through one of us." She turned slightly to look up at her friend. "Now tell me about this Terran female, Miosh," she said changing the subject. "How did she behave while you helped her this evening?"

"She's not used to attendants, that was very clear, but she listened to what I had to suggest—and we compromised." The female smiled at her in the mirror.

"She has a mind of her own, then?"

"Oh, assuredly. She would have none of my suggestions to braid her hair, she preferred to let it hang loose. Nor would she use any of our cosmetics, saying she'd prefer to try them herself another day. She was right," said Miosh candidly as she put the brush aside. "I realized that to make her look like us would be a crime. She is so much more striking as she is."

"She's certainly striking beside my son," said Rhyasha. "They couldn't be more physically different!"

"The Terrans are pleasing to look at, Rhyasha," said Miosh, dividing her hair into three handfuls and beginning to braid it into a thick plait.

"They are, but it will take a little time to get used to her," admitted Rhyasha. "How were they with each other?"

"As any new couple would be, happy to be together. When all is said and done, Rhyasha, no matter their species, they're only young people in love."

"You're right, Miosh. As a telepath, I see the inner person first, not the outer form. I'd do well to remember this now. I hope Konis does," she sighed.

"There, I've finished. Will you take your shower now?"

"No, I think I'd prefer to soak in a bath," Rhyasha said getting up. "The hot water will finish the relaxation you've begun. Then I'll call Vanna."

* * *

The boarding across the bar's entrance was loose, Kaedoe discovered when he touched it. Not only that, but behind it, the door gave. It was open.

"In here!" a voice hissed.

Startled, he looked carefully around; then, pushing the board to one side, he slipped through into the darkened room. For a moment he stood there, his back to the wall, sniffing the air. The walls were so ingrained with the smoke of many years that he could smell little but that. He turned his head slightly, feeling the sudden movement of air passing over the tiny hairs on either side of his nose and brows. A sudden blow to his throat sent excruciating pain exploding through him. His head collided with the wall behind as, gasping for air, he clutched at his neck, doubling up in agony.

Dzaka grasped him by the scruff of the neck with his left hand, pulling him forward onto the blade. It slipped easily between his ribs and Kaedoe was dead before he reached the ground.

Leaving the knife where it was—it was standard issue to all troopers—Dzaka took two drug-laced cones out of his pocket and dropped them beside the body. Turning, he made his way across the room to the bar, going behind it to the sink used for washing the glasses. He held his hands under the stream of water, making sure that any overt signs of blood were removed before drying them on a bar towel. Then it was back out the way he'd come, through the ventilation system.

* * *

Kusac made his way back to the medical area. Kaid was where he'd left him. "It's getting late, Kaid," he said. "Can you organize security so you and the other two get some sleep?"

"I'll see it's done, Liegen."

Kusac nodded and rejoined Vanna.

"You were correct about something happening," said

Vanna, watching the results of the brain scan she was running on Carrie.

"What can you see?" asked Kusac.

"I don't know what I'm looking at, Kusac, let alone looking for. This isn't standard medical information I'm getting, it's something totally new. Increased electrical activity, but nothing that seems to be causing any harm—no fits or convulsions, I mean. You tell me what we're seeing," she said, waving her hand toward the monitor's readings.

"I can't understand those things, I can't even sense what's happening," Kusac said helplessly. "I'm afraid for her, for myself."

He leaned over the cover of the IC unit, touching Carrie's face, his hand dark against the pallor of her skin. "She looks so fragile, doesn't she?" he said softly, moving his hand to stroke her forehead as he glanced up at Vanna.

She looked away quickly. It wasn't good for her to see his emotions so easily in his eyes. "It's time for your tests now," she said, moving over to the other unit a few meters away.

Kusac sighed, turning away from his Leska. "I shouldn't be doing this to you, Vanna," he said, stopping briefly beside her and putting his hand on her shoulder. "I know it isn't easy for you to be so closely involved with us, but I have no option: you're the only person I would trust with our lives."

"Kusac, stop being foolish and get into the other unit," she said, trying to divert his attention away from her.

He went over to the unit, stripping off his clothes and handing them to Vanna. As he settled himself down into the soft foam, he realized Jack was missing.

"Where's Jack?" he asked as Vanna pulled the cover over him.

"He's off getting his first telepathic imprint," she replied, checking the panels before swinging over the other brain scan unit.

"That as well?" he asked, nodding toward the device.

"I want to watch both of you for a comparison," she said, adjusting the position of his head. "Now keep still, or I'll have to sedate you," she threatened as he continued to turn his head.

"What tests are you doing?"

"Don't worry, you won't even be aware of them," she said, lowering the top half of the scanner to about a foot above his head. "I've programmed the body unit to take blood and skin cell samples so I can check your endocrine systems. I'm looking for any alterations in your hormone levels and DNA structure. Since both of you were affected by what appeared to be Carrie's shape-changing debut, I want to make sure that there aren't any other permanent changes in either of you, beyond the shape of her pupils."

"Have you any idea yet why her eyes changed?"

"None, but I have ascertained that they are fully functioning eyes. She can see in the same range as us now. The color of her irises has altered slightly. Where they were brown before, now there is a narrow amber ring around the pupil," said Vanna, pressing a series of buttons on her side of the unit. She watched an ultrasound scan appear on the recessed screen. "You'll be pleased to know that internally everything is as it should be."

"And Carrie?"

"Carrie, too. I told you, the only obvious physical difference is that she now has eyes like us. I have to leave you now, I've got work to do. Try and rest," she said.

* * *

Maikoe liked to have the scouter's engines up and running before take off, especially when her shift started during the Keissian night. She ran through the checks as the rest of the crew boarded. Everything came up green, not that she expected anything else, but Kaedoe's paranoia was catching.

They were using four-person crews now. Shifts were shorter, only six hours, so there was no need for on- and off-duty personnel. They could take their breaks at their controls, they'd done it before.

She turned as the last person boarded. Her eyes widened in surprise. "Chyad! What the hell are you doing on my shift!" she hissed as he made his way over to her.

"I swapped shifts. Kaedoe's dead," he said quietly. "I think our days are numbered."

"Gods! What happened to him?"

"He was found dead inside the smoke bar."

"But that was closed down after Jakule's death!"

"I know. Security were investigating a reported break-in at the place and found his body."

"How was he killed?"

"Knifed. They reckon he was collecting drugs and had an argument with the dealer."

"I didn't know he used illegal drugs," she said, reluctant to believe him.

"Come off it, Maikoe! Don't be so naive. You know damned well Kaedoe never touched the stuff! There's only you and me left now."

"What the hell are we going to do?"

"Can you make it look like we've got engine trouble or something and ditch this craft on the planet? I think our only chance of survival is to lose ourselves on this mud ball."

"I can do it, but the others will tell them we've gone."

"Not if they've been killed in the crash," said Chyad grimly. "If we destroy the scouter, they'll never know we didn't go up with it, too."

"We can't kill them, Chyad!" she hissed, appalled at the idea.

"Don't get squeamish on me, Maikoe," said Chyad noticing her ears were folding over in distress. "You were prepared to kill the telepath and his Leska, what's different about killing these two?"

"Scouter four one, clear for take off," said the communicator.

"Get back with the others," said Maikoe. "We've got to leave."

Chyad gripped her shoulder, his claws puncturing through her uniform into her flesh. "Just remember to fake a crash. I've no intention of dying if I can avoid it," he growled in her ear before releasing her and heading for his post.

They were scheduled to do low sweeps of Keiss over the mountainous terrain around the village of Hillfort. They were on the watch for stray Valtegans. Sholan High Command was desperate to capture as many alive as possible. Those stranded on the planet had either mounted suicide attacks or died within hours of capture. None had survived long enough to be fully interrogated.

Their shift was nearly at an end when suddenly the craft began to weave about alarmingly.

"What's wrong?" demanded the navigator as he fumbled for his safety harness.

"One engine's gone off-line," said Maikoe as she struggled to right the craft. "I'm losing altitude!"

The scouter dipped toward the ground, beginning to roll as it lost stability. Maikoe pulled at the controls as the trees loomed in front of them.

"Gods! We're going to crash," muttered a voice from behind.

"Hang on," yelled Maikoe. "We're going down!"

The scouter skimmed across the treetops, the interior of the craft echoing to the sound of the hull being scraped and banged by branches. Suddenly the craft somersaulted, diving down into the trees, heading straight for the ground. There was no time to react as the craft ripped its way through the branches, ploughing nose first toward the forest floor.

Tallinu came round first, looking groggily about the craft for survivors. Up front he could see Maikoe was dead. A massive branch had penetrated the view screen, forcing its way past the pilot into the main cabin area. He was lucky. It had missed killing him by only a few feet.

To the rear, the navigator's seat was empty. He must have been flung out of it by the force of their impact. To the other side of navigation, Chyad lay in his seat, blood running down the side of his head. As he looked, the male moaned softly. Only injured, then. He reached for his gun and found it missing. He cursed softly, realizing it must have been jarred loose in the crash. He had to get free before Chyad came round.

The scouter was lying canted on one side with the rear end held clear of the ground. The floor under him sloped down toward where the tangle of the tree had breached the front. He looked down for the release on his harness and stopped. A sliver of wood pinned his thigh to the seat. Blood had matted the surrounding fur: obviously he'd been unconscious for some time.

He closed his eyes for a moment, mentally beginning the litany that banished pain. Taking hold of the end of the sliver, he gritted his teeth and pulled. Despite himself, an involuntary groan escaped his lips. Fresh blood began to ooze out, glistening wetly on his fur. He looked around for something to act as a bandage, then saw that Chyad was beginning to stir. He was running out of time.

Pressing open the seal on the front of his uniform, he drew out his knife and stabbed it into the fabric of the seat. Ripping a strip free, he quickly bound his thigh above the injury. It would slow the blood for now. With any luck there was already a craft on the way to check for survivors. He glanced at Chyad again, gauging the distance. Reluctantly he returned the knife to its sheath. At this angle he had no chance of hitting him.

Wrapping one arm through the armrest, he reached for the fastening on his harness and pressed. It flew open, releasing him with a jerk that almost tore his arm from its socket. He swung round against the side of the chair, legs dangling in midair.

The floor of the scouter was smooth, no hand or footholds there. If he let go, there was every chance he would impale himself on the tree beneath him. He heard a sound from above. Chyad. Praying to Vartra, he let go, his hands and feet scrabbling desperately for a hold as he fell. He crashed through the foliage, small branches whipping him in the face as he fell. His hands grabbed for them, but they gave under his weight. Then his fingers closed on a thicker branch and he came to an abrupt stop, fresh agony lancing through his already bruised shoulder joint. He clung there breathing hard, trying to lift his other arm up to secure his hold. At last his claws caught and he managed to haul himself up just enough to wrap his arms around it.

His feet had touched something firm beneath him. Reaching down with his toes he felt to see what it was. There was a broad branch just below. He tried to peer down, but the loss of blood and the pain were beginning to take their toll, and his head began to swim.

From above he could hear Chyad moving about. Looking up, he realized the other male could release himself and land on the back of one of the seats in front. After that he faced the same problems in getting down to the tree. As he watched, Chyad left his seat abruptly, managing to land where he'd predicted.

"What a pity," said Chyad cynically, looking down at him. "All that effort for nothing." He drew an energy pistol from inside his jacket and aimed. "I just can't let there be any other survivors."

Tallinu let go, landing in a crouch on the branch below. His thigh buckled under his weight, almost pitching him forward off the branch. The energy bolt hissed past him, sending the smell of burning greenery wafting up to his nose. Clutching the branch with his hands, he swung himself down, grunting in pain as he took his weight yet again on his arms.

The nose of the craft was only a few meters below him

now and he let go, landing in a heap against the pilot's console. The smell of blood was strong, its taste metallic in his mouth. The hatch was beside him and with a swift prayer, he thumped the release mechanism, dodging aside as another bolt of energy hissed downward.

"There's no use hiding, I can see you." Chyad's voice drifted down from above.

The door remained closed. Reaching for the manual lever, he pulled hard. Slowly the hatch began to slide open. From above came the sound of Chyad crashing down through the tree.

Fumbling in his jacket, he pulled out a small device from the inside pocket. Pressing the button set in the top, he lobbed it toward the bodies of Maikoe and the navigator, then dived through the gap.

He hit the ground hard but managed to roll clear of the hatchway, fetching up against the trunk of a tree. Pushing himself to his feet, he grabbed the trunk for support and began to lurch away from the scouter. Once again his leg buckled under him, throwing him to the ground. Cursing, he rose in a three-legged stance, keeping his injured leg free of the ground. His shoulders felt as if knives were piercing them, but he lurched on. He had to get out of range or he was dead, too.

Every painful step seemed to take an eternity as the seconds raced by. Then a blast of heated air lifted him high, hurling him through the trees till, with a sickening thump, he came to a halt. Daylight dimmed around him and his last coherent thought was that this hadn't been one of his better jobs.

* * *

Kusac was emotionally exhausted by the events of the last few hours, and sleep quickly claimed him despite his fears.

Mid-morning ship time he was jerked violently awake seconds before every alarm on both their units went into alert.

"Vanna, get me out of this contraption," he yelled, straining against the inside of the unit although he knew it was useless. He could sense Carrie again. She had come out of unconsciousness. Her mind was caught in some nightmare, broadcasting waves of fear and terror.

The warning tones dinned in his ears, adding to his urgency. "Turn that damned racket off!" he yelled.

Jack ran over to him, fumbling with the latches while Vanna bent over Carrie, checking her for physical signs of distress. One of the nurses ran to switch off the alarms and silence returned.

"Don't touch her, Vanna," Kusac said frantically, rolling off the bed as Jack finally got his cover free.

"Help me get the lid off!" he said, his hands flying over the catches on his side. As he finished, Vanna pushed the lid back out of the way.

"I need a chair," he said, gently slipping his arms under Carrie and lifting her.

Jack brought one over, placing it behind him.

Kusac sat down, adjusting his hold on her till she was cradled in his arms like a small child.

Vanna held out a blanket. He frowned, looking at it.

"Without fur, she'll feel the cold more than us," she reminded him.

He took the blanket, draping it across her. Closing his eyes, he rested his head on hers. There was no need for even a slight adjustment now; their rhythms were perfectly synchromeshed, and he had no difficulty in reaching her dream world.

She was still reliving the scene with her father at the reception. Kusac found the looped thoughts, parted them, and gradually brought her anger and panic under control until she was breathing gently again.

He rested a moment before opening his eyes. It felt good to hold her again after seeing her locked in the IC unit beyond his help. He rubbed his cheek against the top of her head, breathing in her scent as he felt the familiar pull of their Link. In his arms she began to rouse.

"How is she?" asked Vanna.

"She's fine. Only a nightmare, nothing more," he murmured, letting the hypersensitivity wash through him. This time it was different. Now there was an anticipation that had been lacking before. He felt relaxed yet alert to the feel of her body against his. She moved, unconsciously curling up closer to him.

"Kusac," said Vanna, bringing his attention back to her. "I've got a room ready next door for you. I think you'd better take her there. When you feel up to it, you can return to your suite."

Kusac nodded slowly, disinclined to move.

Vanna leaned forward to touch him, then flinched as the sensations coursing through him hit her. It jolted Kusac out of his dreamy state, making him fully aware of what was happening.

"I'm sorry," he said, getting carefully to his feet as Carrie began to move again in his arms. "With everything that's happened I forgot what day it was. I didn't expect our Link to affect me like this."

"Forget it," said Vanna, tucking her hands under her armpits. "Just take her into the other room now before she wakes. I'll check up on you in a few hours. There's a food dispenser and a communicator by the bed if you need anything."

Vanna watched them leave, trying to forget the sudden surge of heightened sexuality she had felt from Kusac, and the answering one from Carrie.

"What's up?" asked Jack as she went back to the desk where they were correlating the data they'd collected from the tests. "Where's he taking her?"

"To a private room next door," she said. "It's their Link day, they need the next twenty-six hours to themselves."

"Ah, yes. Kusac mentioned it to me yesterday," said Jack. "Their Link is really that demanding?"

"You've read the files," she said curtly, sitting down beside him. "Yes, it's that demanding."

"Excuse me, Physician Kyjishi," said Draz, standing at the door. "Clan Leader Aldatan wishes to see you."

"Tell her she can come in, Draz."

"What are you going to tell her?" asked Jack.

"The truth about their endocrine levels."

"And your suspicions over the genetic changes?"

"Nothing till I have proof," she said, gathering her papers together and putting them in her drawer out of sight. "It might never happen." She stood up as Kusac's mother entered.

"I wanted to see you on your own, Vanna," she said, coming over to her desk. "I'm aware my son and his Leska have other matters to attend to," she said with a faint smile, "so I know they won't be aware of our discussion." She nodded to the Terran doctor.

Jack had gotten up as she arrived and now placed a chair at the other side of the desk for her.

"Thank you," she said, sitting down. "Do you know yet why Carrie changed shape?"

"I'm afraid I have no idea, Clan Leader," said Vanna, resuming her seat. "I take it you've met Jack Reynolds, physician to Carrie's family on Keiss?"

"Under less than ideal circumstances," Rhyasha said. "Do either of you know why her eyes have altered?"

"I'm afraid we don't know that either."

"Then what have you found out?" asked Rhyasha, a touch of exasperation in her voice.

"Clan Leader, you have to understand that we are attempting to understand a completely unknown phenomenon here," said Vanna. "There has never been another telepathic species until now and the Terrans don't believe telepathy exists. Because of this, unlike us they have no body of knowledge about the mechanics of their people's Talents. I'm working blind here. The only people who have a chance of really understanding what's happening to them are your son and Carrie."

"Your pardon, Vanna, but I know all this," said Rhyasha. "You've been running tests, you told me so when I spoke to you an hour or two after this happened. What were the results?"

"They're both changing," Vanna said quietly.

"How?"

"Their endocrine systems are fluctuating."

"Explain it to me, please."

"The Sholan and Terran endocrine systems work on the same principle, but at different levels and proportions. Those levels in both of them are changing in relationship to each other. Carrie's system seems to be tending toward the Sholan balance, and Kusac's seems to be adjusting toward the Terran one," said Jack.

"Are you saying my son is becoming more Terran, and . . ." began Rhyasha, her ears flicking slightly despite her rigid self-control.

"No," interrupted Vanna. "Far from it. We aren't sure yet, but we think there is a trend toward a balance of levels between them. In other words, their systems will match."

"What effect will that have on them?"

"The endocrine system controls a lot of the body's functions," said Vanna. "It affects appetite, thirst, the body's ability to withstand heat and cold, and the ability to sleep amongst other things. They'll have a variety of symptoms including possible dizzy spells, headaches, feeling washed out and tired at the wrong times of day, and may be generally irritable, unable to cope with stress. Basically, adrenaline levels peak at different times for different people. It means their adrenaline and hormone levels will be in phase with each other. The worry is the fact that their systems are changing at all."

"Is this due to their mental Link?" asked Rhyasha.

"Almost definitely. We've no idea what can happen when two different minds blend so completely as theirs have. Like them, all we can do is wait and see while we record what's happening."

"Do you plan to do nothing at all?" asked Rhyasha.

"I don't want to treat them with drugs because I have a feeling this is a process that must be allowed to run its course. We daren't interfere," said Vanna.

"We'll monitor them both to see when these endocrine changes level out, and to make sure that nothing else is happening. Apart from that, I'm afraid there is little we can do," said Jack.

Rhyasha sat and digested this. "What you're saying is that my son and his Leska will feel alert or tired at the same time of day."

"Essentially, yes," said Vanna. "Nothing more dramatic than that."

Rhyasha nodded. "Then there is nothing to worry about."

"Nothing that we can see," agreed Vanna.

"Apart from the change in Carrie's eyes."

"Clan Leader, Carrie can heal. Not every time, but sometimes. I think like you that she identified so much with Kusac that for an instant she appeared Sholan. She can make tissue regenerate, I've seen her do it. Perhaps she used this Talent to change her eyes. Who knows? Probably not even Carrie. It's one of those things about which we may never find an answer."

"Thank you, Vanna, you've set my mind at rest. Now I must go. I intend to remain on board the *Khalossa* for some days to continue the treaty negotiations here rather than planetside on Keiss. If there is any more news, please make sure I'm informed." Rhyasha stood up and took her leave of them.

* * *

Vanna was in the general medical area when the survivor of the crashed scouter was brought in. She glanced at him in passing, then stopped.

"Hey!" she called out to the orderlies who were taking him to one of the emergency treatment rooms. "Wait a minute!"

They stopped, the floater bobbing gently between them. "Yes, Physician?"

She ran over to them and looked closely at the male lying unconscious under the bloodstained cover.

"I'll see to him," she said abruptly. "Take him up to my lab."

"But, Physician . . ."

"I gave you an order," she said.

"Very well, Physician," the orderly said, turning round to tow the floater toward Vanna's lab.

Tallinu came round as Vanna finished spraying his thigh with sealant.

"Are you in pain?" she asked, binding a dressing over the wound.

"My shoulders," he said, his voice barely audible. "I fell through the trees. And my leg."

Vanna loaded her hypo and gave him a shot in the arm, then sat down beside him.

"I want to know exactly what you were doing in that crashed scouter, Kaid," she said.

He lay there silently.

"Don't try to play dead with me. I know you're conscious, I can tell by your readings on the telemetry comm. Give me one good reason why I shouldn't call Security, Kaid. Or is it Tallinu?" she asked, dangling his ID tag in front of him.

"Don't call Security," he said, eyes flicking open. Slowly his head turned to face her. "Was I the only survivor?"

"Yes. The other three died in the explosion."

The tension went out of his face. "Gods, I feel like shit," he groaned. "What's the extent of my injuries?"

"I'm still waiting for my answer, Kaid, or whoever you are," she said, her voice taking on a hard edge.

"It's Kaid Tallinu," he said tiredly. "You're Garras' companion, aren't you?"

Vanna's ears flicked angrily. "Yes, if you need to put it like that."

"He'll tell you. I'm working for your friend Kusac now."

"What?" The shock was evident in her voice.

"Ask Garras," he repeated. "Your turn. Tell me what's broken."

"You know about your thigh injury," she said. "You've cracked a couple of ribs and probably have torn ligaments in your right shoulder as well as a couple of badly broken claws."

"I have to be on my feet again today."

"Forget it!" she said. "My patients stay put till they're capable of getting up. Ultrasound will deal with your shoulder and help your ribs, but your leg isn't going to support you for a couple of days."

He swore graphically for a full minute.

"Have you quite finished?" Vanna asked in amusement.

"Yes!" he snapped. "I've a job to do. I've got to be up today." He struggled to rise, but Vanna pushed him gently back down.

"No, you don't. In another minute the sedative I gave you will kick in. You aren't going anywhere for at least fifty-two hours."

He looked at her, eyes narrowing, then gave a slight grin. "You win. If I stay put, will you get me on my feet as soon as possible?"

"What's so urgent that you need to be up and about? What's this job you're supposed to be doing for Kusac?"

Kaid's eyes began to glaze slightly, the inner lids starting to close. "Ask Garras," he said, his words beginning to slur. "Don't tell your friend Kusac. He isn't to know. See Garras first." His voice trailed off as the drug took effect.

Chapter 8

Vanna had tracked Garras down to his quarters. She pressed the chime and waited impatiently for him to respond. The door slid back.

"Vanna!" said Garras, surprised to see her. He stood aside for her to enter. "I thought you were on duty."

"I've been permanently attached to Kusac's staff," she said, going over to one of the easy chairs. "I'm on call, not on shifts. Did you know that a scouter crashed on Keiss earlier today?" she asked abruptly.

"Yes, I heard it mentioned when I came off duty," he said, returning to his seat. "It went down in the forest around Valleytown—exploded just after crashing. Three lives were lost. What brought it to your attention?"

"I was in the sick bay reception when the only survivor was brought in," she said, watching his face closely.

"I hope he wasn't too badly hurt."

"He wasn't, but that's not what I'm talking about, Garras, and you know it."

"Excuse me?" he said, looking baffled.

"You didn't know your friend Kaid was on board?"

"My friend Kaid?" said Garras.

"He claims to be your friend."

"Does he?"

"Garras, don't mess me around," she said, exasperated. "His name is Kaid Tallinu. He told me he was working for Kusac and that you would explain it."

"Where is he?" asked Garras brusquely, leaning toward her, the polite interest gone now.

"I had him taken to my lab as soon as I recognized him."

"Thank Vartra for your presence of mind! How badly injured is he?"

"Garras, what's going. . . ?"

"Vanna, I haven't time to explain to you now. I need to

know how badly he's injured," said Garras, cutting her short.

"A couple of cracked ribs, a puncture wound in his thigh caused by a piece of wood, and torn ligaments in one shoulder."

Garras got to his feet. "I need to see him now," he said, turning toward the door. "Come on."

"It won't do you any good," said Vanna, getting up. "I sedated him. He'll be out for about eight hours."

"Why the hell did you do that?"

"Because it isn't normal for an adjutant to be on active duty in a scouter! I know nothing about him. He could be trying to kill Carrie or Kusac for all I know."

"Quite the opposite," said Garras, stopping at the door. "In fact, this incident could have blown his cover. Can you bring him round so I can talk to him? I need to find out what has to be done to cover his tracks."

"His system's taken a hell of a beating with the injuries he's sustained, Garras. The last thing he needs is a stimulant. And I certainly won't give him one without knowing what's going on!"

"Kaid's a bodyguard. There's likely to be a search for the missing crewman that you treated, and because he was the only survivor, they'll want to question him about the accident. It won't take Security long to find out he's Kusac's adjutant and that you treated him personally. We could all very shortly find ourselves under a cloud of suspicion. All this can be avoided if you let me speak to him."

She hesitated.

He reached out and took her by the shoulder. "Vanna, trust me on this. I must talk to him now."

"All right," she conceded. "But you realize I'm doing it against my better judgment. And I want to know what the hell he was doing on the scouter!"

Vanna put her hypo gun away while Garras settled himself on a chair beside Kaid.

"Kaid, it's me, Garras," he said quietly as his friend began to stir.

Kaid's eyes flickered open, the inner lids still partially visible. "She's good, that little female of yours," he said slowly, with a wry grin. "Slipped a sedative on me, then threatened me with Security. How long have I been out?"

"An hour and a half."

"Knew you'd bring me round. Contact Draz. Tell him code Three, Seven, Green."

Garras raised an eyeridge. "Flying high."

"Very. That'll cover it. Dzaka's on board, at the temple. Tell him, too. Next, I need to get up," he said, beginning to move fretfully. "I've got to meet the Clan Leader today. It can't wait. Speak to your female. She's got to patch me up somehow."

"She can speak for herself," said Vanna coldly.

"Vanna," said Garras, turning to her. "Do it. There's more at stake than you want to know."

"I'll do it on your risk, Kaid, not mine, and only for two hours. Then I want you back here."

"Deal. Garras, I'll need robes. She mustn't see my injuries. There're some in my quarters in the Ambassadorial Suite. Where're Kusac and his mate?"

"Here," said Vanna.

"Good, then the Clan Leader can come to me, which should please you, Vanna," Kaid said with a half smile. "You can keep an eye on me then."

"Damned right I will," she growled. "For two reasons. I know where you're from."

"Vanna, we'll talk later," said Garras, putting a hand on her arm and squeezing it gently. "Leave it till then."

Reluctantly she nodded.

Kaid met Rhyasha in one of the small side rooms adjacent to Vanna's lab. Shutting the door behind her, she turned to him. "What's been going on?" she asked without preamble. "Your reports have been lacking much vital information. Why? You made no mention of the fact that the Terran girl was also my son's Leska, nor more recently of the attempt on her life."

"It wasn't relevant, Liege," said Kaid. "I told you his association with her had engendered feelings of xenophobia among certain elements of the crew, and this was the truth. As for the shooting, she wasn't the intended target. It happened two days ago and there hasn't been time to report to you. You saw for yourself the female is fine, it was only a flesh wound. I made sure there wasn't a second shot."

"I don't expect economy with the truth from you, Kaid," she said. "It's not what you've been retained to do."

"You know how I work, Liege. I made it perfectly clear from the outset that I would use my own judgment. Those were the terms of the contract. You agreed to it and have no call to question it now."

Only the swiveling of her ears betrayed her frustration. "My husband is being starved of information, too. I hoped this wouldn't be the case for me when I engaged you to see my son and his Leska were brought safely home. Her father had the right of it. There is a conspiracy of silence from everyone involved with them. Why, Kaid?"

"No one wanted to be the first to tell you that your son has an alien Leska, Liege. Especially when the fate of the treaty depends on their parents."

"That explains the Commander and the guild," she snapped, "but not you!"

"I sent you your son's file," he said. "It confirmed your suspicions. You knew then that she was Terran."

Her temper evaporated. "Thank Vartra you did. My son owes his life to you finding that file and sending it to his physician. Without her intervention both of them would be dead. Gods, Kaid. This is a mess!" She moved over to the seat opposite him. "Do you know what he plans to do?"

"Yes, Liege. I learned yesterday when you did," he said ironically.

"He'll give up everything to marry her. Position, family, his hope of children, the lot, all for this Terran female. I don't understand it, Kaid. What is there about her that he feels this strongly? You've seen them together, do you know?"

"No, Liege, but I can hazard a guess. She's unlike anyone else he's ever met. He feels she needs to be protected where our females are independent. Then there're their experiences on Keiss, and lastly the Link. All this has bonded them to each other in a way nothing else could."

She sighed. "Well, it's done now, and I'll do what I can to help them. This anti-Terran movement, what are you doing about it? What was the shooting about?"

"The Commander preempted my plans because of the shooting and had them moved up to the Ambassadorial level. The male involved was one of the dissidents and he was intending to murder their leader because of a personal disagreement. At the last moment Kusac and Carrie came between him and his target and he decided to shoot her instead."

"The situation is far more complex than I had realized," said Rhyasha. "What have you done about the other dissidents?"

"They have all been terminated."

"What? I didn't authorize you to kill people!" Her tone was one of outrage and horror.

"My experience and judgment are why you hired me, Liege. Restructuring their social outlook wouldn't guarantee the safety of your son and his Leska. Termination makes it definite," he said, a note of tiredness creeping into his voice.

"Once Kusac and Carrie are home, then your contract has been fulfilled," said Rhyasha coldly. "I'll have no more killings."

"Would you have left the dissidents to start again?" he asked, raising an eye ridge.

"Of course not! But I didn't wish them killed."

"In my judgment, the risk to your son and his Leska warranted that course of action, and the Brotherhood will back me. I'm afraid that my contract won't be done when we return to Shola."

"What do you mean?"

"When I took your contract it was concurrent with another to guard the same people. That won't expire when we return to Shola."

"You can't accept two contracts at the same time!" exclaimed Rhyasha. "It's against your guild principles. Without that certainty of knowing you will honor a contract, it makes a mockery of what you do!"

"The two are concurrent, Liege, not disparate. My second contract doesn't expire with their return to Shola."

"Who's it with?" she demanded. "You have compromised our agreement and I wish to know with whom."

"I can't tell you, Liege, just as I wouldn't betray you to them," said Kaid.

She searched his face. "Your mind is too still," she sighed. "I can sense nothing on its surface. Will you swear that you have my son's and his mate's welfare as your objective?"

Kaid had been trying to avoid this moment. He knew he was at the decision point. With his mind as bruised and battered as his body was, he didn't want to make this kind of decision now. He hadn't had enough time and he couldn't afford to get it wrong. Tiredly he closed his eyes. "Yes, Liege, I have their interests at heart," he said. That, at least, wasn't a lie.

"Then I'll have to be content with that," she said, getting to her feet. "I'll have to go now. I've a meeting with the Commander shortly." She gave him a last penetrating look. "You're close to my son now. Though shortly you'll cease to be under my contract, keep them safe for me, and you'll have my blessing."

When she'd gone, Kaid slumped down in the chair. This meeting had taken a heavy toll on what little energy he had left. Once again he began the litany to banish pain, pushing the thought deep into his subconscious till his mind repeated it automatically and the pain began to ease a little.

Garras came in. "I contacted Draz," he said as he went to his friend's aid. "He says he'll be along later to talk to you about what happened on the scouter."

"Dzaka?"

"He knows, too. He's insisting on coming to see you as soon as Vanna gives her permission."

Leaning heavily on Garras, Kaid got to his feet. "It wasn't my doing," he said as he limped through the rear door into Vanna's medical lab. "Didn't get the chance to ditch us. I had to wing it. I'm not convinced I got Chyad. I survived, he could have."

"They'll search the wreckage for remains," said Garras.

"Messy job, Garras, not knowing if he's dead. Didn't anticipate this crash and being injured."

"I know you, Kaid. You'd have taken every precaution. Now stop worrying about it," he said, helping him sit on the edge of his bed. "Let's get your robe off."

"He'll probably sleep now till morning," she said, pulling the cover back over him. "It's the best thing he can do."

Garras took her by the arm. "Where do you want to go to talk?" he asked quietly. "It's third meal time. How about coming to eat with me?"

"All right," she agreed.

"Mess or restaurant?" he asked as they left the lab.

"Restaurant, and you can pay," she said.

"At least you've got your sense of humor back."

* * *

Early next morning as Vanna was checking on Kaid, Kusac walked in. He stood by the doorway watching.

"Vanna. Kaid," he said, acknowledging them and drawing their attention to his presence.

Vanna looked up. "Hello there. You're up early," she said.

"I came to see Kaid."

"How did you know he was here?" she asked.

Kusac shrugged. "A knack. Look, Vanna, I need a private word with him. Do you mind?"

"Not at all. I'm finished here," she said, clearing her instruments away.

Kusac waited till she'd left, then moved over to Kaid's bed. Folding his arms across his chest, he stared down at him.

"Are you feeling better?"

Kaid looked warily at him. "Yes. I want to be up and back to work, but Physician Vanna won't let me, sir."

"You'll be back when you're fit. Meral and Sevrin can cope for now. We owe you our lives at least twice over. Thank you."

Kaid's ears flicked in acknowledgment.

"Why kill them, Kaid? They'd done nothing."

"I don't know what you mean, sir."

"You want them catalogued? The oxygen pipe in the aft landing bay, the shuttle engine explosion ... Shall I go on, Kaid Tallinu?"

Kaid regarded him balefully. "Another knack?" he asked.

"No. Our telepathic abilities were enhanced yesterday. You were broadcasting while you spoke to Garras. We couldn't avoid picking you up. Don't worry, your mental training is still more than adequate to frustrate most telepaths."

"Not you, eh?"

Kusac shrugged. "It varies," he said noncommittally. "Why them, Kaid? They'd done nothing."

"They were planning to murder you and they were capable of succeeding."

"I can understand Chyad and Maikoe, but the others?" He narrowed his eyes, studying Kaid's face. "You'd do the same again." It was a statement.

"Yes. Without a second thought."

"Who are you working for, Kaid?"

"From the moment we touch Sholan soil, you."

"Whether or not I want it?"

"Yes."

"If I told you no more killings?"

"Then my job would be impossible, if I agreed to it."

Kusac uncrossed his arms and sat down on the chair by the bed. "Carrie and I talked about you last night. She feels safer with you around."

"And you?"

His eyes took on a hard look. "We're too vulnerable, too noticeable. We need you. I don't like it, but I have to be a realist for both of us now. We can't afford our vulnerability. Kill one of us and we both die, and I want us to live, Kaid." He stopped, refocusing his eyes on Kaid.

"I'll only place one restriction on you. You touch no one we hold dear without our permission. I know that the Brotherhood obeys its own tenets before any contracts if there is a conflict of interest. I want no conflict of interest with us, Kaid."

Kaid hesitated. "I agree, Liegen. I'm glad you see the need for protection. So much is at stake here."

"You mean the treaty," said Kusac. "I'm sick of us being equated with the damned treaty!"

"Not the treaty, Liegen," Kaid said. "You two are important to Shola. You're a new force in our world, a force for change. I can see the God's hand in this."

"Don't get religious with me, Brother Tallinu," warned Kusac. "I've never been at ease with any of your Brotherhood. I'll hear no more about it. Neither Warrior nor Telepath Guild—nor the Brotherhood—will use us for their own ends." He got up to leave. "When Vanna says you can leave your bed, return to our suite. Even though you won't be fit to work, having you there will ease Carrie."

"She fears the Terrans."

"Very perceptive," said Kusac. "Her father's behavior the other night could have destroyed the trust that's taken me so long to build with Carrie. I won't risk him or any other

Terran upsetting her like that again. Apart from certain people, I want them kept away from her."

"It shall be as you wish, Liegen."

Kusac stopped at the door. "Who are you working for, Kaid? I want the truth."

"It's against Brotherhood principles to . . ."

"You're not a member of the Brotherhood, though, are you?" he interrupted.

Kaid pushed himself up using his good arm and regarded Kusac balefully. "Why ask me when you already know?"

"I want to hear you tell me."

"Until we reach Shola, your mother, then you."

"Where does Garras fit into this?"

"You'd better ask him," said Kaid, his tone final. "I'm not in your employ until we reach Shola."

"Who hired you to work for me?"

"That's confidential. Now, if you don't mind, Liegen, I need to rest." With that Kaid lay back and shut his eyes.

Kusac had to turn away lest Tallinu see the half-grin that touched his mouth. Despite everything to the contrary, he liked and trusted this male. Why, he had no idea. Who in their right mind would trust a renegade Brother?

* * *

"Tallinu's report is overdue. I want to know why the delay," said Ghezu.

"I'm not privy to his plans," said Dzaka. "If he delays his report, there will be a reason for it."

"I've heard he's been injured."

Dzaka looked stonily at the image on his comm. "If you know, why ask me?"

"You'll make the assessment of them."

Dzaka betrayed his startlement. "Me?"

"You. We can't wait much longer, we need a decision. Shortly they'll be transferred here, to Shola. If they're a danger to us, I want them dealt with now."

"I can't assess them without observation. I'll need time—which you say we haven't got. Besides, Kaid may already have reached a decision."

"Ask him and send me his report. Then I want yours. You have two days, make the most of it."

"Why do you want me duplicating his work?" Dzaka was baffled.

"That's not your concern," said Ghezu. "Just do your job."

"You don't trust him."

"Just do your job, Dzaka. Need I remind you of your oath?"

Dzaka could feel his hackles begin to rise. "No. You don't," he snapped, cutting the connection. It was happening again. Ghezu had no right to use him against Kaid, no right to make him peer over his shoulders. Why hire him if he trusted him so little?

He clenched his fist till his claws started to cut into his palms. Now Ghezu was making him choose again. He brought his fist down hard on the desk. The pain helped stop the memories, the feelings of his unwitting betrayal of Kaid on that day. And the memory of Kaid's eventual abandonment of him. The only reason he'd stayed then was because Kaid wouldn't take him.

* * *

"The Valtegan prisoner will be here within the next hour," said Raguul, looking round the table at the heads of staff gathered there. "This time I want some information out of him."

"What is his current state of health?" asked Chiort, head of Medical.

"Alive, uncommunicative, but not yet catatonic," said Raguul. "Have you been able to isolate a hypnotic drug that would prevent his withdrawing from reality?"

"I've got one in the developmental stage. It's our best bet yet, but I've only tried computer simulations. I need to test it on a live Valtegan to see if it will really work."

Raguul nodded. "Mnya, can your people work on him if he's drugged?"

"Debatable, Commander. Neither I nor my people know enough about the Valtegan mind to work with it at all except on the most basic level, let alone be able to compensate for drugs. It takes time for us to be able to read a new species, and with respect, Commander, every one of the Valtegans you have had brought on board has been catatonic by the time he arrived. We've done no better than Vroozoi did."

"Commander, the Terrans captured this one and delivered

him to the shuttle holding cell still alert and in his right mind," said Draz. "It occurs to me that we may be missing an obvious correlation between the Valtegans and ourselves. We know they don't become catatonic in Terran company. Perhaps it's exposure to us that triggers their mental withdrawal."

"That's ridiculous!" said Chiort. "Why would exposure to us trigger their withdrawal?"

"The idea's not as ridiculous as you think," said Mnya slowly. "If we continued the Terran contact when they arrive on board, making sure that all Sholan scents are removed from their route to the brig, then we'd have a reasonable amount of proof that Draz's suggestion is at least a working hypothesis."

"Then what?" asked Chiort. "If you're right, we can't examine him either physically or mentally!"

"Not so," said Mnya. "We have a potentially reliable Terran telepath in Carrie. It's time her Talent was actually tested in a real situation. She and Kusac have both been able to enter Valtegan minds virtually from the first. We also have a Terran physician on board who is more than capable of administering your drug, Chiort."

"We'd need communication devices for the Terran physician so we can contact him and advise him as he conducts the questioning," said Draz thoughtfully. "We have something that should work."

"The most reliable of the Terrans are Skai, Anders, and Perry," said Vrail, head of Alien Relations. "We could use them as guards."

"Let's implement Draz's idea," said Raguul. "We've nothing to lose by trying. Draz, you see to the communications devices and getting maintenance to clear the route from the landing bay to the brig. We also need the air purified of any trace of our scent, the same with the brig. Myak," he said, turning to his adjutant, "you contact the three Terrans and get them to report to Draz for a briefing. Mnya, you see to our Leska pair, and Chiort, you brief Dr. Reynolds. We've got just under an hour to get this together, so let's move."

Carrie took Mnya's call as Kusac was still with Kaid. As soon as he left medical, she reached for him.

The Mentor wants us to meet her at the brig, she sent.

They've captured a Valtegan, and they want us to read him. He's the first one they've had who hasn't gone catatonic in custody.

I'll meet you there. Get Sevrin to take you, he replied.

Kusac was waiting for her when they arrived. "They want you to work with the Terrans," he said, coming forward to meet her. "Can you do it?" he asked, his hand touching her cheek. "They think that fear of us is what makes the Valtegans retreat into their own minds."

"Who do they want me to work with?" she asked, trying to keep her anxiety under control as she sensed his concern.

"Mainly with Jack," he replied. "They're using Skai, Anders, and Perry as guards. None of the people involved in the bar fight that first evening. No Sholans will be visible."

She nodded. "Where will you be?"

"In here," he said, taking her by the hand and leading her through the doorway beside them.

The Mentor sat at a desk facing a window-sized viewing screen. Beside her was a high ranking official from the Medical Guild, and behind them stood Draz. The adjacent room was being swabbed down by a couple of maintenance personnel wearing environmental suits.

Mnya turned to them as they entered. "Kusac, Carrie, it's good to see you again," she said, getting up and holding out her palm in greeting.

Briefly Carrie touched her hand to the Mentor's.

"This is Consultant Chiort from Medical," Mnya said, indicating her companion. "Sub-Lieutenant Draz you already know. We thought it time for you to try using your Talent professionally, as it were," she said, resuming her seat. "I take it Kusac has told you the gist of our problem?"

Carrie nodded. "You could be right," she said. "The Valtegans that came to the inn on Keiss were terrified of Kusac. They kept as far away from him as possible."

"That's interesting. Perhaps Draz's observations are nearer the mark than we thought."

You'll be able to cope, sent Kusac, his hand tightening around hers. *Jack will be there, too.*

I'll manage, she replied, aware of his concern.

"Kusac and you have both told me how you've read Valtegan minds before," Mnya said. "We need you to question the Valtegan about why he's on Keiss, where his home world is, and who they're fighting. When you ask the questions, listen not so much to his words as to his surface thoughts. We're recording the interview so that we can make sense of the actual language he speaks afterward. Here's a list of the questions we need you to ask," she said, handing her a piece of paper. "They've been written phonetically in Valtegan by your friend Jo. All you have to do is read them out."

Carrie felt Kusac about to speak. *I'll get the answers, but I'll do it my way.*

Remember, he warned, *only listen to the surface thoughts, don't take from him.*

"We'll be watching from here," Mnya continued. "If there's the slightest sign of trouble, Draz will be in immediately." She looked wryly at Kusac. "If he wasn't, then Kusac would be. Do you have any questions? They should be arriving in a few minutes."

Carrie shook her head. "None. A captive Valtegan won't bother me." She moved away from the Mentor to look through the screen. The room was empty now save for a table and two chairs opposite each other, one being obviously a padded restraint chair.

You know what to do, don't you? Kusac sent. *Match your mind to his, then ask the questions. You should be able to feel his answers as he speaks them. If you need to, use our Link as I showed you to draw on me for extra energy.* He stood behind her and put his hands on her shoulders. *You'll do fine.*

She put her hand up to cover one of his. *I'm not worried,* she sent, aware of his continuing concern. *It's good to feel useful for a change.* She felt his immediate objections and laughed. "You know what I mean," she said.

Her attention was drawn back to the other room as the door opened to admit Skai. Perry and Anders followed, holding the struggling Valtegan between them.

Carrie watched as the prisoner was unceremoniously placed in the chair and the automatic restraints activated to hold him by the forearms and calves. The three then stood back against the wall, waiting.

The Valtegan sat there looking ahead, toward her. With tiny jerky movements he turned his head, eyes flicking in every direction, assessing the room, weighing the odds against an escape attempt.

She watched him almost dispassionately. He was scared, she could feel it even from here. His skin was more than usually pallid, the scales looking dull and lackluster. The whites of his slightly bulbous eyes were red and rimmed with matter; he blinked at the brightness of the lights. His wrists moved, pulling against the restraints, testing them.

"Turn the lights down," she said abruptly. "It's too bright for him."

As the lights dimmed, a little of the tension seemed to leave his body and he sat still now except for the slow blinking of his eyes.

His clothing was mud-streaked and torn. That was to be expected, but there was something unusual about it, and him. Frowning, she stepped closer to the view screen. Under the stains the uniform was slightly different in color from those she was used to seeing around Valleytown. Perhaps he was on active service rather than one of the garrison troops.

It was hard to see in this one trapped soldier the aliens who had terrified her people for years on Keiss. Those nightmare days seemed removed from reality now, belonging to another time.

"I'm going in," she said, turning away from the screen.

She hesitated in front of the door, then resolutely pressed the access panel. It slid open and as she stepped inside, the familiar dry musty smell hit her nostrils, this time overlaid with the sharpness of fear. Memories started to crowd her mind, and she pushed them aside firmly. She didn't want to remember now, she had a job to do.

She walked past their captive on slightly unsteady legs, grateful for the long Sholan robes that she now wore. At least no one could see she was nervous. Stopping between the table and the prisoner, she raised her eyes and looked up at him. He stared back, eyes locking onto her face briefly before he looked away.

The hairless face and head was humanoid, with a forehead that fell smoothly down toward the nose. His bulbous eyes were set in a skin that was scaled an unhealthy shade of pale green. He sniffed, tongue-tip flicking out to taste the air. The mouth opened slightly revealing rows of sharp pointed incisors.

"You insult me," he hissed in badly spoken Terran, pulling again at his restraints. "Not talk to female." He arched his hands, the nonretractable claws puncturing and ripping the fabric beneath.

"You'll talk to me," said Carrie, resting her hands behind her against the table top. "You're not one of the garrison troops."

Hissing, he turned his head, trying to see the Terran males behind him.

"I asked you a question," she said, her voice taking on a hard edge.

He ignored her, continuing to hiss and turn his head. The smell of fear was getting stronger.

Leaning forward, Carrie reached for his jaw, grasping it firmly and forcing his face round to hers.

"You will talk to me!" she said, her fingers pressing into his flesh.

His mouth opened and the tongue flicked out to touch her wrist. He recoiled, trying to pull away from her, his teeth snapping in the hope of catching her arm. His mouth opened wide as he tried to hiss, but his attempt ended in a choking cough.

Carrie, take care! Your hand is too close! sent Kusac.

The Valtegan's eyes were beginning to glaze, and his movements became more frantic as he jerked his head free of her hand. A flap of skin on his scalp raised, forming a small crest that fluttered briefly before collapsing again. He began to gabble in his own language, his eyes rolling up till only the whites showed.

She felt fear welling up inside him, pushing coherent thoughts aside and filling his mind till there was no room for anything else. He was still conscious but not for much longer. There was no time to think, only to act. Reaching into his mind she took control. His body jerked, then his limbs went slack. Where there had been fear before there was now stark terror at her presence, a terror so strong it broke her hold over him.

Surprised she followed, sinking through the levels of his consciousness as he fled her mental touch. Aware of Kusac's thoughts as he tried to stop her, she thrust them aside, intent on the hunt as any Sholan would have been.

The falling sensation stopped abruptly to be replaced by the feeling of floating in a vast cavern, an alien landscape full of shadows briefly illuminated by flashes of brightness that for a split second revealed an image. She knew that if she could but reach the flashes she would have the information she needed.

The myriad of tiny flares were dimming now, fewer each second as his terror extinguished them one by one. Reaching for those few that were left, she memorized them, storing them at the back of her mind for later. No time now to examine them. One by one the lights faded, turning in on themselves till all that remained was his terror and the dark within dark.

She knew reality was nearby, just the other side of the darkness, but sudden tiredness weakened her. She tried to go back the way she had come but now she felt a resistance to her as everything around her started to slow down. It was like moving through a thick, dark syrup. Then slowly she realized something was wrong. Panicking, she reached out for Kusac. His thoughts swamped her, full of anger and fear as he pulled her back out of the Valtegan's mind.

The return to her own mind was so abrupt that it made her reel and she clutched at the table to steady herself, blinking as she realized she was watching Jack monitoring the effects of the drug on their captive.

Kusac's thoughts were blistering. *Just what the hell do you think you were doing? I said read the surface thoughts! I didn't expect you to follow him! You were nearly trapped there!*

I had to go in. He tasted your scent on me and started to withdraw. If I hadn't, we'd have gotten nothing!

You should have told me! We'd have sent Jack in to administer the drug first.

It was the drug that nearly trapped me there. Her tone was sharp and angry. *At least now we have some information from him.*

You took unnecessary risks, you violated our code of ethics!

I don't subscribe to your damned code! I'm at war with them and I'll do what's necessary to get the information we need. I've succeeded, that's what counts at the end of the day.

"Carrie, are you all right?" asked Jack, glancing round at her.

"I'm fine, thanks," she said, rubbing her hand across her eyes as she stood up. "He's gone catatonic. You'll get nothing from him now," she said as she began to walk slowly toward the door. Dammit, Kusac had no right to be angry with her.

As she passed Skai, he flinched and averted his eyes. Puzzled she glanced at him, feeling his shock at the sight of her eyes.

She's not human! His thought echoed round inside her head as she hurried out into the corridor away from him.

Kusac was waiting. He came over and grasped her by the arm. "The Mentor's furious," he growled as he escorted her through the door. "We'll talk later."

Carrie pulled away from him and strode over to Mnya. "Before you start complaining, too, I'm going to tell you just why I did it that way. He was fine until his tongue touched my arm, then he picked up Kusac's scent. That triggered off a terror reaction that's programmed into him and he began to withdraw. I tried to stop it, but he preferred to die rather than be exposed to Sholans."

She turned to look at Chiort. "Your drugs won't stop it, nothing will, the fear of your people is too strong. If I hadn't gone in there and then to take what I could, we'd have had nothing. I did what I had to do."

Her tone became angrier as she looked back at Mnya. "His kind aren't polite in war, I don't intend to be either. They tortured my sister to death. I'll follow your code in most circumstances, but not these. Politeness won't win wars, information will."

Mnya's hard look didn't change, and Carrie could feel the female's hostility washing over her. There was a dislike of the unknown quantity that she and Kusac represented, and a fear of the unpredictable element that Carrie's Link to Kusac had now brought into the Sholan telepath culture.

"Your actions lost us the chance to interrogate this prisoner," the Mentor said. "More than that, because you exceeded your instructions, you are responsible for terrifying him to death. Your undisciplined Terran mind . . ."

"No," interrupted Carrie. "You're wrong. It wasn't my Terran mind that caused this. He went catatonic because something deep in his subconscious recognized the Sholan in me! He believed I was one of you. My mind isn't human any more, Mentor. Even he recognized that."

A stunned silence greeted her remark, then she felt a sharp invasive probe reach for her mind. Without thinking, she fended it off, hearing Kusac begin to laugh quietly as he moved to stand beside her.

"We both forgot something vital, Mentor," he said. "The nature of our Link. What I know, Carrie knows and is learning how to use. She has had the equivalent of an identical upbringing and education to me, including the full knowledge of our code of ethics. Do you know that I'm beginning to think she's got the right of it after all? In a war, only the victors can afford to have a rigid ethical code."

He frowned briefly, putting a hand on her shoulder. Carrie felt the probe at the same time he did.

"No. I won't let you read me either," he said. "My Leska only did what I would have done, given the same circumstances."

"Do you want to know what I discovered?" Carrie asked, aware that Kusac's anger with her had evaporated in the face of the Mentor's attitude.

"Yes," snapped Mnya.

Carrie sat down on the edge of the table. "The Valtegans seem to have a communal inherited memory. If something has affected them on a racial scale, then somehow, I don't know the mechanism, it's imprinted on them and retained to warn future generations. A fear of feline species is what triggers their catatonia—the sight, smell, or worst of all, the touch of a Sholan mind creates a terror so deep they prefer to die rather than face it."

"Since we first went into space there has been no record of a species like the Valtegans," said Mnya, obviously swallowing her anger in her need to know more. "Where have they gotten this fear from? Is there another species like us? Why didn't the Valtegans you and Kusac were in contact with before we arrived react in the same way?"

"They were afraid of Kusac, and of the forest cats, but their fear was controllable. Perhaps their paranoia wasn't triggered until there were large numbers of you on the planet. When we read their minds on Keiss perhaps the presence of a Terran mind—mine—masked Kusac. As for there being another telepathic felinoid species," said Carrie, "I doubt it. That's too much of a coincidence. It was definitely the touch of my mind that was the final straw for him. That's when I took control, hoping to prevent him withdrawing, but his conditioning was so strong that it broke my hold. I followed, hoping either to hold him again, or at the least to gather some of the information we need."

"What did you discover?"

Carrie felt some of the Mentor's hostility begin to dissipate. "Nothing new, I'm afraid," she said. "Their war has been going on for a very long time in his reckoning. The enemy is faceless and unseen, they just attack them when told to do so." She stopped, hesitating before going on. "I don't know if it's relevant, but there was something about a holy object or a relic that he was appealing to. It was on the starship they had orbiting Keiss."

"What's this relic like?"

Carrie shook her head. "I didn't see it clearly, only that it was dark and large."

"Bulky," interrupted Kusac. "It felt as if it had considerable mass."

"You're right," she nodded. "It was over the height of a male and about three or four times as wide. There was no real shape to it, it just was."

"What's this about a Valtegan starship?" asked Kusac.

"It escaped," said Mnya, getting up. "You'll have to ask Draz if you wish to know more. Thank you for what you've done. In the circumstances you've achieved more than we could have looked for," she said grudgingly.

The door opened and Jack came in. "I'm afraid you were right, Carrie," he said. "He's gone. The drug was no help at all. Sorry, Chiort. I did everything I could to keep him alive."

"If the Liegena is correct, then interrogating them is next to impossible," sighed Chiort, pushing himself up from the table. "Even the Terrans can get nothing from them. Still, we're learning much about their physiology."

Carrie glanced at the view screen while the others talked. Already the three Terrans had left and Draz was organizing the removal of the body to the ship's morgue. She turned to the Mentor.

"I'll have the report for you tomorrow," she said, answering the as yet unasked question before reaching for Kusac.

Let's go. I'm tired of being shut in the suite, I want to go for a walk.

We haven't eaten yet. How about going to the concourse for breakfast?

Sounds good. Do we need to take Meral and Sevrin with us?

Yes, he sent firmly. *You were the one who felt happier having Kaid around. Do you now want to be without them while Kaid is bedridden?*

All right, let's just go! she sent, getting off the table and heading for the door.

"Oh, Mentor," she said, stopping for a moment. "This one was an officer, not one of the fighting men. His mind is more complex, and he was actually less susceptible to the fear of Sholans. You should try looking for other Terran telepaths. Perhaps one without a Leska Link to your people will be able to succeed where we've failed."

* * *

Miosh tapped on Rhyasha's bedroom door before opening it. "The Clan Lord is on the comm for you," she said.

"Tell him I'll be right there," said Rhyasha. Taking a deep breath, she got to her feet. This would probably be one of the most difficult calls of her life, and one of the most important for her son.

Resolutely she went through to the lounge, sitting down at the desk in front of the comm.

"Konis," she said, thinking how like his father Kusac was. Same clear gaze, though Konis' eyes were more green; same determined set to the ears and jawline. "How nice of you to call. How are you and the children?"

"We're surviving. I'll be glad when you get back, though. That damned cook of yours won't do what I ask her. Pretends she doesn't understand me. We're all getting sick of fish!"

"Oh, no, not again!" said Rhyasha, trying not to laugh. "I thought I'd broken her of that habit after the last time."

"Obviously not. Anyway, it wasn't to discuss our starvation that I called you. I want to talk about Kusac. He called me up at some ungodly hour the night before last."

"Ah, I rather hoped he might."

"He said his Leska's a Terran."

"Yes, that's right."

"Well, what's she like?"

"Haven't you received the pictorial data on the Terrans yet?"

"Rhyasha, that's not what I mean and you know it," her husband growled.

"She's small and appears vulnerable but is fiercely loyal to him. She was prepared to take me on if necessary," she said with a grin.

"And Kusac? What does he think of her?"

"He's changed, Konis," she said. "Having to look out for both of them has made him grow up. I've never known him feel so content and happy."

Her husband raised an eye ridge. "You surprise me, Rhyasha. To hear you speak so well of her she must indeed be special. I take it you approve of his Leska?"

"Yes, I do. He calls her cub, and she has that quality about her. You'll see for yourself when you meet her."

"What about their Link? Can they work together? Is their Talent similar?"

"What he allowed me to sense of their Link is different from any Sholan Link I've known," she said slowly. "They have a barrier that won't allow one to read anything from them. Yes, their minds are in phase and they work well together, but she has more than one Talent."

"You've noticed the barrier, too. I haven't sensed anything from him since their Link was completed and what I felt then was more the sudden flare of this barrier going up between us."

"You were monitoring him, Konis," said Rhyasha, her tone one of disbelief and anger. "You had no right to intrude on his privacy like that!"

Her husband's ears flicked backward, then stilled. "I wasn't eavesdropping, Rhyasha. I sensed very little from him," he said. "I only did it because I was worried at what I'd been picking up."

"You should have called and spoken to him."

"I did! That damned Adjutant Myak kept giving me the runaround, saying Kusac wasn't available for one reason or another. Don't tell me you didn't try to pick him up, Rhyasha, because I won't believe it!"

"Well, I didn't," she said, "and you ought to be ashamed of yourself."

"At least he'll soon be home," said Konis. "Try and get him to travel back with you. I need to find out all I can about these Terrans and their Talents. If there's been one mixed Leska Link, there could be more. I want to know

what caused it. Perhaps her Talents can be passed to other
telepaths just as we pass on languages."

"Konis, just remember your son and his Leska are people
entitled to their own lives. They aren't to be put under your
scrutiny and torn apart so you can examine what makes
them work," she said.

"Nonsense, it's nothing like that, Rhyasha. At least now
we've found him we can get that marriage settled. News of
Kusac's Leska has been spread over the public information
channels, and Rala's family are becoming concerned. I've
assured them there won't be any problems. They don't know
she's Terran yet."

"Konis, I should go easy on this with Kusac if I were
you," warned Rhyasha. "Now is not the time to talk to him
about marriage."

"Rubbish. Now is the best time. He's found a Leska, and
you say he's happy. What better time? It might have caused
a problem if she were Sholan, but she isn't. Besides, I've already spoken to him about it. He knows his duty to the Clan.
He won't cause any trouble over it."

Rhyasha briefly closed her eyes. There's no fool like one
who refuses to see what's under his nose, she thought, making sure to keep it to herself. He's already left us once because you pushed him too hard, Konis. We could lose him
again, this time for good. You have enough clues, you
should know he won't come to your heel. Already he can
block us out mentally. He doesn't need us any more, and you
could push him till he realizes that.

"Leave it for now, Konis. Believe me they have enough
on their minds with the guild trying to gauge her Talents and
find out how many of them Kusac now has."

"There's no point in me pursuing it now anyway. I'll
leave it until they return to Shola," he agreed. "Now tell me
how the treaty negotiations are going."

* * *

Dzaka had been waiting for upward of an hour before
Vanna allowed him in. Kaid was lying propped up against a
pile of pillows. He looked tired and in pain.

"How are you?" Dzaka asked, lifting the chair from the
other side of the room over to the bedside.

"Annoyed," he said. "I've got work to do, and I feel as
weak as a cub."

"What happened?"

"The craft suddenly went out of control. Either there was something wrong with the vehicle or Maikoe tried to fake it and crashed. Have they examined the wreck yet?"

Dzaka nodded. "The explosion damaged the remains of the crew to the extent that that couldn't say how many bodies there were. Officially, there were no survivors. Three died in the crash, and the fourth in the sick bay."

Kaid sighed. "I was hoping they could tell how many bodies there were. One of them, the ringleader Chyad, could have got away. He and I were the only survivors and he was trying to kill me. He and Maikoe—had she survived—were intending to hide on the planet's surface."

"Did he break your cover?"

"No, thank the God. It was simply that I could have told the authorities he had escaped the crash, too. You haven't heard anything, have you?"

"Nothing. I'll get Rulla onto it. The troopers will know if a stranger turns up in their midst." He looked down at his hands for a moment, reluctant to carry on. "How has the rest of your contract gone? Have you assessed the pair yet?"

Kaid closed his eyes and laid his head back against the pillows. "Ghezu," he said succinctly. "So far, nothing they've done or said leads me to believe they are in any way dangerous, Dzaka, but I need longer. They've only been on board the *Khalossa* for some thirteen or fourteen days, together for six of them. Normally when we do one of these missions, the Brotherhood and the Telepath Guild has been observing them for years. Not this time. Officially, I'm their adjutant, and I'll be returning to Shola with them where I intend to continue my observation. Tell Ghezu that."

"I had to ask," Dzaka said.

Kaid opened his eyes again and reached his hand out to touch Dzaka's briefly. "I know. Ghezu is testing your loyalty."

Dzaka stirred. "I realize that," he said, moving his hand away. "Why did you never contact me?" he asked abruptly. "I wanted to leave with you. You were all I had then. Gods, Kaid, I was almost an adult with the right to choose for myself, and you refused me! You were all the family I'd ever known!"

"I had to leave you. Ghezu made it a condition of my release that you were to remain. It proved that he'd beaten me, and he needed the Stronghold to see that."

"Why did you want to leave?"

"I couldn't stay after what he did to you, and I knew that he'd use you again to get at me." Kaid turned his head to look at his grown fosterling. "The past still lies between Ghezu and me, and it touches you. Be careful of him. The Brotherhood means more to him than anything, even friendship. I'll give him his due, though, he's led the Brotherhood well these past ten years."

"You still haven't said why you never contacted me."

"What would I have said, Dzaka?" There was a touch of anger in his voice. "Having a great time, wish you were here—where you're a target for any Brother who wants to kill you? If I'd have gotten in touch with you, you'd have left—you know it as well as I do. I couldn't let you be killed because of loyalty to me! In his own way he was right. He's made a better leader than ever I would have done. He had the ruthlessness to see it and do something about it."

"And you had the ruthlessness to risk your own life to escape him, and leave me there," said Dzaka bleakly, getting up and turning away.

The door had just slid open when Kaid spoke again.

"Tell me I was wrong, Dzaka. Tell me I should have taken you with me, or stayed at the Stronghold, if that's what you really believe."

"I can't tell you that, Kaid. You did what you did," he said before stepping into the corridor.

* * *

The restaurant Kusac chose was on the concourse near the viewing window. As they left the elevator to cross over to it, Carrie was aware of the many speculative looks cast in her direction, looks that took in her appearance, then backed off. She remembered Skai's reaction to her and the words she'd used to the Mentor—to shock, not because she believed them. Now she began to wonder.

They waited outside with Sevrin while Meral went in first to conduct a security check.

We need to talk, Kusac, she sent.

I know, he replied.

She felt him pull his gaze away, eyes focusing somewhere around the top of her head.

Don't do that!

He looked back at her. *I'm sorry. I'm not used to them yet. It makes you seem more Sholan.*

Meral returned to beckon them in. They followed, only peripherally aware of the stir their arrival was causing.

That's what we need to talk about, and I mean talk.

While we eat, promised Kusac as he moved in to sit at the table Meral had selected.

Automatically, Carrie sat opposite him, sinking down into the soft bowl at the center of the seat. Surprised, she found her feet no longer touched the floor. She took stock of the chair, realizing its cushioned seat curved up to a high back, making it perfect for lounging in. Glancing round the other tables in the softly-lit room, she noticed many of the customers were curled up in their chairs. She could feel their air of studied involvement in their own affairs.

Carrie looked back to see Meral hovering uncertainly. "Where are you sitting?" she asked.

"With us," said Kusac, pulling the chair adjacent to him out. "You need to eat, too."

Hesitantly, Meral and Sevrin sat.

"We'll still talk," Kusac said to her in Terran. "What do you want to eat?"

"Order anything," she said, trying to settle herself comfortably into the chair. She felt dwarfed by it and finally ended up pulling her legs up beside her.

The meal ordered, Kusac gave her his full attention.

"Kusac, have you any idea what's happening to us? Why are we changing?" she asked, leaning across the table.

"Vanna told us about . . ."

"I'm not talking about what Vanna said," she interrupted. "I'm talking about the other changes, ones you've noticed in me."

He stretched out his hand to her. "I haven't noticed any changes in you."

"You keep telling me how Sholan I seem."

"That's just a figure of speech, cub," he said, his ears giving a tiny flick.

"No. Your thoughts give you away. You really did mean it at the time. Today, even the Valtegan recognized the touch of my mind. You've trained in this field, Kusac, you know the feel of a Terran mind and you know mine. They're not the same, are they?"

"No," he said quietly. "They're not." His hand tightened on hers. "I find my own outlook is changing, too. I'm challenging the codes I was brought up to believe. They seem too rigid to me now."

"Where's all this taking us, Kusac? Where will it end? What are we becoming?"

"I don't know, Carrie. The Sholan mind has only ever been telepathic. Yours is much more flexible, not only in what you can do but the way you think. A lot of what we do is dictated by the past, by following guild rules. Now I find myself questioning everything just as you do." His ears flicked again briefly. "Our minds have merged to the point where we're neither of us Sholan or Terran but something else, and I don't know what that is."

"But I'm changing in other ways. Look at my eyes," she said, tugging gently at his hand to make him look up. "Even you're uncomfortable with me now. I'm still the same person, Kusac. Don't make me feel even more isolated than I am," she said, a catch in her voice as she looked into his amber eyes. "I'm frightened, Kusac. What else about me will change, and why is it only me that's changing physically?"

"Carrie, I'm sorry. I don't mean to make you feel isolated," he said, squeezing her hand reassuringly. "Nothing like this has ever happened in the history of either our people or yours. I don't understand it either."

She could feel his helplessness, his frustration at not having an answer for them.

"We don't know that you're changing physically. Yes, your eyes are different, but that was after you triggered the gestalt. I think we should make a point of avoiding using it if we possibly can. Apart from that there's nothing we can do, cub, except see this through together."

"I didn't trigger the gestalt, Kusac. It just happened."

Kusac looked dubiously at her. "The other times it happened, you seemed to do it at will."

"I didn't this time."

"Maybe strong emotions trigger it. I think that if either of us feels it building again, we both have to fight it."

"If we have it and can use it, there has to be a purpose to it," Carrie pointed out reasonably.

"I'm sure there is, but at the moment there's so much we don't know about our abilities that something as wild as the gestalt is better left till after we can control what we know we have. We could end up doing great harm to ourselves or others through ignorance if we trigger it again."

"That sounds fine to me. I'd really rather not wake up out of a faint and find I've acquired a tail!"

"Oh, I don't know, it could be quite fetching," he grinned, ducking when she threw a handful of paper napkins at him.

Chapter 9

Later that day Kusac received a message to report to Tutor Rhuso. While Kusac accompanied his tutor into the less formal inner office, Meral remained in the waiting area.

"Thank you for coming so promptly. Please, take a seat," said Rhuso, indicating the form-shaped chairs around the low table. "C'shar?" he asked, going over to the dispenser as Kusac sat down.

"Thanks."

"You look much improved from when I last saw you," said Rhuso, returning with two mugs.

Kusac took the one held out to him, sipping it as his tutor sat down opposite him. "If you'll pardon me saying so, Tutor, I'm aware of your concern not to offend me," he said. "Perhaps it would be better if you just told me what the problem is." He felt the other's surge of surprise before Rhuso retreated behind a stronger shield.

"I've been asked to speak to you on behalf of the Mentor," said Rhuso, putting his mug down. "We need your cooperation on a matter of some delicacy."

Kusac raised an eye ridge as he took another drink.

"It's with regard to your Leska."

"I rather thought it might be," murmured Kusac.

"We're all aware of her lack of experience and training and are making allowances," said Rhuso, "but we can't go on doing that for much longer. From what happened today with the Valtegan, it's obvious that she has a powerful Talent—in fact, I'd hazard a guess that it was on a level with yours. Given her lack of discipline, and the fact that your Link allows her access not only to all you know but to your power as well, the potential for disaster is immense."

Kusac held his ears still by an effort of will, but on the seat beside him the tip of his tail began to flick from side to side.

"I would hardly say her Talent is potentially disastrous," he said quietly.

"I'm afraid I would. She's been on board some ten days and in that time she's had to be drugged to stop her broadcasting her distress to the entire complement of thirty-five telepaths, and two days ago she drained one telepath completely of energy. She would have affected more people had your mother not been able to prevent her. Then there was today's incident. Her Talent is wild, Kusac. She needs to be trained."

"I wasn't aware any request for her to start training had been made by the guild."

"It's being made now," said Rhuso. "And it isn't a request. She must be brought into line and made to conform."

"Why?"

Rhuso looked as taken aback as he felt. "You're asking me?"

Kusac's ears were beginning to swivel sideward in anger. "The first two incidents were due to fear, Tutor Rhuso. Today, I consider she was in the right. There was no time for her to ask, only to act. I would have done the same. We've been at peace for so long that we've forgotten how to fight. Her people haven't, neither have the Valtegans. Her sister was tortured to death by them, and because of her Link, she was the one who suffered both the pain and the injuries! How can you expect her to show a nicety of feeling toward them? I think she did remarkably well in not causing any injury to the Valtegan!"

"I've read the files," said Rhuso. "I'm well aware of what she suffered."

Kusac looked at him, eyes hard. "You didn't experience her pain. I did," he said coldly.

Rhuso looked away. "Nonetheless, she has to follow our ways; she has to conform."

"She's not Sholan, Rhuso! Why should she follow our ways?"

"Because you made her part of our world, and she accepted it!" Rhuso locked eyes with him.

"Kusac, you're a contender for the Leadership of the Sixteen Telepath Clans," he continued in a quieter tone. "You've also been brought up with the knowledge that one day you will succeed your mother. You've been trained to always put the good of the Clans and Shola first. You must see that your Leska presents a threat to our way of life if she continues like this. She shows no respect for our authorities—dammit, she can't talk to the Mentor like that! Surely even you realize she was in the wrong!"

"Perhaps I don't want to be heir either to my own Clan or the Sixteen," said Kusac evenly. "Maybe that's why I joined the Forces in the first place. There's a lot that's good about the Terran outlook. We've become stale over the years of peace. Just pray that we don't find the Valtegans, because mentally we aren't ready to face the kind of war they wage."

"I'll repeat what I said. You made her part of our world by your own actions," said Rhuso. "If she continues like this, you will both be fighting against everything in our culture. Is that what you want? Neither of you to belong anywhere?"

Kusac made a derisive noise. "Tell me where we'll fit in even if we do as you ask?"

"I don't know, but at least you'll be giving yourselves a chance! All we're asking is your cooperation in getting her to come for training. In a few weeks you'll return to Shola to live at the guild. Think of the damage she could do to our students there, damage to their attitude to authority among other things."

He leaned forward earnestly. "We can't afford to have impressionable younglings turn their backs on the ethics that form the foundation of our place in society, Kusac. One person like Carrie paying no attention to those ethics could lead a generation of young telepaths to believe their judgment is as valid as that of their more experienced tutors. Our young males, particularly, will be susceptible to her influence," he said. "As a potential future Lord of the Clans it makes it even more important that your Leska be brought to heel now while you, at least, can still influence her. Our fear is that her Talent will take her beyond your ability to control."

"Don't be ridiculous! You're overexaggerating her importance, and her ability."

"Am I? Can you honestly say that you'll always be able to influence her?"

"Yes, I can. You don't know her. I do."

"Then see she comes to me for training," said Rhuso quietly. "Do it now, before I have to make it an order."

"She'll come," Kusac snapped. "But not because I believe you. See that you don't use subliminals or blocks on her, because if you do, I'll know instantly and, by Vartra, you'll regret it!"

"No subliminals or blocks, Kusac. That I promise," said Rhuso, watching him get up.

"Is that all you wanted to see me about?" he asked.

Rhuso nodded. "That's it."

"In that case, I'll be leaving, Tutor," he said, ears and tail flicking in anger. "Carrie will be in touch with you either later today or tomorrow."

Kusac had no sooner left than Sevrin came to tell Carrie she had a visitor. It was Rhyasha.

"I hope I'm not intruding," she said as she settled herself in one of the easy chairs, "but I thought we ought to have a chat."

"No, you're very welcome," said Carrie. "I'm afraid you've missed Kusac, though. He's just gone out."

"In which case I'm glad I've caught you on your own. Now, don't look so worried," she said, leaning forward to touch Carrie's hand. "Since you're going to be part of our world, I thought it best to explain something of it to you. I know Kusac won't think to do it! Memory transfers give you the knowledge but not the experience to use it, as I'm sure he's told you," she smiled.

She could feel the young human begin to bristle—if she'd been Sholan, her hackles would be rising. Their bodies were so difficult to read compared to her people! She was still having some difficulty reading her mind, but that was getting easier with every day as her mental patterns moved closer to those of her son. And his closer to hers, she sighed.

"Have you been talking to the Mentor?" Carrie asked, staring her straight in the eyes.

Damn! So much for the subtle approach, she thought. "Actually, I have," admitted Rhyasha. "But I didn't come here to talk to you about your session with the Valtegan."

"I'm delighted to hear it," Carrie said ironically, pulling her legs up onto the chair beside her.

"You have to realize, Carrie, that the real power on our world is held by the guilds. We have a central government comprised of elected members, but the inner council that guides our Governor is made up in the main of the Guild Masters. They decide on the policy. It isn't wise to alienate any of the guilds, and the way you spoke to Mnya today seriously ruffled her fur. She isn't used to people assuming such a high-handed attitude toward her, especially in front of other guild members. It minimizes her position. As Mentor, she has virtually Guild Master status on the *Khalossa*."

"She tried to minimize me," said Carrie. "She asked me to do a job for her, then she complained about my methods. I did my best. I got her the information she wanted despite the Valtegan going catatonic on me."

"You shouldn't have spoken to her the way you did, my dear," said Rhyasha, softening her voice to take the sting out of her words. "You're in an anomalous position, a vulnerable one at the moment. Mnya has been given the task of assessing your talents and reporting on them to the main Telepath Guild on Shola, the one situated at Valsgarth where we live. When you leave the *Khalossa,* you'll be going there. We don't want Guild Master Esken to get a false impression of you."

"Why does it matter what he thinks of me? He's got nothing to do with our life, has he?"

"On the contrary," said Rhyasha. "He'll have to eventually decide where to place you and Kusac—what line of work you are suited for. If you are unable to adhere to the codes of our guild it will make his task the more difficult. Perhaps even impossible."

With an exclamation of annoyance, Carrie got to her feet and began to pace in front of Rhyasha. "I'm sick to death of hearing about your damned code! You all forget that I'm not Sholan, and unlike you, I've personally suffered under the hands of these aliens! How on earth do you expect me to be able to treat them as I would normal, decent people?"

Rhyasha reached out and caught Carrie by the hand, forcing her to stop. "Listen to me, cub. For Kusac's sake you mustn't fight the Telepath Guild. Your Link to him has wider ranging consequences than you can imagine. Political consequences. You need as many people on your side as you can get. Don't alienate the guild, for all our sakes."

Carrie tried to pull away, but Rhyasha refused to let go. "I haven't finished yet. We have abilities the ordinary person is wary of; we don't want their fear to escalate. Seeing one of their telepaths with an alien Leska, knowing the pair are now able to fight, could just turn that wariness into outright fear."

She gently tugged at Carrie's arm. "Come, sit beside me.

Let me explain." She felt Carrie stiffen. "I'm not here to criticize you, cub, I'm here to help you understand."

Grudgingly, Carrie sat down.

"More than a thousand years ago, after the Cataclysm, there was a terror of all telepaths. The ordinary Sholans believed that we had brought about the destruction that raged across our world and they tried to hunt us down and kill us. Only the intervention of our God, Vartra, stopped it. He spoke to the people, urging them to stop fighting each other and instead work together to rebuild our world. It was He who told us to set up the guilds so that in the aftermath of the disaster, no skills would be utterly lost. He initiated a Warrior Guild to protect us from harm, and also to protect our people from any telepaths who would misuse their Talent. This balance has lasted since then. Now, suddenly, there are telepaths who can fight, who may be capable of taking on Warriors and defeating them. Can you see why our guild may be afraid you will upset this balance? Especially when you resist all the ethics they've built up primarily to see that none of us would think of misusing our Talent?"

"I can see the sense in what you're saying," Carrie admitted reluctantly. "But many of your ethics are totally unrealistic. When you're fighting a species with no honor, how can you expect to win if you play fairly with them? They won't respect you for it, they'll only walk over you and laugh while they do it."

"I understand what you're saying, too, but you have to see it from the viewpoint of people like Mnya. They see only that you refuse to live by our codes and that this is a threat to their authority. When you're dealing with Talents like ours, you need to be able to command the respect of the young ones you're teaching so that they will grow up into responsible members of society. If you're seen to flaunt our rules, then our young will want to emulate you. We can't allow that." She reached out to gently touch her cheek.

"You and Kusac can't live unnoticed on Shola. People will see what you do. You need to set an example, to show that your people will honor our customs and protect our society."

Carrie made an exasperated noise. "Is there no place where we can be just us? Will we always be under a microscope being observed and studied? I don't think I can stand it, Rhyasha."

"You'll have to, my dear," she said with sympathy. "I know now is a difficult time for the two of you, but you have Kusac. There's no one better to have at your side for this. Together you'll manage, I know it."

"I wish I had your confidence," Carrie muttered as Rhyasha put a comforting arm around her shoulders.

"I have to go now. I'm supposed to be here on official business after all. If you want to talk, cub, you know where I am," she said, getting up. "You'll be welcome any time."

By the time he reached their suite, he'd managed to shake off enough of his anger to be able to bring down the barrier he'd placed between them. It wasn't an insurmountable barrier, it was more one of politeness that they each used and respected in the other. It gave them a semblance of privacy, something they both needed.

Sevrin was in the hallway. She was in, good. Kusac nodded briefly to him as he went past.

Carrie was in the lounge, curled up on the settee. She'd been watching the entertainment channel on the wall comm and switched it off as he entered.

"Carrie," he said without preamble, "will you contact Tutor Rhuso either today or tomorrow? The Guild wants you to start training with them now."

"I thought you were teaching me."

"Apparently that's not good enough," he said.

"I'd rather not go. Can't you tell them I prefer to learn from you?"

"No, I can't. If you don't go voluntarily, then they'll order you to go," said Kusac, pacing round the room, tail flicking from side to side.

"Order me?" she said incredulously, turning to follow him with her eyes. "They can't just order me to go!"

He stopped in front of her. "They can, and they will. It's for the best, Carrie. You don't take much notice of me, maybe you'll pay attention to the Tutor."

"That's unfair, Kusac. The only thing we disagree on is that damned code of ethics."

"That's what's at the root of this. You've got to realize that the guilds are the real power on Shola. You can't talk to Mentors the way you did this morning, even if you are in the right. Think it by all means, say it to me if you have to, but not to the guild officials."

"Don't you start as well! I've just had half an hour of your mother lecturing me on the importance of your code as well as how to speak to the Mentor."

"Did it occur to you we might be right? I've had Rhuso jumping on me because of what you said to the Mentor. We can't afford to alienate the Telepath Guild."

"I did my best this morning, Kusac. If I'd done it their way, we'd have had nothing," she said angrily.

"Put your shield up, Carrie! You're broadcasting again! Why can't you even do something as simple as that?" he said, equally angry. "It's about time you learned some of the responsibilities that go with possessing a Talent. You can't keep making everyone around you ill."

"I don't believe this," she said, jumping to her feet. "You get a hard time from your Tutor, so you take it out on me!"

"I'm taking nothing out on you," he snapped. "I'm telling you that you've upset the guild and they aren't happy about it. It's up to you to deal with it. I can't spend the rest of our lives apologizing for you because you don't want to behave in an acceptable manner."

"I've had enough of this," she said, heading toward the door. "How dare you talk to me like that!"

"Go where you want," he said, putting a hand up to his forehead as a stabbing pain lanced through his temples. "Just put your damned shield up before you give everyone on the ship a headache like mine!"

The door slammed behind her, and her shield went up.

Minutes later Kusac followed her into the hall, noticing that Sevrin was gone. Muttering darkly, he went to the bedroom to find his spare jacket. In the pocket were the pills Vanna had given him when they first came on board the *Khalossa*. He needed one for the headache their angry exchange had left him with. Getting a glass of water from the bathroom, he swallowed the tablet and returned to lie down on the bed.

He knew he'd mishandled it badly, and that wasn't like him. Come to think of it, Carrie's reaction was equally unlike her. If he was being honest, his anger was with the guild, not her. Feeling through their Link, he tried to reach her, but she'd put up a barrier, the same one she'd had before they'd become lovers. Now he was angry with her. There was no need to take it that far. That was childish, not the behavior expected of a female, even one several years his junior.

He lay there with his head pounding, feeling angry and sorry for himself in turns. He knew that at least half of the headache was due to the fact he'd let himself get so wound up.

A knock sounded at the door. "Come in," he said.

It was Sevrin. "I'm afraid I lost her, sir," he said apologetically.

"Lost who?" Kusac asked, pushing himself up enough to peer at him.

"The Liegena, sir. She went out, so I followed her. She took the elevator down to the fourteenth level, and then she started running and dodging between people. That's when I lost her."

Kusac sat up quickly, wincing at the pain his sudden movement caused. "Then get out there and find her!" he growled. "Take Meral with you and don't come back without her. She's never been down as far as the troop levels before. The God knows what could happen to her!"

"What about you, sir? We can't leave you on your own."

"I'm not going anywhere with this headache, I can't even see straight. Now go!"

* * *

She knew that she'd lost Sevrin almost as soon as she'd gotten out of the elevator, but she kept running until she couldn't go any farther. She stopped at last, chest heaving in an effort to catch her breath as she leaned against the corridor wall. The looks of naked curiosity from the passersby burned her with their intensity. Frantically she looked around for a familiar referent, but nothing was recognizable, not even the Sholans in their strange drab-brown uniforms. Pushing herself away from the wall, she walked on, forcing herself not to run, trying to look purposeful despite her mounting fear.

At the next intersection, cursive symbols were written on the walls but though she knew how to read, she couldn't make sense of them. The words in front of her remained alien. Everything down here smelled and sounded different; strange odors combined with the half-familiar scents of oil and grease. Suddenly the corridor was full of people, all chattering at once and jostling shoulders with each other as they pushed past her. Those few who noticed her stopped to stare in open surprise.

Trapped against the wall by this living tide of beings, real panic began to take hold of her. The audible noise they were making was as nothing compared to what their minds were generating inside her head. She had to get away! They were so large they wouldn't see her, she'd be crushed alive! Then someone bumped into her and as he turned round to apologize, what was left of her self-control snapped.

Terror took hold of her as, bodily pushing people aside, she began to run again, desperate to see an open space among this crowd, desperate for some silence inside her head. Their verbal and mental outrage at being treated so thoughtlessly followed her as she fled round the corner—only to crash straight into a tall male.

"Hey!" he said, making a grab for her as she stumbled against him. "What are you doing down here? Are you lost or something?"

She pulled free, turning frightened eyes up at him as she backed away.

"You're the Terran telepath," he said, understanding dawning on his face as he touched the Leska symbol on her purple tunic.

Carrie turned and fled. All around her Sholans were changing shifts and this corridor was as crowded as the other had been.

"Get out of my way!" she screamed, using her fists to pummel her way through them while ignoring their enraged exclamations.

An arm reached out and tried to bar her way. Trying to dodge past, she lost her footing and as she fell, strong hands grasped her and pulled her up. She began to scream, struggling to escape. The arms pulled her closer, wrapping around her threshing limbs in an effort to contain her and hold her still.

She continued to scream and struggle, turning her head in an attempt to bite at the restraining arms. He smelled of stale air, and sweat. Around them the other Sholans moved aside, giving them plenty of space. They didn't want to get involved.

As her teeth caught his forearm and sank into his flesh, he cursed. This was getting him nowhere. She was beyond reason, utterly hysterical. He had to get her out of the corridor before someone else decided to intervene. Thank the Gods there was somebody he knew on this level. It wasn't the ideal place, but it was better than trying to make it up to his room.

He grunted in pain as he tried to shake his arm free. No good; he needed to get her mouth open first. Lifting his feral bundle, he took advantage of the clear space around them to head for corridor nine.

* * *

Rhuso sat in front of his comm, waiting for the Mentor to answer his call.

"Rhuso," she said as her image came on screen. "I've been expecting you. Have you spoken to him?"

"Yes, Mentor, I've spoken to him."

"And what is your conclusion?"

Rhuso sighed. "It's as you said. He conceals all his thoughts behind a shield. It could be penetrated, but not without alerting him."

"And his attitude to our worries?"

"Your worries, Mentor, not mine," said Rhuso. "I still believe he can control her."

"What was his attitude?" insisted Mnya.

"Angry, as I said he would be. What did you expect, Mentor? Absolute compliance from him? He'd hardly be a fit heir to the Clans if he didn't question us and make up his own mind."

"Did he accept our authority over him and his Leska?"

"Eventually, Mentor. I must remind you that since he came here to escape from his future as heir, he has nothing to lose. Force will get us nowhere with him. You worry about her strength of will, yet you forget his."

"I forget nothing, Rhuso," said the Mentor coldly. "While he will still obey the Guild, I have to bind him to us as best I can. He knows the truth of what we're telling him. She needs to be taught. If she isn't, apart from the dangers she presents to others, he'll become tired of her lack of knowledge. They need to be equals, not teacher and pupil. By insisting that we train her, we're relieving him of the responsibility. I don't think he's likely to miss that point."

"I hope you're right, Mentor," said Rhuso.

* * *

She felt the pressure on the seat beside her and looked up from her comp notepad.

"Mind if I join you?" he asked, putting his mug down on the table.

Somewhat taken aback, Mito didn't have a ready reply.

"Thought you wouldn't mind," he said confidently. "I feel as if I know you already, I've heard so much about you from your friends."

Mito sat back and gave him a long look. He was one of the ground troops from the color of his jacket. They didn't usually come into this mess, and he looked like he'd recently been in a fight.

"You've got the wrong person," she said abruptly, returning to her notepad.

"I don't think so," he said. "My name's Rrael, and you're Mito, right?"

"Your company's unwelcome," she said, not lifting her head up from what she was reading. "Go and sit elsewhere."

"That's not very nice," he said, putting his hand over her pad. "Maikoe said you were a lot friendlier than that. So did Chyad."

Instinctively her ears gave a flick to the side in sudden fear, and she looked up at him again.

He nodded. "That's right. I knew you were Mito. It's good to mourn the passing of friends, but if you can do something to make sure they haven't been forgotten, that's even better, isn't it, Mito? And I know you won't want to forget them."

She heard the implicit threat in his voice as his fingers moved over her pad keyboard.

"I'll see you in here tomorrow at the same time," he said, moving his hand away. "Don't forget. I'd hate to have to go all the way up to your room on the twenty-seventh floor to find you." He slid out from behind the table. "See you tomorrow."

Mito sat unmoving till he left the mess. She looked down at her pad. On it his words glowed. "Message from *Rhyaki* due in your bridge shift twenty-fifth hour tonight."

* * *

In their suite, Kusac's eyes flew open as Carrie's terror flared through her barrier to reach him. Then there was silence again. He sat up, ignoring the pain as he tried to reach her. Nothing. Where was she? What had happened to her?

Crawling out of bed, he made his way to the comm in the lounge.

* * *

Meral and Sevrin left at a run, heading for the elevator down to the fourteenth floor. Once in it, Meral thumbed his communicator.

"Have you alerted Security?"

"Not yet," said Sevrin. "I wanted to tell our Liegen first."

"You've a lot to learn," growled Meral, activating his unit. "Unit one to security. We have a code amber. I repeat, a code amber."

"Repeat that message, unit one," said the voice at the other end of his device.

"Code amber, security."

"Draz here. What's your location?"

"Elevator from the Ambassadorial level to deck fourteen."

"We'll meet you there. Draz out."

The doors finally parted. Draz was waiting with a team of ten males. "Which way did she go?" he asked.

"Down there," said Sevrin, pointing off to the right. "I followed her as far as the first junction then lost her."

"You two take corridors three through nine," said Draz, pointing to his people. "You, corridors two through thirty, ten through sixteen, seventeen through twenty-three. You two," he said to the last pair, "cover the other two elevators. Get to it."

They left at a run.

Draz turned to them. "I take it the Liegen doesn't know where she is."

"No," said Sevrin, looking briefly at Meral. "They had a row, and she left. He's lying down with a headache."

Draz looked quizzically at Meral.

"He'd been to see his Guild Tutor," said Meral. "I'm sure it was something to do with that."

"If he doesn't know where she is, then the chances are none of the other telepaths will be able to locate her either."

"I don't think the Liegen would thank us if we involved their guild," said Meral.

"There doesn't seem to be any point at the moment," said Draz. "Right, let's go back to where you lost her."

* * *

She was unable to shriek with her mouth full of his arm. That, at least, was a blessing! Her cry was piercing to say the least. The door was open as always, and for a wonder, the temple seemed empty. The lighting was still down low and the incense lay heavy in the air, resisting the attempts of the purifiers to disperse it. A service must just have finished. He tried to enter but somehow she managed to get an arm free and grab hold of the doorjamb. She hung on grimly while her teeth tightened on his arm.

He growled in annoyance, risking letting go of her with one arm so he could prise at her fingers.

Her teeth bit deeper, and his growl turned to a yelp as he jerked her hand free and stumbled into the room.

"Dzaka, where the hell are you?" he called. "Shut the damned door and get these bloody lights raised! I need your help!"

Startled, Dzaka appeared silhouetted against the light from his inner room. Sizing up the situation, he keyed the outer door shut from the control panel beside him, then raised the light level.

"The Terran?"

"Later. Give me a hand, for the God's sake!" he said as his feral bundle began to kick and struggle again.

The meditation mats were still out and Dzaka headed over to them, piling a couple of them together. "Put her down here," he said brusquely.

Still attached to her, he knelt down and dumped her on the makeshift bed. "Let go, you stupid female," he growled, trying to force her mouth apart with his other hand. He yelped again as she bit down on his fingers. Her eyes were wild and staring, she was beyond sense.

A band suddenly seemed to form around his throat and start to tighten; he began to choke and gasp for air. No time to mess about. Making a fist of his free hand, he drew it back and took careful aim.

Their search was hampered by the movements of personnel from work stations to leisure activities. Of those asked, no one had seen anything.

"Where would she have gone, Sevrin?" demanded Draz. "Who does she know? Who'd she go and visit if she was upset?"

"Vanna's the only one she knows," said Sevrin.

Draz pressed his communicator. "Unit three, go to level twenty-seven. Secure the exterior of the medical section. No one to enter or leave till I get there."

"Unit three complying."

"Would she go to the Terrans?" asked Draz as they loped round to the nearest elevator.

"She doesn't know where they are," replied Meral. "The Liegen wants them kept away from her because of their attitude to their Link."

Draz growled softly as they got in. "Why these Terrans think they have a right to interfere in other people's lives is beyond me. This should be a matter for them and no one else."

Meral glanced at Sevrin and grinned briefly.

They skidded to a halt outside the medical unit.

"No one's been in or out, sir," said one of the males on guard.

Draz nodded. "Keep a watch for her. Permit entry and exit again."

They headed into the reception area.

"Just what do you think you're doing, Sub-Lieutenant Draz?" demanded the senior nurse on duty. "What's the meaning of this intrusion?"

"Is Physician Vanna Kyjishi on duty?" demanded Draz.

"I've no idea," he snapped. "Physician Kyjishi was removed from the duty roster several days ago. She has her own lab with its own entrance."

"Is she in the medical facility?"

"You'll have to go and look."

"You're not exactly being helpful," growled Draz. "Where's her lab?"

"Down the corridor, second right, along to the end and on the left."

Meral and Sevrin hurried after him, following him into the lab. A nurse sat on duty at the station. He looked up as they entered.

"Vanna here?" demanded Draz.

"No, sir. Only myself and the patient in the next room."

When Draz opened the door, Kaid was already sitting on the side of his bed. "What's up?" he demanded.

"The human female's missing," said Draz. "They had a row and she ran off. Any idea where she might have gone?"

"Who's with Kusac?"

"No one," said Meral. "He ordered us both out to find her. He's flat on his back with a headache. I think she's blocked him out again."

"Dammit! Do I have to see to everything myself?" Kaid demanded as he pushed himself to his feet. "One of you get back up there with him. I don't want him left alone for a minute. I thought I made that clear from the outset."

"If you'll pardon the observation, I think you'd be better going up to Kusac," said Meral, noticing how Kaid was already favoring his injured leg.

Kaid gave him a measured look. "Right. I'll see to Kusac. You check Vanna's room, see if she's there. I take it Carrie went missing on this level?"

"No, on the fourteenth," said Draz.

"Get back down there and check the mess on that level, then check the concourse and the Terran quarters. Contact the Mentor and alert her as to what's happened. Even if the other telepaths can't pick her up, they can report in to her if Carrie is in sight. As a last resort, check her father's suite and the Clan Leader's."

"Can you make it up to the Ambassadorial level?" asked Draz, looking at the way Kaid limped round to the other side of the bed to retrieve his clothes.

"I'll manage. You get going," he said grimly, putting one arm then the other through the sleeves of his robe. Leaving it hanging open in front, he limped through the door after them.

* * *

Kusac was still sitting at the comm when he felt the sudden surge of power pass through him. Not the gestalt again! He felt it grip his mind, this time only tugging at him mentally until briefly they merged, then everything went dark and quiet. Frantic, he got to his feet. What the hell was happening to her to make her so terrified that it triggered the gestalt? He had to find her.

Trying to convince himself that his head felt better, he attempted to walk slowly across the room to the door. Each step made him feel more nauseous as it jarred his aching head. Screwing his eyes up against the light, he opened the door, heading slowly down the hallway. He stopped halfway, knowing he was kidding himself. He wasn't fit to be up on his feet, let alone take part in a search.

His stomach finally began to rebel and he turned, stumbling blindly for the kitchen.

That was where Kaid found him several minutes later, hanging onto the food preparation sink and looking and feeling utterly wretched, his hands slick with sweat.

Kusac looked myopically at him as he entered. "You shouldn't be up," he said.

"Neither should you," Kaid replied, limping across to him. "What caused the sickness? Her blocking your Link?" He turned to the tap and picking up a mug, filled it for him.

"No. She forgets to shield," he said, taking the drink thankfully. "And when she's angry or upset, it causes the headaches. This one is the worst yet." He drank deeply, then put the mug down.

"It's all right when she's experiencing pleasure, I expect," said Kaid with a slight flick of his ears.

Kusac began to grin. "Not so bad," he admitted. "It has its up side too."

"How's the head now?"

"Better," he said, straightening up. "Not good, but better."

"Do you want to lie down?"

"I can't rest. Let's go back to the lounge," he said, offering Kaid a steadying arm.

"Have you picked anything up that might give us a clue as to where she is?"

"She was terrified, that I felt. It triggered the gestalt again, but seconds later, everything went silent. Someone's got her. I saw a room with some kind of a bed in it, then she blacked out. I think she's unconscious. We've got to find her, Kaid," he said urgently.

"They'll find her," said Kaid confidently, opening the lounge door. "Even if they have to do a room by room search, they'll find her."

They made their way over to the settee and collapsed there, their mutual infirmities drawing a grin from both of them despite the circumstances.

"Do you want to tell me what happened?" asked Kaid. "It might help to work out where she was headed."

* * *

Dzaka crouched beside the human female. Garras was calling Vanna. He had her to himself for the moment. Reaching out, he pressed a hand to her neck, checking the pulse. Slow and steady, the rhythm the same as a Sholan's. He saw the torc. The Aldatan cub's intentions were serious, then. It might have been easier to deal with them both had they not been emotionally attached to each other. As it was, given his age, Kusac was likely to be somewhat irrational in his defense of her. He sighed. Then there was his family. Kusac wasn't exactly the sort of person who could disappear without causing a ripple, nor was he the sort of person whose every move wouldn't be watched by the media-nets back on Shola.

Her attempt to strangle Garras had him seriously concerned. That was a Talent destined to cause a disaster, especially if she couldn't control it. He wasn't sure which was potentially more dangerous, her lack of control, or the possibility that she would develop it.

He glanced toward the door. Garras was still busy. There was time for him to solve that problem now. His hand slipped easily round her throat. Just a little pressure in the same area as the already livid bruises and it was over, for both of them. No further need for concern over her strange mental talents, or their ability to fight. He might never have another chance. Unconscious as she was now, she couldn't stop him. If he left it till later, the result could be a battle which he might not survive.

This was the first time he'd seen her close up. Kaid, at least, had been observing them for several days. Like him, he couldn't yet form even a basic conclusion regarding their outlook or their talents. Of the two, perhaps their outlook was more important. While he hesitated, Garras came out of the inner room. Dzaka removed his hand and stood up, moving away to sit on the plinth of the statue.

Garras pressed the towel more firmly against his arm. The wound was still bleeding copiously despite Dzaka's cold water treatment. Who'd have thought she'd have teeth capable of inflicting so deep an injury? He looked down at where she lay sprawled on the mats. He'd tried to place her in a comfortable position, but he didn't know enough about Terran anatomy.

"So this is the Terran all the excitement is about," Dzaka observed from his perch.

Garras nodded, still watching her.

She lay there, her chest rising and falling faintly with her shallow breathing. He'd have been gentler had he known she was pregnant. He frowned, surprised he hadn't heard about her condition. Crouching down, he touched her jaw carefully with his hand. Already an angry bruise was beginning to form. He hadn't realized her skin was so fragile. Remembering the feel of her in his arms as she struggled against him, and the smell of her scent, he could understand the appeal this human female held for Sholan males. He wasn't unmoved by her himself. His hand strayed down to the torc that nestled at the base of her throat. Maybe the lad had more sense than anyone credited him with.

Standing up, he turned around, and, still keeping the pressure on his wounded arm, he joined Dzaka.

"She needs your help," he said abruptly. "She was so terrified even I could feel her fear."

Dzaka stirred, changing his position so he could see her better. "I don't know that I can help," he said. "I need to know what caused her to be so afraid that she tried to strangle you. Her talent is dangerous, you realize that?"

"Don't confuse her with Sholan telepaths," said Garras. "She can, and will fight as I've found out to my cost," he said, looking down at the towel that was slowly becoming dark with blood. "But I don't think she realized what she was doing. It was an unthinking reaction to a situation in which she felt utterly helpless."

"Has she ever done this before?"

He shook his head. "Never. She's alone here, Dzaka, isolated from her own kind because of her fear of their reaction to her Link with Kusac. She needs to learn to cope with that fear. You can help her do that. You're obviously running meditation services here, which means you're authorized to teach."

"I can only help her if she'll cooperate with me," he said, "and if their minds work the same way ours do."

"At least give it a try."

Dzaka sighed. "We'll see."

Draz's call to Vanna's room had proved futile, the same with her personal pager: she'd turned it off. The Terrans had seen nothing of Carrie either. Draz had just received a call from Kaid asking him to avoid contacting the guild and the

Clan Leader if at all possible. Working on the premise that they would have contacted Kusac if they'd been aware of her, Draz was prepared to leave them for the present. He dispatched his men to check out the levels above and below.

The towel was a bloody rag by the time the door went. "Who is it?"

"It's me, Vanna Kyjishi," came the answer.

He opened the door and stepped aside for her to enter.

"What's all this ... Gods, what happened to you, Garras?" she said, catching sight of him standing beyond Dzaka. She pushed past the Brother, anxious to reach him. "Sit down and let me see to it." Then she saw Carrie lying on the mats.

"Just what the hell's been going on here?" she demanded, going instantly to the human girl's side.

"She's just unconscious, Vanna," said Garras, his ears twitching as he tried to prevent them from lying backward along his skull. "I found her down on this level when I came off duty. She was hysterical. I had to do something."

Obviously satisfied by her quick examination of Carrie, Vanna left her to return to Garras. "Tell me about it while I see to your arm," she said, placing her medikit on the floor. "And it better be good!"

Garras sat down on the plinth again, resting his arm on his thighs.

Squatting on her heels, Vanna carefully unwrapped the towel. Blood was still oozing from the crescent-shaped wound.

She glanced up at Dzaka. "Fetch me another towel, please."

When he handed it to her, she placed it under Garras' arm, discarding the soiled one. From her kit she pulled out a container of sterile water and some soft wool and began swabbing the wound carefully to see the full extent of the injury.

"Tell me what happened," she said, reaching for the coagulant spray.

"I'd just come off duty when I saw Carrie running toward me," he said, watching her begin to clip back the fur at the edges of the wound. "That's one hell of a deep bite."

"It is," she agreed, spraying an antibiotic over the whole area. "Carry on."

"I could see from her face that she was in a panic, so

when she drew level with me, I grabbed her. She went berserk, Vanna, laying into me with hands and feet—and teeth."

"So I see," she said, looking up at him before pulling a dressing and bandage out of her kit.

"I've never seen anyone so terrified," he said, glancing over to the girl's still form. "She'd gone feral. So I picked her up and brought her in here to get Dzaka's help."

"Another of your old friends?" she asked, not expecting an answer. "So why did you need to knock her out?" She finished tying off the bandage. "Try moving your arm."

"It's the damnedest thing, Vanna," he said slowly as he lifted his arm and flexed it carefully. "It's fine," he nodded. "I couldn't get her to let go of me, so I dumped her on the mats. As I tried to open her mouth, I began to feel as if I was being strangled. It was as if there was something tight around my neck. I knew she was doing it. There was nothing else I could do but . . ."

"Hit her on the jaw," finished Vanna.

He nodded. "Believe me, I wouldn't have done it if there was another way. Especially since she's pregnant."

Vanna looked at him sharply. "What?"

"Well, it's obvious, isn't it? I have to admit I would never have guessed if I hadn't held her."

Vanna's frown cleared. "She's not pregnant, Garras. Terran females are different from us, that's all."

Garras looked puzzled. "Are you sure?"

"Positive. I carried out the initial medical examination on her, remember? If she was pregnant, believe me, I'd know about it," she said, pulling her hypo gun out and loading it. "I'm giving you a large dose of a broad spectrum antibiotic, and an analgesic, just in case," she said, swabbing down his upper arm before triggering the drug. "You're also off duty for at least a week till that arm begins to heal." She packed the hypo away then got up. "Let's have a look at Carrie now."

She sat down beside the girl, reaching out gently and taking hold of her jaw. "You made a good job of that."

"I didn't realize she'd bruise so badly," he said apologetically.

"Well, she's still out cold," said Vanna, checking the girl's eyes to find the inner lids closed. "and likely to remain so for some time from the looks of her. Have you called Kusac yet to let him know where she is?"

Garras shook his head. "No. I thought it best to contact you first."

"I'd better give him a call. He'll be beside himself with worry. Have you a comm I can use?" she asked Dzaka.

"In the other room," he said, nodding toward it.

Getting up she went over to the room and sat down at Dzaka's desk. She switched on the comm, selecting the vidiphone channel, and keyed in Kusac's number.

The image resolved to show Kaid.

"What the hell are you doing out of bed?" she demanded, then shook her head. "Never mind, just get me Kusac."

Kaid's worried look cleared. "You've found her."

"Yes, we've got her. She's here at the temple with Garras and me. What happened to make her leave there on her own?"

"They had a row," said Kaid. "I've just persuaded Kusac to lie down again because of his headache, and I don't want to disturb him yet. How is she?"

"Unconscious. Garras had to knock her out she was so hysterical. Beyond that, she appears to be fine. Garras wasn't so lucky. She took a chunk out of his arm."

Kaid's eye ridges went up. "She's a fighter," he said.

"I could have told you that," said Vanna. "What's wrong with Kusac? He isn't unconscious, too, is he?"

"No, just sleeping. Give me a moment to contact Draz and call off the search," he said, moving aside from the screen. He was back a moment later.

"This morning Carrie was involved in an abortive attempt to question a captive Valtegan. Afterward she let rip at the Mentor for criticizing the way she'd handled the situation. Then this afternoon Kusac was called down to his Tutor's where pressure was put on him to make Carrie toe the guild line and turn up for training, or else," said Kaid. "The Mentor's concerned that Carrie's undisciplined Talent and bad attitude is a danger to the guild, which is why she wants her brought in line."

"What the hell is the Mentor playing at?" Vanna asked angrily. "I gave her a copy of the current medical data on them both and took the trouble to explain it personally to her. She knows their endocrine levels are in flux at the moment! They can't handle the stress of this sort of pressure! Tell Kusac she's safe here with us. We'll bring her back when she comes round, but I want to talk to her first."

"Oh, almost forgot. Kusac says the gestalt triggered for a few seconds, then she became unconscious."

Vanna nodded. "I'll sort it out from this end. Tell him that he can call her if he wants, but to leave it for about an hour. How's his headache?"

"He took one of the pills you gave him a few days ago, but since then he's thrown up. He seems a little better, but I convinced him it would be wise to lie down."

"I'll turn my pager on. If you need me, call."

Kaid nodded, and she cut the connection.

She turned round to face Garras. "I want a word with you in private," she said.

He followed her to the door and stepped outside. "What is it?"

"Why bring her here? I don't like you involving the Brotherhood, Garras."

"There wasn't anywhere else I could take her, Vanna," he said reasonably. "There's nothing wrong with Dzaka. If I hadn't had to knock her out, he'd have been the ideal person to help her lie down."

"I don't like it, Garras. The Brothers have always been a two-edged benefit that can go either way. I'm afraid for Carrie."

"Look, I'm here, don't worry. I wouldn't let anything happen to her."

"I have to go. Just watch her well because I don't trust Dzaka. She's likely to be out for another hour at least. Can you cope? I have a few words I want to say to Rhuso and Mnya," she said grimly.

"We'll be fine," he said.

"Make sure that if she wakes she can't get out. I don't want us to be chasing her all over the ship again."

"Vanna," said Garras, catching her by the arm. "I didn't know Terrans went feral with fear."

"They don't, as far as I know," she said quietly.

As Garras closed the door behind her, Dzaka got up. "Would you like a c'shar?"

"Please," he said tiredly, returning to his seat on the plinth. He leaned back against the God's knee, glad now for the analgesic Vanna had given him. "You do remember me, don't you, Dzaka? You were a lot younger when we last met."

"Of course. After you left, Kaid was never quite the same. He lost something," he said, coming to the doorway.

Garras grunted, detecting the faint hint of censure. "You know the rules concerning anyone who has to leave the Brotherhood for Clan reasons. They cease to exist outside Stronghold. Those who remain can't have ties to anyone outside." He moved his arm, trying to make it more comfortable.

"I knew Ghezu would give Kaid orders concerning these two," he nodded toward where Carrie lay. "It was a chance I had to take when I called him in to guard them, but I trust his judgment. Don't preempt him, Dzaka," he said, the warning implicit in his tone.

"You called him in?" Dzaka leaned against the door jamb.

"Yes." He turned his head to look at the younger male, noticing the faint creasing of the skin around his nose. "Kaid and I worked together for eight years before you were found. We go back a long way. How does it go? 'Observe, assess, recruit or destroy'? Rogue telepaths always attract the Brotherhood's specialists, so who better to protect them?" He noticed with amusement Dzaka's slight discomfort at the description. Still young enough to have illusions, then.

"I'm not having a group of younglings fresh from their mother's last grooming use their deaths to make a political statement. I also don't want them sacrificed for the Telepath Guild's peace of mind. They're decent people, Dzaka, they only want to be left alone."

"I'm sure Kaid will make the right decision," murmured Dzaka, returning to his c'shar making.

Vanna headed up to the Telepath Guild's office on the twenty-fifth level. "Is the Mentor in?" she asked the secretary.

"Yes, but you have to have an appointment to see her," he replied. "Hey! You can't just walk in like that!" he said as Vanna walked past him to open the door to the inner office.

"Watch me," she said over her shoulder.

Startled, Mnya stood up as soon as she entered. "Vanna," she said. "This is a surprise."

"It shouldn't be," said Vanna. "I could understand your actions if I hadn't made a point of explaining my findings to you in person, but considering I did, your blatant lack of concern for these two people's physical and mental health is beyond my understanding. Why the hell couldn't you have waited a few more days before demanding she attend training classes? Or couldn't you have framed it as a request rather than a poorly veiled threat?"

"Physician Vanna," said Mnya stiffly, "in my opinion . . ."

"Bugger your opinion!" said the enraged Vanna. "How dare you go against my medical advice? I've every intention of reporting this to the Commander! I specifically said they were not to be put under any form of stress for the next few weeks until I gave the all clear. Not only are they at a vulnerable point in their relationship, but Carrie has to cope with the immense problem of leaving her Clan behind to make a new life amongst us. She's faced with prejudice from her own people, including her father, and now pressure from Kusac to conform to our ways because of you!"

"I think you're overreacting, Physician . . ."

"Am I! They both need a period of adjustment, not only to get used to each other, but for Carrie to get used to our way of life. You shouldn't even have involved her in questioning the Valtegan today! How much more plainly can I say it? Their moods are unstable, their adrenaline levels are unstable, they cannot function properly until their systems level out! For the Gods' sake, give them a chance! I've found Carrie cooperative, helpful, and understanding. If you can't find those qualities in her, then perhaps it's you who are approaching her in the wrong way. As for being afraid of her talents, I'll bet you she's more afraid than you could ever be!"

"Have you quite finished?" asked Mnya, her face and tone frozen.

"Yes, thank you," said Vanna, turning and marching out.

A chuckle came from the comm as Mnya stared angrily at the door.

"It seems they already have friends ready to Challenge for them."

Mnya schooled her features into impassivity before she sat down. "My apologies, Master Esken," she said to the elderly Sholan on the vidiphone link. "Physician Kyjishi just rushed in unannounced."

"Her comments were worthwhile, Mnya," he said. "I think that now is too early for you to make a judgment on them. From what she said there are sound medical reasons for the Keissian human's behavior. I appreciate you had to take advantage of the moment, but it would have been wiser, in hindsight, not to have involved our unique Leska pair in questioning the Valtegan. Send me a copy of Physician Kyjishi's report and in the interim, treat them both gently. If she turns up for training, all well and good. If not, send Rhuso to her and let Kusac remain in the same room. I want to be able to study them here at Valsgarth, not have to have one or both of them hospitalized through excess stress."

"I only did what I considered appropriate, Guild Master," said Mnya stiffly.

"I am fully appreciative of your efforts, Mnya," he said gently. "You have put Rhuso in charge of her, now let him do his job. I have to go now, I'm afraid. High Command is restricting the time allowed for essential communications. It was difficult enough to get permission to speak to you at all. Konis Aldatan says AlRel expects the communications block to be lifted within a week. I'll hear from you then."

"Guild Master," she said as the screen changed to show the Allied Worlds logo.

Guild Master Esken sat for a moment regarding the blank screen of his comm. From the moment he'd heard that Kusac Aldatan was the Sholan telepath involved in this cross-species link, he knew there'd be problems. Still, if the Brotherhood passed him, then when they arrived at Valsgarth, there would still be time to make sure they remained true to the guild.

He scratched behind his ear thoughtfully. If he remembered correctly, Kusac had always been one of the quieter students, never exhibiting any rash behavior—until he left home, that was. He sighed, knowing there was no easy solution to his problem. The impact of another telepathic species on their culture couldn't be gauged, even without the added complication of Carrie's and Kusac's Link. He just prayed that it wouldn't awaken the old fears of telepaths.

His thoughts were interrupted by a knock at the door. Senior Tutor Sorli poked his head round. "Master Esken, there's been another find over at the Chazoun Guild. Their Mentor has just notified us."

Esken nodded. "Tell Mentor Khoenga to dispatch his priest and attendants to bless the site as usual. Make sure they check the explosives are laid to destroy all the artifacts this time. Too many of them are being recovered and falling into the wrong hands."

"The excavators are too afraid of the God to steal from the ruins, Master," said Sorli. "I hardly think . . ."

"Some artifacts are turning up," interrupted Esken. "I don't know who's taking them, nor do I particularly care at this moment in time. I merely want it to stop. If the charges are properly laid, then the ruins will be destroyed but the refined metals will remain salvageable. Just see to it, Sorli."

"Yes Master Esken."

* * *

As Vanna rode the elevator to the Admin level, she checked her wrist unit. She'd have to hurry.

As luck would have it, Myak was in the Commander's outer office. "Myak," she said, "I want a word with you."

"Certainly, Physician Kyjishi," he said. "Would it be to do with the Mentor and Kusac?"

Vanna frowned. "Has she been in touch with you already?"

Myak made a noncommittal gesture.

"Fine. Now you can hear my side of it," she said.

* * *

Carrie moaned, putting her hand up to her jaw as she opened her eyes. Her sense of smell, almost as acute as Kusac's now, had already told her she was in an unfamiliar place. She moved her head slowly till she saw the statue with the weapons round its feet. Then she remembered.

Lurching to her feet, she tried to reach the door as simultaneously she sent out a mental cry for help, trying desperately to find a mind she recognized.

Before she'd taken more than two steps, a strange male, one she'd never seen before, was blocking the door. She didn't notice the plain black robe, all she saw was the gray brindled fur, and the green eyes set in a narrow face. Her mind screamed, *Wolf!* She opened her mouth to cry out, then someone touched her from behind.

As she whirled round, Garras felt his mind being probed and winced in pain. "You're going to have to learn to be more gentle, Carrie," he said, his hand closing firmly on her arm.

He could feel the stiffness suddenly leave her body as she recognized him.

"That's what Kusac says."

"Well, he's right," he said candidly. "That was painful."

"I'm sorry," she said. "Where am I, Garras? Who's he?" She indicated the male behind her.

"You're at the temple on level fourteen. That's Dzaka, the lay priest in charge."

"How did I get here? The last thing I remember is someone grabbing me. Oh," she said, as she saw Garras' bandage. "Your arm."

"I brought you here, and don't let anyone ever tell you that you haven't got sharp teeth," said Garras, his mouth opening in a faint grin.

"I'm sorry," she said, her face taking on a stricken look that even Garras recognized. "I didn't realize it was you." She put a tentative hand up to her jaw.

"Don't worry about me, it wasn't serious. Sit down, I want you to meet Dzaka properly," he said, letting her go and indicating the mat beside them.

Dzaka left the outer door and came over to squat down beside them. He held out his hand, palm uppermost, to her.

"I'm Dzaka," he said. "You're Carrie Hamilton."

Carrie touched his fingertips with hers, acknowledging the introduction with a flick of her head to one side.

"I'm a member of the Brotherhood of Vartra. The statue that you see is of Him. Garras brought you here because you were so frightened. He's asked me to help you."

Garras leaned toward her. "What got you so frightened, Carrie? Was it something someone said or did to you?"

"No, nothing like that," she said, keeping her eyes focussed on her hands. "I just needed to get away from everyone, be on my own for a little while. Then I got lost."

"Didn't you see the directions written on every corridor?" asked Garras.

She looked up. "Yes, I saw them, Garras, but I can't read them! No one's taught me to read yet!"

"I thought you knew everything Kusac knows," said Dzaka.

She turned to look at him. "I do, but I can't use it until I've learned how. The corridors were so busy, and everyone was looking at me—when they noticed I was there. You're all so tall! People kept bumping into me. I was afraid I'd get crushed."

Garras could hear the panic in her voice and reached out to touch her hand. "You're safe now. We're waiting for Vanna to return, then we'll take you back up to the Ambassadorial level."

"You arrived on level fourteen at the shift change, Carrie," said Dzaka. "Level fourteen is the dividing line between the starship and pilot crews and the troopers below us. Were they mainly wearing brown uniforms?"

She nodded.

"I expect you've only seen the areas of the ship that V.I.P.s get to see—the concourse and the Ambassadorial levels where you live now."

"And the Admin level," said Garras.

"Exactly. You've only seen the leisure areas of the *Khalossa*, not the working areas. That's why it was so unfamiliar." He shifted, making himself more comfortable. "Vanna told us this is a bad time for you at the moment. You're suffering from all the stress caused by a new environment, a new relationship, and a new Talent. Any one of those is enough at a time, but to have all three together! That's when you need some help, and Garras has asked me to see what I can do for you."

Garras sat back and listened to them. Dzaka might still be young and idealistic, but he was good at what he did. He was giving her no half measures.

"Vartra teaches us personal responsibility for our thoughts and our actions. Being a Telepath, you know thoughts are as good as actions, don't you? We teach meditation techniques that help to control the mind in moments of stress or pain. If you'd be willing to come here once a day, then I could teach you these techniques."

"Would there be other people around?"

"No. I have times, like now, when I can close the temple to others for an hour or two," said Dzaka.

"Yes, I'd like to come," she said, glancing in Garras' direction for his approval.

Fifteen minutes later, with a satisfied look on her face and a promise from Myak to get the Commander to sanction her orders regarding Kusac and Carrie, Vanna headed back to the temple.

"You timed it well," Garras said in a low voice as he let her in. "Dzaka's just finished teaching her a meditation exercise to help her calm down. How did it go with the Mentor and the Commander?"

"Fine," said Vanna. "I told the Mentor exactly what I thought of her, then reported her actions to the Commander through Myak. I've got his backing and a promise he'll see the Commander talks to Mnya and Rhuso."

"Good. Now, what do you want us to do? Make ourselves scarce while you talk to her?"

"What's the point?" she asked dryly, looking over to where Carrie and Dzaka sat talking. "You could get a protein drink for us. I haven't had time to eat, and I'll wager you didn't bother to feed Carrie."

Dzaka excused himself as Vanna joined them. "I've some business I need to attend to," he said. "If I'm not back before you leave, just close the door behind you."

"Well, cub," said Vanna, sitting down beside her. "What put the wind under your tail and made you run away like that?"

"Nothing really," Carrie said evasively, taking a drink from Garras.

"You had a row, didn't you? Come on, you can talk to us, you know. Everyone needs friends. We're here to help," said Vanna, touching her cheek fleetingly for reassurance.

Carrie sighed. "Everyone assumes that because I have a Link with Kusac that I know everything he does. I don't. It's there, yes, but until someone tells me about it, I can't remember!" she said. "I've been pushed in the deep end too soon, Vanna. They expect me to know everything when I don't even know the basics. Kusac complains because I forget to keep my shield up, but it's all new, even that. I can't cope with it all at once! I don't belong here, I just don't fit in."

Her cup began to shake and Vanna hastily reached out to rescue it, putting it and hers down on the floor. She wrapped her arms around Carrie, pulling her close.

"Hey, don't talk like that," she said. "You'll fit in fine once you get used to us. Remember, I told you that for the next few days you'd have mood swings? Well, this is one of them, just like Kusac had when he got angry. It has nothing to do with you, it's because of the chemical balances in your bodies."

"I just felt so isolated, Vanna," Carrie said, her voice muffled against the other's jacket. "Everything was suddenly strange and frightening. I don't want to be dependent on one person. What happens to me if Kusac changes his mind and doesn't want me living with him? Where do I go? What do I do?"

Vanna gave her a little shake. "Stop even thinking like that," she said sternly. "You must know how Kusac feels about you. Believe me, he has no intention of living without you beside him."

"How can you know that if I don't?" Carrie asked, sitting upright again.

"I know," Vanna said. "Trust me. He's spoken to me about what he feels for you. You've got absolutely nothing to worry about."

The comm chimed and Garras got up to answer it. He leaned out round the doorway. "It's Kusac," he said. "Do you want to take his call?"

Carrie looked at Vanna.

"Talk to him," Vanna whispered. "He's come to you this time."

Carrie got up and walked over to the other room. Garras moved out of her way, joining Vanna on the mat.

As she sat down at the desk, Carrie felt Kusac's mind reach for hers.

Cub, I'm sorry. If I come to fetch you, will you come home?

She hesitated, unsure what to say.

Carrie, it wasn't you I was angry with, it was the Mentor and Rhuso. I shouldn't have taken it out on you. I'm sorry. Let me come and fetch you.

She nodded. *Come soon.*

Kusac grinned. *Don't get too comfortable,* he sent as he signed off.

She got up and returned to Vanna and Garras. Garras lifted her drink up and handed it back to her.

"Thanks," she said. "Kusac's coming for me." Her hand went up to her face, feeling the swelling along the jawline. "Ouch. That's sore. What happened?"

Garras' ears flicked. "I'm afraid I had to knock you out you were so hysterical," he said. "I didn't realize how little it takes to make you bruise."

She gave a lopsided grin. "I suppose it's a fair exchange

for your bitten arm. I really am sorry about that. I don't even remember doing it."

"Don't worry about it. I'm just glad it was me who found you."

Carrie sat down and took a drink from her mug.

Garras reached out a hand to touch hers. "Don't ever feel that lonely again, Carrie," he said. "We all went through a lot together on Keiss. It makes me feel we're almost family. Don't forget I'm your friend as well."

Carrie smiled and reached out to gently touch his cheek, a gesture so Sholan it seemed natural until Vanna mentioned it to him later.

"Thank you," she said.

Vanna answered the door to Kusac, moving out into the corridor to speak to him in private.

"Kusac, I have to say this quickly. She's scared. Scared of us and of being without you. She's not adjusting as quickly as we thought. You've got to help her, Kusac. Watch for the mood swings in you both and make allowances. You've the training and experience to cope with it, use it."

"Vanna, I don't know what more to do," he said.

"Take her out among our people. Let her see life, don't spend all your time in that damned suite! She feels isolated. And why haven't you told her about the torc?"

He shook his head. "I had to give it to her too soon. I can't tell her yet."

"I think you should. She needs the security of knowing what it means." She felt the door move behind her. "Leave it for now. We'll speak later."

The door slid open as she turned round. "He's here, Carrie," she said, moving back into the room.

PART 2:

SHOLA

Chapter 10

Anxiously Mito paced her room, waiting for a call from her contact in Security. If it took much longer, she'd be on the bridge before she heard, and she'd have to take the message from the *Rhyaki*. Then the comm chimed. She rushed over to her desk and activated the unit. It was Personnel.

"Sorry to have taken so long to get back to you, Lieutenant, but I've been able to secure you an appointment in Medical. If you report there now, the on-duty medic will examine you for the records. Don't worry about missing your shift, I've allocated a replacement."

Baffled, Mito sat down and blinked at the secretary. She opened her mouth to speak, but she was forestalled.

"You look confused," said the secretary with a frown of concern. "These fevers can take you like that. Have you a companion who can accompany you?"

Mutely, Mito shook her head.

"Is there someone I can contact to join you there? You really shouldn't be on your own for the next twenty-six hours at least."

Then Mito realized what was happening. "Yes," she said with the faintest of grins. "I have a companion. One of the Keissian Terrans. Anders."

Why not? It was worth a try. Because the humans' movements about the ship were still restricted, she'd never had the chance to be alone with him. He was always pleasant to her, ready to accept her invitation to accompany her when she was involved in an outing with Carrie and Kusac. It wasn't exactly a lie. With any luck, he would be her companion shortly.

The young male turned his head, obviously listening to someone out of sight of the screen. Mito held her breath.

"We'll contact him, Lieutenant," he said, turning back to

her. "If he's agreeable, he'll meet you at the medical section."

Mito tried to rearrange her grin as she headed for the door. She was supposed to be suffering a fever, not celebrating.

When she arrived there, she was ushered straight into the physician's examination room.

"Good evening, Lieutenant," he said, scanning his comm. "Take a seat on the examination couch, I won't be a moment. Ah, yes, you were one of the crew that was stranded on Keiss for several weeks." He turned round to face her, getting to his feet.

"Right, open your mouth," he said and gave it a cursory look. "Yes, definitely inflamed. You can close it now." He felt the palms of her hands, then touched her nose. "Palms hot and nose dry; definitely signs of a fever." He turned back to his comm.

"I see your companion is human and has recently recovered from a dose of Terran flu. There's no doubt in my mind that you contracted it from him." He sat down and made an entry in her files. "You'll be quarantined in your quarters for the next five days, but that shouldn't be a problem for you since your companion will be with you. We don't want this flu to spread."

He turned to glance at her again. "Plenty of rest and plenty of fluids. You can eat what you fancy." He passed her a small container. "Take two of these every five hours if you have any aches in your joints or muscles. Come and see me again in five days." Nodding to her, he turned back to his comm.

Dazed, Mito slid off the couch and with a quiet "Thank you," left his room for the waiting area. She barely noticed Anders hurrying over to her.

"What's the matter?" he asked, his tone concerned as he took her by the arm. "They said you were ill and would I come down to Medical to look after you."

Her eyes focused on him and with great presence of mind, she leaned against him. "Thank you for coming," she said in a faint voice. "I didn't know who else to call."

"Don't be silly," he said, supporting her as they made their way slowly to the elevator. "I'm glad I could help."

* * *

The door of her room safely shut behind them, Mito let go of his arm and stood up. Across from her a red light blinked on her comm. Hurriedly, she crossed over to it, switched it on, and keyed in the command to download a hard copy.

"The dispenser is over there," she said, pointing to a covered hatch in the wall beyond her. "Why don't you get us a couple of coffees?" She turned her attention back to the comm.

It was his turn to be baffled, but realizing that there had to be a good reason for her deception, and that he was likely to find out sooner rather than later if he played along with her, he fetched the coffees. He put hers on the desk.

"Thanks," she said, taking the mug and handing him a sheet of paper. "This is for you. It should explain everything."

She watched him read the document through twice before he put it aside.

"Five days' quarantine," he said, "for Terran flu, which I, as your companion, am supposed to have given you."

She nodded.

He finished his drink, putting the mug down by her full one.

"A companion is . . . ?"

"Your partner of the moment."

"Uh. I presume since I haven't been ill, that neither are you."

She shook her head.

"Do I get to know what the security reasons for this are? No? I thought not. Well, five days off is five days off," he said with a slight smile. "It gives me a chance to . . ."

"No more questions about Shola!" she said in mock exasperation, reaching forward to touch his face. "There are things about you I'd like to know."

Anders' arm went round her waist, gently pulling her closer while his other hand stroked her cheek. "I was only going to say it gives me a chance to get to know you better," he said quietly.

The following day Vanna called the suite to speak to Kusac. She got Kaid instead.

"They're out at present," he said. "She's seeing Tutor Rhuso, and he's with his mother."

Vanna grunted. "Well, let's hope Rhuso's less heavy-handed this time. How did things go last night after they got back?"

"I believe they sat up late talking. This morning they both seemed more relaxed. He asked me to fix up a visit to the Storyteller's Theater and to ask you and Garras if you'd like to accompany them."

"That sounds like an excellent idea," she said. "When do they want to go?"

"Tonight. I'll get back to you when I've made the arrangements."

"I hope you're not overdoing it," she said warningly. "I'd prefer you still in my sick bay, but I expect there's no chance of that."

"None," he said, "but be assured, I know the futility of fighting against nature's time scale when it comes to the healing of wounds. I will take proper rest and exercise, Physician Vanna."

"See that you do," she growled. "Ask them to meet me in my lab at the sixteenth hour today. You can come, too. I'll have a look at your leg after I've seen them."

"Wouldn't it be better for you to come here, Physician? I'm concerned about them mixing too much with the rest of the ship's crew. I don't want any more incidents."

"No, it's better for them to come to me," she said firmly. "They need to get out and mix. Carrie has to feel at ease with our people and she can't do that stuck behind the doors of that suite."

"Very well, Physician," he sighed. "I'll pass on your message."

Garras was the next one to call.

"They're out," said Kaid.

"I know. It's you I came to see. It's time we had a chat."

Kaid nodded, and closing the door, led him toward the food preparation room.

"I'll make us a drink," Garras grinned, watching Kaid limp toward one of the tall stools by the c'shar brewing unit. "How's the leg?"

"Sore," he said shortly, moving aside to let Garras pick up the jug. Wincing, he pushed himself up onto an adjacent stool.

Garras filled the jug at the sink then returned to the

counter. "Pass the c'shar," he said, filling the brewing unit with the water.

Kaid handed him a pack of fresh leaves.

Garras ripped it open with his teeth and poured it in at the top of the unit, closing the lid and switching it on. He tossed the empty packet at the disposal unit by the sink then sat down.

"Vanna knows we're ex-Brotherhood," he said. "I didn't tell her, she told me."

Kaid raised an eye ridge. "How'd she find out?"

"She's being catalyzed by her association with Carrie and Kusac but she doesn't realize it yet. She thinks she worked it out by logic."

"Is she going to be a problem?"

"No, I can take care of her. She's suspicious and is watching us, though. Look, Kaid, I need to know how you feel about Carrie and Kusac. What report did you make to Ghezu?"

Kaid's look was thoughtful as he pulled a stim twig out of his jacket pocket and began to chew it. "I gave my report to Dzaka, then called Ghezu myself yesterday."

"What did you tell him?"

He took the twig out. "These are overrated," he said, looking at it briefly before putting it back in his mouth. "Their only ambition is to be together. If they're pushed by one or another of the guilds, then they're likely to become dangerous out of a need to protect themselves. I said I would continue to work with them when we leave for Shola."

"So you said there was no need for any action."

"Ghezu's involved Dzaka."

Garras frowned. "Dzaka? Why?"

"He's Brotherhood. I'm not."

Garras let out his breath in an explosive hiss. "Then we could find ourselves working against him. Ghezu just doesn't give up, does he? Why does he keep targeting you?"

"He needs to know where he stands with Dzaka."

"Where do you stand with him?"

"The c'shar's ready," he said, nodding toward the now-full jug.

"Don't avoid me, Kaid."

Kaid took a couple of mugs off the shelf beside him and passed them over to Garras.

"Kaid!"

He gestured to the brewer. "Pour the c'shar."

Garras' ears flicked in exasperation as he picked up the jug and filled the mugs.

Kaid took his drink and added whitener and sweetener. "Dzaka still resents me leaving without him."

"Will it cloud his judgment?"

"He's a pro. He'll do his job."

"Dammit, Kaid! Will he let it cloud his judgment?" Garras grabbed the arm that held the mug. C'shar spilled over the countertop.

"I don't know!" Kaid said angrily, spilling more of his drink as he pulled his arm free. "I don't know, Garras."

"Is Ghezu likely to order their termination?"

Kaid shrugged. "The Telepath Guild and Ghezu want the same thing—data on human telepaths. At the moment we only have one available. Carrie Hamilton. I think they're safe for the moment."

"Until we have another human telepath," said Garras thoughtfully. "Gods! I didn't know what I was getting us into when I sent for you."

"Vartra knows what they would have done if you hadn't," said Kaid. "They're not safe yet."

"So what do we do?"

"What you asked me to do in the first place. Guard them closely," said Kaid. "It's as well you took Carrie to Dzaka. At least he's got the chance now to see them at first hand."

"Vanna says the meditation is helping Carrie. She's becoming more able to cope, more relaxed."

"Her mind must be very similar to ours, then. I wonder if our techniques would work on a Terran who didn't have a Link with one of our people," Kaid said thoughtfully.

"You know my opinion," said Garras, taking a mouthful of c'shar from his mug. "The sooner the Telepath Guild uses some of our mental training techniques, the better. There's been too much inbreeding among the old families, most of them are way too highly strung. Our litanies would help them handle life outside their guilds better."

"That'll be the day! You were right in your initial assessment of these two younglings, Garras."

"Hmm?"

"They're a true blending of the Brotherhood and the Telepaths. They could mean full guild status for Ghezu, if they survive long enough for him to recruit them, and if he thinks he can control them. They'd be a powerful weapon in his hands. He could break the telepaths' dominance of the World Council with them."

"I know. And if Esken gets them, then he's got his own loyal private army, hasn't he? One that's faithful to his guild and makes him independent of both the Warriors and Stronghold."

"His position on the council would be unassailable," agreed Kaid.

"Then there's Vartra."

"I wonder what fate He's planned for them. Rulla says the God's been walking the halls at Dzahai. Some of the Brothers have been having visions."

"Did he say what they were?"

Kaid shook his head. "No, but he said some of them preferred to follow the God rather than the figurehead. Sounds like there's some disaffection spreading among the Brothers." He sighed, leaning forward on the counter. "I tried to reach the God myself, but He's been beyond me for some time now."

"He'll come to you when He's ready," said Garras sympathetically.

"Can you contact Rulla for me? I want to know if he's picked up anything from the troopers. I'm not convinced Chyad died in the explosion. I want to be sure."

"No problem," he said. Draining his mug, he got to his feet. "I've got to go now anyway. I'll be in touch."

Knowing the personal stress that Carrie and Kusac would face over the next few days, Vanna endeavored to keep them busy recording details not only of their Link but also about Terran life on Keiss. This served several purposes. It provided the Medical and Telepath Guilds with some basic information as well as augmenting Alien Relations' file. It also gave them each a project to keep them occupied.

As well as that, she and Garras encouraged them to develop a social life and the couple began to eat more often in the guild mess or at one of the two restaurants with Vanna and Garras. Kusac's mother helped, too, taking Carrie to the concourse and joining them for meals when her work permitted.

Carrie had a message sent to Meg and a few days later a case of clothes and board games arrived for her. One that caught on with their friends was Rithmomachia, a game of mental agility involving numerical progressions on counters. It attracted Meral's and Sevrin's attention, too, and before long had been adopted by many Sholans.

Finally, Vanna told them that their systems had leveled out as expected, uniquely parallel to each other. By then Carrie's training with Rhuso had progressed to the point where her shield was more than adequate, give or take the odd forgetful moment. Rhuso had also managed to make her aware of at least those portions of their ethics that made it possible for telepaths to live together in a community. Life was beginning to come together for them—among the Sholans.

During this time, Alien Relations had pushed on with their Attitude Indoctrination program, both with the visiting Keissian humans and the ship's crew. The Keissian peace delegation had been given the grand tour of the ship, then over the ensuing days had been entertained by visits to the Storyteller's Theater, a restaurant, and various competitive sports ranging from the Sholan equivalent of unarmed martial arts and weapons skills displayed by the Warrior's Guild, to elaborate games of tag. It culminated with a visit to the Wilderness, an entertainment area unique to the *Khalossa*.

The Wilderness was a piece of Shola designed to cater to the Sholan need for wide open vistas. It was planted with trees and grassy areas, and it contained a river running into a small lake. Using computer enhancement techniques, it could portray any climatic region of Shola's surface. Game could be released for hunting and the lake was stocked with fish. The tree canopy could be navigated using the ropes provided.

It was one of the places Vanna had suggested that they visit. Mito had been invited and had accepted on the proviso she could bring Anders. Though reluctant, Carrie had agreed and found to her surprise that he had been good company and, like her, fascinated by the plants and animals that inhabited the Wilderness.

The tour broke the ice that had settled over the peace talks, and though still not completely happy about his daughter's involvement with Kusac, at least Peter Hamilton no longer make it an issue on which the talks depended.

Kaid had instructed Personnel not to allow any incoming calls from her father, but according to the Mentor, he had now been exposed to enough of the Sholan culture to be able to reevaluate his opinions concerning them. So it was that a couple of days before Carrie and Kusac were due to leave the *Khalossa,* an early morning call came in from him.

Kusac nudged Carrie with his knee.

"Mmm?" she mumbled, snuggling her back closer into the curve of his body, enjoying the silky warmth of him against her skin.

"It's your father," he said, gently shaking her shoulder. "You'd better get up and take the call in the other room."

"Don't want to get up," she mumbled sleepily.

"He's waiting. Asking him to call back will hardly improve his temper."

Carrie groaned and surfaced enough to glower at the screen on the night table. Leaning out of bed, she flicked it on.

With a reproachful hiss, Kusac moved back from her but not before her father's image had appeared.

Peter Hamilton frowned slightly, disapproval evident on his face.

Kusac sensed that she was throwing her father in at the deep end, forcing him to face the fact of their intimacy.

"Good morning, Carrie. Kusac," he said stiffly. "I was hoping to come over and see you this morning."

Kusac could feel her reluctance. She didn't want the repeated hurt of her father's rejection.

Maybe he's changed, sent Kusac. *We'll never know if you refuse to see him. It would be better to try and make our peace with him before we leave for Shola.*

"We'll be up within the hour," she said reluctantly. "If you wish to come, bring the duty interpreter with you. I don't want any more misunderstandings."

"I've seen the telepaths at work," said Peter Hamilton slowly. "I understand more about your Link now. I don't intend to make a scene, Carrie. I love you too much to lose you." He stopped, looking faintly embarrassed. "I'll see you in an hour." He blanked the screen.

Kusac leaned across Carrie, switching their unit off.

You're tracking upwind of him, he warned, sliding his arms round her. *I understand, but I don't think it's wise.*

I won't live in shadows, Kusac, she said, turning round. *Surely I'm no less his daughter for loving you? I won't let him make me feel it's wrong.*

Kusac held her close, feeling her need for him as a person. It felt good. His tail curled protectively round her legs.

An hour later, Kaid showed Mr. Hamilton and the interpreter into the inner lounge.

"Liegen Aldatan," said the interpreter, saluting him with arms crossed over his chest.

Kusac, caught in the midst of brushing Carrie's hair, mentally swore a few choice epithets and put the brush down hurriedly. Why did her father always have to catch him at a disadvantage?

Hamilton hovered near the door, obviously unsure as to how to address Kusac and unwilling to give him the benefit of his rank.

Unable to ignore Carrie's unspoken plea, Kusac reluctantly eased the situation by going to greet him.

"Come in, Mr. Hamilton, Serif. Well come. Be at ease with us, we don't hold with ceremony here," he said, escorting both of them over to the settee.

Mr. Hamilton sat down on the edge. "Is it really necessary for us to have Interpreter Serif and Kusac here?" he asked his daughter. "I'd like to talk to you on your own."

"Even if Kusac left the room, he'd know what you said," she replied, playing with her hairbrush and keeping her eyes down.

"I realize that, but Serif?"

"I've assured the Ambassador that I can only pick up surface thoughts," said Serif.

His mood seems calm. I'll take Serif to the other end of the room. Then he can feel he has his privacy with you, sent Kusac.

Carrie shot him a frightened look. *No! Don't leave me with him, I need you close.*

We're always close, came the reassuring thought.

Serif rose to his feet, following Kusac.

"I find the telepaths a little unnerving," said her father suddenly. "I can usually tell when they're talking to each other."

Carrie wrinkled her forehead in surprise, tucking her legs up into the chair. "Perhaps you should be tested for telepathic abilities then."

Her father shook his head. "No, I'm too old for that sort of upheaval in my life. One prodigy in the family is enough," he said, smiling wryly. "The Commander made sure I realized how important the two of you are to both our species, and I accept what has happened between you."

"I'm glad, but what about us? Can you see us beyond the political implications? Doesn't it bother you that we're important to each other? Where do Carrie and Kusac fit into your life—if at all?" she asked.

"I can't say it's what I want for you, Carrie, it isn't," he said, looking acutely uncomfortable. "I understand your need to be defensive, but if you feel this relationship is right for you, that's all that really matters, isn't it?"

"You don't understand at all, do you? I can feel it, so don't tell me I'm wrong. You think I'm making the best of an intolerable situation, don't you?"

"Carrie, I want you to be happy," he said, leaning forward to take her hand. "I just think that you aren't going to be happy with him. I don't see how you can. Think of all the differences between his people and ours; their customs, morals—everything will be different."

"When our Link was completed, I understood everything Kusac knew as if I was him," she said softly, still keeping her eyes down. "I know what it's like to grow up on Shola, to walk under a sun brighter than ours or Earth's, to run on all fours across the fields of the estate chasing game. I'm no longer just a human from Earth, or a colonist from Keiss. Part of me is totally Sholan, and the Terrans feel as alien to me as you feel the Sholans are to you." She looked up at him, forcing eye contact.

Her father frowned, glancing uneasily away. "You're talking rubbish, Carrie. Just because you know what it feels like, it doesn't make you Sholan."

"Have you seen my eyes, Father?" she asked quietly. "Look at them and tell me again there's nothing about me that's Sholan."

He lifted his gaze to hers, a perplexed frown giving way to an expression of shock. "What the hell have you done to them?"

"They've been like that since the night of the reception. I don't know how or why it happened, but it marks me apart, an external sign of what I feel inside."

"They told me you were all right," he said. "They didn't say anything about this. What caused it? Is it some kind of illness or disease?"

"No, I'm fine. I told you, we don't know what caused my eyes to change, but they're Sholan eyes now. I've never fitted in anywhere before, Father. I belong here, I can have a life of my own with them. I never could on Keiss."

Kusac, aware her mood was becoming too introspective, returned to her side and placed a hand protectively on her shoulder. As he did, he felt her lower her shield enough to let her feelings leak out to her father through their hand contact.

Divining her purpose, he took control, bringing her father briefly into their Link, allowing him for a moment to experience what it was like to share such a mental bond.

White-faced, her father snatched his hand away. "My God! What was that?"

"That's our Link," said Carrie. "Now you know what it feels like."

"I could feel what both of you were thinking, like a constant stream running through my mind. How can you live like that, so aware of each other?" He sat there, face still pale, hands shaking.

At Kusac's unspoken request, Serif brought over a mug of c'shar from the unit on the desk and handed it to him.

Kusac moved to sit beside Mr. Hamilton, wrapping the human's hands around the cup. "Drink this," he said. "It'll help."

Her father took a gulp, then another, the tremors beginning to steady. "I didn't realize people could be that close," he said quietly. "How can you stand it?" he asked, looking up at his daughter. "It's so intense, so . . . dominating."

"Only to you," said Kusac, standing up and moving back to Carrie. "For us, life would be unbearable without it. What we have isn't an ordinary Sholan Leska Link, though. It's more demanding."

"And more rewarding," added Carrie. "Now do you understand?"

"Yes, I understand, and I felt your commitment to each other, but I still can't say I like it," he said, putting down the cup. "What about your father, Kusac? Can you honestly say he's overjoyed? Or your mother?"

Kusac shifted restlessly. "I've told him, and like you he would have it otherwise, but he's prepared to accept Carrie as my Leska," he admitted.

"You can appreciate it isn't an ideal situation," said her father.

"I don't think you can believe that either of us would have chosen this relationship if it could have been avoided, Mr. Hamilton," said Kusac, part of his mind shushing Carrie's mental exclamation.

"Fathers worry more about their daughters," he said, getting to his feet. He leaned over Carrie, giving her a hug. "I do wish you happiness in your new life," he said. "Don't forget me while you're on Shola. I don't want to lose you, Carrie. Call me, or whatever it is they do there."

She returned the hug. "Bye, Dad. We aren't due to leave for a couple of days yet, so I'll see you before we go."

He held out his hand to Kusac who shook it briefly. "We'll see ourselves out," Hamilton said.

* * *

"Here's the report from Intelligence based on Lieutenant Mito Rralgu's findings, Commander," said Myak. "With the help of the human Jo Edwards, she's managed to translate the Valtegan's deep-space message."

"About time," said Raguul, taking the document from him. He scanned it quickly. "This was sent several days before the base was taken. <`Loshul to Ghaikkuir base. Investigation of alien cube continuing (?). Cannot confirm (?) it is a data storage unit (?) at this time. Will keep you informed. (?) > Hm, there are several words she's had to approximate, but it looked like they never did manage to access our code. Intelligence concludes that, in their opinion, it was destroyed when we liberated Keiss if not earlier by the attack on the base. Now that's good news." He handed the document back to his adjutant. "See the information is transmitted to Sholan High Command, Myak."

"Yes, sir." He hesitated.

"What else is there to tell me?" asked Raguul.

"It looks like we may have run into another delay with the treaty."

Raguul groaned. "What is it this time?"

"Captain Jordan and Mr. James Blackwell of the *Erasmus* have been making representation to Sub-Commander Rhuk that they want to be included in the treaty talks."

"Just what I need," muttered Raguul. "What do our current Keissian delegates say?"

"All Hamilton and Skinner are concerned with is having our help to protect their world from the Valtegans. As Hamilton pointed out, Earth's interests are entirely different from theirs, and the people from the *Erasmus* know nothing about life on Keiss or under the Valtegans. They've been in space so long that they aren't even representative of the current Earth attitudes."

"Does that mean they want to exclude them from the council?"

"No. They've no objection to them having a representative—they suggest Mr. Blackwell—so long as it's understood who's in charge. Skinner and Hamilton are more concerned by Earth's attitude that after all they've been through, they haven't the right to autonomy."

"They seem to have settled it between themselves so there's no need for us to become involved. Any news from High Command on that Valtegan craft that escaped? Have they managed to track down where it was headed?"

"Nothing yet, sir. One more thing, Commander. The Brother is waiting to see you."

"He is, is he? Any idea what he wants?"

"You did say you wanted to see him when he was recovered."

Raguul nodded. "So I did. A small matter of seven deaths, wasn't it? Ask him to come in." His ears flicked with annoyance.

Kaid entered, only a slight limp betraying his injured leg. "Commander," he said, sitting down.

The Commander nodded. "There have been four incidents in the last few days that have resulted in the deaths of members of my crew. I don't suppose you know anything about them, do you?" he asked, tapping his claws on the surface of his desk.

"I'm not at liberty to divulge that information, Commander, and you know that," Kaid murmured.

"Dammit, your contract didn't mention anything about killing!" exclaimed Raguul.

"My contract gave me the authority to take what steps were necessary to ensure the safe delivery of Liegen Kusac Aldatan and his Leska to Shola. You wanted me to wind up my investigation of the dissidents. That's what I did."

"I didn't expect you to take the law into your own hands!"

said Raguul angrily. "Those people should have been brought into custody, not killed!"

"Had the movement been more widespread, I would have perhaps acted differently, but there were only a small number of people involved as far as I knew. As it is, I have to report that my undercover contact has been approached by yet another member of this movement. She was due on bridge duty tonight and was asked to intercept an incoming message from the *Rhyaki*—a message that was arranged by Chyad."

"I'll have no more killings," growled Raguul. "Draz will deal with it from now on!"

"That is exactly what I've done, Commander," Kaid said quietly. "Unfortunately, I am hardly in any state to deal with the matter myself. I contacted Draz and he arranged for your officer to be reported sick with some Terran ailment. She's been quarantined for the next five days and her replacement is one of Draz's people. I won't place Lieutenant Rralgu in any further danger. I suggest you post her to Keiss as soon as possible to keep her out of the way of these people. On Keiss she is of no use to them. They play hard, as I found out to my cost," he said wryly. "The scouter crash was none of my doing."

"You planned to kill Chyad and Maikoe," said Raguul.

"I never endanger the innocent," said Kaid stiffly.

"You took the law into your own hands when you decided the others were guilty," growled Raguul.

"Their continued existence constituted a threat to the lives of those I was hired to protect. I assure you my judgment has never been questioned before," growled Kaid. "Check with the Brotherhood if you wish. I had their blessing, and their instructions for this mission, as you well know."

"I want your promise that there will be no more killings on the *Khalossa*," Raguul demanded.

"I can't give you that. If their lives are threatened again, as they were by Jakule, then I will kill to protect them."

"Dammit, you know full well what I mean!"

"No, Commander, I don't. I have my instructions, and you have yours. Let's just follow them, shall we?" Kaid stood up. "If you have a complaint, you know the procedure. Contact Dzahai Stronghold and request a tribunal. Good day, Commander."

As Raguul watched him leave, he realized that the room about him was starting to darken.

"Commander," said Myak, taking hold of his shoulder and shaking him. "Leave it. He's in the right. His primary contract was to ensure their safety."

Raguul took a deep breath, aware that Myak was trying to prevent him from going into a hunter/kill state.

"I know," he growled, "which is why it annoys me!"

"At least he's put Draz in charge now," said Myak. "And he's removed Lieutenant Rralgu from danger. I think it would be wise to follow his advice and have her posted planet-side as soon as possible." He left the Commander's side and went over to the drinks cupboard.

"I think you'll enjoy this, Commander," he said, picking up a small bottle and a glass. "It's from Keiss, a human drink. They call it brandy. I've tried it and it's rather pleasant. It's said to have a settling effect on the stomach."

* * *

"I've seen you about, of course, but if you hadn't come over, I'd never have placed you," said Rulla.

"It's been a few years," admitted Garras, nudging the meat on his plate around with his fork. "What the hell's this supposed to be?" he asked, holding up a piece of gristle.

"The supply ship's been delayed," said Rulla, pushing his plate aside. "We're getting the dregs. They lifted the blackout today, so it should arrive here tomorrow."

"Thank the God for that!" said Garras, giving up on his meal, too. "Tallinu asked me to get a report from you. Anything interesting happening below decks?"

"Depends what you call interesting," said Rulla. "I managed to get some planet leave in, so I ambled over to the shanty bar on the edge of the new space port. Did you know there are Keissian qwenes there?"

"Qwenes? No, I didn't. Wait a minute. I remember Carrie telling us that some of their women went voluntarily to the Valtegan pleasure cities. I expect it's them. They wouldn't have been very popular with their own people after the Valtegans left."

"Well, they're popular with our males," grinned Rulla. "In fact, one or two of the troopers have formed semipermanent relationships with them. All this is beside the point, though. From these females I found out that there's been a spate of thefts recently. Thefts of Sholan property. The qwenes weren't too happy about it as they were getting the blame. Then as suddenly as they started, they stopped."

"Curious. What type of things were going missing?" asked Garras.

"All sorts. Clothing, kit bags, personal mementos. A real mixture of goods."

"Strange. Wonder why?"

"Perhaps one of the females felt she needed the security of possessions she could sell."

"Or someone wanted to create a new identity."

Rulla frowned thoughtfully. "You think so? The thefts were random and spaced over several days. There was no pattern either to the type of goods taken or those they were stolen from."

"Keep your ear to the ground on this one, Rulla. If it happens again, let me know. Nobody's gone missing, have they? No one late back from leave?"

"There are always people who dig their claws into the ground when it comes to returning to duty," he grinned. "That's nothing remarkable. What're you looking for?"

"A male trying to pass himself off as someone else."

"Oh? Who's that, then? This Chyad fellow?"

Garras let his mouth open in a slight grin. "You're sharp today," he said. "Yes, Chyad. He was on the scouter that went down several days ago. He was reported dead, but we aren't so sure. Keep it to yourself, though."

Rulla nodded. "Will do. It's good to see you and Kaid working together again. Tell him to remember what I said. If you're with him, then I'm in too."

Garras felt a shiver run down his spine. On the chair beside him, the fur on his tail started to bush out. With an effort of will, he forced himself to think calmly. "There's nothing happening, Rulla. We're merely doing a job."

Rulla gave a derisory snort. "Don't give me that crap, Garras. Think I'm a youngling, do you? I know what's at stake here as well as you do, and I'm not prepared to back either Stronghold or the Telepaths. Just don't forget me, that's all I ask. You know I can be counted on."

Garras stood up. "I'll tell Kaid what you said."

* * *

Carrie and Kusac were due to leave for Shola that day, on the craft which had brought the Earth dignitaries to Keiss.

The treaty with Keiss was all but complete despite the minor delay encountered from those lately arrived via the *Erasmus*. Alien Relations had agreed to the inclusion of Blackwell so long as it was understood that they would deal only with the Terrans who had been running Keiss from the beginning. Those humans—now commonly referred to by all, including themselves, as Keissians—knew exactly how important the program to arm Keiss was, and they were more than capable of taking the hard decisions necessary to ensure this was done as quickly as possible.

Alien Relations was now prepared to talk separately to the humans from Earth. After being virtually ignored for the last two weeks, Earth was more than happy to talk to them.

Carrie and Kusac had gone down to the viewing gallery in the main landing bay to watch them debark. Kusac noted with interest that like the Sholans, Terrans came in many sizes and colors. On Keiss he had met very few and they had been of the same basic stock as Carrie.

She stood at Kusac's side watching the tiny figures scurrying about loading fresh supplies.

Kusac pointed to the craft, its sharp lines thrown into relief by the harsh landing bay lights. It seemed to be crouching on the pad in front of the massive air lock as if impatiently waiting the command to take off.

"That's the ship we'll be traveling on," he said.

"It looks very small," she said dubiously.

"Only because of the size of the landing bay," he said, putting an arm round her.

She turned almond-slitted eyes to him. "I was just getting used to the *Khalossa*."

"You'll like Shola, and once the Terrans start recruiting their Talented and sending them there, you won't feel so unique."

She sighed. "I'm still not comfortable in human company, Kusac. Among Sholans I'm at ease; they don't judge me."

"Not all humans do," said Kusac giving her a hug. "Look at Mito. She finally got her human male, didn't she?"

Carrie grinned. "Anders? Yes, but it took her weeks of answering his questions about Shola first, and then she still had to jump on him!"

"Ah, your human reticence," sighed Kusac, turning away from the view and leading her back into the main part of the ship. "What's your opinion of the Keissian females, Meral?" he asked.

"Near enough our own kind to be interesting, Liegen. There were a couple I had my eyes on during my one tour of duty on Keiss, but I didn't get the chance to even talk to them," he said regretfully.

"Sevrin?"

"I haven't been down to Keiss, Liegen. The only Terrans I've met are those on the ship. Having read the communiqués on interspecies relationships, I would be cautious about initiating a friendship, even if I did get the chance to meet them socially."

"Wise," said Kusac, as they headed back to the elevator. "I hear they have foul tempers."

"Kusac!" exclaimed Carrie, rising to the bait. Then she caught his mental laugh. "Really," she said, poking him in the ribs with her elbow.

Kusac laughed. "You should know better by now," he said.

Their personal possessions had already been packed and sent to the ship by Kaid.

"We'll be able to have more clothes made for you on Shola," said Kusac confidently. "Clothes that fit you properly rather than just wearing Sholan fashions that are too large for you."

Carrie looked down at the long split-paneled tabard she wore over her trousers. It was the preferred item of casual dress for Sholans when off duty.

"I like these tabards," she said, touching the soft olive-colored fabric.

"They're fine in the controlled environment of the ship," said Kusac looking critically at her, "but you don't need such long splits. In the winter, your legs will be cold."

"What's the climate like on Shola?"

"Where we're going, warmer than Keiss in the summer season, but the winter is bitter. We'll have more of your trousers made for you, and some long robes like those my mother wears. Shoes shouldn't be a problem since we can have your existing ones copied."

"Where exactly on Shola are we going?"

"To the main Telepath Guild at Valsgarth. The town's on the east coast of the major planetary land mass and adjoins my family's estate. The estate actually borders the sea. You'll like it there; plenty of good hunting." He stopped short, realizing she wouldn't be able to accompany him on a hunt.

"There're many ways to hunt," said Carrie, putting a comforting hand on his arm. "My ancestors managed quite well on two legs. We'll work out something."

Kusac nodded, not completely convinced. He tried not to wonder how many more aspects of normal Sholan life would be denied to his human Leska and himself.

He glanced at the timepiece on the wall. "I think you'd better finish dressing for the journey, it's almost time to leave. Wear the purple cloak."

"What will you wear, then?"

"I'll wear the gray one," he said, handing her the cloak from the chair. "They know me. I want them to identify you as a telepath from the first."

She nodded. "Will I be warm enough with just a shirt on underneath?" she asked.

"We've got a couple of the padded jerkins for when we land on Shola. That's when you'll feel the cold. We won't be in the landing bay area long enough for it to matter here. Come on, time to go. My mother's meeting us there," he said, walking to the bedroom door.

Carrie took a last look round the room. He felt her sadness in leaving what had become their home over the last few weeks. He went back, taking her by the hand and urging her gently to leave.

I know, but come, we must leave now.

Meral and Sevrin were waiting for them in the hallway.

"Where's Kaid?" asked Carrie.

"He's on board, making sure the suite is in order, Liegena," answered Meral.

They took the elevator down to the lower levels of the ship, stepping out into the unheated air of the landing bay. The metal floor was icy under Kusac's bare feet and reflexively his claws extended, his footsteps echoing as they walked over to the waiting craft.

Carrie shivered, drawing the woolen cloak tighter.

Once up the ramp and through the hatch, the warm air of the ship was a welcome relief. Kaid was waiting to show them to their quarters.

"The Clan Leader is waiting for you, Liegen," he said.

"I'm afraid it isn't as spacious as the suite on the *Khalossa,* but it's adequate considering we'll only be using it for a week," he said, ushering them in.

Rhyasha got to her feet as they entered. "I hope you don't mind me waiting in here, but I hate the sterile environment of the landing bay. It's so impersonal," she said, coming forward to greet them. She embraced Kusac first, then Carrie.

"I wish I was coming with you," she said, wrapping Carrie's arm through hers. "Unfortunately, I need to remain long enough to get the treaty with Earth off the ground. Once the preliminaries are over, then I can leave it to the AlRel people. Believe me, when that moment comes, I will be on the fastest ship home!"

"How long do you think you'll be?" Kusac asked.

"About another week, maybe two," she said, "I'll have to go now, I'm afraid," she said as they felt the vibration of the engines starting up. "Give your father and sisters my love," she said, drawing them both toward the corridor.

Kusac, see you tell your father all about Carrie. I know you haven't done so yet, she sent as they walked toward the hatchway.

I'll tell him face-to-face, Mother, not from the safety of a comm.

I understand, but I think you'd do better to tell him now.

Rhyasha hugged them both again, then left.

Silently, they made their way back to their rooms.

"When do we leave?" Kusac asked Kaid as he helped Carrie off with her cloak.

"In a quarter of an hour."

"Has Vanna arrived yet?" asked Carrie, wandering around the room and opening the various doors that led off the small lounge.

"Yes, Liegena. She's gone to check what medical facilities the ship carries."

"Let's trust we don't need them," said Kusac. "What sleeping arrangements have you made?"

"There are three bedrooms in the suite, Liegen. I have allowed one for you and the Liegena, one for Physician Vanna, and the last for us." He indicated himself and the two guards. "Your room has been fitted with a psychic inhibitor to make the journey more peaceful for you."

Going to be cozy, Kusac sent to Carrie as he sat down.

Only for a week.

Kusac grunted.

"We have to eat in the communal dining room," continued Kaid apologetically.

"How many passengers?"

"Another ten, Liegen. Those whose tour of duty is over."

The door opened and Vanna entered. She was carrying a portable sampling unit along with her medikit.

"More tests? How much longer will you be taking them?" asked Carrie, curling up beside Kusac on the settee.

"Until I'm sure that your systems have stabilized," she replied, squatting down beside Kusac and opening the lid of the test unit.

Kusac pulled up his shirt sleeve and laid his forearm along the hollowed recess. It fitted snugly against his arm, leaving his wrist and hand free. Vanna closed the lid, latching it in place and resting it on her knee.

"I thought you said we were stable," said Kusac.

"You are. I just want to take a routine weekly test for the next few months," she replied, checking the results on the display.

She released the catch, opening a small panel beside the display to remove a tiny phial which she placed in her medikit. Moving over to Carrie, she held the unit open while the girl likewise bared her arm and placed it in the recess.

"I intend to have some energy scans done using the aura unit at your Guild House," said Vanna, waiting for Carrie's results to appear.

"Why didn't you do them while we were here?" asked Kusac, pulling his sleeve back down.

"They only have that particular equipment in the Telepath Guild," replied Vanna, unclipping the unit and taking out the second phial. "I thought you'd know it takes a medical telepath to interpret the results, and they won't work outside the shielded confines of their guild. We have to send our patients to them. I believe they also use the equipment in the early assessment and training of telepaths, don't they?"

Kusac nodded. "They'll probably use it on us to chart the extent of our Link and Carrie's Talents."

A chime sounded in the suite. "Would all passengers please prepare for takeoff?" said an impersonal voice.

Vanna got to her feet. "I'll take these down to the lab after we're underway," she said, stowing the unit safely in her kit.

The trip was unremarkable except for its tediousness. Eventually, the ship docked at the space station in orbit above Shola. They transferred to a private shuttle and within an hour had landed at the spaceport on the planet.

The hatch slid open onto a covered walk that led to an arrival lounge. Waiting for them was a small party of Sholans. The two in front wore Telepath colors and were flanked by two Warrior guards in full ceremonial uniform. As Kusac and Carrie stepped out into the waiting area, the dark-furred female Sholan launched herself into Kusac's arms.

"Kusac! You're home at last! I've missed you," she said, her voice a velvety purr.

"Taizia, I didn't expect to see you here," said Kusac, returning the hug and setting her down. He was aware of Carrie's reaction—a mixture of jealousy and curiosity.

"Glad as I am to see you, have you forgotten your manners?" he asked the female sternly. "Have you no word for my Leska?"

"I'm honored to meet you," she said, holding out her open palm in greeting while trying to peer surreptitiously inside Carrie's hood.

Carrie lowered the hood, putting her palm on Taizia's as Kusac introduced her.

"You'll have to forgive my sister. She was always the impulsive one," he said, "and short on manners!"

Taizia ignored the comment and stared in frank curiosity at Carrie, who flinched slightly under her scrutiny. She turned to her brother. "You're right. She is pretty despite the species difference, and I like what I can feel of her mind."

Kusac's ears twitched with embarrassment and he aimed a cuff at her. She dodged, laughing.

"Imp!" he growled. "How come Father let you out at this time of night?"

"I'm staying at the Guild House at the moment. I insisted on coming with Senior Tutor Sorli to meet you," she said as the others came up to join them.

"I'll just bet you did," said Kusac, taking Carrie by the arm.

"Welcome to Shola, er . . ." The Tutor hesitated, unsure as to how to address Carrie.

"Liegena Carrie," emphasized Kusac, moving Carrie's cloak so that the bronze at her neck glinted briefly in the artificial light.

There was a shocked silence into which Taizia spoke. "So you've torced her," she said with a grin. "Who're you calling impetuous now, brother?"

As he let Carrie's cloak fall back, she clutched at his arm, her other hand going instinctively to the torc around her neck, realizing for the first time some of the significance of the gift.

"Not impetuous," he denied, staring down the Tutor. "It's what I wish. You'll treat her accordingly."

The Tutor bowed. "As Liegen Aldatan wishes, but have you considered . . . ?"

"I've considered what matters. I'll deal with other issues as they arise. This is my affair," Kusac interrupted, his voice uncompromising.

"It's not our place to interfere, Liegen," murmured the Tutor. "I have transport waiting outside. If you would follow us?"

Kusac nodded, acutely aware of Carrie's withdrawal and confusion.

The Tutor and his companion led the way, the two guards flanking Kusac's party.

"Oh, I *am* going to enjoy the next few months," grinned Taizia, fairly skipping along beside them.

Kusac grunted. "You might, imp, but we won't." He reached for Carrie's hand, sending out thoughts of reassurance but she remained silent.

In the aircar, Kusac sat with Carrie held close by his side. By tacit agreement they'd been left to sit alone, the rest of the group taking seats at the front of the vehicle. Her eyes were closed, and he could feel not only her tiredness but also the underlying worry. He reached gently, searching for the area of her mind that initiated sleep and soothed it until her breathing slowed. Releasing the contact he sighed, closing his eyes, too. He'd promised her time for themselves. So far, the days had been full of commitments to others with no space for them. He intended to keep that promise come what may, starting tomorrow.

The journey took an hour, at the end of which time Taizia gently shook them awake.

She stood looking down at them as they yawned and stretched.

"It's strange to see you with a female," she said, "let alone a Leska. You were always one for your own company, brother. No time for females in your life."

"Events took me by surprise," he yawned.

"You must have crept up on him when he wasn't looking," Taizia smiled at Carrie.

"He wasn't running very fast," she murmured, sitting up.

Taizia grasped her by the wrist, hand around her forearm, and helped her to her feet.

"I do like you," she said. "Should you need a break from my worthy brother, come and find me in the third female's dorm."

"Don't overcomplicate her life, Taizia," warned Kusac, sliding his way out along the seats. "Remember, through me she knows our culture, but she hasn't yet learned to live in it."

"I'll remember, Kusac. I've read Father's notes on what we know of the Keissian human culture. You do realize, don't you, that he expects you to use your knowledge to record a definitive study?" she asked, looking shrewdly at him.

"Does he now?" said Kusac, his hand searching for Carrie's as they walked out of the aircar into the chill night.

They had set down in the inner courtyard. Opposite them one of the huge double doors of the Guild House stood open, a pool of golden light welcoming them.

Kusac led his party into the hallway.

"I have to take you and . . ." Tutor Sorli hesitated, "the Liegena Carrie to the Guild Master immediately."

"I'll leave you now," said Taizia, reaching up to nuzzle her brother's cheek. "Good luck. I'll see you tomorrow," she said, letting him go and hugging Carrie.

Kusac picked up his Leska's surprise. *Taizia is impulsive, no matter what she says, but if she takes a liking to someone, it's genuine. Take her offer of friendship. You'll find her good company.*

She's very different from you.

She wasn't the eldest, nor the heir, sent Kusac resignedly.

"Our guard will see that your staff are installed in the guest house," Tutor Sorli continued, indicating that they should follow him.

Taizia waved before disappearing into the main refectory hall.

"Doubtless a description of your Leska will have circulated throughout the guild before morning," said Sorli dryly as he started up the winding stone staircase.

He stopped outside a plain wooden door, knocking before entering. "Liegen Aldatan and his Leska are here, Guild Master," he said.

"Then show them in," said a quiet voice.

Sorli stood back, holding the door open for them to enter. The room was gently lit by indirect means, a balm to their eyes after the swift changes from the dark of night to the harsh glare in the main area of the building. The Guild Master rose from behind his desk as they entered. Over a plain black tunic he wore a robe of dark purple edged with gold embroidery so stiff that it rustled as he moved around the desk toward them. His fur was a dark brown streaked with gray around the eyes and temples, as was his hair. He held his hand out in greeting to Carrie.

"Well come to the guild, my dear," he said as she returned the gesture.

Through her, Kusac was aware of a feather-light touch to her mind.

"A new telepath is always welcome, but one already bonded as a Leska is a blessing indeed." He flashed a Sholan smile and turned to Kusac.

"It's a year or two since we last met," he said as Kusac touched palms with him.

Again the light probe, measuring and weighing without judging.

"Come, take off your cloaks and sit by the fire," the Master said, turning toward the other end of the room where a log fire glowed gently.

"Sorli, bring them something hot to drink. They must be tired after such a journey."

Carrie unfastened her cloak, trying to tug the neck of her jerkin up to cover her torc.

Kusac frowned, taking her hand away and beginning to unlace the fastenings. *It's meant to be seen, Leska. Unless you want to return it to me?* His hands stopped and he looked questioningly at her.

Carrie put her hand protectively to the torc, her denial instant and loud.

Kusac winced. *Then wear it with joy,* he sent, grinning from ear to ear as he flicked her cheek with a finger. Taking off his own cloak he took hers and put them both over the back of the chair facing the Master's desk.

They joined him at the fire, taking the settee that he indicated.

"You must call me Master Esken," said the Master, settling himself comfortably in his chair. "I know Kusac's family well. I had you here for several years, didn't I?"

Kusac nodded. "Ten years," he said, "then off and on for another five."

"Then there's Taizia. Wild little thing for all she's twenty-five," he chuckled, "not at all like you. And Kitra, your younger sister. She studies hard and will do well for herself when she's older. Now you've brought us your Leska. I like to see continuity in a family. It gives me a sense of tradition."

Kusac shifted uncomfortably, aware of the undertones.

The door opened quietly and Sorli returned with a tray bearing three pottery goblets. He offered them, then withdrew.

Kusac sipped his drink, surprised to find it mildly alcoholic.

"So we have to measure your Talent, Carrie," Master Esken continued after a moment. "Undoubtedly you're a Telepath or you wouldn't be Kusac's Leska. I also hear you have shown an ability to heal. This is a rare gift amongst the telepaths. We shall have to get you to demonstrate this ability. Do you have any other gifts, my dear?"

Carrie cast a frantic glance at Kusac. *What does he want me to say?* she asked, panic in her mental tone.

"You know about our gestalt Link?" he asked the Master, pressing Carrie's hand reassuringly.

"I've had reports about it, and it's a subject I want to examine more closely, along with the shape-changing incident. I believe your medic has come with you. I'll have to speak to her personally. All that is in the future, though. This is just an informal chat for tonight since the hour is late. For tomorrow, Carrie, I'd like you to think of the extent of Terran telepathic abilities. If you are the norm, it would appear that you perhaps have a greater variety of Talents than us."

Kusac stirred. "Not tomorrow, Master Esken," he said. "We need some time to ourselves as well. We've had precious little of it so far."

"As you wish," said Master Esken amicably. "You aren't back at school, after all. Why not take Carrie round the craft quarters of the town? Let her experience a little of the real Shola after the military environment of the *Khalossa*."

"That's what I planned to do," said Kusac, finishing his drink.

"Then I will see you here at the fourth hour the day after tomorrow," said the Master, getting to his feet. "Sorli will be waiting outside to take you to your Leska apartment. It will be yours for as long as you are on Shola. Treat it as your home."

He walked back to the door with them. "I have assigned Sorli to be your tutor. Any problems, no matter how small, take them to him. He lives in the Leska wing, and has worked closely with our bonded telepaths for many years. I would say there are few problems he hasn't come across, but in your case, he'll be breaking new ground, too," he smiled, opening the door. "Good night," he said as they joined their tutor outside.

Sorli led them back down the stairs, then through a labyrinth of corridors until they reached a more modern extension. Up a flight of stairs and along another corridor they went, finally coming to a halt outside one of several adjacent doors. He handed Kusac a flat pass key.

"This is the apartment you've been assigned," he said as Kusac slid the key into the slot, activating the door.

"My personal number is on file in your comm. As Master Esken said, should you need me, call. I'll be seeing you later on in the week when Master Esken has decided how he wants to proceed. If you'll excuse me for now, I have an early start in the morning. Good night, Kusac, Carrie." He nodded his head, then turned back the way they had come.

Kusac pushed open the door. Kaid was waiting for them. He took their cloaks from Kusac.

"I've unpacked for you, Liegen," he said. "There's hot c'shar and some of the Guild's special biscuits for you. At least, they say they're special biscuits," he amended as Kusac and Carrie flopped down exhausted onto the settee.

"Where are the others?" asked Kusac tiredly as Kaid put their cloaks away and bustled around pouring c'shar for them.

"One of the Warriors escorted them to their quarters in the

guest house. If you look out of that window," he indicated it with a nod of his head, "you can see the visitor's block. They're not at all happy about having non-Telepaths inside the guild precinct, but I managed to convince them that you couldn't do without my personal services."

Kusac smiled faintly as he sat up and took a couple of biscuits off the plate, handing one to Carrie. "I'm as tired as you are," he said softly, "but we missed a meal. These have a high protein content and are used to replace the energy we lose while working. You'll feel better even after one."

She took the biscuit, nibbling cautiously at one corner, taking a bigger bite when she found it to her taste.

"How did you manage to convince the guild we couldn't do without you?" asked Kusac, chewing his way through a biscuit himself.

"By pointing out that the Liegena needs specially prepared food and that I alone could prepare it."

Kusac grinned. "Nice."

"I thought so myself," Kaid said, with a slight smile. "Meral and Sevrin will accompany you when you leave the guild, but they'll remain in the guest house till then."

Kusac grunted, finished his drink and got to his feet. Grasping Carrie by the hand, he pulled her up, shifting his grasp to her arm.

"Bed," he said, steering her toward the doors at the back of the room. "You're dead on your feet. Which one, Kaid?" he asked.

"On the left, Liegen."

A subdued light came on as soon as they entered. With a sigh of relief, Kusac shut the door behind them.

"I'm not that tired now," said Carrie.

"That's good," said Kusac, his voice becoming liquid velvet, "because I don't have sleep in mind."

He turned, eyes blazing with a feral glow in the dim light. Caging her against the door with his arms, he lowered his face to hers. She met him halfway.

Chapter 11

Next morning they rose too late for breakfast in the refectory. Luckily, the apartment had its own kitchens which Kaid had ordered stocked. Knowing Carrie's preference for fruit rather than meat for first meal, he'd made sure several varieties were available for her. After a leisurely meal, Carrie stowed a spare pair of trousers and shoes into a bag and grabbed her cloak in preparation to go out.

"You won't need a cloak, Liegena," said Kaid, glancing up from clearing the table. "It's late spring now and the temperature is warmer than on the *Khalossa*. You'll probably be too warm dressed as you are."

You look fine, Kusac sent, eyeing her sweater and trousers critically. *You'll be noticed more in a cloak. If you aren't ready to face Shola as a Terran, then we'll have to try an illusion, but it will seriously drain our energy.*

She sighed, undecided.

Come as you are, he urged. *One day you'll have to. Besides, more than I find you attractive.* His tone was teasing.

What do you mean? she demanded.

Just that if you hadn't been known to be newly Leskabonded to me, there were many on board the Khalossa *who'd have approached you.*

Carrie refused the bait this time.

I don't say you won't face curiosity, but you'll probably see a few Chemer and Sumaan in the town, maybe even a group of Touibans. Shola is used to aliens, and you're much prettier than the other three species!

Feeling her resolve waver, Kusac took her hand. *Come on. We're together, that's all either of us needs.* "Who's on duty today, Kaid?" he asked verbally.

"Myself and Meral, Liegen," said Kaid.

* * *

The guild was quiet as they made their way downstairs to the main doors. Classes were in session and they met only one student who turned to watch them in openmouthed amazement.

They stepped out into the courtyard, and Carrie took her first look at Shola by daylight. The sky was a cloudless deep cerulean blue which contrasted vividly against the terra-cotta stone wall that surrounded the Guild House. Here and there ornamental trees and bushes in huge decorated clay tubs livened up the paved courtyard. The gentle fragrances of the blossoms were carried toward them on the warm breeze.

"Oh, it's beautiful," she said, looking round. "I didn't expect it to be like this."

The front of the Guild House was overgrown with dark green foliage that left only the windows exposed. To one side of the rambling building stood an obviously new extension, its clean white walls as yet bare of the climbing plants.

"It looks so old, as if it's grown up out of the ground," she said, hauling her sweater off over her head. "You were right about the weather, Kaid."

"The original hall is over a thousand years old," said Kusac. "Obviously, it's been repaired and added to over that time, as you can see by the new extension. Round the back is the new wing where we're staying. This area at the front is paved to allow vehicles to land because no traffic is allowed in Valsgarth from around dawn till the twentieth hour. Wait till you see the rest of the guild estate, though. At the back there's parkland—all grass, trees and bushes—space to really run free."

"I'd love to look at it later," she said, experiencing his enthusiasm as she looped the arms of her sweater round her waist.

Meral was waiting for them by the massive iron gates next to the porter's lodge. Surprisingly, like Kaid, he was dressed in civilian clothes.

"We don't want to draw attention to ourselves," said Kaid in response to Kusac's raised eye ridge.

Outside the gates it was another world. The street was narrowed by the profusion of store frontages claiming extra space, their contents spilling through the doorways out onto the paved footpaths. Above them, awnings in faded colors spread their shade, keeping the heat of the sun from the goods below. Mobile counters had been wheeled out, the transparent cabinets protecting the foodstuffs within from the attentions of the insect population.

All was hustle and bustle as a living tide of colorfully dressed Sholans of all ages picked their way between the goods on the street. Some entered the small stores to haggle over prices with the storekeepers, others stopped outside to chat with friends and share the latest pieces of gossip. The air was redolent with the fascinating aromas of food and alive with the low singsong cadence of their voices.

Neither her life on Keiss nor the time she'd spent on the ship had prepared her for this total assault on her senses. She stood there astounded by it all.

Put your shield up fully, Kusac said, taking her by the hand. *You'll soon get used to it.* He pointed to the ground around the store fronts. *If you look between the goods, you can see the mosaics that mark each store's boundary—the area they can use for trading.*

Why the need for boundaries?

We're a territorial species—at least the males are, he amended. *It's not so bad now as it was in our far past.*

Are you one of the territorial males? she asked, looking up at him.

As a telepath, unable to fight, I had it bred out of me but now I'm not so sure anymore, he replied slowly, his hand tightening on hers briefly.

They walked down the street, threading their way between the people, pausing for her to look at nearly every store. Openly curious glances followed them, many of the towns-people recognizing her from the newscasts. Naturally they were interested in their local Liege's family, especially now her son had an alien Leska from the newly-found telepathic species.

Despite her shield, Carrie was acutely aware of the many eyes focused on her.

They're concerned because I'm the heir to the Clan, Kusac sent. *This is our family land and most of the people in Valsgarth are related to us in one way or another.*

I thought your father was Clan Lord.

Lord of the Sixteen Telepath Clans, he corrected. *A position he holds by virtue of being the most powerful telepath on Shola, and being elected to the position by the Council of Telepath Clan Lords. I'm also a contender as heir to that ti-*

tle because of my Talent, along with another six or seven others from my generation.

How did your mother come to inherit the Clan, not your father?

Father doesn't belong to our Clan, he married into it. The firstborn inherits the title and in that generation, it was Mother. I was firstborn this time.

Carrie turned her attention back to the stores. Each one sold food of some description. Savory breads with or without fillings, sweet pastries and cakes, fruit, cooked meats served in hand-sized chunks or grilled on skewers over braziers—the variety was seemingly endless. Despite having just eaten, she found the smells appetizing.

"Students are always hungry, that's why there are so many food stores outside the guild," said Kusac, anticipating her question. "Remember, our towns grew up to serve the Guild Houses."

"Do you have guilds for everything?" asked Carrie.

"Of course. Telepaths, Warriors, Agriculture, Communications, Engineers—the list is long," said Kusac.

"And every one is a mixture of a school and a register of standards?"

Kusac flicked his ears in assent. "Every one."

"There used to be a similar system in our middle ages, but it was too rigid to survive," said Carrie, her attention caught by a high-pitched yowl. Turning to look, she saw a mother hustling two young ones into a fruit store, telling them off for running out without her.

"They're really sweet," she said, grinning as the smaller one continued to yowl and hold its ear. "What age would they be?" As she turned back to him, something small and furry came flying round the corner ahead of them and collided with her knees, making her stumble.

"Hey! Watch out!" she said, automatically reaching down with one hand to scoop up the small stunned bundle. She found herself looking at a very young Sholan. Hurriedly, she brought her other hand up to clasp her more firmly.

"She's about two," said Kusac, watching with a grin as the little one shook her head, then blinked.

Eyes widening in surprise and ears rotating forward, the child stretched toward Carrie, sniffing audibly before her curious hands grasped her hair and she began to purr loudly.

They heard the angry shouts of her mother. "Jaisa! Come back you bad kitling!"

Trying one-handedly to disengage the clutching hands with their tiny needle-sharp claws from her hair, Carrie looked up to see the child's mother come to an abrupt halt in front of her, ears and tail twitching anxiously. Around her she could hear the sudden silence.

"Is she yours?" asked Carrie from behind a curtain of her hair, still trying to disentangle herself.

With a laugh, Kusac came to her rescue, taking the child from her while she freed herself. He held the now squirming and loudly complaining bundle out to her mother.

The mother nodded, taking hold of her daughter. "I put her down to try and get her to walk properly," she said, finding her voice as she tucked the little one against her hip, "but before I could take her hand, she was gone. I'm sorry she disturbed you and your Leska, Liegen," she said, looking anxiously from Kusac to Carrie and back.

"No problem," said Carrie. "I'm glad I was there to catch her."

"Thank you again," the mother said, backing round the corner and out of sight. Around them, conversations began to break out again.

"The child was running on all fours, Kusac," said Carrie incredulously.

"Of course she was," he said with a laugh. "They do until they can walk upright. Don't sound so surprised, you've seen me on four legs. Surely your young go through a similar stage?"

"Not quite like that," she said, aware of a sharp pang of regret from him that he didn't quite manage to block in time as he remembered she was of a different species.

Beginning to walk down the street again, she gave herself a little shake and looked up at him. "We were talking about guilds."

"The guilds, yes," he said, bringing his attention back to her. "Our system is reasonably flexible. You attend a basic school until your particular talent is recognized, then you're sent to the appropriate guild." He drew her down the side street, empty now of the mother and her kitling. "Except for telepaths and Warriors."

"What happens to them?"

"Telepaths mainly come from one of the sixteen Telepath

Clans on Shola. In fact, they and the Warriors are the only Clans with a guild of their own. Our children are tested for a telepathic Talent when young and if they have one, are sent to the guild from the first. The rest of the young people are tested at about ten, and if they show a Talent, or a wild Talent is discovered later, then they're sent to the guild."

"What about the telepath children without Talent?"

"They're free to choose the profession they wish, provided they have the gift for it," said Kusac, as they stepped from the alley into another busy main street. "They tend to prefer to work in the Telepath Guild under another profession though, medicine for instance."

"And the Warriors?" asked Carrie, stopping for a moment to look at Meral.

"Warriors traditionally come from one of twenty Clans, or from the main branch of a Clan—a younger daughter, or a son like myself for instance," said Meral. "We train exclusively in weapons skills, then instead of doing military service, we remain at our guild until we're posted into space to do a tour of duty there."

"What position do Warriors have in Sholan society? What do they do?" Carrie asked as Kusac urged her on again.

"Security work, bodyguards or honor guards to dignitaries and visiting aliens, and representing those who choose not to fight in Challenges, particularly the females' Challenges."

"I thought you had law courts and a judicial system," said Carrie as they rounded the corner into a wider and more formal street.

"We have," said Kusac, "but litigants can choose to settle a dispute with a formal Challenge, letting the Gods choose who is in the right."

"The Challenge is held in front of a judge and witnesses and the outcome is legally binding," said Meral. "Often they choose champions to represent them, and that's where we come in."

"Swords for hire," said Kaid. "Military service is compulsory for males between the ages of eighteen and thirty, unless they're Telepaths. Whether we do it in the Forces or the Warrior's Guild is up to us."

"Vanna mentioned something about it, but I got the impression that you'd lived peacefully within the Alliance for a very long time."

"We're on a war footing now," Kusac reminded her.

"Have you forgotten the Valtegans? We've had compulsory military service for several hundred years, primarily to channel the virility and aggression of our excess of young males. It keeps them out of trouble," he said with a grin.

"Vanna mentioned that too, but I didn't notice any problems from the males on the *Khalossa*. You were in the Forces, so what age does that make you?" she asked.

Kusac grinned down at her, his canines white against his dark fur. "Old enough to know what I like," he said, touching her cheek.

Meral didn't quite succeed in stifling his laughter, even though Kaid frowned at him.

Be serious, sent Carrie.

"Twenty-eight in your years," he said, relenting and squeezing her hand gently. "Now enough of Sholan life, let's find a store that can copy your clothes."

The street they were now on had no goods on the walkways. Though paved, the central area had been left grass-covered; every few hundred meters ancient trees spread their foliage, offering shade to the people sitting on the seats beneath them. Most of the stores had at least half of their frontage open to the street to allow both easy browsing for customers and the passage of air to cool the interior.

This street seemed to be dedicated to either making or selling clothing, Carrie deduced from the goods on display.

Kusac chose a small store that he'd visited once before. As he explained what they wanted, the storekeeper stared at Carrie with a mixture of frank curiosity and appraisal.

"Trousers, eh? New style, are they?"

"No. They're for her," said Kusac patiently, his tail flicking with an irritation he couldn't conceal.

"No tail?"

Kusac kept his face impassive despite his mounting annoyance. "You can see she hasn't. Touibans wear similar garments. Can you make them or not?"

"She doesn't look Touiban," the trader said, eyeing her up and down in a manner Carrie took an instant exception to. "Is she a female one?"

Carrie was losing her temper. She leaned forward until her face was inches from his. "Look, you mangy, point-eared Sholan, I know it hasn't escaped your notice that you haven't seen an alien like me before, so cut the crap! You know damn well I'm not a Touiban! Either you're prepared to talk business or we leave. Understand?"

Meral and Kaid turned their backs, this time both of them exchanging grins.

The storekeeper wasn't looking at her, he was staring at the torc she wore. When she'd leaned forward, its weight had pulled it free of the neckline of her shirt. His ears flicked back along his head as he tore his gaze away from it, looking again at her face, then at Kusac standing beside her.

"Liegen Aldatan?" he said at last, his voice very quiet. "Liegen, I'm sorry. I didn't recognize you without your torc," he said, stumbling over the words in his haste to get out an apology.

"You thought you'd have some fun with students from the guild," said Carrie, still angry, "and mock me into the bargain!"

"A Telepath?" the trader asked, a haunted look coming into his eyes. "Your Leska?"

Kusac nodded. "And a new ally for Shola. There will be more of her kind here soon. They'll be wanting clothing, too," he added, driving his point home.

"If the Liegena wants this garment copied, then I will do my poor best to accommodate her," the storekeeper said, his supercilious attitude completely gone.

"I'm sure you will," said Kusac dryly. "We want two pairs made, both in lightweight fabric. Had you been more cooperative, we might have given you other business. When will they be ready?"

"By the end of the week, Liegen Aldatan. What colors would the Liegena like?"

"Red and a light blue," replied Kusac, aware of what she wanted through their link. "Send them to the guild when they're ready." Taking Carrie by the arm, he turned to leave.

Patience, he sent to her, aware of her continuing anger. *He'll do for now. Later we'll go to one of the major stores.*

Mentally Carrie fumed, sending him images of what she'd like to do to the trader.

"You've got a very graphic imagination," Kusac said, more than a little shocked at some of the imagery.

Meral and Kaid exchanged puzzled glances.

Footwear was next, but this time, Kusac took her to a larger leather workers' store. There they met with deference and a professional sense of challenge in producing a totally new item for the Liegena.

Their immediate business finished, Carrie wanted to wander round the town, stopping to look at a store selling hand-woven rugs, a pottery selling delicately painted bowls and, more to the males' taste, a weapons store.

"Nearly everything seems to be hand-made," she said as they left there and headed farther down the metal workers' street. "Don't you mass produce anything?"

"Not in Valsgarth. Across the bay in Nazule, the Warriors' Guild town, there are some manufacturing areas and larger stores where the goods are sold. Most people want to have something that has been made for them, something individual, with its own character," said Kusac as they came to the jewelry quarter.

They passed by several larger stores till they came to one that took Carrie's fancy. It was small and set back from the main part of the street. The window was full of bronze and silver jewelry, pendants of silver or bronze set with colored stones, earrings either looped or pendant, bracelets and torcs both plain and of differing diameters of twisted silver or bronze wire.

Nearly all the Sholans she'd met wore some form of jewelry, even if it was only when off duty. As they entered, she was instantly surrounded by half a dozen beings several centimeters taller than herself.

Too stunned to move, she stood there while in their high, fluting voices, they chattered back and forth to each other, each one reaching out to touch her hair, her face, her garments. Their movements were so fast, it almost made her dizzy trying to follow them with her eyes. With their long, thin, clawed hands prodding at her, she felt as if she were being picked at by a host of insects.

She didn't have time to panic as Kusac literally barked a few phrases in Traders'—the common spaceport language—at them. They froze, waiting while he made a few choice comments about their behavior and his willingness to report them to their Swarm Leader.

Carrie had never seen anything like them. Dressed in the brightest, most garish colours they could find, their dress sense made her wince. Then there was the jewelry. They obviously believed in wearing their wealth as they were each festooned with gold and silver chains, strings of brightly colored transparent stones, not to mention the brooches and rings.

As to their physical appearance, they were strange creatures, almost apelike in appearance, with their long bodies and short limbs. Their brows were pronounced, overshadowing the small eyes set beneath them in dark-skinned sockets. What hair they had was sparse, though thicker on the crown of the head and the lower jaw. The nose was their least humanoid feature. Long and thin, it was flanged and edged with stiff hairs.

As one, they began to move again, bowing and nodding to her while apologizing vociferously in their fluting voices. Then as quickly as they'd mobbed her, they were gone, leaving a cloud of sharply scented air behind them.

Kusac sneezed loudly, followed by Meral and Kaid. Even Carrie felt her eyes begin to water and her nose smart until the storekeeper pulled out a bottle from under his counter and sprayed the air liberally.

"Thank you," said Kusac, his nose twitching as he tried not to give in to a second sneeze. He lost the battle.

"Being popular with the Touibans can have its disadvantages," the jeweler said. "Their scent will be neutralized in a few moments. Don't let it drive you from my store. I've many lovely pieces for you to consider, especially some delicate enough even for your Leska, Liegen Aldatan."

Sure enough, the air was beginning to clear.

"What on earth was that all about?" asked Carrie, watching the motley colored group as they scuttled off down the street.

"Touibans," said Kusac. "The last members of the Alliance. You've met us all now. They're insatiably curious beings, wonderful with electronics. Nearly all the computers we use were at least partially designed by them."

"What was that smell they left behind?"

"An apology scent. They communicate almost as much by scent as by words. I told them that you were the Ambassador of a new species and deserved at the least the honor accorded to the Leader of a Hundred Swarms. That's why they disappeared so fast," he grinned. "It can be intimidating to be surrounded by a group of them, but the ones you're likely to meet are harmless."

"Do they always go around in groups?"

"Yes. They're a breeding unit, a small clan if you like, but their females don't leave the home worlds."

Carrie shook her head slowly and turned away from the doorway. "Strange," she said.

She wandered round, leaving the males to look at various arm and wrist bracelets. Several pieces took her fancy even though the style tended to be on the chunky side for her because of the larger size of Sholan wrists.

Kusac, what do you do for money here?

He looked up from where he stood at the counter talking to the trader.

What do you mean? he asked.

What do I use for money?

If you want something, I'll get it for you, he sent.

That's not what I mean. How do I go about getting some money of my own? How do I earn some?

Ah, I see what you mean. I should've thought to tell you sooner. When we became Leskas, you were automatically recruited into the Forces with me. They'll be paying you wages, too.

But I'm not doing anything for them.

We're here at the Guild on their orders. I'll check with the commerce center later. There should be an account in your name by now, probably with quite a tidy sum in it. Are you wanting to buy something?

I want to get something for you.

"What?" he asked, surprised, as she joined him at the counter.

"I'd like to get you another torc."

He looked down at her, putting an arm round her shoulders. "That's a nice thought," he said, "but it isn't necessary."

"I thought I was beginning to make sense of the memories I inherited from you," she said. "Isn't it the right thing to do since you've given me yours?" she asked.

"Well, yes," he admitted. "Torcs are usually exchanged, but there's no need for you to get me one. It isn't necessary for me to wear a torc."

Why did you give me your torc, Kusac? came her thought. *Why is it important that I wear it?*

Kusac was startled. He hadn't anticipated her question and had no ready answer.

Carrie let herself be drawn by him to the rear of the store, away from the interested owner and the other customers.

Circumstances forced me to give you my torc sooner than I wished. I wanted to ask you first, but at least I did make sure you were willing to wear it, and that you actually took it from me.

What circumstances, and why was it important that I took it from you? You aren't making much sense, Kusac, she sent, turning round to look at him. *And what's happened again?*

With you and me, nothing happens the way I want it, he replied with a sigh. *That's what's happened again. The circumstances were my mother's unexpected arrival.*

He put his hands up to gently hold either side of her face. *I intended to ask you before we met my family so that if you were willing, you'd be wearing my torc then. The right moment has never arrived, and I think with us, never will.* His mouth opened slightly and his lips curved up in an almost human grin.

Kusac . . .

Hush, let me finish. When I gave you my torc, I couldn't tell you that it was a betrothal gift. There wasn't time. It was more important that I was the one to tell my mother you were Terran, and that she knew how I felt about you from the start. You had to be wearing my torc when she met you for the first time. The night we became lovers, you asked me what kind of life I wanted for us. I said then I wanted you beside me always. I meant it, they weren't just idle words, cub. This is hardly an appropriate place to ask you, but will you take the life-oath with me and become my mate?

She could sense his hopes and fears for the future, and with it his uncertainty that she would accept him.

I wasn't trying to mislead you by not telling you its importance before now, he sent anxiously. *I was trying to protect you. I intended to ask you tonight.*

Are you sure that's what you want? she asked, aware now of what he was prepared to give up, what would probably be demanded of him if he married his alien Leska.

For an answer, he leaned forward to kiss her. "Nothing less will do," he growled as he released her. "I find I'm becoming unnaturally territorial when it comes to you."

"So, will you wear my torc?" she asked.

"You know how much it would please me to wear it," he said quietly as they returned to the counter at the front of the store. He pulled her close, rubbing his cheek against the top of her head.

"The Liegena wishes to buy a bronze torc," he said to the trader. "One bearing the Aldatan sunbursts."

The next couple of hours were spent in one of the larger stores, ordering tabards and long tunics to be made to fit her uniquely human shape. They also picked up a couple of the ready-made shirts and short tunics to do her in the meantime.

Rather than return to the guild, or spend the requisite two or three hours in a restaurant, they stopped for lunch in one of the taverns that served meals for the students.

Like nearly all the buildings in the center of Valsgarth, the tavern was old. Several mutually connecting small rooms gave it the size necessary to host large numbers of students yet still retain its antique charm. At the back was a small room reserved for diners. They pushed their way through the lunchtime throng until they reached it.

For once, no one seemed to notice her, Carrie thought with relief as she sat down in one of the high curve-backed wooden chairs. A large soft cushion compensated for the lack of the usual bowl-shaped seat. In this chair, at least her feet touched the ground!

Tentatively, she let her shield down a little, curious as to what it would feel like to be in such an enclosed area with so many student Telepaths. A myriad of unsubtle probes pricked at her mind. She winced, replacing her shield hurriedly.

Instantly even the echo of their probes was shut out as Kusac extended his own shielding to include her.

Now you know what it feels like, he grinned. *And the importance of shielding and manners in our community! Though I must say, they aren't exactly showing much courtesy to you.*

She felt him send a loud mental reprimand to those who had been too curious. As she watched, several pairs of ears were suddenly laid flat and remained so for a good few minutes.

Was I that unsubtle? she asked.

I'm afraid so, but you've improved immensely, he replied as a harassed waitress came in to take their order.

They'd just finished when Kaid got to his feet. "Stay where you are," he said quietly. "Some public information reporters have just come in. I'd lay odds they know we're here." He moved toward the rear of the room, checking that the exit was clear. Disappearing from sight, he returned moments later and beckoned to them. They rose hastily and with backward glances, slipped out the rear door into the yard.

"I suggest we head back to the guild now," said Kaid, leading the way out into the lane beyond. "They know you've arrived on Shola, so they aren't likely to give up until they draw a blank at the guild. You're going to have to speak to them at some point, but I suggest you leave it until I've checked in at Dzahai Stronghold. I want to see what the official line on your Link is first," he said as they made their way through the narrow back streets to the Guild House.

"Contacting your father would also be a wise idea, Liegen. Leave it to me to talk to the Master, that's part of my job as your adjutant."

As they passed the porter, Kaid stopped briefly to leave instructions that the Liegen Aldatan and his Leska were not willing to be seen by any callers.

Once they were in their quarters, Kusac went to the comm and placed a call to his father.

"Why call him when you can use telepathy?" asked Carrie, moving out of the viewer's range.

"Courtesy and safety," he replied. "I don't wish to intrude on his personal thoughts, especially when he could be involved in important business. He's the head of Alien Relations and as such is a member of the Sholan High Command, as well as doing his duty as an occasional circuit judge. If he's busy he won't thank me for interrupting him. Now hush, please," he said as the Telepath Guild symbol blinked off the screen to be replaced by his father's image.

"Kusac, I hadn't expected to hear from you so soon," said his father. "Naturally, I sensed your arrival last night. I won't ask how your journey was as I expect it was as tedious as they usually are. So to what do I owe the pleasure of this call?"

"The public information reporters, Father," he said without preamble. "I took Carrie round Valsgarth today and they tracked us down to the tavern where we were eating. Kaid, my adjutant, got us out of there without being noticed. What do you want us to do about them?"

"What do I want you to do?" said his father, lifting an eye ridge. "You were the one who wanted to take charge of your own life, Kusac. Are you now asking me for advice?"

"You're head of the Clan while Mother is away," he said, trying not to let his irritation show.

His father regarded him for a moment. "If the decision were yours, what would you do?" he asked abruptly.

Kusac blinked in surprise, ears flicking slightly. He began to run several possibilities through his mind. "I'd issue a statement through Kaid to the effect that we were suffering time lag from the long journey and that my Leska, never having visited Shola before, needs time to adjust. That we'd appreciate being left in peace for the meantime."

His father nodded. "Then say that," he said. "You can add that Alien Relations can supply them with all the details they need about the Terrans, including images of your Leska. You'll have to get used to fending them off for yourself, Kusac. You're the first person to ever have a cross-species Leska. That in itself is newsworthy, never mind the fact that Carrie and her people have lived under the Valtegans for many years."

"Yes, I know," said Kusac. "I assume you've issued a statement regarding both our link and the Valtegans on Keiss."

"Only the barest of facts. I'll leave it to you to flesh out the details." His father grinned, letting Kusac feel his amusement at the situation. "It's good training for your future in Alien Relations. After all, who should know more about intimate relations with the Keissian Terrans than you?"

"Thanks, Father," he said, trying to contain his annoyance yet again.

"I'll look forward to hearing or reading your articles. When can I expect to see you both at the estate? I'm tied up with work on these two treaties at the moment and can't leave here to visit you."

"When we've got any time free from our guild commitments," Kusac replied, grateful that at least he didn't have to worry about his father descending on them at the guild.

"See you don't leave it too long."

"Yes, Father," he said as the screen blanked.

Carrie kept her thoughts carefully neutral, well aware that there was a long-standing unresolved conflict between Kusac and his father.

Kusac got up from the desk and yawned. "I'm afraid that I wasn't exaggerating my tiredness. I don't know about you, but I could do with some more sleep."

"I'll join you," she said, going over to him and tucking herself up against him.

"I'm glad I've got you," he said, wrapping his arm round her and resting his head on top of hers briefly. "Let me go and tell Kaid what I want him to say to the reporters, then we can rest."

Garras finished powering down the scouter, then opened the hatch. It had been a long and tiring shift. Flying low over the forest and swamp around the ruins of the Valtegan base searching for any stray Valtegans was not his idea of stimulating work. Even with the new scanners, it was more reliable to physically keep an eye on the ground.

He sat there rubbing his eyes as the rest of his crew released themselves from their seats and began to move toward the hatch. He acknowledged their leavetakings with a grunt. Maybe he was getting too old for this. He grinned. Better not let Vanna hear him say that. The grin faded. She'd have arrived on Shola by now. Sighing, he released himself from his harness and stood up. He was definitely getting too old for this.

As he turned round, he heard someone coming up the ramp. Draz stuck his head through the hatch.

"Everyone gone?" he asked as he came aboard.

"Yes, Sub-Lieutenant," said Garras, his tail giving a slight involuntary twitch of curiosity. "Can I help you?"

Draz leaned past him and sealed the hatch. "I hope you can," he said. "Are you still in touch with Kaid?"

"I can contact him if that's what you mean," he said.

"I need a line of secure communication to him. Can you set one up for me through your friend Vanna Kyjishi?"

"Easily, but as to how secure the communications would be, I can't vouch. What's the problem?"

"Sit down," said Draz, perching on the arm of the navigator's seat.

Garras sat down again, swiveling his seat round to face him.

"How much did Kaid tell you of what he was doing?"

"Only what I needed to know," said Garras cautiously.

"You knew he'd discovered a small group of dissidents from our two destroyed colonies, didn't you?"

"He mentioned that," Garras confirmed.

"Kaid overheard them try to involve your ex-crew member, Mito, in their plotting. With her cooperation he placed her as an undercover agent among them. When the six dissidents died, we assumed, wrongly as it turns out, that the matter would end there. A few days ago Mito was contacted by yet another dissident. It seems that those six were not the only ones involved."

"What did they want?"

"Mito was told to intercept an incoming coded message from the *Rhyaki* when she was next on bridge duty and that she'd be contacted in the mess the following day to pass it on."

"I'd heard Mito was quarantined because she'd contracted a Terran illness. I take it that's not true," said Garras.

Draz nodded. "We substituted one of my people for her on the bridge and intercepted the message. We haven't been able to find out who it was that contacted her in the mess unfortunately, but we have decoded the message."

"Oh?" Garras waited.

"I need that message passed on to Kaid," said Draz reluctantly.

"It'll take me a day at least to set it up," said Garras. "Vanna will be staying at the Telepath Guild because she'll be working in their medical center. Once I've contacted her I can pass on your message for Kaid. What do you want me to say?"

"I want you to transmit data from your terminal to Vanna. The message will be encoded and included with the medical information. All Vanna has to do is pass on the relevant portion to Kaid."

"Do I get to know what the message is?"

Draz shook his head. "On a need-to-know basis, Garras."

Garras reached into the topmost pocket of his jacket and pulled out a small bronze disk mounted on a chain. It was inscribed with a cursive sigil. He held it out in the palm of his hand toward Draz.

The Sub-Lieutenant leaned forward and, with a sharp intake of breath, reached out for it.

Garras' hand closed over it, claws extended. "No." He put it away.

"Kaid's?"

"Mine," said Garras. "I had to leave for Clan reasons. We're guild brothers. I think you can tell me that message, don't you, Sub-Lieutenant?"

"Captain." Draz acknowledged the other's superior rank, ears flicking in annoyance. "The message said Earth has had no contact with the Valtegans, and Keiss is merely what it seems, a first colony. It continues that another motive for rallying the survivors against the Terrans on Earth must be found. There's a contact address to be visited when the male concerned goes on leave to Shola."

Garras' eyes narrowed as he began to swear softly. "Is there any way to identify him?"

"None, beyond the fact he has to be one of the career people. There are forty-five due for leave on Shola when the cruiser arrives with their replacements."

"When?"

"Within the week."

Garras got up from his seat. "How soon can you get that data ready for me to send to Vanna?"

"It's being processed now."

"I'll be in my quarters. Let me know when it's ready and I'll contact Vanna. What do you plan to do about Mito?"

"Kaid wanted her transferred planetside now. She's scheduled to be posted to Keiss anyway to work on what's left of the Valtegan computer systems. Down there she'll not be of any use to the dissidents."

"Sounds reasonable." Garras' hand hovered over the hatch switch. "You realize that I prefer to keep my past to myself, Sub-Lieutenant. If you choose to keep me informed, though, I could probably be of help to you. The decision is entirely yours." He pressed the switch.

"Now I know why the males on the *Khalossa* stayed away from me," said Carrie with a grin as she stood brushing her hair at the long mirror set into the wardrobe. "Wearing your torc was what you meant when you said there were other ways to avoid me being propositioned."

Kusac remained lying on the bed watching her, still trying to wake up from their afternoon sleep. He was suffering more from the change in his circadian rhythm than she was.

I was jealous, I admit it, which is a totally non-Sholan re-action, but then as I've already said, I'm getting used to having reactions that are alien to me. His tone was wry.

She put the brush down on the table nearby and came over to sit beside him. "There was no need," she said.

He reached out to take her hand. As he did, they felt an echo of their Link compulsion run through him.

"What day is tomorrow?" she asked abruptly. "We're sup-posed to be seeing Master Esken in the morning."

"You're right," he said, sitting up. "I lost track of the days because of the time differences. We'll have to cancel. I'll call Sorli and tell him."

"Kusac, do you think Kaid would mind joining Meral and Sevrin?" she asked. "I'm beginning to feel we have no life of our own. There's always someone else around. It's not as if anyone could harm us here in the guild, and we're so hy-persensitive to anyone around us during our Link day that we'd be sure to pick up any threat."

"When I said the same thing to you on the *Khalossa,* you were the one who didn't mind having bodyguards," he said.

"I don't mind most of the time. I like them, they're good company, more like friends now. It's just that at this time it would be nice to have some real privacy."

"I agree wholeheartedly," he said, pulling her closer.

"Food first," she said, pushing him away. "I'm hungry."

"You're always hungry," he said, swinging his legs off the bed and standing up. "Do you want to eat here or brave the student refectory?"

"Here, please. I'd rather relax than be an object of curios-ity and speculation. Also, I've started getting the odd burst of flickering images. I haven't had that since the first time. With our Link day so close, I'd rather stay in our shielded quarters."

"Our bodies are still working on ship time," he said, checking his wrist unit. "I reckon we're at least twelve hours behind planetary time. For us it's early morning. It'll take a couple of days to adjust, I'm afraid. You get dressed and I'll see to contacting Sorli and talking to Kaid."

After much verbal maneuvering by Kusac, it was reluc-tantly agreed by the accommodation staff that Kaid could move into the empty Leska apartment next door to them. This done, Kaid contacted Meral and Sevrin, alerting them to the fact that he was leaving the premises. He then requested a public aircar to take him to the outskirts of town where the vehicle hire firms were located.

From there he flew southeast to the town of Nazule and the Warrior Guild. Stopping there briefly, he took off again, this time heading inland toward the Dzahai Mountains.

They were expecting him. In the courtyard below, the landing lights were on. Automatically he compensated for the gusting wind as he brought the small craft down to land vertically. It was nearly always blustery at the Stronghold because of the altitude.

Powering the craft down, he released his safety harness. Getting to his feet, he reached for his gray cloak, flinging it round his shoulders and fastening it in place. A traditionalist, he still preferred cloaks to coats in most circumstances. They were more easily taken off and could be used many different ways in both a defensive and offensive manner.

The landing lights flicked off as he stepped out into the courtyard. He closed his eyes, waiting till the eidetic images died before opening them again. The light from the windows threw a faint glow that gave him more than enough visibility. Moving across the yard to the main doors he heard the faint sound of a footfall on the gravel nearby.

He gave a small growl of annoyance. They weren't still playing that old game, were they? In one fluid move, he stooped to pick up a handful of gravel, then swung toward the noise, releasing his small missiles.

A sharp yelp of surprise rang out. Kaid straightened up with a laugh. "Too noisy, youngling. You need more practice."

Still chuckling, he continued walking toward the doors, pushing the left one open just enough for him to slip inside.

The hall was as he remembered it, not that he'd expected it to be different. At the far end sat the massive statue of Vartra, flanked on either side by glowing braziers from which curled opaque coils of smoke heavy with the scent of incense.

His shadow flickering before him, Kaid walked down the length of the hall. On either side, torches set in ancient wall sconces lit his way. Stopping in front of the statue, he regarded it critically for a moment. He'd never been able to decide whether the God was laying down his weapons or was about to pick them up.

Crossing his forearms over his chest, he bowed his head in tribute to the image, then stepped forward to pick up a small block of incense from the stand beside the brazier. Softly saying the ritual words, he tossed the incense into the hot coals. Moving to the right, he stepped past the statue to the great crimson curtain that hung down behind it from ceiling to floor. Twitching at the folds, he found the opening and stepped through into the alcove.

The metal door in front of him slid silently aside, allowing him to enter the brightly lit corridor beyond. Blinking as he stepped through, he was aware of the door closing behind him. He continued walking, coming to a stop at the first doorway. Knocking gently, he entered.

The Leader sat behind his desk. On a chair to one side of him was the head of the cult of Vartra, the priest and telepath, Lijou.

"Leader Ghezu," murmured Kaid, inclining his head toward him as he approached the desk. "Brother Lijou."

"We've waited impatiently for your arrival," said Ghezu, indicating that Kaid should take the empty seat facing him. "What news have you?"

Unwrapping himself from his cloak, Kaid sat. "You've had my reports," he said.

Ghezu made a dismissive gesture with his hand. "You know what we need to hear."

"I don't know that I can tell you, Ghezu," said Kaid.

"What do you mean?" demanded Ghezu sharply.

"He means that his contract is not now under your jurisdiction," said Lijou with a smile. "Isn't that so, Kaid?"

Kaid inclined his head. "My contract with the Clan Leader, and you, is fulfilled. I came to remind you of this."

"There are questions I need answered, Kaid. Your reports were too brief," said Ghezu.

"How so? I told you all that you requested."

"We didn't realize that the matter was so complex," said Ghezu. "Now we're aware of that, we know how much information we're lacking."

"I understand your predicament, but it's out of my hands now," murmured Kaid, examining his claws.

"What about your duty to the Brotherhood?" Ghezu asked. "You know how important this is to us."

"If you remember, I was retired from the Brotherhood

some time ago," said Kaid quietly. "I owe no one anything now, except the client who gave me my current contract."

Ghezu made a noise of exasperation and sat back in his seat. "You always were too much of an individualist, Kaid," he said. "I'd forgotten how much of a mixed blessing your early retirement was for us all. Why the hell did you kill all the dissidents on the *Khalossa?*"

"The Commander wanted the matter brought to an end. I told you in my report."

"You could at least have interrogated one of them before termination."

"Why? I knew all there was to know about them. Again, it was all in my report."

"Softly, Ghezu," said Lijou, smiling again. "You know you can't fault Kaid. He was protecting his client's interests. What we need to discover from him is what he's prepared to accept in return for the information we seek."

Ghezu narrowed his eyes, ears giving one slight flick.

"What is it you want, Kaid?" continued the priest.

Kaid looked up from examining his nails. "A steady source of information in Valsgarth and beyond. I'm not convinced my clients' lives aren't still at risk."

"Ah, here we have one piece of information for free," purred Lijou. "You're still protecting our Liegen and his Leska."

"That was never in doubt, was it?" asked Kaid, raising an eye ridge.

"Very well, what do you wish to know?" asked Ghezu with a sigh.

"Do I get my back-up?"

"Yes."

"What's been the grass roots reaction to his link with the Terran female?" asked Kaid.

"The average person doesn't care one way or the other," said Ghezu. "You know they view telepaths as a breed apart anyway. Everything they do is strange. Granted having an alien Leska is more strange than usual, but there's no undercurrent of feeling beyond curiosity about the Terran and her relationship to Kusac Aldatan. The Attitude Indoctrination program was run on the public channels and seems to have been effective."

"What about the Clans?"

"That's another matter," said Lijou. "There's a lot of muttering among the Clan Lords. The next sitting of the council isn't for two months yet, but by then I predict there will be several complaints about the fitness of Kusac as a candidate for the Clans' Lordship because of his alien Leska."

"Vailkoi has been muttering loudest on behalf of his daughter Rala. He sees this Terran as a threat to his daughter's position and wants the life-bonding date to be set as soon as possible," said Ghezu.

Kaid nodded. "That much I expected. What of the reaction to the discovery of the Terrans and the Valtegans? Does anyone believe the Terrans were involved in the destruction of Khyaal and Szurtha?"

"None that we've heard. Nearly every clan has lost someone on the two colonies, but they hold the Valtegans totally responsible for the destruction. There was no obvious anti-Terran feeling that we noticed, and as I said, the A.I. program would have rectified it if there had been any."

"How did the reporters cover the topic?"

"Factually, for a change," said Ghezu. "Though today when they reported your arrival on Shola, there was speculation as to the nature of their relationship—I don't need to tell you how they love to trivialize things."

Kaid nodded. "Thank you. That answers my most pressing questions for the moment."

"I need to ask a few questions," said Lijou. "My guild is not being forthcoming with information about them. Are they truly Leskas in the sense that we understand it? Do they have a real telepathic Link with each other to the exclusion of anyone else?"

"Yes, their Link is real. In fact it's more demanding and tying than the Links our people have," replied Kaid.

"I've heard rumors to the effect she's more powerful, more Talented than he is."

"As to that, I can't comment. She certainly has more Talents than we have, which is why the Forces have sent them to the Telepath Guild for her to be assessed."

"If they can devise tests for abilities we know nothing about," said Lijou dubiously. "Do they know yet why the Leska Link occurred between them?"

Kaid shook his head. "No, but others of our kind find the Terrans attractive. There have been several nontelepath pairings already. Their personal physician thinks it's due initially to similar pheromones. Beyond that, your guess is as good as mine until your guild comes up with the answers."

"Is it true that the female can fight without any of the physical problems that our telepaths suffer?" asked Ghezu.

"Yes, it's true, and so can Kusac now," said Kaid. "On Keiss he killed four Valtegans without a second thought, and on the *Khalossa* he was involved in a bar brawl in her defense against the other Terrans on board."

"Against the Terrans? What had they done to cause him to attack them?" asked Lijou, ears flicking in surprise.

"Some of them were reacting with species prejudice toward her for having a sexual relationship with one of us." Kaid shrugged. "As it happens, she didn't have such a relationship with him at that point."

"So Kusac is now free from all the inhibitions that prevent us from fighting," said Lijou.

"Yes. There has been a crossover of her abilities to him," said Kaid. "What she can do, it now seems so can he. The Warrior Guild want to study them as well because the Sholan High Command sees their potential for military use. It's my belief that if this Link proves successful and they can isolate the reasons for it happening in the first place, they will try to reproduce those conditions using other mixed species pairs."

Lijou turned to Ghezu. "This will upset the balance between both our guilds," he said thoughtfully. "The potential repercussions of telepaths who can fight are enormous. It will affect our social structure at every level."

Ghezu shifted uncomfortably. "It seems you were right. They are a force for change, whether or not we want it. Vartra knows where this will lead."

"The God's hand can certainly be seen at work here," said Lijou. "There's nothing else we can do but go with it until we see what His plan is, because take my word for it, there is a plan!"

Ghezu stirred again. "You should return to them now. We'll see that you're provided with the information you need. In return, keep us informed on their progress at both guilds. I've issued a directive that we are accepting no negative contracts concerning Terrans or Leska pairs where one partner is Terran."

Kaid nodded and got to his feet, collecting his cloak from the back of the chair. "That'll certainly help. I'll keep in touch through my contact. I take it if I need support, I can call on the Brothers?"

"Of course," said Ghezu.

Ghezu waited till Kaid had left. "Well, I hope you're satisfied," he said. "We could have gotten as much information from our people already on the *Khalossa*."

"Not really," said Lijou, sitting back in his seat with a satisfied look on his face. "We've achieved more than you realize, Ghezu. I always told you that you didn't have enough depth of vision."

"What are you rambling on about?" demanded Ghezu, his tone irritated as he tapped his stylus on the desk.

"While Kaid needs us, we still have someone close to the pair who will feed us information on them. If he wants our help, it'll cost him. Had we used your people on the *Khalossa*, then we wouldn't have that, would we?"

"Very well, I'll concede that." Ghezu's tone was far from pleased. The stylus he was holding broke with a loud snap.

Seeing the thunderous look on his face, Lijou forbore to comment on his colleague's lack of self control. "There's more," he said. "Kaid's let this become personal."

That shocked Ghezu. "Are you sure?"

"Positive. I couldn't pick up any more than that, but it's enough. We know we can use it if we need to. It gives us an advantage over him."

"It's as well we have Dzaka, then."

Lijou frowned. "I don't understand this desire of yours to set him against Kaid. It's foolish in the extreme. You're trying his loyalty to us too much."

"I'm not setting him against Kaid. He's the best we have. He's also the only one who has a chance of besting him if it came to it."

Lijou snorted his derision. "Do you really think he'd terminate Kaid? Then you're a bigger fool than I thought you were, Ghezu!"

"He'd do it, if it's presented properly to him," smiled Ghezu. "You've forgotten how he feels about Kaid leaving him with us when he was expelled."

"That was no more than the hurt pride of a youngling, Ghezu! He got over that years ago."

"Did he?" It was Ghezu's turn to purr with self-satisfaction. "We'll see, Lijou. We'll see. For the moment

I'm content to leave the Aldatan cub and his Leska alone.
Both Kaid and Dzaka said that at the moment they're stable
and have no ambitions. We'll watch and wait. I want proof
that they can fight. When we have it, then we can think
about possibly moving to recruit them. With them on our
side, Esken and his guild won't dare to block our request for
full guild status at the council meeting. Because if we do
manage to pull them to the Brotherhood, they'll be fighting
against the Telepath Guild themselves. We're the logical
place for them to belong. Your guild can't cope with the
mentality of fighters, and the Warrior Guild hasn't the facilities for telepaths. We, on the other hand, can offer them
both."

"Don't risk everything on just one pair, Ghezu," Lijou
warned. "Yes, we want them, but we can't risk generations
of work on just one pair. Wait and see if there are more."

"I'm not a fool, Lijou," said Ghezu, getting to his feet.
"Of course I'll wait."

Chapter 12

She slept lightly, her mind drifting calmly in the gray mists of peacefulness, more secure with her own identity now they had begun to edit their common memories. As always she could feel his presence, relaxed like her in sleep: quiet, quiescent.

In the distance twin flickers of light caught her attention, beckoning her. They flared brightly, then died down again, but in that instant she saw a shape beyond them, a presence that called to her.

Curious, she let herself be drawn toward the lights. Who was it that could touch her subconscious mind? The torches flared again as she drew nearer. Blinking, she tried to peer beyond the glow, straining to make out the details of the seated figure beyond.

With her still new night-sight, she saw the being begin to rise sinuously to its feet, its movement bringing the smell of incense drifting toward her nostrils.

She wasn't afraid, she realized. Whoever or whatever was coming toward her intended no harm. There was a presence, but she couldn't feel the mind: there was no sense of identity, no ongoing stream of conscious thought.

Puzzled, she waited as the figure continued to approach. It stopped between the braziers of fire. The flickering flames picked out a feature here and there—the ears pricked toward her, the nose with the bifurcated mouth below it, a suggestion of high cheekbones—before dying down, once more leaving him anonymous in the gloom.

"You are one, now," said a voice, its tone low, the Sholan strangely accented. "Is it well between you, or do you regret your bond?"

She hesitated before replying. "It's well. I regret nothing. But who are you?"

The voice continued, ignoring her question. "So many

lives changed, so many lost." The voice was a whisper as the reflection of the flames briefly highlighted a face, leaving deep shadows where its eyes should be. "It is good to find the few who are happy from the first. Often the price you have paid for your Talent has been too high."

The voice died to nothing as the figure faded back into the shadows.

"Wait!" She stepped forward, the braziers behind her now, but the presence had gone leaving only a dark form sitting on the ground, the glint of metal by its feet.

The gray mist returned, roiling turbulently around her feet, spreading rapidly upwards, blanking out everything.

"Wait!" she cried, arms reaching out to grasp . . . nothing.

"Where are you?" she cried frantically, looking round the darkened room, terror now beginning to creep into her soul.

A groan from beside her, a sudden movement in the dark as a hand damp with sweat grasped her bare arm, claws pricking her in his urgency to reassure.

"I'm here," said a voice groggy with sleep.

"I can't see you . . . I can't see anything!" she said, turning her head blindly from side to side.

The light came on, its brightness making her cover her eyes.

Strong arms pulled her close, the familiar feel and smell of his damp fur calming her instantly.

I'm here, cub, he sent, pushing aside his own nightmare to reassure her through their link. *Open your eyes, you'll see me now.*

She peered through half-open fingers, letting her hands fall away as she saw his face, brows creased and ears flicking in concern.

Images jostled in her mind for attention. "Where were you?" Her voice held a residue of panic.

"I was here," he said as she clutched his arms for the physical reassurance she needed.

"I couldn't see you through the mist." She was confused, unable to sort between the images. "There were flames, incense . . ."

"A dark figure beyond them . . ." he said, smelling her fear mingling with his own.

"Yes!" she said, turning to him eagerly, "talking about our Link! You saw him, too?"

He shook his head, sensing what she had seen. "My vision

was different. I saw only a shadowy figure who asked if I was content, nothing more."

"Who was it, Kusac?"

"I don't know. I'm not sure . . . I had a friend—Ghyan. He was like a brother to me. He left here for the temple. Perhaps he's still there. Maybe he can tell us."

A shiver ran the length of his body, making his hackles and hair rise. Consciously he tried to relax the muscles, lay his fur flat. He tried to ignore the small voice from his upbringing that still believed in superstition.

Carrie picked it up though. "Vartra? But Gods aren't real, they don't appear to people, do they?" When he remained silent, she gave him a shake.

"I don't know," he said. "I've never believed so." His tone was unsure despite his words. "Likely it was a dream we both shared."

Carrie made a noise of disbelief. "You don't really believe that. You can't, since we each experienced something different."

"I don't know what I believe," he said. Their dream, vision, whatever it had been, had disturbed him more than he was prepared to admit. He bent his head toward her, licking her cheek. She tasted of salt and sweat.

Reaching up, she stroked his face. His head turned to follow her hand, his tongue licking her palm. Amber eyes looked up at her, an opalescence beginning to gather in their depths.

The need for her to understand the dream was fading, being replaced with more urgent matters for both of them. Besides, thinking seriously about anything during this time was difficult. It was better left till tomorrow evening.

"It's not just your eyes that glow at this time, cub, it's all of you," he said, his voice a deep purr as he held her closer and stretched out for the light sensor.

She could feel his warmth against her body, his hands touching her, but she could see nothing. Moving back, she said in a small voice, "Kusac, please put the light on. Your fur's so dark that I can't see you."

He couldn't hide the shock that swept through him. This was totally unexpected, something that had never happened to him before, and a harsh reminder that she wasn't Sholan. His other senses, so much sharper than hers, told him she was there without the need of sight. For Sholans, darkness often enhanced their lovemaking.

"There's no light in the room," she said quietly, sharing his shock as he moved to put the light on again. "I don't need it bright, just ... not dark."

He dimmed it to the faintest glow before turning back to her. Were it not for the demands of their Link, the mood would have been broken for him. Though he pushed the incident aside in his mind, it had hurt.

She held him close, her mouth and hands soothing the pain away till he remembered only the magic they shared.

* * *

Vanna's aircar dropped her in the courtyard of the Guild House.

"Go in the main doors and turn left," the pilot had told her. "The office is down there. They'll show you to the medical center."

She slung her large kit bag over her shoulder and climbed the shallow steps up to the entrance. Through the open doors she could see the large refectory, empty at this time of day. She padded down the left-hand corridor, coming to the office.

The secretary looked up as she entered. A frown crossed her face. "You're a day early. We're only testing the children today. Tomorrow's the day for the adults," she said, "and I'm afraid we don't have the facilities to put you up. You'll have to go to the Accommodation Guild on the outskirts of the town."

"I'm not here for the testing. I'm Vanna Kyjishi, personal physician to Liegen Aldatan and his Leska. I'm going to be working here in the medical center with your physicians."

A surprised look crossed the secretary's face. "My apologies, Physician Kyjishi," she said, after consulting her diary. "We *are* expecting you. If you care to leave your bag here, we'll have the porter take it over to your rooms at the guest house. Meanwhile, if you continue down this corridor you'll come to the door leading to our new wing. That's where the medical center is."

"Thank you," said Vanna, "but I prefer to settle into my room first."

"In that case, I'll call the porter now," she said, pressing a button to summon him.

* * *

Her room reminded her of the one she had lived in at the Medical Guild when last on leave. Leaning forward, she pressed the bed, testing it for softness. She sighed with relief. It wasn't one of the biscuit-mattress types given to the students! This one was fully as comfortable as her bed on the *Khalossa* had been.

Her most important creature comfort assured, she looked round the rest of the room. The walls were a neutral beige color with the carpet and other furnishings in a contrasting dark brown. Opposite the bed a large window overlooked the rear grounds. Sunlight streamed in, accompanied by a gentle breeze bearing the scent of the blossoms on the trees and bushes below.

A desk and chair to the left of the bed formed her work station, and set into the wall to her right was a small screen—the entertainment center.

Vanna reached for the fastening on her bag and began to unpack. The standard wardrobe and drawers were set into the walls, and within a few minutes she had stowed away her clothes.

She surveyed her meager selection, wondering what she should wear. Though still attached to the Forces, there was no need for her to remain in uniform. Taking the easy option, she reached for her blue Medic Guild tunic and began to change. After her time on the *Khalossa,* it didn't seem like the uniform it had been before she joined up.

Taking a deep breath of the fresh air, she stretched from fingertips to tail. She'd only been on Shola for two days and already she was beginning to relax. It was amazing the effect her home world had on her. Limitless space to spread out in, unlike the *Khalossa,* and air that was fresh and didn't smell of chemical cleansers from the recycling plant! Though she wasn't claustrophobic, sometimes even she needed to feel the earth between her toes and the sun on her back—Gods forbid it, but she had even found herself hankering after the rain!

Going over to the window, she leaned out, looking down at the grounds below. The grassland stretched for several kilometers before it gradually turned into woodland. Longingly she looked at it. What she needed was a good run, perhaps even a little hunting. She sighed, wondering if as a guest of the Telepath Guild she qualified for using their leisure facilities.

A gentle buzz drew her attention back into the room. She left the window reluctantly and approached the desk. One of the keys in the keypad set into the surface glowed red, showing that there was a message for her. Activating the monitor key, she waited for the screen to rise from its recess. As it tilted up into a vertical position, the monitor came to life with the logo of the Telepath Guild.

Pulling the chair out, Vanna sat down and began to use the now exposed keyboard. At her command, the logo was replaced with a page of script and diagrams. A soothing voice began to recite the text to her. With a grimace, Vanna hit the volume control and proceeded to read it. She loathed the unctuous voices of the public announcers.

The file gave her a basic tour around the facilities in the guest house, and informed her which areas of the Guild House and grounds she was authorized to use. Wonder of wonders, the grounds were available for the use of guests provided they checked in with the office first. This was so the younger students could be warned to be on their best behavior because of the presence of nontelepaths in unshielded areas.

The guest house had a communal lounge area with a large public entertainment screen catering to several different forms of leisure—music, storyteller theater, interactive games, news—all the usual things. There was also a communal kitchen with a food dispenser boasting a menu as extensive as those she'd seen in the ambassadorial quarters on the *Khalossa*. Or, if she chose, she could cook her own food.

The showers and bathing rooms were communal, too. She frowned a little; she'd gotten used her privacy when off-planet and it wouldn't be easy to recondition herself to the gregarious life that the planet-bound Sholans still lived.

The diagrammatic tour over, the screen reverted to the Guild logo again. In the bottom left corner, a blinking message light demanded her attention.

Keying in the replay, she waited. The screen cleared to reform with the image of Garras.

"I'd hoped to speak to you in person," he said, "but it seems I've miscalculated your arrival time at the guild. They've assured me this will be recorded for you to see when you do arrive." He stopped, looking to one side of the screen before continuing.

"I'm transmitting that medical data you wanted. The labs finished the tests you were running for Kaid yesterday. You know how long it can take for the authorities to process things, so I collected it for you since I knew it was urgent. I'll try contacting you again in another couple of days." His ears flicked briefly in acknowledgment before the screen blanked and the printer began to hum gently.

Confused, Vanna watched the printer disgorge its text. The words "for Kaid," and "urgent" rang in her ears. What was happening on the *Khalossa* that necessitated Garras contacting Kaid? Perhaps she'd be able to tell from the printout.

She took the first page, scanning it quickly for any clues as to Garras' cryptic message. It was only the results of her latest test on human and Sholan pheromones, showing a marked similarity as she had suspected. Certainly enough to account for the attraction between their species.

The second page was merely a report on Kaid's injuries after the scouter crash, and a record of the treatment he'd received plus his response to it. It was all standard stuff, nothing out of the ordinary at all. If there was a message for Kaid in there, then it was cunningly hidden. Probably some code Kaid and Garras had learned at their guild. The best thing she could do was to contact the office and find out where Kaid was so she could pass on this document to him without further delay. If she needed to know more, she trusted either Garras or he would tell her. Her mind made up, she buzzed the office.

It was evening, and with the approaching night, much of their Link's compulsion was fading. Kusac left Carrie sleeping and padded quietly through to the kitchen. He reached for the c'shar, then hesitated and picked up the container of coffee instead.

Heading back to the lounge with his drink, he sat down at the comm unit. The message light was blinking. Not surprising when their public life had been on hold for the last twenty-six hours. He keyed the comm to print the messages.

The first item was a report on the state of the treaty talks. It started with the fact that Shola had requested that Earth send them a selection of people with Talents similar to Carrie's, including telepathy. They also wanted any information they had on how these Talents were tested or measured.

He'd been sitting there reading the same paragraph for several minutes before he realized that with his still-enhanced senses he was picking up something that was disturbing him. He frowned. Their quarters were well shielded, as much to protect those outside as to form a barrier for them. What could manage to penetrate that protection?

He'd just gotten to his feet when the comm buzzer sounded. Sitting down again, he responded to the call. The screen flicked on to show the image of a very harassed female in the office.

"Liegen, I'm sorry to disturb you at this time, but I'm afraid we have a problem that only you can resolve."

In the background he could hear raised voices.

"How can I help?" he asked.

"It's Rala Vailkoi. She's here and demanding to see you. We've explained the circumstances, but ... I'm afraid it only made her more determined. Could you please come down here and speak to her? She's broadcasting her anger in every direction and refuses to enter one of the shielded interview rooms. It need only be for a minute or two. I'm sure that as it's toward the end of your day your state won't affect her."

"I'm leaving now," he said tersely before switching the comm off and reaching for his uniform jacket.

Shrugging his arms into it, he had it sealed and was buckling the belt as he opened the door, almost colliding with Kaid in the corridor outside.

"You know what's happening?" he asked.

Kaid nodded.

"See she doesn't leave our apartment or use the comm."

"I'll make sure she doesn't get involved in this," Kaid said as he stepped past him into the lounge.

Kusac headed down the corridor at a lope, the full measure of Rala's temper, augmented by his sensitivity, reaching him now. He strengthened his shield hastily. Minutes later he was at the office where the staff were still trying to persuade Rala to calm down and to enter one of the interview rooms to wait for him.

Hearing the door open, the young female ceased shouting at the on-duty Guild Mother and pulled herself free of the porter to turn round.

"I told you he'd come when he knew it was me!" she said triumphantly. Then, with a croon of pleasure, she skipped over to him, her hands sliding across his upper arms as she held herself close to him and pressed her cheek against his.

He submitted to the gesture, then moved away from her light grasp, taking her by the elbow and steering her toward the door.

"My apologies for her behavior," he said to the Guild Mother, his tone short and clipped. "You have my word this will not happen again."

He hardly heard the polite murmurs saying he was not to blame as he escorted Rala out into the hallway then down the corridor.

She went willingly, trying to wind her arm possessively around his waist as he stopped outside the nearest empty room. He opened the door and stepped inside, waiting for her to follow. Her arm fell from about him and she hesitated at the door.

Kusac gave a low growl and grasped her arm again, claws just pricking her flesh. He pulled her inside and shut the door.

"Do you really want witnesses to our conversation, Rala?" he asked.

"I don't know what you mean," she said, trying to tug her arm free. "You're hurting me. Why are you being so unpleasant?" she asked, her tone becoming petulant. "I thought after a year apart you'd be glad to see me."

Kusac let her go and stepped back to lean against the door. He regarded her dispassionately. "Why did you come? Have you any idea of how much you have embarrassed both me and your family by your actions tonight?" he demanded. "As for your temper tantrum, you've managed to make your mood known to just about every inhabitant of the guild! If you haven't upset the cubs and caused them to have nightmares, then it's pure luck!"

"I wasn't upset till they wouldn't let me see you," she said, touching her hand to his forearm. "Imagine it! Trying to keep me, your betrothed, away from you just because you were with that female." She moved closer, leaning against him so one leg came free of her robe and pressed against his.

Her artfulness was almost having the desired effect, probably would have had it not been for Carrie. None too gently he pushed her away, annoyed with himself even though he knew full well that his present vulnerability was not something he could control.

"You've seen me. Now it's time for you to leave. Where's your escort? You didn't come alone, I hope."

"I don't want to leave, Kusac," she said, reaching out for him again. "Surely we can spend a little time together? After all, it has been a year since I last saw you."

He brushed her aside. "Leave me alone, Rala. It's time for you to go."

She turned with a flounce, her long split-paneled skirt flaring around her. "How dare you treat me like this!" Her voice had risen in pitch with her anger. "I'm your future wife: I have rights, you know! One of them is the right to see you when I desire it!"

"You have no rights over me yet," he said coldly. "And you certainly would never have the right to walk into my guild and demand my presence when I'm with my Leska!"

Rala made a spitting sound of contempt, a look of fury creasing her face. Her ears lay flat and flicked backward. "Your alien! She's nothing, not a real Leska," she said contemptuously. "I won't be second to her, I warn you!"

Despite his shield Kusac could feel her anger and hatred of Carrie.

"My Leska is none of your concern," he snapped, his own temper rising.

"When you prefer her company to mine, she is! How *dare* you be seen around Valsgarth with her when your first duty is to contact me!" Her tail began to move from side to side in small, angry jerks.

"What I do with my time is my affair." His voice was a snarl now. "How dare *you* come here, where you have no right to be, and purposely use your tantrums to manipulate people! Even though you aren't a telepath, it doesn't excuse you from exercising self-control when mixing with us!"

Her eyes narrowed and with an obvious effort, she stilled her tail and relaxed her ears.

"I'm sorry, Kusac," she said, keeping her eyes lowered. "I just wanted to see you so much. I needed to know that nothing had changed between us." Her hands plucked nervously at the edge of one of the panels of her robe, and she returned hesitantly to his side, her eyes looking up at him through long lashes.

He stared at her for a moment, hardly crediting her duplicity.

"You planned this down to the minute, didn't you?" he said, his voice barely audible as his anger mounted. "You must have buzzed the office earlier in the day to find out."

Real fear crossed her face briefly. "I'm sure I don't know what you're talking about," she said, looking him squarely in the eyes as she tried to brazen it out.

Kusac reached for her with one hand and wrenched the door open behind him. "You're leaving now," he said, his voice cold with rage as he pulled her toward him. "Your little plan failed, Rala. Did you really think you could compete with my Leska? That you could seduce me that easily? You'll not force me into this marriage by claiming I mated with you and made you pregnant! I don't want this marriage at all!"

He pushed her through the door ahead of him, ignoring her loud protestations of innocence as he hauled her back up the corridor.

Outside the office, Meral and Sevrin waited, the signs of a hurried summons evident in their dress which they were still adjusting.

Kusac pushed Rala toward them. "Get her out of my sight," he said. "If she hasn't an aircar and a companion outside, get one of the females from the office to accompany you both and escort her home. The Gods help us, she's the daughter of a Clan Leader and technically betrothed to me; she must be properly escorted."

Sevrin caught her as she stumbled against him.

"I won't forget this, Kusac. You'll pay for this!" Her voice was a hiss of venom.

Kusac turned his back on her and opened the office door as his two bodyguards escorted her outside. He shut the door quietly behind him.

The night staff stood in a huddle next to the desk. They looked toward him as he entered.

"Liegen, our apologies for this incident," said the Guild Mother, stepping forward. "The fault is mine. I should have sent her home as soon as she arrived."

Kusac shook his head. "You could no more have controlled her than I could," he said tiredly. "She may not be Talented, but she does know how to project her moods so she can get what she wants."

The older female hesitated before continuing. "I'm afraid we couldn't help but be aware of some of your discussion," she said apologetically, ears and tail flicking in embarrassment. "This incident has made us realize that Rala has developed her ability to project her thoughts despite the fact that when she was tested as a child, we could find no Talent worth training. The shielding in the interview rooms was just not adequate to contain her. If you wish, we can all vouch for the fact that you were only alone for a few minutes."

"I hope it won't be necessary, but thank you," he said, distinctly aware that if they had followed the discussion, then there was a strong likelihood that it had disturbed Carrie too. He reached for her through their Link but could sense nothing beyond her presence. "I've sent Rala home with my guards. Once again, I apologize for the fact that everyone has been disturbed by her because of me."

"Liegen, she is entirely responsible for her own actions," said the Guild Mother. "May I suggest that we lodge a strong complaint with Clan Leader Vailkoi on both our and your behalf? Coming from me before her arrival home, it should do much to discredit any false claims his daughter may try to make."

Despite his worry at not being able to sense Carrie, Kusac grinned. "I think it's a marvelous idea. I hope that the whole guild hasn't been aware of what happened tonight."

"No, Liegen," she reassured him. "Master Esken is, and myself, but her anger was only felt by the few students who hadn't gone out for the evening and were still in the common lounge. The cubs had long since gone to bed and their quarters are even better shielded than yours. Master Esken is going to want to talk to her father about her mood projections. She must learn to control them. Why her family has let her get away with it this long is beyond me."

"I'm glad the cubs are all right. As for Rala, I'm afraid she knows exactly how to control her moods and thoughts," he said, turning to leave. "I must go. Good night."

Once away from the office, the need to suppress his anger with Rala was lessened, and it began to build again. He had to get out of the guild. Too many people were able to pick him up; he needed to talk to someone, someone he could trust and who could help him.

There had only really been one friend when he'd been

here before. Ghyan. He couldn't face Carrie now. Hopefully, she was still asleep and totally unaware of what had happened. It was a faint hope, though.

He stopped at the public comm unit and buzzed their apartment. Kaid answered.

"Is she awake?" he asked.

"I made sure she didn't, Liegen," said Kaid. "I had made it my business to find out about Rala Vailkoi some time ago, so I took the precaution of sedating your Leska as soon as I arrived." He looked Kusac straight in the eyes.

Kusac frowned. "You did what?" he asked slowly, hardly able to believe what Kaid was saying.

"I gave her a mild sedative," said Kaid. "I had some basic medical training through the Brotherhood, and I've updated it to include a knowledge of Terrans. I knew exactly how much she needed."

"You took a lot for granted," he said, relief countering the anger he knew he ought to have felt.

"It would have served no useful purpose to have had a confrontation between her and Rala," said Kaid.

"I know. My concern now is that Rala may try to harm her. She wouldn't dare do anything to me, but Carrie is another matter. In future I want you to protect *her*, not me. I'll have Meral and Sevrin, but she's more vulnerable. If you protect her, we've both got a better chance."

"If that's what you wish," said Kaid.

Kusac nodded.

"Rala won't get anyone from the Brotherhood to help her," murmured Kaid. "There's a ban on taking a negative contract that involves any Terran or the Leska of a Terran."

Kusac pulled a wry face. "I'm relieved to hear it," he said. "What occasioned such a decision?"

Kaid hesitated. "You won't want to hear it," he said. "Last time I spoke of the God you told me to be silent."

Kusac broke eye contact, suddenly feeling the coldness up and down his spine again. "Let it lie then, Kaid. It's enough that the Brotherhood has made the decision. How long will Carrie be asleep?"

"Only for an hour or two," said Kaid. "I'd like to remain here on guard for tonight. I'm not expecting trouble, but it pays to be safe."

"If you consider it necessary. I'll be back shortly," Kusac

said before cutting the connection. He needed to find Ghyan—now.

Carrie's vision still haunted him. Perhaps the God had been trying to tell him there was a way through their problems. Ghyan, if he was still at the temple, might hold the solution.

He left the guild through one of the rear exits and headed out across the grassland for the trees. The night air was fresh with the scent of damp grass. It smelled comfortingly familiar. Dropping down onto all fours he loped off into the darkness, beginning to run as he felt the anger surge within him.

His vision began to fade at the edges till all he saw was the ground immediately in front of him; all he heard was the blood pounding in his ears as he ran faster, dodging between the bushes and skidding past trees, trying to outrun his rage while still containing it.

Small nocturnal animals scattered in fright as, unmindful of the noise he made, he continued his headlong flight through the woodland. Abruptly the wall loomed ahead of him. He slithered to a stop, ending up with his flank against the rough bricks as he halted just in time.

At a slower pace, he followed the wall round to his right, coming at length to a small iron gate. Bunching his leg muscles, he sprang forward, clearing it with a foot or more to spare and landing in the paved area outside, sides heaving as he began to gasp for breath.

He smelled incense and someone coming. The scent was familiar, yet it had to be an enemy. His vision narrowed even further, the scene in front of him becoming tinged with red. Concentrating on the robed figure, with a snarl he attempted to stand upright. As he did, the world tipped crazily about him and he felt the gestalt flare into being.

Carrie was too far away to touch, yet he felt her presence as acutely as if he had been touching her; he could feel her stirring in her drugged sleep. The energy, unable to reach her, began to build in him, swirling round and round like a cyclone. Unable to escape his shield it exploded, sending him reeling to his knees with the backlash. He fell forward, his forearms barely managing to take the impact as he became hypersensitively aware of every atom of his body. The pain in his knees and arms and the chill air of the night in his lungs, were all equally unbearable. Through their Link he felt her cry out in her sleep.

"I wondered when you'd come. It's been too long since we last saw each other, Kusac."

The quiet voice and the featherlight touch of a mind he knew well gave him something other than himself to focus on; its familiarity reassured him. Gradually the sensitivity eased and breathing became less painful.

"Ghyan," he said, lifting his head and forcing his vision to clear. His friend stood patiently waiting for him to recover. Kusac knew that he had sensed nothing.

"I felt your anger from the Temple and knew that the God would guide your steps here," said Ghyan.

Kusac growled softly as he pushed himself up off the damp stones to sit on his haunches. "Don't talk to me of Gods, Ghyan, I've no faith in them. They twist your life out of shape by giving with one hand and destroying with the other."

"Has the God destroyed something of yours, Kusac?" his friend asked. "I rather thought He had given you a wondrous gift."

Again he growled warningly. "Ghyan, I came to you for help, not a sermon."

"Then you're doubly welcome. Come in and tell me what's angered you so badly." He leaned forward and held out his hand.

Kusac hesitated, then took it, letting his friend help him to his feet. Together they walked down the path to the temple.

"I heard you'd disappeared," Ghyan said. "I wasn't surprised. It didn't take much Talent to know how trapped you felt by the life that your father had mapped out for you."

They'd come to a side door and Ghyan pushed it open for him. "It doesn't lead into the main temple," said Ghyan, forestalling him. "This leads to my own quarters."

Still keeping a tight rein on his emotions, Kusac followed him down the narrow corridor till his friend stopped to open the door to his room. As they entered, Kusac looked around and stopped dead.

"This isn't an acolyte's room," he said accusingly, indicating the expensive but simple furniture.

"No, it isn't," agreed Ghyan with a smile. "I'm no longer an acolyte. You wouldn't be aware of our hierarchy unless you were attending the Temple regularly. There is only one resident priest, and he must be a telepath."

"You, a priest? When you left the guild to come here, you

intended only to serve a year or two as an acolyte. What happened?"

Ghyan shrugged, and indicated that they should move over to the chairs. "I found this was where I belonged," he said simply, sitting in one of the two easy chairs. He watched Kusac prowl restlessly round the room then stop beside the window, leaning on the sill.

"You won't see much in the dark," Ghyan said. "Why don't you tell me how I can help you?"

"Rala Vailkoi," Kusac said succinctly, continuing to look out into the night.

"Ah. Your forthcoming marriage."

"I won't have her, Ghyan. I can't stand the female! She's a spoiled, manipulative brat!" he said angrily, his tail beginning to lash from side to side.

"I wouldn't disagree with you, but you've known this for a long time now. You never seemed concerned about her before."

"I was younger then. There was plenty of time to worry about marriage later."

"Now time has run out," said Ghyan quietly.

"Yes." Kusac turned and began pacing round the small room again. The fire had gone out of his anger, leaving only a feeling of desolation. "I can't marry her, Ghyan." He returned to the window, keeping his back to his friend as he stared out into the night again. "I've met someone else," he said quietly.

"Your Leska." It was a statement.

"Yes," said Kusac. "There must be some way to dissolve the contract."

"Only if your father and Vailkoi agree it should be dissolved, and I don't think they will. Having a Leska that you'd rather was your mate doesn't constitute a good reason, I'm afraid."

Kusac turned round to look at him. "I won't life-bond with Rala, Ghyan."

"You can't bond to your Terran, Kusac. The Council of Clans wouldn't condone it."

"Then I'll not bond at all, no matter what the council says," he said angrily.

"Would it be so bad? It's only a dynastic bonding, you wouldn't have to live with her."

"I can't stand her near me, let alone touching me," he said.

"It would only be occasionally. You have a duty to provide your Clan with heirs."

"Dammit, Ghyan, I know all about my duty!" he said angrily, pushing himself away from the window. "You don't know what I feel for Carrie—what she means to me! I'll have her or no one!"

Ghyan looked him steadily in the eye. "I do know, Kusac. I can feel it, despite your shield," he said with sympathy. "But have you really thought this through? Where would you go? If you flout the law, then your mother will have no choice but to expel you from your clan. The guild couldn't support you. It can't afford to get involved in political or civil matters."

"I've thought it through every way I could imagine," he said, taking a kick at the small waste bin standing by Ghyan's chair. It bounced noisily across the room, shedding its contents before rolling to a stop. "I've got to find a way out of this contract."

Turning, he perched on the arm of the chair opposite his friend. "You don't understand, Ghyan. Our link is far stronger than normal Leska Links, we're more dependent on each other, and I'm all that Carrie has on Shola. If I marry Rala, it could wreck the love we share."

"Surely she understands," said Ghyan.

"I haven't told her yet," he admitted, his ears flicking backward and remaining there. "We've both had to work hard for the relationship we have. I won't risk ruining that. Like I said, the Gods screw your life up for their own amusement. First they give us each other, then they make it impossible for us to be together as mates."

"It has always been impossible, Kusac," Ghyan reminded him softly. "At least Vartra has given you Carrie and your love for each other, perhaps to compensate for the marriage you must make."

At the mention of Vartra, the dream of the night before came forcefully to Kusac's mind and he looked down at the floor.

Ghyan rose, moving past him to where a container of c'shar sat on a heated unit. "Would you like a drink?" he asked, taking a couple of mugs from the shelf behind.

"Please."

"Why don't you tell me about your vision?" he said, pouring the c'shar into the mugs.

Kusac looked up, tail and ears flicking. "Is my shield that bad?"

"It is now," said Ghyan, returning with the mugs. He handed one to Kusac then resumed his seat. "I sensed nothing when you arrived, but you've relaxed a little since then. Now, tell me about your vision."

"It wasn't a vision," said Kusac defensively, "and Carrie saw more than me."

"Then tell me what your Leska saw."

"She saw a temple very like this, with the statue of Vartra," said Kusac reluctantly. "He spoke to her, asking if she was content and telling her that too many lives had been lost because of our Talents." Even as he spoke, he could sense his friend's surprise.

"A vision of this type is often seen by new Leska pairs when they stay at the Valsgarth Guild, but usually the God only asks if they are content," said Ghyan thoughtfully, taking a drink from his mug. "This mention of lives lost is new."

"I only heard Him ask if I was content," said Kusac. "What does it mean, Ghyan?"

"We don't know, I'm afraid. It doesn't happen to every pair, only a few, and only when they are living at the guild. I'm intrigued that He should appear to someone from another species, even though she is your Leska."

"There's a lot of crossover of abilities between us, so much so that it worries me."

"Worries you? How?"

Kusac got to his feet again, turning away from his friend, unsure how much to tell him. He'd already said more to Ghyan than perhaps he should, but he needed someone to talk to. Walking over to the window, he twitched the curtains aside while he considered what to do. Making up his mind, he returned to the chair. "When the Link formed, we exchanged the experiences of our lives up to that point in time. We're linked so closely that I know what she's doing and thinking all the time, as she does with me. Ghyan, I'm finding my outlook is changing. I question everything, especially the things I took for granted before I met her. Nothing is sacrosanct any more, everything has to be proved to me."

He hesitated before voicing his deepest fear. "I'm afraid I'm becoming less Sholan and more like her."

Ghyan was silent for a moment. "I've known you a long time, Kusac. I know the feel of your mind. Yes, you've changed. As you say, your mind is so closely meshed with Carrie's that change was inevitable. But you've always questioned everything, you're no different in that respect. Remember, if you feel influenced by Carrie's human mind, she is equally influenced by your Sholan one."

"I'm not so sure," Kusac said. "It was easier before. I knew that my decisions were made from the foundations of training based on my experience and were not against the interest of our Clan. Now my decisions are based on her experiences and knowledge, too. How can I be sure they're right any more?"

"Was your decision to join the Forces taken for the benefit of the Clan?" asked Ghyan with a smile.

Kusac's ears flicked and he glanced away. Remembering his c'shar, he hid himself behind his mug as he took a drink.

"As I said, the essential you hasn't changed that much," said Ghyan. "The God has given you each other. More than that, He has acknowledged both you and your Leska. There must be a reason for it, and in time we will know. Meanwhile, you have each other, be content."

"What about this marriage? I've got to stop it happening, Ghyan. You were studying law before you came here, can't you see if there's a way we can have the contract set aside?"

"I can check for you," Ghyan admitted, "but I honestly think it's most unlikely. Think carefully before making a decision. If you marry Rala, you'd still be free to live with Carrie. Do anything else and you'll both be outcasts with nowhere to go, nowhere to live. Our civil laws concerning the ruling families of Clans are very strict. You know that."

"There's got to be something I can do," Kusac said, putting down his mug and getting restlessly to his feet again.

"Have you thought of meditating and asking Vartra what you should do?" asked Ghyan, turning round in his seat to follow him with his eyes. "If, as you feel, He has caused the problem, then surely He can provide the solution."

"I've no faith in any Gods at the moment, Ghyan, only in people, and then only a very few." He stopped by the door, hand on the lever. "I've got to go. She'll waken soon."

"I'll check the archives for you, but don't get your hopes

up," he said warningly. "I doubt that there are any loopholes that would fit your circumstances."

"I know you'll do what you can," Kusac said, opening the door. "Thank you for listening to me. I'll be in touch again soon."

When Ghyan knew Kusac was well on his way back to the guild, he activated his comm. The human female's vision had him concerned. She had seen so much more than any of their people ever had. If she was to be believed. But then why should she lie, or Kusac for that matter, since he had experienced at least her memory of the vision. No, it had to be true.

"Ghyan, it's somewhat late to be hearing from you. I trust there's nothing wrong?"

"Father Lijou, my apologies for disturbing you, but you have told me to contact you concerning the God visions experienced by our new Leskas here at Valsgarth."

"The Aldatan cub," said Lijou succinctly.

"Not exactly," said Ghyan. "It was the human female, not Kusac, who experienced the main vision."

Lijou frowned, his brows drawing together thoughtfully. "The Keissian? What did she see?"

"It was different from the usual vision, Father. Kusac came to see me tonight, and he told me that the God said too many lives had been lost. Why should Vartra say that?"

"Offhand, I've no idea, Ghyan. Are you sure he was reporting the vision accurately?"

"Do you doubt my judgment?"

"Not when I have your assurance to the contrary. We haven't been cataloguing the God visions for long, Ghyan. It takes time to build up an image of what really happened in the years following the Cataclysm. All we know for sure is that we've found no records in existence before then, and the legends tell us that Vartra was responsible for uniting those Sholans who survived the planetwide disaster that almost wiped us out. Though it doesn't take long for a charismatic male like that to pass from legend into divinity, we're still no nearer knowing why there are visions and why they only happen at Valsgarth!"

Ghyan sighed. "I know we have to move slowly, Father, but there are times when I despair of us ever finding the answers. It saps the spirit when you hear another ruin has been 'blessed' to prevent unholy items from corrupting our souls. We've lost so much of our past it's a wonder any still remains!"

"Every loss is a tragedy," Lijou agreed, "but the ancient cities were numerous and large. Each time Esken orders a 'blessing' only a small portion of the whole is lost."

"That small portion could contain unrepeatable treasures which would tell us what caused the cataclysm in the first place!"

"Don't get things out of proportion, Ghyan," warned Lijou. "Our past isn't the end result in itself. It's merely a tool to enable us to break the stranglehold people like Esken have on our future. With the discovery of the Terrans, it's even more important that we have the freedom to evolve as a species. If we don't, then these humans with their multiple Talents could end up dominating the Alliance, and they're too young a species for a position of such importance. Dzahai Stronghold is the last hope for us. The Gods help us if Esken realizes the true nature of the Brotherhood before we're ready to reveal it! Your friend Kusac Aldatan and his human Leska may be the key to us attaining full guild status. Once we have that, if there are more like them, then we can Challenge the Telepath Guild with a hope of winning."

"So what do you want me to do?"

"Remain apparently neutral for now. We have agents in the field watching them, passing us information regarding their Link, keeping them safe. We're doing what we're best at, watching and waiting."

"Just remember Kusac is my friend," said Ghyan, an ear flicking in concern. "I won't sit back and see them come to harm."

"No harm is intended toward them, quite the opposite in fact," said Lijou. "Thank you for your report. If you can find out any more from either of them without arousing their suspicions, then let me know."

"Yes, Father," said Ghyan.

* * *

The next morning brought Konis Aldatan two puzzling messages—messages that he accepted on his wife's behalf as surrogate Clan Leader. The first was from Master Esken stating that he was informing him out of courtesy that he'd lodged a formal complaint against Rala Vailkoi with her

Clan Leader about her behavior the previous night. The second was an apology from Clan Leader Vailkoi concerning his daughter's behavior at the Telepath Guild on the same night, and assuring him that it would not be repeated as he had set two more Warriors to guard her.

Perplexed, he decided to call Esken for a more detailed explanation of the events.

"Esken, what happened at the guild last night?" he asked as soon as the Guild Master's face came on the screen.

"I thought I made it clear in my communication, Konis," said Esken. "Rala Vailkoi visited your son last night."

"Alone, at night, without an appointment? What is Vailkoi up to allowing her that kind of freedom when he's pushing for an early marriage between them?"

"You need have no fear, Konis," said Esken dryly. "Rala is no reluctant bride turning to a lover to make her pregnant so the marriage can be delayed. Quite the opposite in fact. Vailkoi had no need to keep her closely guarded—till now."

Konis sat back in surprise. "I'm not sure I follow you," he said.

"She arrived toward the end of Kusac's Link day with the intention of seeing him while he was still vulnerable." Esken's brows met in a frown. "I have my doubts as to the wisdom of your choice of a bride for your son, Konis. The Vailkoi female is unprincipled and manipulative. Hardly a suitable wife for one of the Contenders as heir to your title and position. You'll have trouble making Kusac keep this contract. He is already dissatisfied with her, and with good reason. Her disgraceful behavior last night may well have brought the matter to a head."

"He has a Leska now," said Konis. "He doesn't need love in his marriage. The combination of his and Rala's genes will make it more likely that all their children will be highly Talented, even if she has no usable Talent herself. That is more important to the Clan than whether or not he likes his wife."

"You take too practical a view of life, Konis," said Master Esken sadly. "You are too harsh with his feelings. He isn't like you."

"I brought him up to have a sense of responsibility to the Clan," said Konis. "He knows what he has to do. I have to be hard, Esken, else how could I arrange the marriages within the Clans? Few of them will ever be love matches. At least Kusac will have a wife slightly younger than himself. What of Soola Kayan? She has a husband a good thirty years her senior."

"We'll see," said Esken. "Just remember that when the God takes a hand in our lives, events don't always work out as we planned them."

"Now you're being superstitious," said Konis uncomfortably. "I have to go, Esken. I can't sit here discussing theology with you, I've work to do."

"Before you go, I have some advice for you. Don't push Kusac into marriage yet. Leave it for now until he has forgotten this incident with Rala. Perhaps then you'll find him more amenable."

"Your advice is noted, Master Esken, but I will choose my own time to speak to Kusac about his marriage. Good day to you."

Konis had reason to remember Master Esken's advice later in the day when Kusac also lodged an official complaint about Rala's behavior. It gave him pause to consider that perhaps he didn't know his son as well as he had thought and that the advice was not so misplaced after all.

* * *

Carrie sat at the comm unit reading through her brother's message.

"Kusac, Richard's sent me a copy of the encyclopedia that we had on board the *Eureka!* His message says to check the section on psychics because it mentions all of the gifts that people on Earth were thought to have, and the tests they used to check if the gifts were genuine."

"Let me see," he said, joining her at the desk. "Put the section he mentions onto the screen."

"Hold on. I haven't quite got the hang of this computer yet."

"It's a lot more than a computer," Kusac murmured as he watched her struggling to remember which keys to press. At least physically it was easier for her now that her fingernails had regrown.

She grunted in reply as she tried several key combinations, managing to connect into the library system, then the public news network, neither of which she wanted.

Kusac leaned forward. "Try this," he said, pressing a couple of keys to take them back to the basic function choice and then to the textual message display. "Put your brother's complete message into a memory crystal, then you can access it properly." He reached into the desk drawer and drew out a spare crystal, slotting it into a square aperture at the side of the keyboard.

"I wondered what that was for," said Carrie as the cube was briefly illuminated from underneath.

"Now you can see the contents and choose the section we want," he said, moving back so she could finish.

"I don't remember it being arranged like this," said Carrie as she scanned through the contents.

"It was probably done when your brother had the encyclopedia put into a format we could read. There, that's what we want," he said, pointing.

Carrie turned round to look up at him. "How come you can read my language so easily when I can't read yours?"

Kusac grinned, his lips curving slightly. "I've had more practice with languages," he said.

With another grunt, she turned back to her encyclopedia and selected the section on psychical research. She found it cross-referenced with extra-sensory perception, psychokinesis, psychometry, object reading, dowsing . . .

"This list is huge! I haven't heard of half the things they're talking about," she said. "Where do we begin?"

"Try looking up the first item."

They skimmed through the document, finding it a history of the study of what was termed ESP. It was divided into two distinct skills, PK or psychokinesis, which was the ability to move objects with the power of the mind, and ESP, which included telepathy and the ability to have foreknowledge of events.

"I don't think we should read any further," said Kusac, putting a hand on her shoulder. "We might prejudice the tests."

"How could we do that?"

"By assuming in advance whether or not we can do what they ask us." Reaching into the drawer, he took out another cube and began copying the data from one to the other. "How are we for time?"

"We should leave now," she said, finishing her coffee hurriedly. "They're expecting me for the aura scan in ten minutes."

"I'm finished," said Kusac, switching off the comm and

getting up. He reached for his uniform jacket, shrugging it on over the tunic he wore.

Carrie looked up at him. "You'll need to change your jacket, that one's got mud on it," she said.

Kusac rubbed ineffectually at the mark on his left side. "You're right," he said, taking it off and flinging it back over the chair. "I won't be a minute."

Carrie was waiting by the door for him when he returned, her unasked question loud in his mind despite her efforts to the contrary.

"I couldn't sleep last night, so I went to visit a friend," he said, opening the door for them. "Kaid watched you while I was gone. I went across country and the ground was damp."

"I was only curious. No Kaid?" she asked as they passed his door.

"We decided there wasn't any need for someone to accompany us around the Guild House," said Kusac.

As they headed along the corridor and down the stairs, Carrie looked around her for referents, trying to make sure she could recognize the route back to their rooms. Reaching the ground floor, they made their way past the main hall toward the office, then along the corridor to the new wing.

Ahead of them was a transparent door bearing a sign in the cursive Sholan script.

"It says 'Medical Center,' " Kusac said quietly, pressing the panel set into the wall beside it.

The door slid back, admitting them to a small foyer. Ahead of them was a curved counter behind which two Sholan females dressed in medic blue were working. To their left was an external entrance for nonguild patients.

Old fears returned and Carrie began to walk more slowly, wishing she were anywhere else but here. Hospitals were hospitals to her no matter which world she was on, and she hated them.

An involuntary shiver ran through her. The hospitals on Earth had treated her like a mentally deranged child until they had tested the truth of what her parents had told them about her and Elise.

Kusac's hand touched hers, his fingers curling round her palm as he mentally reassured her. It wasn't enough. The cold feeling continued.

They were directed to the seats nearby and asked to wait until someone came for them. As they sat there, Carrie began to shiver again. Kusac's arm went round her shoulders, drawing her up against his side. She leaned against him gratefully, feeling the warmth of his body through the thin tunic he wore. It helped counteract the chill.

It's all right, Carrie. You're an accepted telepath here. You've nothing to prove to them. Just relax, it'll be fine, he sent.

Vanna's coming, she replied just as the door to the right of the counter slid open.

"Hello again," said Vanna, coming forward to greet them. "I had a feeling you'd arrived." She briefly touched Kusac's outstretched hand as he stood up, but turned to Carrie and embraced her.

"When did you arrive?" Carrie returned the hug.

"Yesterday, but you were busy, so I left it till today. Come with me, they're ready for you now," she said, turning toward the doorway.

They followed her through into the main part of the medical center, turning left down a short corridor to the aura reading room.

"The whole hospital is heavily shielded," she said, "otherwise the telepath medics would find it almost unbearable to work here."

"Is this the main hospital for Valsgarth?" asked Carrie, aware that Vanna was trying to put her at her ease. She moved her fingers slightly in Kusac's grasp, holding his hand more firmly.

"The main hospital is in Nazule," said Kusac. "This facility is here mainly for the guild members, but is also available for ordinary patients who have need of the treatment that they can only get here, like the aura readings for diagnosis of certain conditions."

Vanna stopped outside the last door, opening it for them.

The small room was brightly lit, that was the first thing she noticed; the second was an examination couch. Carrie felt a surge of panic. Here she was, alone among a room full of Sholans with only Kusac and Vanna between her and them. They could do anything they wanted to her.

It's only an aura reading, cub, Kusac reassured her. *Shall I let them take one of me first?*

No. I'm fine, honestly. "What do you want me to do, Vanna?" she asked, determined not to let anyone else know how nervous she was.

"I'm not conducting the test, Carrie. I'm merely here to see how it's done and how they interpret the data. Khafsa is the physician," she said, indicating the medic talking to two technicians by the control desk to their left.

Khafsa came forward, hand outstretched to touch theirs in greeting. Carrie noticed he wore the telepath and medic colors on his long sleeved jacket.

"It's a pleasure to meet you," he said, mouth falling open in the Sholan grin. "We've heard a lot about you," he said to Carrie. "It's wonderful to have found another telepathic species. Makes us feel a little less alone!"

Carrie grinned back, feeling instantly more at ease.

"It's a completely painless experience," he said, taking her by the forearm and drawing her toward the couch. "Just sit up here while I explain it," he said, helping her up.

As she sat down, she realized that Kusac had remained with Vanna. Firmly she suppressed the instant surge of panic at being left alone with this strange male and made an effort instead to concentrate on what he was saying.

"The couch is formfitting, as you'll realize when you lie down," he said, carefully swinging her legs up. "Just lie back and relax. You should find it reasonably comfortable, we're using one of the small couches for you."

Carrie felt the surface of the couch yield slightly under her, adjusting to the contours of her body.

"If you turn your head to the side, you'll see the lid. It's made of two layers of crystal with a special clear fluid between them which enables me to see your aura more clearly. When I close the lid over you, my technicians will put out the lights. In the darkness I'll be able to see the colors that surround you. The next bit's the really clever stuff," he said with a wide Sholan grin. "I use my particular Talent to reproduce those colors around you, so they can be photographed to study later in more detail. There's nothing to it," he reassured her. "It takes about fifteen minutes, so just lie still and relax."

"I'm not afraid," she muttered, turning her head again to look at Kusac who was sending encouraging thoughts to her.

Khafsa lifted the lid over her, closing it carefully. As he did, a gentle flow of cool air began to move round her. Beneath her she could feel the couch beginning to warm gently. As the lights went out, she shut her eyes, gradually relaxing as the chill started to leave her body.

* * *

"Wake up, sleepy one," said Vanna, giving her a little shake. "Before you get down, I want to take my samples."

Carrie opened bleary eyes. Her limbs felt as dull and heavy as her head. Slowly she lifted her arm up for Vanna.

"Your temperature's a bit high," Vanna said, checking the panel at the side of her sampling unit. "How do you feel?"

"Like I want to go back to bed," she said, sitting up carefully when Vanna had finished. "I think I'm coming down with something nasty, like flu."

Kusac was instantly at her side, helping her down. "I'm taking her upstairs now, Vanna," he said, concern in his voice. "I didn't realize till now, but she's right, she isn't well."

"I'll come up when I've finished analyzing these samples. By then I should have some idea of what's wrong with her. Thank the Gods I've been taking baseline tests for so long. It should help me isolate any infection."

Khafsa touched Kusac briefly on the shoulder to attract his attention. "When your Leska is settled, I'd like you back down here to run a scan on you," he said. "I want a current reading to compare with your last one."

Kusac nodded. "I'll come down when Vanna's with her," he said, swinging Carrie up into his arms.

"I can walk," she objected halfheartedly, glad not to have to use her aching limbs.

"I'm carrying you," he said firmly, heading for the door. "We'll be back at our rooms sooner than if you walk."

Vanna watched them leave, then turned to Khafsa. "Was the scan adequate?"

"Yes, we've got the data we need. It'll take some time to interpret it because I don't know what a Terran aura should look like, but on first appraisal, I'd say you're right. Much of the scan has a Sholan look to it, more than one would expect from a different species."

"We need Kusac's as well," she said. "I want you to compare them, see what, if anything, they have in common. Meanwhile, I only hope that Carrie hasn't picked up a serious infection. I've no real idea how our viruses will affect a Terran system."

"I thought that would have been checked out on the *Khalossa*."

"It was, in theory. I was able to give her some shots to protect her against our most virulent infections. Thankfully, the serums worked, but that doesn't mean to say she's immune to everything. A simple infection for us could be serious for her."

"I'll see if our readings show anything."

"Thanks," she said. "I'll be in the lab if you need me."

It was over an hour later before Vanna arrived at their apartment. Kaid let her in.

"You got my message all right?" she asked as she followed him toward the bedroom door.

"Yes, thank you."

Vanna glanced curiously at him, but he said no more, merely opened the door for her.

Kusac was crouched on the bed beside Carrie, trying to calm her as she moved restlessly from side to side.

"Thank the Gods you're here," he said without looking round. "She's been like this for the last half hour. She's burning hot and she's delirious."

"She would be," said Vanna, going round to the other side. "It's nothing serious. She's managed to get a dose of ni'uzu. There's nothing I can do, I'm afraid, but treat her symptoms."

From her medikit, Vanna had taken a smaller version of the sampling unit she'd used downstairs. Unsealing it, she placed it around Carrie's arm and closed it.

"Ni'uzu?" he repeated. "How did she manage to catch that? It's usually a winter virus, not a summer one." He reached out to take Carrie's other arm as she feebly tried to dislodge the unit. "None of us are ill."

"She could have caught it anywhere," said Vanna, noting the readings from the unit in her comp pad. "It's a common enough virus. She'll have aches and pains in her joints, and a high temperature for a couple of days. Hopefully, it won't be severe enough to cause any chest or throat infections. The lab's working on a vaccine now."

Kusac looked up at her, eye ridges creased in puzzlement. "Why a vaccine? Surely it's too late for that."

"For her, yes, but remember her system is different enough from ours to mutate the virus. You'll likely go down with it, too, not to mention anyone else she's come into contact with over the last three or four days. Can you get me some water, please? I've got a rehydration formula here. I want her to drink as much as possible. Make it a whole jug," she called out after his retreating figure.

Brushing back the damp hair from Carrie's forehead, she concentrated once more on pushing the worries she didn't want Kusac to feel deep down into her subconscious. Time enough for them later, if her fears proved to have foundation. There *was* a vaccine, for the purely Sholan virus, not the one Carrie had caught. What neither she nor the lab could work out was how and why the virus had mutated into the form that Carrie had caught.

Once more, she didn't dare treat the human girl. Instinct told her to let it run its course—with both of them, because without doubt, Kusac would contract it, too, if he hadn't already.

Kusac returned with the jug and a glass which he put down on the night table beside Vanna.

"Thanks," she said, tipping a packet of powder into the jug then waiting for the effervescence to subside. She poured a glassful for Carrie. "You go down and see Khafsa, I'll stay with her." She took a couple of tablets from a container and dropped them into the glass. "It's just a febrifuge," she said, picking up his concern. "On you go," she urged, swirling the pills round in the glass to make them dissolve more quickly.

When he'd gone, she lifted Carrie's head and slowly encouraged her to drink the mixture. Replacing the glass, she went to the bathroom to fetch a dampened towel and began to wipe the girl's face in an effort to cool her down.

"Hush, cub," she said soothingly as Carrie's hand plucked ineffectually at her wrist, trying to push her away. "You're safe, I'm here."

Carrie continued to toss and turn restlessly, muttering in a mixture of Terran and Sholan, trying to evade Vanna's touch. Gradually, the drug began to take effect and she became calmer.

Vanna took the opportunity to talk to Kaid and get him to bring in a more comfortable chair for her. She also arranged for him to prepare a meal for them when Kusac returned.

She'd just begun to relax when Carrie began to moan again, her head tossing from side to side on the pillow. Vanna leaned forward, taking one of the girl's damp hands between hers.

"Carrie, it's all right," she said. "Hush, you'll feel better soon."

"It hurts, 'Lise," Carrie moaned. "Don't do it, it hurts me." She began to move restlessly, trying to push the covers aside. "Don't go back to them, please."

'Lise? Does she mean Elise? thought Vanna.

"Don't go back to them. They'll catch you."

Gods, she's reliving her sister's death! Vanna thought furiously for something to say that wouldn't upset the girl even more.

"Carrie, it's over, cub. The Valtegans are gone. You're safe with me."

The girl became more agitated, her movements more determined as she opened her eyes and tried to get up.

"I have to stop her! It hurts me when she's with them," she whimpered, looking round with wide, staring eyes. "If she goes back, I know she'll get caught this time. You mustn't go, Elise! Come back!"

By now, Vanna had her hands full trying to stop Carrie from getting up. The human had very little strength, but she seemed to have more than two arms as she tried to push Vanna away.

Suddenly Carrie went rigid, then began to tremble convulsively. "Blood," she whispered in Terran, looking at her arms and hands. "There's never been blood before!" Tears began to roll down her face as she tried to wipe her hands on the covers.

Panicking, Vanna attempted something she'd never have thought of trying under any other circumstances. She reached for Kusac, crying out mentally for him. *Kusac!*

I'm coming, he sent.

Carrie had begun to struggle more strongly now. "Elise!" she cried, trying to escape from Vanna's grip. "No! I won't go with you! Let me go!" she screamed at Vanna, trying to hit the Sholan female. "Leave me!"

She was so busy trying to defend herself from Carrie's sudden attack that she didn't hear the door burst open behind her. All she was aware of was Kusac reaching in front of her and taking hold of Carrie, imprisoning her flailing arms in his hands.

Go! he sent, waiting for her to leave.

* * *

Carrie continued to struggle with him, but more weakly now. "I won't go, Elise! Leave me!" she whimpered.

Kusac released her, one arm at a time, pulling her close against his chest, reaching for her mind with his.

Carrie, I'm here, He took one of her hands in his, pressing it against his face. *Elise has gone. She's left you with me. Touch me, feel my fur,* he sent, moving his cheek against her hand. *She's gone, cub. You're safe with me now. Safe.*

She became still, her hand curling round his cheek of her own volition. She let it fall lower, moving down his shoulder to his arm before stopping.

"Kusac?" she said quietly.

"Yes, cub?"

Her eyes closed wearily. "She's gone without me?"

"She's gone," he said. "You must rest now."

Her head moved in a slow nod as he laid her back on the pillows. He touched her forehead. It was cooler now. He waited while she relaxed into sleep, ignoring the aches that had begun in his limbs. He couldn't afford to be ill yet.

* * *

"Are you sure you want to see the body, Sub-Lieutenant Draz?" asked the coroner, hesitating before pulling out the refrigerated drawer. "It isn't a pretty sight, I warn you."

"Just let me see it," said Draz impatiently. "I need to be sure that it's a reasonable assumption he's the missing member of the scouter that blew up several weeks ago."

"If you're only missing one male, then it's him." The physician pulled the drawer out, then lifted the foil cover off the corpse.

Draz took a quick look then turned away as the Coroner replaced the cover and slid the drawer back.

"I did warn you. He was found lying in the open on the edges of swampy ground. The indigenous amphibians have been dining off him since the crash. You're lucky," he said, turning back to Draz who was still looking an unhealthy color around his nose and eyes, "you didn't have the smell as well. You think he's a mess now? You should have seen him before I cleaned him up. Funny thing is, though, there was no water in the lungs. You'd think there would be if he was still alive when he hit the ground. Then, maybe he wasn't."

"Are his injuries consistent with being flung from an exploding vehicle?" asked Draz.

The coroner laughed, ears giving a flick of amusement. "They're consistent with having been chewed on by the local wild life! How the hell do you expect me to tell when there's as little of him left as that? As I said before, if you're only missing one male, then it's him. That's what my report'll say."

"Thanks," said Draz, moving toward the door with relief.

A week later, a copy of the report was waiting on Kaid's comm for him. He read it carefully, wanting to believe it was Chyad, but there were too many convenient anomalies. Like the lack of ID tags and the implanted locator device, either of which in the absence of enough physical evidence would have identified him. However, the scenario was believable. It could be the remains of Chyad. Though there wasn't enough proof that it was him, equally there wasn't enough proof that it wasn't. The coroner hadn't ordered a DNA test on the grounds it was unnecessary as he had no doubt as to the identity of the body. Thoughtfully, Kaid filed the report in his desk.

Chapter 13

Though he'd managed not to catch the full-blown version of the fever, Kaid hadn't escaped without suffering some of the symptoms. A day later, though, he was up and about again. With Carrie and Kusac still laid low recovering, he was free to follow up Garras' message. Personnel from the *Khalossa* due planet leave had landed earlier that day, so leaving Meral and Sevrin on duty in their apartment, he left the Telepath Guild.

He threaded his way through the busy streets toward the outskirts of Valsgarth, skirting round the groups of exuberant younglings on their leave day. As he sidestepped one group, one of them stumbled against him, righting himself quickly with an apology. Pocketing the note thrust into his hand, Kaid continued to head for the aircar park.

Once in a vehicle, he fished the note out of his coat and read it. Satisfied, he screwed it up and pocketed it again. It merely confirmed the information sent to him by Garras. Powering up the aircar, he took off and headed for Nazule.

As the bay came into sight, he skimmed lower, listening for the landing beacon in the center of the city. Once locked onto it, he let the city's traffic system guide his craft in to land.

Climbing out of the aircar, he stepped off the conveyor belt, leaving the vehicle to be swept off into the interior parking area. An elevator took him down to the street level. As in all Sholan towns, no traffic was allowed from dawn till the twentieth hour. However, because of its size, Nazule boasted an underground transport system.

Kaid headed purposefully to the ticket barrier and inserted his personal card into the maw of the access machine. Once his details had been scanned and the requisite cost deducted, it spat the card back at him and opened the gateway. Loping quickly down the stairs, he just made it in time for his shuttle.

It wasn't a long ride, but as the ancient monorail jolted and hissed to a stop at each station, he idly wondered if Carrie's home world possessed equally antiquated transport systems. He had a feeling that their worlds had more similarities than they guessed. Funds for civic works were always scarce if one believed the politicians. Earth with its lack of centralized government would probably fare worse than Shola.

With a howl of compressed air the shuttle came to a standstill, doors sliding open to disgorge the passengers. Kaid joined the living tide that swept along the platform and up to the fresh air above.

He hesitated a moment, getting his bearings as he looked along the busy street. This side of the city, so far from the Warrior Guild, the streets weren't restricted to specific crafts. Everywhere was a jumble of different kinds of stores—restaurants rubbing shoulders with clothing and jewelry shops.

Accommodation Guild Houses, catering to those from every guild, were allowed generous numbers of premises since the actual Craft Guilds had chosen to keep to the outskirts of the city, preferring the quietness and room for larger premises. The only exception was the Warriors' Guild situated close to the town center.

The place Kaid was looking for was located in this area. He headed off to his left, looking for the food bar beside an Accommodation Guild House.

It was in one of the more rundown areas of Nazule, not a place where one would expect folk on planet leave to want to spend their time. The food bar's exterior was dingy; sunfaded paintwork on the facade with the awning permanently rusted in an upright folded position. Several letters from the boldly displayed sign above the window had fallen off and never been replaced.

Kaid pushed the door open and entered, making his way up to the seats at the counter. Sliding onto one, he wrinkled his nose as he caught a whiff of stale cooking.

At the far end, the one assistant stood talking to a faded female of indeterminate age. He looked toward Kaid, then returned to his conversation. Kaid sighed, pulling out a packet of stim-twigs. Taking one out, he stuck it in his mouth and put the pack away in his Forces jacket.

After a few minutes, he hit the counter with his fist, glowering down at the assistant.

"Hey! What's a male gotta do to get some service around here?" he demanded.

The assistant looked round and scowled at him before returning to say a few words to the female. With an air of indolent arrogance, he walked up the counter to Kaid.

"You want something?"

"Yeah. C'shar, and make it strong," said Kaid, reaching into his coat pocket for a handful of coins which he flung down on the counter.

The assistant gathered up the coins, then turned to the kettle and poured Kaid his drink. The mug was banged down in front of him, the contents slopping over onto the counter-top.

Kaid picked it up and turning round, surveyed the rest of the bar. There were only a handful of customers. The bulk of them sat at the back of the bar grouped round a table. One of them still wore the uniform of the *Khalossa* and had a kit bag lying by his feet on the floor. The male opposite him wore the uniform of the *Rhyaki*.

Pushing the twig to one side of his mouth, he took a swig of his drink and half-turned back to the bar. He jerked his head at the assistant.

"What y'want now?"

"Plate of stew," said Kaid, putting more coins on the counter. Reaching up, he scratched his right ear enthusiastically. The pickup in place, he could now hear their conversation.

The stew was placed before him. "You on planet leave?" asked the assistant, handing him eating utensils.

Kaid disdained the knife, pulling his own from his belt. "Yeah. Just off the *Khalossa*. What's it to you?"

"Nothing, just curious. We got quite a few Forces people in today."

"So I see," said Kaid, taking the twig out of his mouth and pocketing it before starting on the stew. It tasted rubbery and undercooked, but he'd eaten worse.

"What's going on up there?" the assistant asked, jerking his head toward the ceiling. "Seems like there's trouble from what I hear."

"Who you heard that from?" asked Kaid, looking up at him.

"I keep my ears open," he said evasively.

"And I keep my mouth shut," Kaid said, scooping up a forkful of the gravy-soaked bread.

With a muttered oath, the assistant moved back down to where the female still perched on the bar stool.

"So how're you planning to stop this treaty with the Terrans?" asked the male from the *Khalossa*.

"T'Chezo will tell you her plans when we meet up with her later, Rhudi," said one of the civilians.

"The original idea of taking out the Sholan telepath and his mate is still as good as any," said the other spacer.

"I think so, Niaza. Chyad's plan was to recruit an anti-Sholan Terran. Where can we find one on Shola?" Rhudi asked.

"There's only the one," said Vrall. "Liegen Aldatan's Leska."

"More Terrans are due on Shola in eight weeks," said Niaza.

"Why, Niaza? Why do they want to bring Terrans to Shola?" asked another of the civilians.

"They're Terran telepaths, Faikal, but I wouldn't expect a grounder like you to know that. If they're anything like our telepaths they'll be no use to us," said Rhudi, the sarcasm heavy in his voice.

"How do the Terrans on the *Khalossa* view this alliance?" asked Faikal, ignoring Rhudi's comments.

"The Keissians want the treaty. We don't. A treaty with either Terran world will leave our back door open to another attack from the Valtegans. We need to do something that will enrage either the Terrans on Earth, or our own people against the Terrans, if we're to stop this treaty."

Faikal looked round his little group.

"How many of us are committed to this course of action?" asked Rhudi, leaning forward on the table.

"Considering that nearly every Clan on the planet has lost at least one member of their family from the colony worlds, very few of them are interested in anything but retribution against the Valtegans," said Faikal.

"Don't they consider this alliance with the Terrans a danger? Aliens as potentially powerful as our telepaths mixing freely with our people? Can't they see that we have no reason to trust them? The humans on the *Khalossa* were just as suspicious of us as we were of them," said Rhudi.

"They don't think about it at all," said Vrall. "Most are content to let the Governor and the Council make the decisions."

Rhudi let out a string of oaths. "How many of us are there?"

"About a dozen," replied Faikal. "We'll take you to meet T'Chezo later tonight. She'll bring you up to date on her plans."

"Having a Terran kill the Terran female and her Leska sounds the best way of enraging the Governor and the Council to the point where they at least cut off communications with Earth," said Niaza thoughtfully. "The Terrans have won no friends on the *Rhyaki* with their demands and arrogance. Do we actually need a Terran, though? What if it was merely thought that a Terran was responsible?"

"How do you propose we do that without a Terran?" asked Rhudi. "It isn't as if we can pass any of us off as one of them. They're too physically different. We need a real Terran."

"If we kill the Leska pair already here, wouldn't the Terrans feel their people were at risk on Shola and refuse to let any more come here?" said Niaza. "We could achieve the same object without involving a Terran."

Rhudi nodded slowly. "Possible," he said. "Easier than trying to subvert a Terran. If we're working with our own people, less can go wrong."

"It solves the problem of us only having a month's leave and the fact that the Terrans won't have arrived by then."

They were so intent on their own conversation that they missed the uneasy looks the civilians were exchanging.

"You'll have to try this one out on T'Chezo," Vrall said. "She's our leader after all. I think you'll find she has definite ideas of her own."

"Just what are her plans?" asked Rhudi. "You obviously know them."

Faikal looked uneasily at Vrall.

"Well?" demanded Rhudi.

"She wants to take a less offensive stance, at least at first," said Faikal. "Holding demonstrations and handing out leaflets, only resorting to violence if we have to."

"Then why involve us?" demanded Rhudi. "We've got the

military experience to plan a strike on them and we've told you we're only here for a month."

"You'll have to talk to T'Chezo," said Vrall uncomfortably.

"Let's take you to your room," said Faikal, getting up. "We can't solve this without her."

"Fair enough," sighed Rhudi, reaching down to pick up his kit bag. "Where's this room you've got for us?"

"Just next door," said Faikal, getting up to stand in the aisle between the tables.

As they got up to leave, Rhudi pulled Niaza back, letting the others go in front of them. "If this T'Chezo doesn't see it our way, we'll do the job ourselves," he said in a low voice.

Niaza flicked his ears in agreement.

As Kaid watched them file out, he finished his c'shar and got to his feet. The assistant and the female looked up as he walked past them.

"Finished?" the male asked.

Kaid ignored him and with a swirl of his long coat, swept out of the door into the street. He saw them enter the Accommodation Guild House next door.

He hung around for half an hour looking in the windows of the stores opposite, keeping an eye on the guild doorway, but the group remained inside. He wanted to see the trooper from the *Khalossa* again. There was something about him that jogged at his memory. He needed information, an agent placed within the group. It was something he couldn't do himself because of his need to guard Carrie and Kusac.

He headed back the way he'd come, collecting his rented aircar at the parking lot. This time he headed for the Warrior Guild, landing in their parking area. Flinging off his long coat, he headed into the Guild House, going straight to the office.

The secretary looked up at him, taking in his uniform with the Warrior's flash of red at the shoulder.

"How can I help you?" he asked.

Taking the chain from his neck, Kaid held it out to him.

The secretary reached out and took hold of the disk that hung from it. He let it go as if it had burned him.

"Brother," he said, eyes wide as he tried to move further away from Kaid. "What may I do to help you?"

Kaid watched the young male's ears twitching with a look of wry humor on his face. He put the chain back over his head. "I need a room with a secure comm in it. I want to contact Dzahai Stronghold."

"Of course," he stammered. "Down the corridor, first on the left."

"Thank you."

* * *

Sorli sat with Master Esken in his study. They were going over the results of the last three weeks' tests with Kusac.

"I'd like your opinion on the latest tests first, Kusac," said Master Esken, picking up his comp note pad.

"You have the results, Master Esken," said Kusac. "I don't know that I can add anything to them."

"Our results have been interpreted objectively by the testers. We now need your insight into how you felt about both the tests and their outcome. Many of these include skills we don't have. Whether we ever did possess them is the topic that Sorli has been looking into. We'll hear his results as we go through the list."

"I'll start with divining, then. We tried the metal rods as suggested, and as you see, neither Carrie nor I had any luck with them. What we did find was that if I was in the room when Carrie was trying, the rods swung round to me. When I wasn't in the room, the rods turned completely round and pointed to Carrie. The same happened when I tried it. We seem to create too strong a field for them to work. We obtained the same result when we tried to use the pendulums over maps. This doesn't appear to be a talent either of us possess."

"Sorli? What about the Sholan control group?"

"No luck with the rods, but one of the group had some success with the pendulum," said Sorli. "If one has it, there will probably be others."

Master Esken nodded. "Anything about it in the Guild Archives?"

"Nothing at all," said Sorli.

"Teleporting was next." Kusac looked up at his tutor and the Guild Master and grinned. "We sat there and thought about moving, but nothing happened. If the Terrans could ever do it, they didn't tell anyone how."

"This was an ability mentioned in passing in the encyclopedia," Sorli said hurriedly. "We didn't expect anyone to be able to do it."

"I take it no one in the control group succeeded either," said Master Esken with a gentle smile.

"No, Master Esken. We did verify that it wasn't possible for either species to do it, though."

"If it's mentioned, then some Terran must have appeared to do it," said Kusac. "Carrie is only one Terran after all, and she's hardly representative of her kind now." His tone had become more than a little sharp.

"People have been said to disappear suddenly," said Sorli. "Unfortunately there was no record of them suddenly reappearing elsewhere. It was worth trying since it would be a useful talent to have."

"I think that's a test we can keep on our list for the Terrans when they arrive," said Master Esken.

Kusac's ears pricked forward. "Terrans arriving?"

"Your father sent us word that the first Terrans with Talents similar to Carrie's will arrive from Earth in eight weeks."

"Father's moved fast."

"I believe it was your mother's doing," said Master Esken. "It will be good for your Leska to have people from her own world to speak to."

"Earth is no longer her home world," said Kusac. "Carrie's a Keissian, and I don't think she'll want to socialize with the Terrans."

"What's she doing today?" asked Sorli.

"She's out with Taizia and some of her friends, answering an interminable number of questions about Terrans, Keiss, and how we met. She's getting more than a little embarrassed by their questions, but Taizia is stopping them from getting too personal," he said, returning to studying his comp pad again.

Sorli raised an eye ridge to the Guild Master who acknowledged it with the smallest of flick of an ear.

As you said, their link gives them constant detailed information about each other, Master Esken sent on a tight personal level.

"Distant viewing was next," said Master Esken.

"That was a lot more successful," said Kusac, looking up at them again. "The test was set up as it was in the article, random locations, randomly chosen and in our case, visited by non-telepaths."

"These tests were particularly valid in Carrie's case as she doesn't know our world, yet she still identified the sites in surprisingly accurate detail," said Sorli.

"Hardly surprising, considering what we did on Keiss," said Kusac. "Both of us scored well on those tests."

"I see the distances between you and the target sites were quite varied, ranging from near to the other side of the continent," said Esken. "It seems that distance was no barrier. Were you able to decide whether you saw through the eyes of the visitors or were actually there yourselves?"

"We both felt that we were actually there. We saw things from a bird's eye view as well as from ground level. We could see details of the sites that the visitor couldn't because of their restricted angle of view. I'd say conclusively that our minds were actually there."

"How did our people do?"

"Very well. Everyone picked up something in the test, even if it wasn't enough to absolutely pinpoint the location."

"Anything in the archives?" Esken asked Sorli.

"Nothing."

"With such positive results from you and the controls, this isn't likely to be another crossover talent," said Master Esken. "It's one you used on Keiss before your Link was completed, Kusac. Perhaps it's a Sholan Talent we've been unaware of because we've concentrated mainly on telepathy. The control group also had some success with this talent, I see. I'm sure we'll find a use for it. Perhaps locating missing persons, checking security measures—who knows."

"I'm sure the military will find a good use to put it to," Sorli murmured. "A little extra information on the Chemerians wouldn't go amiss in their eyes."

"Then we do what we have always done, we use our code of ethics to refuse the military," said Master Esken calmly. "It infringes upon a person's right to privacy."

"You'll find the Terrans less ethical," reminded Kusac. "When they arrive, you'll have to impress on them the need to respect each other's privacy."

"We're already working on an induction program for their arrival at the guild, Kusac. Their course of studies with us is already being mapped out with the aid of our colleagues in AlRel. Your father's involved in it as a matter of fact."

"I know. He's requested me to compile a study of the Keissians, with particular attention to Carrie's own skills."

"That should be interesting," said Master Esken. "I trust you'll have a copy for us?"

"Certainly, but I don't know how long it will take. We've both been constantly busy since we recovered from that virus."

"I'm glad Vanna was able to contain the infection. Now is not a good time for the guild to have an epidemic running riot," said Sorli.

"There's never a good time for epidemics," said Master Esken. "Let's move on to the last test. Healing, I believe. Now that's a Talent which we do have, and we used our own testing system. How do you assess the results, Kusac?"

"Of the eight categories in healing, we can both do six. They are, identifying the site of an injury, identifying the type of injury, reducing the pain, reducing the extent of the injury, accelerating the healing process, and healing minor injuries like bruises and pulled muscles." Kusac looked up from his comp. "Carrie wasn't able to duplicate what she did with my bitten shoulder on Keiss. That unfortunately looks like it might have been unique. Likewise, I can't close open wounds at all or heal major injuries like tissue damage and broken bones."

"What about controlling your own pain?" asked Master Esken. "It says you were able to do that, but Carrie couldn't."

"Under lab conditions, and when I was hurt during the crash on Keiss, yes, I was able to control my pain, but not later after the Challenge, or after I was shot in the Valtegan base. Again, it seems to be an undependable skill with us. Carrie can't work on herself at all. The tests showed she has the ability to heal a variety of conditions in others, so perhaps her inability to work on herself is psychological."

Master Esken nodded. "That sounds a reasonable hypothesis. What do you think caused the block? Sorli thought perhaps she'd desensitized herself due to the horrific link she had with her twin sister."

Kusac shook his head. "No. I think it was because her sister prevented her. You have my report on that link. In it I said that Elise pushed all her pain to Carrie, and that because Carrie expected her to do that, and didn't realize her sister was using her, she not only accepted the pain but actually took it from her. There may also have been the fact that she never tried to block either her own pain or her sister's."

"Perhaps she just wasn't aware she could," suggested Sorli.

"Only practice will remove the block," said Master Esken. "What about yourself? You tested negatively on healing both as a child and when you worked with the medics four years ago. Why the sudden change?"

"Perhaps I was approaching it the wrong way. Need is a great incentive," he said. "We all know that each of us is an individual and works slightly differently from the next person. Perhaps I never found the right trigger to release my healing ability until I was on Keiss."

"What about the fact that you'd already touched Carrie's mind and established an early Link with her? Even though the Link was incomplete, could that have been enough to create a crossover of abilities from her to you?"

"I doubt it, Master Esken," said Kusac. "She had never tried to heal anyone at that time."

"She would still have had the ability to do it even then."

"Who knows?" said Sorli. "We can speculate till tomorrow and never know conclusively."

Esken nodded. "You're right, of course." He sat back in his chair and looked across his desk at Kusac and Sorli. "What about Carrie? In your opinion, has she acquired any skills from you?"

"Not skills. I taught her how to use her telepathic abilities," said Kusac. "Once the initial Leska Link was forged, she knew what I could do with my Talent. That gave her the confidence to try what were to her totally new techniques."

"We've also been guilty of failing to push the boundaries of our Talent forward," said Sorli. "It's taken the discovery of the Terrans to make us wake up to the fact that we aren't the only telepathic species and that for too long we've sat on our Talent and assumed no one could rival us. Now we know otherwise. We need to explore our own abilities in the light of these findings."

"It does indeed appear that we've been ignoring a wealth of Talents that we didn't realize existed till now," said Master Esken slowly. "If nothing else, Carrie's link to you has taught us a great deal about our own abilities. I wonder why none of these skills was ever mentioned in the archives. Could it be in their desire to breed for telepaths, the guild ignored these other Talents, considering them lesser than telepathy?"

"Perhaps during the years that followed the Cataclysm only telepathy and healing were considered worth training," suggested Sorli.

Master Esken sighed. "I suspect you're right. What need had they of distant viewing when thoughts were all that was needed to communicate over large distances? What use was knowing an object's past history when they were struggling to avoid starvation? Moving small objects is amusing, but it didn't help rebuild their towns and Guild Houses. I wonder how many more Talents we've learned to ignore in the past thousand years."

"Well, we've two choices ahead of us. Do we start testing everyone in the guild for these Talents now, or do we wait until the Terrans arrive so we can include them?"

"Start now," said Sorli. "We'll have our hands full when the Terrans arrive."

Kusac nodded. "I agree. Not only that, but you can start training our people now. When the Terrans arrive, the system will be in operation and it'll be easier slotting them into a fully integrated program rather than adding on extra classes later."

"Very well, I'll broach the matter tomorrow at the staff meeting. Sorli, can you present a first draft for the proposed course at that meeting?"

"If I can call on the personnel I need, Master Esken. One of those people is Kusac. No one knows more about these skills than he does."

"By all means include him. You're in rather an anomalous position here at the guild anyway, Kusac. Neither a student nor a tutor but a mixture of both. Your Leska is the one we need to teach."

"Tell me about it," Kusac murmured, switching off his comp. "I'm here so you can study me and see what I've become now that my mind is linked with an alien's."

Sorli looked startled. Master Esken merely smiled. "I'd have been disappointed in you if you'd failed to realize that," he said. "Thank you both for your insights into the test results. I'd better let you get on with your work if you're to have it ready for tomorrow."

Sorli and Kusac rose.

"Good day, Master Esken," said Sorli, inclining his head before turning toward the door.

The Guild Master looked up from his comm. "Would you mind remaining a moment longer, Sorli? I need a few more minutes of your time."

"Good day, Master Esken, Tutor Sorli," said Kusac, opening the door and closing it softly behind him.

"Sorli, sit down again, please. Normally we don't involve ourselves in civil matters, but I'm concerned about these two. You're constantly involved with the training of our Leska pairs. Just how close are they?"

"Closer than if they had been born Talented twins," said Sorli. "As you observed for yourself, there is a constant communication between them. Unlike Sholan Leskas, they don't have to search for the knowledge of what their partner is doing, they know."

"That's what I thought from the data I've been sent by their physician and by you. It's a damned shame she isn't a Sholan. If she had been, then there might have been a chance of his father trying to negate this life-bonding contract with Vailkoi. It would also mean we wouldn't have a problem over their ability to fight. As it is, I'm afraid they're both going to be bitterly disappointed. How do you think Kusac will react?"

"I believe Kusac will disobey his father if it comes to it," said Sorli thoughtfully. "He's equally determined to have Carrie as his legal lifemate. Has anyone stopped to consider what the effect would be on the Terran if Kusac does marry and mate with Rala? Since they're bound so closely, I feel sure the effect would be devastating to both of them. She'd be sharing his intimacy while he mated with Rala."

"That's just another problem they'll have to face when they come to it, along with Konis' wrath when he finds out Kusac has given the human his torc," sighed Master Esken. "It's at times like these that I'm glad to take the coward's way out and claim political and civil neutrality. It isn't up to us to inform him about Kusac's unofficial betrothal gift to her."

"Hardly the coward's way, Master, more the diplomat's.

At least she conceals the torc most of the time," said Sorli quietly. "Was there anything more?"

"No. You've given me much to think about."

* * *

Though religion on Shola was a matter of personal commitment and not organized, this wasn't the case with those who chose to live a life of service to their God.

For Ghyan, a telepath and a Priest of Vartra, this meant he owed allegiance to Lijou, head of the cult of Vartra and co-Leader of the Brotherhood of Vartra at Dzahai Stronghold.

Ghyan's position with the cult was high since only to someone of his ability—and commitment—could the running of the Temple at Valsgarth, the main Telepath Guild town, be given. Equal to him in seniority came Joaylah, the priest at the Temple at Nazule, the Warrior Guild town.

Only the senior Priests and Brothers were aware of the true nature of Lijou and Ghezu's program to achieve full guild status, and of their belief in the mortality of their God.

Ghyan didn't have a problem about the duality of his God. Whatever the original nature of Vartra, the fact that He appeared to new Leska pairs at Valsgarth Telepath Guild, and that by following the temple rituals he could achieve a oneness with the God, made Him divine in his eyes. At Dzahai Stronghold, the Brothers often had God-visions of a personal nature—prophetic ones.

Ghyan was taking his turn at trimming back the candle wicks and checking the torches. It was a job he enjoyed doing—probably because it wasn't a regular task of his, he admitted with a grin to himself. Not far from him, one of the younger acolytes was polishing the metal features on the plinth of the statue of the God.

The youngster was handling the task with a lot of apprehension, not completely convinced that standing on the plinth and polishing Vartra's weapons wasn't an act of sacrilege. He was afraid that the God might come to life before his eyes.

"Come on, lad," said Ghyan. "Put some effort into it! The God's far more likely to censure you for not doing the job properly!"

"Yes, Father Ghyan," said the youngling, his hands now scrubbing faster as he burnished the steel.

Ghyan felt the stillness of the mind before he heard the soft footfall. It had the mark of one of the Brothers. "Good morning, Brother. What can we do for you?" He turned round to see a black robed figure approaching him.

"Father Ghyan," the Brother said, inclining his head before slipping back the hood.

He was still young, just entering the prime of life, Ghyan judged. A highlander, his color an unremarkable tan. Wider than usual ears were pricked toward him, and brown eyes regarded him lazily from a rounded, stocky face.

"I requested leave to attend the Temple. Leaders Lijou and Ghezu appointed me to Valsgarth. Until now my posting had been on board the *Khalossa*. My name is Rulla."

"Well come, Rulla," Ghyan said, laying his paring knife down on the bench below where he'd been working. "Leader Lijou had mentioned I might expect one or more of the Brothers." He felt a faint flare of surprise from Rulla. Not an agent, then. Curious.

"Have you luggage?" he asked, going over to join him.

"In the passage," replied Rulla. "I didn't like to bring it into the Temple."

"I'll get one of the younglings to take it to your quarters. You'll join me in a mug of c'shar?"

"Please."

"See to the rest of the candles when you finish, Vrazo," he said before leading Rulla toward the door to his private quarters.

Settled with a plate of cold meats and bread between them, Ghyan sipped his c'shar, eyeing Rulla curiously.

"What do you plan to do with your time here, Rulla?" he asked.

Rulla put down his mug and helped himself to a slice of meat. He placed it meticulously on the bread, then rolled it into a cylinder.

"I'd like to study, if I may, Father Ghyan," he said before taking a bite of his meat roll.

"We do have an extensive library here," said Ghyan with a pleased smile. "In fact, it's my own particular pride that I've been able to add to the wealth of books—real books, not the cartridges for the comp pads. What are you wanting to study?"

"Comparative religions." He hesitated. "With particular reference to the Keissian religion."

Ghyan's mouth fell open in surprise. Recollecting himself, he shut it almost immediately.

"I have to admit I was hoping to be posted here," Rulla continued. "You see, I know you have a friend with an—intimate knowledge—of Keissian customs."

Ghyan frowned. "I can only authorize your use of the facilities here at the Temple," he said stiffly. "We have nothing yet on Keissian religions. As to my personal friends, they remain just that. Personal."

"Oh, I appreciate that, Father Ghyan. I merely hoped to contact a friend of mine who's in the employ of your friend. I trust you would have no objections to me conducting some research outside the Temple, if I can get permission to speak to Liegen Aldatan and his Leska. I would, of course, leave a copy of my studies with the Temple when I depart."

"I think you'll find it highly unlikely that you'll get permission," said Ghyan. "Should you be lucky enough to do so, then I'd have no objection." This was no coincidence, Ghyan was sure. If Lijou hadn't sent him, then who had? A word to Kusac was the least he could do. If he was mistaken, it would cause no harm. If he wasn't . . .

* * *

Kaid accompanied Taizia and Carrie to the inn where they were meeting some of the other students from her year.

"I don't know that this is a good idea," said Carrie as they stepped out into the guild's sunny courtyard.

"Of course it is," said Taizia, taking her by the arm. "Tell her it is, Kaid. She's been shut up in this mausoleum of a guild for far too long. She needs to get out and meet people."

"She's probably right," Kaid agreed, falling into step on her other side.

"Your life is here on Shola with my brother, so you need to meet people and make friends."

"I have friends, Taizia. I have Vanna and you as well as Kaid, Meral, and Sevrin."

"I mean more friends, then! Come on, don't dig your claws in, we'll be late," she chided, pulling Carrie on when she tried to lag back at the main gate.

Carrie allowed herself to be drawn into the street. It was

only her second visit to the town. Over the last few weeks they'd been kept busy with tests for the guild. At least Vanna's tests were less frequent now. Taizia was right; she needed the break and the fresh air.

"Where are we going?"

"To the Green Goddess Inn. It has a wonderful garden out the back."

"Green Goddess?" asked Carrie as they walked past the food stalls. "I thought Vartra was your main God."

"He is, if you're a telepath or a Warrior," Taizia said. "But there are others, lots of them. Religion is up to the individual. Most houses have a shrine to one of the Gods or Goddesses. Our religions aren't organized like yours are." She gave her a quick grin. "I've been reading up on your people. That encyclopedia is fascinating." She pronounced the unfamiliar Terran word carefully.

"How did you manage to see it? I thought it was still restricted."

Taizia gave a low purring laugh. "It is, but Mother let me use her access code to the locked AlRel files. I thought that since my brother's Leska is human, I should learn something about her people. Anyway, I'm officially allowed to have it now."

Abruptly Taizia pulled her over to a stall selling grilled cubes of meat on skewers. "Three, please," she said, digging into the pocket of her tabard for the appropriate coins. "Here," she said, distributing them to Carrie and Kaid. "They smelled so good I couldn't resist them."

"Thank you," said Carrie, gingerly taking a small mouthful. The meat was spicy and tender. She took a larger bite. "I thought you said we were eating at the inn."

"Oh, we are, don't worry," she said, licking the juices off her forearm.

"Don't you get fur in your mouth?" Carrie asked.

"Only if you lick against the lie of the fur," said Taizia, eyes alight with humor. "I thought you'd been with Kusac long enough to learn that."

Carrie decided to ignore the remark.

The inn was near the jewelry quarter, a part of the town she'd visited before. As they made their way along one of the small streets, Carrie stopped abruptly in front of one of the stores.

"Kaid, isn't this the store we visited on my first trip?"

"Yes, I believe it is, Liegena."

Taizia frowned and caught him by the arm. "Don't call her Liegena, Kaid. It'll only draw attention to her. We don't need that yet," she said quietly.

"I agree," said Carrie, turning back to look at them. "Please, call me Carrie, Kaid. I'd prefer it."

"I didn't think you'd hear me," said Taizia, her ears flicking in embarrassment.

"I can hear and smell almost as well as you, Taizia," said Carrie. It was her turn to look amused. "All my senses are sharper since your brother and I became fully Linked." She turned to Kaid. "I need to collect something from the shop. Will you wait outside for me?"

Kaid frowned. "Let me check it out first," he said before biting the last cube of meat off its skewer. Tossing the stick in a nearby bin, he went into the shop. Moments later he was out again. "It's empty except for the storekeeper," he said. "I'll remain outside unless someone else goes in."

Carrie nodded and went in. A few minutes later she returned with the belt pouch at her waist looking a good deal heavier.

"What's all the mystery?" asked Taizia as they moved off again toward the inn.

"It would be wiser to be ignorant in this case," Kaid murmured in her ear as he moved past her to Carrie's other side.

Carrie noticed Taizia give him a sharp look, but she said nothing.

The inn was at the corner of a row of stores. A large, closely cropped, open green swathe was at the rear of the building. On it were set rustic benches and tables round which groups of Sholans lounged.

As Taizia led them across the green toward a table set a little back from the others, Carrie was aware of the curious stares and retreated behind her shield feeling exposed and vulnerable. She straightened her back automatically. Let them look. At least she was getting more used to it. Taizia gave her arm a reassuring squeeze as they approached a group of about half a dozen females.

"You're going to be outnumbered, Kaid," Carrie said, trying to conceal her nervousness. "I hope you don't mind."

"Not when the company is so stimulating," Kaid said with a slight grin.

Taizia laughed. "You've got a rare escort there, Carrie,"

she said. "Few of them are that diplomatic and complimentary at the same time."

Carrie found her arm taken again by Taizia as they approached the table.

"Hello, everyone," she said. "I'd like you to meet Carrie, my brother's Leska, and this is Kaid, her escort."

Carrie looked at the circle of new faces. A wave of panic hit her until she felt her arm nipped by Taizia on one side, then Kaid's comforting presence moving closer to her on the other.

Take a deep breath, you'll be fine, Taizia sent. *We're all students from AlRel. We've actually had some experience with other species. If Kusac has his way and life-bonds to you, you'll have to get used to mixing with other Sholans.*

"Hello," she said, letting Taizia push her down onto the bench.

"That's Taiba next to you," said Taizia, "and Laesu, Vekki, G'hiled and Changu."

Carrie looked at each of them in turn. It was getting easier to tell the Sholans apart these days. She was even beginning to appreciate the Sholan ideals of beauty. Each of the females nodded at her in greeting.

Taiba reached out for the large jug that sat in the center of the table. "Would you like some wine?" she asked. "We ordered enough for all of us."

"Please," said Carrie, pushing her glass and Taizia's forward.

"What about you, Kaid?" Taiba asked as she filled them.

"Thank you, no. I'm on duty," he said, slipping onto the bench beside Changu.

"Isn't it a little ridiculous for her to have an escort?" said G'hiled, lifting her glass for a drink. "Only the female heirs of Clan families need escorts, and then only just before they're married."

Under the table, Taizia's hand clamped over Carrie's thigh, pressing it warningly. "I see the wine hasn't sweetened your nature yet, G'hiled," she said. "If my brother feels his Leska needs an escort, who am I to disagree?"

"Your friend is quite right," said Kaid smoothly as he helped himself to a glass of water. "I'm actually Liegen Aldatan's adjutant. Today I am merely escorting her to prevent the sort of unwanted male attention that she suffered from on the *Khalossa*."

"If you're going to be snippy, G'hiled, then perhaps you'd better leave now," said Changu. "I, for one, would prefer to sit and chat with Carrie rather than criticize her. You're only saying that because your nose is out of joint. You've had your eye on Kusac for a long time now, and he's never even been aware you exist!"

"I think enough private opinions have been aired in public," said Vekki, her tone reproving. "This isn't exactly the way we intended to welcome you, Carrie. I'm afraid you're getting a rather poor impression of us."

Strangely enough, the bickering had actually helped her relax and feel part of the group. It reminded her of some of the teenagers she'd taught back home.

"Don't worry about it," she grinned. "I'm used to it. I was a teacher on Keiss."

G'hiled hissed at the implied insult, then subsided as the others began to smile.

"Have you ordered any food yet?" Taizia asked, taking a sip of her wine.

"Of course. We ordered a variety of dishes for all of us. We didn't know what Carrie likes to eat, so we thought this way she's bound to find something that takes her fancy," said Vekki.

"Good, I'm famished," said Taizia.

Carrie picked up her glass and cautiously tasted the wine. It was pleasantly fruity and not too sweet. Her father would have liked it, she thought.

Then we'll send him a crate of it, sent Kusac.

She grinned as she put her glass down again.

"What is it?" asked Taizia.

"Just a comment about the wine from Kusac," she said, without thinking.

"Your minds are that close?" asked Taizia in disbelief. "What did he say?"

"Only that if the wine was that good, we'd send my father some. He grows vines, you see."

"Vines?" asked Vekki.

"Don't you have vines? What kind of fruit do you use for your wine?"

"All kinds," said Taizia. "This one is made from redberries."

"My mother makes her own wines," said Laesu. "Perhaps

we can exchange recipes. I'm sure she would love to try some Terran wines."

"Not Terran, Keissian," corrected Taizia. "The Terrans are from Earth. If we don't distinguish between the two worlds now, it'll only cause confusion later."

"So I'm no longer a Terran, then," said Carrie in amusement. "I'm a Keissian."

Taizia's mouth opened in a grin. "That's right," she said. "Nothing like having your identity changed for you, is there?"

"Tell me about it," said Carrie with a laugh. "I'm still learning to cope with the Sholan part of me!"

"The Sholan part?" asked Taiba curiously.

"All the memories I inherited from Kusac," explained Carrie.

Taizia gave a loud purring laugh. "You want to be thankful Kusac didn't notice you, G'hiled! If he had, Carrie would know all about it!"

Carrie turned to look at Taizia. "I hadn't thought of that," she said thoughtfully.

There's nothing worth remembering, came the thought from Kusac.

"Kusac again?" grinned Taizia. "These multiple conversations you have must be confusing."

"They've never happened till now," Carrie said. "I've never really been anywhere without Kusac before."

"Then it's definitely a good idea for you to come out with me more often," said Taizia, pouring some more wine into her glass.

"Here comes the food," said Laesu. "I'm surprised you didn't notice it before me, Taizia."

"There's no justice in the world when you two can gorge yourself on food and stay as slim as a reed and I only have to look at it to gain weight," moaned Taiba as the waiter approached with a laden tray.

The meal was one of the long leisurely affairs that the Sholans so loved. With the wine and the warm sun as well, Carrie soon found herself relaxing. The conversation became a little too personal at times, but Taizia deftly steered it back onto neutral ground.

"So, what do you think of Shola?" asked Laesu. "Is it very different from Keiss?"

"Very. We were the advance colonists, setting up an agricultural community to support the next wave. They were the people who would build up the industrial side of our colony."

"Strange way to do it," observed Vekki. "When our last colony was set up, they started simultaneously with the industrial bases on the moons and the agriculture on the planet."

"I believe that's what's happening now, thanks to your people," said Carrie. "We didn't have the technology to send more than one ship at a time, nor to land on the moon and ferry goods to Keiss."

"What else do you find different?" asked Taiba.

"The climate, but that's probably got more to do with being nearer your equator than we were on Keiss. I must admit, I like the warm weather." She stretched her arms, enjoying the feel of the sun on them.

"We had four small villages on Keiss, that was all," she said. "There was an inn in each village, no stores, and our market day was once a month. We lived a very simple life. Here you've got all the benefits of an industrial technological society with none of the problems of pollution and overcrowding."

"Shola's no perfect land of the Gods, Carrie," said Taizia, leaning forward onto the table. "You've only seen Valsgarth. Telepath towns are kept small because of our needs—we don't need the noise of thousands of minds all day and all night. Nazule is our nearest big city, and it's a different matter. There's overcrowding and even poverty there. Not everyone has the pride, enthusiasm, or interest to make their life the best it can be. The central government does what it can, but it can't help everyone."

"I suppose you're right. I'm afraid I left Earth when I was eleven, and I remember very little about it. I remember there was pollution and overcrowding and slums, but that's about all. I've spent more of my life on Keiss."

"How do the Terrans train their telepaths?" asked Changu, picking up her glass and taking another sip from it.

"Didn't you bother to read the files we were given by AlRel?" asked G'hiled scornfully. "If you had, you'd know that the Terrans don't recognize telepathy at all. They don't believe it exists!"

"Some of them do," said Taizia, catching the eye of one

of the waiters. "More iced water, please," she said, then turned back to their group.

"I've seen the encyclopedia they brought with them from their home world. It's amazing. Apart from all the other subjects, there's a large number of articles on their various Talents, including telepathy. The trouble stems from the fact that scientists were trying to devise repeatable tests for a talent they didn't believe existed. Had the telepaths formed their own guild, there wouldn't have been this problem."

"How did you manage to get access to that information?" demanded G'hiled. "Your father shouldn't have let you see confidential AlRel documents."

"Father didn't," said Taizia mildly. "My mother did. The encyclopedia was sent to Carrie by her brother. She gave the guild and AlRel their copies."

"Is it going to be made available to us?" asked Vekki. "It seems to me that it would be good experience for the senior year students of AlRel to study the first new culture that's come along in over two hundred years. Especially when we have a member of that species living in the guild with us."

"I'm way ahead of you, my dear." Taizia's purr was only a shade higher than her brother's. "Father's already agreed. However, it's going to cost us, and you might not like the price."

"You and your wheeling and dealing, Taizia," said Laesu with a laugh. "What have you got us into now?"

"Well, first of all we're studying Keissian humans, not Earth Terrans," she said with a sideways grin at Carrie. "He wants a comparative study of their social customs. He wants to see how far from the Terran norm the colony on Keiss has moved, and whether the changes are due to the lack of influence from the home world or to the domination of the culture by the Valtegans."

"Will you be helping us?" Changu asked Carrie.

"I don't know that I can be much help. I'll certainly do what I can. Kusac says he's working on a similar topic. He'd be glad to make some of his files available to you for cross-reference."

"I thought we'd be looking at the telepaths in Keissian culture," said Taiba.

"There's only one of me," said Carrie, glancing up as the waiter approached with their jug of water.

"That comes next term," said Taizia, nodding her thanks to him and pouring herself a drink. "We've got eight weeks for this study before more Terrans arrive on Shola, then we're evaluating their ability to fit into our culture."

"More Terrans?" said Taiba, her interest caught. "Will they be males or females?"

"Both, I expect," said Carrie. "Our males don't suffer from the same antisocial behavior that I'm told yours do."

"What are your males like?" asked Vekki curiously.

Carrie looked across at Kaid. "Taller, more heavily built than me and their voices are deeper than human females. Some of them choose to grow hair on parts of their faces."

"Are there pictures of them in the encyclopedia?"

"Yes," confirmed Taizia. "If you come back to our room, I can show you."

"We're all finished here, aren't we?" Laesu asked, looking round the group for the chorus of affirmatives.

"Then let's pay the waiter and go," she said.

They each put in an equal amount, Taizia helping Carrie with the value of the different coins.

"Don't worry, I'll remember them now," she said, putting the rest back in the pouch on her belt. "Everything has a familiar look and feel to it, as if I've temporarily forgotten the name. Once I'm told, I don't forget."

As they walked back through the town to the guild, Carrie could feel Taizia's growing desire to ask her something she considered important. When the Sholan female touched her hand and sent her a request to slow down, she knew the question was imminent.

"Carrie, what did you collect from the store?"

Carrie gave her an amused look. *I'll trade you,* she sent. *You tell me why you asked me to cover up my torc, and I'll tell you what I bought. Deal?*

A startled look crossed Taizia's face. *I didn't realize you could send that well to any telepath.*

Don't underestimate her, Taizia. For all her Terran appearance and lack of experience, she's one of us. Be careful what you say, Kusac warned her on the private level they'd used as cubs.

Kusac wants to tell our father about you himself. If you're seen wearing his torc, people will talk and Father will find out before Kusac has spoken to him.

Carrie digested this for a moment.

You're not Sholan, Carrie, sent Taizia. *It's a big step for Kusac to take. Father is bound to be concerned about it.*

Fair enough. When Kusac and I were in Valsgarth before, we arranged for me to buy him a torc. This is the first chance I've had to collect it.

Taizia gave Carrie a curious look, then grinning, linked her arm in the Terran's. *Gods, you've both got it bad, haven't you? I'm glad of that because you'll always have each other.*

"Come on," said Taiba, stopping to wait for them.

"You'll have to wait another eight weeks to see our men," laughed Carrie as they caught up.

Why don't you go with them and show them the encyclopedia, sent Kusac. *I'm busy working with Tutor Sorli to draft out a new course to be presented at the staff meeting tomorrow. I'll be finished by third meal.*

Carrie timed her arrival back at their apartment to coincide with Kusac finishing his work. Sorli was leaving as they arrived. Seeing all was well, Kaid excused himself and left her there.

"We've just written a course for developing three new mental skills," said Kusac as the door slid quietly shut behind them. He draped his arm across her shoulders as they walked over to the settee.

"You enjoyed yourself, I know. Did you like Taizia's friends?"

"Yes, I did. I particularly like Vekki and Laesu. I'm going to help them with their work for the next two terms," she said, sitting down beside him.

"That's good. It'll get you out and about. You need to find a niche for yourself," he said, reaching up to knead one of his shoulders.

"Let me do that," she said. "Turn around."

He did as she asked, drawing his legs up in front of himself.

Slipping her hands inside the back of his shirt, she pushed through his fur and began to work the muscles at the sides of his neck.

"They're absolutely solid," she said. "I bet you didn't take any breaks, did you?"

"No," he admitted, squirming under her hands. "We wanted to get it finished, so Sorli could go over it before tomorrow. Ouch! That hurts, Carrie."

"Sorry, but it isn't easy for me when your shirt's in the way." She leaned forward to undo the first couple of buttons, then returned to kneading his shoulders, gradually working her way across the top then down onto his back just below his neck.

As well as she knew his body by now, the subtle differences never failed to fascinate her. The heavy muscles around his highly mobile joints were designed to allow him to change to four-legged locomotion at a moment's notice.

"What you need is a good soak in a hot bath," she said, aware of his tiredness as she tried to soften the muscles underlying his shoulder blades.

"Later." His hand reached up for one of hers, tugging gently on it. "Come round this side," he said, his voice a lazy purr now that she had relieved the worst of the tension and strain.

She got up and moved in front of him, leaning against the arm of the settee. "I got something for you today," she said, trying to stop him from picking up her thoughts.

He cocked his head to one side, a look of curiosity on his face. "You did?" His ears swiveled round to face her.

She nodded, reaching into her pouch to take out a padded package. Nervously she began to open it, suddenly afraid that despite what he'd said at the time, he wouldn't accept the gift from her.

"If it's for me, shouldn't I be doing that?" he asked.

"No, not with this," she said, trying to control the slight shaking in her hands as she unwrapped the final layer. Keeping it on its bed of soft paper, she held it out to him. "It's your torc, Kusac."

The moment hung there between them, each of them aware of the importance of this promise, both aware of what they were giving up for the other.

Kusac breathed in sharply, looking up at her. He didn't need to see her face to know what she felt for him, he could sense it clearly through their Link. He reached out to take the torc then hesitated, hand poised above it.

"You realize what this signifies?" he said. "The bonding ceremony is only the final seal to our promises. If I take your torc, there's no going back." His eyes searched her face even as his mind searched hers, looking for any trace of doubt. There was none.

His hand touched her face, cupping her cheek. "I'm from the Clan Leader's family, Carrie, and you're my Leska. It means no children for either of us," he said softly. "Neither Terran, nor Sholan. Can you live with that?"

"I know," she said, resting her hands and her gift on her knees. "We'll have each other, that's enough."

Picking up the torc, he spread the terminals and placed it round his neck, the bronze gleaming against his dark fur. "It's warm," he said, surprised.

Carrie grinned. "It would be. I've been carrying it around next to me all day. When you gave me yours, it was warm, too."

He moved his legs, reaching out to pull her closer so he could untie the lightweight scarf she'd worn over her torc. "You don't need to wear this now. I'll speak to Father tomorrow."

As she leaned forward to undo the remaining buttons on his shirt, she felt him running his hand down her side till he reached her bare leg.

"I see you didn't bother with your trousers after all," he said, burying his face against her hair and neck, breathing in her scent. His hand caressed her thigh gently, claw tips tracing intricate patterns.

She'd reached his belt and by the time it fell loose to the settee, his other hand had found the front seal of her tabard and released it.

He tumbled backward, arms grasping her and taking her with him.

"It was too hot today," she murmured, her mouth searching for his.

No more talk, he sent between the small bites and kisses. *Let's seal our betrothal.*

* * *

Kaid threaded his way through the packed inn till he reached the table at the back where Rulla sat waiting for him.

"What the hell are you doing requesting leave at the Tem-

ple in Valsgarth?" he demanded, his voice low and angry as
he sat down opposite him.

"Gently, Kaid," he said, pushing a spirit glass over to him.
"Have this and calm down. I didn't ask for Valsgarth, Lijou
posted me here. I expect he hopes to make use of me at
some point."

Kaid gave a low growl of annoyance.

"Have your drink," said Rulla, edging it closer to him. "I
know you're off duty or you wouldn't be here. It's
Chemerian M'ikkoe. You still like it, don't you?"

Kaid glowered at him and picked the drink up. "You still
haven't told me why you're here."

"I figured that Ghezu will only tell you what he wants you
to know considering you're working free-lance. With me
here, too, he reckons it gives him the edge over you, so I'm
more likely to find out what he's up to." He lifted his glass
and took a drink.

"I'm also in the Temple," he continued, putting the glass
down again. "We know Lijou plays both ends against the
middle and if he's after information on what Ghezu's up to,
he'll ask me since I'm now officially attached to him as a
lay Brother."

Kaid grunted, allowing his brow to relax and took a
mouthful of the drink. "It'll do as a cover," he said. "Now
tell me what you're really doing here."

Rulla sat forward, leaning low across the table. "I told
you on the *Khalossa,* Kaid," he said, his voice almost a
whisper. "Some of us hear the God calling. If you're going
to keep them safe, out of the hands of both Esken and the
Brotherhood, then you can't do it alone. It's too much for
one person."

"Who says that's what I'm doing?"

"Stop messing around, Kaid! You wouldn't do Ghezu's
dirty work for him ever again, nor would you let the likes of
Lijou or Esken call your tune. So what's left? All I need to
know is where we're going."

"I don't know what you're talking about," said Kaid, taking another mouthful of his drink. "We're not going anywhere."

"What are your plans, Kaid, because whatever they are,
I'm going to be part of them. There were a lot of us who dis-
agreed with Ghezu's actions back . . ."

Kaid slammed the glass on the table, sending the contents

slopping over the side. "Forget that day!" he said angrily. "It's gone, over and done with." More quietly, "I have, Rulla. I've no desire or need to pull Ghezu down. Leave the Brotherhood out of this. I'm no longer an active part of it."

"So you've got no plans yet?" Rulla nodded slowly. "Then you'd better get some together, Kaid, because you've already got a following."

Kaid looked up sharply at him, eyes narrowing, ears swiveling forward so he missed nothing. "What d'you mean?" he demanded.

"Exactly what I said. If you haven't realized it by now, then you're slipping, my friend. There's Garras for a start. Then what about those two lads from the *Khalossa* that you brought with you? Meral and Sevrin? Saw them today. Can't you see it's the old days starting all over again?"

"Don't be ridiculous!" he snapped.

"Am I? Like I said, Kaid, you better start finalizing your plans." He drank the last of his ale and stood up to leave. "Remember, you've got me inside the Brotherhood and the Temple now. You've got a following, whether or not you want us, we're there."

He reached out for Rulla, pulling him back down. "Sit down, for the God's sake! You can't help me, you're still in the Brotherhood, still subject to your oath to Ghezu! You know what the penalty is if you break it. Don't be a fool, Rulla!"

Rulla let himself be pulled down again. "Do you remember our oath?" he asked.

"Of course I remember it," growled Kaid. "I still try to live by it."

"How can you do that, when you're no longer one of the Brotherhood?"

"I keep my oath to the God."

"Exactly. The basis of our oath is to Vartra, not Ghezu. How does it go? 'I swear that for the rest of my life I will follow the God's calling, and abide by the rules of the Brotherhood. To this end I renounce all Clan ties. From now till I die, my family is of the Brotherhood at Dzahai Stronghold.'"

"What's your point, Rulla?"

"Merely that I can follow my oath from outside the Brotherhood, too, if our move is made public enough. Now I really do have to go, Kaid. Ghyan is expecting me back. I did tell you that I've asked to study comparative religions, didn't I? Particularly the Keissian one. I'll be getting in touch with your Liegen in a day or two."

Kaid sat on for a while after Rulla had left. He had a lot of thinking to do. An old mirror had been held up in front of him again and he wasn't sure he liked the image in it.

Chapter 14

True to his word, Kusac rose early the next morning and, leaving Carrie still asleep, went through to the lounge to contact his father. He had no real idea of what he was going to say beyond the fact that he had no intention of marrying Rala. What he did next depended on his father's reaction.

Approaching the desk, he saw the message light was blinking urgently. With a sense of resignation, he sat down and keyed in the replay. It told him that because of problems in the peace talks with Earth, his father's presence on the *Rhyaki* was essential. His mother was due home that day, but until then he, Kusac, was in charge of the Clan and all messages would be relayed to his comm. Groaning, he checked the time. Kaid would definitely be awake. Contacting him, he asked him to deal with any incoming calls for the time being.

Switching off the comm, he rubbed his hands across his ears, frustrated at the delay. Having nerved himself up to talk to his father, it was annoying to find that he was gone for several weeks. He padded back to the bedroom, slipping quietly into the warmth of their bed. As he lay down beside her, from the depths of sleep Carrie sensed his return and moved closer to him, matching her body to his. Her hand reached back seeking his, bringing it forward to wrap around herself.

He slid his tail across her legs, feeling the slight movement from her that told him she'd relaxed again. Since the night of their dream, she'd waken suddenly with a start, needing to see and touch him immediately to reassure herself he was still there. Beside him the light glowed faintly for her as it did every night. For himself, every morning that he woke and found her there was a wonder he was afraid wouldn't last.

His eyes began to close as he relaxed into the familiar touch and smell of her body against his.

* * *

As soon as Rhyasha reached her home on the estate, she sent a message to the guild requesting her daughter's presence immediately.

Taizia was there within the hour. "Mother, it's good to see you," she said, greeting her with a hug. Fetching one of the large floor cushions, she planted it and herself by her mother's feet.

"It's good to be home again," Rhyasha said. "C'shar?"

"Please. How are the talks with Keiss going?"

"They're complete," said Rhyasha with satisfaction, handing her a mug. "Even if I do say so myself, your father couldn't have done a better job. We had some interesting news before I left. There's been no sign of that Valtegan ship yet, and all attempts to find their home world have come up blank. However, the Chemerians have suddenly gone absolutely paranoid—even for them—about what they term 'our enemy' being a threat to their worlds. Considering the distances involved between us and them, we're wondering if they know something that we don't. I left Vrail dealing with it. If he finds out anything, he'll let me know." She stopped to pick up one of the biscuits beside her.

"Now tell me about your father. I hear he's headed out to Earth. What's happening there?"

"The Terrans are reluctant to send us any telepaths. They say they haven't got any, so Father's on his way there armed with a copy of Carrie's encyclopedia. You remember, it's that book of knowledge you lent me your access code for. It lists the various centers of learning where they've been studying the Terran Talents for years."

"I remember. Well, your father's sure to enjoy himself," she said dryly. "He always did like the cut and thrust of the diplomatic world. How's your brother and his Leska? Are they well? How are they settling in on Shola?"

"Don't you mean his betrothed?" said Taizia, eyeing her mother over the top of her mug as she took a sip of her drink. "Carrie gave him a torc yesterday."

Rhyasha nodded. "I expected she would. Has Kusac spoken to your father about it yet?"

"Not to my knowledge. You got my message about Rala?"

Rhyasha frowned. "Yes, I did. I've never been happy about your father's choice, now I'm utterly convinced she's wrong for him. The stupidity of her trying that old trick on Kusac! Neither her tantrums nor her ingenuous act will have any effect on him, the opposite in fact, thank the Gods!"

"Frankly, I'm glad. I never did like the idea of having Rala living here as my sister," said Taizia.

Her mother sat and sipped her drink, amber eyes taking on a faraway look. "I knew Kusac's marriage with Rala would give him very little emotional satisfaction and I'd just about given up hope of him ever finding a female he could care for. Then he finds Carrie." She sighed and her eyes refocused on her daughter.

Taizia leaned forward and took her mother's hand, stroking the soft golden fur. "Strange as it may sound, she's right for him. You know he's always enjoyed his studies. Well, now he has a lifetime to devote to studying his Leska's species."

"What about her, though? Do you think she cares as much for him?"

Taizia laughed, giving her mother's hand a gentle squeeze. "She's as besotted with him as he is with her! Never fear, they'll be happy, given half a chance," she said, her tone becoming more somber.

"You've reminded me why I sent for you," said Rhyasha, businesslike once more. "I've been trying to look ahead and decide what's best for the Clan in the long run. Kusac has two choices. To marry Rala, or not to marry her. If he decides to disobey his father and the Council by not marrying her, I'll have no option but to declare him outcast from the Clan. I'm sure he intends to break the contract; therefore, we have to find some reason for it to be dissolved before he does."

"I know," said Taizia quietly. "I've already been thinking along the same lines."

Rhyasha hesitated. "There is something else that has to be taken into consideration. If he does marry Carrie, he can't remain my heir. You'll have to be named."

Her daughter sat there in stunned silence. "No," she said at last. "I refuse."

"You can't. We need a marriage which will give the Clan heirs. Kusac's marriage to Carrie obviously won't, and since she's also his Leska, the duty falls to you."

"I don't want my brother's position," Taizia said. "Why must he lose it? He can lead the Clan just as easily with an alien wife as he can with a Sholan one."

"He can't provide heirs, you know that."

"Then name my children his heirs!" she exclaimed, "but don't take the heirship away from him! It's been done before—in Grandfather's time—why not now?"

"Kusac would gladly give it up," Rhyasha said dryly.

"I'm sure he would, but he's been brought up to lead the Clan one day, I haven't. I know nothing about it."

"You've as much common sense—if not more—than Kusac. Very well, if that's what you want," she sighed. "I'll name your future children as Kusac's heirs. I'd love to know why the Gods should bond him into a sterile link. I just hope he can cope with it. Since he's now behaving like any other competitive, virile male, he'll be experiencing the pull toward persuading her to have his cubs."

"He'll cope," said Taizia. "He learned the painful way to control his aggression, as we all did. He'll probably work harder to compensate. Anyway, the physical shape of Terran females makes them appear to be pregnant all the time. That may in itself be enough."

"Maybe," said Rhyasha. "Meanwhile, we need to find at least one good reason for the marriage contract to Rala to be dissolved. I won't let him be pushed into breaking the Clan laws."

"Surely his Link to Carrie is reason enough. Do you know how close they are?"

"I've a fair idea," admitted Rhyasha. "Enough to be very concerned as to the effects on both Carrie and Kusac if he had to pair with Rala to provide heirs. But his link isn't a good enough reason for the Council or for your father."

Taizia glanced up at her mother. "Frankly, I don't think he'd be capable of pairing with Rala because of the totality of his Link with Carrie. What about using Rala's behavior at the guild as a valid reason?"

"I intend to do that anyway," said Rhyasha, her voice becoming hard. "That's what happens when a female is brought up almost exclusively by a doting father who refuses to listen to his female relatives' advice! I hope to change your father's opinion on the grounds that in complete defiance of guild rules, she is mentally manipulating people around her, and attempted to do the same to Kusac at a time when she knew he was vulnerable. Those certainly are acceptable grounds for annulling a marriage contract."

"I told you that Meral came to find me so I could accompany them to Rala's home. I can certainly testify as to her attitude then. She was projecting a most vile temper all the way back to her father's estate."

"That will certainly help. Another worry of mine is concerned with Carrie. If he does intend to marry her within our Clan system, then she must have an escort when he isn't with her. Despite the fact there's no need to protect her honor until the wedding, all the proprieties must be seen to be followed. I don't want the Clan council to have any grounds for demanding an annulment."

Taizia grinned. "That's the first thing we've discussed today where the news is good," she said. "I've just realized how clever Kusac has been. He had Kaid escorting us yesterday."

Rhyasha looked thoughtfully at her daughter. "Did he? Then he is more perceptive than I thought. Do you realize who Kaid is?"

Her daughter frowned. "What do you mean? He's Kusac's adjutant, isn't he?"

"That, too, but he is one of the Brothers of Vartra."

"Ye Gods!" swore Taizia, her eyes widening in surprise. "She couldn't have a more acceptable escort, but why a Brother?"

"There was an attempt on her life while they were on the *Khalossa*."

"But why?"

"Dissident survivors from the two dead colonies who didn't want the treaty with Earth."

"I knew nothing about this. Tell me more," she said, taking another drink of her c'shar and pulling a face as she realized it was now cold.

* * *

Myak was waiting for him when he came out of the scouter.

"Captain Garras, Commander Raguul wishes to see you. If you would accompany me?"

Garras padded alongside Myak, too tired to be curious. What he wanted was a shower, food, and his bed. Food and sleep would do.

The Commander looked up as they entered. "I don't know when I've had a tour of duty so full of surprises," he said, picking up a small sealed package and holding it out to him. "The Brotherhood has reactivated your status. Your orders are in here, as is the location of your new posting."

Garras took the package. "Thank you, sir," he murmured, too astonished to really take in what was happening.

"Your transport is waiting in the central docking bay. You leave immediately." Raguul nodded toward his adjutant. "Myak had your personal effects packed. They've already been loaded."

Raguul waited a moment for a response from Garras. When none was forthcoming, he spoke again. "Good-bye, Captain Garras. Doubtless your next appointment will be more interesting than the routine patrols you've been flying here," he said with heavy sarcasm.

"Yes, sir," said Garras, finally putting the anonymous envelope into a pocket and turning to leave.

Garras stopped dead in his tracks as he entered the bay. Crouched in the center with the fuel and oxygen lines being disconnected was a Stealth fighter. Dressed in the active service grays of his guild, the Captain stood by the side of his craft keeping a watchful eye on the maintenance crew.

He turned as he heard Garras approach. "Captain Garras," he said, ears dipping in acknowledgement of the other's superior grade. "If you'd like to board, sir, you'll find a uniform and food waiting for you in the cabin area. I'll be with you as soon as I'm finished here."

Garras nodded, letting his eyes rove over the sleek craft, in no hurry to board yet.

"Beautiful, isn't she?" The young Captain's mouth opened in a proud grin. "You can travel up front with me if you like, or you can sleep in the cabin. It's a two man craft but with the space to squeeze in one passenger if necessary. My colleague flew the outward flight, so he'll probably bed down after takeoff."

"Regretfully, so will I," said Garras, finally finding his voice. "I've just come off duty myself." He turned and headed for the steps up to the hatch.

The inside of the craft was compact. The cabin had a table surrounded by three bench seats which obviously doubled as very narrow beds. Set in the wall was a heater unit and in the cupboard above it he found a variety of meal and hot drink packages. Dried protein strips and concentrated emergency rations were in abundance, too.

"Captain Garras?" came a voice from the flight deck.

"Yes?"

"Welcome aboard, sir. Help yourself to a meal. We'll be another ten minutes or so before we lift off. Blankets are stored under the benches along with the safety restraints."

"Thank you." Garras took a c'shar pack and one of the less revolting looking packages of stew and put them in the heater. While he waited for them, he sat down and took out the package containing his orders. Ripping it open, he scanned the page quickly, his feelings ambivalent as he read the letter from the Brotherhood.

He knew exactly who to thank for this. "You bastard, Kaid," he muttered under his breath. It had been fifteen years since he left Stronghold, and now not only had he been recalled to active service by Kaid, but he'd requested him for an undercover job.

The heater chimed. Folding up his orders, he stuffed them into his inside pocket, then got up to collect his food. He bit the end off the drink sachet and poured it into a disposable cup. Sitting down again, he pulled the tab on his meal pack and began to suck the contents. He hated eating processed food. There was no texture to it.

So Kaid would meet him at Nazule Guild and brief him, would he? Well, he had a few things he wanted to say to him, too! Then a slow grin crossed his face. Dammit, but life had grown too staid. After his experiences on Keiss, the routine flights had left him bored out of his mind. The thought of returning to the merchant routes was almost as bad. The skills they'd both learned were never forgotten. They were ingrained into your body, not just your mind. Then there was Vanna. His grin faded. If there was still trouble looming for Kusac and Carrie, then Vanna could be in danger, too.

He heard footsteps on the ladder outside as the Captain came aboard.

* * *

Kusac, accompanied by Meral and Sevrin, was taking some time off to visit his mother at the estate. His father had been gone a week, but there had been no news from him as yet.

They were heading for the vehicle park to hire an aircar, the secondary reason for their journey. Kusac had his own vehicle at the estate and he was intending to bring it back to the guild to be kept there.

Kusac paid the fee, then they followed the assistant down into the bowels of the underground park. Sevrin let Kusac walk ahead of them with the assistant and touched Meral on the arm to draw his attention.

"Someone following us," he whispered.

Meral's ears swiveled round, listening for the slightest sound. He started to shake his head, then he heard it too. The faintest click of claws on metal. As one they loosened their jackets, drawing the slim energy pistols. Meral gestured Sevrin to go ahead and warn Kusac.

He scanned the park in more detail now, checking the pools of shadow at the back of each empty bay, the concrete supporting pillars, the half-height landings fronted with open railings. A few meters ahead was a doorway, another potential hazard.

Sevrin had stopped them and was gesturing for them to duck behind the vehicle in the adjacent bay. Kusac started to move, but the assistant's voice rang out in the silence.

"Don't be ridiculous!" As she stepped toward the doorway an energy bolt hit her square in the back. Without a sound, she pitched forward onto her face, dead before she hit the ground.

Kusac flung himself into the bay, rolling across the ground till he was out of range behind the small private craft. As he came up in a crouch against the side of the vehicle, he heard the sound of another discharge followed by a grunt of pain from Sevrin as he staggered backward. He hit the side of the vehicle, the gun falling from his hand as slowly he slid down to the ground.

Keeping his head down, Kusac inched cautiously back to him, picking up the gun as he came to it. Carrie's presence flared in his mind, then was still. He knew she'd alerted Kaid.

The front of Sevrin's chest was a gaping seared wound and his breath came in short pants. He turned his head toward Kusac, eyes full of pain. Already they were beginning to dim. Kusac reached for his hand, aware of his agony but unable to help. Sevrin's eyes flickered once, then closed, his body suddenly becoming still and limp.

Deep in Kusac's throat an angry growl began to build. Letting Sevrin down to the ground, he checked the gun then mentally sought for their attackers. Meral was three bays away to his left and beyond him he could feel two minds intent on more killing.

Carefully he raised his head above the nose of the aircar, seeing the semi-darkness of the park lit up with flares from the weapons. Meral was pinned down, safe for the moment but unable to reach their assailants on the half-level above.

Measuring the distance to the doorway, he waited his moment then dived away from the aircar, rolling across the open park and coming to rest by the door. A kick and it was open. He tumbled through.

Crouching low he hugged the walls, making his way carefully up the few steps till he reached the next floor. The door opened inward this time, giving them no warning of his location. Keeping his head down, he waited till he heard shooting, then ran for the opposite side, diving between two vehicles. Keeping one vehicle between him and them, he checked for their minds. Awareness of Carrie's passive strength flared within him and using their combined energy, he carefully probed at their two assailants. They weren't yet aware of him.

He ran the length of the vehicle, stopping at the wall. There was a gap just large enough for him to squeeze through. The same with the next aircar. Carefully he moved forward to the front of the craft, looking round it to visually check on their position. Suddenly one of them came into view, backing into the accessway between the two rows of bays.

Eyes fixed on his target, Kusac brought the gun up, pressing the trigger as the male came into range. The beam hit him, flinging his body through the air like a broken toy.

A brief silence followed, then with a blur of movement too fast for him to react, the second male leaped forward from the gap, disappearing between the vehicles on the other side. Kusac heard the hollow metallic thump of someone landing on a vehicle and using it as a springboard, followed by the flash of a body scrambling up to the next level. He was gone.

Kusac stayed where he was, reaction finally setting in as he sat there mentally searching for any more attackers.

"Kusac!" He recognized Meral's voice. Although several hundred meters away, it sounded loud to his enhanced senses. With a brief mental acknowledgment to Carrie, he stopped searching.

"Here!" he called. "I killed one. The other got away."

"Sevrin?"

"Dead."

A short silence. "Stay where you are, I'll join you."

Within five minutes, Meral appeared in front of the adjacent vehicle. "The area's secure now," he said, crouching down beside him. "I checked the body. Nice shot. Pity you had to take his head with it. We'll need a DNA typing for his identity."

Kusac's eyes narrowed. "I wanted to be sure," he said shortly. "We've to wait here for Kaid. The Protectors are on their way."

Meral nodded, squatting down like him with his back to the aircar, gun cradled ready for use. "Who's watching Carrie?"

"Armed Protectors," he said shortly.

They sat in silence. Now was neither the time nor the place for talk. Later, when they returned to the Guild, he'd have plenty to say. For now he was keeping watch with his mind. The skills they'd learned the hard way on Keiss once more were proving invaluable.

It took a lot to unsettle Kaid, but this silence from Kusac had him more rattled than he cared to admit. On the way out, he'd contacted the Brotherhood from the aircar, alerting them to the need to round up all suspects and start a search for the remaining assailant. It had to be one of the two ground troopers from the Forces. No one else on Shola had a reason to do this.

He was blazing with anger himself. He and his two males were supposed to be the final link in a chain of surveillance designed to stop any attempts like this. Instead, they had turned out to be the main defense. He intended to speak to Ghezu about that later.

Meral was flying their vehicle while he sat in the back with Kusac. An escort of two armed Protector craft had accompanied them, circling overhead as Meral brought the aircar down to land in the guild forecourt.

As they climbed out, Carrie came running across to meet them. Kusac had never been more glad to see her. Sevrin's death had reminded them how vulnerable flesh and blood were. They held each other close for a moment, then Kusac turned to Meral and Kaid.

"We're going to talk. Now." He turned, his arm still around Carrie, and started toward the Guild House.

Kusac closed the door and turned on the two males. "Just what the hell is going on?" he demanded. "You told me the attack on the *Khalossa* was unexpected, out of the blue, yet it's happened again. I want to know why. You also said all the dissidents were dead. If so, why were we attacked?"

"The attack on the Liegena wasn't premeditated," began Kaid.

"Don't lie to me, Kaid," Kusac warned quietly, walking past them toward his desk. He turned, leaning against the edge of it. "I'm remembering all the security people that rushed forward when Carrie was shot. At the time it was the last thing on my mind. Not now."

"Normally the people I've guarded don't want to know what's happening around them," said Kaid, equally quietly. "I work better without interference."

Carrie came over to stand beside Kusac. "How many telepaths have you guarded?" she asked. "Enough to know that we can help if we're aware of what we're facing, if we know there's danger around us? Or are you too much of a loner to want any help?"

"The attack on the *Khalossa* was not premeditated," Kaid repeated, "but I was expecting an attack to be made at some point. The rest you know."

"What about this attempt?"

"Two males were involved, one from the *Khalossa,* one from the *Rhyaki.* They were due to meet up with the anti-Terran faction here. They were the two who attacked you today."

"There's still one of them at large," said Carrie.

"Not for long," said Kaid, his voice becoming a low growl. "The Brotherhood and the Protectors are looking for all of them now."

"What of these others?" asked Kusac. "Are they also determined to stop the treaty with Earth by killing us?"

"According to my informant, they plan merely to demonstrate their disapproval of the Earth treaty and would have nothing to do with the two troopers. They only wanted information from them, not your deaths."

"In future I want to be kept informed, Kaid," said Kusac. "I want to know how much danger we're in. It's our lives, not yours."

Carrie indicated the gun Kusac still wore stuck through his belt. "I want a gun, Kaid, and I want to learn how to use it properly," she said. "If there ever is a next time, I want to be able to protect myself."

"The Warrior Guild keeps contacting me, asking when we can schedule sessions with them," said Kusac. "I've been putting them off until now. I think it's become a necessity."

Carrie frowned up at him. "The Warrior Guild? Why do they want us?"

"Part of our orders were to attend their guild to have our ability to fight assessed," Kusac reminded her.

"I think it's an excellent idea, Liegen," said Kaid. "Do you want me to see Master Esken and liaise between here and the Warrior Guild?"

"Please."

"What happens to Sevrin now?" Carrie asked in the silence that followed.

"The Warrior Guild will inform his family that he died in the line of duty," said Kaid gently. "His body will be released to them for cremation on the family estate."

"I'd like to go to the funeral if the family wouldn't object," said Carrie. "I liked Sevrin. I can't believe he's gone."

"I'll contact his parents personally," said Kusac. "You organize the transport, Kaid. Would you also find out what you can about the female who was killed? I want to speak to her family, too."

"I'll see to it, Liegen," said Kaid. "The Commissioner of the Protectorate has insisted in the interests of public safety that greater security measures should be initiated here at the guild. From now on, armed Warriors will be guarding the lower levels and the grounds. Esken will just have to live with it. Snipers and assassins don't care if the innocent are hurt as this afternoon demonstrated."

* * *

The funeral was held the following day at dusk. Sevrin's body lay on a bier in front of them. He looked peaceful, as if a touch on his shoulder would waken him. Carrie shivered. The night air was chill and she stood beside Kusac wrapped within the folds of a woolen cloak. At her side, the unfamiliar weight of the energy pistol on her belt felt comforting.

Even with her shields well up, she could still sense the utter shock that Sevrin's family felt over their loss. Mingled with it was pride that he had died while on duty protecting the life of his Liegen, and that his Liegen was there with them, sharing their grief.

The night was lit by the blazing torches held by the members of his immediate family, and by Kusac and Carrie.

"Who's that?" asked Carrie, nodding toward a figure wearing a simple long brown robe. He was looking directly toward them and as Kusac glanced in his direction, he tilted his head in acknowledgment. Beside him stood another figure in a black robe.

"Ghyan. He's the old friend I spoke of," he said quietly. "He's a priest of Vartra. I don't know the other."

Carrie kept her eyes on him, aware of his curiosity. Then he turned his attention away from them and gestured the gathering to silence. All that could be heard was the sound of the wind whipping the flames of the torches

Flanked by Sevrin's parents, Ghyan stepped forward and said a few quiet words over the bier before turning toward the rest of the family and friends. He called for the blessing of Vartra upon them, and asked that the God receive Sevrin's spirit. This done, he stepped back and took his place amongst the mourners.

Sevrin's father threw the first torch onto the bier, followed by his mother. Then the rest of the family went forward, Carrie and Kusac bringing up the rear.

The wind fanned the flames, making them leap high. As Kusac threw his torch, the last, a low keening began to build around them. It rose in pitch until it became a howl that echoed round the courtyard. Again Carrie shivered. The sound was unbearably sad.

Kusac's arm came round her shoulders, holding them firmly against his side. She felt his sorrow at losing Sevrin, as well as his fierce relief that they would never have to do this for each other. They would live, and die, together. The thought chilled her even as it comforted her and she turned into his arms, pressing close against his chest, aware of how near death had been.

The gathering broke up, following the parents back to the house. The all-night vigil would be kept by Sevrin's fellow guild members, Meral foremost among them. As they turned to leave, Ghyan came over to them.

"Funerals sadden me," he said. "His was a brave spirit from what I sense from his family and friends. He will be missed."

"Yes," said Kusac, "he will."

Ghyan put his head on one side, trying to see Carrie's face within the folds of her hooded cloak. "This must be your Leska," he said.

Carrie lifted her hood back and looked up at him. His ears were smaller than average, yet had the width of Kaid's. Brown eyes set above wide cheekbones regarded her with a faint look of amusement.

"You're from inland, aren't you? One of the highlanders," she said, holding out her palm. "And a telepath," she added, gently touching the edges of his mind before he touched her hand.

Ghyan's mouth dropped in a smile. "You're learning our ways," he said, his fingertips touching hers. "It's a pleasure to meet you, Carrie, though I'm sorry it had to be at a friend's funeral. Kusac has told me a lot about you."

Carrie's eyebrows disappeared under her fringe. "Oh? All good, I hope."

"But of course. Kusac," he said, "you must bring her to see me some day soon."

"I will."

"Have you had your strange dream again?"

"No," said Kusac.

"Yes," said Carrie, glancing sideways at her Leska.

Kusac looked down at her. "You haven't mentioned it."

"I didn't see the point," she said. "The images were all confused, like a memory that's begun to fade. I couldn't make any sense of them."

"Is that why you wake in the night?"

She nodded. "Mostly."

"When you come to visit me, you must tell me about these dreams," said Ghyan. "I must go now, I'm afraid. Sevrin's parents will need to speak to me."

"We'll see you again, Ghyan. Good-bye."

"Good-bye, Kusac. Guard your little cub well," said

Ghyan, his fingers fleetingly touching Carrie's cheek before he left.

Carrie turned to Kusac with a frown. "What did he mean?"

"That he appreciates your qualities," he said ambiguously, and wouldn't be drawn further.

They took their leave and returned to the guild with Kaid.

* * *

Once they had gone to their room, Kaid contacted the office of the Protectorate, the civilian police force on Shola. He was put through to the Commissioner of Valsgarth.

"Any news yet, Commissioner?" he asked.

"Nazule has rounded up all the protesters you spoke of. Their papers have been checked and their files run through the comm. They're all clean. They had no charges on which to detain them, so they let them go this morning after AlRel had a word with them. No sign of this other trooper. We did establish that the dead one was from the *Rhyaki*. I think it's unlikely our missing male will return to the *Khalossa*."

"I agree with you," said Kaid. "Have you displayed his image on the public comm nets?"

"It's going out every two hours with the newscasts. As you requested, we're not mentioning Liegen Aldatan. Someone is bound to have seen our missing male."

"Let me know the minute there's any news."

"I will."

Cutting the connection, Kaid switched off and was about to leave his room to check with the senior security officer when the message light buzzed.

"Kaid," drawled a familiar voice, "remind me to return the favor someday. I really enjoyed my free bed last night."

Kaid's mouth opened in a grin. "I thought you might. See it as my thanks for luring me out of retirement with a job I couldn't refuse."

"Bastard," said Garras without rancor.

"How's it going?"

"No problems. This lot's as innocent as day-old cubs. When the protectors told them that there had been an assassination attempt against Liegen Aldatan to stop the treaty with Earth, they were genuinely shocked. Even the truthsayer—remember old Jorto? He's still around and he recognized me—he vouched for us all."

"Stay where you are for the time being in case our male turns up looking for help."

"Fair enough. I'm involved with this rather nice young female at the moment. How's Vanna?"

"Busy, but fine. We don't see much of her these days."

"I want to see her soon, Kaid."

Garras looked around and called to someone off screen before turning back to him. "Got to go."

Later that night, he called Stronghold. "Ghezu, what the hell's going on? You told me that you'd give me backup. Where was it when I needed it today?" he demanded.

"We can't watch them every minute of the day, Tallinu. That's your job, remember?" said Ghezu. "We do what we can. In enclosed areas like the vehicle park, it isn't easy to have you tailed."

"If you've had a change of priorities, I expect to be kept informed. You do still want them kept alive, don't you?"

"Don't be ridiculous! Of course we do!"

"Then give me some people and I'll take charge of surveillance."

Ghezu only hesitated for a moment. "I'll send four people over to you tomorrow."

"How important are they to you, Ghezu?" Kaid's voice was silky.

"All right, eight, dammit, and no more!" He leaned forward and cut the connection.

Kaid smiled to himself as he switched off the comm.

* * *

It was the following week before Carrie and Kusac's schedule could be adjusted to fit in regular sessions at the Warrior Guild. Meral and Kaid were accompanying them and staying at the guild while they were there.

"Is it really necessary?" asked Kusac. "Surely we should be safe there."

"I'm not prepared to take the risk," Kaid said.

"Neither am I," said Carrie as the small aircar took off. Sevrin's death was still weighing heavily on her spirits.

The flight to the center of Nazule took about an hour. When they arrived, they were taken to Guild Master Rhayfso's private rooms. His study was an armory with a desk in the corner and a variety of swords and knives mounted in brackets on the walls. Two of the four corners of the room contained stacks of every imaginable type of pole weapon.

"Ah, you've arrived," he said, looking up from the two blades he was examining on his desk. "Good to see you again, Kaid, Meral. It's been too long. Now you two," he said, turning to Carrie and Kusac. "What do you think of these? Just arrived this morning."

Carrie stepped forward to look at the swords, putting out a tentative finger. "I won't," she said in answer to his unspoken warning, making him jump. She drew her finger along the single-edged blade just above its surface. "Your son is a fine smith. He's put beauty and strength into these blades."

"No wonder there's a superstitious awe of telepaths when you come out with something like that," said the Master, shaking his head. "Enough of these," he said, closing the lid of their case, "I want to discuss the details of your program with us."

He pushed the case to one side of his cluttered desk and sat down, indicating that they should do the same. Carrie and Kusac took the chairs nearest him while Meral and Kaid moved toward a bench at the rear of the room.

"Since Kaid contacted us, I've spent some time discussing with my staff which skills would best suit your needs. We've compiled a special course to familiarize you as swiftly as possible with the basics in three areas. Modern energy weapons, hand-to-hand combat, and the traditional skills of knife and sword. Once you've mastered them, I want to try you out against some of my students so you can see for yourself how capable you are. Commander Chuz, President of Sholan High Command, wants your capability to fight in simulated real situations assessed. Does that meet with your agreement?"

Kusac looked at Carrie and shrugged. "Whatever you say, Master Rhayfso. It's pretty much what I expected. We're here to learn."

"Good. Meral and Kaid will take you down to the veterans' quarters where you'll be staying overnight, and where your teachers will meet you. Come and see me if you have any problems," he said, standing up to indicate the meeting was over.

"Oh, by the way, you're hardly likely to need Meral and

Kaid as bodyguards while you're here," he said. "I should let them have some time off duty if I were you."

"I'll stay," said Kaid unequivocally. "Meral can go off duty until twelfth hour."

The sprawl of buildings that made up the Warrior Guild seemed to have retained an austere look in comparison to the Telepath Guild. In fact, there was little comparison between the two guilds despite their ancient ties. Comfort here was on a minimal level, even for the Master.

The shielded room they were to occupy on their overnight stops belonged to the guild's resident telepath. He'd agreed to stay at the guild in Valsgarth for that one night a week. There was a bed, harder than they were used to, and the basic storage facilities for their clothes.

Once their small amount of luggage had been left in their rooms, Meral departed for the delights of the city and they joined their first teacher in the staff lounge.

"My name's Varos," said a large Sholan in a dull sand-colored uniform jacket getting up from his chair and coming toward them. "I'll be showing you how to use energy weapons." He towered over both of them before sweeping past them into the corridor. "Well, come on!" he said. "We need to go down to the range to use the guns. Can't have you taking pot shots at the students, can I?" A rumbling purr followed his last remark.

As they turned to follow him, Carrie grasped Kusac's arm. *I've never seen such a large Sholan before!* she sent. *He's huge! Look at the size of his legs, they're as thick as two of yours.*

And it's all muscle, from the look of him, agreed Kusac with a grin.

"So you're one of the Terrans, are you?" Varos said, turning round to look at her from piercing green eyes. "You look better in life than you did on the newscast last week. Too bad about Sevrin," he said regretfully.

The range was indoors in the basement of the building. They entered the rest area first, waiting while Varos fetched some pistols and battery packs.

"I'll probably have a few practice shots myself, if you don't mind, Liegen," said Kaid, looking thoughtfully at the range.

"Whatever you want," said Kusac, "only so long as you

stop using my title! They know you here in the guild, there's no need for it."

"The same goes for me," said Carrie, going to examine the drinks dispenser. "They haven't got coffee in them yet," she said regretfully.

"Hardly. Remember its effect on us on Keiss?" said Kusac, joining Kaid at the transparent window overlooking the range.

Varos returned. "Here," he said, throwing Kusac a battery pack, then another. "Stick them in your jacket. I'm glad to see you all had the sense to come in uniform." He walked over to Carrie, holding out hands as large as plates. "Let me see your hands," he said.

Carrie hesitated, looking up at the intimidatingly tall, tan-colored male standing before her.

"Come on," he said. "I won't eat you. I need to see if your hands can use our weapons properly."

Reluctantly, she held them out. The skin on his hands felt rough as they manipulated her fingers and examined her grip. He let her go and frowned.

"Hm. You're on the small side. I think we'll need to have a gun specially crafted for your own use. Learning to use ours will at least enable you to pick any gun up and use it properly." He took one from his belt and handed it to her, butt first. "We don't load until we're on the range, and we don't ever point it at anyone we don't intend to shoot, got that?" he said.

"I learned some basics from Captain Garras on Keiss," she said dryly. "I also used projectile rifles at home."

Varos grunted as he gave her two battery packs. "I don't assume anything, and I make no apology for it," he said. "That way, no one gets hurt by accident. I'll be showing you how to keep your guns in good repair, all the maintenance tricks the Forces don't teach their people. That's the difference between warriors and fighters. We train you to look after yourselves rather than rely on support personnel expressly trained for the purpose," he said, leading them through to the range.

"We'll start on static targets and then move on to the mobile range. It's set up like a street full of houses populated by warriors, attackers and civilians that spring out at you without warning. The idea is to go in and clear out the attackers without taking out your own people or the civilians. That kind of practical skill is going to be of more use to you. An attacker doesn't usually stand still so you can aim up on him or her."

If they thought the morning was unremitting hard work, the afternoon was no better. This time it was the turn of Shaku, and her specialty was bladed weapons. Using heavy wooden clubs instead of swords—"I don't believe in wasting good steel on beginners."—they were drilled again and again through the basic attack and defense positions until their bodies were one homogeneous ache.

"This will help you to build up those wrist and arm muscles. When I do allow you to use the real weapons, they'll be far lighter by comparison," she said cheerfully.

By mutual consent, as soon as they were through for the day, they headed toward the bath house. Kaid had arranged for them to be given sole use of one of the smaller rooms and gratefully they stripped, lowering themselves into the steaming herb-scented water.

Kusac hooked his neck over the padded edge of the large communal tub, letting his body drift full length just under the surface. He relaxed, letting the heat wash over him, unknotting muscles used far beyond their normal endurance. He could sense Carrie doing the same, feel her pleasure mingling with his own until it was a balm in itself to their tired minds.

I didn't think cats liked water so much, came her drowsy thought.

One of life's luxuries, replied Kusac lazily. *Have you ever tried licking fur? It gets stuck all over your tongue if you don't do it properly. Baths or showers are much more pleasant.*

You still have rough tongues.

Kusac opened one eye. *So we have,* he agreed placidly. *I haven't heard you complain.*

Carrie kicked a feeble shower of water at him with one foot. *If I wasn't so tired,* she threatened.

He laughed and reaching out, caught her by the ankle and towed her toward him, wincing as a pulled muscle in his chest hurt.

"Kusac!" she spluttered, righting herself when her head appeared above the surface again.

He pulled her close, wrapping his arms around her as she lay just above him in the water.

I don't know how we're going to get through tomorrow. Today was bad enough and we didn't ache like this.

Ah, sent Carrie. *I discovered a little trick that might help even things out.*

What's that?

With both our teachers I found that once the lesson had progressed to a certain level, they were mentally accessing their own skills and I could tap into that knowledge, learning it from them. It changes the emphasis from learning a totally new skill, to remembering how to utilize a known one.

I thought you were doing suspiciously well, sent Kusac, letting her go and causing the water to surge as he sat up. "I don't suppose you thought to share the knowledge with me."

Carrie let herself drift as she caught hold of the bath rim. "I wasn't sure until this afternoon, and we were too busy for me to transfer the knowledge then. I'm telling you now, aren't I?" she said, sending him the information she had gleaned from their tutors.

Kusac sorted through it, nodding his head at last. "Yes, I see where I've been going wrong now. You're right, this will make it a lot easier, but I think what you did was somewhat unethical," he added, frowning at her.

"I didn't have to probe for it, and anyway, it makes their job easier as well as ours. Besides, you know I don't share all your ethics," she said primly.

"You've got a convenient conscience, cub. You're infecting me with it, and your enjoyment of the skill involved in fighting."

"I thought you were beginning to enjoy yourself," she said.

"It's a nonreal situation. Skill for skill, as you said. Whether or not I could use it in a real situation is another matter."

"We'll see," she said, reaching for the bottle of soap. "Come here and let me wash you. When I touched you today, I noticed you were shedding."

Kusac grunted, ears flicking as he moved over to sit with his back to her. "Probably the remains of my winter coat, courtesy of Keiss," he grumbled, moving the muscles of his back under the rough massage of her fingers. A deep-throated purr escaped him.

"I like hearing you purr," she said, her hands going up to his head as she began to rub the soap through his hair.

"Don't stop rubbing my back," he said, squirming under her lather-covered fingers. "You've got just the spot where I've had an itch for hours!"

Matters settled down at last into a routine of training shared between the two Guild Houses. The interminable tests were over, and it was now a question of Carrie learning to develop her talents and them pushing their combined abilities in the directions highlighted by the tests. She'd been awarded a level of First Grade like Kusac and at long last, the "L" insignia brooches had caught up with them, identifying them as a Leska pair.

As she pinned hers on, Carrie remembered Rhian from the *Khalossa* and how she'd tried to help her come to terms with her new status as a Leska. Now she took it for granted, part of her life, just as the students and teachers at the guild took her presence among them as unremarkable. The only thing no one suggested they test was the gestalt Link.

Vanna's tests were also less frequent now. They'd seen little of her recently as she'd been working in the labs correlating her results and writing up the information for both the Telepath Guild, and the Guild of Medics. The last time they'd seen her, however, she'd been concerned that she'd heard nothing from Garras.

"I called him on the *Khalossa,* but all they'd say was that he'd been posted. They wouldn't say when or where," she said worriedly.

"I'll see if I can find out anything," said Kusac. "I'll ask Kaid. If anyone can find out, he can."

"Thanks," she said, getting up to go. "Can you drop into the lab later today? It's about time for your tests again."

Carrie sighed. "When will you be done with testing us?"

Vanna grinned, reaching down to touch her hair. "Soon, cub, soon. I just want to establish baselines that we can all rely on. See you later."

* * *

One day a couple of months later, Kusac looked up from the comm where he was working. "Father's back," he said.

Carrie put aside the book she'd been reading. It was Taizia's, one of the rare real ones, not on a comp notebook. "How do you know?"

"I can sense him now. He's not in a good mood either.

It's the Council meeting today and he's having to go straight there."

"What council meeting?"

"The Council of the Sixteen Telepath Clans. It's one of their regular policy meetings."

His comm buzzed and he cycled it to accept the call. It was his mother.

"Your father's back from Chagda Station," she said, "and he's not happy. The Governor wants to keep the Terrans on-station for the next three days till they're sure decontam has worked."

"This is a joke, isn't it?"

"No, they're absolutely serious."

"Surely they realize any infections would have shown up during the three-week flight!"

"Of course they do. Someone on the Council of Sixteen is making life difficult for your father. There's something else," she said, watching him carefully.

"What?"

"A motion has been tabled demanding that you be dropped as a candidate for Lordship of the Clans."

Kusac shrugged. "I expected no less," he said. "How has Father taken it?"

"Badly. He's told me to invite you and Carrie over for a few days. He wants to meet her. Tread warily round for now, Kusac. Stay downwind. Don't issue ultimatums, play for time for the moment."

I can't leave it much longer, Mother.

"He wants you here for third meal tomorrow."

Kusac sighed. "We'll be there," he said.

Don't wear your torcs, Kusac, she warned.

Out of the question!

Then conceal them.

No. It will make no difference. I have a feeling he already knows about them.

As you wish. Perhaps it's for the best. "I'll see you both tomorrow."

* * *

The permanent replacement warrior for Sevrin arrived the following day. Kaid had taken some time to choose, finally deciding on a female from Stronghold. Her name was T'Chebbi. She'd been accepted into their sub-guild the hard way—from the back streets of one of the highland towns. Rough and ready she might be, but she was good.

She was smaller than the average height, only a few inches taller than Carrie, but she made up for it in muscle and energy. Icy gray eyes looked coldly out on the world from tabby colored fur of a slightly longer length than usual. Her dark hair had been grown long, confined at the back in a single plait with the hair at the sides of the neck braided into smaller ones. She wore the ceremonial Warriors' uniform, including the two crossed swords at her back, and a compact multifire energy pistol at her belt.

As they boarded the aircar to leave for the estate, Kusac watched Meral eye her warily. T'Chebbi gave no feeling of needing to make a place for herself on this small team, she knew her own worth; she'd been chosen.

Before the hatch was closed, Taizia came bounding up. "You'll need me," she said cryptically, giving Kusac a long, hard look.

Carrie had continued her friendship with his sister, finding that with Vanna busy in the medical area, she was bereft of female company. They'd gone to the town a couple of times on their own and with other friends of Taizia's. She enjoyed their sense of adventure: life was becoming a little too quiet for her at the guild. She also enjoyed working with them on their report on the comparative differences between Keissian and Terran social customs. It gave her something to do that she felt was worthwhile when Kusac was busy.

Taizia settled herself beside Meral and began chatting animatedly with him.

From the air, Carrie's first view of the Clan estate was breathtaking. The forested land thinned out gradually until the fields and clusters of houses took over. They flew over the estate gardens, both natural and formal, bisected by tiny crisscrossing paths. Set like a blazing jewel in the midst of this was Kusac's home.

Walls of white reflected the sunlight back at them, almost dazzling their eyes. Terra-cotta pillared balconies fronted the two sides of the building facing them. As they came closer, she could see it was roughly square in shape, enclosing an internal open courtyard set with an ornamental pool and trees. As they came down to land in the outer courtyard, Carrie saw the family's double sunburst emblem set above the massive terra-cotta pillars at the entrance. The panic she'd felt, which had receded when she caught sight of the house, now returned in full as she looked out at the imposing facade in front of her.

"Don't be put off by its appearance," said Kusac, unfastening his safety belt. "What you're seeing is the cumulative effect of generations. Our Clan is one of the oldest on this continent, going back at least to the days of the Cataclysm. The house is several hundred years old and each successive generation has added to it. My father had a solar built two years ago."

Your torcs, Kusac, sent Taizia from behind, using a private link. *Is it wise to let him see them right now?*

Not wise, but honest, Kusac replied, turning his attention back to Carrie.

It was well into summer now, and she was dressed in a lightweight purple tunic. Her legs and feet were bare save for the slip-on sandals she'd brought with her from Keiss. The bronze torc glinted at her throat and he'd brushed her hair that morning until it gleamed like spun gold. She looked exotic, and very alien.

As he got to his feet, his hand went unconsciously to his own torc for reassurance.

Carrie rose and followed him out, unable to take her eyes off the building. The entrance was open to the sunlight, giving it a light, airy look. Now she could see just how massive the pillars were. Topping only some twelve feet, they were broad, tapering from wide at the top to narrow at the base. On the steps up to the main entrance, two single pillars were set one behind the other to support the balcony on the floor above.

Movement from the interior of the house caught her eye. A male in long robes was coming toward them—Kusac's father! Once again, the panic returned.

Kusac tried mentally to reassure her despite the apprehension he felt himself. They made their way up the stairs followed by Taizia, Meral, Kaid, and T'Chebbi.

Carrie's fear began to swamp him, but it wasn't until Taizia touched his arm warningly that he realized she was broadcasting.

Shield up, he sent, nerves already beginning to fray.

The tension eased as his father stepped forward, palm held out to Carrie.

There was a strong family resemblance in the line of the jaw and set of the ears, but here and there several white hairs were scattered over his face and hair. As she returned the greeting, she felt the gentle assessing touch she had come to associate with meeting fellow telepaths.

"Greetings, Carrie," he said, his voice low and melodious. "It's a pleasure to welcome you to our estate and to meet you at last in person."

"I'm honored, Clan Lord Aldatan," she murmured.

"Taizia, I didn't expect to see you," her father said, catching sight of his daughter.

"I thought it was time I showed my nose again," she replied.

"Kusac," he said, turning to his son. "I can see for myself that you look well. You've filled out over the last year. Your current lifestyle must suit you."

"It's the exercise," Kusac said.

"Ah, yes. And how is the training going?" Konis asked, gesturing for them to precede him into the house.

"As a discipline, it goes well. Whether or not I can use it if the need arises has yet to be seen. Carrie will have no problem. Apparently she has a Warrior's soul!"

"I wonder if that's a gift to be wished for in a telepath," said his father, leading them through the hall into the colonnaded courtyard. He stopped for a moment, waiting while Carrie looked at the frescoes on the walls.

"They're beautiful," she said, pointing to a scene depicting Sholan hunters in the reeds by a river.

"They are rather pleasant to look at, aren't they? Most telepaths like to surround themselves with beauty in one form or another. It helps relax the spirit and calm the mind," said Konis.

They went through the courtyard and past the pool with its ornamental waterfall before entering a corridor. It was cool and the dimmer light was soothing to the eyes compared to the glare outside. They emerged into a large airy lounge that opened onto the gardens where his mother and younger sister were sitting under the shade of a large leafed tree.

The smaller figure, a miniature copy of his mother, turned round and leaped to her feet with a squeak of pleasure, racing through the room to Kusac and flinging her arms around him as he bent to meet her.

"Kitra, it's good to see you again," he said, picking her up.

"I've missed you," she said, giving him a hug before looking toward Carrie.

"Is this your Terran Leska?" she asked.

"Yes."

She held her hand out to Carrie. "Greetings to you," she said solemnly, her brown eyes wide as she tried not to stare.

"Greetings to you, Kitra," said Carrie, reaching out to touch her hand.

Kusac's mother entered. She, too, was dressed for the hot weather, wearing a short tunic similar to Carrie's.

Carrie turned to meet her as Kusac put his sister down. Rhyasha approached the girl, putting her hands on her shoulders and drawing her close until their cheeks touched. "It's good to see you again, Carrie. You are well come to our home."

She was released as Rhyasha turned to Kusac, hugging him closely before stepping back to look at him carefully. She ran a hand across his cheek, pushing a stray lock of hair behind his ear.

"You look better," she said critically. "You've put some weight on, and the God knows, you needed to!" Surreptitiously she touched his torc.

"Hush," said Kusac, hugging her tightly. "Just wish me well," he whispered in her ear, receiving a fierce hug in return.

"Don't crush him to death," said his father, moving past them to take up his seat in the garden again.

"Taizia, please take the guards to the kitchen and arrange for them to be fed, and order c'shar for us. We'll dine in half an hour," Rhyasha said, giving her daughter a quick embrace.

Taizia moved to do her bidding as Carrie and Kusac followed Rhyasha and Kitra into the garden.

"How did your trip to Earth go?" asked Kusac, pulling a couple of soft cushions up for himself and Carrie. As he squatted down on them, Carrie settled herself next to him.

"I didn't have to go down to Earth," said Konis. "I spoke directly to their negotiators on the *Rhyaki* and by comm link to their leaders on the planet. They were trying to tell us they had no telepaths, so I quoted the names of a few centers of learning where the encyclopedia said they were studying what they call psychic talents. After that, they were quiet for a day or two, then the telepaths started arriving."

"How many are there?"

"About twenty. A couple of families with three or four members, the rest single people, mainly males. They'll be brought down to the guild the day after tomorrow. How are the arrangements going for their accommodation?"

"Fine," said Kusac. "They've erected a semipermanent building for them near the medical facility. It's completely self-contained as you asked, and fully shielded."

"Good. I'll be going over to see them again once they've settled in. The discovery of another species with telepathic abilities is going to affect our culture, not to mention Earth's, profoundly, especially if there are other Leska pairings like yours," said Konis.

"I know," said Kusac. "Carrie and I have been speculating on what the changes could be."

"If there are more Leska pairings, let's hope they're mainly between our males and Terran females, like yours and Carrie's, because we already have an imbalance with our male population," said Rhyasha dryly. "Ah, here come our drinks."

Taizia emerged from the lounge with a large tray of mugs and a jug of c'shar.

"Did you try their coffee when you were on the *Rhyaki* by any chance?" asked Kusac with a faint grin.

"I did, as a matter of fact. Quite nice for a change. I brought a few plants back as a gift for your mother. She likes the odd gardening challenge."

After a leisurely evening meal, Kusac reached for Taizia's mind, asking her to take Carrie off to her room while he spoke to their father.

Keep her occupied. I have a feeling Father is not at his most amenable tonight.

I'm on your side, but you can hardly blame him, can you? she replied.

Kusac glared at her and hurriedly she turned to Carrie.

"Let's leave these gray heads to talk," she said. "Come up to my room. I've got a few things I'd like to show you."

When they'd left, Kusac turned to his father. "I want you to dissolve my marriage contract, Father," he said. "I have no intention of life-bonding to Rala."

"I gathered that when I saw you and Carrie had exchanged torcs," said Konis. "Tell me, what prompted you to make such a foolish gesture?"

"It wasn't foolish. I gave it to her for her peace of mind and protection as much as anything else. Her people have a more rigid sexual code than ours, and I'm well aware that others have found her attractive," Kusac said, looking down at the knife he was toying with.

"As my wife, she would to a large degree be spared the problem of dealing with unwanted lovers. Having seen the Terrans for yourself, you're probably aware that they usually pair for life, taking no other lovers. Carrie will feel more secure if we're life-bonded."

"I suppose your feelings for her never came into it?"

"Of course they did," he said, looking up. "Will you cancel the contract?"

"No," said his father calmly. "You have duties to your Clan that you can't ignore. Having a Leska is not a valid reason for terminating the contract."

"I'd be willing to release him from Clan duties, Konis," Rhyasha said quietly.

"There are specific grounds set down in the laws governing the dissolution of a marriage contract. I can't, and won't ask for a special case to be made for Kusac."

"I can't marry Rala, Father. It would destroy Carrie. She gave up home and Clan—everything for me. I can't do less for her."

"It won't destroy her. Other Leskas cope with their partner's marriage, so will she."

"I don't think you realize how closely we're Linked," said Kusac, trying to prevent his ears from lying flat.

His father stirred slightly, resting his forearms on the table and leaning forward.

"I have a fair idea. I get sent the data from both guilds. There is little about your relationship I don't know."

Kusac's ears flicked with embarrassment. "Then you should know how she'll react to even the news I'm expected to marry."

His father sighed. "You shouldn't have given her your torc, Kusac. You weren't free to give it, and you should have told her you were already betrothed. You've compounded your own folly."

"You betrothed me when I was a child, Father! Circumstances have changed," he said, beginning to lose the battle to keep his temper.

"That's irrelevant. Rala was chosen as a mate for you because of her bloodlines and the political advantages of an alliance with the northern Telepath Clans. I know you dislike her, but you're free to love where you want. You only have to father children on Rala and treat her with the courtesy due to a wife, nothing more."

"What does Carrie do while I'm fathering these children?" asked Kusac angrily. "She's aware of everything I do or say, it's almost impossible to keep anything from her!"

"If she can't cope with the situation, then we'll have her drugged so she's unaware of it," came the calm reply.

"Konis," said Rhyasha warningly, "this isn't a wise way to approach the matter."

"I don't intend to let my Leska be drugged for the sake of some female I can't tolerate!" Kusac exclaimed angrily. "If I have to marry her, then it will be in name only. Or will you drug me into acquiescence, too?" he asked with barely suppressed fury.

"If Carrie was Sholan, it might have been feasible to nullify the contract because of the responsibility of Leska pairs to have children, but she isn't. She can't provide you with heirs, and the Family needs heirs, legitimate heirs, not bastards, no matter whether your mother would allow it or not," Konis said angrily. "As Lord of the Council I can't allow my son to break his contract and if drugging both of you is what it takes, then, yes, I'll have it done!"

"What about Rala's behavior at the guild? The fact that she's misusing a minor Talent to manipulate people? That's grounds for an annulment!"

"Give her what she wants, Kusac, and she'll be easily kept under control," said Konis, his tone more conciliatory. "You're making too much of the guild incident, and too much of this marriage."

"I disagree. Had it been anyone else, you would have taken some disciplinary action. Because it's Rala, you won't!"

"I've had enough, Kusac! You'll do as you're told! Today at the Council meeting I had to sit through a discussion on whether you, with an alien Leska, were fit to remain a candidate. The majority vote was no! It was narrow-minded of them, but they see their comfortable little world threatened by these Terrans. I need you to marry Rala to prove to them that your Link to a Terran doesn't make you unfit for a position of responsibility. Happily Vailkoi doesn't agree with the majority, even if his opinion is affected by the fact that he doesn't want his future son-in-law to lose his candidacy for the leadership of the Clans!"

"Vailkoi will do anything to get rid of his daughter! She's a damned liability to him now with her moods and tantrums!" Kusac's voice had become an angry snarl.

"You'll do as you're told, Kusac," repeated his father in a voice like ice. "Tomorrow Rala is coming here to see you. I expect you to greet her as your betrothed wife."

"I think you're being too hasty about this," said his mother, touching her husband lightly on the arm.

Konis shook her off, getting to his feet. "He marries Rala, Rhyasha. That's the last I want to hear of the matter," he snapped, stalking angrily from the room.

His mother sighed. "I don't know what more I can do. He's adamant, as you can see."

"So am I," muttered Kusac, aware with a sinking feeling that Carrie had heard the conversation. "I have to go to her, Mother. She heard him."

"Go, then," she said. "Don't do anything foolish, Kusac. I'd rather you were happy than have the heirs your father wants."

Kusac touched her briefly on the shoulder as he passed her.

He took the stairs at a lope, heading along the pillared central balcony to Taizia's room. His sister opened the door for him.

"You lied to me," said Carrie as he entered.

"No, I only tried to . . ."

"You lied!" Her eyes were narrowed to slits and her voice was like winter's breath. He'd never seen her so angry before.

"You knew about this marriage all along, yet you purposely kept it from me. I trusted you, Kusac! How could you keep something as important as this from me?"

"It isn't important, Carrie," he said quietly, moving away from the door. "It's only an arranged marriage. She means nothing to me. I didn't choose her."

"It's a marriage, Kusac," she said, cold fury in her voice

as she got to her feet and began to pace between the bed and the window.

"Arranged marriages happen all the time in the Clans. It doesn't stop the people involved from having lovers and living apart from each other, you know that. Even if I have to marry her, it won't affect us."

"Oh, won't it?" She spun round, eyes blazing. "What am I supposed to do while you're screwing that female? Enjoy the secondhand experience? I'm your Leska, Kusac, we're Linked together for life, we belong to each other, or doesn't that matter any more? I thought that Sholans understood about Leskas! Or am I just a working partner, someone else you didn't choose, with nothing to offer in comparison to a wife?" She turned away from him again, sitting back down on the bed.

Taizia, part of her realized, was sitting at the other end of the bed, trying to take up as small a space as possible in her own room. She was wishing she was anywhere else but here with them. Tears of anger and hurt stung Carrie's eyes and she blinked rapidly in an effort to hide them.

She felt his hand on her shoulder and shrugged away from him. "Leave me alone," she snapped. "I trusted you, I came here with you, turned my back on my own people—for what? A handful of lies?"

Through their Link she knew every word she said hurt him, but she didn't care any more. What was his hurt compared to hers? She was alone on an alien world with no way of getting home. She couldn't leave even if the means were available. Her life depended on her physical nearness to him. Anger rose inside her. How dare he deceive her like this!

"Carrie," said Taizia, "Kusac's not like that. He's put it badly, but he was only trying to stop you from worrying needlessly."

"Needlessly?" she said, looking over at his sister. "It's all right for you to say that with the security of your home and family behind you, but I've only got Kusac, and now I find out I haven't even got a right to him!"

She reached up to tug her torc off, but anger made her clumsy. "I can't get this damned thing off!" she cried, jumping to her feet. "I've had enough, Kusac! I wish I'd never met you, I wish you'd let me die when Elise died!"

Tears of anger and frustration began to blur her vision as

she made for the door. Kusac reached out to take her by the arm, but she pulled away. He grasped her more firmly.

"I told you, Kusac, leave me alone! You've no right to stop me leaving, I don't belong to you!" She lashed out with her free hand, landing him a stinging slap on the face.

He snarled in surprise and pain, then grabbed that arm also as she tried to hit him again.

She couldn't see properly, her eyes weren't focusing. Everything looked strange, unreal. His arms moved, encircling her and holding her pressed tightly against his chest. Breathing was difficult, all she could smell was him, all she could hear was the blood pounding in her ears, driving her to struggle and fight against him. Trapped, she opened her mouth to scream her rage only to have his hand clamped across it.

"For the love of Vartra, get Mother," Kusac hissed. "I can't control her! She's hunting! Carrie, for the Gods' sake, stop it! You'll trigger the gestalt!" he said as she tried to bite his hand.

Taizia leaped off the bed and ran from the room.

Kicks rained on his shins, so he lifted her up, hoping that would prevent her reaching him. It only made it easier for her. Her eyes had a red glow to them and the hate and anger that battered at his mind was making him feel ill.

He carried her struggling body over to Taizia's bed and dumped her face down on it, keeping his hand over her mouth as he did. Sitting down beside her, he pinioned her arms behind her with one hand and turned her face so she could breathe.

"Carrie, calm down," he said, trying to keep his voice soothing. "I've never lied to you, believe me." Under his grip she began to struggle again.

Kusac, came his mother's thought. *She's hunting like an angry Sholan female. Treat her like one. Let her go.*

But she'll run off!

She'll fight you, not run. Let her go and block the door.

She's not Sholan, Mother. I don't think Terrans do that. It won't work.

You made her what she now is. Why ask me to help, then ignore my advice? was her acid reply.

Kusac let her go and hastily backed up to the door to prevent her from leaving.

For a moment she stayed where she was, then in one sinuous movement, she sprang off the bed and was running at him. Her fists flailed at him, alternately hitting then trying to scratch him with her blunt nails.

He fended her off as best he could, trying to take the blows on his forearms but inevitably some of them got through.

She spent her fury on him, her movements becoming more and more sluggish till she collapsed on the floor, sobbing.

Squatting down, he picked her up. She no longer fought him, but the desolate sense of loss she felt hurt him more keenly than the blows had. He carried her back over to the bed and was settling her there when the door opened.

"Well, you made a complete fool of yourself over all this, didn't you?" said his mother, coming over. "You should have told her from the first!"

I couldn't. I was afraid of losing her, he sent to her.

Don't tell me, tell her! was the tart response as she sat beside the human girl.

Rhyasha leaned forward and stroked Carrie's head, making soothing, purring noises while Kusac moved back and sat on his haunches nearby, watching them unhappily.

Gradually Rhyasha encouraged Carrie to put her head on her lap while she continued to stroke and soothe her.

"You're not alone, cub," she said, "never think that. You have me and Taizia as well as my fool of a son. You're part of our family now. No matter what Konis says, he knows that, too. You belong with us now."

"He lied to me." Carrie's voice was faint through her sobs.

"He was foolish, he cared too much to tell you," she said. "Think of what he has done, cub. He gave you his torc, letting all the world see it's you he cares for, no one else. In our culture, that's no small act. He's also fighting his father over you, refusing to marry Rala. Would he do all these things if he didn't care?"

A shuddering breath was all the response Carrie made.

Rhyasha tried another approach. "Here I am, trying to persuade my son's alien Leska that he loves her. I, his mother, am encouraging him to turn his back on his own kind, to reject the Sholan bride chosen for him, to give up the right to have children—all this, for what? A female who gives in at the first hint of trouble, who won't fight for him as a Sholan female would? A fine Leska you are!"

"Mother!" said Kusac, getting anxiously to his feet.

It worked, though. Carrie sat up, glaring angrily at Rhyasha.

"That's better. I thought I'd read you correctly the first time we met," said Rhyasha, giving her a hug before she could back away. "Kusac would leave Shola with you before he would marry Rala, and I don't want to lose my son or you. We'll find a legitimate way to dissolve this betrothal, never fear. Taizia and I have been checking through the Clan laws to find any loopholes."

"I didn't realize," said Kusac, taken aback by the support that he'd never known he had.

"There's a lot you don't realize," said his mother. "Since you met Carrie, I swear you've let your hormones do the thinking!"

Carrie couldn't stifle her laugh.

Rhyasha hugged her again. "That's right. You laugh at him! My son, the scholar, not really interested in females, doesn't want to marry, so he runs away. What does he do then? Why, he finds the only female telepath on an alien world and bonds to her for life, losing his heart to her in the process!"

This time Carrie found it impossible not to laugh, a laugh born from despair but still a laugh.

"Carrie, I'm sorry," he said, hovering several meters away from her, not daring to come closer. "You had so many doubts and fears from the start that I didn't dare tell you. It was wrong of me, I know."

Carrie looked at Rhyasha who cocked her head on one side, ears flicking gently. "Well? Have you made him suffer enough?"

"I wasn't trying to make him suffer," she objected, then saw Rhyasha's eye ridge lift. "Well, not intentionally," she amended as Kusac squatted on the floor beside them. She reached down for his hand and found it gratefully given.

"Kusac, Rala is coming for second meal tomorrow. You will see her, and you will be civil to her. We need time. If you give her any reason to complain, she'll be demanding an early wedding. Playing for time includes taking your torc off so she doesn't realize you've exchanged it with someone else already."

"No. Carrie gave it to me, I refuse to remove it. We've been through this already, Mother."

"I know Carrie gave it to you, and so will anyone else who sees it because of the bands on either side of the emblem. It looks like exactly what it is—a betrothal torc, not your family torc. At least turn it around so your hair conceals the motif."

"If your mother needs the time to help us, then do it," said Carrie. "I don't want you outcast from your Clan because of me."

He looked from his mother to Carrie and back. "Very well," he sighed. "I'll turn my torc around, but that's all. I won't lie or mislead Rala about the wedding."

Rhyasha sighed in exasperation. "I've never yet met a male that was any good at dissembling! You're as stubborn as your father!"

Kusac grinned. "Funny, he always says that about you!"

"Insolent cub," she said good-naturedly, getting to her feet. "I think Taizia would like her room back. You two go and get some rest, you both feel like you could do with it, especially you, Carrie. You look as if you could do with several good meals inside you as well! Tomorrow will come soon enough."

Kusac stood up and wrapped his arms around his mother. "Thank you."

"Good-night Kusac, good-night cub," she said, turning to touch Carrie's cheek. "Don't fret. All will work out well, I'm sure."

Rhyasha walked along the balcony to her study where Taizia waited impatiently.

"Well?" she asked.

"He'll conceal his torc, but he won't lie to her," said Rhyasha, sitting down at her desk. She tapped her claws thoughtfully on the surface, looking up at Taizia. "We've run out of time," she said abruptly. "It has to be the Challenge. There's no other way."

"I thought so," nodded her daughter. "I've been talking to Meral. He says their training at the Warrior Guild goes well. Apparently Carrie is a natural with a sword. Their encyclopedia says it's an old Earth weapon, too."

"So Carrie stands a good chance of winning?"

"From what Meral says, yes."

She shook her head, setting the beads in her hair chiming. "I don't like it, Taizia. It's tempting fate. The words she quoted at that reception on the *Khalossa* were those spoken by Khadulah. I thought then it was a bad omen, but Miosh assured me it meant Carrie would have to fight her family. Now here we are contemplating the same Challenge, and using the same weapons that took the lives of two telepaths."

"You're being superstitious, Mother. There's a big difference in what we're doing. For a start, Carrie isn't Sholan and she can fight—has even killed—without the trauma we suffer. That puts her two steps ahead of Khadulah already. She can fight Rala on equal terms. Then, if you want to be religious about it, why would the God put them together just to kill them during a Challenge, a religious Challenge at that?"

"What you say is true, but I still feel uneasy. I can't quite put my finger on it, but something's changed."

"What? A person? Circumstances?"

"That's it, I just don't know and it's annoying me. It's to do with Carrie and I feel it's right in front of my eyes if only I could see it." She shook herself. "Enough of that," she said, opening one of her drawers and taking out a small box. "Here's the key to the chest in the shrine. The swords and shields that belonged to Khadulah are in there. Make sure you aren't seen with them. Until the Challenge is issued, we can't afford to have anyone else but Carrie and her guard know, or Konis and Kusac will try to stop her."

"What about the political implications of Father's argument?" asked Taizia, opening the box and looking at the simple iron key that lay within. "That the Council are afraid that Carrie's mental Link to Kusac makes him unfit to hold a position of authority? Should we be going against what is a very sound point, namely that we need to prove Kusac is still capable of leadership with the Clan's interests foremost in his mind? I have to admit that that thought worries me."

"There are other ways to achieve the same result, Taizia," said her mother. "I will never let any of you be sacrificed for politics. I will also never let my personal opinions cloud my judgment when it comes to Clan matters."

"Very well. I'll collect the weapons later tonight and conceal them. Tomorrow, if Carrie, myself, Meral, and Kaid head off for the coast, we can talk about our plan then and Carrie can start practicing." She leaned forward to nuzzle her mother's cheek before leaving.

Chapter 15

Carrie woke with a start. As always, a faint glow of light filled the room. Beside her she could hear Kusac's even breathing beginning to change, become faster as, aware of her even in sleep, he began to wake. Retreating behind a barrier that made him think she still slept, she heard his breathing slow again.

When she was sure he wouldn't wake, she slipped from the bed and padded over to the doorway leading to the balcony. The two moons were still in the sky, the larger one dipping near the horizon. It was late, then.

The dream had awakened her again, but this time it had been stronger, less confused. There had been a fight, the sound of shots, and the high-pitched yowls of wounded Sholans. Closing her eyes, she tried to consciously conjure it up. It had begun in the room with the flickering torches. There had been a lone figure running, then falling. No, not falling, climbing downward. The image faded. There had been more, she knew there had been more! She frowned in concentration, finally catching the wayward thread of the dream. As she relaxed her mind, the images started to form once more. A large room, brightly lit, and the same male pacing around it.

Too soon. They found us too soon.

She shivered as a breeze swept across her bare skin, banishing the dream images. Opening her eyes, she saw that the larger moon was beginning to dip behind the hill on the headland. For an instant, she thought she saw the ghostly outline of a ruined building thrown into sharp relief, then it was gone. Another shiver ran through her. One day she'd have to go and look on top of that hill, but it wouldn't be today. She turned back to the room and her warm bed.

* * *

Despite her broken night's sleep, Carrie woke at the same time as Kusac. Seeing a square of white lying at the foot of the door, she got up to investigate. It was a note. She read it, then put it down on the dresser.

"What does it say?" asked Kusac.

"Don't you mean, who's it from?" she teased.

"It could only come from Taizia," he grinned. "Has she come up with something? She's usually very good at dreaming up involved plots to get her own way."

"It just says that she wants me to meet her in her room at the fifth hour, when Rala arrives."

"I've half a mind to leave now," growled Kusac, his grin fading.

"You'd only be using half a mind if you did," she responded tartly, picking up her clothes and starting to dress. "We need the time this meeting will give us."

He grunted, unconvinced. "Last night I asked for breakfast to be sent up to us. I can't face another meal with my father."

"Thank God for that," sighed Carrie.

Kusac rose and went through to the small lounge, checking the comm unit in the desk for any messages. Carrie followed him, going across to the doorway that opened out onto the central balcony. She leaned on the balustrade, looking down into the courtyard below. The sound of water rushing over the small artificial waterfall filled the air. It was restful even to her raw nerves.

She returned to the lounge as Kusac, now dressed, re-emerged from the bedroom.

"Are all the rooms like this, with no doors?"

Kusac gave her a baffled look.

She pointed to the lounge doorway. "It opens straight onto the balcony, and the bedroom's the same."

Kusac grinned. "I left the doors open last night because it was so warm. During the day, you'd cook in these rooms if it wasn't for the current of air going through them. There is air-conditioning, but I had enough of that on the *Khalossa*."

"So where are the doors then?"

"On the left-hand side, concealed in the carving around the doorway, you'll see the switch mechanism. Do you like the rooms?" he asked. "When Mother heard you'd admired the paintings in the courtyard, she put us in here. Apart from their suite, these have the best paintings in the house."

Where the walls were bare of furniture, they had been decorated with a frieze of wild animals making their way toward a seated female dressed in green. Clustered round her feet and hands were those creatures which had already reached her.

Perched on her lap was a small, furred animal the painter had caught so well that Carrie held her breath, waiting for it to move. A fine, bushy tail, fully as long as its body, lay across the female's knee. The lithe body was standing balanced on its back legs, paws reaching up toward her face. Bright eyes sparkled against the almost white fur.

Carrie went over to the wall, gently touching the vibrantly colored birds and animals. "I saw it last night," she said, "but daylight brings the colors alive. Who is she?"

"She's the Green Goddess," he said, coming over to join her, "the Mother of our world. She looks after the creatures of nature, and our cubs."

Tracing the outline of the ears and head of the animal on the Goddess's lap, Carrie turned to look at him. "I'm just waiting for her to turn and speak to me," she said. "The artist who painted them has a rare talent. Who is he?"

"She, actually. She's a member of our Clan who belongs to the Guild of Artisans. She works from the estate. Her paintings are very popular and usually command a high fee."

"No wonder," said Carrie.

"The little creature on her lap is a jegget, by the way," he said. "It's the only other truly telepathic species on our world."

"Apart from me," she said.

"Apart from you."

A noise from the doorway drew their attention. An attendant with a breakfast tray stood there casting dubious looks at T'Chebbi who stood beside him.

"Your breakfast, Liegen," their guard said. "I checked him out, he's a member of your mother's household."

"Um. Thank you, T'Chebbi," said Kusac, at a loss to know quite what to say. "Have you eaten?"

"Three hours ago, Liegen, before I came on duty."

"Was there someone outside our room all night?" asked Carrie.

T'Chebbi looked offended. "Naturally, Liegena. Kaid was on duty. He will go with you today, Liegena, and I will remain here with you, Liegen."

"Of course," said Kusac. "Thank you. You can bring in our breakfast now," he said to the attendant as T'Chebbi stepped back out of sight.

Carrie sniffed the air, then followed the tray to its destination on the lounge table. The attendant put it down and hurriedly disappeared, glad to leave the proximity of their guard.

Two jugs sat on the tray amidst the bread and sliced meats. Sniffing again, Carrie lifted the lid of the larger jug.

"Coffee! I thought I smelled it! There's a note here for you," she said, passing it over to him before pouring out two mugs of the steaming drink.

Kusac read it and put it down on the table. "A peace offering from my father."

"Does it actually say it's a peace offering?"

"No, but . . ."

"Then we can drink it," she said, taking a large mouthful. "Come and get some breakfast before I eat it all." She picked up a chunk of newly baked bread and a knife. "Did you grow up here?" she asked, spreading the dressing on it.

"Yes and no," he replied, piling several slices of meat on his plate. "I went to the guild as a day student until I was sixteen, then the more intensive work began and I had to live in." He looked over at Carrie with narrowed eyes, the merest slit of black showing in the amber.

"As homes go, I wasn't here much, despite the fact that I was fairly close to my parents. Neither of us have really had much of a home life, have we?"

"Was your mother's an arranged marriage?" she asked, changing the subject as she sat down.

"They all are in our family. Not out there amongst the Clan," he said, waving an arm in the direction of the bedroom. "They're free to choose, but in here, it's different."

"Tell me about Rala." She felt his surprise and gave a small laugh. "Know the enemy," she said. She couldn't keep the touch of bitterness out of her voice though she knew it distressed him.

He flicked an ear, dipping his head to one side. "What's to tell? She's a couple of years younger than me, brought up by her father and spoiled to the point where if she doesn't get what she wants, she throws tantrums. I dislike her intensely. She isn't Talented, but her bloodlines match well with mine. They—both families—expect to strengthen our telepathic gift until it breeds true for every child in every generation."

"I thought both your sisters were Talented."

"They are, but last generation, my mother's, of four children only she was a telepath. She was one of her generation's candidates for the position my father was finally awarded, Lord of the Clans. She has one of the most powerful Talents around, almost the equal of my father."

"Until now," said Carrie sardonically, helping herself to more meat.

Kusac frowned, then picked up her thought. "The gestalt? Yes, it's far more powerful, but to what end? So far it has initiated some minor body changes in us, and made you briefly appear Sholan. That isn't exactly useful."

"Oh, ye of little faith," she said grinning at him. "I'm sure there will be a use for it yet. Wait and see."

* * *

As the fifth hour approached, Kusac became more and more withdrawn. He was only too acutely aware of Carrie's fear that somehow this meeting could make him change his mind about Rala.

"Believe me, it's not what I want," he said, holding her close before she left for Taizia's room. As she returned the hug and pressed her face against his, he winced.

"What is it?" she asked anxiously, letting him go.

He touched his cheekbone gently with a forefinger. "I think one of your fists made contact there last night," he said ruefully.

"Serves you right," she said unsympathetically.

Taizia was waiting for her. She gave Carrie a shrewd look. "I don't need any talent to know you want to see Rala," she said, taking her by the hand and leading her over to the doorway.

Like theirs, her room had a balcony, but a much narrower one that overlooked the gardens at the back of the house. Below they could see Kusac's parents lounging under the shade of the tree where they'd sat the day before. Beyond them a path led to the less formal area of garden, screened from the house by trees and bushes.

"He'll probably take her over there," said Taizia, pointing to the path. "Whatever he says, he won't want our parents overhearing him. Sit down on the floor and keep your head back or they'll see us," she advised, demonstrating.

"Won't they sense us?"

Taizia shook her head. "No. They'll be shielding themselves from casual contacts. Most people do."

Within a few minutes, Kusac's parents were joined by a female elaborately dressed in a long, embroidered robe of blue and gold that contrasted prettily with her pale gray fur. At each step, the panels of the robe separated to show a brief glimpse of her legs. She was accompanied by a taller male dressed in dark blue edged with the Telepath Guild purple.

There was an ease and a proprietary air about her attitude as she graciously accepted Konis' and Rhyasha's greeting before she settled down in one of the chairs.

"Typical," said Taizia with a low growl. "Overdressed as usual. That's her brother with her. He's quite nice."

Carrie leaned forward, trying to assess every detail of the female's appearance, but right now she knew her judgment was flawed. She turned to Taizia, annoyed at her inability to be objective.

"Is she attractive, young, what? Tell me," she demanded.

Taizia raised her eye ridges, making her eyes appear even larger. "You really have got it as bad as Kusac, haven't you?" she said with a chuckle. Instinctively she put her hand on Carrie's arm.

"She's reasonably pretty, about two years younger than Kusac, and can turn on the charm when she wishes. It doesn't fool a telepath, though. All that is only as deep as her fur, and no one knows it better than Kusac."

Carrie glanced down again. Kusac had joined them by now, and she watched him greet Rala with stiff formality. He hadn't dressed for the occasion, she noticed with a sharp pleasure. He was still wearing yesterday's olive-colored short tabard. The terminals at the ends of his torc gleamed against the short fur at his throat.

"And Kusac?" she asked. "How does he compare with other males?"

Taizia laughed, pulling her to her feet and away from the doorway. "You ask me that when you've been on the *Khalossa* with all those hundreds of males? He'd have broken many hearts if he'd shown an interest in females at the guild. Come to think of it," she said, shutting the door behind her, "he broke several because of his lack of interest."

"How can he prefer me to someone like her, his own kind, who can give him all the things I can't?" she asked, stopping dead. "I don't understand it."

"Why did you turn your back on the Terrans for my brother?" countered Taizia. "What did he have that they lacked?"

"I knew him, really knew him, inside and out," Carrie faltered. "And he's different," she said defensively.

Taizia gave a bark of laughter, pulling her forward again. "He is definitely different from your Terrans! And you are just as different for him. Come on, Meral and Kaid are waiting for us at the aircar."

"Where are we going?" she asked, as Taizia led her downstairs and out a side entrance to where the family aircars were garaged.

"Somewhere we won't be bothered," said Taizia firmly, pushing her toward the waiting vehicle.

As soon as they sat down, Meral closed the hatch and took off, heading toward the coast.

"I'm making for a little cove where we'll be undisturbed," he said, turning to grin at them.

"And what would you be needing an isolated cove for?" asked Taizia archly.

"Come with me tomorrow when I'm off duty and I'll show you," he said persuasively.

"I might, if I have time," she said, grinning back. "First we have business to attend to. Where did you put that bag?"

"Over there, in the back," he said, indicating the direction with a backward jerk of an ear.

"Come with me, Carrie," said Taizia, getting up and heading between the seats to the rear.

"What's going on?" demanded Kaid suspiciously.

"You'll find out when I've told Carrie," she replied, crouching down beside the bag and unfastening it. From its depths she pulled out a book. "This was the only solution Mother and I could come up with, if you're prepared to try it," she said, leafing through the pages until she came to the place she wanted.

"This book contains a history of our family," she said quietly, "and the item we want happened about two hundred years ago. This is why it was declared unlawful to Challenge a telepath." She passed the open book to Carrie. "Here, read it for yourself."

Carrie scanned the page, going back to read it more carefully. At length she looked up at Taizia. "As far as I can see, you're suggesting that as Kusac's Leska, I can Challenge Rala for the right to marry him."

Taizia nodded. "Before you say anything, Rala isn't a telepath, and there's no law that says a telepath can't issue a Challenge."

"Liegena, the whole idea is dangerous in the extreme," said Kaid. "Have nothing to do with it."

Carrie took a deep breath, ignoring Kaid. "A couple of points, Taizia. I saw Kusac Challenged by Guynor. I can't fight like that, I haven't got the claws or the strength to do it," she said. "Second, your ancestor died. I've no intention of risking our lives."

"You don't need claws, it isn't like the males' Challenges; it's a ritual one, so you use weapons. A special long knife and a small round shield. And it's only to first blood, not to the death."

"Then how did Kadulah die?"

"She was accidentally killed by her opponent. Khadulah, being a telepath, had never learned to fight. Her opponent, on the other hand, had. A blow that would only have taken first blood became a death blow when Khadulah panicked and turned onto the blade. Female's Challenges are fought by Champions now. Warriors like Meral will fight for their family or their lover if they issue a Challenge," Taizia explained. "This Challenge," she tapped the page, "has to be fought by the two interested parties, so it does carry a small element of risk. It's an En'Shalla Challenge, meaning the outcome is in the hands of the Gods."

"Carrie," said Kaid insistently, moving to sit at the back of the craft with them, "Kusac will have all our hides when he finds out. Leave it to the Gods to work this problem through in their own way, don't take this dangerous path."

Carrie was aware of his fear, the first emotion she had ever picked up from his usually still mind. "The Gods help those who help themselves, Kaid," she said quietly. "Who's to say that this Challenge isn't their way of helping us?" She closed the book and handed it back to Taizia. "Is the result of the Challenge legally binding?"

"Oh, yes," said Taizia, shocked. "If you win, Rala's contract with Kusac is instantly nullified. Rala can't pursue the matter any further. Her family wouldn't let her, even if she wanted to."

Carrie sat thinking for a moment. "What happens if I lose?"

"You're no worse off, but you won't lose, because Meral, and hopefully Kaid, are going to train you," she said triumphantly. "I knew you'd do it! It is the only way," she said, serious for a moment. "Mother agrees with me. That contract is watertight, and nothing would make Father break it. You win this Challenge, and you've broken it yourself. Kusac will be free to life-bond with you."

"I don't know if I'm good enough," Carrie said. "What's Rala like as a fighter?"

"Middling. Meral checked through the Guild," said Taizia. "All non-telepath females learn some form of self-defense, and traditionally the Clan families learn sword skills. You'll be able to beat her easily by the time we've finished with you."

"This is utter madness," said Kaid, grasping Carrie's arm. "You've no business lending yourself to this folly, Meral. Liegena, you must have nothing to do with this mad idea."

"The decision isn't yours to make, Kaid," said Carrie, shaking her arm free. "I hope to God you're right, Taizia," she said, "because it looks like the only chance we've got. Kaid, either you help train me so I can win this Challenge, or you don't. Either way I'm Challenging Rala."

"You give me a hell of a choice," said Kaid angrily. "Either way I could be responsible for your death!"

"I've got no choice, why should you?" she said. "This isn't a problem Kusac can solve, nor anyone else, only me! I'm not one of your spineless lowland females from Kysubi, I'll damned well fight for what's mine!"

Despite himself, Kaid had to grin. "No, you're not one of the lowlanders," he said. "My job is to keep you safe, and if that entails teaching you how to defeat Rala in a Challenge, so be it."

* * *

Kusac was so tense that he was instantly aware of Rala's and her brother Talgo's arrival. He went downstairs to join his family, preferring to go voluntarily rather than suffer the indignity of being sent for.

He greeted her with a curt nod, taking a seat as far from

her as possible. Despite his heavy shielding, he felt his father's annoyance though Konis remained silent.

Kusac sat through the interminable round of pleasantries and small talk, contributing only monosyllabic answers, barely managing to conceal his impatience with the whole proceedings.

As an attendant came out to announce the second meal at midday, he reached for his mother. *Where are Carrie and Taizia?* He didn't want to open his link to Carrie because of Rala's presence.

They've gone to the coast for the day, came the reassuring reply. *Meral and Kaid are with them.*

"Kusac, verbalize if you please," said his father curtly. "It's hardly courteous to use telepathy in the presence of a non-telepathic guest."

Kusac stiffened, then forced himself to relax. Anger wouldn't benefit him now.

After lunch, Konis claimed urgent work to be done and his mother took Talgo with her to the estate pottery. Talgo had spoken of an interest in setting up such a facility on his family's estate. Kusac and Rala were left to their own devices. So far, Rala had surprised him by behaving impeccably.

Kusac invited her to accompany him into the private garden away from the immediate vicinity of the house. He didn't want any of his family overhearing what he had to say to her.

As he led her along the path to the seclusion of the private garden, T'Chebbi began to follow them at a discreet distance. He'd forgotten she was there, but then she would have been watching him all along. He allowed himself the smallest of grins as he realized her presence would have a dampening effect on Rala should she try her seduction tactics again.

Rala walked silently at his side until they passed the high hedges that concealed them from the house. Ahead of them was a carved stone seat. She stopped and sat down. "We've a lot to discuss, Kusac," she said, looking up at him. She frowned, catching sight of T'Chebbi. "Hasn't she got other things to do?" she asked. "Like polishing her swords or something?"

Kusac looked toward the Warrior, managing to flick one

ear just enough to invite a conspiracy with her as he answered Rala. "She's merely doing her job, Rala. There was an attempt on my life several weeks ago. One of the males is still at large."

"Surely you're in no danger here with me?" she said persuasively, her mouth opening in a smile.

"Not with T'Chebbi here, no," he agreed.

Rala sighed. "Kusac, send her away. I want to talk to you privately."

"She stays. There's nothing we have to say to each other she can't hear anyway."

"Very well," she said, her tone dissatisfied. "My father thinks it's time we formalized our betrothal, especially now you have a Leska, and I agree with him." She waited for a response.

Kusac moved away from her to where an ornamental tree stood beside the hedges. Leaning against it, he picked idly at the flaking bark with one claw.

"After that, we need only wait a couple of months before becoming life-bonded," Rala continued.

Kusac had let enough of his shielding down to be aware of Rala on a basic level and he could feel her absolute confidence. This time she was playing the mature young female, not the giddy youngling anxious to see her betrothed.

"It's all just one big game to you, isn't it?" he said. "What do you expect to gain by marrying me, Rala?"

"I don't know what you mean by a game, Kusac," she said, her tone slightly baffled. "I expect what any wife expects, naturally. To become part of your Clan, and in time have the position and respect due to the Clan Leader's wife."

"And me? Where do my feelings fit into your picture of marriage?"

She shrugged prettily, smoothing a fold in her robe. "It's an arranged marriage, Kusac. You have your Leska for love if that's what you want. I'll run your household and be the mother of your children. We'll do our duty to our Clans."

Kusac's eyes changed, the pupils contracting until almost all the black was gone. "This is very different from what you said that night at my Guild, Rala," he said coldly. "If I marry you, there will be no children. It will be purely a bonding of convenience. If position is all you want and I can't find a way out of our marriage contract, then you can have it, but you'll have none of me."

Rala's eyes flashed briefly. "Our betrothal is irrevocable, Kusac," she said mildly. "I'm sorry you don't want it, but it's a matter apart from our wishes. Once we're life-bonded, I've no doubt I can change your mind. There's no reason we can't have affection in our relationship."

"Any marriage will be in name only," he repeated firmly. "There will be no children."

"We'll see," she said confidently, getting up and walking over to him. "Surely marriage to me wouldn't be that unpleasant? We could even exchange torcs now."

Her lithe body pressed against his and her perfume filled his nostrils. He pushed her aside, aware that for him there was a subliminal wrongness in the feel of her body against his. Only the softness and smell of Carrie felt right.

Kusac moved sharply away from her, backing down the path. "There will be no exchange," he said. "I'll give you nothing of mine save the position you want."

"Kusac, I am entitled to ..." she began.

"No," he interrupted. "You are not entitled to my torc. It's mine to do with as I wish! There will be no exchange."

"I warn you, Kusac ..." she began, her eyes flashing angrily, but he cut her short.

"It'll be as I say," Kusac said flatly, turning away from her, T'Chebbi following him. "I've nothing more to discuss with you, Rala. Good day."

"How dare you treat me like this!," she said, her voice rising in pitch, brittle with anger.

Kusac was out of earshot, but he felt her anger hit him like a wave. Shutting it out, he returned to the house, heading for their rooms. Once inside, he stripped his tunic off, throwing it on a chair. The belt he kept, fastening it round his waist again and making sure the knife was firmly in its sheath.

T'Chebbi would be waiting outside on guard. He couldn't leave that way. He went to the balcony, walking the few meters to where the household shrine roof projected below him. It was a leap of only a meter or so to the rooftop.

He landed with a thump and froze, hoping no one had heard. When there was no response, he made his way cautiously to the edge and looked over. There was no one about. He jumped, absorbing the shock of landing on all four limbs, then ran for the undergrowth nearby, dodging between the bushes for cover until he was in open scrub land. Moving

into a lope, he ran till his ribs ached and his mind was too
numb to think coherently, heading instinctively for the hide-
away he had used in younger days.

It was still there. Limbs trembling with fatigue, he scrab-
bled at the debris covering the entrance—more now since it
hadn't been used in so many years—and pushed his way
through the thornbush into the cave in the rocky outcrop behind. Sides heaving, he flopped onto his side and put a hand
to his mouth to suck out the stray thorn that had penetrated
a finger pad. That done, he curled up, trying to get comfortable.

* * *

The afternoon drew on, and finally Kaid called a halt to
the training session.

"We've made a good start," he said as Carrie collapsed,
panting, in a heap on the sand. "You're beginning to use the
knowledge you took from me in that transfer, but your body
needs to know what to do as well as your mind. You also
need to improve your stamina. You can't rely on skill alone
to beat Rala, you need to be able to stay the course for however long the Challenge takes. Whoever tires or gets angry
first will take the risks and make the mistakes. Don't let her
emotions get to you. Better still, make sure you shield them
out."

"How long does a Challenge usually last?" she asked, trying to breathe deeply and slowly.

Kaid shrugged, wiping down the blades of the short
swords with an oily rag. "It could be over in the first few
seconds, or it could take ten minutes. Who knows? You need
to be at peak fighting performance for as long as it takes. I'd
like to get you to the pitch where you take her in less than
a minute."

He slipped the blades back into their case and closed it,
turning to give each of the small punch shields a wipe, too.

"That means daily training until the day of the Challenge," he said, looking at her. "Can you keep this from
Kusac until you've actually issued the Challenge?"

When Carrie hesitated, Taizia answered for her. "You'll
have to," she said. "He's bound to try to stop it, and it really
is your only chance to prevent his marriage to Rala."

"Can you keep it from him?" Kaid asked again.

"Yes, I can block it, but I'll need you," she nodded to

Taizia, "to help give me an excuse to leave the guild regularly so I can practice."

"No problem," said Taizia, grinning at Meral, "I'll be happy to accompany you."

Carrie pushed herself groaning to her feet. "I'm as stiff as a board again," she complained, grabbing a towel to scrub at her sweating face.

"You can have a shower when we get back," said Taizia, putting the book and weapons in her bag.

"Taizia, what would happen if Kusac and I just got life-bonded? What's to stop us? We're adults after all."

Taizia gave her a horrified look. "You couldn't do that, Carrie! It's a question of honor, Kusac's honor, even though he had nothing to do with making the bonding contract. Even if he did try, the priest at the Temple would refuse."

"I'm not thinking of suggesting it," she assured Taizia hurriedly, "I just wondered what the position was."

"I thought you understood Kusac's position," she said, a worried look on her face.

"I know all that Kusac does about your culture, but I don't understand it until I'm told or I experience it for myself," Carrie said. "I can't explain it any better. I'm sorry," she said helplessly.

Taizia gave her a quick hug. "It's all right. I understand, I think," she said with a little laugh.

Picking up the bag, she headed back to the aircar. Meral ran after her, taking the bag from her and helping her into the craft. Taizia thanked him, her hand lingering in his for longer than was necessary.

Carrie and Kaid exchanged glances, then Carrie linked her arm briefly through his. "Thanks, Kaid. I know you don't approve, but I do appreciate your help."

When they joined them at the hatch, with a flick of her tail, Taizia ducked into the passenger area, leaving Meral to help Carrie up.

* * *

Kusac had awakened and was on his way back to the house. Lowering his shield to a normal level, he sensed that Rala and Talgo were about to leave, and his sister and Carrie were returning. A sudden dread and a premonition of danger filled him and he began to run in earnest.

Meral set the craft down at the front entrance and opened the hatch.

"Keep the bag out of sight at the back," Taizia said to him. "We need to take it with us when we leave. Can you keep it in your quarters? I'm afraid that weapons in the Telepath Guild House are likely to be discovered."

Meral nodded, waiting until Kaid and the two females were out before following them.

Carrie turned to Taizia as they walked round the front of the vehicle. "Do you think the other Terrans will have arrived yet?" she asked.

Taizia grabbed her by the arm, hauling her sharply to one side.

"Hey!" exclaimed Carrie, stumbling against her in an effort to regain her balance.

An angry growl made her turn her head. In front of her stood Rala. Taizia had just prevented Carrie from knocking the Sholan female down.

Carrie stood frozen to the spot, facing a mental blast of rage as Rala took a long look at her and the torc that she wore.

Rala took a step forward. Claws extended, she reached for Carrie.

There was a blur of black and Kusac slewed to a halt, sending a spray of gravel in Rala's direction, making her start back in surprise. He rose suddenly to his hind feet, towering between the two females, making Carrie's senses reel at the sudden change. His mouth opened in a warning snarl and he made no attempt to control the lashing of his tail.

Rala took another step backward. "I see now where your torc is! She's changed you into a savage to come at her beck and call," she hissed.

Carrie stole a quick look at him. There was a kind of barbaric splendor about him at the moment, clad as he was only in the torc and knife belt.

"How could you betray your own kind and place her above me?" Rala demanded angrily. "I thought it impossible for a Clan Leader's son to behave in a way that went against the good of our race and his own honor, but you have!"

"Those aren't accusations for you to make, Rala," said Kusac's father as he emerged from the house. "So far my son hasn't done anything to let either our Clan or Shola down."

Now! now! now! yammered a voice in Carrie's mind, a mixture of her own urgings and Taizia's.

She stepped out from behind Kusac. "I Challenge you . . ." she began.

Kusac, knowing her mind, whipped round to face her. Grasping her by the shoulders, he tried to shake her into silence, but she continued, her voice getting stronger as she feared he would prevent her from finishing.

"I Challenge your right to marry my Leska by the rules of En'Shalla!"

Kusac released her. "You can't," he said flatly.

"Accepted!" growled Rala, seeing her chance for blood.

"Father," demanded Kusac, turning toward him, "tell her the Challenge can't stand."

"I demand that it stands!" said Rala.

"I'm afraid Carrie has the legal right to issue this or any Challenge," his father replied slowly, a concerned look on his face.

"Telepaths can't be Challenged!"

"Nothing says a telepath can't issue a Challenge," said Konis.

"Then she'll have a Champion," said Kusac.

"Oh, no," said Rala, "she's not getting out of it that easily! She issued the Challenge, I demand she fights it!"

Kusac glanced from the unholy glee on Rala's face back to his father.

"I'm not sure of the law in this case, but I do know the last time this Challenge was fought it led to the banning of telepaths being Challenged," Konis replied.

"Then how can she fight Rala?"

"It's an anomaly. Although this incident made telepaths inviolate, the Challenge itself was never removed from the statute books as far as I remember. I'm surprised Carrie knew about it," said his father, frowning thoughtfully at Taizia.

"The law in this case states that the Challenger and the one Challenged must be the ones to fight," said Rhyasha's quiet voice.

"Father, this is nonsense! Stop the Challenge," pleaded Kusac.

His father shook his head. "I can't interfere. As your mother says, the Challenge is valid, and legally issued. It's also En'Shalla—in the hands of the Gods. No judge can stop it, only a priest."

"In that case, I set the date for . . ." began Rala.

Kaid stepped forward. "Liegena Vailkoi, the Challenge was issued by Carrie. She decides the place, time, and weapons." He glanced at Carrie and, receiving the barest of nods, continued.

"It will be held here two weeks from now, and the weapons will be the ritual shield and short sword provided by the Liegena Taizia Aldatan. The time will be the fourth hour."

"Those are the weapons from the shrine," exclaimed Kusac, turning on his sister. "They were used in the original Challenge! How could you suggest she use them when they've already caused two deaths? They're cursed!"

"The weapons sound ideal," purred Rala, ears flicking in anticipation of the fight to come.

"That's superstition," said Taizia. "Surely you don't believe it?"

Kusac turned away from her to Kaid. "Are the arrangements complete?" he demanded, his voice as cold as ice.

"Yes, Liegen Aldatan."

Kusac grasped Carrie firmly, ignoring her pain as his claws dug fiercely into her wrist. "We're leaving now, Father," he said, walking toward the stairs and pulling Carrie with him. He turned briefly to Rala.

"We'll see you in two weeks, Liegena Vailkoi," he said before stalking into the house, dragging Carrie behind him.

"You may win your Leska, Terran, but watch you haven't lost his love," Rala called after her, laughing.

"Damn you, Carrie," said Kusac, his voice harsh as he dragged her along the balcony and into their suite. "Why did you have to do that to me?" He changed his grip to her upper arm as he activated the lounge door. Dragging her over to the settee, he flung her down on it, watching while she recovered her balance and examined her wrist.

Blood trickled slowly down her forearm, making him shiver with an icy premonition of worse to come. Acutely aware of her pain and distress as well as his own, he went over to her, crouching down on the floor. He took her by the shoulders, shaking her more gently this time.

"Don't you realize the risk you're taking, not just for yourself but both of us? I know the Challenge is to First Blood only, but something could go wrong. What possessed you to allow Taizia—and my mother—to talk you into this wild scheme?"

"It's the only way to break the contract."

"I would rather have disobeyed my father and left the Clan than risk you in a Challenge. The only good point, if you can call it such, is that if anything happens to you, I won't survive either," he said heavily, pulling her close.

"Don't say that!"

"It's a fact," he said, lifting her injured wrist and beginning to lick it. "No," he said in response to her look, "I don't like the taste of blood, but it'll help the wounds close. I'm sorry I hurt you."

"I'm sorry if I did the wrong thing, but your mother and sister desperately wanted to help us. They're afraid of losing you if this bonding ceremony couldn't be stopped." She sighed, relaxing against him.

"It was my problem, I should have solved it!"

"Is there any other way?" she demanded.

"No," he admitted, letting her wrist go. "Gods, cub, no one could say life with you was boring. What the hell am I supposed to do with you?"

"Love me?" she suggested, wrapping her arms around his neck and pulling him close enough to kiss.

His canines bit her lip a bit more sharply than usual. "I'm still angry with you." His voice was a low growl. "Come on, I want to be out of here within the hour. Go and pack."

They arrived back at the guild to find it alive with excitement. The Terrans had arrived and were being processed through Medical. A message on their comm told them to report to the Terran quarters to give what aid they could to Physician Vanna Kyjishi.

They found her looking slightly harassed, busily delegating her nurses to record the Terrans' basic medical details using the sampling units.

"An interesting batch," she said in answer to Kusac's unspoken question.

"I'm glad you came. I didn't expect to see you for another couple of days. I have to talk to you when I'm finished here," she said. "Now that Terran over there," she nodded briefly toward a dark-haired male who was staring in their direction, "there's something about him, but I don't know what. Every time I turn round, he seems to be looking at me."

"Strange," agreed Kusac, keeping a straight face. "Perhaps he just likes the look of you."

Vanna shot him a half-angry look. "I doubt it," she said. "It's his turn now. Come over with me."

They accompanied her over to the Terran.

"This is Carrie and Kusac," she said to him, "the Leska pair you were asking about. You're . . . ?"

"Brynne Stevens," he replied, smiling as he stood up.

He was tall, about Kusac's height. Dark curly hair reaching to the neck of his sweater framed a pleasantly featured face. Gray-blue eyes regarded them with interest. His jawline and mouth were outlined by a close-cropped beard and mustache.

"You know what this does," Vanna said, reaching out to position his arm correctly in the molded sampler unit. As she touched him, she flinched, pulling back from him and almost dropping the unit.

"What the hell!" he exclaimed, catching hold of it. "That's some kind of static charge you've got!"

Kusac's arm shot out to steady Vanna. "Are you all right?" he asked as she straightened up.

"I'm fine," she said, passing a hand across her head before giving herself a little shake. "Honestly, I'm fine." With hands that shook slightly she took the unit from Brynne.

"You're overtired," chided Kusac, taking the unit away from her and calling one of the nurses over. "I'm sure you'll excuse us, won't you, Brynne?" he said, handing the unit to the nurse and drawing Vanna away. "Now, where's your office? You need to sit down."

"Kusac, I'm fine," she protested as they went toward her room. While Kusac made her sit down, Carrie went for some c'shar for them all.

"Why are you rubbing your hands?" he asked, taking hold of them. "Is there something wrong? What happened there?"

"Nothing, I just got a jolt of static from him," she said, allowing him to look at her palms. "Honestly, Kusac, there's nothing to be concerned about."

Carrie returned with a tray and three drinks. Vanna took one gratefully. "I am tired," she admitted. "This is the first break I've had since they arrived three hours ago. We've got a problem already," she sighed. "One of our young male telepaths on the *Rhyaki* was assigned to accompany the Terrans to Chagda Station, then return. He formed a friendship with a female Terran, the daughter of one of their telepaths. That in itself was bad enough in her parents' eyes, but they Leska-bonded when only a few days out from Earth!"

Kusac glanced at Carrie then back at Vanna. "So there's another pair like us," he said. "That's not so very dreadful for them, is it? I wonder why my father didn't mention them."

"It is for these two," said Vanna, taking another mouthful of her drink. "Her parents will have none of it. They don't believe it's happened."

"What about the girl? What has she said about it?" asked Carrie.

"Not a lot. Her parents have shut themselves and her away in the Terran quarters upstairs and won't come out, not even for the medical checks."

"Why don't you just go and get her?" asked Kusac. "They can't keep her locked up."

"Oh, they can," said Vanna, "and they are, and we can't do anything about it. The Terrans are totally autonomous in their own section. We can't interfere."

"How old is the girl?" asked Carrie.

"Sixteen."

"Damn. She's underage. Her parents have legal authority over her. She can't make the decision to leave them. Unless she actually manages to escape and ask us for help, there's nothing we can do," said Carrie. "I'll happily go and talk to them and explain what a Leska bond is."

"Thanks. We hoped you would," said Vanna. "We haven't got too long, though, from the state Raill's in. We've had some success controlling the memories with psychic suppressants but he's weakening fast."

"I'll go and see her parents shortly," said Carrie.

"I forgot to ask how your visit went," said Vanna.

"We've had some excitement, too," said Kusac dryly, ears twitching as his eye ridges met in a frown.

"I found out that Kusac was betrothed," said Carrie, casting a frown of her own at him.

"I've been trying to find a way to dissolve the contract my parents made," he explained hastily. "Carrie, however, with the help of my sister and mother, has Challenged my unwanted bride."

"She can't, Kusac!" exclaimed Vanna, a look of sheer terror on her face. "She mustn't fight or she'll lose the child!"

Absolute silence greeted her remark.

Kusac looked at Carrie, noticing that the blood had drained from his Leska's face. "You're saying Carrie's pregnant," he said carefully, his voice questioning.

"Yes," Vanna nodded. "I only found out a day or two ago and I haven't been able to reach you to tell you."

"Then who is the father?" he asked Carrie, stunned. "I'll swear I was your first lover, so that means you've been with someone since then. Why didn't you tell me about it, or your wish to have children?"

He was confused and hurt that he should have missed that need in her and sensed nothing when she took another lover.

"No, Kusac," said Vanna, leaning forward to touch him. "You've got it wrong. The child is yours."

"Mine? Don't be ridiculous," he said, looking sharply at her. "We're too different to breed. It's impossible."

Vanna shook her head. "I've said nothing to anyone but Jack Reynolds, but I've been monitoring for genetic changes in you both since the gestalt link on the *Khalossa*. I knew there would be far-reaching changes, but I never expected you to be able to have children. It's scientifically and medically impossible, but somehow—I don't know how—it's happened."

Kusac looked back at Carrie. "Didn't you know? Couldn't you tell you were pregnant?" he demanded.

Some of the color had come back to her face. She shifted uncomfortably, unable to meet his eyes. "I thought I might be," she admitted, "but I dismissed it as being impossible. As you said, we're two different species."

"You wouldn't have conceived if you hadn't wanted to," he said, his anger mounting. "Knowing you could be pregnant, you still Challenged Rala!" He shook his head. "You're carrying a child that by rights should never have been conceived, and you're prepared to risk it, and us, over a Challenge? Gods, what have I done to deserve a Leska with as little sense as you?" he demanded, getting to his feet and pacing across the room. He stopped by the door, his back to them.

He ached inside. The shock of finding out that he'd fathered a child on his alien Leska—a child that he desperately wanted to have with her—coupled with the knowledge that she was risking everything on that damned foolish Challenge, was too much for him to absorb coherently. He needed to get away from her—from himself, too, if he was being honest—to give himself time to think.

He pounded his fist against the wall, the momentary pain helping to focus the anger which he knew he was wrongly directing at her.

"Damn you, Carrie," he said, his voice breaking, "why must you keep getting me into untenable situations?"

Carrie got to her feet. "Kusac, I . . ."

"Just leave me alone, Carrie," he said, his mind and voice full of pain. "Leave me alone."

"Dammit, Kusac!" she said, grabbing hold of him and pulling him around to face her. "I'm not the only one to blame. You had more than a little to do with it, you know! How on earth was I supposed to know this could happen? It's all right for you, you're not the one who's pregnant! And how dare you suggest that anyone else could be the father!"

He reached out to touch her. "Carrie, I . . ."

"Don't touch me!" she spat, shaking with rage. "Just. Leave. Me. Alone!" Darting past him, she wrenched the door open and fled.

He stared after her retreating figure.

"Nicely handled, Kusac," said Vanna, getting up. "Very sensitive of you. Sounds like Carrie's had a wonderful couple of days."

"What do you mean?" he asked, totally thrown first by Carrie's reaction and now by Vanna's.

"First she finds out you're betrothed, then that the only way to break that contract is for her to fight a Challenge with your betrothed, and on top of it all, she discovers that the impossible has happened and she's pregnant. And who's to blame for all this? She is, according to you."

"That's not what I said, Vanna!"

"Isn't it? It looks that way to me. What about her feelings in all this? Did you think to ask her how she felt? Even, Gods forbid, to say you were glad she's having your child?"

"She knew she was pregnant, she said as much, Vanna! Knowing that, what possessed her to issue the Challenge? That was utterly foolish of her! If she'd only waited a few more hours, none of that would have been necessary. If I can

only father children with her then there's little point in me
marrying Rala! The contract would have been dissolved."

"I need to confirm that yet," warned Vanna. "Carrie certainly can never have Terran children, but I need to run tests
on you to find out if you're still fertile with other Sholans."

"I'm sick to death of these tests, Vanna. Tell me what
good they've done us?"

"Suit yourself, Kusac," said Vanna with a shrug, sitting
down again. "If you don't care, why should I? Tell me,
though, aren't you worried about Carrie rushing off like
that?"

"No," he growled, angry with Vanna now. "She can go
where she wants. You heard her tell me to leave her alone!"

"You're a fool, Kusac, and at this moment I have to say
a selfish fool! That female is your life, she's everything to
you, and I don't just mean your Link. Don't be so blind to
her feelings or you could lose her."

"I don't have to hear any more of this," he snapped, turning his back on her and leaving.

* * *

Chyad threw the wrapper into the garbage bag with disgust. He might have enough rations to last him a month, but
it didn't mean they were edible. They were worse than
Forces' rations, and that was saying a lot! He took a drink
from the bottle of water and almost gagged on it. It had been
tepid that morning, now it was warm.

He'd arrived in the dead of night, managing to find somewhere to land and conceal his aircar till dawn. As the sun
rose, he went scouting round the immediate area, looking for
a better place of concealment for himself and his craft.

As luck would have it, only twenty meters away he'd
found the entrance to a widemouthed tunnel. It was choked
with the God knew how many years of dead growth from the
bushes growing in front of it, but he'd been able to clear
away enough to allow him to drive the aircar into the tunnel
then conceal it again from outside.

His hand went up to his brow and fingered the scar there.
It was a permanent reminder of his crash on Keiss. That
damn-fool she-jegget Maikoe was responsible for that. How
anyone could screw up a faked emergency landing, he'd no
idea, but she had. Just as well she'd died in the crash else
he'd have killed her himself!

Then there was the male who'd thrown the explosive into the craft. His jaw tightened as he remembered him. He'd been lucky to get out alive. He'd risk his last coin betting that that male had been the one who'd killed the others. That had been a big mistake. Now it was personal. Now his sense of honor was involved.

He'd had a long time to plan his revenge. The worst thing he could do to someone hired to keep that damned Leska pair alive was to kill them, and leave him alive to live with his failure. That's why he was hiding out on the Aldatan estate, waiting for his chance. He still believed the treaty with Earth was totally insane, but now, as an added bonus, the death of the telepath and his alien qwene would destroy that treaty.

Leaning forward, he picked up the earpiece for the public info nets and placed it in his ear before switching on the comm. He had several hours to kill before he could risk leaving his cover to go scouting round the grounds. While he listened to the news program, he stripped down his gun, making sure it was clean and ready for use when the time came.

* * *

Carrie hadn't gone far. As she fled out of the Terran area into the guild grounds, she ran straight into Kaid.

"Hey," he said, catching hold of her. "What's the matter?" He saw the tears streaking her face and heard her ragged breathing. He gathered her against his side, holding her face against his chest so it couldn't be seen. "Come with me," he said, taking her across the grounds to the guest house.

When he reached Meral's room, he banged loudly on the door. Meral opened it, stepping back in surprise.

"Out," ordered Kaid. "Fetch a large pot of coffee from their suite. Here's my key, use it."

He took her over to the nearest chair and sat her down in it, pulling up a soft cushion for himself.

"Now, tell me what's wrong," he said, holding her hands. Carrie snuffled. "I need my hands."

He let them go until she'd dug out a tissue and blown her nose, then he recaptured them in one of his.

"It has to be something serious to get you so upset," he said. He frowned, catching hold of her chin and examining her face. "I thought so," he said, letting her go. "You're pregnant, aren't you? It shows in your eyes. I've suspected as much for a couple of days."

"How many more people can tell?" she asked, utter panic in her voice and on her face.

"Only those who know what to look for. You have to be at least three months. At a guess, another week, maybe two, then you'll begin to show." He hesitated. "Kusac's?"

She nodded, tears streaming down her cheeks again. "He blames me for this and the Challenge. It's not my fault, Kaid! He's as much to blame as I am!" Her shoulders began to shake again.

Kaid gathered her close, bringing her down onto the cushion beside him. "Don't start crying again. It's no one's fault, Carrie."

"They'll know, they'll all know as soon as they see me, Kaid, and they'll hate me for it," she wept, clutching at his jacket. "And now he hates me too! What am I going to do? I wish I were dead!"

"Never wish that," said Kaid. "Why should anyone, especially Kusac, hate you?"

"They'll know I'm sleeping with him, that the child's his."

"Of course you're pairing with Kusac, you're his Leska, that's what Leskas do," said Kaid. "Why should it suddenly matter to anyone but the two of you?"

"The Terrans. Don't you see? They'll hate me for carrying an alien child! And he hates me, too. Why, Kaid?" she sobbed. "I know he wanted children, I felt it that day in the market. Why doesn't he want ours?"

Kaid felt completely out of his depth. Armfuls of soft pregnant females were totally outside his experience, especially when they were as upset as Carrie was.

"Carrie . . . I don't know what to tell you, what to say. You don't live with the Terrans now, you live with us. It doesn't matter what they think. Kusac can't hate you, nor your child. It's a shock to both of you—to all of us! Both of you just need time to adjust."

"To adjust to what, Kaid?" Her tearful face looked up at him. "I'm not human anymore! I'm carrying an alien's child, for God's sake! What the hell am I, Kaid? What have I become?" Where she held onto his jacket, she started to shake him. "What has he done to me, Kaid?" Her voice rose in hysteria.

"Enough of that," said Kaid, grasping her hands firmly. "I can't tell you what you want to know, Carrie. All I can say is that to me you're no different than when I first met you." Gently, he unclenched her hand, letting her hold his instead of his jacket.

A knock sounded at the door and Meral cautiously opened it. "Coffee's here," he said, bringing it over to put on the table beside Kaid. "I'll get mugs, shall I?"

"When you've got them, fetch Vanna over here, and if you see Kusac, say nothing about this," said Kaid.

Carrie had quieted to the point where only the odd shuddering breath showed she'd been crying. Kaid carefully extricated himself from her grip and poured the coffee.

"Here," he said, handing her a mug. "It'll help relax you."

Carrie began to laugh, a very wobbly laugh to be sure. "Have I become so Sholan that coffee is an intoxicant to me?"

"Would that be such a bad thing?" he asked. "Would it upset you so much to know that most males have to be careful not to respond to you as they would to a Sholan female? You're becoming part of our world, Carrie. This child of yours and Kusac's proves it. The God moves in strange ways. There's a reason for everything, even if we don't know it."

"There's another mixed Leska pair," Carrie said after digesting Kaid's words.

"I thought you'd not be the only ones. When there are more like you, then the Terrans won't be so intolerant."

"The girl's underage, Kaid. Her parents still control her life. They won't accept the Link and have shut their daughter away in the Terran quarters. Vanna wants me to talk to her."

"Are you strong enough to do that now?"

Carrie cocked her head on one side and looked quizzically at him.

Kaid leaned forward and flicked her nose with a finger. "So Sholan," he said. "Can you now go and tell another Terran how good a Sholan Leska link is, knowing that you are carrying a Sholan's child and that this girl will probably do the same when the God wills it?"

Carrie took a deep, calming breath. "I think so," she said.

"Then you know what to do when Vanna arrives."

"Kaid," she said, putting her mug down. "What are you?"

"What do you think I am?" he asked, amused by her question.

"I know you're a Warrior, but you're more. You give nothing away mentally. Your mind is so still."

He shifted his position on the cushion, making himself more comfortable. "I was a member of the Brotherhood of Vartra," he said.

"The Warrior elite," she said quietly.

"If you like. They have their own sub-Guild affiliated to the Warriors', but our order is also religious. We don't advertise our calling. Those who need us know where to find us, and that is all I will tell you," he said with a faint grin.

The door chimed. "Probably Vanna," said Kaid, getting to his feet.

"Carrie will go with you to talk to the Terran girl," he said, flicking an ear at Vanna as she entered.

"Right," she agreed. "Well, if she's ready?"

Carrie got to her feet and joined her at the door.

"I think we should stop off in my room for you to freshen up first," Vanna said diplomatically.

Chapter 16

"Mrs. Fielding, thank you for seeing us," said Carrie as they stood at the entrance to the family's rooms.

"I only agreed to see you," said the woman, her voice sharp with criticism. "You had no right to bring her with you."

"Vanna's my friend and a doctor, Mrs. Fielding. I was actually hoping to see your daughter, Lynn."

"I know you did, but you'll have to make do with me."

Inwardly Carrie sighed. The woman was exactly what she looked. Middle-aged, belligerent, and set in her ways. There was no flexibility of mind here. Why on earth had they sent her as a telepath? Perhaps it was on the strength of her daughter. She, at least, had to be the genuine item.

"Mrs. Fielding, I've come to talk to you about Lynn's telepathic link with one of our Sholan males."

"Such things don't exist."

"They do, Mrs. Fielding. I'm proof of that. I have a Link with a Sholan too."

Hard eyes raked her from head to toe. "Then you're no better than you should be, miss. If you want to go sleeping with their menfolk, that's up to you, but no daughter of mine's about to do the same if I've got any say in the matter."

Carrie tried not to flinch. "Lynn's ill, isn't she?" she insisted. "Wanting to sleep all the time, not eating, having dizzy spells and stomach cramps?"

"She's suffering a touch of jet-lag, or whatever you call it, that's all."

"It isn't that simple, Mrs. Fielding. She's suffering what we call Link deprivation. When two people are Linked like this, they exchange all their day-to-day experiences. Lynn is as aware of everything Raill does as if she was there with him. It's the same for Raill. These experiences will overload their minds if they aren't sorted out every few days. Your daughter is suffering from a mental overload at the moment, that's why she's so ill."

"There's nothing wrong with our Lynn that a few days rest won't cure," said Mrs. Fielding with finality. "I'm treating her stomach pains with herbs like I usually do. There's no need for you to make more of it than there is."

"Can I ask why you chose to come to Shola, Mrs. Fielding?" asked Vanna.

The woman frowned. "What do you mean? We came because we were asked to come."

"Asked?"

"Yes. My son-in-law is one of the organizers of this project and he asked us to come for a year or two. I'm well known for my herbal remedies and he said you people were interested in that sort of thing."

Mentally, Carrie groaned. Apart from the daughter, this family was probably useless. If she read the woman's character right, it looked as if her son-in-law had seen this as a chance to get rid of her at least for a few years. Fortunately, or unfortunately, there was at least one real telepath in the family.

"Mrs. Fielding, believe me, this Link exists, and your daughter is in real danger if you continue to keep her away from Raill. Will you at least consent to her visiting him in our medical section? In your company, of course," said Carrie.

"Look, I keep telling you people, there's no such thing as a link between my Lynn and this Raill," she said angrily. "I want her to have nothing to do with him. He started getting a mite too friendly toward her on the ship, and it isn't happening again! Now that's an end to it!" The door slammed in their faces.

Carrie turned to Vanna. "Let's leave," she said abruptly, beginning to shiver.

"What is it, Carrie?" asked Vanna, taking hold of her by the arm.

"I need to get out of here," she said. "The woman's projecting ... I don't seem to be able to shield against it, Vanna."

"Come on," said her friend, leading her quickly back to the elevator.

Carrie leaned against the wall as they traveled down to the

ground floor. "She was thinking such ugly thoughts, Vanna. She won't let her daughter near Raill. If you want to help them, you're going to have to get someone with authority to go in and demand her. I'm sorry, I tried."

"You did all you could," said Vanna soothingly. "Look, it's been an overwhelming day for you. Why don't I take you back to your apartment?"

"No. I'm not going back there."

"But why?" asked Vanna, baffled.

"I don't want to see Kusac. He'd no right to speak to me like that. He's shut me out of our Link. I don't want him near me."

Vanna could see her tears were threatening to fall again. "Look, don't start crying here. There's a corridor full of Terrans just outside this elevator. You don't want them to see you're upset, do you?"

Carrie blinked rapidly and scrubbed at her eyes with her hands. "I'm all right," she said.

"No, you're not," said Vanna, putting her arm around her. "That Leska of yours needs a good lesson in manners! You're coming with me. You need some looking after."

Once downstairs, Vanna took her out a side exit to the vehicle park she was using.

"Get in," she said, pulling back the hatch door of an aircar. "We don't want Kaid to see us, do we?"

"Where're we going?" she asked as Vanna took off and headed inland.

"To my home," she said. "If you're determined not to see Kusac for a day or two, you might as well go somewhere where you're not going to brood over your row with him."

The flight didn't take long and soon Vanna was bringing the aircar down alongside several others a short distance from a cluster of buildings.

"Vanna, I'm not sure if I like this idea," said Carrie nervously.

"It's the best one I've had for a long time. Trust me. You'll find it different from Kusac's home," she said as she powered the vehicle down. "We don't belong to the Clan Leader's family so we don't live in the main house. Kara, Tyan, and Kikho, before she chose to have a cub, all work on the estate. Our Clan's specialties are fruit and bread which are sold both in Valsgarth and Nazule."

As they climbed our of the aircar, they saw a female with a mane of brown and black hair come to the open door of the largest building.

"It's Vanna," she yelled, "and she's brought her Terran friend with her!"

Carrie could feel the disbelief in her voice. Within moments, some half a dozen Sholans had surged through the door toward them, all calling out greetings and questions to Vanna.

"How long are you here for, Vanna?" asked the female they'd first seen.

"Carrie, this is Sashti, my sister. I'm here till tomorrow, Sashti, but Carrie's here for a couple of days. I've brought her home to you for some good, old-fashioned care."

"But of course. She's very welcome," said Sashti, mouth open in a grin. She turned to the others and began to scold them out of the way. "Kara, leave her be, let her have a chance to feel her feet on the land again first."

"But she has such lovely hair," said Kara, reaching out a tentative hand to Carrie's hair.

Sashti smacked the hand away. "Later," she said. "Third meal isn't for a couple of hours yet, I'm afraid."

"That's fine. We both need a shower first. Have you any of your special massage oils?"

"Plenty. We made a batch yesterday," said Sashti, leading the way into the house.

Like Kusac's home, the outside of this house was painted white to reflect the heat, but the comparison ended there. Unlike a main Clan home, it was a very comfortable family dwelling. Inside, the main room was large and spacious. A log fire, unused at this time of year, took up the central position against one wall. Several easy chairs were dotted around in a semicircle facing it. At the far end of the room was a large table with padded benches surrounding it.

"Shower first," said Vanna as the others clustered round them again. "Then a massage, if you wouldn't mind, Sashti."

"I'd be glad to," her sister replied.

Vanna grabbed Carrie by the hand and towed her through one of the doorways leading off the main room into a short corridor. Two doors opened off it.

"Toilet there," said Vanna, "showers here." She pushed the door open, waiting for Carrie to enter first.

The room was bright and sunny, the walls decorated in shades of yellow. Benches lined it and in the center were two large padded massage tables.

Vanna unsealed her medic's short coat, looking over to where Carrie still stood. "You can't shower in your clothes," she said gently. "Bathing tends to be communal among us, but being with Kusac I know you haven't come across it yet. I got out of the habit on the *Khalossa,* but family's different."

When Carrie had undressed, Vanna led her through to the showers. There was already someone using them and Vanna was greeted with a cry of delight as the shower was turned off.

"Vanna, well come home! You have a friend with you— the Terran?"

"Yes, Carrie."

"I hope you have a nice visit with us, Carrie."

"Thanks," she said, casting a cautious glance toward the wet Sholan.

"Come on," said Vanna, "we'll use this one." She stepped inside the stall and turned the water on.

Carrie joined her, letting the jets of hot water wash over her. As Vanna's hands touched her back, she jumped, looking over her shoulder at her friend.

"I'm only going to wash you," she said. "I said you were going to have some old-fashioned care, and so you are, Sholan style. Now stand still."

She stood rigid as Vanna began to soap her shoulders and back.

"Relax," Vanna purred in her ear.

Gradually the heat from the fine jets of water and the gentle rhythm of her friend's soothing fingertips combined to disperse the stiffness in her body.

"That looks like fun," said a voice from behind. "Can I help, too?"

"Of course, Jayed. You finish her back for me," said Vanna.

Carrie sensed Vanna moving round in front of her before she felt her begin to spread the soapy lather over her neck and shoulders. "Who's Jayed?" she asked.

"My brother," said Vanna, working downward to cover her breasts.

Carrie stiffened, her hands going up to stop Vanna. "Your

brother! He's a male?" She could feel Jayed's hands starting to rub the soap over her lower back.

Vanna chuckled, gently pulling her hands free. "Brothers usually are."

Carrie was suddenly very aware of the hands that were now gently massaging soap over her buttocks and the back of her thighs.

"Relax," said Vanna, "we're just treating you like one of our family."

"But he's a male!" she hissed.

"So? He's helping wash you. That's perfectly normal, isn't it, Jayed?"

"We always help each other wash," affirmed Jayed. "You help your Leska, don't you?"

"It's like grooming," said Vanna, squatting as she worked the soap over Carrie's belly and thighs. "It's virtually impossible to do it properly yourself, so we help each other. Come on, relax," she said persuasively, looking up at Carrie. "I said this is part of normal Sholan family life."

Carrie tried, but she was hypersensitively aware of Jayed's hands as they curved around the sides of her thighs. His touch became featherlight, holding the promise of sensuality.

"Such a lovely body you have, Carrie," he purred, his hand briefly caressing her right calf. "Nice firm muscles. Do you exercise a lot?" He finished her legs and tapped her ankle indicating that she should raise her foot.

"Um, a fair bit, at the Warrior Guild," she said, standing on one leg.

He turned the sole backward toward himself, rubbing the soap along her instep and between her toes.

Carrie flinched and grabbed Vanna for support as his fingers tickled her foot.

"You're tickly?" said Jayed, surprise in his voice. "I suppose being furless you would be more susceptible than us. Your other foot, please."

She changed feet, still hanging on to Vanna as her friend stood up. This time Jayed did tickle her, making her laugh and try to twist away.

"Now you're relaxing," said Vanna, pleased. "Bend forward a little and I'll do your hair."

Her feet both on the ground again, Carrie bent forward slightly, feeling Vanna's fingers push through her hair to her

scalp and begin working the lather in. She tried to sense
where Jayed was but couldn't. She felt too vulnerable, standing there naked with her eyes closed and soap running down
her face. Then Jayed's hands returned, this time with a
rougher touch.

"I'm using a cloth on you to rub away any dead skin," he
explained. "Not that I think you have any. Your skin's so
soft, so sensual," he purred in her ear.

"Jayed, stop teasing her," said Vanna reprovingly, withdrawing her hands from Carrie's scalp. "This is the first time
she's experienced the intimacy of a family like ours."

Vanna's voice seemed to come from behind and Jayed's
cloth was working its way round her side. Where was he?
Lifting her head, she dashed the water from her face. She
found herself eye to eye with Jayed as he stepped round in
front of her.

"You're pregnant!" he said, mouth opening in a happy
grin. "You didn't tell us she was pregnant, Vanna!"

Carrie pulled back, crossing her arms over her breasts and
cringing in anticipation of his reaction as she looked from
Vanna to Jayed and back.

"That's why I brought her here," said Vanna, touching
Carrie's cheek reassuringly. "To be pampered a little now by
us before her mate refuses to let her out of his sight."

"The child's a Sholan's?" He shook his head, drops of water flying from his ear tips. "The Gods have really blessed
you," he said, awe in his voice as he resumed working the
cloth across her body.

His ready acceptance of her situation and his genuine
pleasure for her were so different from what she'd feared
that it left her totally confused.

"Carrie, I can't reach your head easily," said Vanna
gently.

As Jayed moved to one side, Carrie bobbed her head
down again, then froze as a third person began to rub her
back.

"I've done there, Kara," said Jayed.

"Not with the cloth."

Beginning to panic again, Carrie stumbled, clutching at
the nearest body to stop herself from falling over. A hand
she knew was Vanna's caught her arm.

"Relax, Carrie," her friend said soothingly. "I know humans don't share wash times, but we do. You need to expe-

rience more about us as people. I'd have suggested this to
Kusac earlier, but you weren't ready emotionally for it."

While she talked, Vanna moved round in front of her, lifting her face and wiping the soap from her eyes with Jayed's
cloth.

"Open your eyes," she said, turning her around. "See? It's
only my cousin Kara. Nothing to fear, truly. Do you think I
would bring my friend here, to my family, only to let her be
seduced or raped? Shame on you, Carrie!"

Despite Vanna's humorous overtones, Carrie flushed. She
felt a sense of amusement from Jayed as if he knew what she
was thinking.

"You're one of us, Carrie," she said, cupping the girl's
face with both hands. "You're part Sholan, part human, just
like your unborn cub. You really do belong here on Shola,
there can never be any doubt of that now—not that there
ever was."

Carrie reached up to cover Vanna's hands with hers, feeling the familiar silkiness of wet fur beneath her palms.
"Thank you," she said.

Vanna grinned. "Don't mention it. Now if you have no
further objections, I'll wash the soap off your hair."

Chastened, Carrie bent her head again, feeling Vanna lift
and part her hair, letting the stream of water wash the soap
off. Meanwhile, the other two continued to gently rub at the
rest of her body. She began to relax, giving herself over to
the pleasantly sensual feelings their touch engendered.

Searching her inherited memories, she found similar
scenes from Kusac's life at the guild and at home. His sense
of relaxation and security from those days filled her. This
was an experience only shared with family or close friends.
More often now she was finding that her experiences and his
memories were beginning to overlap. Carrie smiled, suddenly feeling much more at home with Vanna's family.

"Vanna's turn now," said Kara.

Carrie blinked the water from her eyes. Vanna had turned
away from her and Kara had begun to vigorously lather soap
into her fur. Jayed had also turned to help his sister.

"May I help?" she asked hesitantly.

Vanna's eyes lit up as she grinned. "Yes, cub. Join in the
fun. It's one of the pleasures of belonging to a large family."

"Here," said Jayed, handing her his soap bottle. "Use
mine."

Hesitantly at first, she rubbed the soap into her friend's side, pushing the lather through the fur to the skin underneath, massaging it in with a circular motion.

"Kusac showed you how to do it properly," Vanna said, turning her head to grin at Carrie over her shoulder. "Don't stop, Carrie, that feels really good."

Her grin was infectious, and smiling back, Carrie continued to rub the lather over her friend's side. As she worked, she realized that the four of them had formed a natural little grouping of Jayed washing Kara and Kara and herself washing Vanna.

"Don't worry about me," said Jayed grinning across at her. "I'm done. I was just finishing when you arrived."

As she rubbed the soap across Vanna's flat chest and belly, she began to appreciate why the Sholan ideal of beauty was a lean, muscular body. Though smaller and stockier than Kusac, there was little real difference in the physical shape or feel of Vanna's body when compared to his, but a world of difference in the mental feel. With no outward difference between the sexes beyond the colored banding of the female's fur, each admired the same features in the other. To all intents and purposes their bodies appeared sexless to the Terrans who relied only on sight to identify the males from the females.

But you obviously know differently, came the humorous thought. The sending was faint but understandable.

Startled she looked up, catching Jayed's eye. He flicked an ear at her, grinning again. Looking away in confusion, she returned to lathering Vanna's legs.

I'm only a grade three telepath, not as exalted a level as you and your Leska, he sent.

You do all right, Carrie grinned back at him.

Finished now, they all stood for a few minutes letting the water flow sleekly off their bodies. Carrie watched the last of the soap and loose fur swirl around their feet to be sucked down the drain.

"You forgot towels," said Sashti from outside the stall. She was carrying a large bundle of them.

Vanna turned the shower off and as the Sholans began to run their hands down their bodies pushing the water from their fur, Sashti dumped her bundle on a nearby bench, taking one from the top and opening it out.

"Come, I'll dry you, Carrie," she said.

"It's all right, I can do it myself," Carrie said, stepping out into the cooler air of the room with an involuntary shiver.

Sashti flicked her ears. "Why do it yourself when I can do it for you? Vanna said you needed some pampering, so come and be pampered!"

Gently but vigorously she was toweled down. "I'll start her massage now, Vanna," Sashti said, wrapping Carrie in the folds of a fresh, dry towel.

"I'll be through in a minute," said Vanna, her head briefly emerging from her towel.

"I'm sorry to put you all out by being here," Carrie began, but Sashti cut her short as she took her through to the room where they'd left their clothes.

"No. Your visit has made today special for us," she said, indicating that Carrie should get up on the massage table. "When Vanna visited home last, she told us all about you and we longed to meet you. The chances of us being able to do that would normally be very small, yet here we are with you all to ourselves, not just for tonight, but tomorrow as well! This is a treat for us."

She lifted Carrie's legs up onto the table. "Roll over on your stomach first," she said, helping her unwind the towel again. "You see, we can show you family hospitality here, something you can't get from your life at the guild. Tonight will definitely be special," she promised, reaching for her jars.

"Oils? I wouldn't have thought you could use oils," she said, pillowing her cheek on her forearms.

"We need to look after our skins, too, you know," Sashti said, beginning to rub the delicately scented liquid into Carrie's back. "We get dry and sore patches under our fur and a good massage puts back the oils that we lose through washing daily."

Her fingers probed gently at Carrie's back. "Your muscles are quite different. I'll need to feel my way around them for a few minutes."

"Is massage your profession?"

"You could say that," said Sashti with a touch of humor in her voice.

"She runs the largest massage store in Valsgarth, and her oils are bought by even the city stores in Nazule," said

Jayed. "If you give me a jar, Sashti, I'll work on her feet and legs."

Sashti passed one down to him then began gently kneading the muscles across Carrie's neck and shoulders. This time, Carrie found herself relaxing almost immediately as the scent of the oils filled the room.

"You do realize you could end up with a great many Terran customers, too, don't you?" she murmured, giving herself up totally to the soothing rhythm of Sashti's and Jayed's hands.

"So I could, once I've practiced a few times on you."

"Any time at all," said Carrie, her voice almost a purr as she let her eyes close.

Wrapped in a warm toweling robe, Carrie was ushered back through to the main room where the third meal was waiting for them—not on the dining table, but on a low table set in the center of the floor. Large soft cushions surrounded it.

As they joined the others at the table, Sashti looked around the group of expectant faces. "Since we've got Vanna and Carrie with us, after we've eaten, we'll tell stories. I'm sure they have new ones we haven't heard before." This pronouncement was greeted with enthusiasm by everyone.

The meal was long and leisurely, consisting of the usual wide variety of hot cooked meats and vegetables to dip into half a dozen different rich sauces. Unlike those in the restaurants she'd eaten in before, these sauces had a fruity base taste to them. There were several different breads to try, all of them baked on the estate. Afterward there was fresh fruit, including several kinds that Carrie had never seen before. One particular one she found greatly to her liking was a rainbow fruit. Shaped like a star, the thick waxy skin peeled off to reveal a delicately colored flesh that shaded from lilac through to yellow in rainbow hues. The taste was unlike anything she'd ever had before.

"Fruit and bread are our Clan's specialty," said Sashti, passing her another rainbow fruit. "When it comes time for you to leave, we'll make sure you take some of these with you."

Finally the table was cleared and removed, the cushions spread to fill the gap and more wine handed round as they got comfortable for the serious business of telling and listening to stories.

They each took a turn, starting with Vanna and as the evening wore pleasantly on, Carrie's head drooped lower and lower till she was leaning against Vanna.

"Your friend's asleep," said Kikho, looking across at her.

"I know," she said, twisting round and trying to take hold of Carrie's limp body.

"I'll help," said Jayed, leaning forward from his place beside Kikho. He gently took hold of Carrie and laid her down on the cushions. "From the feel of her mind she'll sleep the night through now," he said. "She's a lot calmer than when she arrived," he added, gently touching the sleeping human's face. He sat back, looking quizzically at his sister. "What is it you want us to do for her?"

"I'm breaking up the evening," Vanna said, looking round the others.

"Not at all," said Sashti. "I'm equally intrigued as to why you brought Carrie to us, not that I mind in the least," she added hurriedly, ears flicking.

"She has a problem," said Vanna, pulling her legs up in front of her and wrapping her arms around them. "Imagine you have a lover who's Terran, her kind but male. Jayed, you think of her as your Leska."

Her brother's tail flicked lazily. "I've got the picture, Vanna," he said.

"You remember what it's like to leave the life you grew up with, Jayed, don't you? When the guild found you and you had to leave the estate? Well, Carrie has suffered all that, but in a culture truly alien to her. She's tried to fit in, but found because of her Leska she can only do that by turning her back on her own kind. Then the impossible happens. She finds out she's pregnant and the child is her Leska's, a Sholan child."

"And?" prompted Jayed.

"The Terrans have no time for her because of her relationship with Kusac. They're likely to hurl abuse at her when they know she's pregnant, so she can't belong to them. Kusac is betrothed, so she has no security there, and finally, she's afraid her child is going to be some kind of hybrid monster," concluded Vanna.

"That's some problem," said Sashti. "Is she right about the cub?"

"I can't tell until we've done a scan," Vanna replied. "Carrie's stuck between two worlds, feeling she belongs to neither. For now, she desperately needs to feel she belongs with us."

"Vanna, how did she become pregnant in the first place?" asked Jayed.

Kikho laughed, easing her gravid body into a more comfortable position as she leaned against her companion. "The same way I did, Jayed. Don't tell me you've forgotten what to do since last night?"

"That's not what I meant," said Jayed, ears flicking in acceptance of the general laughter at his expense.

"I don't know the answer," said Vanna. "It should be impossible, yet there's a child on the way, and Kusac is the father."

"You brought her here because of me, didn't you?" said Kikho. "You hope she'll accept her pregnancy better after seeing me."

"Yes, but it's not that simple, Kikho," said Vanna. "I want her to feel what it's like to be part of a family, part of us. All she's known is the starship and the Telepath Guild."

"Where is her Leska, then? He should be with her now, helping her feel part of his life," said Sashti.

"That's another problem. He's equally shocked by the fact she's pregnant. They had a row and she ran from him. I was called to look after her."

"Does her Leska knows she's here?" asked Kara.

Vanna shook her head. "No, he doesn't. He needs a lesson in taking equal responsibility, and to be reminded he had more than a little to do with her condition. She wants a day or two away from him, so I thought here would be ideal."

"A child is a child," said Kikho. "They should be happy at this time. She chose to bear one, after all, despite their physical differences."

"I don't know if she did. As I said, it came as a shock to her, too. I wonder if human females can control their fertility. Because we do, it's natural to assume that they can."

"Is she saying she doesn't want the child?" asked Jayed.

"She's not saying anything about it yet. That's why she's here. I want to help her feel that she isn't some kind of freak. Let her realize that pregnancy is a normal part of life for females, even for her. Just make her feel welcome and part of us, nothing out of the ordinary."

"That part's easily done," said Sashti. "She's pleasant company."

"I have to work tomorrow, but I'll be back in the evening. You don't mind looking after her, do you?"

"I'm glad you brought her," said Kikho. "We'll look after her, don't worry."

"She must have some wonderful stories to tell," said Tyan wistfully, his ears flicking.

"Don't you go bothering her for tales," Vanna warned her young cousin.

"I can ask to groom her," said Kara, leaning over to touch Carrie's hair as it lay spread out on the cushion.

Vanna laughed, leaning forward to flick Kara's nose. "Yes, you can ask her tomorrow," she said.

Carrie woke with a start to find herself still on the pile of cushions. Levering herself up on an elbow, she realized that so were several of the others. Sunlight streamed in through the open door, as did the morning heat. She reckoned it was probably 25 degrees Celsius already. Another hot day. As she sat up, her movements woke the others.

"Good morning," said Sashti, coming through from another room. "You were so peaceful last night that we didn't bother to wake you and ask if you preferred a bed. We sleep in here when it's as hot as this anyway. First meal's on the table over there."

"Did you sleep well?" asked Vanna, yawning and stretching.

"Fine, thank you."

"Good. I've got to go to the guild today, but I'll be back here tonight. Sashti and the others will look after you if you still want to stay for a day or two," said Vanna getting to her feet and checking her wrist unit. "I can't stop for first meal, Sashti," she called out.

"Then remember to eat at the Telepath Guild! I know what you're like," Sashti shouted back from the kitchen.

"I'm not going back yet," said Carrie, a determined set to her face.

"Then I'll see you tonight, cub," Vanna said, reaching down to touch her face before leaving.

* * *

As soon as Vanna had landed at the Guild, Kaid came over to her.

"Where's Carrie?"

"She's safe, Kaid," said Vanna, walking toward the medical section.

"I want to know where she is."

"Sorry, but I'm not telling you. She's resting, on my medical advice."

"Vanna, there's a killer out there after either her or Kusac. He won't give a damn which one he gets. I can't protect Carrie unless I know where she is," he said.

"If you don't know where she is, then neither does the killer."

Kaid grasped Vanna by the arm, pulling her to a stop. "I don't think you realize how serious this is," he said, ears twitching slightly backward.

Vanna looked at the arm holding her, then back at Kaid. "I realize that her medical condition means she needs a break from all this security and special treatment. You're isolating her and making her feel depersonalized and frightened, Kaid. I'm not telling you where she is and you can't make me. Now, if you'll excuse me," she said, looking pointedly at his restraining hand again.

Kaid let her go. She left him standing in the grounds as she entered the medical building. As she entered her office, one of the nurses popped her head round the door.

"The test results are on your desk, Physician Kyjishi. Last night's shift ran them through and gave them to me this morning."

"What tests?" she asked, frowning. She didn't remember leaving anything out to be completed.

"The Liegen's. He came in looking for you last night and the medic on duty remembered that you wanted extra tests run, so he took the samples."

"Thank you," she said, leafing through the papers on her desk till she found the lab report. She read the summary through, then picked up the attached crystal. Activating her comm, she inserted the cube in the reader and called up the actual data from the test. The medic had done a thorough job. His results even included the enlarged slides of the genetic material he'd been testing.

Getting out her master crystal, she transferred the information and checking through all her findings, began a final analysis.

* * *

It was well into the afternoon by the time Kaid had to give up trying to trace Vanna's movements the preceding evening. She'd covered her tracks too thoroughly. He'd only one option left. It meant pulling him out of undercover, but the need to have Carrie properly guarded outweighed that. Using his wrist comm, he placed his call, cursing Vanna roundly under his breath.

* * *

Vanna was duplicating her work when she heard a knock at her door. She turned round to find Kusac standing there.

"Hello," she said. "What brings you here?"

"I came to find out the results of the test," he said.

"Then unless you want me to shout them to you, you'd better come in." She turned back to her desk.

Kusac sat down in the chair beside her. "I feel like a patient, sitting here," he said, shifting uncomfortably.

Vanna turned to give him a long look. "You are," she said. "And I'm about to give you a prognosis."

"Don't joke about it, Vanna. I don't find any of this funny." Where his tail lay on the seat beside him, the tip flicked spasmodically with irritation.

"No, I don't suppose you do," she said. "You've certainly lost your sense of humor."

"What are you trying to do, Vanna? Sweeten the medicine? Don't bother. Just tell me what you've found and be done with it. I must know most of it by now, there's not a lot more that can happen to us."

"When your gestalt Link has been triggered in the past, it's initiated physical changes in you, like Carrie's eyes and the endocrine system changes. Can you remember any other times it's been triggered?"

His eye ridges met as he frowned. "What's this got to do with anything?"

"It's important. Try and remember, please."

"On Keiss, before we met up with you," he said.

"Forget that," she said, making a dismissive gesture. "That was before I started my tests. Any other times?"

"Not that I remember."

"Are you positive? Think hard."

"I've told you, Vanna, not that I can. . . ." He stopped. "Wait a minute, there was another time, but it didn't affect Carrie."

"Don't be so sure. Tell me about it," she said.

He looked away from her. "Rala came to the guild one night, toward the end of one of our Link days. They sent for me because she was refusing to leave until she saw me."

"What happened?"

"I came down, we fought, and I sent her home with Meral and Sevrin."

"Kusac, do I have to drag it out of you?" she asked, exasperated.

He breathed in sharply then looked up at her, eyes narrowed, ears flicking. "I was angry about the betrothal, about Rala. I went to see a friend at the Temple to find out if there was any way to break the contract." He was angry, and it showed now in his eyes.

"I wanted Carrie, not Rala, and as I arrived at the Temple the gestalt triggered. It can't have affected her because Kaid told me he'd given her a sedative so she didn't sense Rala at the guild.

"How long ago was that?"

"Some time ago, about three months, just before we went down with that fever. Look, what's the significance of this Vanna? Are you going to tell me what you've found or not?"

Vanna leaned forward on her elbows, clasping her hands together in front of her. "I can tell you now," she said. "That gestalt triggered more than you think, and it did affect Carrie, too, because shortly after that she became pregnant. You're the one responsible for making that possible, not her."

"What're you talking about, Vanna?" he asked angrily. "You know as well as I do that she chose to become pregnant!"

Vanna shook her head. "Forget that rubbish about her choosing. You chose for her because you wanted a normal family life with her, not Rala. That gestalt changed your reproductive system so you could have that life—it changed you to the point where you're infertile with anyone but Carrie. The tests from last night prove it. Not only that, you changed Carrie's system in a similar way. It's impossible for her to have Terran children now, only yours. If you want to apportion blame, then you'll have to shoulder it yourself, since your Leska was lying doped up to the eyeballs at the time!" she said, equally furious.

"You've treated her like shit, Kusac! How would you feel if you were the one who was expecting an alien child and your Leska turned round and blamed you? That's without taking the whole mess of your betrothal into account! You were a fool to hide that from her. It's time you pulled yourself together and started thinking about her and your cub."

She saw the anger in his eyes fade as he flinched under her words. "Am I hurting you?" she asked. "Good! Someone needed to tell you. You've blocked your Link, cut her out, and left her on her own. What do you think she's feeling? You can pretend to run away from all this, she can't. You'd better do something fast while you've still got a lover and not just a Leska."

"I didn't realize I'd caused the changes," he said quietly.

"Well, now you know. And I also think you'll find that human females can't control their fertility the way we can. Here, have this," she said, taking the crystal from her comm. "I was doing this copy for you. It has all the data on the physical changes in you both and my conclusions regarding them. I'm still working on the hows of the reproductive genetic changes, but that's going to take longer."

He took the cube and sat there toying with it. "She didn't come back last night," he said. "I don't know where she is, neither does Kaid." He looked up at her. "Have you any idea where she could be? I know she's safe, but that's all. She's shut down our Link again."

"Funny, I thought you were the one who'd done that."

"I did, but I attempted to reach her this morning only to find I couldn't sense her."

"Sorry, but I can't help you," she said.

"I need to find her, Vanna. Our Link day starts tomorrow."

"Tomorrow!"

"With the Link shut off and her gone, we'll both start suffering from overload within the next twenty-six hours," he said.

"Damn," she said. "I'll see what I can do. You'll have to excuse me," she said, getting up. "You've reminded me I want to check in on Raill."

"I saw him earlier," said Kusac, following her out. "He's

in pretty bad shape. My father's been talking to the Terran leader, but he doesn't believe him either."

"It seems you were lucky to get the one sensible Terran around," said Vanna, shutting her office door.

"It was seeing Raill that reminded me how lucky I am," he said, before walking back down the corridor to the Guild entrance.

There was little they could do for Raill, except try to keep him alive with drugs in the hope that if the Terran girl died they'd be able to save him. Vanna looked at him lying there in the intensive care unit and roundly cursed the Terrans responsible.

She returned to her office to find she had another visitor. "Garras!" she said. "Where have you been? How did you get here?"

He got up and came toward her. "Later," he said, taking her face in both hands and beginning to bite gently at her cheek and neck. "I didn't think I could miss you as much as I have," he said, his hands moving to press her close against him.

Vanna reached up round his neck, her fingers catching hold of his short mane of hair. Her mouth found his, teeth biting gently at his lips. "Where were you? I've been so worried," she said, nuzzling his neck.

"Don't ask," he said. "I can't tell you. We've got a day, then I have to go back."

"A day! Gods, that's no time at all," she said, pushing him away.

"We're lucky to have that," he said, cupping his hand round her cheek. "It cost me, though."

"What do you mean, it cost?" she demanded.

"Kaid wants me to find out where you've got Carrie."

"You what? You mean you're using. . . ."

"Hush," he said, pulling her close again and covering her mouth with his. He held her like that until his gentle bites and caresses had begun to take the tension out of her body, then he released her gently.

"I told him no," said Garras, putting a finger across her mouth to stop her talking. "So I've been given twenty-six hours to find and guard her before I need to bring her back to the guild. I won't be used by anyone, Vanna, never fear."

"Their Link day starts tomorrow," she said, leaning against him, breathing in his scent while her hands held onto his arms. "She'll need to return tomorrow morning at the latest anyway. How did Kaid get you off the *Khalossa?*"

"Let's just say that the past caught up with me temporarily."

"I knew you two were in the same guild," she said, "So you don't intend to stay on Shola?"

"That rather depends," he said, grinning down at her.

She turned away from him and switched her comm off, pocketing the memory crystal. "Come on," she said, taking his hand. "Let's leave. I'm off duty now."

They arrived at the estate in time for the evening meal. Garras had no sooner shown his nose through the door than Carrie came over to hug him, delighted to see him again.

They sat beside her during the meal and Vanna managed to have a few quiet words with her.

"Why are you blocking your Link?" Vanna asked.

Carrie looked startled. "You've seen Kusac?"

"Yes. He tells me your Link day begins tomorrow."

"That's why I'm blocking," she said, frowning. "I know I'm going to have to go back tomorrow, but I resent the fact that he'll expect everything to be forgotten because of the Link."

"Does he? I made him realize that you aren't to blame for the child."

"How did you manage that?"

"By telling him the results of your tests. I'll talk to you on the way home tomorrow. Just enjoy tonight," she said, patting her hand where it lay on the table. "Think about opening the Link to him. You're hurting each other needlessly."

"If I open the Link, Vanna, then I can't be responsible for the effect it has on everyone else," she said in Terran.

"What do you mean?" asked Vanna, replying in the same language.

"We need to be in shielded quarters during our Link time. We broadcast," she said evasively.

"Broadcast what?"

"A lot of raw sexuality," she muttered, looking down at her food.

"Oh! Well, perhaps you'd better keep the block on in that case," said Vanna.

Vanna and Garras opted to have a room that night. Garras shut the door and took Vanna into his arms. "The rest of the night is ours," he said, his voice low as he picked her up and carried her over to the bed.

"You know, planetside life suits you," he said conversationally as he took her tunic off, before throwing his own aside and sitting down beside her. "I like your hair better this length."

He looped a hand behind her back, drawing her toward him, running his hand across her face and ears till his fingers caught in the short curls. Pulling her head back, he lowered his mouth to her neck, licking it gently.

"Have you thought any more about whether or not I stay on Shola?" he asked, his voice so low she could barely hear him.

Her hands clutched his shoulders, claws extending to hold him. "Stay," she whispered. "Be one with me."

His mouth closed on her throat, canines bruising her in his pleasure at her commitment to him.

* * *

"Ah, Tallinu," said Ghezu. "I was wondering when I'd get your next report."

"I call you when I have news," Kaid replied.

"Well, what's been happening?"

"Have you been able to trace the second assassin?"

"Your news first," frowned Ghezu.

"That wasn't the arrangement," said Kaid softly.

"I've nothing," said Ghezu shortly. "It's as if he ceased to exist. One of our own couldn't have done better."

Kaid was hit by a sensation of having had this conversation before as briefly, the room around him seemed to lurch. "I've a feeling he might be a survivor of that scouter crash I had on Keiss. His name was Chyad, the leader of the dissidents on the *Khalossa*," he said.

Ghezu raised a questioning eye ridge but said nothing beyond, "If he is, and you find him first, Tallinu, I want him alive."

Kaid nodded. "If it's possible," he agreed.

"Make it possible," growled Ghezu. "Now, I want your news."

"The human female has issued the Life-bonding Challenge to Rala Vailkoi."

Ghezu's eyes widened in surprise, and his ears flicked. "She has?"

"Liegen Aldatan intends to marry her, not Rala, but they couldn't find grounds on which to break the contract. This seemed the only solution."

"You say seemed. Why?"

"Carrie Hamilton is twelve weeks pregnant, and Kusac is the father." Kaid had the pleasure of seeing Ghezu stunned. "Before you say it isn't possible, it's been confirmed medically, by genetic tests."

"A new species," Ghezu said quietly. "Vartra has created a new species."

"Rala Vailkoi accepted the Challenge," continued Kaid. "It's due to be fought in two weeks. We have to stop it, Ghezu."

Ghezu's eyes snapped back into focus and he frowned. "Why? It gives us the perfect opportunity to see her fight in real circumstances."

"There's a danger that she could lose the child."

"If the God intends the child to be born alive, then there can't be any danger to her. Besides, it will let us see how Kusac behaves during the Challenge. If he's become like us, then all his natural instincts, stronger at the moment because of his age, and her pregnancy, will make him fight to protect her."

"I think the benefits from seeing if she can fight are minimal compared to ensuring that she and the child are safe."

"I disagree. The God has dealt the tokens for the game, let the players play it out."

Kaid could feel his anger rising. It took all his self-control to stop his body from giving him away. "Females can die, even today, because of miscarriages," he said softly. "We could lose them all if we risk her. Is it worth it just to confirm what we already know? What would Lijou say?"

"Lijou would say that Vartra knows what he's doing," said the head priest, stepping into the range of the comm screen.

"I thought you wanted them alive so that you could recruit them and make your bid for full guild status," said Kaid. "How can you do that if they die?"

"We need more than one freak pair, Kaid," said Lijou. "The Challenge she issued is En'Shalla. It isn't up to us to preempt the God's decision. If they are meant to live, they'll live. If the child's meant to survive, then it will. We can't interfere."

"It is only a minor Challenge, one to first blood. The risks are minimal," agreed Ghezu. His voice became a gentle purr. "You aren't letting this become personal, are you Kaid?"

He'd been trapped, and he knew it. "Personal? I merely report the facts, Ghezu."

"Good. I would hate to think you let your judgment become clouded by feelings. What about the other couple?"

"The male, Raill, is severely ill because the Terran female's mother refused to acknowledge there is a Link. They won't let their daughter be seen by anyone. I think we'll lose them."

"I'm sorry to hear that. At least now we know there will be more. Thank you for your report. We'll be in touch."

When the screen had gone blank, Ghezu turned to Lijou. "Could the bones we've saved from the ruined cities possibly be those of humans? Were they created by Vartra at the time of the Cataclysm?" he demanded.

"Unlikely," said Lijou. "I do know the humans are descended from primates, not felines, and they have a long documented history going back farther than our Cataclysm. However, it doesn't mean that they, or some species like them, were on Shola a millennium and a half ago."

"We need more answers! Damn the Telepath Guild! They've had no right to systematically destroy our past."

"Leave it, Ghezu. One day we'll unravel the mystery, but not today," said Lijou. "It would be a pity if the other mixed Leska pair died. Having two pairs would make recruitment a more viable option than just having the one. I wonder how long before we know if the genetic compatibility is isolated to just Kusac and his Leska."

Ghezu grunted agreement. "How long have we to wait till there are more, though?"

"That, my friend, is in the hands of Vartra."

"I'm sending for Dzaka," Ghezu said. "I want someone I can rely on in Valsgarth."

"There's Rulla in the Temple. He's working with Taizia Aldatan to get access to the Terran books of their past."

"Rulla's officially on leave to you."

"Dzaka's one of my lay-priests, Ghezu," said Lijou gently. "What's the difference?"

"I want Dzaka. He'll make Kaid even more unsettled and on edge. I've told you I don't trust him."

Lijou sighed. "You must, of course, do what you think best."

* * *

It was mid-afternoon of the next day by the time Vanna, Carrie, and Garras returned to the guild. Garras had contacted Kaid on their way in so he was waiting for them.

"I've got you covered till third hour tomorrow," Kaid said quietly to Garras as he came over to collect Carrie. "Take the time off with Vanna."

"Are you sure you're all right," Vanna asked Carrie anxiously.

"I'm fine," she said. "Honestly."

"You have my pager."

"I'll call if I need you, I promise."

Vanna watched them leave then turned back to Garras. "Back to the real world," she sighed.

"Her or us?" he asked, putting his arm around her shoulders.

"I meant her actually. She needs to be surrounded by other people to stop her from brooding."

"Like your family, you mean. She certainly seemed a lot more settled last night, but then I haven't seen her for several months."

"She was. I have to check on Raill before I do anything else," she said, "Are you coming?"

"I'll come."

Konis Aldatan was in the I.C. unit when they arrived. He looked up, acknowledging their presence with a flick of his ear.

"He's in a coma now. I doubt there's anything we can do for him," the Clan Lord sighed. "I don't know what state the Terran girl is in. They'll tell us nothing."

A beeper started up, its insistent tone closely followed by another. Vanna reached for her pager. "Vanna Kyjishi here. What's the problem?"

"They've requested medical assistance for the girl. She's on her way down to Intensive."

"I'm there already. What's her status?"

"I've got the parents here."

"Understood." Vanna flipped off her pager and hurried over to the comm unit mounted on the wall near the door.

"Vanna Kyjishi requesting a security team to intercept the Terran couple accompanying their daughter to I.C. They must be kept well clear of this area. I repeat, keep the Terran girl's parents well clear of I.C."

By this time the warning beeper in the room had drawn the medic on duty and two nurses. Vanna had him brief her on Raill's current status and medication, then ordered him to remove the cover of the I.C. Unit.

"Clan Lord," she said, turning to Konis, "anything you can do on a telepathic level would be appreciated. I'm sure both Raill and Lynn are complete novices."

Konis nodded and stood back, letting the staff get the area ready for the arrival of the Terran girl.

Moments later she arrived on a floater and in a flurry of activity was swiftly transferred to the I.C. unit in which Raill lay. Vanna swiftly neutralized Raill's psychic suppressants, then, checking vital signs, gave him a stimulant in the hopes of bringing him round.

Konis tried to buffer the Terran from the shock of the mental imagery that was coursing through both her and Raill's minds, while at the same time trying to draw her mentally back to consciousness.

"She's too weak for me to use any more stimulants," said Vanna. "She's had no basic medical care whatsoever! They've let her dehydrate!"

Raill began to stir as he felt the physical presence of his Leska. His eyes flicked open, a glazed and distant look in them as he slowly turned his head to look at her.

Konis glanced at Vanna conveying everything in the gentle flick of his ears, then he turned back to Raill. Reaching down, he moved the youngling's hand till it touched the girl's arm.

No good, Raill sent, too weak to even speak. *She's too afraid, her mother made sure of that.*

Konis was suddenly aware of Kusac at his side as the Terran girl began to shake convulsively, her eyes opening to show only the whites.

See to Raill, sent his father, reaching mentally for the girl, trying to control the convulsions. Her fear exploded into the minds of everyone there as her body gave one massive convulsion before falling back limp and still.

Where Konis' hand gripped the side of the IC unit, his knuckles showed white through his fur. As they watched, blood began to trickle sluggishly from the girl's ears and nose, then stopped.

Raill looked as if he was merely sleeping.

I was only able to shield him from her convulsions, so his death was peaceful, sent Kusac.

Konis turned a haunted look on him before abruptly leaving.

"Damn those blind Terrans!" swore Vanna. "They were only younglings, both of them! How can they be so utterly stupid as to let these young people die rather than challenge their narrow-minded beliefs? I thought we'd been sent telepaths, not bloody herbalists!" She threw the hypoderm the length of the IC room. It bounced off the far wall with a metallic clunk and the tinkle of breaking glass.

"Vanna, it's not your fault," said Garras, coming over to her and wrapping his arms around her. "You all did everything you could, right up until the last."

"I know, I know. It's the Terrans' fault, not ours." She pushed him back. "I'm going to have a word with her parents," she said, heading purposefully toward the door.

Garras caught her by the arm. "I don't think you ought to be the one to tell them," he said gently, holding her back. "Not when you're so upset. Let someone else do it."

"Dammit, Garras, they've got to know what they've done!" she said, trying to pull free.

From down the corridor they heard the sound of raised voices, Konis Aldatan's being the loudest.

"I think they're already being told," said Garras. "Leave it to the Clan Lord. It's his place to do it, after all, not yours."

The anger abruptly left her as she leaned limply against him, the tears coursing down her cheeks. "Garras, they were hardly more than cubs!"

"Come on," he said, wrapping a supportive arm around her. "I think we should leave."

As he turned, he saw Kusac still standing by the IC unit, looking down at the two still figures. He thumbed his wrist comm.

"Meral? Get in here and get Kusac back to the guild."

"Will do," came the reply.

* * *

The apartment was empty when they arrived. Sensitive to her mood, Kaid suggested that she might prefer to eat there rather than the refectory.

She accepted gratefully, glad to be alone for a few minutes. Settling herself in a chair and dropping her barrier, she tried to sense where Kusac was. She knew he was nearby, but no more than that. Once again he'd blocked the permanent two-way flow of emotions and thoughts, cutting himself off from her. Despite the fact that she'd been doing the same, she felt angry with him.

When Kaid brought the food, she toyed with it, only too aware now of the cause of the nausea she had been experiencing every evening for the last month. It hadn't seemed so bad when she'd been with Vanna and her family. Now, although hungry, she had no stomach for eating.

Suddenly their Link flared into being, sending the Terran girl's fear exploding like a physical blow into her own mind. It lasted only a second and then was gone, to be replaced by the feel of Kusac protecting Raill's fading thoughts from the fear projected by his dying Leska.

She gasped, the tray slipping from her lap onto the floor.

"What is it?" demanded Kaid, at her side in an instant.

"They're dead," she moaned, her mind still wide open through her Link with Kusac to the reactions of those in the IC room. She felt Konis' anguish and realization that his son had come close to the same awful death, and Vanna's helpless anger with the Terrans for allowing the young couple to die. Then, mercifully, it stopped, as Kusac's barrier snapped back up.

She returned to the here and now of their apartment to find Kaid shaking her.

"Who's dead?" he demanded.

"The younglings, Kaid. Raill and Lynn. They couldn't save them," she whispered, no less distraught at their deaths than anyone present in the IC room.

Kaid released her and leaned forward, wiping a tear from her face with his thumb. "I understand," he said gently, "I felt an echo of it, too, but you can't cry for the whole world, Carrie. They're gone now, at peace. Leave them there."

She blinked, looking at him. "What are you, Kaid?" she asked. "Your mind's always so still, too still."

"Someone who's seen a bit more of life than he likes at

times," he said with a faint grin, bending to pick up the fallen crockery and food.

"Let me help," she said.

"No, you rest. Leave it to me."

Kaid stayed with her throughout the evening, but there was still no sign of Kusac. According to the reports first from Meral, then T'Chebbi, he had requested a study room in the guild and was still there.

At last she gave up and retired for the night, curling up in the lonely hollow at the center of the large bed. She pressed her hands against her stomach feeling for any differences, but there were none yet. No roundness, no tiny fluttering movements such as she'd felt from Kikho. Mentally she'd felt nothing either, but then Jayed had said she wouldn't for at least another month. It seemed impossible, unreal, but her body was telling her she was pregnant even though her mind couldn't accept it.

Their child was an impossibility, Vanna had said. So had Kusac. Jayed and his wife Kikho told her she'd been blessed by the Gods. Whatever anyone said, it was there, growing inside her. Like her, it hadn't been consulted as to its wishes. Had they created a monster between them—something neither Terran nor Sholan—a hybrid? She shivered. Fear of what the child would be was uppermost in her mind. Shying away from the problem, she eventually retreated into an uneasy sleep.

Sometime later the door opened, rousing her briefly. Barely awake, she saw Kusac standing framed in the doorway by the light from the main room. He came in, stopping only to take some blankets from a chest at the foot of the bed before leaving again. It hardly registered in her mind before sleep claimed her again.

* * *

She was torn from sleep by an overwhelming sense of horror and panic surging through her. *Kusac!* She leaped out of bed and ran to the door. Wrenching it open, she looked wildly around the room trying to find him, fighting to stop his panic from engulfing her. She missed him at first, then running farther into the room she saw him lying in a tangle of blankets on the settee.

Although deeply asleep, he was twisting and turning restlessly, making low moaning noises.

She rushed over to him, taking hold of his hand to feel if he was feverish. At her touch he began to mutter incoherently, instinctively tightening his grip on her hand, claws pressing into her flesh. Prizing herself free, she put her hands on either side of his forehead, reaching into his mind with hers. He was locked deep into some nightmarish situation beyond her comprehension. Unable to understand it, she called to him, trying to draw him back to wakefulness.

At length he lay still and a shudder passed through him. As his eyes opened, he found himself looking up into her eyes—Sholan eyes. Linked as deeply as they were at that moment, he sensed her fears concerning the child she was carrying, and the knowledge that unlike Sholan females she couldn't control her fertility. He absorbed the facts, filing them away for later and raised his barrier again, this time to protect her from the remnants of his nightmare.

The dream had been a jumble of memories of the time immediately before they'd become lovers when they'd both come too near to death, and what he'd experienced while trying to help Raill and Lynn. Reaching up for her wrists, he pulled her hands away from his face before pushing her aside.

"Get dressed," he said, untangling himself from the blankets and getting to his feet.

Carrie sat there, her face taking on a stunned look. He knew he wasn't thinking straight right now, but the nightmare had only crystallized his fears. There was only one decision he could make, but he hated the feeling that once again circumstances were pressuring him. He'd taken too many safe options of late, trying do the right thing at the right time. Not any more. For good or ill he'd made his decision and now was the time to implement it. He wasn't waiting any longer.

He went over to the desk, switching on the comm and punching in a code. A sleepy Meral answered him.

"Meral, get my aircar round to the front entrance within five minutes," he ordered curtly, breaking the connection. He crossed the room toward the bedroom door, stopping briefly to look back at Carrie.

"I said get dressed," he repeated. "We're going out."

He was aware of her following him into the bedroom,

watching him as he searched in the wardrobe. "Wear these," he said, pulling out her rich olive-colored robe and an open over-robe of heavy black wool edged with the purple border of their guild.

Wordlessly, she took them from him and began dressing.

Pulling similar clothing out for himself, Kusac dressed hastily, then left the room, closing the door behind him. Kaid was standing in the center of the room, rubbing the sleep from his eyes.

"Meral said you were planning to leave, Liegen," he said.

"I need you to come with us. You've got about two minutes to get ready," said Kusac, going over to his desk again. He looked up briefly at Kaid. "You'll be pleased with tonight's work," he said dryly as he punched in another number.

Kaid looked at him quizzically before leaving.

Meral was waiting for them in the aircar when they arrived at the main entrance. Kusac handed Carrie up into the craft, jumping in behind her. Quietly, he gave directions to Meral before joining her in the back.

He could feel Carrie's unhappiness, but he couldn't cope with it yet. There was still too much hurt and anger inside. He'd spent the best part of the day reading Vanna's data, then going to ask her to clarify what he couldn't understand. After that, he'd tried to put his own feelings of fear and anger aside so he could think. It had proved virtually impossible.

Meral slowed the craft, taking it down to land in an enclosed garden lit by wildly flickering torches.

"Stay with the craft," Kusac said curtly to Meral as he got to his feet. Turning to Carrie, he held out his hand to her.

She rose, refusing the hand.

He shrugged and took hers anyway, tightening his grip as she tried to free herself. He led her out of the craft to where a tall Sholan wrapped in a blanket waited for them.

He searched Kusac's face before speaking. "Are you sure this is what you want to do?" he asked, letting go of the blanket to hug him.

Kusac returned the greeting. "Yes, Ghyan. I'm sorry to drag you from your bed at this time of night."

Ghyan nodded, pulling the blanket around himself again. "I understand," he said. He reached out to take Carrie by the hand. "One of these days I'll get the opportunity to meet you properly," he said, tucking her hand round his arm and turning to lead them into the building which loomed darkly behind them. He led them up the steps and through an archway into the interior of the Temple.

Kusac, walking behind with Kaid, hadn't missed the startled look as the Brother realized where they were.

Carrie stopped suddenly. At the far end of the hall, flanked by candles set into tall holders, a massive stone statue loomed. The figure was of a seated Warrior with his weapons laid in front of him at his feet. His face was peaceful, with the attitude of one who has laid aside his cares. In front of him a brazier glowed.

"This isn't the hall from your vision," Ghyan said reassuringly, drawing her onward with him. "All Vartra's temples are like this."

The four of them walked down between the pillars, Carrie's footsteps echoing in the silence. As they approached the statue, Kusac could see the small table to the right of the brazier. On it lay the traditional book, dagger, and bowl of incense cubes.

Ghyan stopped and turned, waiting for Kusac and Kaid. "You know where you are, don't you?" he asked Carrie.

She nodded, looking up at the statue. "The Temple of Vartra," she said. "I didn't realize it was so near the guild."

Kusac joined them. He wanted to let his barrier down, but his emotions were still too confused, too angry for her to share, especially now. "Carrie," he said, gripping her hand tightly for a moment. "Ghyan is a telepath. He'll need to probe your mind for a moment. Don't resist him." He gave her hand to Ghyan.

He waited impatiently until his friend had finished and turned back to him, a look of utter surprise on his face. "It's as you said," he confirmed. "She is indeed expecting your child. In this case my duty is clear. I'll perform the service with pleasure."

Kusac nodded. "Kaid Tallinu," he beckoned him forward, "will witness the life-bonding." He heard Carrie's gasp of shock and turned to her. "It's what you wanted, too, isn't it?" he demanded. "What you Challenged Rala for?"

"Yes, but . . ."

"Then let's proceed. We've a lot to do tonight. Remember, do what I do." He turned back to Ghyan.

"Wait, Kusac," his friend said. "There's a Challenge?"

"The Life-bond Challenge, yes."

"You know this bonding won't stop the Challenge, don't you?"

"I know, and I also know it may be enough to make Rala cancel the Challenge."

"I can approach Rala and ask her to cancel it," said Ghyan. "She comes to the Temple. She may listen."

"Would you?" asked Kusac, seeing the first ray of hope in the last few hours.

"If Carrie wishes," said Ghyan, looking at her.

She looked at Kusac, then Ghyan, and finally at Kaid. The latter nodded. "Ask," he said.

"Yes, please," she said quietly.

"Do you want to go ahead with the life-bonding now?" Ghyan asked her.

Kusac suddenly found a knot of fear within him as he realized she could be the one to change her mind, not him.

Carrie hesitated, then in the stillness of her own thoughts she heard another mind, a quiet mental voice. *Say yes.*

"Yes," she said, with the faintest of smiles.

Kusac realized he'd started to breathe again.

Ghyan nodded. "In that case, I'll perform the ceremony." Turning to Kusac, he asked, "Have you got the bracelets?"

Kusac took a package from his robe, handing it to him.

Ghyan unwrapped them, laying the bronze bracelets on the table by the book. "Given the hour, and the informality of our gathering, I'm sure we'd all prefer a short ceremony," he said with a smile, holding out his hands to them both.

"Give him your right hand," said Kusac, putting his in Ghyan's right palm.

Carrie put hers in Ghyan's left hand, palm up like Kusac's.

"Do you both want to be made one, of one blood?" Ghyan asked them.

"Yes," said Kusac, looking at Carrie, his ear tips flicking gently. Doubt concerning the wisdom of getting married now had vanished when he'd realized that she might have refused him.

"Yes," she said.

Kaid took up the knife. Before she had time to react, he'd made a small cut first in her palm, then Kusac's. Ghyan pressed their hands together, letting their mingled blood drip down into the bowl of incense.

"Then you are one," he said, holding their palms together for a moment or two before releasing them.

His palm still smarting, Kusac picked up some of the incense and threw it into the brazier, indicating that Carrie should do the same. As she did, the coals blazed brightly, throwing up a cloud of aromatic smoke.

"As an outward sign of your life-bond, here are your bracelets. Wear them with the blessing of Vartra," said Ghyan, picking up the bracelets and holding them out toward Kusac.

Checking them, Kusac picked one of them up and taking Carrie's right hand in his, he slipped the bracelet on her wrist and pressed it closed until it was a snug fit.

Ghyan turned to Carrie. Hesitantly, Carrie reached for the other bracelet, looking to Kusac for confirmation.

Impassively, he nodded, holding out his hand to her.

She placed the bracelet on his wrist, trying to pinch it closed as he had done.

With a flick of his ears and a wry smile, he did it for her.

"May Vartra grant you peace and happiness," Ghyan said, pulling his blanket back round himself again. "I won't ask for the gift of fertility since He's obviously given you that," he said with a smile. "Now if you and your mate would sign the book, the legalities are over."

Kusac stepped forward and taking up the stylus, scrawled his name with a flourish. He handed it over to Carrie.

She looked searchingly at his face, still unable to read anything of his emotions. Moving toward the table, she bent forward and added her slightly shaky signature under his.

Ghyan took the stylus from her, handing it to Kaid. "We need your signature as witness."

"Certainly," said Kaid as he signed the book.

"Thank you," Kusac said to Ghyan, relief sweeping over him.

"I'm only glad that in the end I was able to help," his friend said. "Let's hope this is the last of your problems. I'll talk to Rala for you. I assume your parents don't yet know."

"That's what I've got to see to next," said Kusac. "We must go. My thanks again."

"Don't leave it so long the next time you come to see me," said Ghyan. "But I will insist on a hug from Carrie." He stepped forward, wrapping his arms around her and laying his cheek alongside hers.

His coldness won't last. He wanted this bonding to you more than anything. Just have faith in him. He released her, smiling.

"Remember, both of you, the God has blessed you with this child. Trust in Him and all will be well."

"The Gods' help always costs," said Carrie quietly. "They give you nothing for free."

"Good-bye," said Kusac. "I'll be in touch soon."

"See that you are," his friend said.

Meral took off, heading for the Valsgarth Estate this time. The gray light of dawn was touching the horizon as they landed. Lights began to go on as they got out of the aircar. Kusac led Carrie toward the front entrance, ordering the other two to stay on board.

His face was grim as he pushed the door open and strode into the center courtyard, pulling Carrie with him. The argument with his father some four days previously still rankled. Now he needed a confrontation to get it out of his system.

The night duty attendant hurried forward but was waved back by Kusac. "This doesn't concern you. Return to your post," he said, stopping by the fountain.

"Father!" he yelled at the top of his voice. "I want to see you now!"

His father hurried to the balcony, still trying to put his arms into the sleeves of his over-robe.

"Kusac, have you lost your wits?" he demanded angrily. "It's the middle of the night!"

His mother joined him. "Kusac, what's wrong?"

"I want to speak to you both," he said, lowering his voice slightly. "Come down to the study. You, too, Taizia," he added, seeing his sister come running.

"What's this all about?" said his father when they were gathered in the study. "Couldn't you have waited till morning?"

"No, I couldn't," said Kusac, pulling Carrie out from behind him where she was trying to hide. Her face was chalk white. Despite his block, Kusac could feel her fear and knew that his family could, too. *All to the good,* he thought. *Let them realize what she's suffered since she found out about the betrothal.*

"You wanted me to life-bond and get legitimate heirs on my mate. Well, here she is, as of an hour ago." He pushed her forward, holding up their arms so both their bracelets were visible. "As for heirs, she's carrying your first grandchild now."

He paused, enjoying the shocked silence from his father as a recompense for his refusal to cancel the marriage contract with Rala.

"Our Link has changed us to the point where we're infertile with our own kind. The only heirs you'll ever have from me will be Carrie's children, too."

Feeling Carrie's mind begin to swirl, he grasped her around the waist with both hands. "Don't you dare faint on me," he growled in her ear, giving it a sharp nip with his teeth.

She gasped at the sudden pain and straightened up again.

"Kusac," said his father, sitting down in the nearest chair. "This just isn't possible."

Kusac's anger abruptly evaporated and he put a hand into his pocket, bringing out the cube. "Read this for yourself. All Vanna's tests, kept secret even from us, are there. Check Carrie, you'll see I'm not lying," he said tiredly, throwing the cube at his father.

Konis made no effort to catch it and it fell to the floor at his feet. He shook his head. "I don't need to check," he said. "I believe you."

"Have the data as a present anyway. You'll need it. There's going to be more of us. You've got a new species on your hands, Father. I hope you know what to do with it," he said.

He looked at his mother and Taizia. "An hour, maybe two, and the Challenge would have been unnecessary. Why couldn't you have waited?" Strangely he wasn't angry with them, only confused as to why they had rushed everything.

His mother came forward to put an arm around Carrie. "You were so determined to collide head-on with your father and Rala that you left us little choice. You're right, the Challenge is our responsibility," she said, "but because of your actions you bear as much responsibility for it as we do. Carrie is the innocent one in this tangle, so why are you hurting her? This isn't like you, Kusac." She frowned at him, beginning to turn away.

"We can argue this later if you're so minded. I'm taking your mate to the kitchen. She's had a bigger shock than any of us over the last few days and right now she needs something to eat, then rest, not to mention a small dressing on her palm." With that, she ushered Carrie out of the room.

Kusac sat down in the nearest chair, suddenly feeling drained. "That Challenge has got to be stopped, Father," he said tiredly. "I'm getting images of it going wrong, but they're so vague I can't pinpoint a precise cause."

His father stirred, bending to pick up the cube. "Precognition? A Terran ability," he said thoughtfully, turning the cube over in his hands.

"I don't care what you call it," Kusac snapped, "I just keep feeling a sense of danger. Whatever it is, I don't want it to happen!"

"With the genetic changes, all the reasons for your bonding to Rala are gone," said his father. "Not just that, you're already life-bonded," he said dryly. "Given those two facts, I can't see Rala's family objecting to my officially breaking the contract. The Challenge is another thing," he sighed. "In my position as judge, unless Rala agrees to canceling it, I can't do anything. Only the Temple can order her to drop it since it's an En'Shalla Challenge. I have a feeling that Rala will not cooperate."

"Just try, that's all I ask," Kusac said. "There are three lives at stake now. Ghyan has said he'll speak to her. Apparently, she's been going to the Temple during her stay at Valsgarth."

"In that case, he might be able to sway her. I can't understand why Carrie didn't tell you before now that she was pregnant," said his father. "Or why she issued the Challenge, knowing she was putting the child at risk too."

"Did she know?" asked Taizia. "We've been fairly close and she didn't mention it to me. Mother and I would never have suggested the Challenge if we'd known. As you've said, there would have been no need for it."

"I don't understand it either," muttered Kusac, rubbing eyes that felt like they were full of sand. "I picked up something from her about having no control over when she becomes pregnant, but I don't know." He shook his head and looked over at his father. "I was sure she couldn't be mine at first, but she is."

"An impossible pregnancy. This is where your Link with her has been leading all along. How do you feel about this child?"

"She's ours," Kusac said fiercely. "I want her to live."

"You two have given us a pretty problem to sort out," his father said with a sigh. "The Terrans will have to be told, including her father. What his reaction will be, I shudder to think."

"He doesn't concern us," said Kusac. "He's far enough away not to be our problem; he's yours, and you're welcome to him. We've got enough to do just trying to live our own life. The main problem at the moment is stopping the Challenge."

"We can do nothing about it until morning. I suggest you go to bed and get some rest. Are your people still out in the aircar?"

Kusac nodded.

"Then tell them to turn in for what's left of the night. They can use the same rooms they did before. Now go and collect your mate and let's all get some sleep."

Taizia jumped to her feet. "I'll go and tell them," she said, heading off.

Kusac caught his father's thought and gave a little smile. "She'll be all right with Meral," he said. "He's a good male, and at least you know she'll be safe with a Warrior."

Kusac collected Carrie from his mother and took her upstairs, still keeping the block up. He couldn't face the prospect of opening their Link again until he'd come to terms with all his own conflicting emotions. What should have been a time of wonder and joy for them was being marred by the specter of the Challenge, and that still angered him.

He left her at the bedroom door, unable and unwilling to explain. "I'll see you in the morning," he said, closing the door behind her.

Taizia caught up with her mother on the stairs.

"I should have realized that she was pregnant," said Rhyasha. "It was staring me in the face."

"Who'd have believed it was possible?" said Taizia. "We ignored all the signals because she's a Keissian, not a Sholan. We couldn't have known, Mother." She stopped, reaching out to catch hold of her.

"Their cub, what will she look like, can you tell yet? Will she be one of us or a human? The Gods grant she isn't malformed, a grotesque creature that has no chance of survival!"

Rhyasha's ears flicked backward in distress. This was no time to hide her feelings from her daughter.

"It's too early to tell anything but her sex. Carrie's not yet halfway through her pregnancy. In a week or two I'll be able to sense their cub properly. Even though they can breed with each other, so much could go wrong because they're from different species! Just pray your brother keeps his head if the child doesn't survive to be carried full term, or if she has to be terminated because she's nonviable. I can't begin to guess how Carrie would react to either of those situations! One of us would remain clearheaded enough to make the right decisions, but Carrie?" She shook her head, ears flattening backward.

"How do humans relate to their cubs?" Rhyasha continued. "Are their males as possessive and foolish over their pregnant mates as ours? We don't know enough about them as people!" She clenched her hands in frustration, claws pricking her palms.

"We have Carrie here with us," said Taizia. "There will be other humans soon. We can learn! At least we know what knowledge we lack. Gods! If only I'd never suggested that damned Challenge! There was no need for it."

"There's no point in self-recrimination, Taizia. As you've just told me, there was no way we could have known she was pregnant. The trouble now is we don't have the time to learn what we need to know. We need to know it now if we're to help them."

"Perhaps we're looking into too dark a cave," said Taizia, giving her mother a hug. "Everything may go wonderfully well for them."

Rhyasha took a deep breath, concentrating on pulling her ears upright again. There was nothing to gain from letting herself get so agitated now. "Perhaps you're right," she said, forcing a smile for her daughter's benefit. "Let's take things as they come rather than plan for a disaster that may never happen. You go and see your Warrior," she urged, gently pushing Taizia away. "I'm fine."

"Mother!"

Rhyasha gave a low chuckle. "I didn't pry," she said. "Your interest in him hasn't been exactly subtle."

Chapter 17

Having informed the Protectorate of their location, Kaid initiated the securing of the perimeter of the Valsgarth Estate. No one, not even a jegget, could get into the grounds without security being aware of it. That done, he settled down on the balcony outside Kusac's and Carrie's suite.

Kaid knew what neither Kusac nor the rest of his family had yet realized, namely that each one of them was at risk as a potential hostage or worse. The missing dissident from the *Khalossa* had no scruples about using whoever he could to get close enough to Carrie or Kusac to kill them. As far as Kaid was concerned, he'd rather have them all safe under one roof.

Left on her own again, Carrie began to pace round the room. She felt trapped, caged by the very life she had left Keiss to escape. Though her cage was one of flesh and blood, no bars could have been stronger. With a sharp pang she envied Kusac his ability to run free as the wind across the estate. That was what she needed, to run and run until she collapsed from exhaustion, too tired to think. With an effort she pushed these thoughts and memories aside as she felt her own panic beginning to build inside her mind.

Her footsteps took her to the exterior balcony, and as she looked across the grounds to the wooded land, T'Chebbi stepped out of the shadows. No escape that way either. No matter how grand the jail, unless one wanted to be there, it was still a prison.

With a shiver, she wrapped her arms tightly across her chest and returned to the bedroom, this time noticing that a short robe had been left on the bed for her. Rhyasha's doing.

Picking it up, she ran the silky fabric through her hands remembering Rhyasha's reaction to Kusac's news. Strangely, his mother had been delighted. In fact, everyone who knew had been—except for Kusac and his father who had just been shocked. No one had thought to ask her how she felt, which was just as well, because she couldn't have answered them.

She frowned, remembering Kusac's anger. Well, she was furious with him. Anger didn't begin to describe how she felt, and as soon as she got the chance, he'd find that out in no uncertain terms. Rage burned so brightly that it dimmed the uncertainty and fears, making it impossible for her to think. Tonight's events hadn't changed anything, Kusac's behavior proved that. Why else would he still want to sleep apart from her?

She felt adrift, at the mercy of whichever wind happened to be blowing. The Sholans had another simile for it. Didn't they call it being tempered on the anvil of the Gods? She wished they'd use an ordinary hammer rather than one that felt like a meat tenderizer. She didn't know how much more bruising she could take. With a sigh, she began to undress.

Unable to sleep because of the onset of a throbbing headache, she lay in the darkness fretting: fretting at the heat, the flickering images that flashed through her mind, Kusac's intractability, and the beginnings of the siren call of their Link.

Kusac knew she was still awake. For the last hour and a half he'd tried to sleep but without success. Her proximity was maddening him, particularly since he was the one who'd chosen to sleep apart from her in the lounge. He wanted to be with her, especially now he'd gotten used to the reality of her pregnancy. His whole biological system as a male was geared toward finding the right mate, then helping rear the cubs they made between them. Being a telepath only strengthened this need. The family—his family—was all-important.

As well as that, the physical needs of their Link were making themselves felt in ways it was nigh on impossible to ignore. Coming to a decision, he rose and went to the bedroom.

Hypersensitive, she heard the door opening and sat up. Kusac stood there. With sardonic humor she realized he was having trouble maintaining his barrier against her. She knew why he was here, and for now he was dependent on her.

* * *

With a sinuous grace he came across the room, almost stalking her because of his awareness that she was watching his every move. He stopped by the bed and sat down beside her, ears flicking sideways and back, tail gently swaying. In the semidarkness, his eyes glittered as he reached out for her.

"I need you," he said, aware as he spoke that his voice sounded harsher than he had intended. Almost instantly he released her, shaken by the strength of the anger she was directing toward him.

"No," she said, pulling the covers firmly round herself. "If you want to keep yourself apart, then fine, do so—but don't expect to walk in here and make demands of me without a word of apology!"

"Carrie, you know . . ." he began.

"I know nothing, Kusac!" she said, interrupting him. "You've hardly spoken to me since we found out I was pregnant! You know damned well that nothing is reaching me because you've blocked your mind off. What gives you the right to assume you can walk in here and take me because of our Link? You've taken damned near all of me as it is. Just how much more do you want?"

He was silent for a moment, understanding for the first time that his actions could have completely alienated her. Through the remains of his barrier all he could sense was her anger, none of the gentler emotions he had come to associate with her in the past months. Sudden fear gripped him in the pit of his stomach again as he realized that his behavior in the last few days would have driven many a Sholan female away from him let alone her, a human, Clanless, and pregnant by her alien lover.

"You know what I feel for you," he said, ears flicking backward in acute distress as he touched her bracelet with his forefinger.

"Not any more," she countered, pulling away from him. "For all I know, Rala could have been right. Why did you marry me anyway? If it's going to change what we feel for each other, then you can have this damned thing back!" She tugged futilely at her bracelet, unable to either open it or slip it off her wrist.

Kusac's hand closed over hers. "Don't," he said quietly, raising his eyes to hers and trying not to flinch from the hurt and anger that he saw there. "Forget Rala and what she said. I'm sorry for all the pain I've caused you, I should have told you about the betrothal from the first."

"So why didn't you?" she demanded, keeping her hand still.

"I was trying to find an honorable solution, you know that," he said. "One that didn't make us outcasts on Shola. If you'd only waited another day, the Challenge would have been unnecessary. As soon as it was known you carried our child, I'd have been free."

"And just how was I supposed to know that?" She tried again to pull her hand free of his.

"How was I to realize you'd be foolish enough to issue a Challenge?" he demanded, tightening his grip on her till he felt his claws begin to extend. "Why didn't you tell me when you suspected you were pregnant?"

"Because I thought it was impossible! Even you refused to believe Vanna at first!"

His ears flicked dismissively. "You were still willing to risk our lives on the outcome of a combat!"

"What are you really angry about?" she demanded. "The Challenge or the baby? You don't want this child, do you?"

Kusac growled, eyes flashing angrily as he grasped her firmly by the upper arms. "Don't even think of getting rid of her," he snarled, shaking her till she fell backward, her weight pulling him down, too. "She's already as precious to me as you are!"

"How dare you accuse me of that!" She struggled against him, trying to push him away. "You were the one who said she should never have been conceived, not me!"

As he tried to hold her still, Kusac felt the sudden flare of raw sensuality triggered by their physical contact. The remaining shreds of his barrier disintegrated abruptly as he felt it course through her, too, bringing them back into full rapport. The reasons for his anger suddenly dissipated as he sensed for himself the sheer terror she was still feeling over the tiny scrap of life they'd created between them. All her anger and sense of betrayal surged through his mind, leaving him in no doubt as to how badly he'd behaved. He realized now that nothing had ever mattered but her and their cub.

At the same time his body had responded instantly to the flood of sensations that had spread rapidly through them both—there was nothing subtle about the biological demands of their Link. He needed to show her that he loved her the only way he, as a male Sholan telepath, knew how.

Mentally he tried to hold back the Link's compulsion while at the same time projecting images of their lovemaking to come—a task made doubly difficult by the fact she was still struggling against him. He transferred his grip, pinning both her hands in one of his, his superior strength more than a match for hers.

Lowering his face to hers, he began to lick round her neck and ears.

"Kusac! Don't!" she said angrily. "This is unfair!"

He ignored her protests and continued his gentle seduction, easing the covers away from her till his hand closed gently over one breast. His mind—hers as well now—was filled with his wonder and joy over the cub that she carried and the fact that her body now truly reflected her status as a mother—feelings he knew she'd caught glimpses of before but he'd never allowed her to experience till now. Beneath him, her movements changed, slowing till she no longer tried to twist away from him.

We've made a cub, Carrie, he sent, his mouth seeking hers as his hand moved to touch her belly. *Ours! That was all I regretted when we became Leskas, but the Gods have given us even that!*

The hurt and fear that had dominated her mind began to dissolve as she experienced the shock and disbelief he'd felt at the news, and his fears for the safety of her and their child. The anger that his earlier reactions had caused began to dissipate.

You're pleased? she sent, but no answer was necessary as he finally lost control of the compulsion and their minds synchromeshed.

* * *

Morning came and with it Garras' departure. Having seen him off, Vanna headed thoughtfully to her office. She didn't regret her commitment to him, quite the opposite in fact. She knew that what she needed now was someone with whom she could have a dependable relationship. Just those few years older than her, Garras was that person, and he had no illusions about being the primary focus in her life. Conversely, he also knew she would never measure him against any other male.

She sighed as she opened the door to her office. Garras was right about Kusac; she should have spoken sooner, but then Mito had been in the way. Now, because she cared for Carrie as well, it was unlikely she'd ever feel easy about making an approach.

Settling herself in front of her comm, she set about contacting Chagda Point to request that they patch her through to Keiss via the *Khalossa*. As she waited, she couldn't help feeling there was a certain inevitability about the way their lives were so tightly bound together.

Half an hour later, after being passed from department to department as each one claimed they couldn't authorize the call, she finally cut the connection and contacted Alien Relations, asking for Clan Leader Aldatan. Within ten minutes of telling Rhyasha what she wanted, she had the suitably chastened head of communications on the space station calling her to tell her that the Sholan HQ on Keiss was waiting to accept her call.

Her efforts were frustrated once again. Dr. Reynolds wasn't at Seaport. They thought he was in Valleytown but couldn't confirm it as they had no comm link to the Terran physician. A scouter would be immediately dispatched, and they would call her back when they had the Keissian in Seaport.

With a sigh, Vanna called the medical facility's main office, informing them of the call she was expecting and requesting that they page her when it came in. That done, she called up all the files Medical had on Sholan obstetrics. There hadn't been much call for that branch of medicine on the *Khalossa* as those females on board who chose to become pregnant usually requested down-time on their home world first.

She then called up the files on Terran physiology that she and her team had compiled on board the *Khalossa*. It gave her some, but not all the information she wanted. She needed to speak to Jack Reynolds. In frustration, she checked the time, finding to her surprise that if she wanted second meal, she would have to leave for the mess now. Closing up her office, she headed down to the basement.

In their wisdom the Telepath Guild had decided that until the Terran integration program was complete, the most appropriate place for their visitors to eat was in the hospital mess. As Vanna joined the queue at the counter, she noticed one or two small groups of Terrans sitting eating. Despite the fact it was nearing the end of the meal time, the hall was crowded but there were a couple of empty tables over in the far corner near the elevator.

As she waited for her choice to be served, she glanced around again, looking to see if there was anyone she knew. As she did, a figure passing in front of her caught her eye. The Terran opened his mouth in a careful smile and nodded before joining the end of the queue.

She frowned, trying to place him. Obviously he knew her, but she couldn't remember him. Then her attention was claimed by the server and she forgot about him.

While she ate, she used her comp pad to review the notes she'd made so far. It came as something of a surprise to find herself being suddenly addressed in Terran.

"Do you mind if I join you?"

Startled, she looked up to see the male who had smiled at her from the queue. "Please do," she said, switching off her comp.

"Thank you," he said, sliding into the seat opposite. "Aren't you the doctor who's considered to be the expert on Terrans? I remember you from the other day. I'm Brynne Stevens."

Vanna's frown deepened. An errant memory plucked at her mind. So much had happened in the last few days. He did look familiar, though.

"We gave each other a static shock, remember? Your friends took you off to sit down. One of them was a Terran girl," he said, picking up his fork and spearing a chunk of meat from his plate.

Vanna's frown cleared. "I remember," she said. "That was Carrie and Kusac."

"The first mixed Leska pair."

"That's right. You'd been asking about them."

"Have you found out yet what caused their Link?"

Vanna shook her head. "No idea. I don't think any one guild can answer that question. If we do find out, it won't be due to us at Medical alone."

"Any idea of how common these Links are likely to be?"

"Again, I've no idea. There have been two in the five or six months since we first contacted your people."

Brynne's empty fork paused in midair. "Then any one of us could suddenly find himself with an alien Leska?"

Vanna's eyeridges rose as she regarded him. "So far it has been female Terran telepaths who've acquired Sholan Leskas, not male Terrans. I should think you've nothing to worry about."

"I didn't mean it quite like that," said Brynne, having the grace to look embarrassed.

"I'm sure you didn't," she murmured, concentrating on her own meal.

Brynne broke the silence that followed. "Look, I haven't exactly made a good impression, have I? It's just that having some medical knowledge myself, I'm naturally interested in these Links. Can we start again?" He held out his hand toward her.

Vanna hesitated, remembering the last time she'd touched him. "We don't shake hands."

"So what do you do?" he asked.

"We touch palms," she admitted.

"Then let's do that as a sign of good faith," he said, turning his hand over so his palm was extended toward her.

At her side, Vanna's pager began emitting an insistent tone. "I've got to go," she said, acknowledging the signal before grabbing her comp in one hand and getting to her feet.

"No hard feelings?" Brynne insisted as he rose, too.

"None," said Vanna distractedly. She turned too sharply, stumbling as she became entangled in her chair.

"Careful," he warned, reaching out to catch her.

With a small cry of distress, Vanna wrenched herself free. Eyes wide, she backed away from him. "Don't touch me!" she hissed in a low voice before whirling round and running for the stairs, aware as she did that she'd attracted the attention of nearly everyone in the mess.

* * *

"I see you made it in time for third meal," said Taizia, looking up from her book as Kusac and Carrie came into the lounge.

"Cheek," said Kusac, cuffing her gently as he passed.

"Let me see your bracelets," she demanded, reaching out to grab his wrist. "Mother says they're beautiful. When did you get them made?"

Kusac stopped, ears flicking ruefully at Carrie. "I ordered

them the same day that Carrie ordered my torc," he said, letting his sister turn his wrist this way and that.

She let him go and reached for Carrie's hand, examining her bracelet "Mother was right," she said, "they are beautiful. Why has Carrie's got you hunting on it when yours is only portraits of you both?"

Kusac grinned at Carrie over Taizia's head. "A private joke," he said. "Not for your ears."

"Spoilsport," she said, letting Carrie have her hand back. "Don't worry, I'll worm it out of her before long."

"No, you won't," Carrie said, moving away to sit on one of the adjacent chairs.

"Do you know where Father is?" Kusac asked his sister. "In the shrine."

That startled him. "What's he doing there?"

Taizia shrugged. "He's been there most of the day. I thought it wiser not to disturb him; so did Mother."

"I think I should join him," he said, heading out of the room.

"The shrine?" asked Carrie. "Kusac mentioned the other day that the weapons were from there."

"It's the household's private room of prayer to Vartra," Taizia said. "The ashes of our ancestors sleep there. If you want to see it, I'll take you later."

"Exactly who is Vartra? When I check through my inherited memories of him, I find it almost impossible to work out what he was supposed to be the God of."

"Essentially He's a Warrior God who fights for peace when the need arises. He's the father figure of all our Gods," Taizia replied, putting her book down. "Some of the older stories credit him with saving our people from the Cataclysm."

"Kusac's mentioned that before. What actually happened?"

Taizia's ears flicked briefly and her eye ridges met in concentration. "Well, according to the stories, there was a global war—Clan fighting Clan—until everything was destroyed and few survivors remained. Vartra called those that were left together and ordered them to set up the guilds and rebuild Shola. Some even tell of him leading bands of Warriors against the lawless ones who tried to prey on the newly formed guild towns. In other versions, the people turned on the telepaths, blaming them for starting the war, and Vartra set up the Warrior Guild to protect them. The stories are supported by the fact that all over our world are the remains of devastated towns."

"You must have some fascinating treasures from those days in your ..." She searched for an appropriate Sholan word but couldn't find one. "... museums."

"Museums?" Taizia repeated the unfamiliar Terran word carefully.

"Where you display objects from your past so people now can enjoy seeing them," said Carrie.

"Why would we want to look at things from the past? Anyway, our guild discourages it."

Carrie could feel Taizia's genuine bafflement. "Why should your guild forbid it? Aren't you interested in how your ancestors lived?"

"Why should we be interested? Our guild teaches us that life now is far superior to anything we could have achieved then."

"But I've seen old vases and ornaments not only here but at the guild!"

"Every family has its share of relics kept by our ancestors," said Taizia. "They get bought and sold like anything else unless someone in the family really likes them."

"Don't you have any records of your past?" Carrie was utterly bewildered. This was a side to Sholan culture she hadn't realized existed till now. How could they be so incurious about their race's history?

"Of course we do! The guilds record our achievements and most families keep their own archives, but what we achieve in our own lifetimes is far more important."

"Aren't you at all curious about how they lived just after the Cataclysm? Or how the towns were destroyed?"

"Not me," said Taizia firmly, shaking her head. "There's enough to be done today without worrying about our past. The stories tell us all we need to know about our ancestors and Gods."

Carrie realized that Taizia had said all she was prepared to on the subject of the Cataclysm.

"Have you've got a lot of Gods besides Vartra?" she asked, returning to the original conversation.

"More than you could count! Most people aren't bothered one way or another, religion being a personal matter, with the priesthood to help when needed, but every now and then there's a renewed interest in a more formal belief system. Vartra is the most enduring of the Gods."

"Ghyan, the male who married us last night, is a telepath, yet he's also a priest in the Temple."

"You had a temple wedding?" Taizia grinned. "All the way along the trail Kusac's done what the Clan laws demand. No one will be able to fault your bonding on any grounds! Mother will be delighted."

"Excuse me?"

"In the Clan families it isn't enough to be life-bonded, you have to have observed all the proprieties, like the exchange of torcs, having an acceptable escort to protect your honor if you're female, and then the temple wedding."

"I thought you could pair with anyone you wanted," said Carrie. "Why should escorts be so important because you're betrothed?"

"The succession, of course. The families need to know your children belong to your husband. Even though with you two there could be no doubt now, unless the rules had been followed, then the Council could call your life-bonding into question and have it annulled. Kusac has made sure that accusation can't be leveled against you."

"Ah," said Carrie, digesting this for a moment. "And Ghyan?"

"He's a friend of Kusac's from way back. He's head of our temple at present. He organizes the work of the lay brothers and conducts any services that need to be carried out."

"I thought that the Brothers were those from Kaid's guild."

Taizia looked distinctly uncomfortable. "That's the Brotherhood of Vartra. They're a sub-sect of the Warrior Guild, and they're entirely different from the lay brothers."

"I see," Carrie said slowly, confused over the subtle differences. She gave up trying to understand. Kusac or Kaid would be able to explain it to her. "Why have a telepath in charge?"

"Don't you know nontelepaths believe we can see into people's souls?" Taizia said, adopting a mock serious voice. "Actually, they're not so far wrong, but there aren't very many of us telepaths, so we're spread thinly among the various guilds that need us, which means only one for the main temple in each city."

"Why bother with a shrine in the house if you've got temples, and why the special bond between the Warrior and the Telepath Guilds?"

"You're full of questions today," Taizia said. "As I've already told you, the shrine is where we place the ashes of our family for Vartra to look after. It's also believed by some that we can access the telepathic energy from our forefathers, but I've never come across anyone who can, or who knew anyone who could. As for the relationship between Warriors and telepaths, since we're physically more at risk because of our talent, the Warriors protect us. Ghyan believes that at one time telepaths could fight and that Vartra was a real person who was both a Warrior and telepath, but his views are considered eccentric." She uncurled herself and got to her feet.

"Now enough of the questions," she said. "I'm starving. How about we go and raid the kitchen? Third meal won't be served until Father and Kusac come out of the shrine and that might be some time. Besides, it's been Mother's baking day, so there's bound to be something nice to eat."

Carrie grinned. "Brilliant idea," she said.

* * *

The shrine was a small building set onto the exterior of the main house with its entrance in the corridor outside the lounge. It was kept well tended, but unless there was a funeral or someone wished for the God's intervention, rarely were candles lit and incense burned.

Kusac smelled the incense as soon as he stepped into the corridor. Walking down to the doorway, he pushed the door open. His father was sitting on a bench at the back of the room. Between them stood the carved stone altar. The single candle set in front of the incense burner flared briefly.

His father opened his eyes, ears flicking in acknowledgment of his son's presence. "I knew you'd find me here," he said tiredly.

"You look as if you've been awake all night, Father," said Kusac, remaining by the door.

"I should have had more faith in you," Konis sighed, leaning back against the wall. "I saw only the needs of the Sixteen Clans and conveniently assumed you were exaggerating the depth of your bond to Carrie when it threatened to upset my carefully laid plans. I forgot you were never one to exaggerate, quite the opposite. No, let me finish," he said, knowing his son was about to speak.

"The facts were all there for me to see had I but used half the application I tried to bring to bear on you over that damned marriage. I knew you loved Carrie, but not the depth of that love."

Konis raised his head and looked Kusac straight in the eyes. "I know about the sacrifice you were prepared to make for her on the *Khalossa*. That had been kept from me until you gave me Vanna's files."

Kusac looked away. "I didn't read the early stuff," he murmured.

"Hindsight is a wonderful thing. It lets you know just how much of a fool you've been. While we tried to ease Raill's and Lynn's deaths, I was briefly included in your Link with Carrie. Its intensity shocked me. For what it's worth, Kusac, I'm sorry. Had I realized before then what exists between you, I would have broken the contract when you first asked."

"You did what you thought was right, Father."

"Thank you for having the forbearance not to say 'I tried to tell you,' " Konis said with a strained look on his face. "Come and sit with me."

He waited until Kusac had joined him. "I like Carrie, you know. Despite the obvious physical differences, she's very like us. She's brought you out of your shell and taught you what it means to be an adult male. I've a feeling you'll get your wish. You'll never find life dull again."

Kusac grinned. "Not with Carrie."

His father was silent for a minute. "I contacted Rala's family," he said. "The contract has been dissolved. I had to mention the genetic changes, but that will be common knowledge before long anyway."

"I can live with that," said Kusac.

"Rala was present during the discussion, as was her right, but when I mentioned dropping the Challenge she went into a rage. She claimed she'd been insulted by both of you and refused to allow it to be nullified even though now she'd gain nothing by winning."

"So there's no way out."

"I'm afraid not," said his father. "I tried every argument I could think of to persuade her to change her mind. Then,

I regret, I made a tactical error. I told her Carrie was pregnant."

"Ah," said Kusac, ears flicking backward along his skull.

"I'm afraid I've made the situation worse. I explained to her father the implications of the pregnancy, and the danger to Carrie if she fights. He said he would try to induce Rala to drop the Challenge but that he didn't hold out any hope. She's of a legal age to make her own decisions."

Kusac felt a cold shiver run down his spine as his premonition of danger suddenly returned.

"What is it?" said his father sharply, sitting up and looking at his son.

"I don't know," said Kusac helplessly. "Something and nothing. I'm just terribly afraid for her, and she mustn't know that."

"She'll be fine," Konis said reassuringly, reaching out to touch his son affectionately. "If we can't stop the Challenge, we'll bring Vanna and anything she needs over here. Any male whose mate was facing her first Challenge would be worried, whether or not she was pregnant. I'm sure what you're experiencing is just your obviously natural concern for her."

"You're probably right," said Kusac, getting to his feet. "I'm sorry that the council dropped me as a contender for the Clans' Leadership, but I honestly never wanted it. When this is over, I intend to step down as heir in Taizia's favor, presuming I'm still . . ."

"You'll all be fine," interrupted his father. "Warning or no warning, I'm sure of it. As to the succession, your mother has decided that matters remain as they are save that one of Taizia's children, when she marries, will be appointed your heir."

Konis got stiffly to his feet. "Come, let's leave. I've been here long enough. I wonder if there's any way Carrie could claim diplomatic immunity," he said. "I think now would be a good time to contact her father. You can come with me."

Before they left, Kusac lit a candle and placed it on the altar next to his father's. Carrie's words at the temple continued to echo in his mind. The Gods' help always costs. He shivered, turning to leave as quickly as possible.

* * *

"There's the settlement," said Nikuu, slowing down the aircar. "Are you still picking them up?"

"Yes, but hurry." Khalmi's voice was taut with agony that was not his own. "I don't know how they've managed to stay conscious."

"We're nearly there," she said, risking a sideways glance at him. Her Leska's face was creased with the pain. "Are you and Zsyzoi ready?" she asked Naira. "We'll probably need to use force to get them away from their Clan. We have in the past."

"We're ready," said Naira, glancing over to his partner. Zsyzoi had just finished checking her battery packs once again. Last assignment she'd been given a dud and hadn't realized it until almost too late. Since then she triple-checked everything.

They skimmed over the tops of the outlying adobe houses until the village center was ahead of them. Nikuu slowed the craft till it hovered a few meters above the ground, then brought it down to land.

As the dust settled, they saw the villagers approaching them. Nikuu released the canopy, letting it slide back. The hot, arid air of the desert hit them like a physical blow, sucking the moisture out of their lungs almost immediately.

The two Warriors got out first, rifles ready as they stood on either side of the hatch. Nikuu climbed out and waited for Khalmi to join her.

"We've come for the new Leskas," she said, looking round the sea of tan-robed people, their heads covered by matching elaborately wound lengths of cloth. "Where are they?"

A commotion at the rear of the crowd drew Khalmi's attention. *Over there,* he sent. *Their priest is coming. He's angry.*

The crowd parted rapidly as they realized their priest was trying to come to the front. As a path opened up, Nikuu saw a Sholan of middle years, probably about seventy, striding toward them dressed from head to toe in flowing white robes.

He's new. Don't recognize him, she sent to Khalmi.

"What do you want with my people?" the priest demanded, coming to a stop in front of them.

"We're here to collect the new Leska pair," she said. She

felt an immediate wave of fear from the villagers as their priest turned his head toward her and raised his arm.

Naira stepped in front of her in time to ward off the blow with his forearm.

"You dare to stop me striking an unbeliever?" the priest thundered, turning on the Warrior. "No female should dare to speak unless she's given leave to do so by her mate!"

"No one is allowed to strike a telepath," said Naira, taking up a defensive position. "If you attempt to harm her again, I'll take you into custody. We've come here to collect the two new Leskas, nothing more. Bring them to us and we'll be gone."

"There are no new Leskas in this village."

"Over there," said Khalmi, pointing down the still-clear pathway through which the priest had approached. "That house there." He started walking toward it followed by Zsyzoi.

"Stop! I have said there are no new Leskas in our village."

The priest's voice had a tone of command so strong that Khalmi stopped and hesitated, turning back to face him. "I can sense them," he said. "They're in great pain, they need treatment." He held up his medikit.

"There's no one there but two evil younglings who have been punished for their crimes. They do not deserve anything to alleviate their pain. They must learn that to disobey our laws means to suffer."

"I'm treating them anyway," said Khalmi, turning away. In front of him, the crowd had closed, blocking his way to the house.

The crowd's turning nasty, sent Nikuu. *Watch out.*

The priest strode forward to stand between Khalmi and the crowd. "Leave our village. You have no right to be here since there are no telepaths involved."

Khalmi regarded him calmly. "You're lying. Why are you preventing me from seeing to these two?"

"They aren't Leskas. You have no jurisdiction here. I'm trying to tend to the souls of those two youngling and the people of my village. You come here with your immodest females and insult us by their very presence!" He raised his hands above his head, speaking now to the crowd, not just to Khalmi.

"Society is tumbling down about our ears because of females like those with you! Can't you see we must stop the rot before God returns us to the days of the Cataclysm? Believe me, that will be our punishment, and He will show no mercy to those who've been unfaithful to Him!"

"You're talking rubbish," said Naira, moving past him. Slinging his gun to the side, he drew one of his swords and advanced on the crowd. "Now which one of you will try to stop me?" he growled, showing his canines.

Nikuu had been looking carefully at the people gathered around them. The majority were males, with one or two older females standing at the edges. They stood nowhere near the males. She looked back to Khalmi and Naira.

"They're going to attack if we try to reach the house," she said quietly. "Can you and Naira take hold of the priest as a hostage? We've got to pick up those two. Khalmi says they're badly hurt."

Zsyzoi called a phrase to Naira as she unslung her rifle. As her partner swung round on the priest, she stepped forward, putting the barrel of the gun in the small of his back.

"Let's all stay calm," she said to him. "We don't want anyone to get hurt, do we?"

The priest stiffened with rage. "You'll burn in hell for this," he hissed. "Your soul will be forfeit for all eternity!"

"I think not," she said, moving aside so Naira could put a pair of restraint cuffs on his wrists. "Tell me, which God do you follow?"

"There is only one God! Kezule, God of the sun!" said the priest, struggling against the restraints. "How dare you lay hands upon the sacred person of His priest! He'll take revenge on you, never fear!"

"I'll keep that in mind," she said, grasping him by his cuffed wrists and pushing him forward. "You're one of the Modernists. Who appointed you a priest anyway, eh? Don't bother telling me, I'm not interested. Now, how about you take us to these telepaths that you're holding," she said conversationally.

Naira had returned his sword to its scabbard and was covering the angrily muttering males with his rifle. He aimed at the ground in front of the foremost male and pressed the firing button. A bolt of energy hit the dirt, kicking up a plume of dust.

Coughing and spluttering, the crowd began to back away

and part. As it did, a figure came flying toward them and landed in a heap at Khalmi's feet.

"Vartra be praised," she said, reaching out to touch his tunic. "You've come for them! I thought he'd kill them with his beating. They're not more than kitlings! For the God's sake, take them away from this evil place!"

Nikuu moved forward to the woman, bending down to help her to her feet. *See to the young ones, Khalmi. Quickly, then we can get out of here. The crowd is in an ugly mood.*

"Come with me," she said, leading her alongside Naira while Khalmi walked in front. "Are you the mother of one of them?"

"Of Rrai. He's my son. But the priest beat Jinoe so badly, I don't know if she'll live," the female said, wiping her forearm across her face to dry the tears. "The priest, he said they were evil but it wasn't their fault they were so young. They couldn't help it that the God chose them, could they? You'll take them with you," she said anxiously. "You won't leave them here?"

"They're coming with us," said Nikuu. "You, too. What about the female, Jinoe? Where's her mother?"

"Dead this past year. There's only her father and he said the priest was right to beat the evil out of her."

They'd reached the house and leaving the mother outside with Zsyzoi and the priest, Nikuu followed Khalmi inside.

"Oh, Gods, no," she said, as she caught sight of the two small bodies lying curled up on blood-soaked rugs at opposite sides of the room. "Are they still alive?"

Yes, sent her Leska. *Just. Send to Valsgarth Guild and tell them to expect us. I don't know if the female will make it.*

Nikuu went over to the male child, bending over him. *What about the priest? If we take him in, we can't take the mother, and if we leave her she's not going to survive long.*

We'll report him once we've taken off. The Protectorate can deal with him. We'll also report to Brother Lijou that there's at least one non-telepath priest out here. He loaded his hypo, placed it against the young female's neck and gave her a shot, then held it out to Nikuu.

"Here, give him some of this. Antibiotic and a heavy analgesic. It's going to hurt like hell when we lift them."

Nikuu came back over and took the hypo.

"Don't cover his wounds," her Leska warned. "It'll only have stuck to his flesh by the time we get to the guild."

She pocketed the hypo and carefully eased the young male up against her chest, trying to get him partially over her shoulder to balance him. Holding him by his side and across the top of his thighs, she managed to stand up. He whimpered as she shifted her grip, but there was nowhere she could touch him that wasn't covered in bleeding open weals.

As they came out with the younglings, Zsyzoi took one look at them and prodded the priest in the back with her gun. "Don't even think about moving the wrong way," she growled, pushing him ahead of her back toward the aircar. "Modernists like you make me sick with your crazy ideas! We taking him in, too?" she asked.

"We're taking the mother," said Khalmi.

"You idolaters! God will punish you for what you've done today! You perpetuate the evil He despises!"

Zsyzoi jabbed him in the back with her gun and twisted the chain joining his wrist restraints till he yelped at the sudden pain. "Just shut it, unless you want some real trouble!"

The mother followed Nikuu, tentatively reaching out to touch her son then backing off whimpering for fear of hurting him. Around them the angry muttering rose in pitch.

Gods, I hope we reach the 'car before this lot explode! Just keep calm, sent Khalmi. *We'll do it.*

The crowd sullenly opened up again for them. Nikuu could hear the low-voiced comments about them not having the right to interfere in village business, but she ignored them and concentrated on trying to walk steadily toward their vehicle. Her burden was getting heavier with every step and it was with relief she finally leaned against the hull of the aircar.

Naira slung his gun over his shoulder and took the young male carefully from her. He climbed into the 'car and placed him stomach down on one of the two floaters strapped to the side, then went back to take the female from Khalmi. That done, he returned to help Zsyzoi release the priest.

Nikuu had the vehicle fired up and ready to go as soon as they jumped in. The priest's parting words were lost in the roar of the engines and the cloud of dust she made sure the vents kicked up.

* * *

Even after her call to Jack was over and she'd received the data he'd downloaded from the *Eureka*'s computer,

Vanna was still shaking from her experience in the mess. Taking repeated deep breaths and trying to convince herself it was only the adrenaline wasn't helping a lot, but at least the buzzing in her ears had stopped.

Contacting the front desk, she told them she was in to no one but the Liegen Aldatan and his Leska or Jack Reynolds, the Terran physician. She then requested a lab technician be assigned to help her.

Soon she was completely immersed in her work, comparing the Sholan and human data on gestation as she tried to find enough parallels on which to base what at best could only be an educated guess.

Her technician was run ragged because Vanna had no intention of leaving her office for anything. Finally, as Vanna had just about worked herself to a standstill, the younger female broached the subject of time.

"Physician Kyjishi, I should have gone off duty an hour ago," she said quietly. "You should rest, too. You've been working without a break for the last five hours."

"I hadn't realized it had been that long," said Vanna, checking her wrist unit. "You're right. Off you go, I'll finish up here. I'll see you again in the morning."

"The front office sent the list of the calls that came in for you," she said, handing Vanna the comp pad she'd been using. "Good night, Physician."

"Good night," said Vanna, putting the comp down on her desk and running her hands across her ears and head. She began to massage her temples, hoping to alleviate the headache that had been threatening all afternoon. At least now she was on her own it was so much quieter.

She looked across at the couch on the other side of her room. She didn't need to go back to the guest house to sleep, she could stay here in her office. The couches were intended to double as beds and in the drawer underneath it were several blankets and a pillow.

Sighing, she took another couple of analgesics from the bottle on her desk, pulling a face as she washed them down with some disgustingly tepid water from the jug.

There was a light tap on the door before Khafsa came into the room. "I thought you'd still be here," he said. "I called you a couple of times, but the office refused to put me through so I thought I'd come in person."

Vanna smiled tiredly up at him. "Sorry, Khafsa. I've been busy and I didn't want to be disturbed."

"Well, since you're obviously finished for the night, I won't feel so guilty about taking you to see a patient of mine."

"Khafsa, I've got a splitting headache. I don't feel like looking at patients at this time of night."

"I really think you should come," he said, walking into the room and leaning past her to switch off her desk light. "Besides, it's on your way back to the guest house."

"I was going to sleep here tonight," she objected.

"You need to get away from your work, Vanna," he said, helping her to her feet. "A change of scenery will do you good. You'll be able to come back to it tomorrow with a fresh mind."

Despite her protests, Khafsa gently but firmly led her out of her office and down the corridor toward the wards and single rooms.

"Who is it you want me to see?" she asked, too tired to feel anything but relief that the buzzing in her ears that she'd experienced earlier in the day hadn't returned. "Why is it so important that I see them?"

"You know quite a lot about these sorts of cases," he said, stopping outside one of the rooms adjacent to his department. "I'd value your opinion." He opened the door and ushered her inside.

As the door closed behind them, she realized she'd been tricked and that Khafsa had been shielding her mind until now. The full pain of her headache exploded behind her eyes, making her feel sick and giddy.

"Damn you, Khafsa!" she said, trying to push past him to get out. "This has nothing to do with me!"

"But it has, Vanna," said Khafsa quietly, taking hold of her and turning her back toward the room's interior. "You know you're the other half of the problem. It took us quite a long time to work out it was you. Full marks for hiding yourself so well."

Weakly, Vanna tried to pull herself free. "I don't need this, Khafsa! I don't want it!"

"I'm afraid you have no choice," he said.

The strength of Vanna's mental call for help shocked him but it took the last of her strength. Moments later, she collapsed against him.

* * *

Konis led the way through the corridor to his study. "Did you know that the Sholan translator on Earth has also found a Leska?" he said, sitting down at his desk and keying up his comm screen. "I received the news yesterday morning. He and his partner are being shipped out here immediately. I'm issuing instructions to make sure they are kept as free of stress as possible so their relationship can develop at a more normal rate. At least they didn't have any psychological or physical problems in consummating their Link."

"I'm glad," said Kusac. "Maybe it'll get easier the more mixed Leska pairs there are like us."

"Perhaps," said Konis, turning round to look at him. "You probably haven't heard yet, but there's been a third anomalous Link on Shola. This last Link was two younglings barely old enough to pair. That wasn't the worst of it, though. All three pairs come from tribes within the Ghuulgul Desert region. Khalmi and Nikuu—have you met them yet? No? You will. They were sent out from Laasoi Guild to fetch them in. We have to keep a mental watch on the villages in that region because they don't report anyone developing telepathic talents to us. Khalmi picked them up as soon as their Link started, so they took two Warriors with them and went out to collect them. It's a couple of years since we were last out there and they found that a new priest had installed himself in the village. He's yet another of this new religious movement that's suddenly started to gain ground out there. They call themselves the Modernists."

"Modernist? What's that?"

"Aspects of their beliefs are fairly predictable for people living out in the desert. They believe in only one God, Kezule, the God of the sun. The rest of us are idolaters who worship false Gods, of course. They believe that females should be subservient to their male relatives, and should only have the one mate for life. They're completely against females in any occupation outside the home, more so since the destruction of Khyaal and Szurtha and, I'm sorry to say, your Link to Carrie."

"What do the females say to that? I can't see them being any too happy to accept such a restrictive religion."

"That's one of the worrying aspects of this movement. The females are agreeing to it. It's based on the premise that the days of the Catacylsm are returning and all nonbelievers will perish at the hands of their sun God. The other worrying aspect is that when our team arrived there, they found that because the new Leska pair were so young, barely old enough to pair as I said, the priest had ordered them to be beaten until the evil left them."

"You can't be serious," said Kusac, a stunned look on his face.

"I am. I was called in to witness their arrival. They were brought in just after dawn and quite honestly, we thought we were going to lose them. However, they're bedded down in a Leska unit, on drips with constant I.C. nursing and so far, they're holding their own."

"I take it that they were found trying to pair."

Konis nodded. "They're still virgins, but thank the Gods their Link compulsion is minimal and we're managing to keep them psychic stable with psychic suppressants. The male, Rrai, his mother refuses to leave their sides. She said she and her son had been here some three months ago and they'd gone down with that ni'uzu virus you had a few weeks later. Now this. I wonder if there's a connection. It was a mutated virus after all, and we don't normally have as many Leska pairings in a year on the whole of Shola, let alone in that desert region."

"There could be. You'd have to ask Vanna about that. What happened with the priest?"

"The Protectors went out to pick up this self-appointed priest, but he'd disappeared and the villagers won't say where he is. I'm concerned that they're going to see him as some kind of martyr figure and the whole thing's going to blow up out of proportion. That area's ripe for it. We've had several seasons that have brought droughts there and despite the aid they've been sent, the people are dissatisfied. I don't want to see a Modernist anti-telepath movement starting to build."

"We'll be having a plague of snakes followed by locusts," said Kusac darkly.

"Excuse me?"

"Oh, something from Carrie's Terran culture," Kusac said. "Their God called these plagues down on unbelievers. I think it's worthwhile getting Vanna to follow up the virus idea, Father. I suppose if they were carrying the virus, Rrail and his mother could have spread it through the desert community. That doesn't explain the translator on the *Rhyaki*, though."

His father turned back to the comm. "It could, if I had become a carrier through picking it up from one of my guild contacts before I went out to the *Rhyaki*."

Once he'd reached the *Khalossa*'s comm office, he asked to be put through to the Terran Ambassador on Keiss, Mr Hamilton.

"He's no longer the Ambassador, Liege, he's their Prime Councillor now," replied the adjutant.

"Put me through to him anyway," said Clan Lord Aldatan.

"It's the twenty-first hour, three a.m. local time on Keiss, Leige," said the adjutant carefully.

"I said put me through." Konis' voice brooked no argument.

"Yes, Liege."

It took some five minutes until Carrie's father appeared on the screen. He frowned, obviously trying to place the Sholan.

"Clan Lord Aldatan? Aren't you Kusac's father? What can I do for you at this late hour?"

"Yes, I'm Konis Aldatan. I'm sorry to disturb your sleep, Mr Hamilton," he purred, "but the matter is somewhat urgent. I'm sure that as Carrie's father, you will share my pleasure in hearing that my son and your daughter have become life-bonded."

Peter Hamilton frowned in puzzlement. "Do you mean married?"

"That's right. Frankly it's the best thing that could have happened to Kusac," he continued, glancing at his son over the top of the unit. "It's brought out qualities in him he didn't know he possessed. Your daughter, too; she's become a brighter and livelier person since she's been with us."

Peter Hamilton ran his hand through his hair, obviously unsure as to what to say. "I hope they'll be very happy," he said at length.

"I'll pass your wishes on to them. However, I didn't disturb you at this time of night just to tell you that. It's the news that we are to become grandparents that has me more worried."

"Grandparents? You aren't saying she's pregnant, surely," said Mr Hamilton, disbelief on his face.

"I'm afraid I am. You are, I know, aware of some of the

changes that their Link has caused, but apparently there have been some far more far-reaching than any of us thought possible—with the result that Carrie is expecting my son's child. My concern," he continued, drowning out the other's exclamations of shock, "is for the child. I think it wrong and unfair to bring into the world a new life that will be neither Sholan nor Terran. What will this strange offspring of theirs look like? Should they have the child?"

"What does my daughter want?" Mr Hamilton asked in a strangled voice.

"She and her mate want the child, of course," he said. "But what, as loving parents, should we do? Should we advise them of the problems, or leave them to decide on their own?"

"Let them decide," her father said firmly. "If they can't live on Shola with their child, there's always a home for them here on Keiss."

Kusac's father sighed. "You're right, of course. Their decision is the one that matters, but we have an even more pressing problem than that to deal with."

Peter Hamilton winced visibly. "What else has happened?"

"Your daughter has foolishly issued a Challenge—a duel by combat—to one of our females. Despite our efforts we have been unable to get the Challenge dropped, even taking Carrie's condition into account. If she fights, at the least she could lose the child. At the worst, we could lose all three of them."

The Clan Lord leaned forward. "We must stop that combat, Mr Hamilton. I intend to try to claim diplomatic immunity for your daughter, but I'm concerned that our Governor and the council of guilds won't allow it because of her bond to my son."

"What do you want me to do?" Mr Hamilton asked, concern written on his face.

"I want you to contact the Terran/Sholan Council on Keiss and demand that the Challenge be canceled. Say you refuse to let your daughter's life, and that of her unborn child, be put at risk. Tell them this new species is too precious to risk over a squabble between women—anything—so long as they cancel it."

"How long until the Challenge?" Mr Hamilton demanded.

"Two weeks. It's on the morning of the third day of that week."

"I'll get onto it now." The screen went blank.

Kusac just looked at his father in awe as the comm unit slid back into the desk.

"I'm not the head of Alien Relations for nothing," murmured Konis, sitting back in his seat and folding his hands in his lap. "I think that with her father petitioning the council on Keiss as well as us petitioning the Governor, we might get some action."

Kusac shook his head. "I don't believe how easily you manipulated him," he said. "Now all he cares about is saving Carrie and the child. He hasn't stopped to think about me being the father."

"Nor will he, until he has accepted his own desire for his granddaughter to survive. Carrie should have fewer problems from him." He glanced at his wrist unit.

"I think we'd better go and see your mother now. She's likely to have our hides for delaying third meal for so long, especially now she's looking out for Carrie's health. I remember what I was like when your mother was carrying you. I got it all wrong and would let her do hardly anything. She got so exasperated she finally resorted to cuffing my ears soundly when I began to fuss over her too much." He chuckled at the memory before looking up at his son.

"I know I don't need to tell you that Carrie will need a lot of support from you." It was his turn to shake his head. "I don't know how you both cope with a Link like that. For me it would be like living without my hide. Its intensity is frightening, almost as frightening as how easily our males are being attracted to the females of Carrie's species."

"I wouldn't know about normal Leska Links," Kusac said. "I only know I couldn't be without her. Given any choice, I would still have chosen Carrie as my Leska."

"You have changed. I told her father the truth. You were too insular, too academic. Your mother and I despaired of you getting emotionally involved with anyone, let alone Rala."

"Rala was a mistake."

"I admit that, but when the betrothal was arranged, you were only children. I had no idea she would turn out to be the vacuous and spiteful young female that she is now."

Kusac gave a little sigh. "I'm well rid of her, but at what cost?"

"Don't talk up trouble," warned his father as he got up from his desk. "Let's assume that either the Challenge will be canceled or all will proceed well and Carrie will win easily. Now, in the name of the Gods, let's go and eat!"

Third meal had finished and while Rhyasha, Taizia, and Carrie sat in the garden enjoying the cool evening breeze, Kusac and his father were busy in the study looking up the various Challenge precedents regarding non-Sholans.

Kusac froze as the cry for help echoed inside his mind. It was so raw and unfocused that even his father had picked it up.

"What in all the hells?" Konis exclaimed.

"It's Vanna," said Kusac, mentally reaching out for her. Knowing the feel of her mind, he was able to lock on to her thoughts only to feel the contact dissolve as she slipped into unconsciousness. "There's something wrong. She needs my help," he said, pushing his chair back and getting up.

"But Vanna's no telepath," said his father. "How could she possibly send to you?"

"She certainly is now," said Kusac as he headed for the door.

"You're not going without me," said Carrie, meeting him in the hallway.

Kusac stopped, reaching out to touch her gently on the cheek. "Not this time, cub. You stay here," he said. "If her Talent has wakened, then your presence will make it harder for her. Remember, she'll know nothing about shielding. It's hard enough for her to have her feelings laid bare without you there to sense them. I'll be back as soon as I can."

Carrie nodded slowly. "She's been a good friend to us. I wouldn't hurt her for the world."

Thank you, he sent, bending to lick her ear. *You've nothing to fear, cub. I'll give her the help and privacy she needs, then come back to you as soon as I can.*

Take care, she sent as he held her close, rubbing his face against hers.

"Meral, get the aircar and meet me at the front of the house," he said, letting her go and turning to the waiting Warrior.

"Do you need any help?" asked Konis.

"I think not, Father. This is a personal matter."

As soon as he got into the craft, Kusac took over the controls from Meral and within a record forty minutes was landing illegally in the guild grounds opposite the medical facility. During the journey, he'd tried to maintain a light contact with Vanna's mind. He'd felt her return to consciousness, but with a sudden flare of fear from her, the contact had been severed as a psychic inhibitor more powerful than any he'd come across before cut in.

He knew exactly where she was, and as he rounded the corner to the aura unit, ahead of him he saw Khafsa and a Warrior on guard outside one of the patient treatment rooms.

"We've been expecting you," said Khafsa as Kusac stopped in front of them.

"What's going on?" he demanded. "I want to see Vanna." He tried to push them aside, but though Khafsa let himself be moved, the Warrior stood firm, glancing apologetically at Meral where he stood behind Kusac.

"She's fine, but you can't see her yet. Sorli's with them."

His reply stopped Kusac in his tracks. "Not Vanna," he said, the shock evident on his face. "At best she's a latent. You must have made a mistake."

"Why do you think we've got the room heavily blocked? Working so closely with you two must have catalyzed her latent ability, and believe me, she's not got a minor Talent. It took us several hours to locate who he was paired with because she'd managed to hide herself mentally from us. She's already triggered the gestalt that's worried you so much." He took Kusac by the arm, turning him slightly away from the door.

"Look, my office is opposite, why don't you and Meral come and wait with me? There's nothing you can do at present."

"I'll wait outside, Liegen," said Meral quietly.

Kusac accompanied Khafsa into his office.

"Please, take a seat," said Khafsa, indicating the couch as he went over to his desk and picked up a thermal jug.

A familiar smell made Kusac's nostrils twitch. The physician held out a mug toward him.

"Coffee. I said we were expecting you," said Khafsa with

a slight smile before he turned away to pour himself a c'shar from the hot plate.

Cautiously Kusac took a sip. "You've even got it the right strength," he said, the surprise evident in his voice as he took a larger mouthful.

"I should have. Vanna's made me the occasional mug of it when we've been working late in the labs. At this strength it seems to lose most of its intoxicant values." He pulled his chair out and sat opposite Kusac.

"You said Sorli was with them. What's happened that necessitates his presence?" asked Kusac.

"She has a human male Leska."

"That makes four pairs," Kusac said quietly. "We really are looking at the emergence of a new species."

"I doubt it, Kusac. Even though the Gods give us Leskas to improve our children's talents, it can't be the same with you mixed pairs. Our species just isn't that compatible with the humans."

Kusac said nothing. They'd learn soon enough.

"Neither of them have taken it well, I'm afraid. We may have trouble with them," Khafsa continued.

"What sort of trouble?"

"The Terran is refusing to acknowledge the Link."

"It's always the humans, isn't it?" said Kusac with a rumble of anger. "Why do they always let their restrictive sexual code get in the way?"

"With respect, I heard that was what happened to you." Khafsa's tone was deferential.

"Then you heard wrong." Kusac's tone was cold. He didn't appreciate the liberty Khafsa had taken. "I no longer have a human Leska, you should know that from the aura readings that you took."

"I think you're splitting hairs, Kusac. Anyway, this time it was Vanna who first refused the Link and we had no intention of losing her or her Leska. Master Esken ordered that we were to make sure their Link was completed in the hope that after their initial pairing, there would be no further difficulties."

In one fluid movement, Kusac had leaped to his feet and taken the older male by the throat. Khafsa's hands came up to clutch at Kusac's forearms, bracing himself to take the pressure off his neck.

"Just what have you done to her?" Kusac's voice was a

menacing growl as he dispassionately watched the physician's eyes dilate with fear.

"In Vartra's name, Kusac, let me go!" gasped Khafsa, his voice strangled as he fought for breath.

"Tell me what you did to her!"

"We drugged them." Khafsa's ears were laid flat and his breath was coming in gasps. "We can't afford to lose her, Kusac, you should understand that!" He clutched at Kusac's hands as he dangled helplessly in midair.

"You took their right to choose away from them! You used them, Khafsa! You let them both be raped! What right do you have to do that?" he demanded, shaking the physician angrily. "We're people, dammit, not animals to be experimented on!" With a final growl of anger, he opened his hand and dropped the other male, turning his back on him in disgust.

At the door he paused. "You can all thank Vartra you're telepaths, Khafsa," he said, showing his teeth in a snarl, "because if you weren't, I'd kill you for this."

In the corridor, Meral was waiting for him, his energy pistol already drawn.

"We're going in," said Kusac, striding over to the door opposite. "Stand aside," he ordered the Warrior.

The guard hesitated, weighing his orders against the fury evident in the set of the Liegen's ears. Reluctantly he stepped aside. Kusac slammed the door open, taking the scene in with a single glance.

Ignoring Sorli, who was bending over the human lying on the bed, he turned to where Vanna sat huddled protectively against the wall. Now inside the damped zone, he was able to tell instantly that she was still heavily under the influence of the drugs.

"Vanna," he said, squatting down beside her and laying a gentle hand on her arm. "I'm here. It's over now."

Slowly her head raised and she looked up at him. Her eyes were half covered by the nictitating lids and it was with an obvious effort that she focused them on him.

Through the hand that touched her, he could feel none of the highly charged sensuality nor the compulsion that accompanied his Link time. Vanna's drug-induced pairing had at least satisfied the needs of her Link this time.

"Vanna, it's over now," he said quietly. "In a few minutes I'm going to take you somewhere safe. Do you understand!"

She nodded slowly.

Kusac turned to look at Sorli. "This isn't the end of it, Sorli. My father shall hear of this." His ears were still flat with anger, and on the ground, his tail flicked rhythmically.

"I was against this from the start, Kusac," said Sorli, moving away from the bed where the unconscious Terran lay. "I persuaded them to only use a hypnotic to make them more susceptible to their Link, nothing more."

"You were all so terrified that Carrie or I would corrupt the guild's principles," said Kusac, his voice a low snarl. "It seems to me that you're the ones who've corrupted our way of life. If this is how the Telepath Guild behaves toward mixed Leskas, then I for one have no further wish to belong to it! What's wrong with the Terran?"

"He was given a dose sufficient for a Sholan, but it was too high for him. His breathing has become too shallow. He needs the antidote to prevent his autonomic reflexes being affected any further."

The Tutor shook his head worriedly. "I told Khafsa we didn't know enough to do this. The only one who does is Vanna, but obviously they weren't about to ask her. This was ill-considered from the start."

"Meral, get Khafsa and enough of the antidote for both of them," ordered Kusac, turning back to Vanna.

"She needs to be in shielded quarters, Kusac," said Sorli. "We had to use the maximum damper because of her. She triggered the gestalt when she called for you."

"So it begins again," Kusac sighed. "She's coming back to the estate with me," he said abruptly. "We'll see to her there."

Meral returned with Khafsa who warily squeezed past Kusac to get to Vanna. After giving her the antidote, he went over to the Terran.

"I'm taking him, too," said Kusac, watching the physician. "Get him ready to travel."

"He needs to be kept under observation tonight, Kusac," said Khafsa, his voice coming hoarsely from his bruised throat. "If you take him to the estate and he has problems with his breathing, we may not get there in time to treat him."

Kusac glanced at Sorli who confirmed Khafsa's words with a nod.

"Then keep him here, but I expect to be kept informed of

his progress," Kusac snapped angrily. "Remember, Vanna's life depends on his survival."

"We're not likely to forget that, Kusac," said Sorli.

Kusac turned back to Vanna, sensing that she was now beginning to throw off the effects of the drug. Her inner eyelids were receding as her mind began to come back into focus. He helped her to her feet, supporting her as she swayed unsteadily.

Now that she was standing, her distressed condition was more evident. Her fur had become dull and lackluster and every line of her body was slumped in defeat. Kusac reached for the spare blanket on the end of the bed. Unfolding it, he wrapped it around her. It hurt him to see her indomitable spirit so badly damaged.

"Get her clothes, Meral," he said, swinging her up into his arms.

Despite the blanket, the fresh air made Vanna shiver. "I can walk, Kusac," she said, her voice slurred by the remains of the drug.

"I know you can."

"Please. Walking will speed up my circulation and help the antidote rid my system of the hypnotic."

Kusac stopped and lowered her to the ground.

"I think I'd be better going to my own home," she said, refusing to look at him.

"You can't go there, Vanna. You need to be in shielded quarters until you've learned to protect your mind from others. My home is shielded and we can teach you everything you need to know."

"Please, I don't want to talk about it," she said, closing her eyes.

"You don't need to, I'm afraid. I can feel it from you," he said gently.

Her eyes flew open, wide with fear. Kusac wrapped his arms round her, pulling her close and rubbing his face against hers. "Hush. You've nothing to fear. We've both known how you feel for a long time. Carrie understands. It's not a problem for either of us. Even now Carrie and my mother are getting a room ready for you."

Tears began to spill out of her eyes. "Why this, Kusac? My life is complicated enough without Brynne."

He continued to hold her close, stroking her head gently

as he felt her continue to shiver. "I don't know why, Vanna. We're no nearer an answer either. All any of us can do is look on it as following an unknown and exciting scent."

"He's a stranger, Kusac! I don't know him at all, yet I know everything about him from the moment he was born! He doesn't want me as a Leska. We'll never have what you and Carrie share."

"What we have grew between us before the Link, Vanna," he said quietly as he broke the gentle rapport with her. "Not all Leskas are lovers, some are merely working partners, you know that. At least he's attracted to you and not prejudiced because you're Sholan."

"It's not him I want, Kusac," she said, her voice muffled against his tunic.

"I know, and I'm sorry, Vanna. There's nothing I can do, you know that," he said, letting her go to lead her over to the waiting aircar. He purposely closed his mind, not wanting to sense these emotions and feelings she would normally have kept to herself.

"Will you let me shield your thoughts for now so you can have mental privacy again? Tomorrow I can teach you how to do it for yourself."

Having left Vanna with Carrie and Taizia in the main bathing area, Kusac headed for his father's study, finding both his parents there.

Kaid had left Meral and T'Chebbi guarding the three females and followed Kusac. Unremarked, he slipped into the study behind Kusac and concealed himself in one of the darker corners of the room.

"Well?" said Kusac, crossing over to where his parents sat. "You heard?"

"I've just spoken to Esken," said his father. "He said he'd told them to only use drugs as a last resort and claimed Khafsa and Sorli had liberally interpreted his orders."

"He would," said Kusac, his tone derisive. "They'll cover for each other because guild interests come first. No one wants to admit responsibility. This can't be allowed to happen again, Father."

"Both of them are complete novices, Kusac. Until today, Vanna didn't even show any strong telepathic abilities. They were only trying to prevent another pair of deaths like Raill's and Lynn's. At least Vanna and Brynne will live long enough to learn what their telepathic Link entails and make a second, informed choice of their own."

"Are you condoning it? What would you have done if you had discovered that Carrie and I had been drugged by the Mentor on board the *Khalossa?*" he demanded.

"She'd have lived to regret it," Rhyasha said, her tone a deep growl of menace. "Kusac's right. This must never be allowed to happen again, Konis. Sholan Leskas have never had the right to choose taken from them before. The guild has overstepped itself. This is a matter for Alien Relations."

Konis moved uncomfortably on his chair, the flicking of his tail tip betraying his mood. "Sholans know what's involved: there's never been an incident of a Sholan refusing a Link within living memory. The guild has naturally assumed responsibility for the mixed pairs and made their plans accordingly."

"Considering there are aliens involved, the matter must include us," said Rhyasha. "We need to intensify our Terran orientation program to deal with the matter of our differing sexual customs once and for all."

"How?" Kusac demanded. "This time, as far as I can gather, it was Vanna who refused to have anything to do with the Terran. Each case needs to be dealt with individually, not seen automatically as a Terran problem. Even I've been guilty of that. The guild can't be allowed to misuse its power like this. What will happen to our cub? Will the guild demand that we raise her there, or worse, demand that she be raised by a team of their specialists so they can study her?"

"Our granddaughter will be raised on the estate." Now Konis' voice was a growl. "The guild wouldn't dare interfere in that."

"How can you be so sure?" countered Kusac. "They've dared to drug Vanna and her Leska, something that up until now would have been unthinkable. I've no wish to belong to the guild if it can rule people's lives like that! The Terrans don't belong in the Telepath Guild anyway, and neither do I now. I was within a heartbeat of killing Khafsa for what he'd done to Vanna."

Stunned silence greeted his statement. "I think you're overreacting," said his father. "You'd never kill anyone, it's not in your nature."

"I've killed several times already on Keiss, Father. I'll do it again to protect Carrie and our child, or our friends." His voice was as hard as ice.

Kaid knew the tone, and could almost feel the threat behind the words. He nodded to himself. Events were moving as he'd predicted. He ought to get in touch with his own guild. His sub-guild, he corrected himself. They didn't merit full guild status in the eyes of the guild council. Now he had to decide what to do. His responsibility was clear—inform Ghezu—and let the Brotherhood use them instead of the Telepath Guild. He heard Kusac's next words with a shock of premonition.

"If I have to, I'll declare our cub En'Shalla," Kusac continued. "Outside the guilds, a child of the Gods."

"No!" exclaimed his mother. "That's too drastic, Kusac!"

"And too late," added his father. "The rules governing En'Shalla are specific and rigid. Your daughter wasn't conceived in accordance with the old customs, so she's not entitled to the protection of the Gods. At the moment we have more pressing worries than the guild, namely this Challenge. It may even be that the guild can find a way to stop the fight. If you alienate yourself any further from them, they may be unwilling to intercede for you."

"Esken wouldn't be so stupid," said Rhyasha. "It's in his interests to see our granddaughter brought safely into this world."

"Is it?" asked Kusac. "I've told you, the guild sees us as a danger to the Sholan power structure, a new force they can't control. It won't be long before the other guilds are seeing us in the same light."

"You're being overly pessimistic, Kusac," said Konis.

"Am I?" Kusac turned round to point at Kaid. "Then tell me why his Brotherhood have issued an edict banning any contracts involving Terrans or mixed Leska pairs, unless they're protective contracts."

Kaid blinked in surprise. He hadn't realized that Kusac had been aware of his presence.

"A brake must be put on the Telepath Guild now, before it's too late. I know more about our Leska Links than they do," said Kusac. "Our daughter isn't going to spend her life having her mind dissected and analyzed to please them, any more than we are. It's over, Father. You can tell them. We'll no longer cooperate with them." With that, Kusac turned and strode out of the room, Kaid following hastily after him.

"He's right," said Rhyasha as the door closed behind them. "You weren't on the *Khalossa*. Mnya was terrified that Carrie would be uncontrollable. I don't say Esken is equally worried, but he'll certainly protect the guild's interests first, and controlling the Leskas like our son and his mate will be high on his list of priorities. For their own protection, we need to place them under the jurisdiction of Alien Relations. One of our people, a telepath naturally, should be in charge of their training at the guild. Someone forceful, who will make sure their rights are respected."

"Perhaps you're right," said Konis, thoughtfully rubbing one ear. "The next All-Guilds' Council meeting at the Governor's palace is due to be held in a few weeks. If you'll assist me, we could perhaps have a feasible solution to bring before the council by then."

Chapter 18

Kaid's room was on the ground floor at the back of the house. Unable to settle, he went outside into the gardens. Coming to the large tree outside the lounge, he squatted down under it, resting his back against the bole.

"Are you actually off duty, Kaid? I don't think I've ever seen you relaxing before."

"Occasionally even I take a break, Liegena Taizia," he said, pulling a stim twig out of his top pocket and putting the end in his mouth. "Waiting for Meral?"

"Actually, yes," she said, dropping down from the branch above him where she'd been sitting. "Carrie's lying down and Kusac's waiting for Vanna to finish bathing. T'Chebbi's on night duty for them, so Meral's free."

Kaid looked up at her, his mouth opening in a slight grin as he flicked an ear at her. "I'm not worried about him shirking his duties, Liegena. He's free to do what he wants in his off-time."

"Don't you have a companion, Kaid? Isn't there a female somewhere whose heart beats faster for you?" she asked.

"No one special, Liegena."

"I expect it's difficult to find someone with the right . . . Talents to suit you."

"Meral's coming, Liegena," he said quietly, taking the twig out of his mouth and regarding her unblinkingly.

"I know. We'll have to talk again," she said, moving away from him toward the house.

He put the twig back in his mouth, waiting till their footfalls died away. He needed the peace to think. Now that Kusac had voiced his decision to break with the Telepath Guild, he should put forward the case for the Brotherhood. It was the sensible option for telepaths who could fight.

Lijou ran the Priesthood of Vartra from Dzahai Stronghold

as well as being co-leader of the Brotherhood with Ghezu. They had the facilities which the other two guilds lacked. It wasn't the only option, however. Kusac had put a name to what had been troubling him for weeks. En'Shalla. It was a risky path, especially when you took the opposition into account. They'd be fighting against fifteen hundred years of tradition, not to mention the Telepath Guild and the Brotherhood.

So far, events had followed the path he'd anticipated, the one the God had shown him only a few days before he'd heard from Garras. What did Vartra want of him now? He had no idea because since that night, the God had remained unreachable. If Carrie and Kusac could have visions here, then surely he could.

Getting up, he walked back into the house, heading for the shrine. There, if anywhere on this estate, surely the God would be reachable.

* * *

Vanna had preferred to shower on her own. It seemed to take forever to rinse the loose hair off her body—a by-product of the drug that Khafsa had given her. Turning the water off, she reached out for the large towel that Carrie had left for her and began to rub off the worst of the water.

She tried to remember what had happened but from the moment Khafsa had taken her into the room with Brynne, it was all very hazy. She remembered the slight sting of the hypo against her neck and the feel of the drug surging straight to her brain, making her feel even more disoriented. What with that and the nausea caused by the Link, it hadn't needed much strength on Khafsa's part to pull her across to the bed where a naked and equally disoriented Brynne was sitting slumped against Sorli. They'd been literally flung together and from that moment onward, neither of them had had any control over the situation.

Phrases she'd used to describe Kusac's Link with Carrie came into her mind as she realized how inadequate language was to describe that initial moment of the meeting of their minds and bodies. It had been heaven and hell at the same time.

She shook her head, trying now to rid herself of the shards of memories as she discarded the towel on the bench opposite. Gods, had it only been someone she knew, someone she cared about, not a stranger, then ... She sighed and turned on the hot air. Having experienced something of what they shared, she knew Kusac would never come to her.

As she left the bathing room, she found him waiting outside.

"You look a lot better," Kusac said, looking at her critically. "Your eyes are clearer."

"I feel better," she admitted as he took her by the arm and drew her along the balcony. "Thank you for lending me the robe."

"Don't mention it. Taizia's picking out one or two things for you to wear while you're here. How's Brynne?"

"He's asleep," she replied without thinking, then stopped dead, eyes wide with fear as she clutched his arm.

Kusac smiled down at her and urged her on. "You'll get used to it," he said reassuringly. "It's always there, that knowledge of what your Leska's doing, but after a few days it doesn't seem to occupy quite so much of your conscious mind." He stopped in front of a door and hesitated. "Vanna, I'd better tell you now. Carrie and I were life-bonded last night."

"I'm glad," she heard herself say as if from a great distance. "Carrie will feel a lot more secure."

"We both do," he said, opening the door. "The betrothal contract was cancelled and even if Carrie should lose the Challenge, there's no question of me marrying Rala now."

Stepping into the lounge, she held onto the doorway as the world jerked back into focus.

"You'll find everything you need in here. Do you want to join us in half an hour for something to eat before you settle down for the night?" he asked as he moved away from her.

She shook her head. "I think I need sleep more than anything else."

"If you change your mind, use the comm. There's always someone on duty in the house in case my parents are needed. You're welcome to stay for as long as you like," he added before turning to leave.

"Kusac, I need to speak to Kaid," Vanna said.

"I'll ask him to come up."

She knew it was Kaid before she opened the door. "I have to see Garras," she said, steeling herself for an argument.

"Word has already been sent, Physician Kyjishi. He'll be here by morning."

"Thank you," she said, relief sweeping through her. Garras was the only stable factor in a life suddenly gone mad around her.

"Is that all?" Kaid asked.

She nodded.

"Then good night, Physician. T'Chebbi will be outside Liegen Kusac's room if you should need her."

* * *

Once he'd left Vanna, Kaid headed downstairs to the kitchen to get a cup of c'shar. He didn't hurry, making sure that he wouldn't be needed again before he finally decided he could take the time he needed in the shrine.

The light came on as he entered, but once he'd lit a candle and placed it on the altar, he turned it off. Settling himself on the bench, he relaxed, concentrating on the flame and letting his mind drift.

The mist thinned and parted, coalescing into a room he'd never seen before. A real fire of logs burned in a corner and he could almost feel the heat. He stood at a doorway looking in. Before him, obscured by a pool of shadow, a male sat in a chair. He broke off talking to shudder and look around the room.

What is it, Vartra? a voice asked.

A shadow walked by me, he said, *nothing more. The world we knew has changed, especially for us. The old ties of family have broken down and we must survive as best we can. Your loyalty can only be to each other, no one else. Those of you who survive will write the rules for the future. They found us too soon. Too many of us have been lost, too many deaths.*

The voice and the vision began to blur and he had to strain to hear the last words.

On you few depends our survival.

The mist writhed and twisted, parting again to show the temple he knew so well, the temple that didn't exist in this world.

This time there was only the voice from the flickering lights that alternately showed and hid the statue of the God.

So many of you calling on me. I tire. Even the Gods need

to rest. Don't come to me. Look to the God within you for the answers. *

With a jolt he was awake again, his hands damp with sweat, his head aching, and his limbs trembling. He rubbed his palms against his jacket to dry them while trying to force the fur around his neck and shoulders to lie flat again.

He'd never had a vision like that before. His hand shook as he raised it to smooth down the hair on his head. It had been so real, the room with the fire, as if he'd actually been there! Inside his mind he almost heard a faint, mocking laugh as the memory of how it had been a few months ago and how it was now came to the front of his mind. He couldn't ignore it any longer: his sensitivity—he hesitated at calling it a Talent—had been enhanced. Why, or how, he had no idea. A thought came rushing forward. Maybe it seemed so different because the visions were stronger at Valsgarth. After all, it was really only here or at the guild that the new Leska pairs had their visions, and until Carrie, always the same one. He closed his mind. He didn't want to hear the mocking laugh again.

Still shaken, he stood, and picking up his candle, put the light back on and blew the flame out before leaving. This time the God had told him to think for himself, and by God—he grinned mirthlessly at his unintended pun—he meant to do it.

* * *

Vanna woke to the gentle touch of someone stroking her cheek. Garras' mouth opened in a faint grin. "Good morning, pretty one," he said.

"You're here so soon?" she said, confused. "I didn't expect you till morning." She pushed herself up into a sitting position. "What time is it?"

"Around twenty-fourth hour."

She rubbed her hands across her eyes and ears, trying to wake up. "It's the middle of the night! Have you eaten? Do you want a drink?"

"I've eaten and drunk," he said quietly. "Kaid met me when I arrived. Stop worrying about me. How are you?"

"Tired," she said. "Garris, did you know that I'm a telepath?"

"Yes, I know. Kaid told me what's happened. I can't say

I'm surprised at the telepathy. I've always thought you might have some Talent in that direction."

Her ears flicked backward. With an effort she pulled them upright again. "Then you know about . . ."

"I know all about your Leska," he said, interrupting her as he once again reached out to touch her face. "I'm back now, to stay with you if that's what you want. I seem to remember we made a commitment to each other, unless you've changed your mind?" He put his head on one side and regarded her quizzically.

"No. No, I haven't," she said, relief plain on her face as she reached out for him.

* * *

In the morning, Vanna insisted on returning to the guild.

"I'll be all right," she assured Kusac and his parents. "I've got work I have to complete. Now Garras is with me, I don't think I'll have any trouble from Khafsa or Sorli." She hesitated, looking from Konis to Rhyasha. "What is our world coming to when we need to be protected from the very guilds that have by tradition been almost a home to us?"

"The existence of our Leska Links with the humans threatens to upset the established order, Vanna," said Kusac. "The guild needs to control us because they're afraid of what we could become."

"I think you're seeing too many jeggets in the shadows," said Konis. "I do, however, intend to take this matter further. This must never be allowed to happen again."

"When do you plan to return to the guild?" Garras asked Kusac.

"Not in the foreseeable future," he said. "We've that damned Challenge in thirteen days. Carrie can't train at the Telepath Guild."

"I'll be in touch in a few days," said Vanna. "I need to run some checks on her."

* * *

Ghyan watched the young female as she lifted a piece of incense and crumbled it into the glowing coals of the brazier. The pungent smoke rose in a thick cloud, making her cough before a draft of warm air from outside caught it and lifted it toward the rafters where it dissipated.

His Talent was in being able to assess people and their needs, a skill admirably suited to his calling as a priest. He knew Rala, knew that the weaknesses in her character had been allowed to flourish by her doting father. Now the elderly male had, to his cost, discovered that he had a virago for a daughter. Ghyan had seen enough of her over the last few weeks to realize that though her moods appeared to fluctuate with the wind, they were actually carefully calculated to make sure she achieved exactly what she wanted.

The set of her ears as well as the tone of her mind was smug, yet he sensed an anger behind it. Her head turned sharply toward him as he came out of the shadows by the door to the private quarters of the temple.

She tipped her chin up, baring her neck by the minimum needed to show respect for his position. "Father," she said, her eyes flicking away from his as he approached her.

"I was hoping you would come today," said Ghyan. "I think it would be wise for us to have a talk, don't you, Rala?"

Her ears pricked forward to face him. "About my forthcoming bonding?" she said brightly. "There's a lot to discuss."

Direct, if nothing else, he thought. "No, about your Challenge," he said, taking her by the forearm and steering her back toward the temple entrance.

"It's a mere detail, Father," she said confidently as they passed through the curtain and out into the hallway. "I shall win and Kusac and I will be life-bonded as was intended."

Ghyan opened the door to his office, gesturing for her to precede him. He waited until the Warrior accompanying her had also entered before following them.

Rala had seated herself in the chair by the low table, ignoring the more formal one at Ghyan's desk.

So she thinks to dominate this meeting, does she? He strolled over to the bookcase behind his desk and appeared to search for a volume.

"You'll be able to see what I have to show you better from my desk," he said, keeping his tone mild. He smiled to himself as he felt the flash of her anger quickly suppressed, then heard her stand and walk over to the desk. Now that she was seated where he wanted her, he pulled the book off the shelf and turned to face her.

"How charming," she purred, "you still use books. I

would have thought your records would be on your comm like everyone else's."

"Naturally they are," he agreed, sitting down. "However, I prefer to have the feel of the original volume in my hands when I'm looking up points of law and precedent. This small portion of the temple's book collection that you see behind me is priceless."

"I'm sure it is." Her tone was just short of snappiness. "However, I am rather busy. What is it you want to talk to me about?"

"The Life-bonding Challenge, being En'Shalla, falls within my jurisdiction," he said, opening his book at the place he'd marked the day before. "Now that your betrothal contract has been dissolved, there is no need for the Challenge to go ahead."

"The Challenge came first, Father, and I accepted it. Even though the contract was later canceled by my father, that takes precedence."

"That's true," he agreed, "but there have been cases like this before where the families have dissolved the contract rather than risk their children in a fight. For example . . ."

"I don't care about them, Father," she interrupted, leaning forward to place her hand over the page Ghyan was looking at. "Even though they are life-bonded, I wish the Challenge to go ahead. When I win, I can have their bonding annulled and demand that ours take place!"

"You have no grounds for doing that, Rala," said Ghyan, removing the book from under her hand. "The temple will not support you."

"Oh, but I have." The purr in her voice had grown louder. "While betrothed to me, he got his alien playmate pregnant and then married her. That he preferred her to me is now public knowledge. I have been insulted in such a way that only the reversal of his bonding will satisfy me. He was promised to me, and I will have him." The purr ended in a low growl.

"You realize that Liegena Aldatan has empowered me to tell you she withdraws her Challenge?"

The growl became menacing. "She has no right to the title! I refuse to accept her withdrawal."

"She is his Leska, and his mate. Because there is a cub on the way, he has a duty to support them both, and they have a duty to their guild to provide more Talented children. Revenge against them is all that's on your mind, Rala. Why?" Ghyan was genuinely bewildered. "You would gain nothing by forcing Kusac into a life-bond with you. He couldn't give you children, he doesn't love you, so why do you want him?"

"My reasons are none of your business," she said, surging to her feet, tail lashing and ears set back in anger. "The Challenge stands!"

"What if you do win? Would you like it known that the only way you could get him was by force?"

"That matters little to me," she spat, but he could sense her uncertainty.

Ghyan stood. "And what if I order you, as the Priest of Vartra in Valsgarth, to drop the Challenge because it goes against our creed, what then?"

"You think I care about your orders?" She flicked her hand at him, claws extending in a gesture of defiance as her resolve hardened once more. "I care that much for them!"

"Then I hope the God can soften your heart, Liegena Vailkoi," said Ghyan, his tone as cold as ice. "Since you refuse to obey me, the Voice of Vartra, you will have to find Him yourself because you are no longer welcome within His temple. Now leave!"

"With pleasure," she snarled, canines showing. "I'll be glad to shake the dust of this place from my feet!" She turned and stalked out of the office, her Warrior guard trailing apologetically behind her.

Ghyan watched her leave, his tail twitching despite his self-control. He growled deep in his throat. That female could be the destruction of not only his friend Kusac and his Leska, but of the manifestation of the God's will—their cub. It was out of his hands; he'd done what he could. Only Vartra could intervene now. This was truly an En'Shalla Challenge.

* * *

When Vanna arrived at the guild and checked in at the office, she was told her belongings had been moved to her new quarters in the Leska wing. One of the older students was asked to show her the way.

She could sense Brynne nearby, still in the medical section from the feel of his mental state. Kusac had shown her how to shield her mind from the "noise" generated by the people around her, but it was taking a great deal of her concentration. It would be quieter once she was in her new quarters.

Her rooms were identical to Carrie's and Kusac's and only a few doors down the corridor from them. She'd no sooner finished prowling round checking her clothes and other personal items when Garras came to tell her Tutor Sorli was there and needed to speak to her.

"I hope you've forgiven me for my part in last night's proceedings," Sorli said, eyeing Garras carefully. "I was concerned about what Khafsa would do if I wasn't there to oversee matters."

Vanna sighed. "Kusac told me what you said, Tutor. I'll reserve my judgment until I know you better."

Garras got to his feet and, tail swaying gently, walked round behind Vanna's chair and stood there, his hand on her shoulder. The gesture was not lost on Sorli.

"I'll be here with Vanna, Sorli," said Garras, his voice low and resonating deep in his chest. "If ever the guild tries to repeat its actions of last night, they'll have me to deal with."

Sorli's ears barely twitched. "And you are?" he asked.

"Captain Garras, lately of the *Khalossa,* Vanna's mate. We're pledged to take out a bonding contract." He felt Vanna shift slightly in surprise and increased his grip on her shoulder reassuringly.

Sorli nodded. "I see. You do realize that we don't allow weapons within the guild premises, don't you?"

"I saw armed Warriors on our way in, and Kusac told me they now patrol the corridors at night. I'm here to protect her from now on. There's still one of the troopers that killed Sevrin out there. They were after Carrie and Kusac, but he may decide that Vanna or Brynne would make a good substitute. Your Guild Master has been informed of the possible dangers."

"Then doubtless Master Esken will confirm this. In the meantime," he said looking back to Vanna "he's asked that you visit him this afternoon at the ninth hour."

"I'll be there," she said.

"Your Leska, Brynne Stevens, has also been asked to attend," said Sorli. "You need to meet each other properly and come to an arrangement about your future."

"I said I'll be there," snapped Vanna. "Now, is that all?"

"Almost. I think it would be wiser if your mate didn't accompany you," he said.

"I'll wait outside," said Garras. "If she needs me, she can call."

"As you wish," said Sorli.

Vanna waited till he'd left before turning to Garras. "A contract? Are you sure about this, Garras?"

"Positive," he said coming round in front of her again. "That's what a commitment means, isn't it?"

"Yes, but . . ."

"You want practical?" he interrupted, squatting in front of her and taking her hands in his. "As your mate, no one can gainsay my involvement in your life, and your Leska can't object to my presence apart from the days when you need to be with him. On the other hand," he said, pulling her toward him, "it's the only way I can ensure that you'll stay with me. You see, I care about you too much to lose you." His hands encircled her waist and the next moment she was lying on her back looking up at him. "Now, do you have a problem with that?" His voice was a low purr as he nuzzled her cheek.

"I don't have a problem with that," she said with a chuckle, reaching up to pull at his ear. "But I do prefer the bed, you know."

"Then it's time you were more adventurous," he said, one hand snaking round the back of her neck to grasp her by the scruff. He stopped dead. "If you and your Leska are constantly aware of each other," he said, "then that makes this somewhat voyeuristic."

Vanna's ears flattened and she pushed him away, scrambling to her feet, the mood broken. "I can't cope with this, Garras," she said. "It's all right for Carrie and Kusac, but I want a life of my own!" She flung herself down on the settee.

Garras turned to face her but remained where he was. "We'll find a way," he said quietly. "Kusac and Carrie seem to be able to keep some part of their minds separate from each other. What about a few days ago, when Carrie stayed with your family? Kusac didn't know where she was then. Ask them how they do it."

"I don't want to talk about it," she said, her voice muffled by the cushion. "I'm sorry, but I need to be alone for a while."

Garras got to his feet. "Kaid said I could use his room. It's three doors up from here. I'll be there if you need me."

"I'm sorry," she said.

"Don't worry about it, Vanna. I knew it would be difficult," he said, touching her gently on the head as he left.

Later that afternoon, escorted by Garras, Vanna turned up at Master Esken's study. She knew Brynne was already there. Throughout the morning and afternoon she'd been aware of his mind clearing as he gradually threw off the effects of the drugs. He studiously ignored her as she was ushered in by the Guild Master and invited to sit with them at a low table. She took the remaining chair rather than sit beside the human.

"It doesn't seem so very long ago that I welcomed another Leska pair like you to the guild," said Esken, handing Vanna a mug of c'shar. "And there's yet another couple on their way here. It seems that the Links between our people are going to be stronger than we thought." Picking up his mug, he sat back in his chair, his gaze going from one to the other.

"You must both find it terribly disorienting—not to mention frightening—to suddenly become not only full telepaths, but ones with an intensely strong bond to each other. Then to add the final irony, it's with someone from another species. Believe me, I do have sympathy for what you're both going through."

She could feel Brynne's anger mounting until it burned high in both their minds.

"What you did was despicable," said Brynne coldly. "You had no right to kidnap me, drug me, and force me to have sex with this female."

"You weren't kidnapped, Mr. Stevens," said Esken mildly. "You were found wandering in the guild grounds, loudly broadcasting your extreme mental confusion. You were quite rightly brought to the medical center."

"I didn't want to go there!"

"I dare say you didn't, but you were judged to be in no condition to go anywhere else. I must apologize for what happened after that, though. Physician Khafsa had no right to administer the mind-altering drugs which rendered both you and your Leska susceptible to the mating compulsion of your Link. He has been severely reprimanded for his actions."

"I don't want a Leska. I refuse to be physically tied to one female, especially one not of my choosing."

"Your Link with Vanna has been consummated, Mr. Stevens," said Esken, taking a sip from his mug. "You now have access to all her memories so you know that a Leska Link cannot be reversed."

"Don't give me that line of rubbish! It's all a matter of willpower and self-control. I have my own ideas about what I want to do with my life, and it doesn't include being heavily involved with any female, Sholan or otherwise."

"You think it a matter of self-control?" Esken asked, mouth opening in amusement as he replaced his mug on the table. "Then touch her. You'll soon find out differently. Go on," he said as Brynne looked taken aback. "Just touch her hand."

Vanna moved slightly backward in her chair. "Master Esken," she began, then Brynne leaned forward and touched her. She gasped as their bodies instantly responded to the pull of their Link and she remembered in crystal clear detail the events of the night before. Worse, she felt his mind share that memory.

He snatched his hand back, looking shaken.

"You see?" said Master Esken. "That's at the end of your time together when the compulsion is passing. It isn't a question of self-control, is it? You are like one person with two bodies, each storing up your own experiences and constantly replaying them to the other. By the end of four days you've absorbed as much as your minds can hold and you need to come together to sort through those memories. Mating is the vehicle which enables you to do this because then your minds are more in tune with each other than at any other time. But you know all this because Vanna does."

"You're all mad," Brynne said, but his voice lacked conviction. "There's no such thing as this Link you're talking about."

"We lost Raill and Lynn because her mother refused to believe in the Link," said Vanna, addressing him for the first time.

"I don't know that," he said, turning an angry face to her. "I'm sorry, but I have no intention of starting up a relationship of any kind with you. I'd like to think that you're as innocently involved as I am, but after last night, I can't afford to trust any of you."

"I'm not exactly overjoyed about our Link either, but I'm adult enough to realize that we have to deal with it, not refuse to acknowledge that it exists. Are you?"

He glowered at her, his eyebrows almost meeting. "What the hell do you mean by that?" he demanded.

"She means that every five days you'll find you need to get together," Esken interrupted smoothly. "By that time, if you try to ignore the mental call of the Link, you'll find that the memories you've acquired from each other start to replay themselves in your mind. If you keep ignoring it, you'll start to experience stomach cramps, nausea, and headaches as your mind begins to go into overload. If you continue to refuse the Link, you'll become weaker, then go into a coma and die. Vanna knows the pattern because it was only due to her intervention that Carrie and Kusac are still alive."

Brynne looked from one to the other of them but said nothing.

"Leskas needn't be more than working partners," said Esken. "There's no necessity for you to live with each other so long as you spend every fifth day together. Once you're both fully trained, then we can see what kind of work your Talents are suited to. I'd like you to report to Tutor Sorli every afternoon at the eighth hour for tuition. The rest of the time is yours. Vanna," he said, turning toward her, "You've been acquiring data from Dr. Reynolds on Keiss."

She nodded.

"Have you done any tests on Carrie yet?"

"Not yet. Did you know they were life-bonded two nights ago?"

Esken raised an eye ridge in surprise. "No. The Clan Lord didn't tell me that when we spoke last night. I suppose it's only right when you consider their genetic compatibility with each other."

"Wait a minute," said Brynne. "Are you telling me that this Link screws up our genes, too?"

"That is what happened with Carrie and Kusac," agreed Esken. "We have no reason to believe it will happen to any of the other mixed Leska pairs though. Time will tell."

"That's just great," said Brynne, turning angrily to Vanna. "Thanks a bunch, honey. You're the most expensive lay I'll ever have! You probably just cost me everything!"

Vanna felt his anger like a physical blow. She shut her eyes, willing him to leave.

"Don't worry, I'm going!" he said, getting to his feet and striding out, slamming the door behind him.

"Being a telepath means that not only can you hear people's thoughts but other telepaths can hear yours," said Esken. "I fear you're going to have trouble with that young male."

Vanna opened her eyes and got to her feet. "I'm sure I am, Master Esken. I'd be surprised if I didn't the way things are going at the moment. Now, if you'll excuse me. I need to see to some of that work you mentioned."

* * *

As he signed in at the Warriors' Accommodation Guild House in Valsgarth, Dzaka couldn't help the slight grin of amusement at the reaction to his uniform. No longer a lay priest but back on active duty, he wore the gray of the Brotherhood with its red and black flash over the shoulders. Their response was compounded half of fear, half of awe.

"You're on the second floor, corridor seven, room forty-nine," said the clerk on duty. "Do you need someone to show you the way?"

"No, thank you. I know my way around." He picked up his kit bag and strolled off toward the stairs.

He was far from pleased to be back on Shola, because Ghezu, once again, had him following Kaid's tail. He was beginning to wonder why. In two minds whether or not to contact Kaid, he'd decided to wait and see what Kaid did once he knew he was back.

* * *

"Dzaka's here," said Rulla.

"I know. You and I need to talk. Meet me tomorrow at the Limping Jegget, ninth hour. Ask Garras to join us."

Kaid broke the connection and sat back thoughtfully in his chair. His mind had cleared over the last few days. Vartra had been right. He had needed to look inside himself for the answers. The mixed Leska Links were here to stay. There would be more of them, and there would be children. Not all would survive, but enough would to ensure a future generation of these new people.

Absentmindedly, he took the well-chewed twig out of his pocket and began to nibble at it. If this new species was to be given a fair chance, it couldn't be at Stronghold. It had been bad enough trying to bring up Dzaka and he'd been around five years old when he'd been found.

The cubs had to be free to grow and develop naturally, which meant the Telepath Guild was also out. They'd do nothing but run interminable tests on them and get their "experts" to raise them instead of their parents. That left only one feasible solution. They had to break away from the guild system and go it alone. This was what he was going to propose to Garras and Rulla. Once they'd talked it through, then they'd approach Carrie, Kusac, Vanna, and Brynne, and pray that they agreed.

That left Dzaka. The chasm between them had to be healed—one way or another. He'd talk to him after he met with the others.

* * *

Carrie's training was scheduled for a couple of hours each morning and afternoon. Meral and T'Chebbi worked with her while Kaid supervised. Kusac watched anxiously, joining in when asked.

Kaid had been carefully analyzing their techniques and by the end of the first hour had seen a basic flaw in their methods. He called a halt to the practice, taking Meral's weapons from him. Sword in one hand, he slipped his arm into the buckler straps.

Dropping into a low crouch, he slowly began to circle her. He maintained eye contact, the shield held close to his body, sword tip projecting just above it in direct line with her eyes.

Her body tensed as she turned on the same spot, following his every move, waiting for his attack.

With a sudden loud yowl, he leaped forward, sword coming down in a deadly arc toward her head.

She blocked it—just—staggering back under the force of his attack. He followed up his advantage, raining down a fusillade of blows on her from every direction until he broke through her guard. Stopping immediately, he pulled back several meters and waited in the guard position, keeping both her and Kusac in sight.

Kusac's low growl had built in volume until now it was clearly audible. Meral held him by the arm, and it was clear he'd had to prevent him from intervening.

Panting, Carrie looked at the thin line of blood beginning to well over the edges of the cut on her sword arm. "What the hell was that about?" she asked angrily, looking across at him. "Why come at me like that?" Sweat was running into her eyes and making them sting. She wiped the back of her hand across her forehead, annoyed that Kaid wasn't even out of breath.

"I wanted to see if you could fight for your life," he said, standing up and beckoning Meral over. He handed the weapons back to him. "My cut was in line with your heart: I could have killed you had I wished. These two have been training you to fight one Challenge to the first blood. Once you're out there in the circle, no one can help you. What happens if Rala decides not to fight by the rules? You need to be able to cope with the unexpected, to fight to stay alive if need be."

He stepped back out of the sanded arena. "Teach her how to kill," he ordered Meral and T'Chebbi. "This isn't a match combat, it's for real. If only one of them walks out of the circle, I intend it to be you, Carrie."

Meral glanced apologetically at Kaid as he took his place opposite her again. "We've been doing what we thought best, given her condition," he said.

"Rala won't be so thoughtful," Kaid replied shortly. "We've just over a week to turn her into a Warrior. A few minor cuts in practice will make her keep her guard up all the more."

"Thanks a lot, Kaid," Carrie muttered, readjusting her grip on the buckler.

"Would you rather die?" he countered, moving round to stand beside Kusac.

With a noise akin to a Sholan growl, she launched herself at Meral.

* * *

Garras was the last to arrive, threading his way through the last of the lunchtime students to the tiny side room.

"We've none of us got long," said Kaid, indicating the glass of ale they'd gotten for Garras. "I'll be brief. My contract with the Brotherhood was over when I landed on Shola. Garras, I reactivated your status myself, it hasn't been done through Stronghold. You're still a free agent. Rulla, you're not. I know this, and before I begin, if you choose not to get involved, I understand."

Rulla shot him a look from under lowered brows. "Cut the crap, Kaid. You know I'm in, whatever the cost."

Kaid sighed. "Kusac intends to leave the Telepath Guild after the Challenge."

There was silence for a moment or two. To be guildless was to be isolated from one's peers, and for the Sholans it was tantamount to being exiled.

Garras nodded slowly. "It's no less than I expected. Vanna would prefer not to belong either, after what Esken had done to her."

Rulla took a swig of his ale. "We're going it alone," he stated. "It's no less than I expected, Kaid. What took you so long to come to the same decision as us?"

Kaid looked sharply at the other two males, catching the faint glint of amusement in their eyes. "The responsibility of making the decision," he said. "It can't be made lightly. I know, I've been guildless for ten years."

"I passed over my merchant responsibilities to my nephew several weeks ago," said Garras. "He's old enough now, and he's been doing it since I was called up by the Forces for active service."

"We've already had this conversation, Kaid," said Rulla. "More important now is when we'll make the break, and what role you see for us in the future."

"We keep things as they are for the moment. None of the guilds must know what we plan. I'll tell you when we're ready to move. You're covered by your leave for a good few months yet, aren't you, Rulla?"

He flicked his ears in assent.

Kaid moved restlessly, the brief motion of his ears showing his uncertainty. "As for our role in the future, we must continue to protect them. There are only two mixed pairs on Shola as yet. Garras, you're involved with one of them. I'm working with the other pair. When the interpreter from Earth and his Leska arrive, we'll need to place one of our people at their side."

"That's easy, I'll do it," said Rulla.

Kaid's ears flicked again.

Garras reached out and touched his hand. "Let me, Kaid. It's not that easy, Rulla. We," he looked at Kaid then back at Rulla, "think that we're being ... called ... to protect certain people. We can't tell yet, we'll have to wait and see. Until then, yes, you'll protect the new pair."

Rulla raised his eye ridges. "Called?"

Garras nodded. "If we're right, you'll find out. We can't tell you any more since it's speculation at the moment."

Rulla looked from one to the other, noticing Kaid's ears. "You're working as one," he said abruptly. "What's happened to you?"

"Speculation," said Kaid. "We need a control to test the theory. You're it, Rulla, I'm afraid."

Rulla shrugged and took another mouthful of the ale. "So be it."

"The Brotherhood want the Challenge to go ahead," said Kaid, taking up his glass again. "They want it proved they can fight. We can't move yet. I'm training her and if all proceeds normally, she'll win."

"Any element of risk is too much," said Rulla.

"I know! Don't tell me!"

"We have no option but to play this hand out," said Garras. "No one likes it."

"I'll be calling you in to help guard the grounds," said Kaid, his voice quieter now. "That trooper is still on the loose. The Challenge is an ideal opportunity for him to make his hit."

"You know where to find me," said Rulla.

* * *

From the Inn, Kaid went to the Warrior's Accommodation Guild House on the outskirts of Valsgarth. Dzaka was waiting in the common room for him.

"You're no longer attached to Lijou, I see," said Kaid, taking the chair beside him.

"No. I'm back on active."

Kaid nodded. "Do you know about the Challenge Liegena Carrie Aldatan is to fight?"

"I've been briefed. They're bonded, then?"

"Yes. I was the witness. Ghezu said I could call on the

people I needed. I want you with us on security at the estate in the days leading up to the Challenge."

"The missing trooper?"

"Yes. I'm not convinced Chyad died on Keiss. He'll make his move during the Challenge."

"You can reach me here. Let me know when you want me over at the Aldatan estate."

Kaid nodded. The silence lengthened between them.

"Was there anything else you wanted?" Dzaka asked.

"You asked me before, on the *Khalossa,* why I had to leave the Brotherhood," said Kaid.

"It's none of my business, Kaid. You don't owe me an explanation," said Dzaka.

"Perhaps not, but it still lies between us. I can't tell you the details, Dzaka, much as I want to, because I gave my word. In return Ghezu promised to treat you fairly. I may have had to leave you behind, but I did keep an eye open to ensure you were safe."

"How would you have helped me if I hadn't been?"

"I'd have been there."

Dzaka gave a snort of disbelief. "Easy to say when you didn't have to do it!" He leaned forward, crowding Kaid. "Why didn't you let me leave, too? Why didn't you give me the right to choose?"

"You had your life ahead of you!" he hissed, pushing him back. "Mine in the Brotherhood was through, finished! What do you think these last ten years have been like for me, Dzaka? Guildless, not able to speak to those I'd lived and trained with? Have you any idea? I doubt it!"

He could read the thoughts flitting across Dzaka's face.

"I never thought . . ."

"I know you didn't. Trust, that's what it's all about, isn't it, Dzaka? That's why Ghezu has you back on my tail again. What is it this time? To kill them if she survives the Challenge, because they've too high a profile? Because Vanna and Brynne, complete novices, will be easier for both sides to control?" He watched Dzaka's ears start to move backward then stop.

"You'll be at the Challenge, Dzaka. A front seat," he said, his voice becoming cold and impersonal. "All you need to do is let the trooper make his shot. I needn't know, need I?" He got to his feet and leaned forward, putting his hand over Dzaka's arm where it lay on the side of the chair.

"Trust, Dzaka." His claws extended, digging into Dzaka's flesh, stopping just short of puncturing the skin. "Show me some, and next time I leave, I swear you'll come, too, if that's what you choose." With that, he turned and left.

* * *

Brynne hadn't shown up at Sorli's classes for the last few days. Vanna didn't expect to see him today either. When she arrived, she collected a mug of c'shar first before settling herself at the table. The classes were small and informal, the only other students being a young Sholan couple.

The door opened and Brynne sauntered in, his exterior attitude at odds with the pounding headache and thoroughly disgruntled mood she knew he was hiding. He took a chair at the far end of the room and slouched there, lighting one of his cigarettes. Sorli glanced at Vanna, raising his eye ridges at her but saying nothing.

Vanna glowered back at Sorli, her ears flicking in annoyance. She wasn't responsible for Brynne's behavior.

The lesson progressed until early evening when they dispersed to the refectory for third meal. Brynne was the first to leave. Sorli, however, held Vanna back.

"I assume you haven't had a chance to talk to him yet."

Vanna shook her head. "This is the first time I've seen him since we met at Master Esken's."

"Your first Link day starts tomorrow. How are you managing?"

She flicked her ear in feigned surprise. "And I thought you were getting reports from Physician Khafsa!" she said. "I'm restless and edgy, but there are good medical reasons for that."

"Don't let the medic overrule the telepath," warned Sorli. "Some of the effects of a Link can't be rationalized away and you must be able to recognize them. You haven't had any memory flashes yet, have you?"

"Nothing like that," she said, following him out.

"If he doesn't come to you before you start to experience them, let me know and I'll do something about it," said Sorli as they walked down the corridor to the refectory. He glanced toward her. "I give my word we won't use drugs again."

"I wish I could believe you," she said. "I'll handle things

myself. I don't think it would endear me to him in the long
run."

"You're probably right," he said, stopping by the mess
doorway. "Are you eating here?"

"No. I think I'd prefer to eat in my room."

Sorli nodded. "Remember, even if Brynne doesn't come
to you, stay in your quarters tomorrow. Our students don't
need any extra encouragement to form pairs!"

"Don't worry, I will," she said, turning toward the stairs.

She prowled round the apartment, feeling tense and unsettled. It was partly due to the endocrine changes, but there
was also Garras. Over the last four days, he'd always been
there, asking nothing of her, patient, protective. She knew
where she was with him, unlike this Terran male. Thank the
Gods, she'd persuaded him to take today and the next day
off!

She could sense Brynne skulking around the refectory
looking for a partner for the night. He was determined to
show Vanna he didn't need her, that any female would do.
She sighed. It looked as if she was in for a repeat of last
night. Another helping of secondhand sex was not what she
needed, especially when she was too inhibited by the mental
closeness to pair with Garras.

By late evening, Vanna was suffering from a headache and
nausea. She'd tried taking medication for them and found
out the truth of Sorli's words. The symptoms persisted. Sen-
sitized as they were to each other, she knew most of it was
due to Brynne's determination to stay away from her.

She could feel the pull of their Link, the compulsion getting stronger as the night wore on. Despite his charm, he'd
been unable to find a partner, probably because of the mixture of signals he was projecting—anger coupled with a
highly charged sexuality was not a combination that would
attract even a non-telepath and he was looking for a female
in the Telepath Guild! At least she had the benefit of
Kusac's advice on how to go about building stronger shields
than they were being shown by Sorli. She needn't let everyone know exactly how she was feeling.

Balked of his chosen diversion, he'd gone out drinking
with his friends. That in itself wasn't a problem, but he'd
continued to the point where she was beginning to feel as
bad as he did.

The whole situation was ludicrous. She'd sat here for the last four hours experiencing his anger and every objection he could think up for staying away from her, and none of it mattered a damn except whether they wanted to live with the Link, or die without it. She was going to live, and she was no meek Terran female to sit and wait for the male to come to her.

Grabbing her jacket, she opened the door, coming face-to-face with her bodyguard.

"Where are you going, Physician?" Lhea asked, falling into step beside her.

"I'm going to get Brynne," she said, ears set to the side of her head and tail flicking with anger. "I've had enough. We've got to sort this thing out between us now."

Lhea, sensibly, made no comment.

They made their way out of the gates and into the narrow streets surrounding the guild. Vanna knew exactly where he was, at a small inn not far from the temple. As they entered, she saw that the Terran males seemed to have made it their meeting place. There were a few ribald comments as she went over to where Brynne and his friends were sitting, but she ignored them. Brynne was slumped over the table nursing his head.

Sitting down opposite him, she reached for his glass and moved it away. "You've had enough," she said firmly.

He looked blearily up at her. "Oh, it's you, is it? What d' you want?"

"You're coming back to the guild with me. We have to talk this thing over."

"I'm not going," he said belligerently, sitting up.

"Look, you can do what you damned well please for the rest of the week, but tonight you'll talk to me!" she snapped. "Being Linked to you isn't exactly my idea of fun either, and I object to suffering from your hangovers!" Just being this close to him was upsetting her already jangled nerves.

"I think you'd better go with the lady," said one of his friends. "You don't look too well."

Vanna got to her feet, fighting to control her own stomach as his began to rebel. "Come on," she said, reaching out a hand to pull him up, but his friend forestalled her.

"I'll help you get him back," he said, getting up and hauling the protesting Brynne out from behind the table. "You

don't look too well yourself. You're his Leska, aren't you?"
He frowned over the strange word. "You're called Vanna."

Vanna nodded as Lhea moved closer to help him.

Once they hit the cold air outside, the argument left
Brynne and he began to droop between them. His friend and
Lhea linked arms with him and marched him along at a rea-
sonable pace while Vanna loped alongside.

"He's not a bad sort once you get to know him," the
Terran said, glancing across at her. "We worked together for
two years on the Cassandra Project back on Earth. That's
how we come to be here. I'm Terry, by the way," he added.
"Who's your friend?"

"Lhea," she said, looking at him more closely. He was
about the same size as Brynne but fair where he was dark,
and clean shaven where Brynne was bearded.

"Cassandra?" she asked.

"We belonged to a group of people who worked for the
police, finding missing persons and stolen goods," he explained.

"Sounds interesting."

"It's not bad. Beats sitting in an office all day," he grinned
as they entered the guild gates. "Where do you want to take
him?"

"My quarters," she said, leading the way.

She pushed the door open, standing back for Terry and
Lhea to take Brynne in. "In the kitchen, please."

Terry gave a low whistle as they half-carried Brynne's in-
ert form through the lounge into the kitchen.

"This is luxury," he said. "Not that where we are isn't
nice," he added hurriedly.

Vanna managed a small grin. "These are the Leska quarters. You'll be in one of the dorms, I expect."

Terry and Lhea sat Brynne down in a chair at the table.

"Yes, we're all together. Well, the men are," he amended.
"The two women are in the dorm next door. I'll leave you
to it, then. See you again, I hope. I'll see myself out." With
a friendly smile he left.

"Can you manage?" asked Lhea.

Vanna nodded.

"I'll be outside if you need me."

Vanna sighed and took off her jacket, flinging it over a

chair. She looked at her Leska and sighed again. Brynne had slumped over the table, his head resting on his forearms.

"We'd better do something for you, hadn't we? I'm afraid you're no use to anyone in this condition." She pulled him up into a vertical position. "Oh, no, you don't," she said, sensing his stomach starting to heave. Hauling him out of his chair, she shoved him over to the sink, holding him there until he'd finished throwing up. Then she pulled his unresisting body to the bathing room.

Propping him against the shower wall, she started trying to undress him, but his knees gave under him and slowly he slid down to a sitting position on the floor. He sat there motionless, his eyes closed.

With an exclamation of annoyance, she turned to the cupboard set above the basin. From it she took out a glass and a sachet of detox. Half filling the glass with water, she ripped the sachet open and poured in the contents. Swirling it around, she turned back to Brynne and squatting down, took him by the chin and shook him.

"Wake up, Brynne," she said in Terran. "Come on, drink this."

As his eyes opened and he tried to focus blearily on her, she found herself very conscious of how soft the hair on his face was. For some reason she'd expected it to be coarse.

"Come on, drink this," she repeated, taking his hand and wrapping it around the glass.

"Hey, 'nother drink!" he said, his voice slurred as he gripped the glass tightly. He tossed the contents off in one swallow then pulled a face as the taste hit him. "God, that's vile," he said, shuddering and shutting his eyes again.

"Never mind that, it'll make you feel better," she said, taking the glass from him and putting it on the side of the basin. She took hold of his sweater and started to haul it off over his head. "Help me, for God's sake," she snapped as her claws snagged yet again in the garment.

"Leave me alone," he mumbled, lifting his arm and trying to fend her off. "What you tryin' to do?"

The sweater finally wrestled off, Vanna gave up. "Damn you," she said, her voice close to a growl. "Shower in the rest of your clothes for all I care!"

Standing up she leaned into the cubicle and switched the water on, letting a burst of cold hit him first.

Brynne gave a yell as it hit him and he began trying to

struggle to his feet. "Bloody hell, woman! What're you trying to do? Kill me?" Then warm water sluiced over him and he gasped again at the sudden change in temperature.

It had some of the desired effect: he was fully conscious, but he was mad. He lunged out of the shower toward her, grabbing her by the arm.

"Just what the hell do you think you're doing?" he demanded. "Look at me! I'm soaked!"

Vanna pulled her chin in and stared up at him. "You feel better now, though, don't you?" Then she began to smile at the sight of him standing there, water streaming off his hair onto his back and shoulders, his saturated trousers and shoes making puddles on the floor.

His eyes narrowed, brows meeting in the middle of his forehead.

Where he held her by the arm, it was as if a static charge was passing between them. Every hair on her body began to tingle and rise. She knew he could feel it, too.

His other arm snaked round her waist, pulling her a little closer. He was studying her, gauging her against a mixture of Terran and Sholan values. Leaning forward, he sniffed at her. "You smell nice," he said.

"You're drunk," she retorted.

He smiled beatifically at her. "That's right," he said, slurring the words.

Vanna was acutely conscious of his presence. She could feel the tension building in their bodies as he released her arm to put his hand up to her face. His fingers gently touched the soft fur there, then moved on to caress her ear.

She looked up at him. He wasn't so different from Sholan males—at least as far as his face was concerned. The dark hair covering the lower part of his face was not unlike their fur.

Where her hand touched his chest, she could feel the warmth and softness of his skin through the fine covering of hair, could feel the compulsive pull of their Link increasing as it swept through them both. Deliberately she ran her hands across his chest, making sure her claws stayed retracted. "We've unfinished business to attend to," she said quietly.

"I know," he said, no longer quite so drunk. His fingers pushed through the short curls on the back of her head, tightening in them as he matched her body to his, unconsciously pulling her head back to expose her throat.

* * *

"You seem singularly unsurprised at the course of recent events," said the younger male as they strolled across the courtyard toward the small formal garden.

His companion made a gesture of dismissal. "When we can clearly see the hand of Vartra at work, nothing should surprise us."

"Well, it surprised me," Ghyan said. "The temple couldn't influence Vailkoi's daughter. She's determined the Challenge will go ahead. How real are the risks to the human girl?"

"Real enough if anything should go wrong," said Kaid, stopping to examine a low fruiting bush. "You'll have a good crop this year," he observed, gently feeling the weight of one of the dark red globes.

"Never mind them! What actions are your people taking to protect her?" he demanded, thrusting his thumbs through the narrow belt that encircled his robe.

"She's being taught to fight." He was surprised to be asked that.

"What of their cub? Will she be affected by this?"

He regarded the younger male, a brief of expression of humor crossing his face. "You're asking me for predictions? She should win easily, with no harm to her unborn cub—if all proceeds as expected."

"The Clan Leader is to petition the Governor, asking him to stop the Challenge."

"Let him. If the God wills it, the Challenge will be stopped. Bring no more pressure to bear on Vailkoi or his daughter as it suits our purposes to see the fight go ahead. We need to know how both of them will react to a real combat situation."

"I don't like it. Too much is being left to chance."

"You call the God's will chance?" His eye ridge rose questioningly as he noted the other's ears flick in concern. "I thought you at least would have perceived the matter differently."

"Don't play semantics with me. There's a lot at stake here, not least their lives! Do you realize that because of the investigations into the Terrans' abilities, my guild has all the information it needs about the lack of minor Talents amongst their members? It's going to draw the obvious conclusion."

"We're aware of that," Kaid said imperturbably, turning to regard the building in the distance. "More important now is the need to know what the Clan Lord plans to do to control the power of your guild. We're aware of what happened to the latest pair. Though we deplore it, at least it ensured they survived. This must not happen again."

"Everything's so cold and calculated with you, isn't it? All you're concerned about is that the outcome is favorable for you. What about them? What if Kusac can't stand there and watch his Leska fight, perhaps even get wounded? Then what will happen to your bid for independence?"

"They have to be tested," he replied, voice and body emotionless. "We have to know once and for all. I know they can do it. He's no longer merely a Telepath, he's more now, more like us—as she has always been."

Ghyan pulled his hands free of his belt. "They chose the right person for the job," he said coldly, turning away from him. "I'll do as I'm ordered, but under protest. You've not a shred of compassion for them, have you? Nothing touches you, only duty. Don't contact me again unless you have to," he said, turning his back on him and walking away.

How wrong you are, Kaid thought, watching the retreating figure. *The God mocks me at every turn, stabbing a knife in my side whenever I think of the Challenge and the risks she faces. You'd laugh if you knew that, little priest.*

He sighed, turning toward the rear exit. It was time he left. He'd been gone too long.

* * *

Vanna contacted Carrie and Kusac midweek, full of apologies. "I would have been in touch earlier, but this last week and a half have been rather difficult."

"Troubles with Brynne?" asked Kusac sympathetically.

"Yes and no. He still resents the physical tie of the bond and hasn't come to terms with the fact that we need each other every fifth day. He still tries to satisfy his frustrations with other females before he comes to me."

"You should return the compliment," said Kusac frowning, annoyed that she was obviously linked to someone so insensitive.

"Actually I did," she admitted, flicking her ears backward,

"with Garras. Brynne didn't appreciate it. Fortunately, his resentment vanishes as soon as we touch. Even though we have no relationship to speak of, the physical side of our Link is more than satisfying."

Kusac grinned. "Well, there have to be some advantages, don't there?"

"Look, I didn't call you up to talk about my problems," she said with a sudden change of mood. "I'd like you to come over to the guild this afternoon. There are some tests I must run on Carrie. If I don't, I'll have Khafsa breathing down my neck and threatening to take over your case."

"What time shall we meet you?"

"Tenth hour, in the reception area of the medical center."

"We'll be there," he said.

* * *

"Once again, confirmation of these rumors eludes us as both the Telepath Guild and the Guild of Medics hold their peace. All we can say for sure is that a Challenge has been made by our Liegen's Leska and was duly accepted by Liegena Vailkoi, heir of the Vailkoi Clan from the Vrusa estate in the northern continent. It is interesting to note, though, that there is a strange silence from the Aldatan Clan who refused to accept any calls from us at Infonet. Should our informant be proved correct, I'm sure you'll join me in expressing concern over the alleged genetic changes that may have made it possible for the increasing number of mixed Leska pairs to breed."

The screen faded to show Kusac and Carrie standing in one of the small central parks in Valsgarth, listening to a public storytelling performance.

"This is Rhaema Vorkoh, your reporter for Infonet News."

Seeing Carrie's face begin to pale, Rhyasha switched off the leisure comm unit.

"Don't worry, cub," she said soothingly. "They love to speculate. I'm sure your people are no different."

"That was taken yesterday," said Carrie, her hands clenching into fists. "We only stood there for five minutes! They're always following us. Why won't they leave us alone? Now everyone knows!"

"No, they don't," said Rhyasha firmly, putting her arm around Carrie's shoulders and giving her a comforting squeeze. "Without proof they won't dare voice their suspicions. The Challenge is only a few days away now. Once it's over, what could be more natural than that you should take an extended rest on the estate?"

Rhyasha leaned forward to pick up the drink that sat half finished on the table beside them. "Come on, drink this down before Kusac arrives. You know how he's worrying about your health. Vanna won't be pleased either, considering the bother she went to in checking out the vitamins and minerals needed to concoct this supplement drink."

Carrie took the mug from her and pulling a face, drank the contents.

Rhyasha laughed. "It would have tasted better if you hadn't let it get cold," she chided as they heard the noise of the aircar landing outside under the window.

"I don't want to go to the guild," said Carrie, reluctantly getting to her feet. "I'm afraid of meeting any of the Terrans."

"There's nothing to fear," said Rhyasha as she linked arms with the girl and led her to the study door. "Kusac and Kaid will be with you. Vanna needs to do this checkup, you know that. Are you sure you don't want me to come, too?" she asked as they walked along the inner balcony to the stairway down to the ground level.

Carrie shook her head. "No, thank you. I know you're busy with estate business today."

Kusac met them at the foot of the stairs. "Don't worry about the newscast," he said, taking her by the hand. "Most people at the guild will be in classes and won't have heard it. As Mother said, once this is over, you won't need to leave the estate until you're ready to do so."

* * *

In his aircar, Chyad turned off the comm. So there was to be a Challenge, was there? They'd just played straight into his hands. Hiding out on their estate had been a long shot that had paid off. Security would be intense, they knew he was still out there, somewhere. He grinned. They didn't know he was so close to them, though. His tail twitched with pleasure. He had a fair chance of escape afterward, but that wasn't important any longer. He was sick of living on the run. So long as he got them, he'd have beaten that bastard hired to guard them, and that was all that mattered now.

He reached for his pulse rifle and began checking it out,

making sure it was ready. The battery packs were still good and he had three of them.

* * *

Vanna met them as arranged and led them along the corridor to the rooms housing the scanner units.

"Jack Reynolds sent me some data on Terran physiology about two weeks ago. Apart from the obvious physical differences between our species, there are several developmental ones," she said, opening the door and ushering them in.

"Gestation time for humans is forty weeks. For us it's twenty-four. I need to take a scan so we can measure the size of your cub's head. Once I have that, then I can make a reasonable prediction as to when she'll be born."

She took Carrie by the arm and led her over to an examination couch set beside the far wall. "Up you get," she said, pulling a low step from underneath the couch.

"Hey, don't worry," she said, sensing Carrie's dread. "There aren't going to be any unpleasant surprises. That's a viable cub you have there, you know that already."

Kusac helped her settle herself on the couch and remained there holding her hand as Vanna reached up to swing the scanner over her.

Carrie lay there, looking at the narrow bar of light as Vanna moved over to her monitor.

Though Kusac was trying hard to block them from her, she could pick up enough fragments of his worries to know that he was as reluctant as she was to see what their child would look like.

Her hands moved instinctively to clasp over her stomach. As Kusac's hand followed, icy fear swept through her. She looked up at him, then to Vanna, suddenly seeing their faces as more feline than humanoid. Kusac's dark-furred face with the impossibly amber eyes. The light caught the tips of his canines where they showed beneath the bifurcated mouth, making them shine white against his darkness. God, what was she doing here with these alien people? What was she doing letting his child grow inside her?

Her stomach lurched as she pushed the fear aside, praying that he hadn't noticed.

He hadn't; something else had claimed his attention. His hand released hers and spread across the gentle swell that lay protected beneath her hands.

"She moved," he whispered. "Carrie, I felt her move!" His eyes, the amber almost opalescent, looked intently at her, all his fears now gone.

"It's too soon," she said, her senses swamped with Kusac's feelings of pleasure and pride.

"Not if we're looking at a Sholan gestation," said Vanna as she activated the unit.

She turned round to look at them, adjusting her scanner monitor so they could see it too. "You'll have to move your hands," she said gently, "otherwise we won't be able to see her."

Carrie moved her hands, holding them clenched at her sides. She could feel Kusac's eagerness now to see their daughter, followed by his realization that she was still afraid.

His hand closed on hers once more, opening the fingers and lifting it up to his cheek. *Everything will be fine,* he sent.

"It's just as well you're staying with your parents," Vanna said, activating the unit, "since I expect that, like me, they've been fending off requests for interviews and tests from various people. After this Challenge is over, I think the two of you should go away for a few weeks, somewhere no one can find you."

"It's already been arranged," said Kusac.

"Good," she said, looking back at them as the scanner bar passed slowly above Carrie toward her head, then began its journey back. "You're definitely beginning to look pregnant now," she said, reaching over to gently touch Carrie's stomach. "I have a feeling we're looking at a Sholan gestation."

She looked back at the monitor, noticing Carrie's knuckles begin to whiten as her grasp tightened on Kusac's hand. She could feel her panic at the thought of any outside interest in her and their child.

"Don't worry," said Kusac. "Once we get back home, you needn't leave there again until after she's born."

"I'm all right," Carrie said, only a slight quaver in her voice. "Why are you working anyway?" she asked Vanna. "I thought you'd be given leave because of your Link. I remember how difficult it was for us, and we were kept secluded in the suite on the *Khalossa.*"

"I promised you I wouldn't allow anyone else to do tests," she said, fiddling with the controls until a picture began to form on the screen. "Besides, I prefer to keep busy."

"There you are," she said, moving back so she could point to the screen. "That's her heart that you can see. It's beating normally, and there's the extra valve that you humans lack."

She touched the controls again and the image changed to show a full-sized picture of the baby. "It looks like your children will be essentially Sholan," she said.

Kusac felt the instinctive side of Carrie's mind begin to react in fear and mentally he reached out to her, trying to reassure her. He bent down to touch her. "Don't be afraid," he said. "She's our cub, our daughter. How can she be alien to us when we made her?"

Carrie reached up and pulled him down, clinging to him, drawing on their Link while she fought to let her intellect take over. His physical and mental presence steadied her, and the fear began to recede as she felt his pride in her.

"Look, Carrie," said Vanna, drawing her attention back to the screen. "Her hands and feet look slightly more like yours, but they're still clawed. Her legs are straighter, too. I have a feeling she'll walk predominantly upright." She adjusted the view again. "Ah, I've got her head now," she said with satisfaction. "Don't worry about it looking out of proportion at the moment because it is at this stage of development."

"Well, there you have your Leska love child," a male Terran voice drawled from the door. "I hope it's what you want."

Vanna rounded on Brynne. "What the hell are you doing here?" she demanded. "You've no business barging in here while I'm with patients! Get out!"

"I've every right," he said. "I've got all your medical knowledge, my dear, and, no, I'm not an ignorant voyeur. I want to know what our child will look like."

"What do you mean?" she asked, stunned.

"Have you checked yourself lately? No? Well, I suggest that you do, then you and your little friend can attend Mothercare classes together. Besides, I wanted to meet Kusac again and see just what sort of male you judge me against. I would have assumed it would have been Garras considering he's your mate, but then you people have no sense of loyalty to one partner, have you?"

Vanna ignored the last remark, hoping Kusac was too busy with Carrie to have heard what Brynne said.

"I'm not pregnant," she stated flatly. "There hasn't been enough time for the genetic changes to reach that stage yet."

"You said that because of the gestalt the whole process was accelerated in our case," Brynne said. "If I were you, I'd check more than my endocrine levels today. We human males have a way of knowing these things. You're pregnant." He gave her an indolent wave and left, letting the door slam shut behind him.

Kusac was too busy attending to Carrie to be other than peripherally aware of Vanna and Brynne's interchange. At Brynne's comment, reason had left her to be replaced with an overwhelming terror. Primal instincts came to the fore, telling her that this child was not like her, was not of her species. It was alien through and through, despite the fact that it carried her genes, too. Hysteria took over, and she tried to push Kusac away and get to her feet. She wanted to run and keep running until she left all this far behind, but a small corner of her mind told her that where she went, this problem went, too.

Kusac shoved the scanner aside, grasping Carrie tightly so that she couldn't move. He felt the gestalt start to build and mentally wrenched the control from her, using its power to subdue her.

Through their Link, he forcibly reminded her of their times together, times when they had laughed, times when they had been joined against a common enemy on Keiss, times when they had loved, and fought with each other. Gradually the terror began to fade, leaving her sobbing against him.

Hush, I know. Believe me, I do understand, he sent. *Forget Brynne and the other Terrans. We live here, on Shola. What they think doesn't concern us. We can't live our lives by what others want of us. We've got each other and a place here to belong. That's enough.*

Take me home, Kusac, she sent, tears still streaming down her face. *Take me home.*

He helped her down and keeping his arm tightly around her, led her to the door. He turned back to Vanna. "We're leaving," he said. "Any more tests can wait." He hesitated. "Until Brynne gets himself straightened out, I'm sorry, but I want him kept away from Carrie."

"Yes, of course," said Vanna, still in shock from what Brynne had said. "I'm sorry. I didn't expect this of him."

Kusac shrugged. "We all react differently to the realization that we've helped create a new life. Look at how I behaved. He is right, though."

Vanna stared after him as he left. She gave herself a little shake. There was a lot to do, she'd better get on with it.

Chapter 19

"Esken, I demand to know what the hell is going on! You told me you had this matter of the alien telepaths under control. An isolated incident, you said! Now I hear that the pair who landed here a few days ago have died, that your top interpreter on Earth is on his way here with a human Leska, and under your own noses a link has formed between one of our female medics and a human male! To cap it all, the first pair are now expecting a cub!" He stared angrily out of the comm screen at Esken.

"I'd hardly call that being in control, would you? I have the Council Administrators demanding answers, and Konis Aldatan contacting me every three hours over this damned Challenge his bond-daughter has gotten herself involved in! What do you suggest I tell them?"

"Governor Nesul, I admit that I was wrong about Kusac Aldatan's Link to the human female being an isolated incident," Master Esken said stiffly, "However, now that the medic who was doing most of the research into this has a human Leska of her own, perhaps we'll have a better chance of finding out what causes these links."

"What you're saying is you don't know."

"We've got several working hypotheses, Governor, but at the moment . . ."

"You don't know," interrupted Nesul, impatient with Esken's evasiveness.

"We are having all the mixed Leska pairs brought to the Guild," said Esken frostily. "The situation is contained. With more cases to study, I'm sure we'll reach a conclusion sooner."

"If you can't solve this problem, then I'm going to involve someone who can. You've had long enough. As to this cub that Kusac Aldatan's Leska is expecting, I suppose there's no doubt that it's his, is there?"

"None, Governor," said Esken, his tone still cool. "Tests show otherwise. The cub is his."

"I want to know how this happened. I was told that these Terrans weren't genetically compatible with us. If there's one cub, there will be others."

"There's no reason to believe that, Governor."

"Don't give me the wrong scent, Esken! You don't believe that any more than I do! What do you intend to do about this child? And this damned Challenge? I presume Konis has contacted you about it, too."

"It's an En'Shalla Challenge, Governor. I've refused to get involved," said the Guild Master. "As for the child, it's a hybrid, neither Sholan nor Terran. Perhaps it would be for the best if it didn't survive."

Nesul's ears flicked contemptuously. "You want it to die, don't you? It's only the first, Esken, mark my words on this. You won't be so lucky a second or third time. One of them will survive."

"Governor Nesul, I've been given my instructions by Commander Chuz, President of the Forces High Command. The pair were sent to me to have their Talents assessed. They were also to attend the Warrior Guild for the same reason. Now that a situation has occurred when their potential to fight can actually be tested, the female will fight the Challenge. Even if I could interfere, I have been ordered not to."

"Since when did you take orders from the military on a guild matter?" demanded Nesul.

"This has been designated a matter of planetary security," said Esken stiffly. "Every guild is cooperating, including the Brotherhood."

"Then why was I not informed?"

Esken began to smile. "Only those guilds involved needed to know, Governor," he said, his tone silky. "There was no need to involve you before now."

Nesul's anger flipped from hot to deadly cold. "Who made that decision?" he asked quietly. "You, I suppose."

"As the primary guild, it was left to my discretion," he admitted with an air of condescension.

Nesul took a deep breath. "Then I suggest that you prepare some answers for me to give my administrators; otherwise, Esken, I will refer them to you personally!" With that he blanked the screen.

His exchange with Esken had annoyed him more than

usual, reminding him yet again that he might be the elected governmental head of Shola, but that a great deal occurred of which he was unaware. He picked up the latest message left by Konis and reread it thoughtfully. Planetbound he might be, but he wasn't the fool that those involved in off-world politics thought him. He could see the wind of change coming as well as the next person, and to his mind it was simple. Either one went with it and thus shaped it, or one opposed it and was trampled in the rush. And cubs born of these Leska pairs were that future.

For too long now the Telepath Guild had dominated politics both on and off world. Telepaths, although few in number, generated uneasiness among those who were unTalented in that direction. Telepaths were vital at every level of society, ensuring the honesty of people in business and civil life, and Leska pairs could communicate instantly with other Telepaths over great distances. The one thing that offset their powerful Talent was their inability to cause pain or to fight. These mixed pairs of fighting telepaths challenged that guild's power by their very existence.

Putting the message down, he scratched his chin thoughtfully. Esken was laying down what amounted to his own private army, setting up a situation for future Guild Masters to have the wherewithal to challenge the elected government. Konis was right, the power of the guild over the mixed Leskas had to be curtailed now, before the other guilds and Clans unquestioningly accepted them as part of Esken's Guild House at Valsgarth.

He started to smile as a plan began to formulate in his mind. The fact that it would coincidentally let him best his old adversary was absolutely irrelevant. Besides, he happened to believe in the sanctity of the family, something that didn't affect Esken since he had chosen to remain childless.

* * *

As soon as Carrie and Kusac had left, Rhyasha went indoors looking for her mate. She found him in his study. "We've got to stop that Challenge," she said, pacing round the room. "There must be something we can do! This should be a time of happiness for them, a time of pride when Kusac can look after her in such a way as to show her how good a father he will be—all the normal things that make up any family's life, be they Keissian or Sholan. Instead, you can cut their fear with a knife!"

"I know, Rhyasha. Do you think I'm insensitive to what they're going through? I feel almost as strong a need to cherish the mother of my granddaughter as my son does! Like him, I'm afraid to do so in case she loses the cub. It would only make her pain worse, especially if the child isn't viable."

"She's viable. You don't think I'd let her go to the guild for a scan without me if I didn't know the outcome, do you? I sensed the cub for the first time today."

Konis frowned up at her, his face a mixture of joy and concern. "You did? Why didn't you tell them? Why let them continue to worry?"

"An hour wasn't going to make much difference and Carrie wouldn't have believed me anyway." She stopped by the desk, turning to look at him. "She's so fragile emotionally, Konis, still so afraid of the cub. She's taken it surprisingly well. I'm sure that only the more imminent fear of the Challenge is keeping her going. If only Taizia and I hadn't suggested it!"

"We've been over that several times, Rhyasha. The suggestion in itself was reasonable, if only Carrie had waited for you to tell her when to do it instead of going along with Taizia's premature enthusiasm. As for stopping the Challenge, I don't know what more to do. The guild won't help. Esken says it must remain a religious matter and he can't interfere. You told me Ghyan approached Rala and he said she refused to either cooperate or obey his orders. Kusac's commanding officer says he's officially on leave and therefore it's a civil matter. Governor Nesul's aides say he's too busy to be disturbed. There's no one left we can contact." His ears were lying backward as he spoke.

"No one wants to get involved! Rala's bent on revenge. I'm sure the only reason this became public knowledge is because Rala herself told Infonet," he finished.

"Then we'll contact them, too, and tell them the truth of the matter!"

"Rhyasha, we can't . . ."

"Why not?" she demanded leaning imperiously over him. "The Clan knows the truth, why not everyone else? Maybe it'll still this fear of our telepaths bonding with Terrans once and for all. What our son and his mate have done is no mean thing. To win the respect and love of someone who is alien, whose whole background is totally different from their own, is a unique achievement that none but our son and Carrie have attained."

Konis regarded her thoughtfully. "You could be right," he said, the tips of his ears flicking slowly. "What better way to deal with it than to bring the whole issue out into the open so it can't be decided in the darkness of closed rooms. Perhaps if we can win that reporter over, then public pressure can achieve what we can't, a cancellation of the Challenge."

"I'll contact them now. What about Carrie's father? Have you heard any more from him?"

"Nothing. I intend to speak to him again this evening."

"We haven't got long left," she reminded him, "only four days. I'll contact this journalist, Vorkoh, and see what I can arrange."

* * *

As Kusac hurried Carrie along the corridor toward the exit, they passed a group of Terrans on their way to the refectory. While they stood back to let them pass, the hysteria started to rise in her again, coupled with a fear that they could tell she carried an alien child. Almost brutally, Kusac forced her mind into a state of immobility, and while Kaid pushed a path through for them, Meral fended the Terrans off with the excuse that they were late for an appointment.

Once they were safely aloft, Kusac gradually relaxed his mental grip, trying to tell her that they were safely on their way home, but he couldn't reach her. Her mind was locked into an ever tightening spiral of rejection and self-hate that he couldn't even penetrate, let alone break. In desperation he reached out and again took control, aware as he did that he was breaking one of the guild's most sacred taboos—not to control another person mentally.

Her eyes glazed over, then closed as she slumped back against the seat, barely conscious.

Distressed and knowing he was out of his depth, for the first time in many years he reached for his father, asking him for his help. The response was instant.

You've taken the right action. I'll be waiting for you, I can do nothing from here.

Though the flight was short, it was one of intense worry for Kusac. She'd seemed to be doing so well. Granted, she hadn't been as enthusiastic about their cub as he would have expected a Sholan female to be, but then the circumstances were very different. Sholan females chose to become mothers, Carrie had not, and most importantly, Carrie wasn't Sholan. Was species isolation the problem? Did she need to talk to another human female? Yet the presence of other humans terrified her. He hadn't realized that her fear of their relationship, or of their cub, was still so strong or went so deep.

Konis was standing in front of the house when they arrived. As soon as the aircar had landed and the door was opened, he jumped in, moving swiftly to take the seat beside Carrie that Kusac had just vacated.

"Release your hold and let me use your Link," Konis said, taking Carrie by the hand.

Obediently, Kusac released her, widening the Link to include his father. Carried stirred but remained unconscious.

She's retreated deep within herself, said Kusac. *I'm afraid that if she continues like this, we'll be unable to reach her at all.*

Let me work with her, said his father, gently pushing back the hair that had fallen over one side of her face.

He reached into her mind, entering the dark cavern where the essential Carrie had retreated. Ignoring the faint flashes of light that signaled the workings of her autonomic functions, he searched for the dim glow that was her, the essence of her being. Eventually he found it within the image of a frightened child hiding in the darkest corner. Mentally he took hold of the child, forcing the contact that she was afraid to give.

You hurt me! she sent, her physical body flinching. *Leave me alone! I don't want to be with anyone.*

I'm sorry, Carrie, I didn't intend to hurt you. You're home now, he sent. *You're among your family. There's no need to be afraid of us, no need to hide yourself from us like this. Your child is part of us all, part of our Clan.*

No, she's not! She's alien! She should never have been conceived, came the fearful denial.

But she was, and she's a gift to you both, someone rare and precious because she's so different. The tone was gently persuasive.

She's taken the last scrap of my humanity from me! There's nothing left, it's all been taken! I'm nothing any more.

You're still human, Carrie, a special human who's carrying the first of a new race. You're a bridge between our people, the only one who understands us both. Your Link to my son has made it possible for there to be peace between your world and ours, possible for Keiss to gain its independence. Because of you, we now have allies to help us protect our worlds from the Valtegans. We have a lot to thank you for. No one else could have done all this.

The Terrans don't thank me, they just despise me. They'll despise me even more when they know about the Sholan cub I'm carrying!

The cub is yours, too, Carrie. She's half Terran. Once they understand, the Terrans will be pleased for you, too, came the reply. *I don't deny that it'll take them longer since the child doesn't look Terran, but they won't think less of you for bearing the first of her kind.*

You're not alone, Carrie, sent Kusac, his mental tone a caress. *Vanna's pregnant, too.*

This shocked the child-Carrie out of her self-pity. The hand that Konis held stirred and her closed eyelids began to move as her mind began to surface. *Vanna's pregnant?*

His father echoed the question.

Kusac nodded. *It seems the females in our Leska links have no choice over whether or not they conceive. There has to be a breeding imperative within the Link that's overriding some of our basic functions.*

"This bears thinking about," said his father as he retreated from Carrie's mind, guiding her back to consciousness.

Her eyes opened, gradually focusing on Konis.

"Yes, you're home, back on the estate," he said, continuing to hold her hand encouragingly as he got up from the seat. "Come, my dear, the rest of your family is indoors waiting for you," he said, helping her to her feet.

Carrie flung her arms around Konis, hugging him tightly.

Kusac gave his father a puzzled look just as he sensed the answer from Carrie herself.

You're the first people who've ever accepted me as I am, she wept. *I didn't realize you even liked me,* she continued, burrowing her head against his robes. *I thought you were just tolerating me as my father tolerates Kusac.*

Konis returned the hug, as stunned as his son that she'd not realized how he and Rhyasha felt about her. He gave her another hug, then released her, wiping her tears away with his thumb while tilting her face so he could look her straight in the eyes.

"Carrie, we see your mind before your outward form. "You're precious to me and Rhyasha because our son loves you, and because you are yourself. In time your people will look at strangers the same way, but they're a much younger race than us. Now go to Kusac," he said, "and join us in your home as the wife of the Clan Leader's heir."

He gave her cheek a gentle stroke, then turned to make his way out of the craft, cutting himself out of their Link as he did.

Kusac took her hand, stepping in front of her to help her down from the aircar.

See, your fears are groundless, he sent, putting his arm around her as they made their way up the steps into the house where his mother waited anxiously.

Rhyasha took Carrie's other hand, drawing her into an embrace.

"Carrie, you mustn't be afraid. We're here to help you. You won't be left to cope alone. You've both brought nothing but honor to our family by your actions. The way you've both faced so many changes not only in your lives, but in your minds and bodies—I know I couldn't have coped so well," she said frankly.

"I haven't coped well," said Carrie, her voice unsteady.

"Yes, you have," said Rhyasha, drawing her toward the central courtyard. "All first-time mothers go through a period of fear and doubt. Believe me, even I experienced it when I carried Kusac. He was an alien presence, something not belonging to my body, not completely of my flesh. It passed, though, as does the initial excitement. Then as you get toward the end of your time, there's just the impatience to be done with it all and actually be able to hold your own cub. Let's leave these males for the moment," she said, her voice fading as the two of them went up the stairway to the floor above, "I know exactly what you need. A little pampering in the form of an herbal bath, followed by a massage. Miosh has a magical touch."

Kusac watched them go, feeling strangely bereft after the intensity of the last couple of hours. His father took him by the arm, urging him along the colonnaded walk to his study. "She'll be fine," he assured Kusac as he closed the door behind them. He indicated a chair for his son, taking the one opposite him.

"You'll need to keep her away from the Terrans until the cub is born," he said. "Among us she feels safe and protected; among the Terrans she fears criticism and censure, even if at the moment it's imagined. After the birth she'll be fine because she'll belong to herself again, a separate entity, not sharing her body."

"Do you doubt her sanity at present?" asked Kusac, fingertips tapping unconsciously on the chair arm as his tail tip flicked.

"Unless she stays here, frankly, yes. How could her father have been so unyielding, so lacking in understanding toward her?"

"The consequences of losing a wife and daughter through taking a chance for a better life," said Kusac. "I can see his point of view, though I don't agree with it."

"You're too generous," growled his father. "I had word from the Alien Relations Council while you were at the guild. They aren't prepared to grant Carrie diplomatic immunity. They argue that because she's life-bonded to you, she's now a Sholan citizen rather than a Terran visitor."

"It's no more than I expected," said Kusac with a sigh. "It looks as if she has no option but to fight the Challenge."

"If you remember, I'm hoping the newly formed Keissian and Sholan Council will prohibit the fight on the grounds that she's still a Keissian subject and as you're the first Leska pair of your kind, Carrie's life and that of your child are more important than the law in this case."

"I assume you haven't heard anything yet."

"Nothing. I plan to contact her father again later today when he's available. I believe we may be lucky since I'd be surprised if the Keissians would want Carrie to be put at any risk at all. However, you know how things move through diplomatic channels—with the greatest resistance."

"I won't build up our hopes, then," said Kusac.

"I think you're wise. Now about Vanna. You said she's pregnant?"

"Yes, by Brynne."

"That's impossibly fast. Even detecting a pregnancy chemically takes longer than a week from the date of conception."

"All I can tell you is that once Brynne told her, I checked and it was obvious."

"So why didn't you know with Carrie?"

"She's not Sholan. I'd be able to tell now that I know what to look for in a human. There were little differences about Vanna, things I can't name. I just knew," he said, shrugging his shoulders.

"How could it have happened so fast?" asked Konis, ears flaring slightly so he picked up every nuance of what his son was saying.

"The call for help that we heard owed its strength to the gestalt that Vanna triggered. She believes that when we've triggered it in the past it's initiated the changes in us. If she's right, then it must have accelerated them to the point where they were fully compatible almost from the first."

"I presume Vanna knew nothing about it."

Kusac's tail flicked. "No, it was a shock to her. If she'd considered it at all, she would have thought it far too soon."

"Well, at least Carrie is no longer unique, which should be a comfort to her. I wonder if the Sholan interpreter from Earth and his human Leska will find themselves compatible so quickly. They're due to arrive within a few days. I issued instructions that they were to be kept from as much stress as possible so as to avoid triggering the gestalt. Dammit! I want to know why, and how, we're losing the breeding capacity of some of our best minds! If this goes on we could end up with no pure Sholan telepaths at all!"

"I think that's unlikely, Father," said Kusac, ears flicking uncomfortably.

Konis grunted, his tail tip rising and falling rhythmically. "We'll see," he said. "That's my worry, not yours. You go and join your mate. Forget about training, take the rest of the day to yourselves, it'll do you both more good in the long run. Go on," he ordered, feeling his son's hesitation, "be a family. Show her how we males feel about the females who choose to bear our cubs. She needs the reassurance. After I've contacted Mr. Hamilton again, I'm going to see Governor Nesul personally. His aides can't put me off so easily when I'm standing there."

* * *

"Rhaema!"

She looked up from her comm unit as she heard her section head call for her.

"What're you working on?"

"Not a lot. A couple of court cases, one of them to be decided by a Challenge at twelfth hour today."

"Give it to Druthi. Momma wants you downstairs. Move your tail!"

"What's all the fuss about?" she asked as she dug hurriedly in her desk drawer for her audio-comp pad.

"You've landed yourself a juicy little job," he said as she hurried toward him. "Special interview. The Liege refuses to speak to anyone but you."

She came to an abrupt stop beside him, the claws on her toes catching hold of the wooden floor to give her greater purchase. "The Liege? Literally a Liege?"

"Yep."

"So tell me who!" she demanded, ears fully swiveled toward him so as not to miss a word.

"Only Clan Leader Aldatan. Seems you made an impression with your article earlier today. This puts us ahead of Centralnet."

"Doesn't it just," she purred, mouth opening in a huge grin.

"So what're you standing round me for?" he demanded. "Get going! Momma doesn't like to be kept waiting!"

"I'm gone!"

* * *

Immediately after he broke the connection with Kusac's father, Peter Hamilton contacted his friend Jack Reynolds.

Jack's tousled face appeared on the screen, yawning hugely.

"This is an uncivilized hour to pull a fellow out of his bed, Peter," he complained. "What's so urgent at this time of night?"

"I need your help, Jack. Carrie's got herself into some sort of bother—a challenge or something—which is complicated by the fact she's pregnant. There's a real fear she could miscarry."

Jack's face froze.

"Pregnant, you say?" he repeated cautiously.

"Something wrong with your hearing, Jack?" Peter asked caustically. "Yes, I said she's pregnant. It's this fight that's the problem. His father just called me to say he's been unable to get the authorities on Shola to intervene and stop the challenge. I've been trying to bring the matter up in the

Council since he first contacted me last week, but the Sholans keep giving me the runaround by saying there are more pressing matters than the outcome of one civil challenge. I need the medical evidence for tomorrow. I presume that doctor of theirs—what's her name?—has been keeping you informed."

"Vanna," said Jack. "She contacted me about a week ago for some human medical information, but she didn't mention anything about Carrie being pregnant. I'll have to get in touch with her to get the current notes on their case."

"Do it. I need something concrete to put before the Council tomorrow."

"Peter, I can't possibly have the information ready for you for tomorrow," protested Jack. "I've got to call Shola and get them to send the data before I can even begin to correlate it!"

"Just call her now," insisted Peter. "Get it to me as soon as you can. We've only got three days left."

* * *

Rhaema towed her autovid out of the aircar, then released it to bob behind her at head height as she walked up the covered staircase to the entrance. An attendant was waiting for her, and he escorted her to Rhyasha's study. The Clan Leader sat in a comfortable chair, a mug of c'shar on the table by her elbow.

"Well come, Rhaema Vorkoh," she said, indicating the reporter should take the other chair.

"Clan Leader Aldatan," said Rhaema, "it's very good of you to talk to me like this."

"C'shar?" Rhyasha asked, pouring a mug for the reporter when she nodded in the affirmative. "There's nothing so destructive as speculation. I thought it time that the facts were known. Now, how do you want to conduct this interview? Do you want to ask me questions, or shall I tell you the facts as we know them?"

"It would be easier for me to ask questions," said Rhaema, taking the proffered mug from her.

"Then, whenever you're ready."

As Rhaema pressed her wrist unit, the autovid began to hum gently and a small red light set on the top began to pulse.

* * *

The interview took perhaps half an hour, at the end of which time Rhaema switched off her autovid.

"Thank you for your cooperation, Clan Leader," she said, finishing off the dregs of her drink. "I don't suppose there's any chance of speaking to either Kusac or Carrie, is there?"

"None," said Rhyasha firmly, getting up to escort Rhaema down to the waiting aircar. "As I explained, today has already been stressful enough for them."

Rhaema shrugged, her ears flicking her acceptance of defeat. "I had to ask," she apologized.

Rhyasha smiled. "Of course, and I had to refuse. When will you broadcast this?"

"On the late news tonight," Rhaema replied as they walked along the balcony to the stairs.

From below them in the central courtyard, squeaks of delight drifted up to their ears. Rhaema turned a curious face to her hostess.

"My youngest, Kitra, and unless I'm mistaken, Carrie and Kusac playing with her."

Rhaema was at the rail and leaning over it before Rhyasha could stop her. The two adults were throwing a soft ball over Kitra's head while the kitling jumped up, trying to catch it.

"Why, she's not so very different after all," said Rhaema, surprise evident in her voice.

"Of course not," said Rhyasha, joining her. "What did you expect?"

"I've never had the opportunity to speak to any of them," she said. "The males go out into the town, but they won't let any of us reporters near them. The females never seem to leave the guild, except for your son's mate, and she's so well guarded, no one gets near her!"

"As I explained earlier, no matter how adventurous their souls, it can be terrifying at times to realize just how alone they are on our alien world."

"I hadn't thought of it in quite that light before," Rhaema said quietly, watching while Carrie held the ball up in the air and Kitra danced round her trying to reach it.

As she turned around, keeping the ball at arm's length, Carrie looked up, her eyes locking onto Rhaema's.

"That's enough for now, Kitra," said Kusac, reaching out to take the ball from his mate. "Carrie's been energetic enough for today. She needs to rest."

"Can we play again later?" the young female asked hopefully.

"We'll see," he said, putting a protective arm around Carrie as he looked up, too. After the flick of an ear to the two on the balcony, he drew her away out of sight.

"I guess that's a no. How can he let her fight a Challenge?" she asked, turning back to look at Rhyasha. "She's so vulnerable, so easy to hurt. All this Rala needs to do is hit her once with her hand and it would be over."

"We know. That's why we need your help. Not just for Carrie, but for all the mixed pairs. The Challenge has to be stopped. Their unborn cub mustn't be put at risk, and never again can the Telepath Guild be allowed to wield the power they did when they drugged Vanna and Brynne. People like you shape public opinion, so make the people aware of what is really happening."

She hesitated, then gave a small smile. "My son says you may use the images you recorded of them playing with Kitra for your broadcast, but they would have appreciated being asked first."

Rhaema's ears lay back in embarrassment. Damn, but he was good! She'd not felt anything when he'd probed her mind. "I triggered it without realizing, Liege," she said in apology. "I'll certainly do what I can to help."

As she left, she gave herself a mental shake in an attempt to dispel the look of fear she had seen in the human female's eyes.

* * *

Back at the guild, Vanna had long since finished processing the data she had obtained from Carrie's scan. Ahead of her lay the task of collating it. There was no need for her to remain in her office. She could do it just as easily, and more comfortably, in her apartment.

She found it empty as she had expected. The last two Link days, Brynne had come over late, stayed only as long as was necessary, then left until the next time. At the moment she could sense him in the refectory with the other Terrans. This suited her since their relationship was very basic: he stayed with her only long enough to satisfy the demands of their Link, then he left for the more pleasant company of one of his Sholan bed companions. She didn't mind that either as only then did she feel comfortable being with Garras.

She set about making herself a meal. Something elaborate for a change, she thought.

Very shortly she lost herself in the task and while she waited for the food to cook, she loaded Jack Reynold's data into her comm.

After she'd eaten she returned to her studies, comparing his data with hers. Every now and then a stray thought about what Brynne had said would force its way into her mind only to be banished as being his idea of a cruel joke. Some time later she got up to make herself a cup of coffee, noticing with a start that it was very late. Filing her work, she switched the comm off and began to get ready for bed.

As she dropped off to sleep, her mind, unguarded for the moment, turned to Kusac and Carrie. It was enough that he had found a Leska he loved, but now that Carrie could bear his children, that small place that might have been hers was irrevocably gone. That she herself should now have a similarly compatible human Leska—and not one who loved her—was the final irony. As tears began to form in her eyes, sleep gently claimed her.

She woke suddenly, blinking because of the unexpected light. After a moment's confusion she sensed Brynne sitting beside her. Trying to sit up, she found herself pushed back on the bed by his firm hand.

"Lie still a minute more," he said, not unkindly. "I'm taking those tests you conveniently forgot to do."

Looking at her left arm, she found it encased in the test unit.

"What do you think you're doing?" she asked, trying to push him away. "You've no idea how to use it."

"Patience, Vanna. I've been learning to use the knowledge I got from you," he said, checking the readings and moving her arm so she could see them, too. "There you are, the proof that you're pregnant."

Angrily, Vanna sat up and snapped the unit free from her arm, setting it aside on the bed. "Not for long," she said flatly.

Brynne shook his head slowly, an amused look on his face. "You've lost that convenient ability. I checked out the standard female Sholan physiology and compared it to yours. That's another area of change. Your mind can no longer affect whether or not you conceive or remain pregnant in the first few days. You're as trapped as I am, Vanna."

For the first time she felt his sympathy for her.

"Poor Vanna, the career medic caught in the oldest human trap, and not even by the male of her choice." He gave a short, dry laugh. "Pity you carry a torch for Kusac; it doesn't exactly give us much of a chance even if circumstances were different. I can't say I enjoy living in an accelerated relationship with a female who loves someone else, and who has yet a third male for a mate!"

Vanna pulled her legs up, wrapping her arms around them protectively, her ears flat against her skull. "You've no right to pry into my private thoughts or life," she said angrily.

He reached out to touch her face, stroking the short fur. She jerked her head away, but his hand followed. Cupping the back of her head in one hand, he ran the fingers of the other gently through the cropped curls that grew down the sides of her neck.

"I'm afraid you're not very good at blocking your thoughts whenever he's around. I'd be very surprised if he isn't as aware as I am of how you feel."

Vanna's pupils widened as her panic increased.

"Pity," he continued, "you're really rather beautiful. Huge green eyes and amazingly soft fur. It's such a waste."

He leaned forward, pulling her face closer and kissing her.

She put up her hands to push him away, but they were grasped and held firmly by the wrists.

He continued, forcing her mouth open, his tongue flicking across her lips and teeth, then just as abruptly he released her and stood up.

"Sleep well," he said, leaving.

Vanna put a hand to her mouth, utterly surprised, unable to sense anything of his feelings through their Link. He had never kissed her before. Stunned, she sat there for a few minutes, then got up to check whether he had really left. Perplexed, she locked the door on the inside then returned to bed. As she lay there in the dark she began to panic anew, trying to recall if she'd been too obvious to Kusac about how she felt.

He's got no illusions about your feelings for him, came Brynne's amused thought.

* * *

"The Leska Link has always been considered a gift from the Gods," said Rhaema Vorkoh as she looked out at them from the main comm screen, "so what justification have the authorities for treating these young telepaths from both our species as if they were experimental animals? After seeing Liegen Kusac Aldatan and his human Leska, even I could feel the touch of the God on them and I'm not a religious person. To be able to truly experience what's it's like to have been born and grown up on an alien world, to win the trust—perhaps even the love—of someone from such a radically different background is an achievement of no small order. Those whom the God chooses to do this are indeed special." Rhaema paused and her image was replaced by that of Carrie and Kusac playing with Kitra.

"Every mixed Leska pair is another strut in the bridge between our worlds, allies who stand between us and the Valtegans, helping prevent tragedies such as those on the colony worlds of Khyaal and Szurtha from ever happening again. Their children will be equally important to us, a sign that the God trusts us to build for the future, a future which includes these children."

Once more, Rhaema returned to the screen. "Let your displeasure be known. Tell your guild representative how you feel about these people being kidnapped and drugged, about the life of the first of these cubs being risked in what is now a pointless Challenge. You have the power to change all this. Do it now, and work toward a better future which honors those brave enough to take up the God's challenge. This is Rhaema Vorkoh of Infonet."

Konis switched the comm off. "Well, she certainly did her best," he said, looking over to where his wife sat. "That reporter knows how to deliver an impassioned speech."

"That's because she spoke the truth," said Rhyasha.

"You really believe what she said about your God," said Carrie from where she sat curled up beside Kusac.

"Of course. How else could all these impossible things have happened to you?"

Leave it, cub. Let her believe it's the work of Vartra, sent Kusac.

At the far side of the lounge, the comm unit began to beep, making it unnecessary for her to reply.

Konis got up and went over to answer it. "Governor

Nesul, what a pleasure," he said, his voice a purr of almost-contempt. "I take it your meeting is over?"

"Subtle, Konis, very subtle," said Nesul. "I detected Rhyasha's hand behind that broadcast, by the way. Compliment her for me."

"How can I help you, Governor?" Konis' voice was silky now.

"I've got a job for you," Nesul said. "You want these Leska pairs under the jurisdiction of AlRel, don't you?"

"Yes." Konis was puzzled. What was Nesul up to?

"Then I suggest you take on the job personally. You base yourself at the guild and monitor the progress of these pairs. You wanted someone impartial who was prepared to gainsay the dictates of the guild, someone to protect the interests of our mixed Leskas? Who better than you?" Nesul grinned, teeth showing whitely. "After all, you have a vested interest in preventing the guild from monopolizing these people and their cubs."

Konis stood there, his face frozen in a polite mask. "I don't think . . ."

"Good, then I'll tell Esken to expect you tomorrow. Good night, Konis." The screen went blank.

Uttering a few choice epithets, Konis turned and headed for the door. "Excuse me, I'm going to call that toothless, tree-climbing bastard back!"

Kusac watched his mother's shoulders start to shake as she hid her face behind her hands. Finally, the laughter escaped her.

"I think your father has overplayed his hand this time," she chuckled. "However, I can't think of anyone better to fill the post. Neither Esken nor anyone else will intimidate your father. I think they'll rue the day they put him in charge!"

We're still no nearer getting the Challenge stopped, sent Kusac.

Maybe. With AlRel in charge, and your father head of AlRel, he can perhaps pull a few strings by himself now. We'll see, sent his mother.

* * *

It was well into the next day before Jack was able to locate Vanna's whereabouts on Shola. Last time they'd been in touch, he'd never thought to ask for her address. There was more delay while Vanna had to request the main guild office to send the data transfer. By the time he was able to actually sit down and examine her findings, it was getting on toward evening and Carrie's father was beginning to get extremely edgy.

"Damn it, Jack, couldn't you have done it quicker?" he demanded, pacing round his friend's now enlarged office in Valleytown.

"Have you ever tried to locate one person on a planet larger than Earth when you only know their first name?" said Jack. "Even the fact that she was with Carrie and Kusac on Keiss wasn't any real help. I was as quick as I could be. If it hadn't been for that Myak chap on the *Khalossa,* I'd never have found her."

"We've got to have it ready for tomorrow. The Council is heavily committed, but I intend to bring this matter up first thing and get it over and done with, so we can contact Kusac's father and get this fight stopped." He snorted. "The whole concept of a combat duel is barbaric!"

"No more barbaric than some of our sports," said Jack, marking areas of text on the screen that he wanted to print out later.

"This isn't a sport. Win or lose, it's got legally binding consequences."

"Not essentially different from our martial arts competitions."

"People don't get hurt on Earth!"

Jack looked up, his eyebrows raised. "You're forgetting the boxing matches, to say nothing of some of the forms of contact karate. To my mind they're far from civilized."

"Dammit all, Jack, my daughter's life is at stake!"

Jack heard the fear in Peter's voice and turned around to see the older man slump down into an easy chair, his head in his hands.

"Come on now, Peter," Jack said, getting up and going over to him. "This isn't going to help Carrie, is it?" Awkwardly, he patted him on the shoulder. "Where's Richard tonight?"

"Looking after the inn," said Peter, his voice muffled by his hands.

"You need to rest, or you'll be too worn down with worry to handle the Council meeting tomorrow. You're overstretching yourself, Peter. I'll get Richard to come over and take you home for an early night. Will you promise to rest?"

As Peter nodded, Jack gave his shoulder another pat. "Good man. Try not to worry about this, I'm sure everything will be all right and the Council will cancel this Challenge. I'll work through the night on this. It'll be ready for tomorrow, I promise."

* * *

The next day, Kusac called Vanna at the Guild.

"You know that it looks like the Challenge will have to go ahead," he said to her.

"I gathered that when Jack Reynolds contacted me last night," she said, ears flicking backward despite her efforts to stop them.

"What did he want?"

"The results of the genetic tests I ran on you. Apparently Carrie's father needs them to put before the Keissian/Sholan Council in an attempt to get them to overrule the law on Challenges."

"If they needed medical evidence, why didn't they get back to us?"

"You go to a medic for medical evidence, Kusac, not usually to the patient," she said dryly.

"Personally, I think they're wasting their time," he said. "I can't see that Council helping us any more than the authorities here. I've actually called to ask you yet another favor," he said, tilting his head slightly to one side, unable to look her straight in the eyes.

"I'll be there," she said. "I hope I won't be needed."

Kusac's ears twitched slightly in surprise but he said nothing. "Father has asked me to request that you bring another medic with you, and everything that might be needed."

The physician in her noticed that his eyes were almost completely black with the white of the inner lids showing at the edges.

"I anticipated this. I've already got permission from the head surgeon to take what I need from the guild hospital. I had some trouble convincing him that I should come at all since he would rather handle the matter himself." She hesitated. "You might be better having someone more qualified than me. All the top medics at the guild now have a working knowledge of Terran physiology."

"No. I don't want anyone else," he said in a rush, afraid she wouldn't come after all. "I don't like imposing on you, especially when things are ..." he hesitated, "difficult, but I'd rather it was you. We trust you. I don't trust anyone else from the guild."

She nodded.

"If you have any trouble with your surgeon, tell him to contact my father as head of AlRel."

She nodded again, aware that an awkwardness was developing between them. "What time is the Challenge?" she asked.

"Fourth hour, the day after tomorrow."

"I'll be there," she said, "without Brynne."

"Thank you," said Kusac. "I'm sorry I have to involve you yet again."

"I'm beginning to think I was born involved. I couldn't leave it to someone else," she said, distress showing on her face and in the set of her ears. "Until I knew you were both all right, it would be like living through hell."

Kusac's ears went completely back and he opened his mouth to speak.

"I'll see you then," she said hurriedly, breaking the contact.

He sat looking at the blank screen for several seconds before leaning forward to switch it off. Inwardly, he cursed whatever cruel trick of fate had decreed that the three of them be so closely involved with each other.

* * *

The day before the Challenge came, and there had still been no word from Keiss. The house seemed to be full of tension despite the fact that everyone tried to behave normally. By mid-morning, Kusac could stand it no longer and announced that he and Carrie were going to town.

Taking a small aircar, he flew them there, parking in the Telepath Guild grounds. They spent the day wandering around the shops, Kaid following them like a silent shadow.

By some unconscious mutual consent, though they stopped several times to haggle over prices of items they liked, they bought nothing. When night fell, they went in search of food, preferring to sit and eat on a seat in the corner of some parkland rather than in one of the many restaurants the town had to offer.

When they finally returned home, Kusac left her at the foot of the stairs while he went into the kitchen. He emerged carrying a large jug of wine and two glasses. Taking her by the hand, he led her upstairs to their rooms.

"Tonight," he said, shutting the door, "we're going to get drunk. Don't worry," he added, feeling her surprise and concern for the morning, "it's early yet, and you won't get a hangover with this wine."

He put the jug and glasses down on the table beside the settee, pulling her closer.

"I'm sure everything will go well tomorrow," he said, stroking her hair, "but this could also be our last night together. I want us to enjoy it."

"Please God, it won't be," she murmured, putting a hand up to either side of his face and drawing it down to kiss him.

* * *

Vanna knocked on the door, waiting for Garras to answer. She knew she had to talk to him, but she wasn't looking forward to it.

"Vanna, this is a surprise," Garras said, standing back for her to enter. He frowned, noticing the nervous set to her ears and the flicking of her tail. "What's wrong?" he asked as he shut the door behind her.

"Nothing, I just needed to talk to you," she said, walking into the center of the room.

Garras already knew what she needed to tell him, and had since she'd first found out. He was prepared to wait for her. She'd either tell him or not in her own good time. "Want some coffee?" he asked, going over to the kitchen area.

"Please," she said, following him. "I thought you didn't like it."

"I've gotten used to it because you like it," he said, pouring out two mugfuls then adding whitener and sweetener to both.

"Garras, I'm carrying Brynne's cub." There, she'd said it. He continued to stir the sweetener into the mugs.

"If you want to get Kaid to choose someone else to watch over me, I'll understand," she said in a small voice.

Garras turned and handed her a mug. "Why should I want to do that?" he asked, leaning back against the counter, watching her carefully. "I already knew, Vanna. I've only been waiting for you to tell me so I could reassure you that it makes no difference."

She looked up, eyes wide with shock. "How did you know?"

"If you had a Sholan Leska, it'd be no different," he said, ignoring her question. "You'd be expected to bear his cubs, too, whether or not you were bonded. What's different, except that you and I can't ever have cubs?"

"Nothing, I suppose."

Growling deep in his throat, he leaned forward and took the mug away from her, slamming it down on the counter. Shaking the spilled coffee off his hand with an exclamation of annoyance, he stepped forward and took hold of her.

Holding her close with one arm, he used the other to lift her chin up until she couldn't avoid looking at him.

"Dammit, Vanna, I've spent too long looking for someone like you to let anything or anyone come between us. Your relationship with Brynne isn't one of love, you've told me that and I can see it for myself. Ours is. Your cub will need a father and I intend to be that father, not Brynne, your five-day wonder! As for what I want to do," he said, lowering his face to hers and beginning to nuzzle her ear, "I intend to guard your body intimately until morning, and I don't care whether or not you have any objections," he said, swinging her up into his arms.

"I don't," said Vanna, wrapping her arms around his neck. "I do need you, Garras."

"And I need you, too, pretty one," he said, his voice a low purr.

* * *

"Before business begins," said Peter Hamilton, looking round the table at the assembled Sholans and humans, "there is a personal matter I'd like to raise. One involving Sholan law."

The Sholan Chairman, Sub-Commander Vioshi, stirred in his seat. "Mr. Hamilton, we have a great deal of civic business to attend to first. As I've said before, personal matters will have to wait, even for you. In fact, I suggest that the Council chamber is not the place for such items. As Planetary Governor you should be aware of that. We've already set up a perfectly adequate complaints procedure."

"The matter does concern this Council," argued Mr. Hamilton, "and it has a time limit to it. We need to discuss it now."

"If you feel so strongly about it then, if we have time, we'll consider your problem after the day's business is over," the Sholan sighed.

"I must insist that the Council does find the time," began Carrie's father.

"Raise the matter at the end of business, Peter," said Captain Skinner, the Keissian co-Chairman. "I understand your concern, but not now."

Peter Hamilton subsided, an angry look on his face as he glanced at the clock.

It was nearing seven at night before he was able to put his case to the Council, by which time it was too late to make a decision without reference to the full facts. A series of notes compiled by Jack Reynolds was given to each council member and a firm promise given that the matter would be looked at again the next day and some decision taken.

Once again there were delays. Some urgent local incident on Keiss needed to be discussed and he was asked to wait while that was dealt with. By late afternoon, they were ready to consider his case.

"You've all read the documents," he said. "The medical facts are simple. If my daughter fights in this Challenge, she could lose the child. If she does, that could put both her life and that of her Leska, the Telepath Clan Lord's son, at risk. Since they are the first Leska pair of their kind, and their child is unique, I suggest that the law governing Challenges be put aside in this case and the Challenge be canceled."

"Sholan law cannot be put aside every time a Keissian is involved, Mr. Hamilton," said Sub-Commander Vioshi. "Your daughter knew what she was doing when she issued this Challenge, and she knew she would have to fight it personally. It's also an En'Shalla Challenge, and not in the civil law domain."

"She didn't know she was pregnant."

"That is immaterial as far as the law is concerned, but the fact that she carries the first child of a new species bears thinking about."

"One of the other Sholan/Terran pairings is also pregnant," interrupted another of the Sholan councilors. "The child is not unique."

"That may be so, but is there really that much of a risk to the mother?" inquired Vioshi.

"According to two medics, yes," said Mr. Hamilton. "It's in my notes." Frantically he searched his mind to see if there was anything else he could say that would sway them.

"One other thing," he said hastily, just as the Chairman was about to speak. "She's a healer, too. Your people regard healers highly, don't they?"

"A healer, you say?" Vioshi sat up and took note. "You should have mentioned this earlier because without a legal ruling on this matter, we can't intervene. Healers are too rare to risk in any circumstances. If such a decision was in your favor, is there anyone on the Council who would block there being a cancellation of the Challenge in this case?"

He looked round the room, receiving negative shakes of the head from all present. "No? Then I suggest we leave this matter till tomorrow when I have had time to contact a judge and get a ruling on it," said the Chairman.

"I'll second that," said Skinner.

"We haven't got until tomorrow," said Carrie's father. "The Challenge is at ten o'clock tonight our time. I need action before then."

"In that case, I suggest we close our business for today so that I can contact the judge on the Khalossa and see you get your ruling as soon as possible."

Peter Hamilton sat down, almost light-headed with relief.

* * *

It was dawn when Brynne strolled out into the small courtyard outside the guild medical center. Vanna and her assistant were busy loading a recovery aircar.

"Today's the Challenge, then?" he asked.

Vanna stopped to look briefly at him. "Yes." She turned to the other female. "Chena, bring me the refrigerated box next. Check that it contains the Terran whole blood, type O, and the plasma. The amount should be as per the label."

She climbed on board and began checking her equipment. Brynne followed her.

"Quite comprehensive, isn't it?" he said, looking round. "Everything up to and including a mobile intensive care unit. There's been no stay of execution, then?"

"Not that I'm aware of," she said, loading her hypoderm

and placing it along with several spare ampoules into pouches on her belt.

Brynne leaned against the counter and, taking his hands out of his pockets, handed her several dressing packs.

"You may need these in your medikit."

Vanna took them from him and was about to lay them aside, then changed her mind and placed them in one of her jacket pockets.

"You could be dealing with either deep cuts or stab wounds," he said. "Pressure dressings are invaluable."

"I know," she said, turning toward him. "How did you?"

He shrugged. "I did a paramedic course back on Earth. I've mentioned before that because I have your medical knowledge through our Link, I'm being allowed to study it here when I've time."

"No, you can't come," she said, knowing what he was about to say. "Kusac wants Carrie kept away from Terrans just now. Your little outburst did her a lot of damage, so stay away from her."

"I had no intention of upsetting her," he said.

She grunted disbelievingly.

"Suit yourself," he said, moving toward the doorway. He stopped beside her, putting a hand on her shoulder.

"I hope everything goes well for them, but remember, if it doesn't, your life needn't end, too." He gave her a gentle squeeze before leaving.

Taken totally by surprise, she stood there in a daze until Chena returned with the refrigerated box.

"Everything's there," Chena said, latching it into its fastenings against the wall. "Aren't we being a little overcautious taking all this stuff?" she asked. "It's only a Challenge to first blood, after all, quite a common occurrence."

Vanna rounded on her. "Do you know who is fighting?" she demanded. "Liegen Kusac Aldatan's Leska! Would you be prepared to risk their lives by not having the necessary equipment if anything went seriously wrong?"

"No, of course not," she stammered, tail and ears flicking in distress.

"Damn!" swore Vanna, looking out the doorway past her toward a small group of Sholans who were heading their way.

"That's the head surgeon and his minions. I'd hoped to leave before they arrived. Go out and meet them, see what they want and try to head them off, Chena. Garras should be along any minute now. When he arrives, he'll send them packing."

Vanna hurriedly went back to checking her medikit.

* * *

"You've checked that the Protectorate's got the estate perimeter and the entrance covered?" Kaid asked T'Chebbi.

"Checked, and we've got the eastern coastline covered," she said. "Everyone is in position and knows what to do."

He turned to Rulla and Dzaka. All four of them now wore the Brotherhood grays to identify themselves immediately as the inner guard. "We're only waiting for Garras, and he's on his way."

He looked up at the roof of the house where a couple of snipers were strategically placed. He activated his throat communicator. "Position Delta. Confirm visibility and reception."

"Confirmed, Alpha."

Still looking at the front of the house, Kaid addressed the little group behind him.

"T'Chebbi, I want you with Meral at the edge of the circle. You'd better get into position now."

"Aye, sir," she said, walking away from them.

"Rulla, Dzaka, you'll be on the hundred meter mark, facing the house. Garras and I will be beyond you, covering the area between there and the treeline. I don't need to tell you what to look for, do I? If in doubt, shoot first. We can sort it out afterward." He turned round, his gaze pinning Dzaka for a long moment. "Positions, then. Keep an eye out behind you as well until Garras and I take up our positions."

"Are you sure you want me that close to them?" asked Dzaka.

"Only people I trust are in the immediate vicinity of the Challenge circle," said Kaid. "Trust, Dzaka." Once again he gave him an uncompromising look before turning and walking away toward the house.

* * *

Carrie paced around the kitchen, unable to relax.

"Eat something," urged Kusac, trying to follow his own advice though the food tasted like sawdust in his mouth.

"I can't," she snapped. "I feel like I'd throw up if I tried."

"Then leave the eggs and meat. Have some bread at least. You can't fight on an empty stomach."

"Cub, you must have something," said his mother, fetching a container from the cupboard. She opened it and offered her one of the ubiquitous energy biscuits that were always plentiful in telepaths' houses.

Reluctantly she accepted one, taking a small bite.

Kusac handed her the mug of coffee, grasping her by the hand and pulling her down onto the bench at his side.

"Now sit still for a moment," he said. "You'll be worn out before you begin."

She took a larger bite, and a drink. "Taizia says there'll be other people there. I didn't realize we'd have an audience."

Kusac glanced at his mother.

"We've insisted on the minimum number of people necessary to satisfy the legal requirements," said his mother soothingly, coming to sit on Carrie's other side. "Kusac will be there, of course, and his father to act as judge in the matter. Rala will be accompanied by her older brother and two Warriors. T'Chebbi and Meral will represent us."

"Why the Warriors?"

"To make sure neither Kusac, nor Rala's brother, interferes, and to judge when the first blood is drawn. Then it will all be over," she said, patting Carrie's hand.

"Is there any chance it will be canceled?" asked Taizia from her corner of the table.

Kusac shook his head, looking at his wrist unit. "There's not enough time left now for that."

Kitra came rushing in. "Your friend Vanna is here," she announced as Vanna, Garras, and Chena followed her into the room.

Kusac's mother got up to greet them. "You've time for some c'shar?" she asked, ushering them to the table.

Vanna checked the time. "We should have," she said, sitting down beside Taizia.

Carrie got up and began pacing again. "I can't stand the waiting," she muttered.

Kusac rose and went over to her. She evaded him, walking over to the window.

"There's another craft arriving," she said. "It feels like Rala."

"They'll call us when they're ready," said Kusac soothingly as he followed her, only too aware of how nervous and jumpy she was.

A few minutes later, his father came in. "Taizia, I've got a job for you."

His daughter looked up unhappily.

"I need you to stay in the study by the comm in case a message arrives from Keiss. If it does, you're to bring it to me immediately."

"Yes, Father," she said. *If it hadn't been for me, she wouldn't have Challenged Rala. This is all my fault,* she sent on their private wavelength.

Tazia, we've been all through this before, sent Konis. *You weren't to know the Challenge wasn't necessary. It's no one's fault.*

Kitra grinned from ear to ear. "Good! I can watch the fight."

"You will be keeping your sister company," her father said sternly.

"But, Father!"

"No arguments. You stay with Taizia. Off you both go."

He noticed Vanna and her two companions and nodded cordially to them. "I think it's time for you to join the others outside now, Vanna."

As they left, Kusac moved away from the window, still following Carrie.

"They're not ready for you yet," Konis said to his son. "I'd like to speak to you both first," he continued.

Once the room was empty except for his wife, he put his hands on Carrie's shoulders. "Whatever happens today, remember that we love you as our daughter. No one blames you for Challenging Rala. The idea in itself was a good one, it's just a damned shame all this is so unnecessary now. Forget us, forget Kusac, forget everything but the fight. Don't let yourself be distracted by anything. You will win, I'm sure of it," he said, hugging her.

She returned the hug and he released her, turning to his son and putting a hand on his shoulder.

May Vartra and all the gods be with you, he sent, the message aimed only at Kusac.

Kusac put his hand up and squeezed his father's arm affectionately, unable to say anything. Then, taking Carrie by the hand, they went outside to be met by Kaid and Garras carrying the weapons.

Kaid looked Carrie up and down with approval. "You remembered," he said, pointing to her loose-fitting, sand-colored trousers and shirt. "With those on, you'll present the minimum target possible. I would fasten your jerkin, though," he warned, leading the way round to the combat circle at the front of the house.

"She'll do fine, lad," said Garras, touching Kusac briefly on the arm. "Don't worry."

"I'll try not to," he said.

Carrie stopped when she saw the knot of people, panic flooding through her. *I can't do it, Kusac,* she sent.

He sensed her fear and put his arm around her, pulling her forward with him. *Yes, you can,* he replied.

Rala turned round and saw them. As she caught sight of their bracelets, they felt her hate like a physical blow. *I know you can hear me, Terran. By the end of this fight, he'll be mine again!*

"The bitch, she's sending to me!" Carrie muttered, pushing Kaid aside as she picked up more thoughts pertaining to her alienness and corruption of Kusac.

Kaid held her back.

"Patience," he said. "Remember what we've taught you. Keep your emotions out of the arena. The first to lose her self-control will lose the fight. Remember that and you'll do all right." His fingers touched her cheek fleetingly, then were gone.

Once again she heard the quiet voice in her mind, this time wishing her luck.

Kaid beckoned Meral over. "I'll leave you with Meral for now," he said. "I have to see to security. We don't want any journalists here, do we?" He hoped she'd forgotten the second killer was still at large.

Meral stood back a little from them, giving them a last moment of privacy. T'Chebbi was already standing beside Rala and her brother while Rala's two Warriors waited for Kusac.

Kusac pulled Carrie around to face him and began to lace up her leather jerkin, the only form of body protection the combatants were allowed.

"Shield yourself fully from her," he said. "Don't let her use her hate to distract you. Stay calm and think of it as a practice with Kaid or Meral."

Carrie could feel Rala's anger mounting because of

Kusac's obvious partisanship. She risked a glance round Kusac's shoulder at the Sholan female. Rala's face was contorted in fury. Her ears were flat, and at her sides her hands clenched into fists as the hair rose on her neck and shoulders. Her tail swayed like an independent entity, bushing out to twice its normal size.

Enjoy it while you can, Terran, because it's the last time he'll touch you! came the vitriolic thought before Rala pointedly turned her back on them. *He'll be mine five minutes from now!*

Ignore her, Kusac sent as he reached the top of the jerkin and tied off the cord, tucking the ends safely away before looking at her. His arms went round her and he held her close, almost crushing the breath from her. His mouth found hers in his equivalent of a kiss. *Remember you are as precious as life to me. Do whatever it takes to win.*

He released her reluctantly, going over to Rala's warriors and her brother.

She watched him walk away, suddenly realizing that in this crowd of furred Sholans, she was the only human. She began to panic as she rubbed her hands together. They felt strange to her, lacking a covering of fur. Her thoughts began to fragment into his/her reactions, then Meral came up to her with the weapons.

With an effort, she forced back the panic and tried to focus on the task ahead of her. Her errant thoughts wandered again, this time worrying how Kusac would react if she did lose the child. Instinctively, she tugged at the jerkin, easing its fit across her stomach.

You are the important one, was the fierce reply as he turned to look at her.

Meral handed her the shield, his presence pulling her back to the moment. "You're winning already," he said quietly. "Look at her. She's hyping herself up with anger. She's going to make mistakes. Don't worry." He helped her fasten the shield on and handed her the short sword.

She balanced it in her hand, giving it a quick spin to loosen her wrist. It was a vicious weapon, resembling a reversed claw. The spine of the blade went from a T-section near the enclosed handle to a diamond shape at the tip, with a secondary cutting edge on the upper surface. The blade extended along the base of the grip, again with a razor sharp edge to it.

No delaying it any more, she thought, stepping onto the sand. She waited for Rala, realizing that most of the fear had gone now that the adrenaline was beginning to take over. Similarly equipped, Rala stepped into the circle.

Carrie remembered what Kaid had said. "Don't see her as a person, see her as an obstacle between you and your Leska."

Carrie moved nearer the center, crouching down and watching her opponent. At a signal from Kusac's father, Rala took a guard position and began to pace around her.

Chapter 20

The stone was really beginning to hurt now, its jagged edges cutting into his hip. It was no good, he had to move. Everyone's attention was focused on the combat circle anyway; he was unlikely to be seen. Cautiously, Chyad eased his stomach and hips upward, shifting his legs a few precious centimeters to the right. His movements disturbed the bird that had been perched in the bush. Shrieking and scolding, it fluttered angrily up through the branches above him and flew off.

Chyad's head sank back down on his forearms as he cursed quietly to himself, waiting for the inevitable. Nothing, not a sound. They'd not noticed. He began to breathe again. He raised his head, looking out through the foliage. No chance for a clean shot yet, everyone was milling around.

There was the male from the *Khalossa,* their bodyguard. So, he was one of the Brotherhood, was he? So much the better. He'd stick to his original plan and take one of them out during the fight when perhaps his shot would go unnoticed. His revenge against him would be even sweeter. He'd have to live with knowing that he'd been beaten by an ordinary Forces male.

Now that the damned bird had gone, he could move a little more freely. He reached down and scratched at a half-healed thorn cut on his leg. He'd been here for the last week, living rough off the land out by the ruined temple until a couple of nights ago. Knowing they'd step up the security in the days before the Challenge, he'd managed to find himself a lair in the middle of this thornbush. It was an ideal location for what he had in mind. Thumbing the power on, he lay there, cradling his pulse rifle, watching, ready to spin the wheel of fortune one final time.

* * *

Kaid turned his back on the circle, walking the couple of hundred meters toward Garras. There he had not only an uninterrupted view of the combat, but also of the cleared area around them.

"Everyone's in position," said Garras quietly. "Anything moves, we'll see it, and they've got instructions to shoot down any autovids."

Kaid nodded, grateful for his friend's presence. Garras' ability to follow his thoughts was even more invaluable now.

"Was it wise to place Dzaka so close?"

"I've snipers on the roof. One way or another, I find out today if I can trust him." Kaid's voice was bleak. He thumbed the communicator clipped at the base of his throat. "All units, report in."

The males and females he'd requested from Ghezu reported in one by one. There were ten in all, scattered throughout the grounds and at the entrances to the estate. His people were taking no chances with the renegade male from the *Khalossa* still at large.

* * *

Carrie turned to keep Rala in sight, allowing the other to do the work while assessing her movements. The Sholan seemed to have poor shield control, as if she disliked it or had spent more time learning to use the sword.

Deciding she couldn't tempt the human into attacking, Rala suddenly rushed toward her, sword raised, aiming for her head.

Carrie blocked using her shield, pushing the Sholan back while cutting with her blade to Rala's left side. It bounced off the other's shield and she pulled back to feint at Rala's right, changing direction at the last minute for a shoulder level blow. Rala turned just in time, managing to take it on her sword. Using her greater strength, she pushed Carrie's blade aside, ramming her in the stomach with her own shield.

Staggering back, Carrie recovered her balance, managing to get her weapons up in time to block the flurry of blows Rala rained about her upper body. As Kaid had warned, she was having to work hard just to defend herself. Waiting for a chance, she shoulder-charged the female backward, rushing in to punch Rala's shield aside while the other was still off balance. It gave Carrie the opening she needed and with a single cut to Rala's side, she had taken first blood.

Rala looked at the rent in her jerkin, seeing the blood beginning to seep out. Going down in a crouch, her face contorted by hate, she moved closer to Carrie as Kusac's father turned to the watching Warriors, waiting for them to declare First Blood.

"If I can't have him, then neither will you," she growled. "You may be a telepath, but you're not Sholan! I call the Blood Rite on you!"

Oh, God, thought Carrie, an icy wash of fear running through her, *not that, not the death Challenge!*

As Rala ran toward her, Kusac moved forward, only to be grabbed by one of the Warriors.

"No!" he yelled, sheer terror in his voice. "Stop her!"

He turned on the Warrior, trying to pull free, but was firmly grasped from the other side as well. Caught between the two, he was unable to move. He felt the gestalt snap into being and hadn't the time to even curse before he saw Carrie stagger backward under its power.

Meral and T'Chebbi stood frozen, unable to intervene for fear of distracting Carrie. Then it was too late.

Rala's cut to her thigh went home, leaving a long slash that began to bleed instantly. The shock jerked Carrie back into control of herself just as Rala, seeing her standing wide open, lunged forward with a stab aimed at her heart.

There wasn't time to block, only to avoid. Carrie turned, taking the blade in the upper arm. It sliced into the tricep muscle, tearing the flesh as it was ripped free.

For Kusac it was as if everything was happening in slow motion. He experienced the hot flare of pain along her thigh as if it was his, then the agony of the wound in the upper arm. He sagged briefly against the males holding him, then fed the power of the gestalt to Carrie, hoping it would give her the strength to continue. Saving just enough for himself, he turned on the Warriors. The one he had stumbled against had relaxed his hold enough for Kusac to pull free. He turned on the other, hitting him full strength across the side of the head with his free hand. Suddenly he found himself in the midst of his own battle as the first one leaped on him.

* * *

Kaid kept turning his head to look at the fight, mentally
sharing every blow given and received by Carrie. He tried to
remember he was supposed to be guarding her, but his eyes
kept returning to the combat. That was where her most
pressing danger lay for now, and in the circle, he couldn't
protect her. He turned away again, scanning the open area
around them, looking for the slightest of movements that
would betray the presence of a sniper.

A shout rang out and he looked back at the two females.
It was over, and Carrie had drawn first blood. He sighed.
Vartra be praised! His mind at ease now, he turned to look
back at the surrounding woodland. A glint of light over to
his left caught his attention.

Simultaneously, he heard more shouting followed by a cry
from Kusac. Around him, all was still. He risked a quick
glance back and saw Rala hit Carrie.

Instinct made him look back at the bushes even as his
chest tightened in fear for her. There was someone there, he
knew it. He scanned the undergrowth, looking for a repeat of
the flash. Now was when he'd attack, when they were both
made vulnerable by her wound.

Carrie gave an involuntary cry of pain as the blade was
wrenched free. She staggered back, aware of a sudden heat
running far too quickly down her arm. Risking a glance at
her injury, she gasped, realizing by the amount of blood she
was losing that a major vessel had been severed. Clamping
her arm quickly against her side, she looked for Rala. There
was no time for fear.

Her vision blurred briefly as the gestalt surged through
her again. This time she realized Kusac was not controlling
it. She reached out, harnessing the power, using it to stave
off the shock to her system and found her dizziness beginning to fade. Keeping her left arm pressed tightly to her
side, shield up at chest level, she waited for the Sholan. She
didn't have the strength to waste on going to her.

Rala, knowing that the blow hadn't been fatal but that
Carrie was seriously wounded, came rushing in to finish her
off. Carrie blocked with her blade, noticing that Rala's
shield had dropped. Risking everything, she stepped forward, using the gestalt energy to shield-punch at the female's face with the rim of her shield. The moment she

moved her arm, blood began to stream from her wound, falling to be absorbed by the sandy floor of the arena.

Rala whipped her shield up, throwing her head back to avoid the blow, giving Carrie the chance she needed. With the last of her strength, she lunged forward, stabbing up into the other's rib cage.

The blade penetrated to the grip, stopping only as it hit Rala's spine. She gave a high-pitched scream of agony and toppled forward, wrenching the blade from Carrie's hand.

Kusac had laid out one of the warriors with his first blow. The other proved more tenacious and he received a couple of head-numbing hits himself before landing a hard enough blow to keep his opponent down. He swung around just as Rala fell dead at Carrie's feet.

He ran toward his Leska, seeing her stagger, blood pouring from her arm as he tried to catch her before she fell. Something punched him hard in the shoulder from behind and he stumbled, unbalanced by the dead weight of Carrie in his arms. He crashed to the ground, landing hard on his knees, Carrie cradled close to his chest. Oblivious to his pain, he sat back on his haunches and felt for her wound with his hand, trying to stem the continuous stream of blood. The gestalt was fading now and his head began to swim with her pain and loss of blood. His shoulder ached, too, for some reason he couldn't comprehend.

Taizia came running up, shouting for her father. She slowed as she saw Kusac bending over Carrie.

"Father," she said quietly, "the message just came. The Council on Keiss has canceled the Challenge."

* * *

Kaid began to run even as the pulse of energy spat out from the assassin's cover. No time to check who'd been hit. It was too late now anyway. Either they were still alive, or they were dead. Anger burned within him as he retaliated with a strafing burst of fire that ignited the bushes.

There was an explosion of movement and a figure broke from the undergrowth to dash four-legged toward the deeper cover of the nearest treeline. Kaid shot again, hearing the communicator at his throat issue orders in Garras' voice. The sound had an eerie quality, alerting him to the fact Garras was close behind.

* * *

Chyad had made it to the woodland. As he plunged headlong through the bushes at least he had the satisfaction of
knowing that he'd hit the male, Kusac. With the trauma from
her wound, all it needed was a push in the same direction for
him and they'd be caught in their mutual pain. There was no
way they could possibly survive. The double shock alone
would kill them.

He heard the sound of pursuit crashing through the bushes
after him. They'd have to be a lot quieter than that if they
planned to catch him. Branches whipped him in the face,
tearing at his ears and nose. He ground to a halt as one
smacked him across the face, its sharp thorn drawing blood
from his forehead and leaving a thorn or two embedded in
his nose. The undergrowth was too thick for him to run like
this. Rearing up, he swung his rifle off his shoulders and
shifted it round into a ready position as he loped off to the
right.

The trees were thinning out as he saw the hill looming up
ahead of him. Once across the clearing, his aircar waited
under the cover of a spiky wintergreen tree. Then he was
clear and free.

Kaid heard Garras crashing around just behind him. The
old magic was still there: Garras had read him and knew exactly what was needed. They'd always made a good team.
He took off to one side of the trail, moving quickly and silently. He had a major advantage over their sniper: he knew
every inch of this woodland.

His quarry was sweating profusely, and he could smell it.
From the direction he was heading in, it was a safe bet he
was making for the hill. The woodland petered out there,
leaving a clearing of some thirty meters to the bushes at the
base of the hill. He increased his speed, playing the hunch,
determined to get there in time to stop the assassin.

The clearing came into sight and with it a running figure.
Kaid used his powerful leg muscles to propel him forward in
a leap that took him a good five meters into the clearing. As
he landed, he fired, aiming a slicing burst of energy at the
male's legs. Chyad went down as if poleaxed, the rifle flying
from his grip as he landed.

Kaid remained where he was, crouching down, ready to
fire again if necessary. The sniper lay there making small
mewling noises of pain; he wasn't going anywhere. Kaid

stood and walked over to him just as Garras emerged from the trees.

"He's mine," said Kaid shortly, gun trained on his captive. "Go back, help the others check the area in case there're more."

Garras hesitated, looking at the hideous burns on the sniper's legs. "Kaid, don't you. . . ."

"I said go!"

Garras nodded and left them alone.

The male on the ground looked up at Kaid, face contorted by pain, ears invisible against his skull. "Damn you! Aren't ... you going ... to ... ask ... why?" His voice was distorted by his clenched teeth.

"No, Chyad. This time I'm going to make sure I kill you," said Kaid, his voice like ice as he flicked off the safety switch on his rifle. "Eventually."

* * *

She was losing too much blood and he couldn't stop it. Dazed, Kusac lifted his head and looked around. "Help me," he said.

As if in a dream, the figures around them suddenly began to move. Vanna was first over, followed by her assistant. She handed Chena the hypoderm, ordering her to give Kusac a shot while she pushed his hand out of the way, applying a pressure pad to Carrie's arm wound. Holding it tightly in place, she ripped the sleeve open with her free hand so she could work on the injury.

"You faint on me, Kusac, and I'll kill you myself!" she growled. "I need you to monitor Carrie." As she fastened the bandage, she spoke to Chena. "Check the other female when you're done."

Kusac flinched when the hypoderm was fired against the inside of his thigh, but as the stimulant began to take effect, his head started to clear slightly.

"I can't give you a psychic suppressant since we need to use your abilities," she said, working quickly to bind the wound on Carrie's thigh. "You're going to have to block her pain yourself." She glanced up at him. "Kusac!" she said sharply, reaching out to pull hard on his ear.

He flicked it away from her, eyes beginning to focus again.

"Block it, Kusac," she ordered. "You've done it before, do it now."

Moments later, she sat back. "Can you carry her?"

He nodded, accepting her help as they lifted her between them.

"Keep her injured arm around your shoulder and take her to the aircar," she said, moving aside.

Kusac started walking—toward the house.

"Damn you Kusac! The aircar," said Vanna, pulling at him, trying to make him change direction. "I can't treat her in the house! All my equipment's in the aircar."

He pulled free, continuing to walk to the house.

"Do you want her to die?" Vanna shouted, dancing beside him in anger.

"If she dies, it'll be in our home."

She whirled round, turning on Chena and anyone within reach. "What the hell are you standing looking for? Get my bloody equipment! Get everything since His Lordship wants me to treat her in the house!" She turned to run after them, slowing long enough to shout over her shoulder, "Get the blood and the drip set up first!"

Taizia, Meral, and T'Chebbi raced after Chena, taking the equipment she handed them and heading for the house at a run.

Kusac's father watched bleakly as his son lifted Carrie. Both of them were drenched with her blood. He knew she was still alive, but for how long? They had all felt Rala's death agony and that psychic shock had been severe enough without the addition of Carrie's pain. He gathered his thoughts. There were things he had to attend to now. There was an eternity for grief later, if grief was needed.

He went over to where Rala's brother, Talgo, was bending over his sister. One of their warriors had removed the sword and tried to arrange the body. He stood up as the Clan Lord approached.

"Clan Lord Aldatan," Talgo said, schooling the grief from his face. "I had no idea my sister intended this. To lose the fight then illegally re-Challenge was utterly dishonorable of her. She was only using the Challenge to hide her desire for revenge. It won't help, I know, but we apologize for what she's done."

"No blame is placed on your family. Your apology is accepted. Neither my bond-daughter nor my son has done anything to warrant facing a Blood Rite Challenge from anyone. Just take Rala's body and go." He gave a brief bow and left him to see to his sister's body.

Entering the house, he called for the main attendant.

"Get that arena cleared," he said, his voice harsh with grief and anger. "I want no trace of it left. Plant it with something, anything, so long as it ceases to exist!"

He found his wife in the study, curled up in one of the chairs, crying.

They're still with us, he sent, placing a hand on her shoulder. *We'll wait here, out of the way. If they need us, we'll know.*

* * *

A quarter of an hour later Kaid arrived back at the Challenge circle. Already two Clan members were removing the blood-soaked sand with shovels. The metallic tang of blood permeated the air: she'd lost too much. He knew she still lived, but it would be touch and go.

Garras moved forward to meet him, reaching out to touch him on the shoulder when he saw the narrowed eyes and the gray skin round his friend's nose. "She's still alive," he said. "They took her upstairs into the house. Vanna's working on her now."

Kaid nodded, face and body impassive.

"The shot missed her, Vartra be praised. I think it may have hit Kusac, though." Garras hesitated. "I'll send a couple of people to fetch the trooper."

"No need. I destroyed the body."

Garras felt ice run down his spine. This wasn't like Kaid. "Because of her?" he asked, suddenly defining what was different. There was no response. He took a deep breath. "Go inside," he said. "I'll take charge out here." When Kaid still hadn't responded, he pushed him toward the house. "Go. I'll keep watch outside with the others. At least you'll know sooner if you're in there."

"There aren't any more of them," Kaid said. "He couldn't get anyone to follow him."

"Can you be sure?"

Kaid looked round at him, eyes bleaker than midwinter. "Oh, yes," he said softly. "I can be sure."

"Kaid, while she's still alive, she needs you guarding her. Go."

Kaid went, heading up the stairs at a run. He reached their lounge in time to have a quick glance through the door before it closed. She was still alive.

Taking a deep breath, he sank down into the nearest chair and began the litany to focus his mind. He needed to think clearly, not be distracted by feelings he'd learned long ago to live without. Ghezu and Lijou had their proof now and the cost had been too high. Anger started to rise within him and he stilled it, concentrating only on the litany.

* * *

Carrie was whiter than the sheets that Kusac had laid her against. As Vanna went into the bathing room, she shielded her anger at having to treat Carrie up here, knowing that more guilt was something Kusac didn't need. The minute or two she had lost wouldn't really make much difference one way or the other now. She dried her hands and returned to the bedroom where Chena had finished cutting Carrie's clothing free of the wounds.

Getting Chena to hold the bag until the portable stand arrived, she started the blood transfusion. The girl's pressure was dangerously low.

Kusac sat on Carrie's right, out of Vanna's way, holding her hand. Now that she was unconscious, her pain was not affecting him so strongly, but he was swaying again despite the stimulant. He moved his shoulder, trying to ease the discomfort there, confused that it hurt.

"Monitor her, Kusac," said Vanna, laying out her suture equipment while Chena carefully released the bandage and wiped the area with an antiseptic.

"Why not use a plasmagraft?" Chena asked, belatedly putting a pad under the wound to catch the flow of blood.

"Clamp the arm above and below the injury," ordered Vanna, turning to check the oxygen and gas mixture on the small anesthetic tank. "We haven't used plasmagrafts on Terrans yet. I can't be sure it'll be compatible."

"She's slipping away, Vanna," said Kusac. His voice was full of fear as he felt Carrie's presence getting weaker and weaker. "I can't hold her much longer."

"Yes, you can," Vanna said savagely, swabbing the blood from the wound and starting to work on the severed artery. She spared a glance at her monitors. "Use that damned gestalt if you have to, I'm not having her die under me!"

Kusac tried to trigger the gestalt, his fear mounting when nothing happened. At last it began to build slowly, its power a fraction of what they had experienced before. Using it, he strengthened their Link, trying to draw her closer to him, willing her to live.

Vanna finished on the artery and ordered Chena to start using the anesthetic while she released the lower clamp first. The joining held, and Vanna sighed with relief, turning her attention to the rest of the wound.

She was only halfway through stitching the torn muscle when the door opened quietly. She looked up to see Brynne.

"What do you want?" she demanded, turning back to her task. "I told you to stay away."

"You're going to need me," he said, stepping up to her and looking to see what she and Chena were doing.

"I haven't the time to argue. Just leave before Kusac notices you're here," she said.

Kusac was sitting as if in a trance, ears back, eyes closed, the visible flesh on his face gray and drawn.

"She's going into shock," said Chena quietly, "and it looks like she's beginning to abort."

Vanna swore. "Just what we need!" She looked at Brynne, a question forming in her mind.

"Yes, I can handle the anesthetic," he said, moving round to Chena's side and taking her place.

"Chena, get Kusac out of here," she said, "then get back and deal with this miscarriage. I have to finish closing her wounds."

The door opened and Taizia stood there. "I brought Brynne upstairs," she said quietly. "I was waiting in case there was a problem with him being here. I'll see to Kusac."

Vanna nodded. "Take him downstairs and see he stays with you," she said abruptly.

Taizia went over to her brother, taking him by the arm.

"Kusac," she said, shaking him gently. "You have to come with me."

Carrie began to move, trying to curl up as her abdominal muscles started to contract.

Kusac's eyes opened wide in fear as they all felt a tiny presence that was barely there cease to exist.

"I know," soothed Taizia, "but you can't help. Come with me. They can work more easily without you here." She pulled him gently, urging him to his feet.

"I can't leave," he said brokenly. "My fear caused this to happen, I can't leave her now."

"You must," said Taizia, leaning forward to unfasten his grip on Carrie's hand. "You can still sense her from downstairs, you know that. They have to stop your emotions from affecting her now. Don't let her feel your sense of loss on top of everything else she's suffering."

Kusac allowed himself to be led from the room. His father was waiting on the stairs for him. He was taken to the study, sat down in a chair, and a drink placed in his hand. He sat looking at it, ears now lying flat against his head.

"It's my fault," he said, his voice low and taut. "If I hadn't triggered the gestalt with my own fear, then she wouldn't have been injured and lost the cub"

"You can't say that, Kusac," said his father, pushing the glass toward his mouth and making him take a drink. "Your fear was perfectly natural."

Kusac coughed, tears streaming from his eyes.

"What's this?" he asked, looking at the glass for the first time. "What are you giving me?"

"Neat arrise."

"I don't want any more," he said, trying to hand the glass back.

It was pushed toward him again. "Drink it," his father ordered. "You need it. We haven't any medics to spare for you. As for the gestalt, obviously I wasn't there the other times, but from experiencing it today, I'd say that the initial effect is lessening. I expect that in time there will be no disorientation at all."

"But if it hadn't happened, she wouldn't have been injured."

"Undoubtedly, but do you really want to go through the rest of your lives blaming yourself for the loss of this cub? If you do, you'll also be constantly reminding Carrie that she should never have Challenged Rala. Can she live with that? Leave it alone, Kusac. You're not to blame, the circumstances are."

"I don't know," he said, putting down the glass and burying his face in his hands. "I'm just so afraid, and there's nothing I can do to help! With all our abilities, I have to sit here and wait!"

His mother got up and went over to him, wrapping her arms around him. "She's not going to die and neither are you," she said, hugging him fiercely. "You've faced death before, on Keiss, and coped with it."

"That's just it!" he said, pushing her away. "I'm not the one facing it this time. She is, and that makes it worse for me."

"Take your drink," said Rhyasha, putting the glass in his hand again. "It'll numb your mind just enough to be able to cope. It was used before we developed suppressant drugs."

He tried to fend the glass away, but she grasped his hand in hers. "She'll live, I tell you! I can already feel her strength coming back. When she comes round, she'll need you there to give her the will to go on, not suffering from useless self-recriminations."

She sat back on her heels, letting his hand go.

"Now drink it. It helps no one for you both to suffer the same pain." She looked at her hands and frowned, then reached out to touch his shoulder. He flinched, spilling a little of the drink.

"You've been hurt," she said, disbelief in her voice.

"He was shot," said Kaid's voice from the open doorway. "It was one of the assassins who killed Sevrin. I've got a medikit here if you'll let me use it."

A moan of fear escaped Rhyasha as she got to her feet and moved aside for Kaid.

"He's dead, Clan Leader," said Kaid, kneeling down in front of Kusac and opening the kit. "It's over. There are no more of them."

* * *

More than two hours passed before Kusac was allowed to rejoin Carrie, the longest two hours of his life. Vanna was in their lounge talking to Kaid, taking a well earned break.

"Good God! What happened to you?" she demanded, seeing the dressing bound round his shoulder.

"It's nothing. How's Carrie?"

"She's stable, and conscious. You know she lost the child." It was a statement. They'd all felt the cub's death. She hesitated. "I need to take the body back to the guild to study it. Do you mind?"

"No, she remains here," he said flatly. "I'm sorry, Vanna, but she'll be cremated here on the estate."

"As you wish, of course," she said. "Will you at least let

me take blood and tissue samples? I promise I'll do it gently."

He hesitated then nodded.

"Thank you. Now, what happened to your shoulder?"

"There was a sniper, the one that got away when Sevrin was killed. We were lucky. He shot me as I ran toward Carrie. Kaid killed him." He stopped, unsure how to put what he wanted to say. "Vanna, thank you," he said simply.

She got up, turning away from him and going toward the bedroom. "I saved her, that's thanks enough," she said tiredly. "You'll find her in a bit of a mess," she said. "We haven't had time to clean her up properly. Speaking of which," she said, glancing back over her shoulder at him, "you could do with a shower and a change, too."

"Once I've seen her. If it's safe, I'm sure Taizia and my mother would help with Carrie."

"If they could, that would be wonderful. Chena and I are dead on our feet." She stopped outside the door. "Brynne's here," she said. "Without him she could have died. He handled the anesthetic when she started to abort."

Kusac frowned. "Does Carrie mind?"

"Funnily enough, no, she doesn't seem to mind, and he's been marvelous with her."

"Then what I think is unimportant," he said as she opened the door.

Carrie was lying propped up against several pillows, her eyes enormous against the pallor of her face. Her injured arm was held elevated in a sling across her chest. The other was firmly bandaged over the site of the drip catheter. Vanna had managed to find a fresh shirt for her to wear.

She smiled faintly as he came across to her. "I'm afraid I've really been in the wars this time. What happened to you?"

He found a space beside her on the bed, leaning forward to stroke her hair. "Nothing worth talking about," he said quietly. "I'm just grateful you're all right." He touched his cheek against hers, gently licking her ear.

"I can't touch you back," she complained. "I need to hold you."

He laughed, feeling a sudden relief from the fear and grief that had gripped him far too tightly these last three hours. Carefully, he put his arms behind her and moved closer until she could put her head on his uninjured shoulder.

She rubbed her face against his neck, taking comfort from the feel of his fur and his warmth. "Did Vanna tell you I lost the baby?"

"Yes, but we still have each other and that's more important," he said quietly. "For the last five or six months we've led a life with very little privacy. I promise you that once you're well enough to travel, we're going away somewhere on our own with no Kaid, Meral, or T'Chebbi. Much as I like them, I want you to myself for as long as possible. Whenever we're among other people, all my plans concerning you go wrong."

"What plans?" she asked, her voice sounding drowsy.

"Those concerning our betrothal and life-bonding for a start," he said, grinning. "I'd planned it very differently, then we ended up in circumstances that gave me little choice but to do it quickly."

She chuckled. "I don't think I could ever forget either of those two occasions even if they didn't happen according to your plans. We got there in the end, though," she yawned.

Vanna came over. "If she's going to have that wash, and some clean bedding, it had better be now. I want her to sleep for the rest of today."

Kusac gently hugged Carrie again before carefully letting her go. The fingers of her sound arm reached for his hand and he held them briefly before getting up. "I won't be far away. Send if you want me," he said, giving her cheek a gentle lick before leaving.

Kusac left her, following Vanna back into the lounge where Brynne and Chena were replacing the equipment that was no longer needed. He staggered, feeling suddenly weak and faint, reaching for Vanna to steady himself.

She caught hold of him, realizing as she did that he was beginning to shiver convulsively. Feeling his palm, she called for Kaid to help her. Between them they guided him to the settee and made him lie down.

"Brynne, get a couple of blankets, please" she said, propping Kusac's feet up with a cushion. "There's a chest full of them at the end of Carrie's bed."

A quick check of his eyelids while she took his pulse told her what she'd suspected. "Don't worry," she said, "you're only suffering from shock, a compound of your own injury and Carrie's. You'll be fine and it won't affect Carrie." She wrapped one of the blankets round him when Brynne handed it to her. "I thought we'd gotten off too lightly with you. Rest and warmth is what you need. We'll a bed made up for you here. Does your shoulder hurt?"

He nodded, teeth chattering as he tried to keep his limbs still. He nodded again, jerkily, clutching the blanket closer.

Vanna threw the other blanket over him. "Chena will give you something for it while I go down to see your mother. Kaid, will you get him out of those clothes, please? He can't be comfortable in them. I'm afraid your shower will have to wait."

She left him with Kaid and Chena, going downstairs to arrange with his mother about getting a bed made up for him as well as organizing sleeping arrangements for herself and Chena.

Taizia was sent for the housekeeper while Rhyasha accompanied Vanna back upstairs.

"Of course Taizia and I will see to Carrie. I'll have an extra bed made up in Kusac's lounge, and you and Chena can have the guest room you used last time you stayed with us."

"I'd prefer an extra bed in the room with Carrie," said Vanna. "Chena and I will take it in turns to stay with her to make sure she's all right."

"I'll see to it at once." Rhyasha prevented Vanna from opening the door. "Thank you, my dear. Both my son and his mate are very dear to us."

Vanna gave a wry smile. "Think nothing of it, they're my friends, too. I just hope life settles down for them now. They seem to go from one crisis to another."

Vanna left Kusac and his mother together for the moment, going over to Brynne.

"Thanks for coming, and for helping," she said. "I'll have to stay for a few days." She hesitated. "I think it would be better if you returned to the guild."

Brynne nodded. "They've got enough on their hands for the present," he agreed. "Will you need the aircar or can I return with it? I came in a public vehicle."

"I've everything I need here, so take the aircar."

"I might as well leave now. There's nothing more for me to do, and I'll just be in the way." He went toward the door, giving her a nod as he left.

She frowned, surprised at his easy acceptance of the need for him to leave, but she could sense nothing untoward through their Link.

* * *

Kusac's father had called Mr. Hamilton back with the news of Carrie's condition. He then called the judge on the *Kahalossa* who had issued the interdiction concerning the Challenge, demanding that steps be taken to make all Challenges involving telepaths illegal. It was agreed this matter should be put before the Sholan World Council at the soonest opportunity. All the laws of Challenge needed to be reviewed to make sure no more such loopholes existed. Sholan telepaths were too rare and too valuable among all the Allied worlds to be risked in the Challenge system because of ancient laws still on the statutes.

A new department would be set up specifically to mediate in matters arising out of a conflict concerning any telepath, whether it was personal or legal. They agreed that an arbitration system was needed to deal with circumstances such as Kusac and Carrie had found themselves in. That done, Konis finally began to relax, knowing that never again would any parent have to face the possible death of both his son and his bond-daughter because of a Challenge.

* * *

After Kusac had been settled upstairs, Kaid called Garras, Meral, T'Chebbi, Rulla, Dzaka and Lhea to the small in-house staff lounge for a conference.

"It looks like the current threat to them is over now," he said. "We've got the last of the two killers, and all reports from Nazule and other major cities show that on Shola, at least, there is no fear of a treaty with Earth. Similarly, reports from the *Khalossa* and *Rhyaki* show that the crew orientation program is now working. However, we aren't going to relax our vigilance yet." He looked round them all, making sure each one thought he or she was the sole focus of his attention.

"As new mixed Leskas occur, they will be assigned bodyguards until we are sure there are too many of them for them to be satisfactory targets for any dissidents."

"You expect there to be that many?" asked Meral.

"Yes, I do. Your dues to Stronghold will continue to be paid for you all as well as a basic wage. Where you're living on an estate, the estate will pay you and feed you. This is the arrangement that has been decided will be the easiest to implement. We'll rotate you, so you can have some time back at Dzahai for training. Any questions?"

There were negative headshakes and murmurs from two of the four Warriors.

"Who are we working for, Kaid?" asked T'Chebbi.

"Me."

"Not the Brotherhood?"

Kaid shook his head slowly, eyes locked on hers.

T'Chebbi's eyes narrowed as she met his gaze. Abruptly, she nodded once. "I'm with you."

"Anyone else have a problem?" he asked, looking straight at Dzaka. No one had.

"Good. T'Chebbi, take over command of the troops outside. Stand half down now for a meal and rest period, then rotate them in for the night shift."

"Aye, sir," she said, getting up and leaving.

"Lhea, you're on duty with Vanna till tomorrow morning. Stay near her and rest when you can. I'm sorry you have a heavy duty, but I need Garras for something else. Is Maylgu still watching Brynne?"

"Yes," said Lhea.

"When you leave here, contact him and tell him he's on the same shift length as you. You can go."

"Aye."

Left with only Garras, Rulla, Dzaka, and Meral, Kaid looked over to his old friend, "Well, Garras?" he asked, raising an eye ridge, his ears pricking toward him.

Alone of the five, Garras had relaxed back into his chair from the beginning of the meeting. "Considering his companion is Liegena Taizia, I think it would be a wise move," he drawled, watching Meral with an amused look on his face. His tail tip flicked lazily from its position on the chair.

Meral's ears went back apprehensively.

"If we adjust the shifts, can you cope?"

"Depends how quickly he learns. We'll need some time at Stronghold, or do you intend to dispense with that?"

Meral was looking from one to the other of them. "You're not talking about the Warrior Guild, are you?" he asked.

"This conversation hasn't happened, Meral," said Kaid sternly, his eyes locking on the young male's. "We'll observe the rules for now, Garras."

"No, sir," said Meral, obviously fighting to keep his ears as vertical as possible.

"You can't join the Brotherhood, you know that, don't you? You must be invited in. You've probably seen us visiting the Warrior Guild to recruit."

Meral nodded.

"We pick likely candidates, ones with the right talents, and then approach them. Your guild doesn't like us doing that, but we have the right. Each person is handpicked, either as a child or at around your age."

Meral's ears had risen again. "You're not ... asking me, are you?" He looked from one to the other.

Garras nodded.

"You have qualities we need," said Kaid. "Are you interested?"

"Yes," he said. "But why me? There's nothing that special about me."

"Telepaths don't tend to choose companions who are Talentless," said Garras. "Now what have you got planned for me to do, Kaid?"

Kaid flicked his ears in recognition of the point Garras had scored. "You and Meral are leaving for Dzahai Stronghold. I can't leave them now, and I want a message delivered in person to Ghezu. You can enter Meral's name on the role of members while you'll there. He'll need a sponsor."

Garras nodded. "I'll sponsor him. What's the message?"

"Tell Ghezu I said he's had his proof now. I won't allow this to happen again. Remind him I owe them nothing, all debts are now paid."

Garras got slowly to his feet. "Come on, lad, we're leaving," he said. "I think I'll see the clerk before I give Ghezu your message."

Kaid's mouth dropped in a rare grin. "It would probably be best," he agreed.

As the door shut, Kaid turned to look at Dzaka.

"You're planning to break from Stronghold," he said.

"I'm not with Stronghold," Kaid reminded him.

"But the others are. You said next time you left, I could choose to come."

Kaid nodded, watching Dzaka carefully through half closed eyes. He was deadly tired now. He needed to sleep. "When I'm ready, I'll tell you."

"What happens if Ghezu calls me back?"

"That's your decision, Dzaka," he said quietly.

"You expect me to decide to disobey Stronghold without knowing why?" he asked in disbelief.

"The rest of us will," said Rulla. "What makes you think you deserve an explanation when we don't?"

"Trust, Dzaka. You either trust me, or you don't. You have to decide. You wanted the right to make up your own mind, well, you've got it now." Kaid got to his feet. "I'm leaving you on duty, too, Rulla. Dzaka, too, if he's staying. T'Chebbi will tell you what needs doing. I need to sleep."

* * *

Both Carrie and Kusac slept for the remainder of that day and through the night.

By morning, Kusac had recovered from the shock. He was only marginally blocking Carrie's pain because she was under such a heavy dose of analgesics that they were affecting him. As a side effect it was lessening the pain in his shoulder.

Vanna was using Kusac's desk comm to call up the Medical Guild to speak to one of the research doctors there. She was explaining her theory that once the Leska Link was established between a Sholan and a human and the pair were fully compatible, there was a biological trigger that forced them to reproduce immediately. She was hoping that after that first child was born there would be a decrease in that dependency and fertility, or a return to the normal Sholan voluntary control over conception. Whatever else, some provision had to be made for the Terran females who had never had the option to voluntarily control their fertility.

Kusac left her to it and went for his shower. As he passed through their bedroom, he saw Carrie was still asleep. He stopped to check on her, finding that the blood transfusion was finished and her color had improved. She no longer looked like she was at death's door. He gave an involuntary shudder, aware of how close to death she had come. Trying not to disturb her, he reached out to touch her face, needing to make sure she was really there and alive before going into the bathroom.

Once in the shower, he had the grisly task of washing her blood and his out of his fur. A good portion of the left side of his body, from shoulder to knee, was stiff with blood and the water ran red for several minutes as he worked his matted fur loose. The last moments of the fight when his fear had triggered the gestalt Link forced themselves through his mind again, and he leaned against the cubical wall while guilt and grief finally caught up with him.

He was aware of nothing until a hand touched his shoulder from behind. Startled, he turned round and, blinking through the spray of water, saw Carrie. The color was draining from her face as slowly, despite her grip on the shower door, she slipped down to the floor. Jumping out, he grabbed her around the waist and lifted her to her feet before carefully swinging her into his arms. Shaking his head to clear his vision, he ignored the water he was dripping everywhere and carried her back to the bedroom.

"What in Vartra's name do you think you're doing?" he demanded, trying to put her back into the bed.

She clung to him, refusing to be put down. Her weight was pulling on his injured shoulder and finally he sat on the bed himself, holding her on his knee.

"I'm getting everything wet," he said reproachfully, looking at the water spreading from him onto the bed and soaking her lightweight sleeping tunic.

"I felt you," she said, tears beginning to roll down her cheeks. "You mustn't blame yourself, Kusac," she said, the fingers of her good arm clutching the fur on his back. "I was just as terrified. It could just as easily have been my fear that triggered the gestalt. We'll never know for sure."

He held her closer, resting his head on hers. "You mustn't cry, Carrie. I thought you were asleep or I'd never have let myself get upset. I'm sorry, Leska."

"She was so beautiful, Kusac, so tiny and beautiful. It wasn't hard to love her," she sobbed. "I wanted her then."

"You saw our cub?"

"I asked Vanna this morning. I couldn't bear to have never seen her."

Kusac picked up the image, Carrie's grief amplifying his own.

"We mustn't, Carrie," he whispered gently, trying to control their emotions. "She's gone. We'll have to let the grief go, too. I know you wanted her, I could feel it in you. You were just afraid."

"I want my baby back, Kusac," she wept, burying herself against the damp fur on his chest.

Kusac heard the door open behind him and it was with relief that he sensed Vanna coming in.

"Hush," he said, holding her tighter and rocking her gently, trying not to let her utter sense of loss dominate him, too.

Vanna came round to his side, applying the hypoderm to Carrie's right arm where it was wrapped around Kusac's waist.

"Just a mild sedative," she said quietly as Carrie's sobs slowly decreased. "You'll be able to put her back on the bed now."

Kusac could already feel her drifting off to sleep. Getting up, he turned and carefully laid her down on the dry side of the bed, pulling the covers over her.

"I don't know how long she'll grieve like this," Vanna replied to Kusac's unspoken thought. "With us, the body goes into a state of rest for what would be the remainder of the pregnancy, but Terrans can apparently conceive again shortly afterward. According to Jack's data, they also brood more over other people's cubs until they either have a full-term pregnancy or their hormone levels return to normal. But us," she sighed, "we're almost that new race, neither Terran nor Sholan. There is no one who knows what will happen. She could come to terms with it tomorrow, or still be desperately wanting a cub next month."

"The solution is with us, then," he said, checking to make sure she was asleep before following Vanna back to the lounge.

"I wouldn't come out here like that," she said with a faint grin. "You're still dripping wet."

Kusac looked down at the floor. There were wet footprints all across the carpet and a small puddle was developing around him.

"Go and finish your shower," she said. "Carrie will sleep for a couple of hours and it's what she needs most at the moment. I'll give her something to help cope with the grief when she wakes. Not drugs, something more natural."

* * *

"Carrie's not up to attending the funeral, Kusac. Be reasonable," his mother said. "She's not even had a full day to come to terms with her loss."

"I am being reasonable, Mother. The funeral will release Carrie from her grief because she'll see our cub is dead. She needs to let go of her, put her to rest. She can't do that while she knows her child lies in the shrine."

"This argument has gone on long enough," said Konis. "See what Vanna has to say."

When Vanna joined them, surprisingly she shared Kusac's view. "I agree with Kusac. Granted she's still extremely weak, but she does need to start coming to terms with the death of her cub so that the healing process can start."

"I'll contact Ghyan, then," said Kusac, going over to the comm unit.

It was mid-afternoon when Ghyan arrived. The tiny funeral pyre had been laid at the front of the house, not far from the newly-planted flower bed. A chair had been brought out for Carrie to use and Kusac had carried her downstairs and settled her in it.

The gathering was small, only their immediate family plus a representative from the estate. Silent tears stole down Carrie's face as she held on tightly to Kusac's hand. She didn't hear a word that Ghyan said. When it came time to light the bier, she roused, rubbing her hand across her face and demanding that she do it.

She struggled one-handedly to get up, pushing Kusac's restraining hand away. "I'm doing it!" she said fiercely.

"Then let me carry you over," he said quietly. "You can lean on me while you light it."

She nodded and he lifted her up, carrying her over to the bier. He set her down, holding her waist while she tried to get her balance without putting any weight on her injured leg. The effort it took for her even to be downstairs was telling on her face.

I'll manage, she sent, knowing she didn't even have the energy to hide her pain from him.

His mother handed her the torch. *She's not strong enough for this. You're pushing her too hard.* There was censure in her mental tone.

I have to do it, Rhyasha, Carrie replied on their private Link, rendering them both speechless. She clutched the torch, finding it too heavy for her to hold up. "Help me, Kusac," she said, looking up at him.

His dark-furred hand closed around hers and together, using his strength, they lifted their torch and thrust it into the heart of the pyre. The flames licked upward, almost invisible in the strong sunlight as they cradled the tiny body in their midst.

Kusac picked her up again, stepping back from the bier so his parents could place their torches. As they did, Carrie felt the presence of Rhyasha's mind at the edge of hers. Konis' followed, to be joined by Taizia and Kitra.

The keening started then, as low as the sighing of a breeze through the trees. As it grew in volume, she became aware of the dozens of minds that hesitantly touched theirs at the edges of perception.

Tears were rolling down Rhyasha's cheeks as she leaned forward to touch Carrie's face. *It's the tribute of the Clan, Carrie. They're sharing your grief, hoping to lessen it by their presence. I've only experienced it once before. They're telling you that you're part of our Clan.*

Carrie lay back against Kusac, resting her head against him. She could feel the rise and fall of his chest, the smell of his fur and the feel of his arms enfolding and protecting her. She closed her eyes.

"*What is a Leska?*" she'd asked.

"*It has to do with our merging,*" he'd replied. "*We are as one—Leskas to each other. Now sleep.*"

It had been so long ago—a world away and a lifetime in the past. She was tired, so very tired, and cried out of tears. He was right, sleep was what she needed. She relaxed, letting herself drift, feeling warm and comfortable in his arms.

She was jolted out of this warm haze as feral eyes, black as night with only the narrowest amber ring glittered down at her.

"*No. You *chose* to stay!*"

She moaned, eyes flicking open as the pain of loss returned. Kusac tilted her back in his arms, lowering his face to hers, his eyes as dark as she'd remembered. His mouth closed on hers, his kiss both frantic and compelling.

You promised to stay with me, he sent fiercely. *Don't you dare try and slip away from me again! Gods, Carrie, I can't bring her back, but I'll give you as many cubs as you want!*

He released her as she started to cry again. This time the grief seemed to come from deep within her. She clung to him as he carried her back into the house and up to their room.

Gradually the hurt began to diminish and she realized that she could still sense the Clan—worried and concerned about one of their own—hovering at the edges of her mind. Satisfied that all would now be well, their presence faded, leaving the Leskas alone.

She looked around the room at the anxious faces of her family and realized at last that she had come home. At the back of the room stood Kaid, and in his eyes and mind she saw approbation.

Vanna pushed past Konis and turned to shoo them all out. "Carrie needs to rest now," she said firmly as they began to leave. "You, too," she said to Kusac.

"No, I want him to stay," Carrie said.

"I want you to rest, cub. You'll heal faster if you do."

"I'll rest better knowing he's beside me."

Vanna sighed. "You're as bad as each other," she grumbled as she and Chena settled Carrie back into bed. "You can stay," she said to Kusac, "but only if you persuade her to sleep."

"We'll both sleep," he said, lying down on top of the bed beside Carrie. He curled himself round behind her, carefully stretching his injured arm across her body to hold her hand. His tail flicked protectively across her legs. *Sleep, before Vanna scolds us both,* he sent as he gently nuzzled the back of her neck.

By evening, Carrie was more like herself, still subdued and saddened but no longer broadcasting a terrible sense of loss.

As Kusac sat beside her and took her hand, he felt a familiar flare of desire that he swiftly blocked, annoyed with himself for responding to the demands of their Link rather than the needs of his Leska, especially when there was no similar response from her. He remained with her for some time before she finally persuaded him to go and eat with his family.

While Vanna changed her dressings, Carrie was aware that her friend was preoccupied and she gently probed to find the underlying cause. What she discovered gave her cause to think.

Her task completed, Vanna said good night and went off duty, leaving Chena to hand Carrie the light meal that had been brought up to the bedroom for her.

She toyed with the food, eating about half before she

knew Kusac was on his way back upstairs. She handed the tray to Chena.

"I've had enough," she said, moving restlessly. "My leg and arm hurt and I can't get comfortable. Can you give me something to help me sleep? Something stronger than I had this morning so I don't wake up during the night."

Chena put the tray on the chest at the end of the bed and went over to the dresser where Vanna kept Carrie's chart and drugs. She checked the chart, then picked up one of the bottles.

"No problem," she said, coming back over to her and pouring her a glass of water. "This should help you," she said.

Carrie smiled her thanks, taking the tablets and washing them down with the water. She returned the glass and let Chena settle her more comfortably.

Kusac came in, a book in his hands. "I thought I'd read to you," he said, making himself comfortable on the bed beside her.

Chena went out, gently closing the door.

"What a nice thought," Carrie said. "I'm afraid I've just taken a sleeping pill, though. Perhaps tomorrow?"

"All right," he agreed, putting the book aside. "I'll just talk to you till you fall asleep." Already he could sense her mind becoming fuzzy.

"I didn't know they worked so quickly," she agreed sleepily. "I'd like you to talk to Vanna, Kusac. She's troubled at the moment and I think you could help each other."

Kusac frowned. "Troubled? How?"

She's unhappy. Go and talk to her. She was beginning to drift into sleep.

All right, but how can she help me? I don't understand what you mean, he replied, concerned.

Go and see her, she sent, waving him away with a limp hand. *She's in the garden.*

Kusac sighed, leaning over to kiss her on the forehead. "I'll go. Sleep well."

She murmured good night as he left the room.

Kusac headed downstairs, reaching out mentally to locate Vanna. As Carrie had said, she was in the garden, sitting on the bench. As he came between the high hedges, Vanna looked up, startled to see him.

"Is something wrong?" she asked, concern on her face.

"Not with Carrie," he replied. "She wanted me to come and see you."

"Me? Whatever for?"

Kusac sat down beside her. "She said you needed to talk to me."

A frown creased Vanna's nose. "I don't know where she got that idea from," she said, beginning to look uncomfortable.

"Is Brynne with someone just now?" he asked abruptly.

"Yes, but what has . . ."

"Carrie's been picking you up," he said angrily, "and doing a little probing on her own account. I'm sorry. She had no justification for prying, and no right to ask me to speak to you at this time."

He put a sympathetic hand on her shoulder, only to snatch it back as the sudden shock of their physical contact jolted through him, so highly sexually charged were they to their separate partners.

"We've been set up by Carrie, Vanna," he said grimly, trying to sense his Leska. He could feel her faint presence but before he could let her know how angry he was, she was sending to him.

You and Vanna both need someone now, came the very faint thought. *What better way to show her that what she has with Brynne is better than anything you two could have, than to spend the night with her? It will also make Brynne more careful of her.*

Kusac's reply was a white hot fury of rage. *I won't be used, Carrie!*

You're making an exchange. Your need for hers. The thought faded as she drifted beyond him into sleep.

"What is it? What's happened?" demanded Vanna, grabbing him by the arm and triggering the same response again. It left neither of them with any illusions about their present physical or mental state.

"Carrie got Chena to drug her up, then sent me to you, knowing that Brynne was with another female," he said angrily. "She must have sensed me earlier this evening. She's throwing us together. I apologize for her, Vanna. Good night." He got up and turned to leave.

Again Vanna grasped him by the arm, this time refusing to let go when the reaction surged through her. "Wait," she said, her ears flattening. "Why not, if Carrie's willing?"

"It would be a mistake, Vanna. What about Brynne?"

"What about him? If he can go off with another female, then I'm free to please myself. But I don't understand why Carrie would do this. Terrans don't have our attitude toward pairings."

"Her attitudes are becoming more Sholan," he said slowly, thinking over what Carrie had actually said and realizing there was some sense to it. He tried to block the resonance building between him and Vanna, but found it almost impossible to ignore.

He turned. "It's too easy for emotions to get involved, Vanna, especially for you."

"I know. If you stay, I realize it's only because Carrie's ill." She was projecting so much hope that mentally he backed away, wondering if Carrie's plan could possibly work. His need for hers though: it was the Sholan way. Before he'd met Carrie he wouldn't have thought twice about it.

"Come with me, then," he said decisively.

"Where are we going?" she asked as he took her arm and led her into the darkness.

"Away from the house," he replied, waiting a moment for his eyes to adjust to the night. As they made their way through the shrubland and across the fields Kusac sensed several of the watchers including T'Chebbi. He reached again for Carrie, but she remained deeply asleep.

At length, a barn loomed in the near distance and he headed toward it.

"A barn!" said Vanna, slightly aghast as she realized where they were going.

"Yes. It was the regular meeting place for couples when I was young." He grinned, his teeth a flash of white in the dark. "I only went there a couple of times myself, but I know Taizia uses it fairly often."

He felt her slow down. "It's all right," he reassured her. "There's no one there, and we won't be disturbed." He pushed the door open, standing back for her to enter first.

"A barn with well oiled hinges," she murmured, shaking her head as she looked around.

Kusac moved toward the few bales of last year's straw that were piled in the far corner. He scrambled on top of them and crouching down, held out his hand to Vanna.

"It hasn't changed," he said, pulling her up and steadying her.

She stumbled, swaying for a moment before she lost her balance. With a sharp cry of fright, she went crashing down onto the straw on the lower level behind them, dragging Kusac along with her.

He landed on top of her, knocking the breath from her lungs.

"I suppose that's one way of getting down here," said Kusac, raising himself on his forearms and shaking his head to rid it of straw. He reached out to unfasten her coat, letting it fall open behind her.

"Another time, another place, isn't that what we once said, Vanna?" he asked, touching her cheek as her arms came up around him.

The pull of their separate Links surged through them, but this time neither of them let go. Their minds met as telepaths' minds did, but it held little of the magic they shared with their Leskas. Through Vanna, Kusac sensed Brynne push his partner aside as the human felt Vanna's response to him. With a thought, Kusac blocked Brynne out and turned his attention back to Vanna.

She was breathing so rapidly now that she could hardly catch her breath. Her hands clutched at his tabard, claws coming out in her almost frantic need to touch him.

He caught her hands in one of his, lifting them to his mouth as he moved to kneel beside her.

"Not so fast," he murmured, licking her fingers. "We've all night." He leaned forward, unfastening her jacket while against his mouth, her fingers trembled.

He let them go, urging her to sit up while he pushed her coat and jacket free of her arms. Again, she reached for him, taking hold of his tunic.

"Still too fast," he chided, pushing her hands away, unfastening it and taking it off himself. "I can't see Garras being so quick. Brynne, perhaps, but not Garras."

She gave a short laugh. "It's just that I need to feel you warm and alive! You came so close to death again."

"Shh, I know," he said, lying down beside her again and beginning to nuzzle her cheek and ear. "Tell me," he asked between licks, "does Brynne give you Terran kisses?"

"I don't know," she said, sighing as finally her hands were

able to touch him. *Show me,* she sent as his mouth covered hers.

A false dawn lit the sky as Kusac left Vanna in the garden by the house. He was glad Carrie had pushed them together. Vanna was sweeter than any Sholan female he'd known, and he was pleased to have had the opportunity to know her body and mind better.

He padded silently upstairs into their rooms, nodding to Kaid as he passed him. Carrie was still fast asleep, as was Chena in her makeshift bed. A note lay on the drawer unit and he stopped to read it.

"Brynne called at the sixteenth hour, asking for Vanna or Kusac. When I said neither of you was available, he broke the connection. He seemed displeased over something."

He shrugged, screwing up the note and throwing it in the bin nearby. He had expected as much. That was something Vanna would shortly be sorting out for herself. Heading for the bathroom, he took a quick shower, luxuriating in the warm water. The walk back had been chilly.

Going over to the bed, he checked Carrie again. She was beginning to stir. Her hand reached unerringly for his, giving it a gentle squeeze.

You're back?

I'm back. He sat beside her.

Not there. Come in beside me, she sent sleepily, moving over to make room.

He got up and crawled in beside her, sliding an arm under her neck and her uninjured side.

You feel better now, more relaxed, and you smell nice. She wriggled closer to him, pillowing her head on his chest.

Strangely enough, I am. From what Vanna and Brynne have experienced, I didn't expect it to work for me. He relaxed against her, enjoying being close to her again. There was a rightness about the feel of her both mentally and physically, something that Vanna, being Sholan, had lacked for him.

Brynne hasn't been with someone he cared about. I know you don't see Vanna as a lover, she sent hastily, feeling his rebuttal, *but I know that, like me, you feel something special for her.*

Kusac subsided, knowing she had correctly sensed his feelings for their friend. *I don't think it eased Vanna's pre-*

dicament, he sent. *She was more tense than before when I left her. It was dangerous to pair with her, she believes herself to be too much in love with me. I think your plan could go wrong.*

We'll see. Remember, Brynne was experiencing what she experienced, and from what you say, her physical need hasn't been diminished, nor will it be until she's with him.

Kusac yawned. *We'll see. I cut Brynne out at the start because I don't appreciate an audience. He called earlier. When I left her, Vanna was going back to the guild. I hope she can handle him after this. It won't exactly endear either her or me to him.*

When she realizes you can't satisfy her, that only Brynne can, she continued, ignoring his protestations, *her attitude to you will change, you'll see. Not that I mean to infer you're lacking as a lover,* she added hastily, running her hand across his chest.

"Honestly, Carrie," he murmured, wrapping his other arm around her waist and hugging her as tightly as he dared, "first you throw me at Vanna, then you try to arouse me yourself! I've had enough excitement for one night. Let's just hope you're right. Now go to sleep," he said, relaxing his hold on her.

Do you regret not having a Sholan Leska? came the wistful thought. She felt the equivalent of a mental laugh.

Jealous? Don't be. I'm not in love with Vanna, and we both discovered that even leaving the Leska bond aside, a Terran lover has something no Sholan could ever have, he sent sleepily.

What's that? she asked, but he was already asleep.

* * *

Kaid woke to someone shaking him. He reached out and grabbed at him just as he realized it was Rulla.

"Kaid, it's Dzaka. He's gone, and he's taken Vanna with him."

Kaid sat up, blinking. "What d'you mean, taken Vanna?"

"I was on patrol near the garages when Dzaka came up behind me and knocked me out. I came to just in time to see him lifting Vanna into an aircar."

Kaid began to swear as he pushed the covers back and got up. "Are you all right?" he asked, throwing a quick glance at Rulla as he pulled on his jacket.

"I'll do," he said, gingerly touching the back of his head. "It happened about an hour ago. I've no idea where he was taking her."

Kaid fastened his belt, pulling his gun from under the pillow and pushing it into the side holster. "Tell T'Chebbi what's happened while I try to contact Brynne. He must have some idea of where she is. Dzaka will regret this night's work," he said coldly."

* * *

Vanna was just beginning to come round as she felt the aircar being buffeted from side to side by heavy winds. An involuntary groan escaped her before she could stop it.

"I'm sorry I had to treat you so roughly, Physician Vanna, but I needed you to come with me, and I knew you wouldn't come voluntarily."

She recognized the voice. It was Dzaka. Groggily, she pushed herself up into a sitting position. Her head ached, and as she put her hand up to it, she realized why. There was a lump on the back of it where Dzaka must have knocked her out.

"Don't bother trying to reach your Leska, Vanna," he said apologetically. "I gave you a dose of one of your suppressant drugs. You won't be able to use your Link."

"What the hell are you doing, Dzaka?" she demanded, bracing herself as the craft was hit by the crosswind yet again. "Why have you kidnapped me? Where are you taking me?"

"Kidnapped's a harsh word, Vanna. I'm merely borrowing you for a few hours."

She could feel the craft starting to descend.

"We're almost there."

"Where the hell is 'there'?"

"Dzahai Stronghold," he said. "Now I'm afraid I must ask you to be quiet while I concentrate on landing. The wind's unusually strong tonight. It might be wise if you took one of the seats and fastened the safety belt."

She sat silently till the craft came to a stop and Dzaka had turned off the engines. "Why couldn't you have just asked me to come here with you?"

"Because Kaid wouldn't have allowed it," said Dzaka, turning round and getting out of his seat. "Now if you would be so kind as to come with me without making a fuss, I'd appreciate it. They are expecting us."

Realizing there was no point in struggling or trying to run from him, she left the craft peacefully. Holding her by the arm, he led her across to a side entrance then up the flight of stairs till they came to a wooden door. Knocking first, he pushed the door open and took her in.

A figure dressed in long purple robes rose and came over to greet her. "Thank you for accepting our invitation, my dear," he said, holding his palm out to her. "My name is Lijou. I'm head of the Priests of Vartra. My colleague is Ghezu, Leader of the Brotherhood."

Vanna ignored the outstretched hand. "I've been brought here against my will, and drugged so I can't reach my Leska," she said, her voice low and angry. "I demand to be taken back to the Aldatan estate immediately."

Lijou turned and walked back toward the desk set in the center of the room. "Oh, I think you'll be glad we ... persuaded you to come when you've seen what I want to show you," he said. "Bring her over, Dzaka, if you please. You see, Physician Kyjishi, we have need of your experience, and your professional eye."

Despite trying to dig her claws into the thick carpeting underfoot, Dzaka urged her over toward where Ghezu sat. A white cloth covered the desk, concealing what was on top of it.

"In return for identifying these objects, we're prepared to offer you something we hope you will consider carefully," continued Lijou.

"We're offering you membership in the Brotherhood," said Ghezu. "With us you needn't fear that we'll treat you the way the Telepath Guild did. We've more respect for our members. Since you and your Leska can fight, here you can train those skills without the mental discomfort you would suffer at the Warrior Guild."

Vanna looked at them in disbelief. "You've had me knocked out, drugged with psychic suppressants, and kidnapped here, and you say you'll treat me better than the Telepath Guild? Do I look like a congenital idiot?" she asked angrily, trying to pull away from Dzaka, who continued to hold onto her firmly.

"I regret the necessity for our less than gentle treatment," said Lijou. "However, it will not be repeated, I assure you.

We want your cooperation not your fear. Will you look at what we have to show you now that you're here?"

"Forget it! I refuse to help you at all! If you want my cooperation, return me to the Aldatan estate then invite me here. I might just come, but I wouldn't bet on it," she said sarcastically.

Lijou lifted the cloth off the table. "Just look, Physician Kyjishi. We needed someone with a medical background who could identify these remains."

Despite herself, Vanna looked. With a hiss of indrawn breath, she moved closer to the table, reaching out to touch the bones lying there.

"Where the hell did you get these? They're Valtegan bones!"

"They were found in one of our ancient ruined cities," said Lijou. . . .

Lisanne Norman

☐ **TURNING POINT** UE2575—$3.99
When a human-colonized world falls under the sway of aliens who have already enslaved many another race, there is scant hope of salvation from far-distant Earth. Instead, their hopes rest upon an underground rebellion and the intervention of a team of catlike aliens, one of whom links with a young woman gifted with unique mind powers.

☐ **FORTUNE'S WHEEL** UE2675—$5.99
Carrie was the daughter of the human governor of the colony planet Keiss. Kusac was the son and heir of the Sholan Clan Lord. Both were telepaths and the bond they formed was compounded equally of love and mind power. But now they were about to be thrust into the heart of an interstellar conflict, as factions on both their worlds sought to use the duo's powers for their own ends . . .

Charles Ingrid

PATTERNS OF CHAOS
Only the Choyan could pilot faster-than-light starships—and the other Compact races would do anything to learn their secret!

☐ **RADIUS OF DOUBT: Book 1**   UE2491—$4.99

☐ **PATH OF FIRE: Book 2**   UE2522—$4.99

☐ **THE DOWNFALL MATRIX: Book 3**   UE2616—$4.99

☐ **SOULFIRE: Book 4**   UE2676—$5.50

THE MARKED MAN SERIES
In a devastated America, can the Lord Protector of a mutating human race find a way to preserve the future of the species?

☐ **THE MARKED MAN: Book 1**   UE2396—$3.95

☐ **THE LAST RECALL: Book 2**   UE2460—$3.95

THE SAND WARS
He was the last Dominion Knight and he would challenge a star empire to defeat the ancient enemies of man.

☐ **SOLAR KILL: Book 1**   UE2391—$3.95

☐ **LASERTOWN BLUES: Book 2**   UE2393—$3.95

☐ **CELESTIAL HIT LIST: Book 3**   UE2394—$3.95

☐ **ALIEN SALUTE: Book 4**   UE2329—$3.95

☐ **RETURN FIRE: Book 5**   UE2363—$3.95

☐ **CHALLENGE MET: Book 6**   UE2436—$3.95

Kate Elliott

The Novels of the Jaran:

S. Andrew Swann

☐ **PROFITEER**   UE2647—$4.99
Book One of Hostile Takeover
In the 24th century, the Human race spans 84 worlds. All but one accept the rule of the Terran Confederacy . . . Enter now the world called Bakunin, where anarchy reigns and power belongs to whoever can seize it. With no taxes, no anti-trust laws, and no governing body, Bakunin is the perfect home base for both super-corporations and ruthless criminals. But now the Confederacy wants a piece of the action—and they're planning a hostile takeover!

OTHER NOVELS
☐ **FORESTS OF THE NIGHT**   UE2565—$4.50
☐ **EMPERORS OF THE TWILIGHT**   UE2589—$4.50
☐ **SPECTERS OF THE DAWN**   UE2613—$4.50